Heirs to the Kingdom

Book Three

The Darkness of Dunnottar
(Revised Edition)

Robin John Morgan

www.heirstothekingdom.com

For
My Father.

The Darkness of my youth, was lifted by your Light.

Maybe now he had a better idea of who the hooded man was, and what the hooded man should do. Robbing the rich and saving the poor had always seemed such a fantasy notion, but now it was real. Knox would continue to murder, maim, and terrorise the people into submission, and he had now seen the direct results. It had to stop, and for the first time in a long time, Robbie knew what the hooded man really was.

He looked at Rune who was looking at him with a concerned look. "Are you alright Robbie, you look terribly pale?"

"I am fine Rune; I had very little sleep last night as I tried to work out what truly is the hooded man."

"And what is it you have come up with?" Everyone was watching and listening.

"Us…All of us…Not just me, but everyone who pulls up a hood and loads a long bow, and says here I am. Here is your hope. I will defend you because you cannot defend yourself. That is what all of us are, and what all of us will do."

(Extract from the diary of Runestone Sapphire Loxley 15-04-2038)

CHAPTER ONE

A TIME OF HARD DECISION

It was still very warm for September, as the pale light of the sun, glinted its first rays off the clear smooth surface of the Mere. The dark tired eyes of Lord Loxley watched as he lifted his cup to his lips, he had a lot on his mind as he tried to think of the coming month, the last nine had been hard, and he had grown into a very different person.

It seemed like a long time ago that the young boy of almost seventeen had sat in a greenhouse not that far from here, and battled with the restless feelings inside him. The mantle of lord had been thrust upon him, he had not been prepared, and had struggled under the weight of responsibility.

Robbie had been forced to look deep inside himself, and find the courage and the strength to lead a small group and seek the truth. Surrounded by the love of his comrades, he found something inside himself that he had never been aware of, and with pride, he pulled up a hood and became another person.

The hooded man had led the quest for truth, and the crown of the king had been saved, he smiled almost in disbelief, as he remembered standing high in the balcony of Canterbury Cathedral, challenging the power of Mason Knox. He had indeed done it and surprised himself.

The backlash had been swift, and people all over the south had been brutally punished by the anger of the Knox Empire. Their loved ones died, and their land was burned, as they fled to the only standard of hope they knew. He remembered the pain and anger that had washed over him, as he looked on the masses of the wretched, as they looked to him for leadership.

He had for some time felt like it had swamped him, and he had feared he would not cope, but the support of his friends once again proved vital, as he used those with talent around him to help guide him. Everyone who fled had found help and support, and suddenly he found that not himself, but his hometown of Loxley had become the centre of the woodland people's world.

Once again, he had looked into the eyes of Mason Knox, and this time it had been the pain and anger at the injustice of the man that had fuelled his power to bring justice back to his people. Robbie had risen to the challenge, and with the Sword of Truth in his hand, he had dealt the heavy blow of justice, and ended the life of Mason Knox.

It was enough for one man's life, but as before, he now stood and faced another task that had been set for him. Armed now with the Sword of Destiny, the sister sword of Excalibur, he had to fight again as the line of Knox brought forward another heir.

The Dark One, whose son Mason, he had killed, had other grandchildren, and one especially was a force to be reckoned with. Billy had been corrupted by the introduction of the Dark One's first born; Mordred the evil slayer of King Arthur had been brought back from the death of a thousand years, and poured into Billy through the Black Blade of Dunnottar.

Robbie now faced a mighty enemy, and he fought with his apprehensive feelings, for he knew that somewhere inside that evil enemy, was the soul of a boy he once called brother. This was not a fight he would relish, but everyone looked to him.

His greatest hope lay in love. Throughout all he had done was the girl he had loved since he was a small boy, she had been by his side and supported him. His love for Runestone was strong and fierce, and with her at his side, he had found hidden depths that had driven him forward.

He smiled, as he thought of her asleep in bed just a moment away, in the home they shared behind him, he knew soon she would wake and he would see the love and the trust in her eyes. Those sapphire blue eyes that burned so bright, in a pale white face, dusted with the faintest of freckles. He knew as she woke surrounded by the fiery red hair that glistened with gold, he would gaze down at her, and from deep within him, he would find the power to face his next daunting task.

He thought of the black rock to the far north. Somehow, he would have to enter and fight, to free the old wizard and defeat Mordred. His life felt like the table of swords, he had sought the truth and dealt out justice, now he had to gain knowledge, for that would be the only way to defeat the dark family that wanted to kill all he believed in.

His dream to save the green world he knew and loved was not over as long as the name of Knox was spoken, bricks and stone would fill the land, and trees of green would be cut down and burned. His fight continued and his search for a true king of the Britons would wait a little longer.

The lake mirrored yellow as dawn broke above him, and he headed slowly back up the glade to his wooden home. Wearily he climbed the stairs, and walked into the bedroom where Rune was sleeping. She opened her bright blue eyes as he slipped under the warm sheets and she smiled at him. "Hi gorgeous."

He smiled back. "Hey beautiful."

Toby breathed hard as he walked down the road. It was hot for September, and he wiped the sweat from his face, as he came trudging down past the small stone cottages, with their old wooden doors and rattling windows, and headed along the harbour to the far end, where he saw the mast bobbing about as the water rose and fell.

"Bout bloody time, I don't know what the hell you're playing at, you should have been here three weeks ago.... Who the bloody hell are you?"

The tall woman with long flowing blonde hair looked up at him, her violet eyes shone deep in her bronzed face, she smiled, she was good looking there was no doubt, and shapely. His eye wandered across her small pale blue crop top, which did not hide the secrets of her bosom, the pants were just as tight and fitted against her, showing the shape of a fit and well toned woman. She gave him a large smile that would melt the heart of any man.

"Hey there, are you Toby?"

He just nodded, momentarily lost for words at the sight of such a stunningly beautiful woman. She jumped on to the ladder in her bare feet, and shot up the harbour wall.

"I am Amethyst; I believe Sapphire has mentioned me. Mum's in the cabin waiting." She looked around the small harbour. "Cute place this... well are you all ready we are running a little late you know? It is going to be a rough sea." She gave him another wonderful smile, and he knew if she told him to jump in the sea, he would.

Her violet eyes danced as she looked around. "So, where are they?"

"Who?"

"The kids, they are coming with you I take it?" Toby gasped.

"Bloody hell yes, I will get them." He turned as Amethyst started to laugh, and he ran up the small harbour, and back up the small cobbled street to the cottage at the end of the lane.

Robbie sat at his desk and looked at the sword that lay across it. The blade shone brightly in the sunlight now streaming in through the window. There was a bright glow about it, as if the rays of the sun were absorbed into it and shone brightly back. Compared to the Sword of Truth it looked plain and quite ordinary, except for the runes that were carved into one side of the blade, and the words 'Destiny will prevail,' carved down the other side. The moonstone, like the line down the centre of the blade, shone with a silvery essence. Robbie raised his hand above the sword palm down, and he felt the power of the sword surge towards it, the hairs on his arm rose with the electric energy that seemed to radiate around it.

He looked across the room at Rune who was sat sideways on, drawing at her desk. Light flooded in through the window, and shone through her hair creating a radiant copper autumnal aura around her, and smiled watching as her blue eyes darted across the drawing following her pencil. She glanced up and smiled as she caught him staring at her. "What you looking at?"

He blinked, and gave her a grin. "The woman I love."

Rune lay down her pencil, and slowly rose from her seat, she crossed the room smiling. "You are so smooth at times Lord Loxley." She came around the desk and dropped into his lap, she giggled as he kissed her slowly. He pulled her close as she rested her head on his shoulder, and he squeezed her tight. "You know Rob; if you stare at the sword much longer it will probably move."

He chuckled. "Sorry... I feel its power, it's weird. It looks like such a plain sword, and yet I know there is something woven into it that almost gives it a life of its own, does that sound odd? I wonder if the Harry side of the family isn't starting to come out of me?"

Rune sat up, and swung round on his lap. "This is the sister of the one sword, it has untold power woven into it. The runes carry the qualities it defends as do the five swords."

"Is that what the runes say, Truth. Justice. Knowledge. Courage. Honour?"

She nodded. "It holds true all the qualities the swords of power have, for this is the mistress of those swords, as Excalibur was their master." Rune slid out the intricately engraved Sword of Knowledge and placed it on the table at its side.

Robbie stared amazed as he saw Rune's sword slide over towards his, as if it wanted to be close. She looked at him and giggled. "I think my sword likes yours." He looked up at her.

"What just happened?"

"Rob, you hold a sword to command all swords, even mine, see how it kneels to its mistress?"

Robbie stared at the golden sword with its long golden rune encrusted blade as it shone in the sunlight, he noticed the handle with its sapphire encrusted hilt, and the finely tooled hand guard with butterflies engraved on it. "What do those runes say?"

She gave him a smile; "It is a very old language spoken long before the age of man." She leaned forward and read it to him.

"Te wak thy pat nay lif, ent hant thy wold en blance. Gant hit nowled ist thy scal ont with al well bo mesurd. Larn by stody yon craf, ent opin yur mynd, ent hert fa on thee kan I bern te brin blance bak te thy wold."

"What?" Robbie looked more confused than ever. "How can you just read this stuff anyhow?"

Rune giggled. "You are funny at times." She kissed him sweetly on the nose. "This is the ancient language of runes and creation. We all spoke like this in the very beginning." Rune ran her finger along the blade of the sword. "To walk the path of life, and hold the world in balance. Know that knowledge is the scales on which all will be measured. Learn by studying your craft, and open your mind and heart, for only then can I burn, to bring balance back to the world... It's quite easy once you get the hang of it."

Robbie stared at the sword, and then back up to her. "I can see why you got it, I did not understand a word of what you just spoke, it is sort of spooky though. You sounded like the Dark One when she spoke the words over the black sword when we watched on your table."

"Well of course I did, it was the same language. It's a bit like the powers we use, neither are good or bad, we both channel the same power, it's just our intentions are different."

"So, she does not have black magic in her?"

Rune smiled sweetly at him. "No Rob, if I sucked out her power it would not corrupt me; it would be made as good as my intention. If I chose to do good; then the power is perceived to be good.... The Dark One has an evil heart, she feels no love, and so her magic contains no love." She kissed him. "I have a lot of love inside me, and I wonder why that is?" She smiled a warm and radiant smile at him. Robbie smiled back at her, as her eyes danced with delight.

"Is that why your Granddad thinks you will become more powerful, because you feel love?"

"No.... It's because the love we hold between each other, is greater than any love known before, even Arthur and Guinevere did not love each other as much as we do."

He gave her a huge smile. "I really do love you Rune."

She kissed him. "Oh, I know." They started to giggle as he pulled her closer. Destiny burned bright in the room with a golden light, Rune lifted her sword, and slid it back into its sheath. "I have a lesson with Jett in a while, what are you going to be up to today?"

He leaned back and stretched. "I want to see Skip later; we are waiting to hear from Angus and his sister. I want to know what is going on in Scotland; I am not keen on heading to that Black Rock place without knowing just what is going on first."

She nodded to him, and he saw her face, he knew she was worried about her grandfather, it had been two days since they had heard from the Dark One, and Rune had not been able to contact him, the table had not been able to show her where, or how her grandfather had been caught. Jade had wept all the previous night, and Rowan had sat with her in his arms and rocked her gently.

He slid his arm around Rune as they descended the stairs of the office; he pulled her close. "I will get him back Rune, I promise."

She smiled weakly. "I know Rob, I worry about him, this is the second time she has found a way to snare him. She caught Gwendolyn who was the fairy queen and very powerful, I just hope she comes for me, I will give her a fight she never expected."

Robbie stopped and looked at her. "What do you mean comes for you?" Rune gave him a sweet smile.

"Rob, she trapped Hearne, Opal, Gwendolyn, and my grandfather to create the age of sleep, they all represent the greatest powers, she has the black book don't forget, there is magic in there from the start of time, I do not underestimate her at all. I am ready for her if she does come."

"You think she will, or do you think she has learnt not to mess with you?"

"I have veiled Loxley to her, I told you, I have also learned the secrets of the black veil, the wheel of Runestone is the most powerful table ever created, apart from one which is not used, and that one lies at the heart of Camelot. Loxley is safe Rob, there are charms of protection placed by myself and by my woodland lord to keep her away, she will never be able to enter here. Everything I love is here; I will not let her harm it." Robbie seemed relieved to hear her say it, his mind had drifted on many occasions to his home and how safe everyone would be. Alice had been snatched right out of the centre of Loxley, it did concern him.

Arm in arm, they walked out on to the front porch of the house, Jade waved as she appeared with Jett and Rowan on the path through the trees. She beamed, and even though they were on the other side of the glade, he knew those bright green eyes danced under her long curly blonde fringe. Jett waved. "HEY ROBBIE, HEY RUNE!" Rune smiled as she squeezed him.

"There is the end of your peace and quiet." She started to laugh; Robbie shrugged.

"Maybe you should have learned to fight with the pole; I could have got Ruby to give you nice quiet lessons." Rune started to giggle, as the group got nearer, Robbie smiled at Jett. "Maybe I should get you a pair of those golden spiked heels."

Rune raised her eyebrows. "I don't need gold feet to raise me in the air." He smiled at her; he knew that with the power now channelling through her, she would have a trick or two for Jett.

Jade gave Rune a hug, and Jett beamed with her usual delight. "So, are we ready for a little dancing with our blades?" Robbie saw the Sword of Truth hanging on Jett's belt; he had always admired the way she had fought with her replica of the Sword of Knowledge. It would be interesting to see how she handled a sword of power. It had certainly helped him against Mason Knox, he had found skills and abilities he had never thought he had.

Rune walked out on to the grass, with her long flowing violet velvet skirt swishing around her legs. The sword hung on her golden belt of oak leaves; he was quite excited as he sat down and nodded his head at Rowan, and sat back in the chair to watch. Jett walked beside Rune talking softly to her, Rowan sat down in the chair next to him, as Jade sat cross legged on the floor. Jett drew the glowing Sword of Truth out, and rainbows glinted across the grass, Rune drew the long golden

Sword of Knowledge out into the sunlight.

Jett in her tight black pants, and long boots with golden spiked heels, faced Rune and raised her sword; she bowed as Rune brought her sword up. The spar was soft to begin with, as Jett worked out what level of skill Rune had with a sword.

They faced each other smiling as Jett picked up the pace a little, Rune parried very well, her wrist flowed smoothly, and the sword swept nicely through the air as Jett picked up the pace, she cut and sliced two very quick blows, Rune stepped back and blocked them easily. Robbie sat forward in his chair; he almost held his breath, as Jett whispered something to Rune. Jett spun on her heels, and unleashed five fast swerving volleys of power. Rune's blade ignited, and she spun round out of the way, bringing her sword across Jett with great agility. Jett whooped loudly. "Go Rune girl."

As Jett spun back round, Rune made her first assault, Robbie gasped as her wrist twisted, and she lashed out at Jett with a series of incredibly fast shots, she almost caught Jett off guard. Jett beamed as she took a new measure of Rune and giggled. "You been hiding your talent Rune, let's see what you really got?"

The real sword fight began, and Jett showed no mercy, she screamed, and spun into the air as her blade moved like lightening. Robbie jumped to his feet, and Rowan grabbed his arm, Rune moved with Flash like response, as her blade of flame blurred with a skill and speed to rival Jett. She spun and wove, her full circle skirt opening out as she spiralled with grace and agility. The bright red long hair flowed behind her like a sparkling cloak, her sword burning bright matching Jett shot for shot. Rune's eyes burned brightly as she smiled and giggled, as Jett whooped and screamed with her strikes and lunges, working faster and faster. Both blades were now a blur as Jade jumped up on to her feet.

"GO RUNE!" She bellowed, as she jumped on the spot, Rune was now almost a blur of violet she was moving so fast, and Jett seemed be just a black streak, flashing and spinning. Robbie could hardly tell who was who, or where they were as they fought faster and faster, black and violet were becoming one, as gold and fiery flame flickered from their blades.

The three watched in disbelief, as Rune vaulted into the air, and landed on her feet behind Jett, who spun round laughing wildly, and she raised her sword and bowed to Rune. They dropped their swords into their sheaths, and hugged each other, then turned laughing and smiling to the group on the porch; all three of who stood looking shocked.

Rune smiled brightly her eyes dancing a bright happy blue, as slightly breathless, she came up the steps, and pulled Robbie into an astonished hug. "I enjoyed that." She kissed his cheek. Jett walked up and breathing heavily she patted Robbie on the shoulder.

"The girl can fight." She giggled looking at his bemused face. Robbie looked at Rowan, and he shrugged and smiled, Robbie looked into the house where Rune was coming out of the kitchen with a tray of tall drinks.

"How the hell did you just do that?" She smiled sweetly as she gave him a glass of lemon grass cooler.

"Robbie I am of the line of Opal and Merlin, of course I can fight. My grandfather is an excellent swordsman, and so was Opal in her time, it looks like I have inherited a little of their ability."

"That was not a little ability Rune, you matched the most impressive swordswoman I have ever seen strike for strike."

Jett beamed, stood up, and kissed Robbie on the cheek. "Hey Robbie, that is such a cool thing to say, thanks." He looked at Jett.

"You knew, didn't you?"

Jett beamed at him. "A little bit... Yeah... Opal taught my mum, so I did think Rune would have good ability, I loved it, and she gave me a better work out than Blades."

Rune slipped her arms around him. "You wanted to make sure I would be able to take care of myself, well sweetheart now you know. Rob, I carry the Sword of Knowledge, it would not come to me if I could not wield it." She kissed him softly and giggled. "You do look funny... come on sit down and have your drink."

He sat down as the three girls smiled at him, and took a long swig from the glass, and looked at Jade who gave him a big grin. "You too?" She giggled as she slid on to Rowan's lap.

"I prefer my knives and bow, but I can handle a sword if I have too."

He sat back in his chair, and looked over at Rowan. "You ever think we are being ganged up on?" Rowan began to laugh.

"Robbie my good friend, we chose sisters of a powerful family, I can't believe you are surprised."

Robbie nodded to himself as Rune slid onto his lap and hugged him. "You are so lovely at times you know?"

"I sometimes wonder what I got myself into?" She giggled as she nuzzled into his neck.

The morning passed slowly, and soon the time came to head for the Village Hall. Robbie and Rowan sat with Robert Lox at Robbie's desk, which had now become the centre of the woodsman world. Beside the large map of the country, which showed the huge walls and the concrete behind them, that was the Knox Empire, sat Skip and Treen.

Robbie looked at the map of Scotland rolled out across his desk. The area around Aberdeen, which had been where Alice had been kept prisoner, was now swamped under new buildings, and it seemed that new work was being undertaken to push north and west across Scotland.

"The Dark One has been busy since we were last there Robbie." Rowan looked carefully at the map as he studied the long new wall that ran down past Stonehaven, and the coastline where Dunnottar Castle perched on the small island, just off the headland.

He sat back in his chair and looked at his father. "The whole coastline has now been rebuilt, and I cannot see how it will be possible to gain access to the castle without being detected."

Robert nodded. "That is a rough sea according to Skip, I am not sure you will be able to just row up there and throw up a rope lad. That is a rough bit of rock, and I will bet you your last bit she will have this place guarded better than any of Mason's hold ups."

Robbie nodded, he knew she was waiting, and possibly expected an attack before the month was up. It seemed impossible; once again he felt the sinking feeling of needing to know more about the place he needed to get to. This was not going to be the sort of place he would find out about easily.

The Dark Rock had just appeared almost overnight. It was a tall castle heavily fortified and built using magic, very few crossed the long black bridge that stretched out across the crashing waves from the mainland. Robbie knew the only way he would find out enough to find a way in would be to actually go and look at it. So far, the only ones who had seen it were Sinclair Forbes and Rose Macintosh, and their reports were late arriving at Loxley. Skip had not said much, but Robbie knew he was worried about their lateness. Angus had sent word that he had not yet met up with them, and was waiting for them at the rendezvous.

The room buzzed with activity as Robbie sat back and watched. Lucy appeared with a bag full of letters, which she handed to Treen, she waved from the other side of the busy room, and he gave her a smile as he waved back. He watched, as Treen sorted the mail and passed half to Skip, while she handed small bunches to many of the women working on the long desks.

All this work and activity he thought, as his eyes slowly wandered around the room. If he did not find a way to free Merlin, he knew it would all be for nothing. It felt once again like the pressure was mounting, and every time he seemed to finally reach a goal, another even harder task was suddenly presented to him.

Robbie sighed and looked at Rowan who was watching him. "It just seems to get more and more difficult my friend; I have no idea where we go from here."

Rowan leant forward in his chair. "Maybe we should go and see this Black Rock for ourselves. It will save a lot of wasted time Robbie."

Robert Lox slapped the desk hard. "Great idea my boy, I am in."

Robbie looked to his father. "You want to come with us?"

Robert smiled, and leaned back in his chair. "Rob, I have sat and talked till I am blue in the face, while you risk your life for me and everyone here, I want to do more, the way I see it, a small group of us could sneak up and have a peep, then get back here with a much more informed idea. I think it will save time now and later if we look this place over."

"I am not sure Dad; I have always relaxed knowing you were here to run the place if anything happened to me." He looked at Rowan.

"I think if we are careful and just have a quick look round Robbie it can't hurt, although I don't want to be there when you tell Jess." His slate grey eyes turned to Robert, who gave a nod.

Robbie knew his mum was not going to like it at all; he had always been kept separate from his dad, so at least one of them was always safe. Jess was not going to be very keen on the idea at all. Robert Lox leaned forward in his chair and clenched Robbie by the shoulder, the light shone in his dark eyes from a tanned caring face. "Let me talk to her Rob, she will understand how important this is."

Robbie looked at his father's reassuring face. "Alright Dad, have a talk, but please do not go making her more upset than you need to. Tell her we will be looking from a distance."

Robert nodded. "Alright son, leave it with me."

It was a lot later when Rowan and Robbie crossed the glade, to see the smiling Rune and Jade, who sat with Una and Crystal. Jett could be heard in the kitchen as she made drinks, and called back asking who had what? As always, her voice was louder than it needed to be. They came up the steps and Robbie flopped down with the others, Robbie told Rune of the plan and her face narrowed. "You three are not thinking of going alone are you, because we have been talking, and have had an idea?"

Robbie looked round at the group of determined looking women, and then back at Rune. "What exactly have you got in mind?"

Rune moved in her chair. "We do actually agree with you about taking a closer look, and we feel the group must be small. I am going to ask the table what our best options would be, and then we just slip off without saying anything. Under the veil, we will be able to get very close to see what is going on. Rob this is a magical place and you will need some of us because we will see things you don't." Rowan nodded as Rune spoke.

"It does make sense Robbie, we could not see the wall at Liverpool, and yet Crystal could, the Dark One might have something there to catch us, if she does, I would much rather avoid it."

Rowan made sense. "Alright then, just us plus my dad and that's all, this is one trip I want to keep as quiet as possible. I will let dad know in the morning, and we will go as soon as Rune has worked out from the wheel, our best options."

They all nodded in agreement, and Jett smiled up at him. "Cool."

Robbie stood and looked out across the afternoon sun on the Mere. Una and Jett were in the house making a meal with Crystal, and Jade was curled on Rowan's knee in the chairs on the porch. Robbie felt Rune's arm slide softly round him. "What you thinking?"

He raised his arm over her shoulder and pulled her close. "I love this place, for the first time in as long as I can remember I feel at ease inside. She threatens this, and it is getting harder every day Rune. I am finding it hard at the moment to work out what the hell to do. I have to stop that whole family somehow, there are dark times coming, I feel it."

Rune watched quietly as he stared out across the Mere and spoke. She pulled him close and rested her head against him. "I will always be here with you Rob." He squeezed her tight, and turned to look at her. Rune raised her head and he smiled as he saw those two bright blue loving eyes sparkle. He bent down and kissed her softly.

"I know, I love you too."

She smiled, and they both stood and watched the water reflect the pale sun as it drifted lazily over the trees. "We will have to be very careful Rune; I don't want any mistakes like last time."

The small group had a sunlit meal on the lawn and talked quietly, they all seemed a little restless, and the memory of their last trip to Scotland was in the back of their minds. It had almost cost the lives of Saff and Robbie, and it had been a time of great anxiety and worry. Scotland was a wild and barren place now, which still held many secrets, and the uncertainty of it worried Robbie more than he was willing to admit.

As the sun faded into the trees, Rune looked up at Jett as they sat on the grass. "You are a sword bearer and heir now Jett." She smiled as she looked down at the bright sword in her sheath at her side; Jett gave a big smile and nodded as her eyes moved to the Sword of Truth in its sheath. "Jett, I want you to pass the pendant of the sword of knowledge to Crystal. I want her in the inner circle of swords, I want to increase the table of Runestone to bring more of us into the fold and protect everyone. Pass the pendant, you have the sword."

Jett seem to hesitate as she touched the pendant she had worn since birth. Her eyes gave a little flicker of lilac, Rune understood her attachment but now the time of war was coming, Rune knew that her table was going to have to play a greater role, and she wanted all her sisters under its full protection, she had no feeling for attachment, this was going to be a matter of survival.

Jett saw the look on Rune's face and nodded. She carefully undid the chain and slid it off her neck, and looked at it sadly, and then she handed it over to Crystal. Crystal seemed reluctant to take it seeing how precious it was to Jett, she knew Jett's copy of the sword now lay in the room of Rune's table, and now the pendant had been taken from her.

Rune leaned forward and patted Jett on the knee. "I know it means a lot to you, and I am sorry." She raised her arms to her neck and undid one of the many chains she wore; Rune slipped the chain off and handed it to her.

Jett opened her hand, and her eyes gleamed as she saw a small golden butterfly with a runic 'R' on each wing, and was covered in tiny sapphires. She looked at Rune and smiled. "Rune you cannot give me this, Opal gave it you the day you were born."

Rune smiled at Jett. "It means as much to me as your sword pendant, it is a fair exchange, it will give you protection and keep you close to me when you travel home again. I love you cousin, you are precious to me, and this will keep us close at all times."

Jett looked lost for words, which was a first; she looked down as tears formed in her eyes. "I love you too Rune, I love all of you. This has been the happiest time of my life." Robbie smiled and lifted his arm around her, and gave her a squeeze as she fastened the chain around her neck, then wiped her eyes on her sleeve.

The night slowly crept in, and Rowan with Jade on his arm, hugged them all goodbye, as did Jett who was spending a few days with them, while Ruby spent time at Harry's. Robbie headed back in with Rune, he pulled the glass doors closed as Una, and Crystal came inside, and Rune went down to her table to add Crystal as a member of the inner circle of swords. Robbie wandered round as he organised his things, and then quietly made his way down the steps to the table of Rune.

Rune sat with her eyes burning violet at her table. He leaned on the wall just at the bottom of the steps, and watched as the multi coloured star on the white background faded, and a new star appeared. Rune muttered a strange language, and a deep twenty-pointed sapphire blue star slowly appeared on the surface of the white table. The silver rune in the centre glowed brightly, as she spoke names and placed others into her protection. Crystal was added, as was Scarlet; Rune waved her arms as the points glowed deep and then back to sapphire blue. Amethyst and Gwinne were then added, and he silently watched fascinated as she sat alone with her eyes glowing violet.

A picture rose out of the table of a young boy walking towards Opal. He had long brown hair with streaks of red running through it, Robbie watched as the small boy turned and he saw the face with the bright blue eyes. Rune stared at the boy as tears ran down her face; she laid her face in her arms and wept.

Robbie walked up to the edge of the table; his heart fluttered as he looked upon the face before it turned. Was it him as a young boy? Rune shook as she wept, and he walked slowly and quietly round the table. Rune noticed the movement and looked up through tear filled eyes at Robbie, as he stared at the small child in Opal's arms. She gasped a huge sob, and jumping up, she ran round the table to him, and threw her arms around him. "Oh, Robbie I am so sorry, I cannot live with my choice... Oh please forgive me." She collapsed into his bewildered arms, and sobbed with terrible grief, as she shook in his tight embrace.

Robbie stared at the table and the pictures. "What is this Rune?" She pushed her head even harder into his arms and wailed even louder with large sobs of extreme grief. The picture shimmered and faded as a new picture grew above the table, Robbie watched as Rune rushed into Hearne's cave with the limp Jade in her arms. He watched as Rune shook and trembled in his arms, and then Opal and Gwendolyn came into the cave. His eyes fixed on the view as the voices resounded around the room.

It was like watching a dream. A painful horrific dream, as he saw Jade on the edge of death, and Rune pleaded for Jade's life. Gwendolyn gave Rune the option, and he saw the horror on her face, tears filled his eyes, and he watched Rune fall pleading to her knees as the arrow withdrew out of Jade. The arrow was almost at the tip, and he knew within seconds it would hit the floor, he closed his eyes and the tears still flowed on his cheeks as Rune gasped her scream to save her sister.

She shuddered in his arms as he pulled her tighter to him. Robbie knew the love of her sister, and the pain in her voice as she cried into Hearne. His heart broke as he watched his son walk into the other realm with Opal. Rune wept harder as he held her in his arms, he pulled her back and lifted her head, as the tears flowed down from her red eyes. "Rune... You should have told me." His voice was raised more than normal.

She shook in his arms. "I am so sorry... How could I?" She sobbed hard. "How could I tell you I have ruined your life?" She shook as she spoke, and gasped deep violent sobs. "I have lost the one thing you have always wanted." She fell to the floor and wailed in pain and grief. "I have destroyed everything."

He knelt on the floor and lifted her into his arms, Rune clung shaking and sobbing, as he pulled her close. He felt utterly wretched as his insides churned, seeing her this way was unbearable. "We will have Iona and her sisters Rune." His voice was soft and quiet, and it held a great deal of inner pain. "Please Rune, don't blame yourself, they gave you no choice." He held her tighter than he had ever held her, as his tears mixed with hers.

Rune gasped from inside his chest. "I hid it from you, how can you love me now?" She sobbed even harder.

He pushed his head on to hers. "You are my world, my life, my dream Rune. I will always love you. You were cheated as you fought to save your sister, what else could you have done?" His quiet words, softly spoken into her red and golden tinted hair, soaked slowly into her as she trembled.

Rune lifted her face, and her eyes seemed dull with the pain he saw inside her. He stroked the wet hair from her face. "You should have told me Rune... there can be no more secrets between us ever... not ever." Rune slid her arms around his neck and pushed her face into the side of his.

"I am ...so... so... sorry, I have wanted to tell you, but I could not find the words. It was tearing me apart, how could I do that to you also?" Robbie now understood as he knelt on the floor with Rune in his arms, why she had been so melancholy and quiet over the past month. He understood the pain she had suffered torturing herself alone. He lifted her face to his and he kissed her softly and he raised his hand and wiped her eyes.

"No more tears now... and no more lies or hiding, we are strong, and there is nothing we will not overcome if we stand together. I will have six beautiful daughters who will all be as beautiful as their mother, and I will love and adore them all my life. And I will always love their mother more, for the joy they will bring me."

She gasped a smile and hiccupped as her lip trembled. "I have been so lonely and afraid. I thought you would hate me; I love you so much I was terrified you would leave me."

He pulled her close and hugged her. "You should not have had to suffer alone Rune, promise me you will never suffer like this again, you must talk to me always."

He kissed her damp face. "I am sorry Robbie, I promise." He gave her a squeeze.

"Alright then, no more tears. It has happened and we cannot change it, the past is past Rune, no more torturing yourself down here, come on lets go up to bed and put this behind us." He lifted her gently into his arms and carried her up the white steps; Rune clung to him, her head on his shoulder. Robbie carried her up to their bedroom, where he gently laid her on the bed. She quietly sniffled as he pulled the covers over her.

He lay in the dark for a long time with Rune curled tightly around him. The pictures of his son stayed in his eyes, even though he had closed them. He felt a deep tight feeling inside, knowing he felt a deep loss for a child not yet born. He stroked her hair down her back as she lay watching him, her head on his chest, Rune felt his loss and the grief, and she felt his love for her. It was hard for him, and she knew it, and yet he had surprised her, she now felt ashamed that she had hidden it from him and regret flooded through her. Rune had tested the love between them more than she would ever realise, and they had survived. He looked down at her eyes glinting in the dark. "Hey... you alright?"

She crept up and looked down into his eyes in the deepening darkness. "I am sorry Robbie. I really do love you."

He pulled her close and kissed her. "I love you too Runestone Sapphire."

She smiled, as she looked down into the eyes of love glowing before her. "I will make it up to you Robbie."

Hearne stood at the water's edge in front of the house. Behind him the water of the mere gently lapped onto the stony shore, and he raised his hands to the stars, and softly spoke with a gruff voice. "I am the creator of all, and she is life, and should not suffer the rule of such cruelty." His hands glowed violet. "Take the one life that was sacrificed, I command you divide one and bring forth two lives, to reflect the sun and the moon of this day, and renew the life that was stolen. Once in the past, a life was given as forward payment, and now shall be the time for its use." He waved his hand across the house and smiled. The house glowed with a faint shimmer of pale violet light, and as Robbie and Rune made love and repaired the hurt between them, one seed divided into two, and the seeds of new life began to grow.

Hearne smiled as he turned and walked into the trees and out of sight as the whole house shimmered in the darkness. The hooded man would have his dreams complete, and he would do battle for all of them. He was the hope of the world and Hearne gave him his second gift; Nature would now bring forth life renewed. The time of the Violet Stone and the Bright Stone was about to begin.

CHAPTER TWO

LEARNING FROM THE PAST

It had been a month earlier, when Rune raised her arms, and commanded the land around her, and she began to show the true power that nature held. The land rose to her command, and then fell into the sea, as the long wretched line of weary woodsmen had appeared at the gates of Loxley.

That day had been the hardest that either Robbie or she had faced, and she had sat at her table several times over the following month watching the events of the day over and over again. The destruction of Liverpool had taken thousands of lives in one almighty surge of power, and Rune had wiped the whole city away, and the sea had rolled inwards, changing the coastline forever. She reflected many times about the loss of life, it was hard for her to accept that she alone had been able to take so many in a single moment.

The table was now her primary source of information, and she was beginning to refine her talents, and work out what was going on all around her. Robbie had many questions, and now in the early hours of the morning, Rune sat and asked the table to show her past events, her eyes glowed with deep violet light and she focused. Her powers had grown and her command of the table was now total.

"Tell me of Lance Knox?" Her voice carried around the chamber, as she commanded the table.

Robbie had spent the day sat with her and Judy as he asked about Lance. Rune now needed to know if she could help Robbie discover the fate of the boy with the long blonde hair, who had fallen over his legs in the corridors of the building at Liverpool.

The violet light spilled out of her eyes and on to the table, it swirled around and then began to clear into the pictures she would be able to read. Slowly they appeared out of the swirling light, and she saw Mason Knox sat in the room where she had watched him fight Robbie.

He sat by the fire with his son as he sipped from his glass; the light bounced off his face, and flickered with yellow and orange. He smiled at his son. "Sound." Rune commanded the table, and the voices echoed around her.

"You must not concern yourself with your sister, she has left us forever. We need to look to the future and the line of Knox, you are still young, but never ever let anyone gain the upper hand on you Lance, remember you are my son, and a Knox. You hold your head high and bark out your orders, and believe me boy; they will do as you say, you have the power I have built here, use it. I am proud of you; above all of them you are most like me."

Lance sat back in his chair and watched his father with pride and adoration. "What do we do about Billy? He is in there somewhere, I miss him, he was funny, and that one is nasty and bloody miserable."

Knox smiled. "Not much of a fan of your uncle then? I have no idea, what the hell does she think she is doing bringing him back? I suppose she has some idea, just as long as she keeps him up there and out of my hair, I don't mind. He is a creepy bastard that is for sure."

"I like mum, she is nice to me. Mac's a bit stupid, but he has been helpful. He is not happy about me bossing him around, but he does get things done." Mason smiled more to himself as he sipped on the whiskey.

"You will be the future of this family Lance; you must remember that the power of our line runs in the female. You must have a daughter to enforce your position, I want you to leave here and go back to the house in London, I have matters here to finish, and then I will join you. Take your new mother and care for her, she has the seeds of our future in her. You must protect your new sister and keep her hidden, leave your dear uncle to the hooded fool and his witch; we can progress faster while he keeps them busy."

"The hooded man is growing stronger, are you not a little bit worried about him dad, you know what the prophecy said? Even Gran takes him seriously especially considering the group he has around him."

"Opal can breed as many offspring as she wants, she has never had enough little witches to protect him. I will be happier letting Mordred deal with him for now, if needs be I will deal with all of them when the time comes. You just get to the manor house with Dana and keep her safe for me."

The door opened and Edgar came running in, he looked fearful, and his eyes were wide. "You told me they would never find out?" His voice had the tones of accusation, as he glared across the room at Mason.

Mason looked at his younger son. "Go my boy, I will come along shortly." Lance looked from Edgar to his father.

"Is everything alright dad?" Mason gave him a broad smile, and took a large swig of his drink.

"Everything is fine Son, go on and take your mother to her new home." Mason pulled Lance into a hug, and patted him roughly on the back, Lance smiled as he made his way towards the side door, and Mason turned on Edgar. "What the hell are you whinging about now?" Lance slipped through the door and into the long corridor.

He walked quickly down the steps and along the passageway to where he knew his stepmother was, a voice screamed out somewhere ahead. "You promised you would not do that." Lance slowed as he cautiously listened.

He watched the corridor ahead, somehow, he knew there was trouble, and as he listened to the sound of nothing, he thought it better to get a move on. He picked up his pace and began to run, getting out of the place quickly was probably a good idea if there was going to be trouble. His job now was to protect his stepmother and her child, until his dad got to London to meet him.

He ran down the corridor and round the corner, and by the time he realised someone was there, he had hit their outstretched feet and felt himself fly through the air. "HEY!" The floor came upwards, and he hit it sliding on his front for several feet. Lance twisted back as he sat up and looked at the figure dressed in all green sat leaning against the wall.

It was only for a moment, and yet he noticed everything. The hood that hung pressed against the wall, the slim green pants and green waistcoat, the long golden handle to the sword in his belt. The brown laced suede boots, but more importantly the golden leaves of the ring, and the bracelet of silver leaves, handmade to the highest quality, and worn only by a lord. He stared at the surprised face with long brown wavy locks of hair, and the warm featured face with intense brown eyes. The eyes seemed to look inside him and recognise him; Lance knew that this was him, it was the hooded man.

The eyes burned with life and Lance realised why he was here. He looked back up the corridor to the wall at the corner, to where he knew his father was. Should he try to run back and warn him? The figure turned slightly and glanced back at the corner, and Lance felt fear begin to rise, he twisted back to his feet and with his heart pounding in his head, he ran.

He ran for all he was worth, straight down the corridor away from the figure in green, he ran for his life, on feet that pounded down hard on the floor, driven by the need to be free of the fear that the hooded man brought. He flew round the corner, his eyes fixed on the end of the corridor, and as he reached it, and darted round, he looked to the brown door where he knew his stepmother waited.

She sat with Mac, who was staring out of the window. Dana Knox was a dark haired woman of about 35 years old, her pale blue eyes set in her white soft face, watched the empty space in front of her. She wore a long jacket of black velvet, with a satin top and long dark cotton pants to her delicate black boots. She was an attractive woman, and for many it had been a surprise that she suddenly appeared on Mason's arm. She was bored and breathed a long sigh as she waited.

The door burst open as Lance exploded in; she jumped with surprise as he slid his back up against it slamming it closed. His breath came in gasps as he gulped air; he looked across at her as she leaned forward alarm in her eyes. "What is it?" Her voice did not seem to carry the elegance of her outward appearance; instead, it was hard and cool.

Lance looked at Mac, and then back over the room of dull furniture to her. "He is here in the building.... The hooded man, dad says we should leave now."

Mac seemed more concerned than she was. He grabbed all their coats and bags as she rose quite coolly. "It will be alright Lance honey." She walked calmly towards him and pulled him close, "you lead the way, and we will follow." She took the long heavy black cloak from Mac, and swung it around her shoulders.

Rune sat back at her table; she was more than surprised at seeing that Mason had married again. She could see the coolness of the woman, and she understood the woman craved power. She leaned forward to get a closer look as the woman carefully controlled the situation, and helped Lance out of the door and down the long corridor. She barked her orders to Mac, who jumped about with each command and nodded politely.

Rune could see the woman was in complete control. "Hold." The picture froze, and Rune stood up and walked slowly round her table, her tired bright blue eyes absorbing the frozen face pictured on her table. This was a face Rune would not easily forget, she took the measure of the woman, and could see the authority in her face. Mason knew what he was doing when he picked her. "Resume."

The figures hurtled through two large brown doors, and down a long set of stairs. Rune worked out quickly that this would lead them to a back entrance, and she watched as a man in uniform opened the door to a black carriage waiting in the snow, at the bottom of the stairs.

Mac threw the bags inside, and helped the lady in and then held the door for Lance, he barked a thunderous order to the soldier, and jumped in. The carriage moved off with speed, as the picture seemed to rise in the air and look down from above. Rune watched as the ships in the harbour exploded. She saw the light bounce off the carriage, as it headed at high speed away from the city centre down a long wide road, the horses were lashed to push forward harder through the deep snow, they gasped and strained as they rounded a long bend, and finally Rune had her questions answered.

At the end of the road was a private dock. A long boat was anchored surrounded by soldiers, and she now understood how Mason had intended to come and go from Liverpool unseen, just like Robbie and the group had in Caerleon. The skipper called out his orders, and the crew prepared the vessel, the carriage came to a sliding halt, and the group bolted up the plank on to the luxury cruiser.

It was minutes before the boat left the dock, and with the driving wail of the motors, the boat picked up speed and headed out to sea. It drove with high speed away from the dock, and then the whole picture turned white, as the flash from the oil refinery lit up the sky.

The small figure of Lance stood on the back of the boat and looked back towards Liverpool, as the white light covered the whole bay. Rune knew as she watched him cover his eyes, that he knew that Robbie was now sat on the balcony talking to Knox, and was about to administer justice for his people.

By the time that Rune stood deep in the woodland on the edge of Liverpool and raised her arms in the air, the boat at high speed would be well out to sea across from North Wales. She sat slowly back onto her chair, and rested her tired head on her arms. "End." The pictures faded from view, and the light on her table faded away.

Disappointment welled inside her. Rune knew that secretly Robbie had hoped that Lance had also been caught in the destruction of Liverpool. He still had another member of the family to fight, and she gave a long sigh as she rubbed her eyes and sat back in her seat.

The line of Knox would continue, and now it looked like future generations of the family would be brought forward, Mason had married, and once again it looked like he had produced another heir. This one was female, and Rune knew that as with Judith, the females of his line would have powers. The seeds of the line of the Dark One were going to be sown and grow, Rune would have to find her and destroy her. It sent chills down her spine, Dana was with child, and deep down inside the words of Robbie reverberated around her. "I will never blame a child for the sins of the parents Rune."

The room was dark and eerie, just the faint glow from the tall crystal, cast a brownish yellow gleam over the dust and debris on the floor. The circle of white with the red star was dull on the stone floor, the furnace had been shut down, and the whole room cleared. Now as dawn rose slowly the pale light filtered in through the slit like windows at the top of the wall. Narrow beams hit the tall column of brown crystal, and an earthy glow emitted around the entombed dark figure. The only sound was the dull crashing of the waves below as they drove hard into the rock of the island of Dunnottar.

Merlin hung limp as if sleeping, hung from a hook. He was suspended above the floor, inside the thick casket of crystal, his body was paralysed, and yet his mind was active. His eyes flickered as he searched his vast memory of power and magic, to find the incantation he knew Gwendolyn had once found.

The door at the top of the stairs opened, and the light rushed in. Fragmented shafts of brownish light danced on the walls, and were extinguished, as the door slammed closed. The tall blonde figure walked slowly and arrogantly, down the steps towards the crystallised captive. The smirk on the pale lips and the glint in the black evil eyes surveyed the room with a sinister humour.

"Well... Well... we meet again in another lifetime, and still, you are the fool of old Merlin. How little things have changed in a thousand years." The voice was as cold as the eyes, and malice oozed off his tongue as he spoke.

His pale fingers softly stroked the crystal walls of Merlin's prison, and he walked slowly round watching with glee, a happy sinister smile on his face. "I know you can hear me Old Man, I want to talk with you about the others."

Merlin remained unmoved, the mention of his daughters resounded through his head, and yet he was not foolish enough to let Mordred know. Merlin watched through his closed eyelids, he had the sight, and he knew the Dark One knew it. Had she told her spawn of evil? He was not entirely sure, as Mordred stared through the brown glass of crystal at him hanging inside.

"It will not pay to ignore me Old Man; you should be wise and help me, for refusal will bring pains beyond even your time of creation." Mordred stared with the cold eyes of darkness, yet Merlin remained calm and quiet inside. He knew that for now he was safe, she would need the black book, and then it would be hard for her to touch him. She had tried for almost a thousand years, yet she could not break him. During the age of sleep, he had fought her, as had Gwendolyn and Opal, and now it seemed she would try to pick up again where she had left off.

Mordred walked around the block of crystal and Merlin noticed how he skirted the red star on the floor, Mordred seemed to fear it. He felt a surge of peace grow inside him; the symbol of his line still frightened the boy, as it had all those years ago.

Mordred slammed his arm into the crystal. "Answer me Old Man when I speak to you. You are a captive of the Black Rock; I command you now." His voice was deep with anger, and yet Merlin smiled inside, Mordred was still the attention seeking brat he had always been, Merlin knew how to deal with that.

Mordred seemed angry with the captive, and it showed in his face, he kicked out at the wall of crystal, and side stepping the circle on the floor he stormed up the stairs, and the door swung open casting a moment's light across the floor. It slammed shut cutting the light away, and returning the room to the dim light of the pale sun.

Merlin's green eyes shone in the dark as he smiled. He hurriedly began to whisper the strange words of an old language and his hands twitched. A butterfly with purple wings flew into the room through the window; it fluttered across to the wall of crystal and landed directly in front of Merlin's face. The green of his eyes seemed to intensify as he hurriedly continued to murmur his strange language, the butterfly flapped its wings slowly, the small markings of white flickering in the dim light.

He finished and nodded to the insect that flapped its wings hard, and took off out of the window. It lifted into the heavy breeze blowing in off the sea, and carried by the wind, it blew past the tall tower of black rock, over the sinister black bridge, back onto the mainland. It began its journey, as it lifted over the endless lines of concrete and stone, and headed southwest to the trees and the safety that would take it to its journeys end.

Rune sat at her table with a blue twenty-pointed star and smiled. She had awoken in the night and felt life burning around her, she was nature and sensitive to these things, and she had felt the power of her grandfather of the woods around her house. A happiness rose inside her like she had never known, and now in the middle of the night she sat at her table, as Robbie slept upstairs.

The purple mist twirled up into the air as she thought, her eyes flashing violet and spilling out on to the table. Pictures started to form in the swirling cloud; Merlin stood on the mainland side of the long black bridge and looked out across the water to the castle. His long white hair blew in the breeze behind him; his pale green eyes stared into the darkness of the island of black rock. Rune watched closely, why was he even there? He was supposed to be in London, and he knew it was foolish to go so close, and she could not understand why her grandfather would do something so stupid.

A white hand appeared on his shoulder, and Rune relaxed to see Opal behind him. Opal opened her arms to embrace him and Rune smiled to herself, she knew how hard it had been to let Opal go, and how much he had missed her. Merlin turned, and smiled as he embraced his wife, the white figure of Opal reared up and turned black, and Rune jumped from her seat with fright, as she saw the Dark One engulf Merlin, and fly across the long black bridge with him to the black castle.

Her heart pounded as she realised how easily her grandfather had been caught. She dropped to her seat with a bump, and put her head down as the pictures faded from the table. She sat quietly for a long time as she realised she now had the confirmation she needed to know, her grandfather was indeed a prisoner on the black rock, using the simplest of means, she had trapped him, and now he was hers to torture until Rune could find a way to free him. The joy she had felt subsided, as the reality of the situation washed over her, they had no choice now, they had to go and she had to prepare for battle with the Dark One.

It was an overwhelming feeling, and very like the feelings she had sensed over the past few days in Robbie. Was she strong enough or prepared enough to fight the Dark One? From the moment her table had been built, she had practiced to control her powers and abilities, but she was not foolish enough to realise that Morgan le Fey had been around for a very long time.

Her time of trial was coming and Rune was very aware that failure would cost her Robbie and Loxley. Now was a time where mistakes were no longer an option, she waved her hand across the table, and the lights dimmed as she left, and headed up the stairs. She felt isolated and nervous as she slid back into bed and rolled over to see Robbie fast asleep.

Very carefully, she slid up against him and softly pulled him to her. Rune lay awake and watched him sleep; he had surprised her a great deal, her biggest fear had been to tell him about her sacrifice for Jade, and now he knew, and had felt terrible pain inside. She had expected him to grow angry and explode and leave her, but he had not and she was at a loss.

Rune was now starting to understand the real depths of the power of the love between them, it was easy now to see why her grandfather had wanted to study it, and unravel the power that lay between the feelings of two people. In many ways, it gave her some relief to know that such a strong force was there, and maybe that would be the help she would need to increase her powers and face the Dark One. Robbie disturbed in his sleep and her eyes flicked to him, he breathed a long sigh and opened his eyes. She gave him a huge smile. "Hi gorgeous." He smiled as he blinked, his head on the pillow.

"Hey beautiful." She slipped forward and kissed him. He slid his hands around her and pulled her close; Rune took his hand in hers and pushed it down on to her warm tummy. She smiled at him and his eyes widened, she quietly nodded. She felt his hand push against her; his voice was happy, surprised, and very quiet. "Iona?"

The happiness inside her flowed to the surface as she smiled and saw the joy pass over his face. "Iona cannot wait; she wants to see her daddy."

Robbie beamed, as he pulled her close and hugged her; she felt the tears rise in her eyes, as she pushed her head into the side of his. Rune whispered quietly. "Robbie... she is not alone; she has the company of her twin brother." Rune watched as he slid back and lifted up in the bed covers above her, and stared down at her, she smiled at his gloriously dark eyes and nodded.

"But the sacrifice.... a life for a life... my son?" Tears welled into his eyes.

"Robbie the Lord of the Woods came by last night as we slept, he brought the life to me, and this is his decision. I have no idea why, and I do not care, I want your son and your daughter, and I am happy that now I know you will have all you have ever dreamed of."

Robbie sat up, and placed his hand on her stomach and looked down at it. She watched with care, as his face seemed to lighten and glow with joy. He slid down the bed and rested his head on her stomach and she held it and smiled with great happiness, she was nature personified in a human form and suddenly with Robbie, she felt complete.

Nature was the bringer of life, and she now contained life. She wanted to scream with happiness as he slid up and looked down into her bright shining eyes, and she began to giggle. "I am going to truly be the mother of life Rob. Your life, let's keep it quiet for now and just enjoy it between us."

He kissed her and laughed as he pulled her close. "Oh Rune, I love you, anything you want, I don't care, I am going to have my children." She giggled as she held him and felt the joy flow out of him and into her; it was the happiest moment of her life.

Robbie smiled as Robert Lox came down the glade with his sword and his long green cloak. He beamed with delight as he hugged his dad and told him how much he loved him.

"I am pleased too Robbie, we can do something together." He embraced him and patted him heavily on the back; Una watched and looked over at Rune.

"Robbie is happy this morning, what have you two been up to?" Rune beamed at Una.

"I told him the truth, and we sorted it out." Una looked flabbergasted as she looked over at him and back to Rune.

"Wow... you must have given him one hell of a convincing argument." She smiled. "I am really happy though it is out, and you have sorted it; I have been so worried about you recently. Oh, Rune I am so glad you have been able to get through this, I can't believe he has taken it so well."

Robbie came laughing with his dad up the steps into the house, and took him up to the office as Rune beamed with delight. He sat at his desk with his dad as he unrolled the map; Robert looked down at it and traced a line with his finger. "Ok Rob... if you look at the terrain here opposite Stonehaven, you can see it's so uneven and rocky, it has given them problems." He looked up at his son. "It's hard to build on... too uneven." Robbie looked down at the arrow shape that the wall of the black city ran round, it pointed to the old city of Stonehaven, below which he saw a few miles south was Dunnottar, with its small island on which he knew the castle of the black rock had been built.

His father ran his finger back to a large hill called Trusta. "There is an old ruined sheep herders hut about half way up here, which is where Angus should be waiting for his sister, we need to get there so we can have a chance of meeting either him or her. They know a route into the city that will get us close enough to see the rock; it's all woodland here so we should have good cover."

Robbie studied the map carefully. "We have to enter a city, isn't that going to be a bit tricky?"

Robert Lox shrugged. "They have been getting regular reports to us, so it must be safe. They must have some way in and out, because Angus has been to Loxley twice now with information from inside." Robbie sat back in his chair and stared at the map. He was not convinced, he knew too little about the Scottish side of things, and it had always worried him. Robert smiled.

"Look Rob if it is too risky, we will just come straight back, Ok?" Robbie gave a big sigh.

"I must admit their lateness has bothered me; I am not keen about walking into a trap Dad."

It was an hour later when they all sat on the porch as Rowan and Jade appeared through the trees. They happily walked across the glade followed a few moments later by Rafe and Jett, the group gathered on the porch, and prepared for their trip. Robbie smiled at Rafe, he had not accounted for him and yet he should have known Jett would not go alone. It was surprising how long the two had been together; he smiled to himself as he remembered the field outside Avon and the jokes about Jett eating her prey after the third date.

Everyone was checking their kit and almost ready, when Rune looked up and saw a purple emperor butterfly, Robbie watched as it fluttered in front of her and then settled on her shoulder. Rune seemed to understand the insect, and turned to walk into the house, Robbie touched her arm. "What is it?" She smiled at him.

"I have a message from my grandfather; I must go to the table." Robbie looked at the butterfly perched softly flapping its wings on her shoulder.

"I will come with you." He followed her across the room to the panel on the wall under the stairs; Rune passed her hand across the symbol of the star in a circle, and the door opened leading down the white stone steps to her table.

The giant circle with a twenty pointed blue star on it seemed to glow slightly as she entered the room and walked round to her seat on the wheel of Runestone. Rune sat quietly as her eyes flickered from lilac to violet. The butterfly fluttered to the centre of the star, and as it landed, bright blue light streamed out of it into the centre of the wheel. It rose like a column of thick light and formed into the shape of Merlin.

He turned and looked at her and smiled. "Hello Granddaughter, I am glad my messenger has reached you safely. I know you and your hooded man well enough to know that you will be preparing to come and find me. I am caught on the black rock and this is not a place you should come to."

Rune looked at the old face and she smiled. "I will not leave you in her grasp Grandfather, no matter what you say. You are family and Robbie and myself are as you put it, preparing already."

He looked around and saw Robbie staring into the centre of the table. Robbie nodded at him, and he turned back to her. "Runestone, she has grown very powerful, you must take care, although she has made one very big mistake. She has a wheel of Carnac here on the floor; it's part of your circle and you can use it to travel here. I cannot warn you; I am in a prison of Crystal, and unable to move out of it. She is trying to hold my powers in until she can find a way to drain them, but she will need more than mere study of the black book to steal my power, I have power from the Whitelines of time, and she will not overcome me as she did my gentle Gwendolyn."

"Can I use this wheel to protect you grandfather? If it is of our line, will it not give you the same protection as it does my sisters of the circles?"

"Runestone please do not worry, I would have to be contained in the circle and I am not, but I have other ways of protecting myself. You must understand that she has placed protection you will not see around the castle. I did not feel anything and walked into her trap. You must not cross the bridge, as you approach, she will know you have entered her realm and she will lie in wait for you."

"Grandfather we will find a way to get you out, she has given us a month to let her know what our terms are so we have the time to help you, we will find a way to get to you do not worry."

"Runestone the butterfly will show you the way, watch it on your wheel and it will guide you." The picture of the old man faded, and the blue light swirled on the table, as the room containing Merlin appeared. Rune gasped as she saw the tall cube of brown crystal, Robbie recognised it instantly, as it had lined the cave he had been trapped in at the side of the river. Now he understood, as did Rune why she had not been able to contact her grandfather, he was contained.

Rune studied the whole room carefully; it was the same room which Victor had made the sword of Dunnottar in. She saw the red five pointed star contained within Gwendolyn's white circle, Rune smiled, she saw the mistakes of the Dark One and it gave her hope.

The pictures faded and the butterfly fluttered off the table and up into the air, Robbie watched as it flew past him and up the stairs back to the outside. Rune smiled sweetly as she walked up and slid her arms around him. He pulled her close. "He is alright for now Rune?"

"I will find a way of getting him out of there Rob. She is already making big mistakes; it will take her a long time to overcome grandfather. Come on let's go and have a look at her house, and see if we can find a way in." She kissed him softly and smiled sweetly. "Are you happy?"

He pulled her close and looked into her bright blue dancing eyes. "I am very happy, and I love you more every moment we are together." She slid her head into him.

"I truly am sorry for my mistakes." He kissed the top of her head.

"We have learned a great deal from it, so let's put it behind us Rune, we have a future with our children." She pulled back and he kissed her as his eyes danced with happiness. They walked arm in arm up the stairs and gathered their bags. Robbie lifted his bow and looked at the group. "Are we ready?"

They all nodded and he gave them all a smile. "Let's go." Rune walked in front as they made their way across the grass to the edge of the trees. She waved her hand, and two trees leaned over to meet in the centre and form a large archway. Her eyes began to glow, violets ran up the tree and round the archway and down again to the floor, the centre shimmered lilac and she stepped through, everyone followed and found themselves in a tree clad area in the pale cloudy light.

It was chilly, and a strong breeze blew across the sky stirring the tops of the trees. Far off in the distance, the sounds of screeching seagulls could be heard, and Robbie smelled the familiar smell of sea air and pine. He looked back at his dad. "Welcome to Scotland." Robert Lox gave him a broad grin.

The group were all close together crouched low, as Robbie scanned through the long rows of trees. The pines were dense and the light levels low for the time of day, Robbie took a deep breath as the deep carpet of needles crunched under his foot, and the damp sticky resin filled air flowed into his lungs. The feel and smell of the pine forest was much heavier than that of his woodland at home.

Rowan and Jade were alert, ready for their commands. Robbie looked to Rune. "Anyone around?" Her eyes closed as she scanned the area, he watched with a smile as faint lilac flashes bounded from under her eyelids, and flashed across her white cheekbones.

Robert Lox watched his son for the first time in a situation of control and authority, John had already spoken to him a great deal about Robbie, and had been very impressed with the way in which he led from the front, and had the respect of everyone.

Rune looked up. "Two hundred yards up front there is a single person, they are quite still, so I would imagine they are hidden and waiting."

Robbie looked at Rowan. "Angus?" He pointed, and Rowan instinctively knew. He slipped off with Jade out of view. Una and Crystal slid into the bushes, as Jett and Rafe melted across the gap on the opposite side of the trees; Robbie looked back at his dad. "Won't be a minute, better make sure before we head on off." Robert smiled, and nodded to his son.

It was ten minutes later when Jade appeared next to Robbie. "Rowan is with Angus just down the path. There is a large group of tall holly bushes next to an old shed thing, and he is under them, he has dug out a little sort of bunker, it's quite cool although it only fits two." She smiled her green eyes dancing.

Robbie looked at the others. "Ok we will move down towards him and see what he knows." Robbie gave the hand signals and they moved forward keeping within the cover of the trees. There were large areas where the pine thinned and light streamed brightly down towards the floor, holly and birch with the odd beech raced up to the canopy trying to get a foothold, before the pine grew back and stole the light.

Rowan and Angus stood out in the open with their backs to the trees, and Angus bowed as Robbie approached. "My Lord Loxley it is quite a surprise to see you here." Robbie took his hand and shook it warmly.

"I thought we would come and do a little exploring ourselves, I am glad to find you well my friend."

Robbie and his father sat with Angus to find out what they could about the current situation. It did not take too long to work out that the Dark One was taking a back seat as her son contained within Billy was now in command of the soldiers.

Mordred was building up quite an army. Men were being drafted from all the cities of Scotland, and dressed in all black with the now familiar crude red raven crest on the front. Robbie was very interested to find the biggest and toughest were being given extra training, and now formed a very elite group.

The Black Guard as they were known were ruthless and aggressive, and there had been stories of brutal butchery and sadistic rape and violation of women by them all over the area. Fear amongst the wood folk was high, and more and more were now migrating west to the outer fringe of the Scottish coast, where he had recently been trying to convince them to return and help.

Angus was getting concerned for the safety of his sister and her partner. They were two days overdue, and he was visibly afraid for them, they had one of the most difficult and dangerous jobs, and Robbie knew from previous conversations with Angus how much he had tried to convince his sister to let others do it. She had always refused, explaining how it had been herself that had set it all up, and she was trusted above all others with her contacts.

Robbie looked at Rune. "Is there any way you can find out where she is?" Rune shrugged.

"Not from here Rob, I would need the table. From here I can only tell you how many people are in the area." Robbie looked at Angus, who looked down at the floor. He put his hand on his shoulder.

"Do you have any idea from which direction she will come? There might be a chance of meeting them on route here." Angus scratched at his stubbly chin as he thought.

"They come up from a town called Elf Hill, it is south east of here down the pass, all I know is that it is on the edge of the wall and they have a secret route into the city."

Robbie looked around at the group who were sat listening as they all kept a watch on the woods. "It seems to me that if she is in the area or in trouble, we would be better off trying to see if we cannot find her trail and give her a lift." Everyone seemed to agree, so Robbie nodded. "Ok we will make for a south east direction down the pass, and see if we cannot find our missing pair of spies. Rune keep scanning and if you get anything let me know."

Robbie stood up and lifted his bow as he looked at the sky. "The weather is on our side for now, although it looks like rain later, so let's move before any tracks get lost. Rowan, Jade, take the point and scout wide of the trail. Dad, Rafe cover the rear. Jett run wide left, Una and Crystal you stay central and I will run wide right. Angus you guide Rowan and Jade. Ok people let's move with some purpose."

Rowan and Jade slipped off ahead and the group moved on through the trees. The woodland was very thick in parts and they moved like shadows along the trail, Rune smiled to herself to see Robbie back out in the woodlands with the trees by his side and the leaves above his head. He moved with skill, and she felt a joy rise inside her, it felt like a long time since her first ever hunting trip when she had marvelled at how he became one with the woods, now she saw him through the same eyes as she followed his lead. Rowan was right; he really did not leave footprints.

They moved down the tree lined valley out of the mountain range towards a fast flowing river, the noise of the water left a slight chill in Rune's heart as it brought back memories of that terrible day. *"Hi gorgeous."* She saw him slightly twitch as he heard her voice in his head.

"Hey beautiful. Are you doing alright?"

"I am fine and feeling happy to see you back in the trees."

"I have missed it; I will look forward to teaching my children these skills."

Rune beamed as she walked along behind him keeping low. *"They will be as good as you, with you as their teacher."*

"Rune you have made me happier than I have ever thought I could be, I have been thinking of names, have you?"

"Robbie I only realised this morning, slow down will you, we have months to wait before they are here."

"I can't wait." Rune giggled as she walked, and Una smiled as she looked across, she knew that Rune was blocking her from her conversation, but she could see by her face, it was Robbie she was talking too.

The valley suddenly fell away sharply and they found themselves heading down through thick trees at a steep fall. Robbie slowed as through the trees he could see the start of the large wall that defended the city around Dunnottar. Rune's eyes began to flicker as she sensed others in the area. She signalled, and Robbie brought everyone to a halt, they melted into the background, as Rune lowered herself down into the undergrowth to try and work out what was ahead. Robbie sat beside her and waited.

Robert crawled over and watched Rune, John had told him all about what it was like to be around the mystical family, but this was his first chance to really see it close up. He watched Rune with great interest, she opened her eyes and he jumped a bit, as the violet light flooded out of her. They faded to lilac, and she smiled sweetly at him and turned to Robbie. "There is a group of about twenty just up ahead, it looks like a deep sort of pass, they have something cornered and trapped at the bottom of it, it could be Rose, I think you need to check it out."

Angus came over as Robbie signalled. "Do you know this deep pass and how to get there quickly under cover?"

Angus pointed through the trees to the rocky outcrops just outside the walls. Robbie pulled out his telescope and expanded it out; he put it to his eye, and looked down the side of the valley.

Black vests stood out against the grey of the granite stone, dried in the sunlight. He could see the pass and the soldiers that seemed to be lined along the top of it looking down, they were big men and very muscular, he handed the scope to his dad, as Rowan and Jade slipped back toward him. Rowan sat and filled Robbie in; he had crawled down with Jade and had a closer look. "I could not see for sure who is in the pass, but looking at the green I glimpsed, it is definitely woodsmen. They are caught behind two large rocks and pinned in place, the soldiers are scattered across the top, we could get most of them with bows, but one or two will need prising out of their holes. Jett grinned and looked at Rafe.

"Hey honey pie, fancy a little rumble with a sword?" She blew him a kiss across the group; Crystal shook her head and laughed, as Jett beamed.

Rowan worked at the detail with Robbie, as Robert sat and watched, Robbie looked up at his dad. "What do you think Dad?" Robert leaned over and looked at the layout drawn in the dust and he nodded. "You have it all worked out Son, let us get on with it." Robbie smiled a huge smile, and his dad winked at him.

The group set off having been briefed. The group of four on the top of the cliff edge were Jett and Rafe's; the rest who were in the rocks would be for the rest of them with their bows. The group came down the rough path, and broke apart as they headed left and right, Rune would co-ordinate, and when everyone was ready, they would attack.

Robbie and Rune slid in behind a large rock, where he could see the whole of the pass. Two soldiers fired, and he saw the shadow of movement, whoever it was had been caught right at the far end and was trapped. They could not easily be taken, and it looked like the soldiers were waiting them out, a good dozen soldiers lay dead scattered around the rocks. Whoever was caught had put up quite a fight, Robbie noticed Rowan slip silently into place over on the far side of the pass, and he smiled. "Rowan is getting really good you know?"

Rune smiled as she watched Jade slide under a log and move into place. "He wants to be as good as you Rob."

"He will never do it." He raised his bow. "The only ones who will ever be as good as me will be Iona and Halbert." Rune looked at him with a smile on her face.

"Halbert... That means bright stone in old runic, how did you know that?"

Robbie winked. "I talk to Hearne as well Runestone Sapphire." She giggled and raised her bow.

Robbie aimed his bow on a group of five. "Ok Rune I will take the left side you take right, and I will meet you in the middle, let the others know." Rune's eyes flickered.

"They will go on your first arrow." Robbie took the shot, and the arrow flew like lightening at the large soldier. Rune released, as Robbie's bow came back up for his second shot, the first soldier took the hit right in the back of his neck, his shoulders snapped together and he fell off the rock he was perched on. Rune hit her man in the chest and he lolled forward. Robbie fired as the others looked up to see where the arrows had come from.

The huge soldier took the hit and much to Robbie's surprise he fell backwards, and then sat back up and pulled the arrow out of his chest. Rune gasped and released her arrow, which hit him right in the skull and the rock sprayed red behind him, as he flopped forward. The other two guards slid down behind the rock for cover.

Jett and Rafe came out of the trees with their swords glinting, the soldiers spun as the golden Sword of Truth flashed and they fell, the third guard who was a giant of a man drew out a huge sword and Jett smiled an evil smile as he headed towards her. Robert Lox pulled back on his string and released two arrows; they shot forward at huge pace, and split in mid-air hitting the two who were sheltering from Robbie and Rune.

Jett clashed with anger and aggression, and the giant soldier, who had laughed at the small black clad figure of Jett, with her golden high heel boots and her twinkling scorpion brooch, was surprised as she brought her blade up at him with an unexpected force. He stepped back with the power of her blow.

Rowan and Jade fired with force, and black clad figures slipped off the wall and fell onto the ground in front of Rose and Sinclair. Rose peered carefully round, and looked at the long white arrow of Loxley. She smiled. "Sinclair darling, we have friends from royal places to aid us."

He popped his head up fast had a look, and then bobbed back down. "Only took him three days to get help here, that's no so bad from Yorkshire." She smiled as another hefty body crashed into the floor.

Two were held fast, as Rafe took on two at the top, and Jett spun with wild whoops as she twisted around the huge soldier with her sword crashing down and swiping across him. He now had several large slices across him that oozed blood, and she seemed to be playing with him, rather than just defeating him with her usual brutal attack style.

She spun around in front of him and blew him a big kiss, as he lifted his huge sword, Jett saw her moment, and with lightning speed she took it. The golden blade twisted in her wrist, and drove up through the soldier's chin, he seemed to shake in spasm, and then he fell shuddering backwards, his legs twitching wildly, he rolled off the rock and fell down into the deep pass. Jett peered over the top, and flinched as he hit the floor with heavy impact.

She turned and watched as Rafe lunged into one of the soldiers and pulled out his blade twisting at the other. "Are you alright Honey Pie?" Jett called over.

Rafe smiled, as he slid his blade across the stomach of the other soldier. "Won't be a moment darling." Jett smiled and wiped her sword clean on the shirt of one of the dead.

Two soldiers remained hidden in amongst the stones, and so low down it was impossible to get them with an arrow. Jade peered down and rolled over to talk to Rowan. "I could drop down from the other side and get them with a knife."

Crystal came up at their side. "Let me convince them." She brought her silver bow up, and fitted her long silver arrow. The arrow sped like a flash across the pass; it hit the wall and vibrated, before spraying snow into the gap behind the stone. The two figures jumped, but froze in mid-air, their clothes hardened by the creeping white frost that covered them. Crystal smiled. "Bout time this lot chilled out." She winked at Jade who beamed a huge smile, and looked back across at the frozen soldiers.

Robbie appeared at the top of the pass, and as he looked around, the group all signalled the all clear; he nodded to them all and looked below him. "This is Lord Robert of Loxley woodsmen, you are safe to move out, we have you covered."

The voice of Rose came up from the bottom of the pass. "Show yourself Loxley and I will judge my own safety."

Robbie moved forward. "Very wise of you Rosie, but make haste we have little light left."

Rose peered over the stones, and saw at the head of the pass stood silhouetted, the hooded figure of Robbie, Angus walked up to his side and waved. She gave him a huge smile and stood up. "Greetings My Lord, and welcome to Scotland." She walked smiling up the pass, followed by Sinclair.

They came up the side of the rock together, and Angus snatched his sister into a warm embrace, Robbie offered his hand to Sinclair who bowed. "My Lord I am honoured." Robbie grabbed his hand and shook it vigorously.

"Me too... It's not every day I get the chance to personally thank the two people who take the greatest risks for my cause." Rune smiled at Robbie, she loved to see him completely wrong foot people by being everything you would not expect of a lord. He turned to her and winked. "This very stunning woman here Sinclair is the Lady Runestone, Oh and this chap coming up the path is my dad." Sinclair bowed to Rune not entirely sure how to react. Robbie beamed a huge smile as he looked around the rocks. "I am becoming really fond of Scotland."

CHAPTER THREE

COMING FULL WHITE CIRCLE

As the light began to fade, and if you had keen eyes, you would only just notice the dark hooded figures that wove through the tall large rugged boulders, and rocks towards the remains of the small town of Elf Hill, right at the edge of the large black wall of the Dark City.

Elf Hill consisted of a few houses, which were mainly inhabited by the elderly who were of no use to the army of Knox. They scratched out a poor living on what little soil they had, and it was the resistance movement of the woodsmen, who helped keep them alive. This small group of elderly members of the resistance were vital in the link between the city and the green world.

Rose led the way, as they headed into a small grove of young sapling trees, which was obviously going to be an orchard in the future, as Robbie noticed the rows of cherry, damson and apple. They came to a halt behind an old stable, and Rose signalled to wait, she scurried across the yard to the half dilapidated old cottage.

Robbie watched through the dim light, as Rose tapped out a signal on the door. It opened a nick, and there were soft whispers, the door swung open and the lamp was turned down as she gave the signal, and they began to move quickly across the yard and in through the door.

Robbie entered the old kitchen, and peered round at the aged smiling face of a woman who must have been at least eighty. She gave him a big smile and pointed to another door, and a set of steps that led down under the house. "This way Laddie, and mind yeah feet."

Robbie headed on to the stairs, and moved down slowly into the basement where Rose was undoing her cloak, her long black hair flowed down the back of her shoulders. She turned and looked up with pale blue eyes and smiled. "This is our first safe house My Lord, we will eat and rest here while I contact the other members of the group and find out who got away."

Robbie reached the bottom of the stairs, and looked around the large room of the cellar. The walls were polished like glass, and he knew well the crystal that prevented power from passing through, the room looked like it was used a lot, with rows of small beds and a few old wooden tables. Extra swords and arrows were stacked in a corner, and small candle holders had been fashioned out of old tins and hung on the beams that supported the floor above them. He undid his cloak as Rose busied herself, and he sat down at the table as the others came down one by one.

Jett looked around with an air of disapproval at the conditions. "Cosy," she sarcastically smirked as she sat at the table with Robbie. Rune slid down at his side and looked round as she dropped her hood and her bright red hair spilled out over her shoulders

"Well, this place is safe enough; she won't see us through this stuff.... Although I won't see her either, which is not the best of things?"

Robbie took her hand in his. "She will not be looking here for us; I would think she will be looking to Loxley for some time to come."

Robert Lox flopped on to one of the beds and lay back; Crystal dropped her green cloak and relaxed as she sat on the bed opposite Robert. Rafe and Rowan both sat in chairs and faced the stairs, Rowan was not the most trusting of strangers, and wanted to keep an eye on who was coming in. Jade slid down next to Jett. "So what now guys?"

Robbie looked up at Angus and Sinclair. Angus smiled. "We will all eat, and then when we know who made it away from the attack and all is clear, we will then move on to the next outpost... Let your people relax a while My Lord, you are in safe hands." Rowan shifted in his seat.

The food came in the form of a hot broth like stew. It was a little pale in colour and very thin, although it tasted surprisingly good, and Robbie dipped his cob into it and made the most of hot food. After the meal, they all waited around in the dim candlelight, Robbie moved over to one of the beds, and sat with his back to the wall as Rune curled up and put her head on his lap.

He pulled his cloak over her and sat softly stroking her hair absentmindedly as he waited for Rose to return with news. His eyes seemed to flicker and he put his head down as tiredness overtook him and he drifted into sleep.

His mind filled with pictures of two laughing children, both with long brown wavy hair with red and gold streaks and bright blue or violet eyes. He saw them run around the glade back at Robbie's Mere laughing and screaming with fun in their eyes, and he felt a joy inside him grow with each moment. The feeling of Rune passed through him, and he felt her inside him, her love mingled with the love he now felt all around him. Faint lights fluttered around the tops of the trees and he looked up and smiled.

"Robbie.... Robbie, come on it's time." He jerked out of his dreams and opened his eyes; the clear happy eyes of Crystal looked at him. "Robbie you and Runestone need to get ready, Rose is back and we are leaving." He nodded to her and began to stir.

Two bright blue happy eyes looked up from his lap, she smiled at him and he leaned down and kissed her softly. "I felt you."

She gave a small giggle. "I sensed your dream and wanted to see it. You are the biggest softy I know," she giggled as she sat up and pulled him into a hug. "It's only been two days, what are you going to be like in nine months?"

He smiled at her. "That's easy.... Very happy."

Rune dropped her legs on the floor and stretched as she smiled at him. "Let's sort this lot out first."

He dropped his legs at her side, and aching he stood up. Everyone was stretching and being organised by Rowan as they prepared to move out. Una yawned as she picked up her holly staff and bow. Crystal already stood at the bottom of the steps as she watched.

Rowan pulled Jade into a hug and kissed her, as she smiled happily up at him and Jett smacked Rafe on the bum as she passed and laughed. Robert adjusted his belt with his long sword, and lifted his bow off the bed, where he had slept with one hand on it.

Angus turned to Robbie. "We will no be going too far, but we need to move swift and quiet, there will be guards on the wall, and it is better they do not notice us." Robbie nodded.

"Have no fear we will keep out of sight." Crystal swung the green cloak of Loxley over her shoulders to hide her dazzling white of her clothes; she slipped up the hood to hide her main of long white feathery hair.

It was not quite dawn and the air was cold as they stepped outside into the yard of the old cottage. Robbie took deep breaths, as he cleared his head and looked up at the clouds blowing fast across the moon, driven on by the winds from the sea, and rain hung heavy in the clouds above them as they moved out. Robbie followed holding Rune's hand in the dark behind Rose. She moved with great skill and agility, and he was impressed with her woodsman skills. They wove past the cottage and down a small track by the hedges of beech; he could see the dark oppressive shadow of the wall as it loomed above them for one hundred feet.

At the bottom of the lane stood an old tavern; a large wooden signboard creaked in the wind as it swung, Robbie looked at the dirty glass and crumbling plaster of the walls. Ivy grew along the roofline and hung in scruffy bunches from the eaves, its long trailing stems looking for purchase to pull itself further along. The uneven stone floor was slippery with wet moss from years of lack of use.

Rose moved quietly up to the door under the rotting wooden porch, which showed the signs of once being ornate and decorative. The last rose of the summer broke as Robbie brushed past, and the petals scattered in the breeze and floated softly to the floor, the rest of the plant was being strangled by the leafy grip of bindweed.

Rose tapped a dull code on the door, and it creaked and groaned as the others pressed themselves into the shadows of the old tavern wall. Robbie heard the whispers, and the door slowly swung open, and she entered. He pulled on Rune's hand and he felt her follow as he nipped quickly inside followed by the rest of the group.

The old tavern smelt musty and damp, the dust in the air from the movement could be tasted in his mouth as he crossed the room filled with silent tables and chairs. Shadows glinted on a large mirror that had not seen a cloth in many years, the pale light of the back room guided Robbie with Rune across and in through the old wooden door with thick white paint.

Rose stood by yet another door, and this one too led to the cellar and they hurried down to a room filled with the scents of stale beer from a past time. Large silver barrels were stacked and covered in cobwebs, and Rose skirted around them, as they all filed down the stairs behind her. She stood next to another very old wooden door, the planks looked black with time, and the pattern of the grain seemed to stand proud with age, she smiled at Robbie and Rune. "This is the biggest kept secret in Scotland, only you Lord Robert have access to this information so all of you guard it well, because many lives hang on the knowledge of this place."

Rose pulled open the door and slowly walked onto the steps. Robbie felt the chill of the breeze blow across him from up the passage that seemed dark and brooding, Rose started to descend the stairs into the darkness, Robbie tried to see what lay ahead of such great importance, and Rune tapped his shoulder. "Robbie this whole place is a thick wall of crystal."

He looked up at the dark smooth surface, but there was not enough light to truly see what the walls were made of, so he lifted his hand and felt the smooth glass like texture. The stairs seemed to go down very deep, and a strange orangey brown light seemed to glow up from the base of the steps and he watched as the hood of Rose bobbed in front of him. No one was really prepared for what they were about to see as they came out of the tunnel at the base of the steps, Robbie walked onto a long wooden balcony and gasped as he looked out, Rune came up at his side and stared in disbelief.

Rose gave a chuckle. "Takes a bit of getting use to doesn't it My Lord?" Robbie turned slowly to her and she gave a broad grin as her pale eyes twinkled at the surprise on his face, Jett and Jade both squealed with delight and Jett laughed.

"How cool is this, Robbie?" Robbie looked out across a huge tunnel of smooth brown glass crystal, it was at least two hundred feet high and below him on the ground was what only could be described as a city of wooden houses, Sinclair patted him on the shoulder.

"Now you see why the woods are empty My Lord, we have moved for a short while. I do not know about this place being called Stonehaven; I think Glasshaven would be more fitting.... Come My Lord, I feel your subjects would like a wee word."

The enormity of the place was too much, Robbie felt at a loss for words as he walked down the long wooden stair to the floor, where row upon row of timber houses had been erected, and woodsmen went about their duties.

He looked around at the sword makers and bow makers, and the arrow producers; it was like a huge encamped army preparing for the last war on earth. Balconies ran down the sides of the walls suspended fifty feet up where homes had been carved into the rock, children ran around playing, and women attended large pens filled with hay where animals fed. The group walked slowly; their eyes wide with disbelief as all of them absorbed the view. Robbie looked at Rose as she walked at his side. "How long has this taken, it is incredible?"

She gave him a soft satisfied smile. "The cave has been here for thousands of years, it is two and a half miles long, and Sinclair's dad, who owned the tavern above owned all of this. When the Cutters started coming about twenty years ago, we pulled a lot of the people from the countryside down here to protect them. The huts came about four years later, and we have just been building it up since, it is a good job considering the black witch decided to move into the neighbourhood a short time ago. We have an old Celtic chieftain here and he told us she couldn't see through the crystal, so it just seemed to make sense to live down here until we can find a way to defeat her. When we heard of the prophecy, we figured if you wanted to kill her, one day you would come here, so here we are My Lord waiting for your command."

Rune gave Rose a warm smile. "This is unbelievable, you have done wonders to protect your people, and we will do everything to help you." Rose smiled back at Rune as she walked along the road at the bottom of the steps. Everybody turned and bowed to Robbie and his men and the children gasped and pointed at him and giggled.

Robbie bowed back, and smiled to all as they walked down the long road to a four storey wooden building at the very centre of the town. Robbie looked up at the large balconies that ran round the rooms of the top floors, and he could barely find the right words to express himself. Rose turned as they approached the Lodge, as it was known. "We have prepared for a long time My Lord; the whole top floor is for you and your men; I assume you will want to bring others at some point; we have prepared the space in advance. There are many who wish to speak with you, and Angus will advise you with Sinclair on who are the best to give you advice. The Celtic Chieftain especially wishes a meeting, he is special to us, and I would strongly advise you meet him before any others. Today I think you should all settle in, and then tomorrow we will plan with earnest."

Rose ran up the steps as the doors were opened and the young woodsmen bowed to him as he passed. All the staff stopped and bowed their heads, as Robbie who wanted to stop and talk was swept past them and up the wide wooden staircases to the top floor.

The place was as big as a London hotel. At the top of the stairs was a long wide corridor with doors leading off either side, Rose led them down the corridor to a double set of doors at the bottom, she swung them open, and they walked into a long oblong room that stretched the whole width of the building.

Brownish light came in through the glass wall at either end, and in the centre was a long wooden table that would seat at least seventy people. A huge brass oil lamp burned brightly, and all the walls around the room were lined with softly covered wooden chairs. Rose pointed to the corridor they had just walked down.

"All the doors off that corridor are for your own people; they will find all their needs will be met." She walked around the big table to the long wooden wall that ran parallel to it; she stood by the door in the centre, and swung it open. "This is your private rooms My Lord; you may hold meetings and relax here. The two doors either side are for your most trusted advisors, I believe Rowan of Loxley is one?"

Jade squealed with delight, and pushed on the door, then slipped in. Happy giggles and laughter emitted from deep inside as Rowan poked his head round to have a look, two small hands grabbed him, and he shot through into the room and the door banged shut, Robbie started to laugh. "That's him gone for the day." Rose smiled.

"With your permission My Lord I have many duties here, please be at home and settle in, you will find food brought up here whenever you will require it. It is simple food I am sorry, but we do have to be careful about what we bring in."

Robbie smiled. "I am overwhelmed at your hospitality, and I can assure you I am very much a simple man of simple tastes. Please thank all of your people for their kindness." Rose bowed and headed out of the door; Robbie turned and looked at the group, they all seemed to be overcome with the size and scale of everything. "Find your own rooms and settle in, we will meet here in one hour."

Jett gave Robbie a huge smile, and somehow, he knew what was coming. "Hey Robbie, technically I am the ambassador for Wales am I not?" Rune started to giggle, and Robbie lifted his thumb and pointed behind him to the other vacant room on the other side of his.

"You only get it if you keep the noise down... Go on Lady Jett, but I mean it, I want you out here in one hour."

Jett reached up and with a huge beaming smile, she kissed him. "I love you Lord Loxley. You do know that don't you?" Jett grabbed Rafe and pulled him to the room; she opened the door and pushed him smiling inside. "Oh, wow how cool is this?" The door slammed shut.

Rune slid her arms around him and smiled. "Jett on one side, Jade on the other, I will never sleep." She giggled as she pulled him to her side, and grabbed the door handle. They stepped through and into the modest rooms. They stood in what was obviously a large living room; at the far end was a large glass window that led onto a balcony. There were two long tables and comfortable chairs dotted all around the room, a door on each side of the room led to a bathroom, and on the opposite side a bedroom. Robbie looked at the large wooden bed and the small dressing table with two wardrobes, all made out of finely carved wood. "This is crazy Rune, have you seen this place? I always thought Loxley was impressive but this place, its mind blowing."

She slipped off her cloak and sat on the bed; her long red hair fell onto the sheets and gleamed. "I will never get used to this life you know; it never feels right that we get all this when you have all those out there living under here when they should be up in the woods."

He sat beside her and took her hand in his. "Maybe one day they will return, when we place the king and the walls crumble, these people will have their lands back. That is why we have this life, Rune they expect us two to do it for them. Did you hear Rose? Tomorrow we plan with earnest."

"Oh god Rob don't... I feel enough pressure just knowing she is somewhere above me, please don't add to it." He pulled her close and held her.

"Somehow, some way, we will find a way to stop her and all her family, I think that as long as we stay side by side, we will do it. I have faith in all my people." He lay back on the bed and kicked his boots off. "We have one hour to think and then we will have to start planning, I want the rest of the team from Loxley with me before I try anything."

It was a little over an hour later when Robbie stepped bare foot out of the room into the large central meeting room. His men were walking in slowly, and they found seats by the window to look out on the vast cave, Robbie sat down next to his father. "It's a lot to take in, isn't it?"

Robert looked up at his son. "That is no life for a woodsman Rob lad, look at em? They are trying their best, but they miss the leaf and the fields. I have no idea how you can help these people, but it seems to me that they think it is your job. I have never seen anyone pushed as quickly as they did you."

The door opened and a young woman pushing a trolley walked in, she looked around at the group. "I have refreshments for Lord Loxley, is he here?"

Robbie stood up. "Thank you, please would you bring it over here." She wheeled the trolley, and looked at Robbie with his shirt unlaced revealing most of his chest and his bare feet. She blushed as her eyes swept over him and he smiled. "That is very kind of you thank you... what is your name?"

She turned scarlet. "My name, My Lord?"

Robbie smiled at her. "Yes, your name, I assume you have one?"

She gave him a small curtsy as her face went a deeper scarlet. "It's Grace My Lord."

Rowan smiled at Robert, as Rune came out of the room. "Well Grace thank you, myself and my people appreciate your efforts."

She gave a very embarrassed nod and turned. "Thank you, My Lord," and she hurried across the room, and out of the door. Rune slid her arms around him and put her head on his shoulder.

"Another fan?"

Robbie smiled as he pulled her arms round his waist. "Not really, Rags is my number one." Rune giggled and picked up the pot and started to pour. Jett appeared looking red in the face, and beaming with delight.

"Oh wow Robbie, this place is so cool, there is a thing in the bathroom that rains on you with hot water." Robert Lox burst into laughter.

"It's called a shower Jett, have you never used one? It's like having a bath stood up."

She beamed with delight. "It is so cool, I am definitely having one of them put in back home, there is loads more room for Rafe than the bath." She flopped down on the chair, and beamed at Una, who shook her head.

"You have no shame Jett Amber." Jett beamed at her.

"Possibly not, you want to try it Una, you know slip Angus in when no one is looking, with a big soapy sponge." She raised her eyebrows. "I am clean all over, and I mean all over."

"JETT!" Una seemed to glow pink as Rune bit her lip and Crystal turned away to hide her smiles. Robbie sat down and sipped his coffee, as he swallowed his smiles. Jade chuckled and looked at Rowan with a glint in her eye.

Robbie sat with the group all around him, and began the process of working out what could actually be done to help. The Dark One was the obvious focus, and they knew that a very large army was also stationed at the castle.

Rune explained her grandfather's comments about the bridge, so a full-scale assault across the bridge looked out. Rowan was keen to spend as much time as possible observing, but he agreed that a small party should head back to Loxley and bring the whole team back together. Robbie wanted to meet this chieftain, and find out what he knew, and so slowly, the first plans for the assault on the black rock began to form.

Robbie sat back in the chair. "After we have had something to eat, it might be nice to have a wander round and get the lay of the land. Let's see if there is anything here that can help us, Rowan I want you and Jade to look into finding us some way of getting on the surface close to the castle, I want to see this place up close."

Rowan nodded and pulled Jade close. "Fancy a stroll in the sea air darling?" She gave him a huge smile and her eyes danced under her long curly fringe.

Dinner was served, or was it breakfast? With no sunlight Robbie was not sure, Rune giggled at his side as he pulled the bowl of thick stew over to him. It was meat but he was not sure what, Robert Lox looked down at the bowl.

"Maybe we should just eat and not ask." He took a small taste; shrugged, and slipped the rest of the spoonful in; he seemed to enjoy the taste and carried on.

"It's been nice having you here dad." Robbie looked up at him, and Robert gave him a big smile.

"Aye lad, I have enjoyed watching you work. You have done well Robbie; these people around you are good folk. It has put my mind at rest being here and seeing how it all works. Rowan is a good lad, I really like him, bit quiet at times but when he talks, he is worth listening to. I thought Jett was a bit flaky, but when I saw her fight, she is impressive, I can understand why you have brought this group together. You got a hard fight coming Lad."

"The odds have always been against us Dad, you know that all we can do is plan carefully, and do our best not to lose too many? I see Rose has the same command and respect as I do, she leads quite a team of her own, I think that is why she wants me to bring in my own. Rose will lead her own group, she will not want us telling her troops what to do, I can respect that."

Robert put his spoon down in his bowl, and looked his son in the eyes. "You are right to trust to those you know. There is little room for error here Rob, your old granddad was the same, and I learned it from him. No matter what the job was, he always had the same people around him, I loved my dad, but I respected him more, I see a lot of him in you Rob; you have no idea how many times you give me the goose bumps when you sound just like him."

Robbie smiled. "He died when I was so small, I don't really remember that much of him." Robert patted Robbie's hand.

"He loved you lad, doted on you he did, every day when he got back from the wall, it was you he would visit first, he always said to me. This one is special lad." Robert gave a soft smile as he remembered his own father, and Robbie felt a surge of happiness to be able to sit and share stories over a meal with his own father. It seemed like it had been such a long time since he had been able to.

Rune sat quietly and watched the moment of care pass between them. Robert treated his son as an equal and more than just his boy. It was a clear sign to her of the respect and the love that he felt for him, would she one day get to witness Robbie be the same with his own son; she smiled to herself with the happiness of the thought.

Two hours later, Robbie walked down the steps on to the ground floor of the

Lodge house. He had left his cloak behind, and chose to walk with just his sword, and leave his bow. Rune had braided her hair back and now walked down with her arm in his. He walked with his team out on to the steps, and once again he was caught in the wonder of the large brown crystal cave. Rune and Robbie walked into the small streets, and looked at how everything worked.

Most of the people knew that Lord Loxley had arrived, but none of them really knew what he looked like. The entire group were treated with reverence, which thrilled Robbie, and Rune smiled, as she knew how much he liked equality in his group.

The set up was well thought out and very impressive. Just down from the large Lodge was a deep well and three large bulls walked round on a wheel pumping the water into their system. All the houses were laid out in straight rows, and some of them were small shops. Rune admired some of the thick winter clothing and the tartan shawls. A small canal had been cut out of the stone and boats were drawn along by horse from what Robbie assumed was the sea end of the cave. It looked like some goods were brought in by boat, and then pulled up the canal to the lodge end of the city.

The air felt fresher, as they had walked for almost an hour stopping and looking at the workings of the city under the stone. The breeze seemed to pick up, and Robbie could hear the waves crashing up in front, he picked up his pace. The cave came down to a long narrow tunnel with two huge wooden doors that were currently slid open, he could see the light of day about five hundred yards down along the canal. Two guards stood with long spears guarding the path.

"Sorry sir this part of the cave is out of bounds. You need special permission to pass." Robbie looked past them at the daylight in the distance. The feeling of a fresh breeze on his face was nice and he felt Rune take deep breaths.

"Tell me woodsman what is it like at the other end?" The guard looked at his colleague and shrugged.

"There is a large fork either side in the cliffs that block out the city to the left, and her castle to the right. The black wall is just above your head so no one can really see the cove. That's why we use it to bring goods in at night."

"Smart thinking, I am very impressed with your operation here, I always thought Loxley was well organised, but you men have something of great wonder."

The soldier swallowed hard as he realised it was not one of the men of Loxley he addressed, but the man himself. "Excuse me sir for asking, but are you him?" Robbie smiled and held out his hand to the soldier.

"Oh sorry, Robert of Loxley." The guard swallowed hard.

"My apologies My Lord I had not realised, you may pass if you please, you have unlimited access to these caves." Robbie took his hand and shook it.

"This is Lady Runestone, and yes my good man I would like to have a little look at the sea and the rocks, that is very good of you." The guard stepped back having shook Rune by the hand; he gave her a big smile as they passed.

The cave was quite narrow at the very end, and Robbie stood with Rune leaning against a small rail. The sun was getting high in the sky, and he now realised it was after midday. There was a large bay surrounded by rough heavy rocks, which towered hundreds of feet into the sky on either side, and the sea pounded and crashed into them. Robbie looked to the southern side of the headland; behind that he knew the tower of hard stone was Dunnottar and her black rock castle.

Rune pulled at his arm. "We must be careful Robbie; there is crystal in those cliffs but not in large sheets, she will have some view through them; we must not stray too far out. If she found out about this place, she would devastate it."

Robbie moved back inside the cave, and leant on the wall. The smell of fresh sea air was wonderful, the breeze was quite heavy, and feeling it blow through his hair made him feel alive and happy, Rune sensed the pleasure he felt and stood quietly by his side as he breathed deeply.

He had been there sometime talking quietly with her about the sea and the waves and the breeze, when he noticed she was shivering, he smiled at her and pulled her close. "Come on let's get you inside, it's getting cold. I will take you back and warm you up. Maybe we should try that shower thing out." Rune giggled and pulled him close as they headed back down the tunnel, and into the large cave and the glass city under Stonehaven.

Robbie walked out of the steaming shower and grabbed a towel. He came out of the bathroom and crossed the room rubbing his hair dry. "Wow that shower thing is quite amazing." He stopped and looked across the room. Rune lay across the bed fast asleep, he smiled and slowly took hold of her boot and gently slid it off. He placed it quietly on the floor and pulled off her other one, she had spent long hours sat at the table of Runestone, and now it had caught up with her. He pulled the covers round her and kissed her softly on the head, she made little noises as she moved, and he smiled.

Robbie sat on the balcony rail with his back to the wall and his legs crossed along the long rail, three feet away sat Rowan on top of his balcony rail. They looked down on the city of huts and the high ceiling of dark glittering stone. Jade stuck her head out to talk, saw Robbie and squealed as she ran back in. "God Rowan you could have told me Robbie was there I would have put some pants on."

Robbie smiled as Rowan giggled. "So my friend, how is married life?"

Rowan leaned back and the happiness in his eyes showed. "Robbie my friend, I have found a joy in my life I did not know could exist."

"Not as quiet as it was then?" Rowan burst in laughter.

"She does have the odd quiet moment I can assure you." Robbie nodded as he sipped from his cup.

"I am happy for you both, she is very special."

Rowan breathed a long sigh. "I like it here, but without trees it feels foreign."

"I hope we will not be here too long, finding a way into that castle could take time, I hope we can move quickly once we have a plan. I want Rune back in Loxley before..."

Rowan noted his sudden and abrupt stop and turned to look at him. "Before what?"

Robbie felt awkward he had almost said, 'started to show.' He looked at Rowan and it was hard to hide the delight in his eyes. Rowan stared and smiled as if reading his thoughts.

"NO?"

Robbie nodded. "We have told no one not even Jade. I only found out yesterday."

Rowan stood on the rail, and jumped over, his face filled with joy, as he pulled Robbie into a big hug and squeezed him tight. "Robbie my friend this is wonderful news, I am so thrilled for you both." He laughed with joy, as he patted him on the back. Robbie had never seen such an outburst of happiness from Rowan.

"You saw the little girl in Rune's table? She will be first, and then will come her twin brother."

Rowan held his mouth as he danced holding in the scream of joy he felt, he grabbed Robbie by the shoulders. "A son to a woodsman, this is the best news my friend, I can barely contain myself. Robbie my friend you must tell Jade soon, she knows of what Rune did, and both of us have been devastated. Jade heard everything after she woke up; she has cried for hours at night; this will heal her in so many ways. I beg you tell her soon."

Robbie felt the tears in his eyes as he watched the sadness and haunted look that had crossed Rowan's eyes, it had reminded him a great deal of the look he wore when Robbie first met him. "We will I promise Rowan." Rowan pulled him into another huge hug.

"There is power around you my friend and it works for the good of us all."

Rowan jumped back to his balcony, and sat back on the rail and smiled as he talked, Jade came out and sat on the rail and they talked for a long time. Robbie felt a little homesick as they talked of Loxley and Harry and all the others, it had felt strange not having them around. Robbie heard Rune as she stirred and walked into the living room. She looked pale as she rubbed her eyes, and as she looked at him, she smiled.

"There you are? I woke up alone and I missed you."

Robbie walked into the room. "I am out on the balcony with Rowan and Jade... Rune I let it slip by accident, Rowan knows, but not Jade. I am sorry I thought of them and with the excitement it just slipped."

Rune pulled him close. "I did not expect you to hold it in for too long, I am surprised you lasted this long." She smiled and kissed him softly. "Will you tell her, or shall I?"

Robbie smiled. "You tell her, she will love hearing it from her sister."

Robbie came out with Rune, and they sat together on the rail. Jade bubbled happily as she chatted endlessly about home and her sculpture. Rowan mentioned what they had in mind for a nursery, Robbie noticed the look of apprehension on Jade's face. She looked up at him and he felt the concern in her, Rune smiled at Jade. "You will make such a wonderful mother Jade; I cannot wait until you make me Auntie Runestone. Although you will be Aunt Jade long before either." She beamed a huge smile at her and Jade seemed confused for a second. She lifted her head slowly, and looked at her sister, tears welled in her eyes, and Rune nodded. "Yes Jade, twins, a girl and her twin brother."

The mass of blonde hair shot passed Robbie with a wail and into Rune's arms. Rowan smiled as he watched Jade weep uncontrollably into Rune. "I thought it was my fault, you had lost your son, I heard Hearne tell you."

Rune realised and felt the pain come out from her sister; she held her tight and stroked her hair as Jade wept.

"My Lord Hearne has found a way Jade to undo what was done. Robbie will have a son and heir to the hooded man." Jade lifted her head and looked at Robbie's smiling face.

She slid over to him and he pulled her into a hug. "Everything works out if you trust it my sweet Pebbles." She smiled up at him as he wiped the tears from her eyes. "So, Auntie Pebbles, I hope you will not lead my children astray?"

"Wow, are you joking? I can teach them to shoot, and throw knives. I will take them into the forest and show them how to hunt. It will be great. I can even teach them to weld and make things... Oh this is going to be so cool, me and Rowan can have them stay over at our place and you two can sneak off and be rude in the woods." She burst out laughing and he pulled her back into a close hug and reminded her to breathe.

The community of the cave city prepared to settle down for the night, and those who looked up saw four happy friends sat on the highest balcony rail of the lodge, talking and laughing into the early hours. No one realised the time, as they had no sun to remind them, and exhausted but happy they fell into bed and were asleep in minutes.

Robert Lox was the first one up, and called to Robbie's private rooms, the cat was out of the bag, because now Jade knew, he figured soon everyone would. Robbie looked at his dad and smiled. "I saw the night I was born in Rune's table.

You raised me up at the sacred oak and presented me to the woods, why did you do that?"

Robert Lox smiled and looked at Rune. "It was something my old pa told me about, every Lox since the time of the hooded man has done it. To my pa it was the most important thing when it came to birth, I felt silly about it at first, but when I took you in my arms Robbie lad, and I showed you to the woods and all the spirits, I felt a pride and joy inside me like I had never known. I felt like you truly would become a woodsman of high value, and I was right."

His manner was fierce with pride as he spoke, and Robbie beamed with delight. "Dad will you stand by my side and show me in nine months when my twins are born?"

"Of course Son, I would be proud... Nine months.... Twins.... Bloody hell Runestone, has he gone and done it?" Rune giggled and nodded at Robert who suddenly beamed with delight, he snatched Robbie into his arms dragging him off the floor, and held him in a hug that would kill a bear. All the time he held him, he smiled at Rune with tears in his eyes. "Another line of Loxley, oh Robbie lad, Oh Rune I cannot tell you how mad Jess will be."

He dropped Robbie to the floor, Robbie's face clouded with confusion. "Why will mum be mad? She was two months pregnant when she got married."

Robert laughed loudly. "She told you about that did she?" He smiled with an air of nostalgia. "Your mum will be mad as hell if she finds out you told me before her Robbie; she prides herself on spotting it long before others do, look at Alice, she knew right away. Beth had not even seen it."

Robbie and Robert Lox were in high spirits when Rose arrived to take him and Rune for his first meeting of the day. They walked down the long stairs back to the ground floor and round the stairway to a back room. The Celtic chieftain was old and so it was easier for them to visit him in his own rooms. Rose tapped gently on the door and slipped in. Robbie heard her voice from the other side of the door speaking quietly, and then she reappeared. "He will see you now; keep it short he gets tired very quickly these days."

Rose opened the door and led them in. The room was neat and orderly.

Bookcases lined the walls, filled with ancient books, Robbie was reminded very much of Sister Mary's office. Rose spoke clearly and loud. "Gwynfor Lyle Osborn, I present to you Lord Robert, and Lady Runestone of Loxley."

The old man with long thin white hair, stood up and smiled, he was of a great age and his face was lined with the years of his summers. He wore long white robes with a pale blue cloak, and for his age he was tall, but his eyes were that of a young man and Robbie felt at ease the moment he saw them. He stepped forward to the desk and took the hand of Gwynfor. "I am very pleased to meet you sir."

Gwynfor looked to Rune and his smile widened. "My Lady of the Woods you honour me." His voice was soft and loving, as he bowed slowly with great reverence, Rune smiled and took his hand, she felt his power run through her and thought of Gwendolyn. She smiled, as he looked her directly in the eyes, as if they were actually talking to her.

"My Lord of the Isle, you have long been hidden." Robbie looked at her, as he noticed the recognition between them, Gwynfor gestured to the seats and then he sat down in the chair behind his desk.

"Well my hooded friend, you have lived beyond the life of my boy, although I must admit you are his double there is no doubt. It is uncanny how alike you are; it gave me quite a flutter to say the least."

Rune smiled at the look of surprise on his face. Robbie looked from one to the other, and Rune took his hand in hers. "Robbie this is your oldest living relative, he was the first Robert of Loxley's grandfather; he is also Gwendolyn's brother."

Gwynfor gave a happy little giggle. "I think my nephew of old needs a little time to soak up the moment." He was right, Robbie was at a complete loss for words, his brain seemed to swirl and then stop as everything crashed into itself.

"Are you telling me I am from the same family as Una and Maddy and Mel?" Rune smiled at him.

"It looks that way Robbie, I must admit I was not sure at first neither was grandfather, but when the white bracelet glowed and you received the sword, that's when I knew for certain.... Oh, and also Iona, that was a big clue." She gave him a sweet smile.

Gwynfor smiled at him. "It is true, let me elaborate. As the good lady of the woods has already said, you are my descendant, and I am the brother of the queen of the fairies Gwendolyn White Circle. She of course, married Merlin and died to save her children from the witch Morgan le Fey. You see young Robbie, it was my daughter who married the Earl of Huntingdon, and gave him a son. She died alas not long after the birth; the line you know today is the true line of half of the family of Gwendolyn."

Rune turned to the stunned looking Robbie. "I met with Gwendolyn when Maddy arrived, the night we stayed at mum's old house in Avon. She told me she had given me the last of her gifts, and when she slipped the white bracelet on to my wrist, I thought she had given me a powerful magical object, which in turn I passed on to you. But she hadn't, she gave the gift of Fae."

"What?"

Gwynfor smiled and nodded. "A bit too fast for you lad, it's alright I will explain. In the old language of the runes, Fae means fairy. My sister passed her crown to Runestone to hold until the true new queen of the fairies could come. Iona is the Violet Isle, and the home of the violet stones. It is the seat of the fairy queen, and one day your daughter soon to be, will sit in her rightful place."

"But Iona will be born of the line of nature, not knowledge and spirit. She is from Opal's line." Robbie had just thought he had figured it all out and now this new old man had completely confused him.

"Also, she is of my line do not forget, I am also from the same line as Gwendolyn, and her power runs through the females of my line as well. My dear hooded man your daughter will become the most powerful force the violet isle has ever seen. The power behind the magic in this world works in ways of mystery, only two nights ago the balance of life was restored after hundreds of years. The daughter I lost after the birth of a hooded man was a high price to be paid to ensure his line. She gave her other child's life knowing one day a new hope would arise, and be put at risk by the dark forces. The Lord and Creator could not interfere, he had to let your good lady here make a terrible choice, and she made it knowing she would risk your line forever. She was very brave; it was too much for my daughter who died of her grief." His eyes twinkled as he paused to let Robbie absorb what he was telling him.

"It was a cruel twist that she suffered, for the Green Lord knew of the life out of balance, but that life was saved for you and you alone my boy. The Green Lord could only use it when he knew your line was at threat. Two nights ago, the balance was redressed and the two lines are now linked together forever, which has made a magic so deep none will truly know its full depths, for nature and knowledge are now one."

Robbie absorbed all he was told, and still found it hard to squeeze into his brain; Rune smiled and kissed him on the cheek. "I know it is a lot Robbie, but it also explains a great deal as well."

"I would have thought that Alley, Saff or Treen would have been the rightful heirs to the isle?"

Rune breathed slowly out. "Robbie Saff was to be the centre of her circle, and by right she should have been. However, my grandfather realised just before she was born that Gwendolyn had not passed on the mark of Fae. When I was born, he saw it on the back of my neck, and he realised that Gwendolyn had marked me and given me some of her powers. She placed her trust in the line of Opal, because she realised that it would increase the power, and also there was a big risk that the Dark One would seek out the others at the stones and kill them all."

Rune lifted her long hair up and turned to him, as she lifted the hair, he saw the Celtic 'R' on the back of her neck, it was almost identical to the scar on his shoulder.

"But that is the letter 'R' for Rune not Fae?"

Gwynfor nodded. "You are right, but in the old languages from before time, that would also be pronounced in certain circles as 'F'. Merlin was clever, and took it as the sign of the rune and named his granddaughter after one stone that was not actually a natural stone. The rune stone is seen as the centre of all life, it is round and used to divine the future, he was clever; I laughed so much when I saw what he had done. I knew then how incredibly smart he was and had created the perfect cover to hide the line from le Fey. Although my sister was equally as clever, for she learned something of the line of the moon and their deep magic, for she was able to pass on a great power to the Green Circle to hold in keep."

Robbie was not exactly sure what the old man meant, but Rune appeared to understand. "It has always been rumoured that she spoke with the seer Sequana before she left, but my grandfather always thought it was just rumours." Gwynfor gave a knowing nod.

"The passage of that kind of power is not a gift of the White Circle, I am convinced my sister secretly met with Sequana and learned some of the secrets to the line of the moon, how else could she mark you with the sign of the Fae to mix with my line and create her successor?"

Robbie shook his head; it was making some sense but was hard going. Rune held his hand tight. "I think it is all very clever. Gwinne said on the night she gave you the sword. 'What was taken would return by other routes,' well it has, and now we will have two very exceptional children. I think it's perfect." She glowed with happiness.

"Alright my children, we must move on to business. Runestone you now carry the seeds of the future; we must act before the word gets out. At the moment of birth, you will be vulnerable to the Dark One; she must not taint this child. You must go to the isle of Iona to give birth, and stay there for a full twenty-four hours to protect the child. It has a powerful magic, and she will be safe, the Dark One cannot enter that realm without being killed. Isolde and Filomena will be there to receive you have no worries they will know what to do."

Gwynfor reached into his pocket, and pulled out a small pouch. "When your son is born, tie this around his neck, it is the Sapphire of Thorn. This amulet has the power to protect, and is linked to the heavens and the realm of Gwendolyn, it is the bright stone of old and has many powers, it will lend itself well to the name of Halbert."

Robbie and Rune both gasped. Robbie looked at the old man. "How could you possibly know that? I only considered using that name yesterday, and I have not even spoken the name out loud."

The old man laughed. "We are kin, I see things in you that no other will see, I am unveiled to you as you are me. If you need me my hooded kinsmen then think of me and we will speak." His eyes sparkled with delight as he looked at Robbie and a sense of understanding formed between them. Robbie nodded. Gwynfor moved in his seat and leaned back. "Have you found a way into her lair yet? For there are two ways she will not see." Robbie's eyes widened.

"You know of these ways and can tell me?" Gwynfor nodded and smiled.

"I am hidden to all but you two. There is a circle of my kin built by her friend the sword maker. He was no fool, and knew what was in the dark thoughts of the sword. It is a doorway to those who wield the blue star of all circles. Now is the time Runestone Sapphire and Lady of the Woods, to bring forth the talismans you have hidden for so long, and as for you my young woodsman and kin, you have the talents of ice at your side, crystals stick together be they ice or powder. Frost has always been good glue to old bridges."

He gave them a big smile. "I do rather like the idea of sounding like my old friend the Green Lord; you will work it out easily enough. I will watch over you from here for now." He gave a broad cheeky smile as he sat back in the chair. "Well I must say, it has been very exciting tonight, but alas I need to rest, my bones are so old they are almost powder, I have but a short time before I am replaced, and I will sleep at my sister's side in the happy realm. Go in peace my kin and prepare, we shall talk more in time."

Rune leaned over the desk and kissed the old man on the forehead. He smiled happily, and took Robbie's hands in his. "Go in peace my kin, I am proud of you and will tell my son of the honour you have shown him when I meet him."

"Goodbye for now Gwynfor, I will speak with you again have no fear." They left the old man to doze in his chair, Robbie pulled Rune close as they walked back to the stairs and she giggled.

"He was so sweet; I hope you look like that when you get that old."

"Hearne, I hope not, he even made Hearne look like a youngster." Rune started to laugh as she headed up to their room with him.

"You are funny at times."

CHAPTER FOUR

THE HOODED FAMILY OF LOXLEY

Arm in arm they walked into the long room expecting to see the group waiting for the day's events. Robbie was a little taken aback to see so many faces look up at him. Sinclair was stood near the door and quickly stepped up. "My Lord we have several leaders of local groups to see you, if I could have a brief word first in your private office?" He steered Robbie quickly by the arm around the long wooden table, and in through the door of his rooms. "Terribly sorry for that My Lord, but I felt it more prudent to keep you clear until you are ready." Rune looked very flustered at being dragged around the room, as she was pulled through the door and Sinclair closed it quickly.

Robbie sat down at the table in the centre of the room. "What do all these people want?" Rune slid down by his side and watched Sinclair.

"My Lord you must understand how hard it has been for everyone here. These people have reached breaking point and have lost all hope; they have come here to seek your reassurance that you will help them."

Robbie seemed surprised. "Sinclair the whole point of me being here is to find a way to defeat the Dark One, why else would I be here? Do they not understand that?" Rune touched his hand.

"How long have these people waited Sinclair?" She smiled sweetly at him as she held Robbie's hand.

"At most My Lady a few weeks."

"Please ask them to wait a little while longer, and we will address them all as a group shortly. Please could you ask Robert to come in?" Sinclair bowed, and left the room, as Rune turned to Robbie.

"Let Una and me deal with the group outside, Rob talk to your dad, some of us must return to Loxley and prepare the others and bring them here. I have to return to my table, there are now things I must do before we approach the black rock. I need to talk to my grandfather. Leave Rowan here to scout, you two will have to decide who goes and who stays." She gave him a soft kiss. "Bye the way... I love you."

He smiled as she stood up, and his father came in through the door. Rune beamed a smile as she passed through the door, and out into the large meeting room. Every face in the place turned to her, and Rune looked out on a sea of all shapes, sizes and shades of green and brown.

"Good morning Ladies and Gents. I am Lady Runestone of Loxley, if you would all please be patient, I will speak to all of you in one moment. My Lord Loxley is very busy as we have just arrived, and there is much to organise. He asked me to please express his apology to you all. If you would all care to be seated at the table, we will commence presently. Thank you."

The assembled group seemed a little surprised that the wife of the lord was to address them; they quietly rose from their seats around the room, and moved to the long wooden table and seated themselves. Rune walked to the tall windows where Angus sat with Una and Crystal. "Where are Rowan and the others?"

Angus rose from his seat and quietly spoke. "They have been taken up into the city My Lady to have a scout about, and look at the castle."

Rune smiled. "Good." She softly touched Angus on the hand. "Please don't leave me, I am terribly nervous." She looked at Una and Crystal. "How are your diplomacy skills?" Una smiled as she stood up, and gave Rune a gentle hug.

"You are doing fine; don't worry we are at your side."

Rune stood at the end of the long table, where sixty faces stared at her. Una and Crystal sat to her left, and Angus remained sat to her right. Rune swallowed hard and took a long deep breath. Her face seemed paler, and her bright sapphire blue eyes sparkled. Her hands slightly shook, and she pressed them into the table surface to keep them still. She took a long deep breath and swallowed. Rune looked up at the assembled faces. "Members of our woodland family, thank you for your patience, it has been a busy time and we have much to put into place. The Lord Loxley and hooded man is very aware of the situation here and across all of England. He has worked constantly over the past months to organise and bring together all of the woodland people of this land."

"Cleared England first though, didn't he?" Rune stumbled a little on her words, as the old woodsman with long grey hair stared with mistrust at her. He seemed to scowl at her from under his thick white bushy eyebrows, as he muttered under his breath. She felt a little anger surge up inside her, and just for a brief moment her eyes flared to pale violet. The old grey haired woodsman jumped back in his seat. His eyes widened by surprise.

Una gently took Rune's hand and held it. She calmed herself, and looked at him. "My Lord Loxley was given the specific task of preventing Mason Knox from being crowned king of all Britain, by his lord, the lord of the woodland realm. If sir, you object with that I can arrange for you to personally visit the High Lord Hearne, and you can complain to him directly." Her bright blue eyes narrowed as she spoke with a slightly sharper edge, her defence of Robbie was fierce. Everyone saw it.

Crystal lowered her head and smiled, as everyone gasped at the revelation that the Lady Runestone could actually arrange a meeting with the High Lord. The old woodsman with long grey hair shrunk back in his seat, as the whole room scowled at him. He lowered his head as the guests smiled. Respect was suddenly abundant and everyone looked with kinder eyes on Rune as she cleared her throat.

"Lord Loxley is but one man with a highly specialised team, you will have noticed but a few of them here with him these past few days. Under his lead, we have destroyed Tintagel, the home and bastion of Knox. We have destroyed his weapon making plant, blown up Windsor where he was planning his seat of power, and disrupted his supply lines across the south. Lord Loxley personally planned and oversaw each of these attacks. It was very dangerous work that cost us dear friends."

Rune took a breath and looked around slowly. "Working closely with Caerleon and the seat of Wales, we have been able to protect Bristol, and planned the attack to recapture Gloucester. From that seat, my lord planned the attacks that saved York and ensured the survival of Loxley, which has become the centre of the woodland people's attention in England. We have fed, housed, and reorganised over fifty thousand people from the south, who have been displaced by Mason Knox."

Una noticed the slight tremble in Rune's legs and squeezed her hand. "You are doing fine, go on," she quietly whispered.

"Lord Loxley was here in Scotland two months ago; having a look round to see what could be done, where I might add he was badly wounded. I am sure Angus here will confirm that to you all. Since that time, he has been in constant touch with Loxley, who have been gathering information that could help all of you. We would have been here sooner, but as you can see, he is very busy and there is much to do."

"Your no kidding girl?" A short dark haired women at the far end of the table nodded her head and everyone laughed. It helped break the ice a little and Rune relaxed and smiled. Her voice softened a little as she looked around at the entire assembled group.

"We would have liked to have been here a lot sooner, we were called back to Liverpool where Knox was building a secret refuelling station, and so we had to take care of that first. My Lord felt it important to prevent Mason Knox from sending his ships with goods and weapons up here to Scotland. It was during that operation that he fought with and killed Mason Knox."

The room was suddenly filled with large gasps and loud hurried discussions between close sitting associates. News of the death of Mason had not reached the isolated Scottish. Rune stood tall and proud, the dim light flowed in behind her back lighting her fiery red hair. Her face seemed paler in the dull light, and yet her eyes burned with life and pride. She stood straight and erect, and all that viewed her saw the elegance, and the refined stature of a very young, and yet very powerful woman with authority. She looked at Una and Crystal, who smiled, as she waited for quiet. The murmur slowly died down, and she looked back up at all of them.

"It has taken longer than expected but we are now here, and looking at ways of helping you all. As I speak, we have four of our most specialist team up on the surface looking at the black rock. It will have a weakness and they will find it. This type of work is slow and highly dangerous, so I would ask all of you here to help this team in any way you can. Very shortly, some of us will depart to gather the rest of our team, who at this time are tying up a few loose ends and will be joining us shortly. You will notice these people amongst you, they are the best at what they do, so please help them if you can, and some of you will be asked to help either Lord Loxley, or some of the other teams that currently operate in this area. We are fighting for you, Loxley is safe, please remember that and try to understand the wealth of work that goes on behind closed doors. It might not always look like a lot is happening but believe me, there is not one single day when my lord is not helping someone. Thank you for your patience, if you have any more questions, my colleagues here, and myself will try to answer them."

A loud rumble began as the whole room began talking. Rune walked over to the window and sat down, she gasped with relief. Una and Crystal flanked her with Angus, and so it began, the next hour passed slowly by as the group sat with endless woodsmen and women from all over Scotland and discussed their situation.

Robbie had sat with his father and talked of Gwynfor and the revelations he had been told. His father listened carefully and gave what little advice he could. Robbie voiced his concerns, which were now growing inside him, about how he was sure that the Scots just expected him to waltz into Dunnottar and kill the Dark One. Robert too felt very much like everyone here seemed to think they would have their freedom in just a couple of days. He felt his sons' concerns, and reassured him that he had to make it clear to everyone this could be a very long operation.

Angus provided paper, nibs and ink, and Rune sat in the centre of a group of woodsmen, and took notes as she spoke. Robbie and his father peered through the gap in the door. Robert patted his back softly. "She has some pluck Rob lad that is a fine woman, and a true Lady of Loxley. She has a lot of Jess about her; you picked a good un there that's for sure." Robbie smiled as he watched her.

"Shall we join her for the last?" Robert Lox smiled, and nodded.

Robbie came out with his father, and she looked up from her conversation, her bright sapphire eyes twinkled, and she gave him a huge smile. The three women who Rune was talking to turned and saw him as he walked up; they rose from their seats and bowed. "My Lord."

"My good ladies, I see that the Lady Runestone is taking good care of you, I can assure you that you are in very capable hands."

The small women who had made the quip that broke the ice earlier smiled at him. "Aye My Lord, we have seen her in action, she gave old McDonald a real reason to think before he spoke, nowty old bugger."

Robbie smiled and moved around the room, he watched as Rune continued with her group, and Crystal and Una, handled several others. Angus talked rapidly, to two large northern Scotsman in the corner. Everyone appeared to be happy and very efficiently handled. He poured a coffee and leaned against the table.

It was a big success thanks to Rune's fast thinking, and he was really proud of her, her group finished and rose from their seats, they waved good-bye and Robbie raised his cup and with a beaming smile, Rune crossed towards him. He slid his arms around her. "You are a big success my darling, I am very impressed."

She smiled, as she pulled closer. "I was terrified. Oh, I do not fancy that again, my legs were shaking for the whole time." He gave a soft chuckle.

"We need to talk about heading home; I want to come with you, I have asked dad to watch here while we are away. I thought we would take Angus and Crystal, and leave the rest to get things moving, what do you think?"

Rune nodded. "I think you are right Rob, when do you want to leave?"

"It is possibly better if we go as soon as we can, I need some time to understand what Gwynfor has told me and you will need to sort out your table. I will organise the group ready to leave. I also do not want us separated for a moment; I have two more to watch over now." He smiled as he spoke and she cuddled into him.

"Rob, you have to calm down it's going to be months yet."

He kissed the top of her head. "I know I am just so very happy."

The preparation was made quickly. They travelled back up to the old tavern, and there in the dust covered main bar, Rune opened her violet window, and they quickly stepped through on to the glade of Robbie's Mere. Rune focused her mind as she walked, and she contacted Melanie and Saff, and told them of the plan and to gather everyone back up at the house by the evening. Rune went immediately to her table.

Robbie welcomed Angus into his home. "Make yourself at home; there is little we will be able to do until this evening so just relax." He went up to his office and sat alone, where he could finally think about the words of Gwynfor. It had all been a big surprise, and he found a lot of it hard to understand. Crystal gave Angus the tour; he was greatly impressed with the house. She sat with him on the seats at the front of the house and filled him in on more of the detail of the events of recent times. News of Robbie's team of specialists had reached the Scottish, and he wanted to learn more about their abilities, his short time with them earlier in the year had been quite a learning curve.

Rune sat by her table and took a deep breath. "Show me the star from Carnac," her eyes burned a deep violet, and she closed them.

The room was very dim even with the sun high in the sky. The large brown block of crystal glowed dimly. On the red five-pointed star on the floor, a faint lilac light appeared in the centre of the star; it burned brighter as Rune rose up out of it. Merlin opened his eyes as a violet coloured Rune stepped off the star, and onto the floor of the dungeon of the castle at Dunnottar. She swept to the front of the crystal. "Oh Grandfather, are you alright?"

Merlin nodded hung inside the crystal prison, he spoke but she could not hear him. Rune stared at the old face and nodded. "I cannot hear you Grandfather."

Merlin closed his eyes, but she already knew that she would not hear him, as she could not hear Saff or find Robbie when he was trapped under the rocks. There had to be a way to talk, but she had no idea of how. She stared through the brownish rock.

"Help is coming, Robbie is here with the group, hold on and I will find a way to get you out." She smiled, as she raised her hand and touched the cold clear surface of the crystal, just in front of her face, and Merlin smiled back at her. Rune blew him a kiss, and then headed back to her circle. Slowly she sank through the floor, and the room seemed duller. Merlin closed his eyes, and carried on his search for the missing incantation that Gwendolyn had found. He knew it, he was sure. Rune opened her eyes, and looked around; she thought for a moment and then focused her mind.

"Robbie hear me."

"Hey beautiful, I am here."

She smiled to herself. *"Hi gorgeous, I want a quick word."*

"I will come down, won't be a moment."

It was a few minutes later, when she heard his feet on the steps, and he came around the corner smiling. "What's up?"

Rune looked up at him, as he came and sat beside her. "I want to put Judy onto the table to protect her."

Robbie nodded. "I understand why, but isn't she tainted with the Dark One?"

Rune shook her head. "She has power, but the influence put on her is inside me, I took it when Maddy pulled it out of her. I shall release it when the time is right, for now it is safe and protected. Rob, Judy has the power of her line, it is neither good or bad, it is up to her how she uses it, I want to begin teaching her how to use it for good. I am a little nervous that is why I am asking you."

He shook his head. "You know how little I understand of all this Rune. I think she is a good kid, and I feel she will be safe. With us, she has felt love for the first time in her life; Maggs has been like a mother to her, and Jess and Beth spoil her and Blades rotten, I think it is up to you, but I think she will be alright."

Rune slipped her arm round him. "I trust your instincts that's why I asked. I will place her on the table as soon as she arrives."

Rowan and his party were taken up on to the long wooden walkway, which ran along the southern side of the cave. It was amazing to see the craftsmanship of the way the houses had been carved out of the crystal walls. In many cases a thin coating had been applied inside to create an opaque effect, to prevent people outside seeing through the dark transparent crystal into the small houses.

One house in particular had no windows and was impossible to see into, this was the one the small group had entered. Sinclair showed them the long wooden stairway that ran up through the ceiling to a wooden door, not un-similar to the one in the tavern.

The door opened into the cellar of another building on the surface. Rowan carefully stepped through to see the long shelves of bagged products. This was the cellar of a small General Store that catered to many of the poorly paid workers of the stone city. There was bag after bag of dried goods, such as lentils and barley and oatmeal, which as Sinclair explained made up the main diets of all those who worked the stone. Many of them hated Knox, but had settled out of fear, more than the wish to live in a world without plant life.

Jett and Jade had a good look around at the foods on offer, many of them were well known to them as woodsmen, but the thought of living on just this without meat, was too much for them to contemplate. Sinclair smiled at the screwed up faces of Jett and Jade as they wandered round. He headed quietly up to the top of the steps and listened at the door. He slid back a small piece of wood that revealed a peephole, and he could see inside the shop.

Two tired looking woodsmen picked up their bags and left as the small bell above the door pinged. Sinclair opened the door and signalled to the shopkeeper, who nodded. The group came up the stairs, and hurried through into the back room, where a small middle-aged woman, stood stirring a pan of stew. Rowan smiled and nodded, and Jett and Jade beamed as the woman turned round, nodded, and then turned back to the pan, and added some small bits of meat.

Sinclair whispered with the shopkeeper, and then came into the room. "You will have to remove your cloaks; woodsman cloaks have been banned. If you are seen wearing them you will be stopped, we have some grey coats here that you can wear, they are long and will hide your weapons, they too are banned."

They undid their cloaks and handed them to Sinclair, who placed them carefully on hooks behind the cellar door. They put on their coats of grey, and fastened them up. Then they were given straw hats. Jade laughed as she put hers on. "Whoa I bet I look like Mel now?" Jett chuckled, they had often teased her about her old battered hat, and had even offered to buy her one on the market at Loxley; she had refused, as she loved the one she had. Mel had told them; someone special had given it to her.

Once they had all got ready, Sinclair opened the back door, and they stepped out into the sea air. They had come up just short of the southern outcrop that blocked the view of Dunnottar Island from the mouth of the cave. The streets were very narrow, and they all followed as Sinclair led the way, Rowan looked round at the cold pale cement that had been used to build the small compacted homes, which were now the only living spaces of the many workers.

They looked and felt drab and miserable; Jade could not understand how anyone could choose to live in such a horrible place, when there were still mountains filled with trees and life. Sinclair now spoke very quietly as they walked close together.

It was hard to walk two across, as the passages were so narrow. The houses were tall three storey buildings, in which a family lived on each floor. The height reduced the light, and so the whole place felt dim and very depressing. Sinclair turned to Rowan. "The whole idea is that if you pack everyone in close, and create a very oppressive atmosphere, it will generate fear and keep everyone in line.

Believe me, it really works well; these cities are havens of fear and terror. The soldiers are ruthless, and will mutilate for sport, so please keep your heads down and out of trouble when we near the wall. You will see it in about twenty minutes."

Rafe leaned over Jett and Jade and whispered to Rowan. "Get a few hooded men up here with bows, and I would bet my last bit fear would soon fade." Rowan smiled and nodded.

They approached what felt like an endless line of long alleyways, and they looked out on an open square. It went right up to the cliff edge, and had a white metal rail running along it. Sinclair turned to face them. "Alright this place has been designed to instill terror. You must not linger, walk alone, and do not speak to each other, do not smile, look terrified as you look upon it, walk to the far end slowly, and then head back here." He pulled out a piece of chalk and quickly drew a cross on the wall. "This will make sure you all get the same alleyway. Walk into it without looking back, and walk very slowly until we all regroup. If there is trouble, head up the alleyway to the house with a black door. Knock four times and wait, the pass word is rose flower."

Everyone gave a short nod, and now began to feel really nervous; the fear in Sinclair's voice was quite real. He turned and led the way, walking at a very slow pace across the wide open square, towards the start of the rail. Jade gasped as the cliff and the sea came into view, it was a drop of several hundred feet, into a bay filled with large jagged brownish rocks, which were battered and smashed constantly by the rough sea. The wind blasted over the edge, and into her face, she quickly lifted her hand and grabbed at her hat to hold on tightly.

There off the coast, was the rough island of dark brown rock, and on top of it was a massive castle of shining black smooth stone. She shuddered as she saw it, and it was easy to understand the fear that people felt. The black castle of Dunnottar was in itself very sinister, and frightening to behold. She sensed pain inside her as she looked across, and without having to ask, she just knew many had died behind the walls of the castle.

Her boots dragged on the floor as she walked her hand on the rail to steady herself from the buffeting wind. Her eyes filled with tears as the wind tore at them, and yet she found it hard to remove her gaze from the evil work built by the Dark One. Jade had always been frightened of the Dark One, it was a joke around the group about how she peed herself when confronted by her, but she really did scare Jade in ways she had never discussed or would ever admit to them.

The tall black tower that grew out of the dark brooding building on its own was enough. The large black raven of cold stone that was the top of the tower instilled her with tremendous fear, as she looked at the pale blue windows for eyes, which seemed to look right into her soul. The beak was open, and in the depth of the throat a dark sinister red light seemed to glow, through two tall arched windows, and cast an eerie light onto the base of the beak, which had stone shard like teeth, and created a wide balcony, which she assumed was where the Dark One would view her prey.

She had always been tough and afraid of nothing, Jade had faced death and looked it in the eye without a care. The Dark One had a cloud of coldness and evil around her that Jade sensed, like her sister she had the ability to see deep inside to the heart of evil of Morgan le Fey, and what Jade saw, was a terror so evil her own heart seemed to freeze. She had spent hours alone with Rune talking about it, and on every occasion, she had shaken and cried with the fear it brought up in her. The Dark One was Jade's only real fear.

That fear returned to her, as she looked out knowing that she was inside that dark tall tower, she looked up at the shoulders of Rowan in front of her. The darkest fear in her heart was that he could be killed, and once again, she would return to the life of a misfit and loner. Her quiet companion had filled the large empty hole inside her with love and warmth, he was the only reason she now wanted to live, and every moment alone with him, had made her life so much more complete and happier. Jade feared that one-day the fight to remove the Dark One would cost him his life.

Every night as she lay by his side, she knew it could be her last and she made the most of her life with him. The Dark One threatened his life, and from that, all her fear was borne. Jade moved slowly forward following Rowan, who looked from the castle to the long black bridge that spanned the stretch of cold rough sea to the headland. Row upon row of soldiers in black walked out from the dark rock castle towards the base of the cliff and a wide deep cut ravine.

They reached the end of the rail and passed the stern looking soldier with their heads down, slowly they crossed the square, and walked back down the street as the long line of viewers broke, and walked off in different directions. At the alley with the cross, they turned in. Rowan walked a few yards and then stopped by a door. He pulled Jade into his arms as she walked up. "I love you Jade of Avon, oh god that place is terrible, how the hell will we get into there?"

Jade tried to smile, but her heart was heavy. "I love you too, get me away from here Rowan, I hate this place." He pulled her close and kissed her, and then slowly they walked a few yards. There was a horrible scream behind them, and they stopped and turned round. Jett stood watching from the corner.

One of the guards had decided to take a dislike to a man and he began to beat him severely. It was vicious and brutal, and the man's wife screamed and pleaded for the guard to stop, he turned and began to beat up on her, as the other guards crowded round, and joined in the attack.

Jade's eyes flickered green. "JETT NO... YOU MUST NOT DO IT!"

It was too late. Jett stood at the corner with rage in her heart, her eyes flickered deep blue, and the screams of the guards began. Their hands snapped to their heads, and they screamed in agony as the pain intensified. Seven of them fell to the floor as their eyes began to bleed.

Rune looked up quickly from the table, her eyes exploded in violet light and Robbie jumped back in his seat.

"No Jett you must not!"

Jett flew back up the alley as if thrown by a heavy weight, she landed on her back and it winded her. She gasped in pain as Rowan snatched her up off the floor, and half dragged her down the alleyway. "Jett you fool, if she has felt you, we could all be in danger."

Jett held her side as she fought to get back her breath; Rune found the guards with her mind, and then focused her thoughts. The guards screamed out in more pain, and staggered around the square, their faces twisted in torment. The workers in grey fled the scene in panic and fear, as a black cloud rose from the dark castle below.

Rowan and Jade flew at high speed, dragging Jett down the alley. Rafe looked backward, watching the square as it grew smaller, a black door flew open, and Sinclair's long arms grabbed Rowan by the front of his coat, and dragged him inside, the others followed, and the door banged closed. Rowan lay sprawled on the floor gasping for air; he looked up at the walls of polished crystal.

Sinclair looked down through the gloom. "Bloody hell that was close, she is in the square. We are safe here; she cannot see us."

Robbie watched, as the pictures appeared in Rune's table, he saw the soldiers screaming in pain, as blood now ran from their ears, nose, and eyes. The Dark One landed, and looked around through her narrow evil eyes. Her voice rebounded around the inside of the room. "I feel you flower girl; think you are oh so clever to reach so far. Enough of your party tricks." Bright light flashed in the picture above the table, and the pictures disappeared. Rune gasped a long breath and opened her eyes, the violet light stopped, and her eyes returned to their usual bright blue with lilac whites. "Wow Rob that was a close one." Robbie swallowed hard, uncertain of what was happening.

"What the hell just happened?" He looked shocked and a little shaken.

Rune took a deep breath. "Jett got upset and lost it for a minute. The Dark One sensed her and came to investigate. I blocked Jett, and carried on with the pain she was inflicting, the Dark One thought it was me all along, we were lucky; Jett could have got all of them caught, I will be having serious words with Jett Amber when we return."

Rowan sat up on the floor and looked at the very pale face of Jett. "WHAT THE BLOODY HELL WERE YOU PLAYING AT?"

Jett looked sadly at the floor. "I am really sorry Rowan; I was filled with fear and pain looking at that horrible place. When those guards picked on that man and started laughing as they battered him to death, I just lost it, I wanted them to stop, and could not use my sword." She started to cry, and tears rolled down her face, her voice rose higher. "They were beating her so hard, and all she wanted to do was protect the man she loved, I just hit them with my gift and hoped they hurt as much as she did." Her shoulders shook as Rowan got up off the floor. Jett never cried, and never showed fear; it was something he had always marvelled at.

Rowan put his arms around her and pulled her into a hug as she wailed into his chest. "It could have been you or Jade or Rafe, I messed up I am so sorry Rowan." Rowan put his head down on hers. He just held her close, Jade watched with tear-filled eyes, as she realised that the Dark One frightened Jett just the same, it was a thought that had never occurred to her before. The skill of the Dark One was to instill your worst nightmare, and Jett loved the friends and family she now had after years of being very lonely at Caerleon. Jett lived in fear of losing those who she too loved dearly.

Rowan whispered quietly to her, and she sniffled in his arms. He looked over at Rafe, and he nodded, Rafe took her gently out of Rowan's arms, and turned her into his. Jett sniffled as he pulled her close; her voice was very quiet and squeaky. "I really do love you Rafe."

It was a long wait, sat in the corner at the table, drinking water and waiting for the all clear; Jade curled up on Rowan's knee and began to calm down. "I am so glad I didn't pee this time Rowan."

Jett gave a soft giggle, and lifted her red eyes out of Rafe. Jade smiled at her. "I didn't bring clean pants; I did ask Rune to get me some just in case." Jett gave another soft giggle, and sat up; Rafe gave her a kiss, and hugged her. The room slowly came back to life, as the oppression of their spirits began to lift. The Dark One had left and gone back to her castle, and Sinclair slipped out of the door and went to look around. Jett's soft voice could be heard in the gloom.

"I really am sorry guys; it won't happen again." Rowan looked across at her.

"It is forgotten Jett, don't think of it anymore, that is how she wins." He nodded and Jett gave him a big smile.

The group began to arrive in the glade with their kit, and waited happily smiling and laughing. For most of them, they had been doing very little, and so the call to arms had come as a relief. Robbie smiled as he saw Maggs with a bag on her shoulder and a bow, Harry stood at her side with Blades and Judy.

"Harry you old maniac, it's great to see you, and Maggs I must say I now feel the team is complete with you back amongst us." Maggs seemed suddenly quite embarrassed and laughed her usual long gasping laugh like a strangled donkey, her teeth dropping down the front of her lip, as her jewellery rattled and jangled in tune with her movement.

"Oh Robbie sweetheart, you are such a doll, isn't he Harry pops?"

Harry beamed at her side. "Yeah man he is like totally beautiful man." Blades and Judy both giggled.

Bear walked slowly down the glade holding Alice by the hand, Jess dropped down from her cart and walked behind them. Rune ran up to Alice and gave her a huge hug. "I wish you were coming; it won't be the same without you at my side with your bow." She gave Bear a kiss on the cheek, and he knew Rune and Alice would talk, so he walked over to John and Martin. Alice patted her now quite large belly.

"I am starting to look like you John." She rubbed her belly like he did when he knew a pint of ale was coming, and all the team laughed. John beamed a smile and then rubbed his belly back at her. Alice chuckled with glee.

"Take care of yourself and Robbie for me Rune. Watch over Mickie... Oh, Rune I really think I am in love with him, you have no idea how hard this will be for me. He is so tender and gentle with me; I am going to really miss him."

Rune pulled her into a hug. "I always watch over my children of the woods, you know that. Don't worry I will bring him and Robbie back."

Jess looked at her son with concern. "Is he safe?"

Robbie pulled her into his arms. "I have him in a deep cave well out of sight bossing people around my headquarters. He is almost happy." Robbie leaned back. "He misses you too."

She gave a weak smile, and bit her lip as she filled up. "He belongs here, but he loves you, and after last time, he just wants to be there to protect you. What can I do, I love you both?" Robbie hugged his mum tight.

"It has meant a lot to me mum having him at my side, I want him to be proud of me, and I really think he is. I am watching out for him, so please don't worry so much."

Jess sniffled. "Just do me one favour Rob?" He leaned back and looked at her damp eyes. "Just kill that bitch so I can have my family home." He smiled at her.

"You swore, that mum is naughty, you took my pie off me when I swore as a kid, so it's no pie for you when I get back." Jess gave a giggle and nodded.

"I love you Robbie, please take care."

He kissed the tip of her nose. "I will."

Rune took Judy by the hand. "We need to talk a minute." Judy looked a little worried and Rune smiled. "Come into the house for a moment." Rune led Judy into the house and walked to the side of the stairs, she waved her hand across the symbol of the five-pointed star and the small door opened.

Rune led Judy down the stairs, and into the lower chamber, Judy gasped at the sight of the table of a white circle surrounded by black, with a large sapphire blue twenty-pointed star in the centre.

"Do you know what this is Judy?" Judy walked round, her eyes were opened wide and a smile on her face, she ran her hand across the surface and small violet flashes jumped from her fingers.

Judy looked up at Rune. "This is a table of power, is it yours? It is beautiful."

"I am Runestone Sapphire a daughter of Hearne, Lord of the woods, and I have succeeded Opal the white. Now is the time of Runestone Sapphire the daughter of violet." Rune watched carefully as Judy looked across at the large silver rune in the centre of the table. "Judy this table is only for the purpose of good; no one can sit and live if their road is for black."

Judy's eyes sparkled. "Can I sit at this table? I have a little power, and I am sure it is not dark."

Rune smiled. "Your power is not good or bad Judy, none of us have a dark power or a white, we just have power. It is what we do with the power that is important. I have brought you here to ask if you really will help Robbie and join the power of good? You cannot lie to this table; it will know and you will be hurt if you try to fool it."

Judy looked up. "I want to do good; I really do... I would love to put right the wrongs my father has done to the people of the woods, who have been so kind to me."

Rune walked around the table and took Judy by the hand; she led her to the seat with a number four on the back. Rune stood her behind it, and then walked to her chair and sat down. "Judith if you join my table and accept me as the centre of your power then I will become your teacher, and as your power grows, I will guide you in the ways of the violet circle. If you join me, then you must lose the name of fear and pain and give up the name of Knox forever. I wish you to take your mother's name and become Judith Hargreaves. If you agree, then take your rightful seat and I will join you, if you cannot, then leave this room and we will remain friends."

Judy nervously slipped into the seat, and raised her hands above the table. Rune nodded as her own hands lay flat on the surface. Judy lowered her hands and they stuck fast. Her whole body shook for a moment, and she glowed violet. Rune nodded and her hands came away. "Welcome to the table of Runestone Sapphire, and the Lady of the Woodland Realm, you are one with us and I am now your centre. You are now under my care, and from this moment only tread the path of the violet circle, the table will know if you deviate and act accordingly."

Judy looked very pale, and swallowed hard, Rune gave her a sweet smile. "Do not be afraid, I have watched you closely and see your heart is good."

Judy smiled. "I love living with Harry and Maggs, they are completely bonkers, but they are so nice to me Runestone, I really do love them, and Blades is like a real sister." Rune gave her a smile.

"I am happy you have found the true meaning of family. We have a busy time ahead of us my sister, we have a hooded man to help and then when we get back, you have a book shop to clean and re-open."

Judy gave her a huge excited smile. "That is mine?"

Rune nodded as she got up and walked over towards her. "You are the last of the Hargreaves family, and Oscar bought it outright. It appears now it has passed to you, his will left it to your mother, and you are her only daughter so it is yours, your brothers will never be allowed on this land. Robert has agreed to hand you the keys when we return."

"Oh wow Rune, that will be so cosmic." Judy pulled her hand to her mouth and giggled. Rune winked at her.

"And radical," they both giggled, as they came up the stairs to the group who were almost ready to leave.

Everyone stood waiting as they came out. They picked up their bags and walked to the trees, where holding Judy by the hand, Rune waved her arm across the trees and they leaned over and formed an arch. The violets ran up and over, then back to the ground and the shimmering light appeared. Rune stepped through into the bar with Judy, the rest followed.

Rune leaned down to Judy. "Go with Blades now and I will see you soon, I have other business to attend to." She stood up and smiled at Robbie; Crystal came up and kissed her on the cheek.

"Tell mum I love her." Rune nodded, as Robbie looked puzzled.

Crystal waved everyone through to the cellar, and they all followed leaving Rune and Robbie alone in the bar with the shimmering curtain of light. "What is going on Rune?"

She gave him a soft kiss on the cheek. "We have another stop before we come here, it is important to us both, Gwynfor asked me as we left the office, he blocked you out, you trust me, don't you?"

"Of course I do, what kind of question is that?" She waved her hand over the pale violet mist, and it sparkled brightly. She took his hand and stepped through.

Robbie stood with Rune in front of a large stone Celtic Cross. He looked at the intricate carvings of knots and dots, with interwoven flowers, just in front of them was an old stone built abbey with a small out building. A figure in all white came out of the door and he recognised her from Rune's table. A tall blonde girl in a very tight fitting set of pale blue clothes, and bare feet walked out behind her, she smiled a bright attractive smile. She ran across the grass, and threw her arms around Rune, whilst the woman in white came forward smiling. Rune hugged her with happiness.

"Oh Amethyst, it is so nice to see you at last." The lady in white bowed.

"We meet again Lord Loxley." He looked at the sword of destiny and then back at her.

"You are Gwinne right? It's just there are so many of your lot, I frequently get lost."

She smiled. "You are quite right My Lord, and do not worry, I get just as lost as you do."

The words of Runestone had very quickly gone around the city of crystal, and her use of the word 'Specialists' had been on everyone's lips. The first group to appear with Lord Loxley had not caused that much of a stir; after all, they had all looked like woodsmen in green with their cloaks. Jett had drawn comment about her black tight fitting clothes tinged with lilac. Crystal had been the talk of the city. Her bright white with small-embroidered snowflake design had drawn a lot of comment, especially with her long snow-white hair and clear eyes that appeared to have just two black circles with a black dot in the centre. The silver bow she carried was the cause of a great deal of talk amongst the men.

As the new arrivals filed down the stairs the word 'Specialists, was again on everyone's lips. It was hard not to stare, as the happy smiling group walked through them smiling and gasping at the sight of the city underground.

Crystal led the way and everyone stood lost for words as the likes of Harry who was tall and in all black, with crossed golden swords on his back and a black wide brimmed hat passed by. He was also holding the hand of a woman in all shades of green, as Maggs wore her best green tie-dyed pants and top under her cloak.

Judy carried the crest of an angry looking hornet on her cloak, and that was a crest no one knew. Blades at her side looked like a small version of Harry with her crossed swords. Her short spiky hair, and her crossbow now slung on her hip with the addition of four silver daggers looked forceful for one so small.

John and Martin looked quite normal, as did Fish and Keith. Saff in all white with a blue cloak stirred rumours as she wore the same colour as the old Celt, and Ruby with her grey clothes and red mirror glasses got everyone's attention. Her hair gleamed like fresh snow, and with her long white pole, most could not understand how a blind person could help.

Jaz in his burgundy and brown with a deep violet cloak looked lordly as did Skip with his new long burgundy cloak bought for him by Treen. The crest of a Unicorn's head was not one any had seen before. The golden sword on his hip gleamed even in the dim light, and he walked with authority, and all knew he was a man of good education.

Treen walked with a smile her arm in his, in her long flowing robes of dusky browns and orange, her belt of orange leaves caught everyone's eye for many did not recognise the plant. Maddy chatted with Mel in her grey cloak with a Morbihan crest of a stone circle in a white ring. Her long velvet violet skirt and blue smock was a favourite amongst the women. These people knew her white bow, and they gasped at the sight of it, for it was a bow of legend, and they all still told the stories of it sat at home round the fire at night, telling the tales of Gwendolyn the high queen of the Violet Isle.

Mel smiled as her long brown hair flowed from under her battered straw hat, the all pale blue of the skies, and the golden belt of eagle feathers drew bows from some of the north. Callanish was indeed a very sacred place to many of the lines of Scots. There before them was the woman that had been spoken of often; they knew she was truly the queen of the Callanish eagles.

Smokes and Steph wore the true colours of Loxley accept that Steph had taken to wearing one of Harry's old hats, her belt of acorn leaves signalled her high rank in the Loxley lodge of the fellowship, and the ring of violets on her hat, made everyone wonder if she was connected to the woodland lady.

Bear followed at the back, and talked with Angus, he was large and impressive, in his frilly white shirt and his black heavy pants and coat, with the golden sword that was something to behold. He walked like a pirate, swaggering with immense power and the men had to admit that for an Englishman, he looked a worthy man indeed.

The crowds parted as everyone watched the long line of Lord Loxley's Specialists arrive. Rose stood up on the steps and watched, and as they approached, people started to bow with respect. Crystal smiled as they came up the steps towards Rose. She gave her a huge smile. "They all thought I was the weird one until this lot arrived." Rose laughed at her.

"I will give Lord Loxley his due, he knows how to pick em, this lot are hero's before they even start. You have certainly brought colour to the place... Come on let's get you all settled in and feeling at home, we have a banquet planned for tonight."

The group marched into the Lodge and up the long stairs to their floor. Una and Robert smiled with delight as the Loxley family of the hood were welcomed. Jett squealed with delight at the sight of Ruby and Judy with Blades. "Hey guys come and see mine and Rafe's room it is so cool. We have a great balcony for dropping water bombs off."

Rowan looked round at the crowd coming in; he grabbed Crystal as she passed. "Where are Robbie and Rune?"

She smiled at him. "They are safe, they had to make a quick visit for an old friend, they will be back before the banquet."

Rowan frowned and gave John and Martin a hug. "I thought I told you two not to let him out of your sight?" John shrugged at Rowan.

"Rune slipped him off before we realised, she knows you know? We cannot hide anything from her, she really can look right through us."

Rowan patted John's arm. "Alright then, go and sort your rooms out, I want you two at the very end of the corridor. You check out anyone who passes, if in doubt shoot them, and we will sort out the questions later. I want Robbie on a twenty four hour guard you understand me?"

John and Martin nodded and picked up their bags, Rowan smiled at Jade who looked worried.

"Why are you so protective of Robbie all of a sudden Rowan, you are never this tense?"

"I am English, I do not trust the Scots or anything that can frighten you, I almost lost him once Jade, it will not happen again. Trust me.... Come on grab your bow."

"Where are we going?"

"To the tavern to wait for them, they will have a guard with them always from now on." Jade collected her bow, and followed Rowan out of the room, as they headed for the tavern.

Gwinne hugged Rune and laughed. "Welcome to Iona My Lord and Lady of Loxley, you bring two gifts to this realm, and much joy to our hearts." Robbie looked stunned.

"How do you know that, it's just days?"

She smiled. "You are on the isle of the people of Fae, your lady carries their next queen, and your excitement inside My Lord is equal to the people here. You will be much loved here... Come we have but a short time and there is much to discuss."

Amethyst smiled at Robbie and put her arm round his shoulder. "Rune seems to have cheated all of us out of a good man." She winked and then raised her eyebrows. "Tell me of this man they call Fish, I love the water and the stories I have heard from sweet cousin Ruby interest me greatly." Robbie smiled at Rune. "You know Ruby is the only thing I know faster than Rags."

Rune began to chuckle as they followed Gwinne in through the door to the smell of fresh coffee and fresh baked bread.

CHAPTER FIVE

FUTURE PLANNING

Everyone sat together at the table as Gwinne smiled across at Rune. "You have been in my thoughts so often Runestone, I know it has been hard for you, but you have done so much already, and now you sit before me shining with the power of the woods. I see my Green Lord so strongly in you, my mother would be so proud if she could see you now."

Rune smiled a sad smile. "I really miss her, I wanted her to stay and share the power, I understand why she had to leave, but it has not stopped me missing her though." Gwinne reached over and took her hands in hers.

"You will bring life renewed and complete the white circle Runestone. Be happy for there is so much joy in your future."

Rune gave her a smile. "I am happy, and Rob is going to explode I think." She giggled as she pulled him close. It showed in his face, he had been so desperately disappointed when he had learned the truth of the life for life exchange. Even now, he still felt anger at the Green Lord for not giving Rune a greater explanation. Robbie had seen the sadness inside her for over a month, and he had been sure that there had been terrible moments of tears at her table in the basement.

To him she was everything good, bright, and happy in life, and the fact that they had taken the joy from her was a source of great pain to him still. He remembered the hours she had spent looking out of the window at the mere, a haunted look on her face reflected in the glass to him, as she leant on her loom. It was cruel, and although he knew that life and nature could be so, he felt she alone in this world did not deserve that. He had not spoken to Hearne, and it was possibly a good thing. He now knew that Gwendolyn had been aware all along of the sacrifice made by her niece, and yet she had still given Rune no option but to choose to trade to save her sister.

It made little sense but he felt what he felt, and even though he now knew it had been a test of Rune's faith and she had been granted the child, his happiness at knowing he would have a son was tainted by the pain he felt for her suffering. Gwinne looked at him with the same blue eyes as her mother, Robbie knew she sensed the anger he felt towards the Lord Hearne. She smiled at him and nodded, she knew his defence of Rune was total, and even the Green Lord himself would not hurt her and be free of him.

Amethyst leaned forward; her bright violet eyes sparkled. "It is almost time Mother; we must get ready and prepare." Gwinne nodded and turned to Robbie.

"My Lord we have little time so we had better get ready, just follow my lead and all will be well."

Robbie looked bemused, as Rune pulled on his hand, and he rose out of his seat. She slid her arm round him and chuckled as they headed out of the door and back into the small yard, shaded by the abbey walls. They stood on the grass in front of the large carved stone cross, the sky was darkening as the sun slipped gently down.

Gwinne looked up at the sky. Robbie felt nervous as he held Rune's hand; she could sense it and smiled at him. "Don't be nervous, this is a very mystical place, it is said that here on Iona there is a meeting of the two worlds of the mortal and the eternal. Here is the centre of many faiths Robbie; it has long been a place of high worship, for the old faiths and the new. This cross before us may seem like a sign of the Christian world, yet it is decorated with the runes and patterns of our own earth faith, and has the circle of life on it. The land below is very sacred, and this is an important realm for us now."

Robbie looked at the tall carved cross; he saw the circle of stone, which encircled the centre of the cross. He had not noticed it before, and he thought of Sister Mary and her worship of two faiths, had she known of this place of dual beliefs?

Amethyst stood by his other side, and she leant slowly into him, her voice seemed calm and quiet as she spoke. "This land was once home to Colum Cille; he was the last of the old lines of great Celtic kings who came here from the land of the shamrock. He joined the two faiths of earth and the Christ, and brought a love of nature and the circle of life to all of this land. He was a great man My Lord. It was his sister Bridget Violet that brought forth the power of the Fae in her two sons from those isles across the water; it was here that her grandchildren Gwendolyn and Gwynfor were born."

Robbie was slowly putting the pieces together. "This is the start of my family line; I am the descendant of the kings of Ireland and the Fae?"

Rune smiled at him, and her blue eyes danced. "You now understand why Iona will rule here, she will be the first child that will be everything Colum Cille strove so hard for, the line of Fae will join the line of Hearne, and the two circles will be forever one. It will be here where the lines of all the old kings were buried that the power of the old world will unite with the new, and become the foundation, that leads to the dawn of awakening in the new age to come."

Gwinne turned to face them. "It is time, and the powers of the past will meet the powers of the future, be prepared to be honoured by the line of kings, and begin the new start to the age of Iona Queen of Fae"

Robbie stood and watched, nervously holding the hand of Rune, as within the stone shrine, set back behind the cross, a bright bluish light appeared. He tensed as the shadowy figures of the past began to appear. Out walked the ghostly figures of old men with long beards and long braided hair. They wore old styles of dress that were brightly coloured, and carried large swords, highly decorated with ancient runes and interwoven patterns. He watched as they all stopped in front of the cross and bowed; they turned, and smiled, then bowed to Robbie and Rune.

Robbie unsure of just what was happening, bowed back to the kings of old, and they passed on with joy in their faces. The procession continued as Robbie and Rune received the honour of the past generations. Over a hundred misty figures of old kings and queens walked up. They bowed, and moved on fading into the darkening sky behind them, Rune squeezed his hand, and he looked to the doorway and there stood Gwendolyn pale and transparent holding the hand of a very frail old man in robes of white and blue.

She walked slowly with the old man who had snow-white hair almost down to his knees, his beard was so long it hung from his belt, and his eyes of dark brown burned with the fires of life and knowledge. Robbie felt the strong presence of the old lord; he realised to be Colum Cille. As the old lord bowed, he felt humbled, and bowed back at him.

Gwendolyn smiled; her voice seemed distant and soft. "Greetings my hooded man and daughter of life, I am happy to see that you have reformed the white circle, and created life anew. You have done wonders Runestone Sapphire, and have added great gifts to the line of my fathers." She bowed before Rune and gave her a huge and happy smile. She turned to Robbie. "Heir of my house, the High Lord of the White Circle has awaited this time with you. It can only be short as the last rays of the sun will return us to the other realm, be at peace in your heart, and heed well his words."

The old man stepped forward, and gave him a huge and bright smile, which reminded Robbie a Little of Gwynfor. His voice was cracked and distant, yet it carried love and affection. "Son of the old I am pleased with your progress. It was never seen that your line would meet with that of the woods and life. I rejoice that you have achieved what we have all worked so hard to bring together, and you have shown us, who have watched for thousands of years, new ways to live. I am very proud of you. It is now your task to help rekindle the line of the people of Fae, and your daughter will return to the violet isle, and take her rightful seat. My children of Fae will shortly arrive, and prepare the way for your child; you must bring her here for her birth, for it will seal the strongest magic and protect her always."

He gave a long swooping bow and smiled as his hand passed across the stomach of Rune, and her eyes flared a bright Purple. "She grows strong with her brother. She is protected, have no fear when you meet with the black one of old, your fear is unfounded, be at peace child of life."

He looked back up at Robbie. "Your son will be bright stone and lord of this Isle with his sister; he will be a jewel in the crown of your woodland realm. You have honoured us son of my line, the isle of Erin will be forever blessed."

He turned to Gwendolyn, and she looked from him to Robbie and Rune. "You have much work to do now, but soon will come a time when you will find and restore the King of this land. You must take the Destiny Stone on the day your daughter is born. Without it, you will not seat a king of power, heed these words well my hooded kin." She began to break apart, and although Robbie wanted to ask more questions, he knew it was too late. The old man turned and waved a hand.

Colum Cille bowed again, and then slowly dissolved into the last rays of the day's sunlight. Gwinne came forward and hugged Rune and then Robbie. "I feel the honour of just seeing that, it has been a thousand years since the kings of old came forth to greet the start of a new queen of Fae"

Robbie felt humbled and confused, so much had happened in the past few days it felt like the weight of knowledge he had would pull him down. Rune slid her arms around and smiled. "It's a lot to think about, isn't it?"

"It is your fault; your lot are so confusing it makes my head spin." She started to giggle as she pulled him close and kissed him. "They are our lot now Rob."

It was time now to depart, and return to the crystal caves, Gwinne, and Amethyst gave them both a huge hug. "Oh Rune, I wish we could have had longer, I have so many things to talk about, and cannot wait for your return." Rune hugged Gwinne and kissed her cheek.

"I will return before the birth, and we will have time, have no fear.... Goodbye Amethyst, take care of your mother, and I will send your love to Crystal." Rune waved her hand and the shimmering violet light appeared before them. They smiled at the two women stood by the old cross in the dim light, and stepped through into the tavern at Stonehaven. Rowan leaned off the bar.

"Why did you leave without a guard?"

Robbie looked at the angry face of Rowan. "I had a guard, we have been protected at all times, I just used an older guard than those of Loxley. Is that a problem?" His eyes flashed at Rowan.

"Robbie you are my friend, but also my lord, your safety is my concern whether you like it or not, you cannot ask me to stop for three hours because it does not suit you, I should have been told of your plans." Rowan seemed un-phased by Robbie's anger, and Rune stepped between them.

"We are sorry Rowan, you are right, I am at fault, for I had to take Robbie to the Violet Isle, you have my assurance he was protected more there than anywhere else on this earth."

Rowan nodded and walked to the door. "There is to be a banquet in honour of all the party of Lord Loxley, we must hurry." He slipped through the door to the cellar, and headed onto the long steps. Jade giggled as she walked with Rune, and looked at the furrowed brow of Robbie.

"Men are so daft, why didn't Rowan just hug him and tell he had been worried like we would. He has driven me mad pacing around all night." Rune giggled at her bright face.

"Robbie knows, and so does Rowan, they just like to stamp their feet a little sometimes."

Robert Lox greeted his son with a hug, in the room filled with the happy banter of his group; he walked into his rooms and collapsed on the bed. He closed his eyes and lay still. His head spun with the day's events, Rune moved round the room and hummed as she unpacked the second bag she had brought from the house. "Come on Rob and change, you are guest of honour tonight and you should look the part." He opened his eyes, and looked at the deep velvet cloak and the dark green clothes she was laying out on the chair.

"Oh Rune, do I have to? Why can I not just stay here and curl up beside you. I feel exhausted."

She began to laugh. "Oh, come on Rob, I know you hate all the lordship duties, but it is the life you have now, I have made these especially for you and I have made a new dress just for tonight. Don't you want to be seen with me at my best?"

He sat up on the bed and looked at the sapphire blue dress that sparkled as she held it against her. "I will be too fat to wear this soon."

"That's not fair, you are just trying to make me feel guilty, so I will go to this stupid thing."

She smiled. "Is it working?" Her bright blue eyes shone with mischief.

He pulled off his shirt and smiled back. "Yes, I feel awful now." Rune giggled as he walked to the bathroom for a wash.

"I love you Lord Loxley." He heard her giggling as he closed the door.

The banquet was held on the bottom floor of the Lodge, in the large hall behind the stairs. It was a very large room, and was laid out with one long table running across the top of the room, where all the group of Loxley were to be seated. Four long tables ran down the room away from the main table.

Considering they had been underground for some time; they certainly had a lot of style.

Long heavy green cloths covered the tables, which were decorated with ornate candle stands. Row upon row of bright cutlery lay ready, with crystal goblets neatly placed. Small decorative cards had the name of each guest neatly written on it. Staff in bright green tartan, ran around the room preparing and ensuring that everyone was adequately taken care of.

Two woodsmen in tartan stood by the door, and announced the guests as they arrived; the names were echoed loud across the room. Rose Mackintosh sat on the high table with Sinclair Forbes. The room was slowly filling up with guests, and dignitaries from the whole of the Scottish woodland, most of who were now living in the crystal cave for protection. The loud voice from the door called out. "Lord William McDonald." Rose looked up as the grey haired frowning old Scot walked in through the doors.

A young woman in a pale green tartan kilt and blouse guided him to the table. "Lord Harold and Lady Margaret Olivia Pickles of Loxley, escorting Lady Katherine of Loxley and Lady Judith Hargreaves." Harry walked in with pride escorting Maggs who wore a very pale tie dyed red dress. Rose smiled to Sinclair.

"Oh good, they are finally arriving." Harry's tall frame could be seen, being guided to his seat; Maggs was so small she was barely visible above the turned heads. "John Albert Sykes of Loxley and Martin Reef of Hope." The two men walked with their heads high and smiled as everyone nodded at them.

"Lord Peter and Lady Stephanie Lane of Avon." Steph beamed on the arm of Smokes in a long blue sequined dress. "James Ashford of Church Hill and Hope." He made his way as the guests all nodded, as they were finally putting names to faces. "Sir Brandon Berkley 79th Duke of Gloucester." There was an audible gasp, and even Rose was surprised.

"Lord Robert has some very important friends." Skip looked the part with his golden coat of arms on his long flowing heavy burgundy velvet cloak.

"Lady Jett Amber, and Lady Ruby Moonstone Bedivere of Caerleon," again the room gasped. The Specialists were proving more surprising than ever. "Captain Rafe of New Avon, Keith Sherman of Loxley." The two men smiled as they headed joking down to the table, Rafe waved to Jett, as he got closer.

"Lord Jacques Michael Giles Phillips, Ambassador to York." The tall pirate looking character of Bear, cut a dashing display as he walked down the centre of the room. He strolled with authority and power, Sinclair leaned and quietly spoke to Rose.

"They call him Bear, but I had no idea? This is becoming a meeting of the nation."

"Lady Crystal Onyx Rimmer of Glastonbury." She glowed in the bright light, such was the white of her garments, and her feathery hair sparkled as small crystals glinted on the tips. "Lord Jasper Verdite, and Lady Sapphire Turquoise Tor, of Callanish." A deep rumble went round the room. Many had seen the belt of Mel, and now they realised her children were amongst them. For many years, there had been stories of the Queen of the eagles, and her children, who lived at the sacred stones. Here they were in person; many in the room turned, stood up, and bowed their heads, as the brother and sister walked smiling past.

"Lady Madeleine Willow Du Luc and her daughters, Alexandrite and Citrine Du Luc of Carnac, Morbihan." The gasps were becoming louder with each announcement; Carnac was a sacred place to all Celts. The Lady of the stones was a line of huge power connected to Fae.

"Lady Melanie Birch Tor, of Callanish." The rumbles were building higher and higher in the room, the talk was now flowing wildly, as families from the history of the whole realm seemed to be visiting the lodge that evening. "Lady Una Holly Rimmer, of Castleriss, Derwent. Lord Robert Jake Loxley, Wolveshead of the fellowship of Loxley Bowmen."

Many of the woodsmen stood up and bowed, as Robert walked down the room a large an impressive figure, and a man who was used to being shown great respect. He walked and bowed back to those who saluted him; Robert carried the true authority of a king.

"Lord Rowan, and Lady Jade Opal, of Loxley." Rowan looked as uncomfortable as ever in clean un-scruffy clothes. He looked the part and Jade who had borrowed a pale lilac dress from Rune having heard about the ball, looked like an angel with her hair tied up. She beamed with delight as she walked on Rowan's arm.

"Lord Robert John Loxley 51st Earl of Huntingdon and Hooded Man returned, escorting The Lady Runestone Sapphire of Loxley and Lady to the Woodland Realm of the Green Lord."

Robbie and Rune stole the show, Robbie in his dark green velvet shirt, and pants with his heavy golden sword, and long dark green velvet cloak with the golden emblem of Loxley on it, looked truly like the most powerful lord in the room. He walked with pride, as the beaming slender figure of Rune in sapphire blue, with a cloak of violet, was covered with silver and golden glittering jewellery, and had the impressive golden sword hanging on a belt of gold oak leaves. She walked elegantly, the golden tiara of Hearne on her head, her long red hair was braided, and the golden butterfly sent red flashes into the air around her braids, which were surrounded with violets.

If the group had wanted to impress, they had just achieved their goal. Robbie sat down next to Rose, and Rune was seated beside him, next to Rowan at the top of the long table. The whole room faced their way, and they smiled and nodded to the mass of strangers who nodded their greetings.

Rose looked fairly shocked. "When you said specialist My Lord, you were not kidding, you keep quite remarkable company." Rune giggled as Robbie looked up and down the table.

"What this lot? They just tagged on for the fun of the fight, we are just good pals who like a little sword and bow play, we have no use of these titles, we just share the same goal of protecting those who cannot protect themselves." John and

Martin grinned and slapped the table.

Row upon row of waitress's flowed into the hall, and bottles opened, and food was whisked at high speed around the room, a slender figure with a silver plate leaned over Robbie and he leaned back to allow her access. "Hello Grace, why thank you, have you met Lady Runestone?"

Grace went beetroot, and gave a small curtsy. "My Lady." Rune gave her a smile.

"Ignore him Grace, he loves to show off." She winked, and Grace gave another curtsy. "Yes, My Lady." She flew off down the table the colour in her face deepening.

The room was soon filled with the sounds of rattling knives and forks, and the hum of conversation. The topic of the Specialists was in the air, as everyone looked at the smiling happy group sat high on the top table. Robbie and Rune looked like a powerful couple, and they were the topic of most of the conversation. Robbie leaned over as she smiled and he talked softly with her. She smiled at Rose as she commented on her dress.

The meal went down very well, and soon the air was filled with polite conversation, as the plates were whisked away, and everyone relaxed. Robbie and Rune had spent most of the evening talking with Rose and Sinclair. Robbie was keen to learn as much as he could about the operation of the Knox Empire here in Scotland and it appeared Rose knew more than most.

Angus stood up and banged a glass rapidly. "My Lords, and Ladies, your attention please. Your host Lady Rosalind of Aberdeen, and heir to the throne of Scotland."

Robbie started to laugh. "You call my lot impressive; you hide a secret or two yourself Rose."

Rose stood up as the whole room applauded her. She smiled and waited for silence. "My Lords and Ladies of the woods, we find ourselves in impressive company tonight, and I find not only do I address the powers of the Scottish resistance, but also the powers of all Britain. We welcome our respected guests to our table, for we all share the same common enemy." There was respectful applause as the Specialists were acknowledged, and they nodded in respect. Rose gave a slight cough and the guests became silent.

"Shortly we will finally see the days we have prepared for, and under the guidance of My Lord Roberts Specialists, we hope to vanquish the powers of the dark tower from our lands. We have hard and painful times ahead, for this will be a hard fight, and all houses of this realm will lose kin. But I am sure our guests will guide us to a new future, sooner than expected. It is my hope that tonight will be the start of the new age for this realm, so I would ask that you all raise a glass and toast... The Future."

Glasses rose into the air. "The Future." The noise thundered around the room as everyone toasted and then began to applaud as Rose sat down. Rune looked at Robbie whose face carried a look of abject surprise.

"Robbie are you alright?" He looked at her and spoke quietly.

"What the hell are they talking about Rune? The Dark One is not just going to pack up and leave now we are here. They have no idea...?"

"My Lords and Ladies, Lord Robert of Loxley 51st Earl of Huntingdon."

"What...?"

The whole room looked at Robbie, who had not even realised he had to give a speech, he looked at Rune and then Rose, who smiled and raised her palm to the assembled guests. He turned and looked out across the sea of faces, and back to Rune who smiled.

"Tell them how it is sweetheart." She gave him a huge smile, and pushed him upwards. Robbie let out a long gasp and smiled as he stood up.

"Lords and Ladies of the Woodland Realm. I am not quite sure where to begin, I had not expected this." He thought for a moment, and raised his glass to drink.

"You all call me Lord Robert, nevertheless, to my associates I am just a simple woodsman who loves the trees and the life below them, who just happens to be known to most as Robbie. I never asked, or wanted the role of hooded man, or earl, or lord."

The room gasped in shock; how could anyone not want the honour? Robbie smiled at the idea of shocking so many, and Rune gave a quiet giggle, she knew how much he hated the lordship side of his life. Robbie thought, and then having made his decision, he began to speak. He was not aware at all of the attention, or how powerful he sounded. He had no idea at the authority in his voice. He was simply being himself.

"Earlier this year, I walked into a room at my lodge in Loxley, having been told one hour earlier, that my distant ancestor was the original Robin in the hood. I was given a cloak and a ring and a very nice bracelet, and given the task of helping woodsman in this country beat the house of Mason Knox." Robbie formed his thoughts and words.

"Since that day I have fought constantly to try and help those who I have seen suffer. The only reason I have been successful, is that some very wonderful people who stand alongside me have shown me the meaning of respect and loyalty, and the love of their lord. Two very special people lie buried in a quiet woodland glade in Caerleon such was their love to me, and my good lady Runestone. It has been hard and painful, and at times I was not sure if I would live through the day."

The room was so quiet you could hear a pin drop. Rune slipped her hand across the table, and placed it on his as he leaned forward on to it.

"I hate to disagree with your leader here, because I really hold a lot of respect for her, hiding you all down here was the best thing anyone has ever done." The silence broke, as furious murmurs rattled up from the tables, Robbie continued as the noise rose. "This is not going to be like any battle you may have witnessed, or read about in the past." Angus jumped up and banged on the table. The angry voices continued.

Robbie looked around at what was starting to look like an angry shouting mob. The old figure of William McDonald jumped up and screamed at Rose, as he pointed a long white finger at Robbie. "I told yeah he was nay good, I told yeah he would nay stand for us."

Robbie drew out his sword, and slammed it down on the table with a mighty crash, scattering candlesticks and glasses everywhere. He pointed his sword south and screamed at the top of his voice as his face reddened with anger.

"DO YOU REALLY KNOW WHAT LIVES IN THAT CASTLE? HAVE YOU ANY IDEA WHAT YOU FACE? BECAUSE I DO, I HAVE LOOKED HER IN THE EYE, AND CUT TWO FINGERS FROM HER HAND, AND I AM TELLING YOU ALL, THAT YOU ARE NOT GOING TO JUST WALK INTO DUNNOTTAR WITH AN ARMY, AND WALK OUT WITH HER HEAD. DO YOU EVEN KNOW HER NAME?"

The whole room fell instantly silent as Robbie's eye's flashed, and his voice carried above the noise. Rune squeezed his hand, and he felt her calmness flow into him. He breathed as his eyes glared at William McDonald, and his voice lowered in tone, and he pointed the long golden sword towards him. "You do not even know me, and yet you dare stand in front of me, and squeal like the wounded rat you have become. I know what you face because I was the one who pushed a sword through the chest of her son, and watched the evil power drain from him. How dare you, who hide in this glass hole, sit in judgement of me?"

William McDonald shrunk back into his seat, and the room all stared at the angry eyes of the hooded man. Rose breathed very deeply at Robbie's side.

Robbie looked left and right at his group, who all stood with their hands on the hilts of their swords. He waved them down, and looked out at the gathering. "I did not ask for this role, but I have lived it, and my companions and I are the only ones here who know what you face, and have seen what they wish to achieve here. If you are smart, you will listen now, but do not expect me to stand here and pretend to you that this will be easy, I won't."

The assembled guests seemed to relax as Robbie searched the eyes of each and every one of them; his anger was now quite visible. "The Castle of Dunnottar contains a form of evil that has lived and prepared for this day for over a thousand years. I faced her once, and it chilled me to my bones with fear. My good lady has fended her off four times, and such was the fear that most of us quaked in our boots, and even wet our trousers. Tell me now that you won't?" He looked around the room at the faces of horror. He lifted the sword and pointed it back behind him, in a gesture towards the dark brooding castle. "That castle contains the evil life form of Morgan le Fey, and her reincarnated son Mordred, who is currently contained by a mystical power, within the body of my brother."

Fear lifted into the air, as he spoke. "You will be lucky to survive her, and if you listen to the good advice of my Specialists, you might have a slim chance of victory. I am here and have never once turned my back on any who have asked for my help, and I will work to rid the world of her and her evil spawn, because her aim is to kill everything in this world that I love." Along the tables, some of the Scots felt ashamed and dropped their heads.

"I love my people, and the realm they live in; I love my lord and master the Green Lord whom I have spoken to many times. I am the hooded man returned, and I have fought none stop, but I will not have any here think this will be a fast or normal war. To rid this world of the Dark One could take years, so dig in for the long haul. I thank you for the hospitality you have bestowed on my group, show them the respect they have earned."

Robbie dropped his sword back into its sheath, and pulled Rune up at his side and placed his arm around her, turned, and walked down the back of the table. Together they headed without speaking towards the door.

"My Lord.... Please My Lord wait I am an old man." Robbie turned as the silent guests watched shocked. William McDonald ran up the side of the long table to Robbie and went down on one knee. "My Lord, I beg your forgiveness, I was rash and insulted you're honour, I see how wrong I was, please accept me in your service, and use my bow and sword as you see fit."

Rune smiled, and knelt down to face the old man, with many summers and winters on his face and long thin grey hair.

"My Lord of Loxley is honoured to accept the hand of any friend. I am touched by your honour Lord William. There is a role for us all, and you too shall play your part, thank you."

Robbie looked down and offered his hand. "No nobleman will kneel to me, stand like a woodsman and take my hand in friendship Lord William."

William McDonald stood and took Robbie by the hand.

"I thank you Lord Loxley."

He smiled as he shook the old Scots hand. "Call me Robbie, you work with me now, I am the hooded man of all our realms." William smiled.

"Aye Laddie, I ken see that." Robbie patted his shoulder, and left the room with Rune smiling on his arm. Rose leaned across the table and looked at Robert Loxley.

"Just what the hell actually happened then?"

Robert burst into laughter. "You just witnessed the biggest fear of the Dark One, which is the power of my son The Hooded Man." She nodded and looked back at the crowd of quiet guests.

"I will think twice about asking him to talk again, he scared the hell out of me."

Robert laughed loudly.

"You should see him with Rune; he is really quite a pussy cat."

Rowan and Jade had already left the room as it returned to normal; Martin and John were several paces ahead of them. Jett beamed down the table. "God Robbie just gets cooler; talk about raising the rafters, that guy has more power than all of us in just one finger. God, I love him."

Many of the group of Specialists stayed to continue talking until the early hours. Melanie suddenly found herself surrounded by men of the highlands, who were loyal to the old clans of the Callanish eagle men. She was treated with the highest courtesy and reverence. Many asked questions about their exploits with Knox, and many expressed their regret at offending Lord and Lady Loxley, who had now proven beyond doubt their commitment to the people right across the whole country. Robbie had risen considerably higher in everyone's esteem.

Rune walked out of the bathroom and came into the bedroom. Robbie was already in bed, his eyes closed; she slid into bed at his side, and leaned on his chest. He opened his eyes, and looked down at her two bright blue eyes staring back at him. She smiled. "You can be quite the rebel when you want to."

He pulled his arm around her, and she snuggled close to him. "I realised that they just have no idea at all what they are facing, this is not Mason who will die by a sword, this is a woman who could take my children and tear out their goodness, and fill them with pure cold evil."

Rune squeezed him tightly. "I will never let her do that Rob; you must not think such thoughts."

"She scares me Rune I will not deny it. In that dream, I thought I was dead, I will never forget the hopelessness I felt as I faced her, she sucked every happy thought I have ever had out of me."

"She will never harm you Rob; I will never let you face her alone again. We will fight her, and kill her side by side."

He looked into her sad eyes. "I have no idea how to actually kill her, do you?"

"There are ways of the old, I have seen some on my table, but yes you are right. It will be the hardest fight we ever have; I am under no illusions Rob."

Robbie closed his eyes. "You know she will have to be the last, don't you? I will have to kill Mordred first, and then it will be her turn."

"All you have to do is draw him into the dagger, let me handle him after that, believe me I have plans for that one."

"I think I should leave speeches to you; I do not have your calm way of expressing myself. Oh Rune, they will certainly remember me in the morning."

Rune started to giggle. "They will remember you for many years have no fear. Although I thought you were fantastic, and Jett was bouncing about loving every bit of it."

"Jett is as mad as a wild boar; you are not helping Rune."

The bed shook as Rune laughed; he opened his eyes, and looked back down at her bright laughing face. "Oh come on Rob, it wasn't that bad, I thought you spoke with authority and experience. You should have seen the horror on their faces when you mentioned cutting her fingers off. It was quite cool, and of course, how you looked Mason in the eyes when you ran him through. That had them cringing, it made great watching I can tell you. I was impressed; you were very sexy and powerful."

"Really?" He smiled; she gave him a happy giggle. "How powerful?"

Her sapphire blue eyes twinkled with delight. "Oh Robbie, you were very, very powerful."

"Wow." He pulled the sheet over her and slid down. She giggled with delight.

Robbie sat at the long table. It was early morning, and Grace had delivered the coffee and toast as requested. He had bare feet, and his shirt hung open, as he looked at all the papers Rune had written the previous day. Rowan and Jade gave him a blow by blow account of the previous day on the surface. Robbie knew the feelings of loss and pain, and the complete hopelessness that radiated from the Dark One, and he knew now that this would be his biggest difficulty.

"How do we get an army close to her without all of them going mad with despair? And where the hell are all those soldiers going if this city is full of them already? We need more information Rowan; we do not have nearly enough."

Rowan sat back and lifted a piece of toast. He took a large bite, as Jade poured out another cup of coffee; she had an odd look on her face. Robbie looked into her green eyes and she smiled. "This might sound daft Rob, but is this the only cave like this around here?"

He shrugged. "I am not sure, why what's on your mind?" She passed him a steaming cup.

"Well, we are all fine down here; I just thought if there were other caves, we could sneak up on her without her knowing, or without any of us getting affected by her."

Robbie looked at Rowan as he put his toast down on the plate. "It's not a bad idea Robbie." Jade beamed a huge smile.

"I thought you would have thought me as mad as Harry." Robbie smiled at her.

"That seems to be Jett at the moment, but Pebbles you might be on to something, what if Dunnottar is as hollow as the rest of this place? We could sit right below her, and she would have no idea."

"You are forgetting one thing Robbie; we have to cross that bridge. There is no way we can cover the amount of open space there without being seen."

Robbie took a large swig of coffee. "That is no problem, a quick word with Crystal and that will be sorted out. There is a way in I just know it... No, my worry is once we are in; we will not have plans like Tintagel or Canterbury, we will be going in blind. Stealth and caution will be needed. She will not make it easy for any of us."

Jade flopped into her chair and munched on her toast. "We will need to create one hell of a big diversion; it's a pity we don't have two Rune's, one outside to draw her out, and one inside to get my grandfather out."

Rowan looked at her with disbelief. "We do." He grabbed Jade, and lifted her long fringe back and then kissed her. "You look so like your sister at times."

Jade dropped her toast. "You can bugger off, one look at her, and I just know I will pee myself."

"Oh it's alright honey; we will stand you in a bucket." Jade looked white and very scared.

"You are joking aren't you...? Please Rowan, I am not like Rune, I cannot face her, she terrifies me."

Robbie leaned forward in his chair. "If you are in the white circle she cannot harm you, we will just need to disguise one so she does not see it, you know Pebbles you might be on to something. I really think we could have what we need to actually make this work."

Jade jumped up out of her chair. "Oh God I am going to pee myself." She fled through the door to her room. Rowan laughed at Robbie.

"Now she knows how poor old Harry feels."

Robbie looked at him quite seriously. "What... are you joking?"

Rowan suddenly looked very serious. "Yes... Robbie that's my wife, please tell me you were as well?"

"Rowan in a circle, and channelling Rune, she could really pull it off. Think about it, if we could change her hair colour and dress her in some of Rune's things, she could really look the part, it would be enough to get her out of her hole where we could see her."

Rowan looked shocked. "No way, you are not putting her at risk like that, are you mad? I will not risk losing her."

Robbie shrugged. "Anyone who enters that castle will be very unlikely to come out, with you two up on the rocks you will be a hell of lot safer than Rune and me. Think about it Rowan."

Robbie could see the fear and the doubt in Rowan's face, the plan did seem very bonkers at first, but with thought, it did look more like a plan that would work, and keep them protected. Robbie got up and patted him on the shoulder.

"I am going to get Rune up, Rowan it is one of many ideas to start with, I want a way that keeps us all as safe as possible. We will keep thinking until we have something that works. Find out if you can, if that lump of rock in the sea is hollow, there was once a big stronghold on it; someone must know what is under it."

He sat on the bed, and looked at her slender form under the soft white silk sheets, as she lay asleep. He understood the look of worry on Rowan's face; he felt the same about Rune, she was even more precious to him now. He placed his hand softly on her flat tummy; she smiled as she felt his hand rest on her. "They are safe," he smiled as she opened her eyes, and looked up at him. He leaned forward and kissed her.

"Hey beautiful mother of my children," she pulled him close as she smiled and held him tight.

"Hi my gorgeous father of my children, what's rattled Jade I can feel her?"

"I thought I could dress her up like you, and use her as a decoy to get the Dark One out of her castle, she almost peed herself again."

Rune sat up and looked at him seriously. "You are joking? That's my sister, I almost lost her once, I am not risking her again Rob."

"It was one crazy idea that's all."

"It had better be Rob, there is no way she will face the Dark One as long as I breathe, Jade is no match for her. That is my job."

"Rune calm down, we were looking at as many ideas as possible, you know like climbing the tower of the cathedral in the dark?"

"Well, that idea sounds a hell of a lot safer than sticking my sister out in the open for target practice with the Dark One."

"We have to find a decoy to get her out of her castle so she won't feel you enter to get your grandfather out."

"You leave it with me, I will find you a way, which keeps us all safe, you focus on getting us in and dealing with your new brother."

She looked very serious and he knew not to push it further, he pulled her back into a hug. "I do not want to lose anyone Rune, but this will not be easy whatever we do."

"We all heard you last night, we know the risks, but we will not easily commit suicide, so don't ask us to." He squeezed her tightly.

"I am not."

She softened. "Please Robbie be careful, I have almost lost you once. I want our children to grow up with their father. Play it as safe as you can, my heart would break and I would die without you."

There was a sadness to her voice, which frightened him. He felt a cold shiver run down his back. It stayed with him all day as he sat in thought in the many meetings that followed. Jade was very quiet, and he felt sorry for her, he had to find a way and he felt a dread on his heart, because this was not going to be easy.

There had to be a way he could get her out without losing anyone. It occupied his every free thought; if she were not in the castle, then he would be able to get things done a lot quicker, and keep Rune safe and his children away from her. What he needed was an area of trees; he needed to talk to the Green Lord. There must be a way of using magical power to fool her and draw her out. If there was, Hearne would know it. Robbie made the decision to find a way of ducking his guard, and sneaking off to consult with Hearne. If only he had the power, to transport himself like Gwendolyn had, and appear somewhere else.

The idea hit him like a bolt of lightning. Alice? Rune made Alice appear somewhere else, she could send him to Hearne, it was so simple. Maddy was talking and he had not heard a word, he jumped up out of his seat, and noticed her jump. "Sorry Maddy, I have just had a crazy idea, and I must see Rune straight away."

She nodded looking very bemused. "Yes Robbie of course."

Rune was sat on the balcony with Jade, when he entered the room. Jade gave a sheepish smile; he ruffled her hair and she gave him a grin. "Don't worry Pebbles we will find you a safer job, it will be too hard to disguise the bucket, it will give you away."

"I am sorry Robbie, I would, but she really does frighten me. I try so hard, but she gets inside me and makes me feel all sad."

He patted her shoulder. "I know, she scares me as well, I have no idea how we will get her, but we will think of something." He looked to Rune who was watching him; she knew he wanted something important. He knelt down, and looked into her bright eyes. "You know that thing you did with Alice? You sent her to John and me, and we spoke to her." Rune nodded. "Could you send me to talk with Hearne?"

"Not from here Rob, I am hidden by the crystals, we would have to leave here, and even then, she could pick up on the power and focus in on us. It would be dangerous; you would be better off going up to see him. The doorways are veiled and she cannot detect them."

Robbie felt himself sink, he could not easily leave, as he knew Rowan was tailing him everywhere he went, and Robbie wanted to keep everyone as low profile as possible. "Every time one of us leaves we take the risk of being caught out in the open, I want to avoid it as much as possible, sending Rowan up top is dangerous enough."

It had felt like a long day. Robbie sat at the table in his private rooms as more and more people came in with new facts. The Scots were now pooling all their information, and life above them was starting to form a fuller picture in his mind. It was very disturbing to hear that there were twelve large five storey orphanages in the city. These were being used as part of a captive breeding program, as women had been captured, raped, and then their children were raised as the new line of the Knox Empire. It sickened Robbie to hear it; once again, the coldness of the whole family became apparent.

Rowan returned from the surface, he had been able to weave his way across the city, and look at the rock from the safety of the safe house. He was concerned about the number of soldiers still pouring out of the castle. Rowan was now convinced that Mordred was planning a war.

Robbie sat back and looked at his worried friend. "Scotland is almost clear; most of the woodland people are down here, who could he be going to war with? They must be reinforcements for other cities."

"What if they are not Robbie? What if they are heading for York, or even Loxley? Robbie there are thousands of them, and if they have as many at Sunderland or Newcastle, we have got one hell of a big problem."

"We have always expected a war Rowan; maybe this will be the start." Robbie stared out through the window at the two quiet figures sat talking on the balcony. He felt the pressure more and more, he needed to free Merlin, and protect Loxley. What he wanted more than anything was to protect Rune. He looked at Rowan and he wore a very serious face. "Do you honestly think we can do this and survive?"

The understanding between them grew. "Robbie my good friend, I honestly do not know, I just want Jade to live."

He nodded. "We have to keep them as far out of this as possible. Rowan, I have a really bad feeling about this, I don't think I will leave that castle if I enter it."

CHAPTER SIX

RETURN OF THE VIOLET BOWMAN

Robbie needed air, the cave felt stale and foreign to him, and he had walked down to the large gates at the end of the cave, and down the long tunnel to the open sea air. Rowan was a few feet behind him with Bear and Skip.

He sat on the edge of a large rock, and breathed the clean salty air deeply, and just enjoyed the sensation of fresh air in his lungs and nostrils. He had felt down all day, and knew he missed the trees. The sea exploded up the cliff and sprayed a fine cool salty mist across his face. He lay back and enjoyed the late afternoon sun.

Rowan sat beside him, and he too made the most of the fresh air. "What is it Robbie? You have seemed very low today. Tell me and I will help." Robbie sat forward and patted his friend on the leg. Skip and Bear leaned on the rail in front.

"We face an unknown enemy my friends, and it is hard for me to confront it. Our team hide their fear well, but I see it in all of you. I will not deny that I fear her as much as all of you do, I meant what I said the other night."

Skip, crouched low to come face to face with him. "They miss the woods and the spirit of adventure that we have all grown use to around you. This place has saved many lives, but these people here have been under the ground so long, their morale has been sapped, what we need Robbie is to boost them up, and give them a reason to live."

Rowan nodded. "I could use a good laugh and no mistake, and looking at those poor sods up on the cliff top, I would say that they could do with something to give them a lift."

Robbie's mind began to slowly plod the idea around. "You are suggesting something that will give everyone something to be happy about, well that's easy we just kill the Dark One."

Skip smiled. "Or we could pretend for a while she is Mason and make her life hard as we did his."

Robbie gave a shrewd grin. "You mean like blow up her supplies, and terrorise her men?"

"That is exactly what I am thinking. Why not? She has had it all her own way for too long, are we not experts in stealth My Lord of the trees? It would seem to me that now is the time to start a few rumours."

Robbie gave a huge grin. "When I was a kid, we had this great story about a haunted part of the woodland near the northern borders of Loxley. They said if you walked alone in the woods after dark, you would be shot dead with a violet arrow. If you had someone with you, then one of you would die and one of you would live. The Violet Bowman always caught the one who lived. He would sneak up on you and grab you from behind and whisper into your ear. You live only by the right of the Violet Bowman, leave now or die." Robbie beamed a huge smile. "I followed Billy one night and really freaked him out with it."

Rowan nodded. "That is so strange, we had the very same folk tale, except he would threaten to visit you in bed and kill you, saying I know where you live."

Bear stood up and looked across the water. "A few visits in the night in that confined place could cause chaos, and make her life very unsettled." Skip straightened up.

"Robbie my friend, think about it, it would also remove your presence from the equation, and how hard would it be in the darkness to navigate the roof tops, they are all flat?" Skip began to chuckle as he spoke. "We would of course have to keep this very quiet, and not tell a soul; just keep it in the Loxley camp."

Robbie felt a little violet ray of hope rise in his heart. "This could work if planned right, we will need violet dye, I mean if we are going to do it, let's colour our arrows. The last thing I want will be the white arrows of Loxley shot all over the place."

Rowan sat back against the wall. "Maggs will know all about dye, if she cannot find us some, no one can, and looking at the clothes she wears, she will not be suspected for buying any."

Robbie felt excited and jumped up. "Ok let's go to work, I want the first strike tonight. The sooner I know her life is harder, the quicker I will feel happier." Laughter sprouted amongst the group as they headed back to the lodge down the tunnel.

Robbie worked fast, he found Rose very quickly. "I need somewhere private for my team to rehearse and practice their routines; do you have anywhere that would suit our training needs?"

Rose thought for a moment. "There is only one place I can think of. It is the large warehouse cut out of the rock under where we enter the old general store. It is quite large, and you would have plenty of space to use swords, possibly not bow practice. I will have Sinclair show you the place."

Robbie drew the plan in his mind, as Rowan visited Maggs and spoke quietly, and then disappeared with her, Robbie returned to the room where everyone sat bored, with a huge smile on his face. "We have a new training facility, grab your kit and follow me."

Sinclair had to be brought in on the plan; Skip made him swear to secrecy before he would reveal anything to him at all. Sinclair was the contact with the surface, and so he would be required to set up the times when the group sneak out on to the roofs.

Finally, after much debate, as Sinclair did not like the idea of hiding things from Rose he did agree, and was brought in on the plan. Rune and Jade squealed with delight and were soon playing their role within the group.

Robbie knocked on the door to the large storage house, and whispered.

"Rebirth." The door opened and Rune giggled, as her eyes danced. The entire group gave each other strange looks. Robbie slipped into the large empty carved space and looked around. Maggs and Jade were in the far corner being supervised by Rowan. Maggs slowly stirred the contents of a large pot whilst Jade swept long sticks through the boiling liquid, and giggled. She passed them to Rowan who laid them out on the floor to dry. The group slipped in through the door and gathered round waiting to see what was in store for them.

A very tall ladder led up to the roof, where a hole had been cut in it, and a trap door fitted. Robbie looked up and then back at Rune. "Nice work." She smiled

"Even crystal reverts back to nature." Robbie looked at the damp puddle on the floor, and the dry dusty compounds. He turned to the puzzled group, as Rune and Bear stood either side of him.

"Well my band of Specialists, we came here to do a job and found that fear is being employed to suppress the people, so, a few of us have thought about using a similar tactic. However, I warn you all now, no word of this is to leave this room. Only the group here is to know, and I will come down hard on any who let this slip."

They all nodded and tried to look past Robbie at what the others behind him were doing. "So Robbie?" Jett smelt fun and adventure. "What is this secret plan, and what do we have to do?" She beamed a big smile at him, as Rune grinned.

"Oh Jett, you will love this... we are going to bring to life the Violet Bowman."

Jett gave a mischievous look of fun. "Oh cool! We get to freak the guards upstairs. Wow Robbie this is going to be totally wicked." Jade giggled from the bottom of the room, and ran up with the first dry violet arrow. She handed it to Robbie.

"This is the first one, the others won't be much longer, Maggs says they are alright, but she will have them spot on by tomorrow."

Robbie held the arrow with deep violet feathers out in front of the group. "Here is what we will do. We cover the city using the darkness and the rooftops, hoods will be essential. We will work in groups of three. One shoots, one grabs and talks and the other one will paint."

Jett looked confused. "Paint what?" Rune gave her a deep and naughty glance.

"He who helps the house of Knox will suffer the Violet Bowman's shots." She gave a giggle. "It will tell the guards to beware, and get the workers panicked; fear will breed a lot of trouble."

"Oh wow, you guys are so crazy and cool. I am so goin to enjoy this. It is about time we started to cause some mayhem." Jett bounced on the spot, itching to go.

Maggs dried out the arrows, and the shooters filled up their quivers with the long violet arrows. Sinclair handed out a paint like substance in jars with string handles and spring-loaded lids, with paintbrushes. Skip, Bear and Robbie worked out the teams and prepared. It had been decided to use different teams over successive nights, so that they would take it in turn to go up on the rooftops. Robbie thought this would also give everyone the chance to get use to the city, and learn it's lay out. The teams prepared on the ladder and Robbie gave the signal. They shot up the ladder, and through the trap door into the room above.

They climbed up to the General Store, and came out in the kitchen. One by one in the dark, they climbed up the pipes to the roof. Robbie pulled them all close, he looked up at the dark sky and the clouds floating quickly past. "Ok are we ready?" They all nodded. "Bear. Jett and Rafe go north. Harry, Rowan, and Jade, south. Dad, Martin, and Fish, head east, and Jaz, Keith, and Saff you handle west, all of you stay alert and make sure you leave enough alive to spread the word. Good luck you have two hours, then meet back here." Robbie rose slowly up, and shot an arrow into the floor. It stood proud in the soft cement. "Don't get lost and use your heads."

The groups scattered silently across the rooftops, Robbie leaned over the edge of the roof and signalled to Sinclair. He gave him the thumbs up, and Robbie turned back to Rune and Big John. "I have something a little special in mind for us. Follow me."

Robbie slipped up his hood, and ran silently across the roofs. The streets below were so narrow everyone had no difficulties in jumping the gaps. He followed the line of the passage the others had taken only the day previous, and slowly he made his way to the viewing rock face.

J ade slipped quietly down the wall; her green eyes glowed in the dark as she peered round the corner. Harry stood on the roof with his bow ready, as Rowan slipped down beside her. The two guards came nearer, and Jade shot across their path into the alley on the other side. She reappeared in the shadows, and leaned forward as Harry took aim.

The guards walked past as she slipped back into the shadow. She stepped out behind them, drawing her knife as Harry released his arrow. It hit the guard to the left in the back, as Jade grabbed the guard to the right. Her Knife slid to his throat, and he froze with fear as he saw his friend fall with the long violet tipped arrow sticking out of his back.

"You know who I am, don't you?" Jade whispered in a deep and sinister voice in his ear.

The eyes of the guard widened in panic, as his childhood fears crept back into his mind. "It cannot be true; you are a myth." His voice was high and filled with disbelief.

Jade pulled the blade tighter on his throat. "Do I feel like a myth, your friend does not think so? I could kill you, or I will let you live."

The soldier shook from head to foot. "Oh, please let me live."

"I will let you live if you leave here. If you don't, I will find where you sleep, and you know the price?" She felt the weakness in the young soldier's knees and thought for a moment he would faint. "Run home, and if you look back, you will see death is behind you." Jade released the soldier, who stumbled and then fled at high speed up the street.

She turned and beamed a huge smile at Rowan, who was now painting on the wall. 'HE WHO HELPS THE HOUSE OF KNOX, WILL SUFFER THE VIOLET BOWMAN'S SHOTS.'

Jade crept up holding her mouth, as she tried to suppress the violent fit of giggles she was having. The wet letters dribbled down the wall, in horrible violet streaks, it glistened in the moonlight. They finished, and climbed back up the drainpipe, to wait for the next group of guards. Rowan pulled her close to stifle her giggles as they waited.

Harry watched from the edge of the roof, he whispered back. "Hey man you don't like think the real bowman dude will get like bad vibes, and get heavy on us. That will be totally uncosmic man; he lives with uncosmic things you know?"

Jade shook harder and little squeaks emitted from around Rowan's chest, Rowan fought hard to swallow his laughter and as he shook, Jade shook even harder. Her legs came around him and she hugged him harder, as she tried to bury her laughter. Rowan pushed his head into her and silently giggled. They both shook as one quaking mass on the floor. Harry peered around nervously in the dark, he was sure the real violet bowman would not like this.

J ett sat on the edge of the roof and looked down; the two guards walked slowly past; she slipped down the drainpipe to Rafe. He loaded his bow and signalled to Bear across the way, they leaned into the shadows.

The guards turned at the end of the street, and walked slowly back. The arrow came out of the alleyway, and hit the first guard in the chest. He dropped to his knees as his companion jumped back with fright. Two blue eyes suddenly gleamed bright in the dark alley, and Bear snatched him from behind. "You may die or not tonight, will you leave this place, or shall I hunt you in the dark another night?"

The puddle on the floor spread wide from his feet, and he struggled to speak. How could those eyes have got round him so fast, he fainted, and Bear chuckled as he fell to the floor in his own urine.

Jett staggered out holding her sides with Rafe's socks stuffed in her mouth. Rafe grabbed the brush off her, and hurriedly began to paint, as Jett rolled around in silent hysterics. Bear snatched her off the floor, and ran with the quaking mass on his shoulder up the narrow street. Rafe sealed the paint jar and then followed.

Robbie looked across the viewing square. "We take all of them for this one." Rune and John nodded, and loaded their bows. The shots were swift and silent, the guards dropped to the floor and before the others could understand what was happening, and another three arrows came out of the darkness.

They dropped quickly to the floor and raced across the square, Rune stood guard as Robbie and John dragged the bodies and sat them against the rail. The long violet tipped arrows stood out of their chests. John took his bow and stood beside Rune, and Robbie pulled out the paintbrush.

BEWARE THE VIOLET BOWMAN WILL VISIT YOU ALL, AND HE WILL SEEK HIS REVENGE ON THE HOUSE OF KNOX. YOU CAN CHOOSE WHEN YOU DIE. He sealed the lid, and tapped the two of them on the shoulder and they left. Into the shadows they silently went with a bright smile, Robbie ran up the drainpipe on to the roof. They made their way slowly back to the roof of the store, any pairs of guards they saw, they took one of them out leaving the other to stare with fear. It was just under two hours later, when the group sat smiling on the roof, having had a night of murderous rebellion. They waited for Sinclair who came out and stood watch, he gave the signal, and like dark shadows they slipped down, and in through the door.

Maggs had Blades and Judith helping her, and the others sat around drinking coffee and waiting. The trap door opened, and the howls of laughter could be heard as the group descended. Jett still chewed Rafe's socks, as she hit the floor, she turned and pulled them out of her mouth and beamed at the others. "That was so cool. It was the best, Robbie you are a genius." Jett went into the story of the guard who wet himself and then fainted, and howled with laughter as she described the scene, Jade rolled around as she gave her story with the deep voice and soon Robbie watched as the smiles and giggles spread from one to the other.

Rune slid her arm round him and passed him a drink. "You are clever Rob; you ridicule what they fear the most, is that why you sent Jade and Jett, because you know how deep their fear of her is?" Robbie pulled her closer and whispered.

"Tell me you are not terrified of her, because I am Rune, I need to keep this lot happy, because if I don't they will never make it through. A few nights of this and they will start to believe they are winning. If they do, they will fight like winners. I want them to win; I have no intention of placing a Loxley grave yard here too."

It was a very happy crowd that walked into the lodge that night. Rose looked up from her desk, and looked out of the window. The group came noisily up the steps and in through the doors. She walked out of her office, and watched as the group rowdily made their way up the stairs. Robbie and Rune came smiling and talking through the doors, Rune beamed as Robbie looked across and nodded at Rose.

"Your group are in very high spirits tonight My Lord?"

He looked up the stairs, as his group turned to go up the next flight. "They have had a very good training session tonight, I believe in letting them celebrate their achievements, it raises morale."

"Maybe I should let you train some of mine; I have seldom seen such a close group of fighters."

Rune gave a small giggle. "That is what makes them such Specialists."

Rose looked unsure. "Their achievements to date speak volumes; I am pleased everything is going so well." Robbie gave a smile and walked past Rose holding Rune close, it had been a long day, and he was tired, but deep down inside he felt a little calmer, knowing his team were beginning to conquer their fear.

Fear is a strange weapon, yet it is effective. Dawn brought unexpected scenes to the viewing square. The group of dawn shift workers screamed like children and pressed themselves against the wall. The soldiers who should have beaten them for it, stood still and white faced, as they saw their colleagues, they too thought that what they faced was myths of childhood. Their dead friends said different. The captain of the guard screamed at them. "Get those bloody workers moving, ignore this children's prank. There is no such thing as the Violet Bowman." The long violet arrow came from nowhere, and hit him deep in the throat. The onlookers turned to see an empty alleyway as the captain slipped dead to the floor.

The women screamed, and ran leaving the men. They looked to the empty alley and they all screamed, and ran after the women. Two green eyes giggled as they came over the wall, and on to the roof towards Robbie. He chuckled as the two of them keeping low ran back to the General Store.

Soldiers panicked across the city, and workers became mysteriously ill, the gossip and fear came back to Robbie via the talk in the General Store, which was just about the only place you could meet and talk. The storekeeper fuelled the flames, as he exaggerated the stories he heard, and soon the whole city was living in fear of the dark.

Robbie and Jade came smiling into the meeting room. Rose stood and looked him in the eye. "What colour are your arrows?" Robbie slid one out from his quiver, and handed it to her.

"Everyone knows a Loxley arrow is white, it is the sign of the hooded man, you knew that didn't you Rose?"

"You have not heard what they are saying up top then?"

Jade slipped past Rose, into her room as Robbie looked at her. "No, we have not sent our crew up yet. They go after breakfast." He looked so innocent it made the whole group blush. "Why is there something we should know?"

Rose somehow knew he was not being honest, and yet she could not prove it. "What do you know of the Violet Bowman?"

"The Violet Bowman...? That old myth to frighten kids...? Actually, you know, there was this really great time when I took Billy out on his own, into the woods."

"LORD LOXLEY!"

"What Rose?"

"This is not the time for old tales of fun and jokes, the Violet Bowman whom you think is a myth struck killing four dozen guards last night."

Robbie looked shocked. "You are joking?"

Rose seemed to deflate. "I wish I was, but I am not, the whole city is feeling somewhat terrified at the moment, they are more scared of him than they are the Dark One. It's chaos up there."

"Well correct me if I am wrong Rose, but isn't that a good thing? Shouldn't we find him and thank him." Robbie smirked, and the group put their heads down. Rune turned away behind Rose, and slipped quietly into her room.

"Lord Loxley the man is a ghost, a myth, how can you thank a spirit?" She seemed like she was about to unravel.

Robbie looked at Jaz. "You can talk to the dead can't you Jasper...? Have a quick word and tell him we are grateful."

Rose stamped her foot on the floor. "Oh!!!" She turned and walked out slamming the door.

Rune fell out of her room with tears in her eyes. "Telling Jaz to thank him, oh Robbie you are so wicked." She howled and everyone started to laugh.

Robbie shrugged as he smiled at her. "That was very good work last night guys, who is up for tonight?"

Rose sat at her desk fuming at Sinclair. "I bloody well know it was him. Bloody smart arse, stood there like butter wouldn't melt. Mind you he is a clever bugger; got us all thinking it's ghosts, while he runs about in his hood and knocks em off one at a time." She glared at the back of Sinclair. "You keep a close eye on him. I want that entrance on the balcony watched all night. He cannot slip up there so easily. It is right out front, if a single person goes through that door, we will know. You know the cheeky bugger actually asked one of his men to contact the ghost and thank him. He is some sort of clairvoyant or something. Can you believe the nerve of the man?"

Sinclair bit his lip and tried not to shake.

The training day in the old warehouse went well. The sound of swords clashing, and shouted instructions came through the doors on the many occasions that Rose walked past. Jett and Skip put everyone through their paces. Robbie wanted everyone at their peak.

Down the side of one of the walls where there was a very wide gap. Robbie roped off a long area, and using large bales of straw, he built a firing range of three hundred meters. Most of the Scottish woodsmen were very interested, as they had never used longer than two, and there were few who were that accurate at such a distance. Robbie and Rune supervised their group.

Blades and Judy had improved a great deal; Maggs was coming along nicely, as was Bear. They shot well, and everyone who stood and watched smirked and nodded. They all knew they could match them arrow for arrow.

Robbie cleared the range, and called up Maddy and Crystal, they moved back to the two fifty mark, the Scots watched carefully. Maddy and Crystal took bulls. The audience were very impressed and politely applauded. Martin and John fired next and met the sides of the girl's arrows. They were not easy shots and the nods from the crowd acknowledged that. Rafe and Keith matched their shots, and the locals were again suitably impressed.

One woodsman looked at the three hundred meter mark. "What's tha point in that if your no gonna use it?" Robbie looked at the marker and then winked at Rune. Crystal pulled all the arrows from the target and stepped back, as Robbie and Rune walked to the three hundred meter mark.

They stood side by side, their movements were fluid, and in perfect timing with each other. Together they slid their white tipped arrows from over their shoulders, and fitted them to the strings. Both bows came up together and they aimed. Rose watched with Sinclair from the balcony on the opposite side of the wide cave. "There is no way you could hit bull from that far."

The arrows released at the same time, and shot down the range at a horrific rate, there was a loud thud, and the crowd roared. As they looked back, Robbie and Rune raised their bows and fired. The arrows hit and split the first two. Rose stared in utter disbelief. Robbie and Rune walked backwards aiming their third arrows, slowly they moved back and Robbie spoke. "Say when sweetheart." The target was getting smaller and smaller.

Rune smiled. "Ok big head that's far enough." They fired and planted their arrows right in the bull, the crowd went insane and Rune beamed as Robbie kissed her on the cheek.

"See practice makes perfect, want to go for the title?" She beamed at him.

"You are such a show off at times," she started to move backwards, as she loaded her arrow. Rune stopped and took aim. Robbie watched her focus; she released the arrow and it hit just inside the ring of the bull. The crowd roared louder and she giggled, Robbie walked back another ten paces, and Rune stepped out of the way.

He was around three hundred and seventy five meters away from the bull. The whole crowd held their breath; Robbie took his time to draw out the suspense. His arrow came like a missile; it passed in a blink, and hit his last arrow splitting it right down the centre. Rose leaned so far over the rail she nearly fell off as Sinclair snatched her back quickly. "BLOODY HELL!"

Rune walked up and gave him a kiss. "Oh you are such a flirt, god that was sexy."

He winked and smiled. "You're my girl, I want to impress you." He put his arm round her, and they walked back to the happy cheering crowd. Rowan and Saff took aim from three hundred and the practice continued. The Scottish woodsmen loved it and soon a few found the courage to ask Lord Loxley his advice.

Very soon, Robbie and Rune were talking tactics and showing the Scottish bowmen a few tricks, all of them improved instantly. Rose smiled as she watched from the balcony opposite. "You can see why they love him, just look at him? Who would think that quiet and calm boy was a lord? How the hell did he learn to shoot like that?"

Sinclair watched at her side. "You should see them up top, they move like shadows and do not make a sound, and you saw them fight in the pass. They really are specialist; they took that whole group of soldiers out in just a few minutes. I tell you what Rose love, if they do get inside that castle. The Dark One will meet her match, they are better than even they realise."

The arrival of Jett and Skip to the range brought another attraction, Rune seized on the opportunity to show the skills of the team. She cleared the range of the bowmen and Blades slid off her top, and pulled her two swords. She wore her tight fitting vest, and was ready to work up a sweat.

Jett unbuttoned her oriental jacket, and slid it down her arms, she was slender, but her arms showed the power in them, Rune smiled at the surprise of Robbie to see a scorpion tattooed on the top of her arm. He had never seen her swimming, unlike the other women. The sting of Jett on her arm looked fierce and menacing. She turned to hang her jacket on the post and he saw on her other arm the sword of truth.

"Now you know why she was your guardian, and that is her sword. It is the one she always found the most beautiful." Rune smiled. He had no idea at all.

Harry drew his blades, and passed them to Jett. She wiped them together and spun them in her hands, a smile crossed her lips as she prepared and licked them. Blades spun her blades faster, and stamped on the floor. The audience gasped as it began; there was a glint of light, and then the clash, and song of steel on steel.

No one in the cave had ever seen the Samurai sword in action, not that you could see the blades because they were just a blur. Jett laughed, and threw back her head. Blades squealed with delight, and the whoops and cheers of the fighting duo sung into the air, it was an unbelievable display. They both had two very different fighting styles, and yet they were evenly matched. Blades bounced into the air somersaulting, still clashing her blades, as she leapt over Jett's head, she landed like a cat, her arms still whizzing with her golden swords. Jett screamed with laughter, as she spun with the grace of a ballerina, her own swords moving with such speed it was hard to know how she focused and screamed with such pleasure.

"Go baby girl," she shouted, as Blades back flipped out of the way of Jett, and vaulted up into the air, landing back in the midst of the glinting steel, she laughed with the joy of the fight, and the crowd gasped in shock and amazement. They fought hard and fast, and as they reached their point of no return, Blades came back flipping out of the midst and up towards Robbie, where she landed in the split's, swords up, and bowed to Jett. Jett spun her swords, and bowed back to Blades, smiling and gasping for breath.

The audience screamed, and whistled and yelled their praise as the two great friends hugged each other, and then bowed to the crowd. The Specialists had done well, and truly stamped their mark on Scotland. Jett spun the swords and happily passed them to Harry. Jett and Blades shone with sweat, and beamed with delight, everyone wanted to shake their hands, and Robbie stood with his crew around him and his arms folded, he looked at Rowan. "Rest those two tonight, take the rest out, and do as much damage as you can. Rose is on to me, so I will lead her around for a while. Slip out at ten and be back here by midnight." Rowan nodded, Robbie looked up at the balcony across the cave, he saw Rose talking to Sinclair, and she turned and looked right at him. Robbie nodded his head and she replied.

The captains of the guards were very worried. No one was about to face Mordred and inform him of the loss of the guards. They had spent all day trying to get the violet letters off the concrete. It was porous, and had soaked in deep. Workers with tears of fear in their eyes scrubbed with all their might, but it was too deep. The guard was tripled, and now all areas were filled with groups of six. Many were white faced, and very worried. The moon was hidden, and all was quiet. Guards stood in the light towers waiting to illuminate anything that might move.

Rowan sat with seventeen companions on the roof. He handed out the violet cloth masks that Maggs had made. "Just in case they use the lights, keep your hood up and let them see the violet in your face. Shoot the lights out and kill the guards. No one goes down on the floor; we all stay on the roof tonight and keep as low as you can. Ok you all know your places, back here in two hours, take as many as possible."

The group fitted their masks and then faded into the dark. It was a night of fear and terror. The biggest game ever known of cat and mouse began, Rowan was fast and furious; he hunted the guards in the light towers. So fast was his bow that as he hit the first man, he was firing at the second. Jade backed him up, and as she ducked behind the wall, and he brought up his bow, a large light flicked on.

Rowan spun, and unleashed his arrow, in the second that the guard saw the violet face, before the light exploded showering him in glass, his heart had frozen with fear, and he jumped from the tower and died on the rocks below.

Those guards on the floor who had seen the violet face, had dropped their weapons, and ran screaming into the alleyways. They ran for all they were worth until they looked up ahead and saw the violet hooded face looking down at them. Fish laughed as he fired and the arrow hit its mark. The group skidded to a halt, turned and ran back towards Rowan.

Jade heard them and prepared, she leaned over the wall and screamed as she fired. Two fainted, and one took an arrow in the chest, the few who remained had no idea how the phantom that stalked them could move so fast, and they fell to the floor and wept in fear.

Crystal dropped her hood and looked over the wall. The bright violet face surrounded by white, bright, ghostly feathered hair, froze the guards where they stood, and she fired, and hit them as they shook with fear. She pulled up her hood laughing and ran across the rooftops.

Eighteen Specialists went on to the rooftops, and two hundred guards died in two hours of terror and hell. The streets were littered with the dead, and the workers of Knox sat huddled in small groups in their homes, and cringed in fear as they heard the terrified shrieks from outside. Fear stalked every street and room in the whole city that night, Mordred still had no idea, but so high were the numbers that there could be no way his officers could hide it for much longer.

Robbie and Rune walked up the street arm in arm, and talked and laughed and kissed. Rose followed in the shadows along the balcony. They headed for the steps up to the tavern; he did not look back because Rune knew she was there, as he stepped onto the first step and started the climb, he leaned over and kissed her softly. "Is she still with us?" Rune giggled loudly, then whispered.

"Twenty feet to your right, eight feet up." She kissed him back very softly on the neck.

"Oh, don't do that now." She laughed quietly. They came to the door of the tavern and slipped through. Rune sped up the steps into the bar, and in a flash; she opened the window of shimmering light. Robbie came up to the side of the door and waited. Rose felt her excitement grow, she knew it was him, especially after the display he had given, she peered through the gap in the door, and Rune had her hand through the window. "Hurry I will wait here please be careful Robbie." She pulled her hand out as Rose opened the door.

A hand with a silver bracelet of oak leaves grabbed her tunic, pulled, and she flew through the air, and straight through the shimmering window, as she squealed with fright. Rose fell headfirst sliding on the grass of Robbie's Mere. Robbie and Rune came through, and the window closed in a shimmering flash behind them. "Welcome to Loxley and my house Rose. If you had wanted an invite, you only had to ask."

Rose was furious as she glared up at him. "What the hell are you doing? And why have you kidnapped me? Take me back immediately." There was fire in her blue eyes, but also a little fear.

Robbie crouched and offered his hand. "You have not been kidnapped, we needed to pop home for a few things, you seemed so keen on coming, I thought I would let you see where I live, you know repay the hospitality. I also am very interested in knowing why you are so keen to follow me, when I know that my own men are watching me."

She took his hand and he pulled her up. "I don't trust you Loxley, you are way too smart for your own good, and way too good to be trusted."

Robbie smiled at Rune. "You and her will make great mates one day honey."

Rune giggled and took her arm. "Let's go in the house and talk, our lord will not be here for a while, we can have a good chat."

Rose looked scared. "The Green Lord comes here?"

Robbie smiled at her. "It's quite safe, we are neighbours... He has a very nice cave over the fence in the woods; he likes to pop in for a chat or a conception." Rune started to laugh as she looked back at the shock on Rose's face.

"Ignore him he thinks he is funny... Come on, I will show you our home. Robbie put a pot on."

"Yes sweetheart." Rune linked Rose by the arm, and led her up the glade, to the house. Rose looked in wonder.

"You live here? Oh my, this is fantastic."

"We like it, there is plenty of cupboard space, and I have my table in the cellar and my loom in the back room. Robbie obviously has his desk in the office in the attic. He never stops working, I have to jump on him just to get him to come and eat with us. Jade and Rowan are the closest neighbours, just through the wood, but apart from them we have the place pretty much to ourselves. It suits us well."

Rose looked back at Robbie and then very nervously she looked into the warm happy eyes of Rune. "Is he serious about the Lord Hearne? I thought that remark you made to old McDonald was just a joke to prove a point."

"Oh no Rose, the Green Lord is actually part of my family, he calls me daughter, but technically I am his great granddaughter. It all confuses Rob a great deal, but he puts up with them. He has banned walking through walls though."

Rose stared at Rune with slight horror on her face. She smiled. "You are joking and making fun of me, aren't you?"

Rune looked quite serious. "Oh no it really is all true, I am the new daughter of the woods, Opal has retired and gone to the other realm, she was over a thousand years old, she needed the rest, although I do miss her." Rose looked even more afraid and looked back to make sure Robbie was still following.

"You know Rose, Robbie does not like being followed, it makes him a little irritable. He will risk his life for your people, you should trust him; you have seen how his team fight twice now. You will not find better, when you talk to the Green Lord, you will see the truth and learn the knowledge of who Robbie is. He is the kindest and most caring person you will ever meet."

Rose looked at Rune with wide frightened eyes, the colour seemed to be draining from her face. "Rune please stop, I am not strong enough to talk to the Green Lord, I am not worthy of him."

Robbie put his hand on her shoulder as they came in through the glass doors. "Rose you have fought tooth and nail for your people. They also happen to be his, you are more worthy than you think, and you should have no fear of him. Come on we will have a coffee or herbal tea while we wait, maybe some sweet jasmine, it has a good calming effect."

Rune showed the very nervous Rose around the house. Rune was bright and happy, as she picked out a clean set of clothes for Robbie. Rune showed her the bedroom for her daughter, and then the room for her son, Rose was not even aware that Rune was pregnant. It had remained a Loxley secret. By the time, they came and joined Robbie out on the porch she had started to calm down.

"I am sorry Robbie, I have become so secretive with the way I guard my people, I should have been a lot straighter with you, although you have not been so straight with me either. I know you either know, or have something to do with this Violet Bowman thing, you cannot deny that?"

He looked at her. "We keep all our work secret not because we have no trust of you Rose, we have suffered two spies in our camp and it has almost lost us some of our best. I now run a very tight outfit, and what happens between us stays between us. You can only be part of the loop if you show your trust in us."

"So, you do know something?"

"Rose what I know is this. Knox was an expert at using fear to defeat his enemies. We have used fear once already to put doubt in the minds of his Cutters, if I can achieve the same goal again I will."

A glimpse of recognition passed over her face as she looked up at Robbie. "So, the rumour of those you wounded and would not kill is right. You maimed them and left them to die?"

"We do not see it that way and you did not see what they did to the women and children, which we buried at Hornsby. I will not talk of it as it disturbs my dreams still. I gave them all a chance to live and think of the horrors they did. Many of them took their own lives, and some lived to remember, and from what I have heard, they left Mason forever. That has saved lives." Robbie sat and looked at the Mere in the dark. "I love this place, it's so peaceful." He sipped his drink and relaxed.

Rune stood up and smiled. "Here he is, right on time." She waved, and ran beaming down the grass. Rose watched in disbelief as Rune was swept up into the arms of the Green Lord. Robbie stood up and looked at Rose.

"She loves her old granddad, come on I will introduce you." Rose stood up as Robbie pulled her hand. Rose blanched with fear almost rooted to the spot.

Hearne looked down into the happy face of Rune. "Oh my daughter, changed is the face since our last meeting; you glow with the flowers that grow inside."

"Oh father of all creation, I am so happy, I was in such pain to know my Robbie would suffer, thank you for the gifts of new life." Hearne smiled and pulled her close and hugged her. His arms seemed to creak like old bark and his robes rustled like the leaves of the winter beech.

Robbie walked up with Rose. "My Lord Hearne happy am I to see you, I have a guest of high honour to present to you." Robbie bowed to his lord. Hearne looked into the frightened eyes of Rose.

"I find it hard to reach you my lady under the stones, long have I waited for this meeting. You have done well for your people; you will return to me the lands of your fathers if you truly trust my grandchildren. You have given much to your land and I thank you, the realm of the woodland folk owes you much."

Rose bowed. "My... Lord, I am unsure what to say, I have never dreamed I would meet you in person." He smiled, and his eyes twinkled like summer berries on the bush. He placed a long twig like finger filled hand on her shoulder, as she looked down at the floor. The lord of the green realm lifted her face to his and smiled.

"The violet arrow has aided your cause, to fight fire with fire can be useful, but now you must crush the stones and enter the castle, time is not on your side. The black son has gathered a mighty army, and soon my son of the woodland must leave to fight in other places. You have a cave filled with men who are standing idle. Give them the joy of the fight and surround the city. The black son will not expect you to lay siege to his land. The tree can grow in strange places."

Hearne looked to Robbie. "I see you are still angry with your lord, My Bowman. You feel I was unjust with the mother of your life. You have a tongue use it, and release what festers inside."

Robbie looked at the old man and he felt the anger. "You gave her no choice at all. How could you, the father of nature and all life rob her of the very essence of who she is, knowing the pain you would cause one whom you say you love? Your choice was cruel and wrong. She is your line, and yet you allowed the cruellest of pains and let her suffer, I would never treat my children with such coldness."

Rune looked shocked and grabbed his arm. "Rob this is your lord, please I beg you. You cannot have these words with him."

Hearne laughed loud, and it boomed like a sound exploding from an old trunk. "My sweet Runestone, do you not see the power of his love. It is such he would risk my anger, but I am not angry and will say this to you bowman. The sacrifice made long ago was for Runestone alone. I could not give that life for any other, I took no pleasure in the rules we made long before time. I took some relief knowing I had the means to correct her decision, but do not think that I found it easy. I walked your woods waiting for her to tell you. For only with your knowledge could the balance be restored. Be at peace together now my children, and enjoy the pleasure that will come of this."

Hearne pulled Robbie forward with Rune, and hugged them both. "My children listen carefully, now is not the time of her death; you can force her back south, and help restore the north. Seek to destroy what is in the sword; you both have the tools now so use them. Butterflies Runestone can speak through all rock. Family I find My Bowman have the answers to questions not asked yet. I will leave you for now, but look to the north."

The Old Lord turned, and the breeze blew happily round him. Robbie smiled as his hair lifted, and he watched the trees bend to greet their creator, and the white mist swirled in around him and he disappeared inside it and was gone. Robbie stood holding Rune's hand and watching the trees sway.

"Robbie, I cannot believe you tried shouting at him, he could just blink and kill you... Although I am so thrilled you had a go at the Lord Hearne to protect me, which was so sweet, I do love you." She pulled him close and gave him a huge slow kiss.

"Wow, I need to get you back to Scotland."

They turned to the pale face of Rose. Rune smiled. "Isn't he sweet? See I told you he would be nice."

Rose was lost. She had spoken to the creator of all things. She felt privileged and honoured, and completely overwhelmed. She had no words to express the emotions flowing through her.

Rune ran up to the house and grabbed her bag. She blew out the candles and closed the doors, she came down the grass to the pair of them, waved her hand as the violet light appeared, and shimmered in front of them. Robbie and Rune stepped through. Robbie reappeared and grabbed Rose, he gave her a tug and she went through as the violet light faded, and quiet descended on Robbie's Mere.

They all stepped through into the tavern, and Robbie looked at Rose. "Are you alright, you seem sort of distant?"

Rose looked dazed as she looked at them. "I honestly thought it was all a joke, but it wasn't. You two really are the real deal, I have just peed myself for the first time in almost thirty years."

Robbie looked at her. "Not you as well, what is it with all you lot peeing at the sight of a lord or dark witch. Rowan was right; I need to get more buckets."

Rune giggled as she slid her arm around him. "Let's get back and have a bath and then slip into bed, we need to start a fight for our lives tomorrow."

The group of happy smiling faces sat on the steps of the lodge as they walked up. Rowan nodded at Robbie, as Rune guided Rose to her room. Rose watched as the two of them walked smiling up the stairs with their crew.

Sinclair came out and smiled at her. "I have been looking for you, where have you been?" She stared at the happy loving pair as they climbed the stairs together.

"You really have no idea how incredibly special those two are. Pull all the watches off them, and let them have free run of the place. I want every resource we have at their disposal." She turned to him and gave him a weak smile. "I have just met with the Green Lord.... Runestone is his great granddaughter for real. She ran up the grass, and jumped into his arms as I would my father's, he kissed her. Anything you hear about myths coming alive, take it from me, they are for real... I need to go to bed now."

Rose walked quietly back into her room, as screams echoed all over the dark stone city. Dead soldiers and violet arrows littered the place. The city beyond the dark rock now lived with a fear greater than the Dark One, she could be seen, this fear hid itself in the mind, and it grew with every quaking moment.

CHAPTER SEVEN

BUTTERFLIES AND TREES

It was shortly before dawn, and the soldiers walked in groups of four along the wall. They were more alert than they had ever been; their eyes darted from left to right, and every sound made them jump. The gloom of the previous night was unbearable as they walked as quietly as possible, keeping low, and trying not to draw attention to themselves. The plan by the hooded man had worked as effectively as the Dark One's. Both sides' now battled fear, and the screams from the darkness as more bodies were discovered, increased the fear now growing in the minds of the guards and workers.

The dawn shift was half what it had been, as more of the captive woodsmen hid in dark corners, afraid they would become the targets of the Violet Bowman. Gossip was rife amongst the early shift, as the reports of a hooded figure with a bright violet face circulated. The guard had been trebled, and yet the Violet Bowman had appeared out of nowhere and taken two hundred souls.

The General stood on the wall with his officers, and looked at the parade square in front of the large wooden gates to the stone city. Row upon row of bodies lay covered in bloody sheets, bright violet tipped arrows were piled in a wooden tub besides them, it was not a sight he had ever expected to see.

General Martin Harold Jarrod looked down at the bodies, and thought hard about the situation. "This is not good, how the hell can there be so many? Are you telling me all of this was done by one man in a night?"

Captain Gregory shuddered, as he watched the dead being laid out, and the violet arrows snapped off. "The men believe it was a spirit Sir; they are as jumpy as hell. It appears that this Violet Bowmen has been spoken of for years."

"I know of the story, it is a myth to frighten young children, I have to report this to the Black Lord, what the hell do I tell him, you tell me that?" There was worry and concern on his face, he knew only too well, what came with failure.

The captain swallowed hard. "You should tell him Sir; the hooded man was also a myth and they have seen what he has done. No ordinary man could have done this sir."

The General looked down at the dead. "I cannot believe this is the work of a spirit, there are men behind this, I just don't know who. Oh well, I do not really have a choice, he is not going to like this right on his own door step, especially when he is preparing to strike elsewhere." He gave a long deep sigh and lifted his hat to scratch his short grey hair. The captain could see the worried look on his face, and he knew delivering bad news to the Dark Lord was not something he would want to do.

Lord William had for a long time served in London, and out of all the family had been the most liked. He had been fair, if not a tough and disciplined ruler. Since he had arrived in Scotland, there had been a notable change in him. General Jarrod had spent a great deal of time with the young lord, and had on many occasions asked if he had been all right. There was a brief period where Lord William would visit the castle at Craigevar, and for many days later, he would be very quiet and withdrawn.

It had been after his final visit to the castle that Lord William had seemed to change overnight. He had now become the most hated member of the family, and everyone out of his earshot called him the Dark Lord. His temper was ferocious, and the coldness he showed was terrifying. The Dark Lord had built up his own fleet of guards, and he actively encouraged them to be brutal and sadistic. Even the Cutter Brigades that the Knox family used were fearful of him and his guard. They were supposed to be the most feared, everyone knew of the Cutters, but his guard were something quite different.

Everyone knew his black sword, many good officers had died at the hands of Lord William, and he was fast to use it when displeased. General Jarrod knew this kind of bad news could go one of two ways. He looked at the young captain. "You have served me well, so listen carefully to me, for this may go against all I have taught you, but it's the best advice you will ever hear. If I do not return, slip over the wall, and get your family as far away as possible. I tell you this as a friend." The captain looked shocked, but General Jarrod just smiled, and turned and walked away down the battlement wall. He walked like a man condemned, and the captain realised that the burden he carried could one day be his. His bright blue eyes shone as they watched the kindly old General walk possibly to his death. The captain looked out over the wall at the scorched earth and gave a long depressed sigh.

The sun was just starting to rise, and the sky above the sea was pale below the dark clouds. At first, he thought he was just seeing things, and he blinked, rubbed his eyes and leaned right out over the wall. The captain stared in disbelief. He looked down the battlement towards where the General walked slowly away. Captain Gregory turned, and began to run along the wall. "General wait you must see... General please wait." He ran as fast as his legs would carry him, and panting he caught up with the General and pointed over the wall. "General.... Look... The trees?" The captain gasped for air, as he turned and leaned over the edge of the long battlement wall.

General Jarrod and Captain Gregory stood stunned as they watched the large cleared area around the castle fill with fast growing small saplings. Tiny green shoots came up through the floor, and raised the height of ten feet. They exploded with side shoots, and within minutes, they were fully expanded small trees. Large bunches of strong smelling deep purple flowers burst into bloom, turning the long stretch of burned and clear dirt into a sea of lilac.

The guards leaned over the wall, and watched as the life spread turning green. They gripped the edge of the stonewall with fear; this was not the work of a normal man. Their minds began to run rife, as comments swept down the wall of spirits and mystical powers. The soldiers of the city who had always seemed mighty and powerful, now seemed sickly and very scared.

The black walls of the stone city now wore a collar of rich deep violet. Where the violet finished, tall trees shot up at high speed, and a thick forest of ancient looking trees spread backwards. It was like watching a carpet unroll, as the green moved back away from the stone city, and up to the mountains. It spread around every wall, and the city was now caught in a sea of green life. Blue and violet butterflies by the million rose into the air, and a powerful voice rose into the sky. All over the city of stone, the troops fell to their knees and screamed in terror.

"Hear me killers of woodland, hear my voice for I am the voice of life and the giver of that brought before you by the high Green Lord. You have felt the hand of the violet one; and you have angered the hooded one. Surrender and release the dwellers of my woodland realm, or suffer the wrath of the hooded man."

Rune lay quite still, her eyes burning deep violet. Robbie watched her looking worried, he sat by her side, and held her hands as she lay in front of him. He could not understand how her eyes could be open, and yet she was not seeing or hearing him, he leaned over her and whispered. "Rune, are you alright?"

The violet light suddenly stopped, and the room darkened, he watched the lilac flowing around her bright sapphire eyes, she focused on him, and her eyes danced as she smiled. "Hi gorgeous."

He gave her a smile. "Hey beautiful... I was worried, you went rigid and then your eyes went purple." She reached up and kissed him.

"I am fine I was just helping my grandfather."

"You were helping Hearne... what doing?" She slid her arms around him as she sat up. "I have a wonderful surprise for you. I would think it would be a little bit of a bigger surprise for the Dark One. Today my darling we start to fight back properly, come on get dressed we have to see Rose."

Rose had not had the best night's sleep. She yawned and stretched, as the images of Loxley and the large walking tree like man had gone through her mind over and over again. She looked up at Rune and Robbie. "Ok I will come to the tavern, but please do not whisk me off to meet any more myths or high lords. You two are used to all this, I am not. The Green Lord up here is a god of huge power, and you just invited me into your home to meet grandpa. Hell you two, it scared the life out of me. A stag at five hundred feet that talks in my head I can live with; we have all heard those tales. Giant walking, tree like men, now that is a whole other level."

Robbie smiled as Rune giggled. "My grandfather really liked you, he was sorry he made you so nervous. He told me next time he will be gentler and in less of a rush. Really Rose, you have nothing to fear, you fight for the same ideals as Rob here. You are highly favoured by your lord, he told me so."

Rose still looked very nervous as she grabbed her cloak. "Just where exactly are we going?"

Rune took her hand. "You can trust us Rose, we will not let anything harm you."

Rune was very excited, and she giggled and smiled all the way down the cave to the wooden staircase that led up to the old tavern, Robbie gave her a shrewd look. "You are very happy this morning, just what exactly is this surprise?"

Her eyes sparkled and danced as she smiled, and he had not seen her this happy since she had told him about Iona. She stretched up and gave him a big kiss. "Trust me."

They entered into the dusty tavern bar, and Rune waved her hand in the air, the shimmering window of violet appeared. She took Robbie's hand and then the hand of Rose. "You are really going to love this." She stepped through, and they followed her into an old and ancient woodland.

Robbie smiled as he saw the trees. He breathed the deep scent of the damp earth and leaves, Rose looked through what was an endless woodland for as far as her eyes could see. It was thick, lush and very beautiful. The sun was just rising, and the pale light of the day came in shafts through the dense canopy. Grasses and ferns grew in tufts across a wide expanse of rock and soil; it was woodland of great age and majesty. Rose stared at the lines of rough barked heavy trees, with a look of confusion on her face. "Rune I have no wish to appear rude, but what are we looking at?" Rune took three steps back.

"Turn around." They both turned as she burst into a huge smile, and they gasped with surprise.

Robbie looked out from the edge of a high outcrop on the city of stone. Rose fell to her knees with her hands to her mouth. The trees ran across the lower plain into a thick violet band that surrounded the city completely. "How is this possible?"

Rune turned, and took Robbie's hand as she looked out over the scene.

"Grandfather found the spirits of all the dead trees, and I gave them life again. Together we have restored the ancient forest of the time of the Celts. The Lilac was my little tribute to the Violet Bowman. I thought it would add a little more fear to those already afraid. It has done the trick; I think it looks very pretty as well."

Robbie pulled her close. "I think it is really beautiful, it is the nicest surprise I have ever had, oh Rune I have missed the feeling of leaves above my head." She gave him a big smile and kissed him on the neck.

"I knew you would like it." Rose walked up to Rune's side, and looked at the city of stone being strangled with green, the air around her felt alive with electric, her voice was quiet and controlled.

"We can use this to our advantage. I have thousands of woodsmen at my fingertips. The Green Lord did say that a tree could grow in strange places. He also told me to lay siege to the city, with cover like this, nothing will come in or out of that city."

Robbie turned to Rune. "How could you do this when you are surrounded by crystal? I thought your magic was confined under the rocks."

"I had a few thousand hibernating friends in the crystal cave." Rune waved her hand, and thousands of butterflies lifted into the air out of the woodland. "My power travelled with each one of these, they flew out of the mouth of the cave to my High Lord, and gave life to the new spirits of each of the trees. Now this will be their realm, and it shall be named The Violet Wood."

Robbie pulled out his telescope and pulled it apart. He looked down at the city and smiled. "They are a little upset." He watched as the guards ran along the walls filling the whole length with bowmen. They were panicked and feared attack. "Rune I need to get back; it is going to be a busy day today. Rose, we have men to prepare, you will have your war of the dark rock, it started at dawn, let us go and prepare. The three of them stepped through the violet window, and came out in the tavern. Within twenty minutes, Robbie had an operations room set up on the long table in the meeting room.

Rowan and Skip stood with Robbie and his father, as they sifted through all the information they had. Rose and Sinclair worked out which clans they had, and what would be the best places for them to be deployed. It was a busy and very hectic morning as slowly a plan came together to cut off and control the city.

Robbie studied the huge map now spread across the table, as Rose and Skip marked areas to place groups of men and prevent anyone from leaving.

Rune and Una worked with Jade in the tavern, as they cleared all the furniture out of the way. The troops would come up to the tavern, and go through windows created by Rune to be deployed. All were given full instruction to hide and remain in cover until they saw the violet signal of the bowman.

Commanders ran from the room with their instructions, and in the street of the cave, the Specialists of Loxley walked up and down giving orders. Long lines of green clad woodsmen with tartan sashes nodded in respect to the Specialists, as they walked along wishing everyone luck, and passing out good advice.

Robbie stood flanked by his father and Rose on the top balcony of the lodge. He yelled at the top of his lungs, and all the prepared woodsman turned and looked up at him. "Woodsmen of Scotland." The noise fell, and he looked down.

Robbie climbed up on to the balcony rail; he wore his hood up and held out his bow in salute. "My brothers and sisters of the woodlands of Scotland. Long have you waited for this moment. You stand before your lord and Hooded man, and he feels your pride to be back in green." All of the woodsmen smiled and straightened. "I have spoken with the Lord of the Green Wood, and you will see that he has given you back your realm, the trees of your land grow green again and the dark burnt land of Knox has been pushed to his walls." His voice was loud and bounced off the crystal cave echoing through the whole of the wooden city.

"Today my friends we will start the pushing of stone into the sea, follow your commanders, go, and protect what has been restored. Fight with pride for your land, your kin, and your freedom. I will see you shortly under the fair leaves of this land. I salute you."

He thrust the bow high into the air, and the cave was filled with the roars of thousands of proud voices, and the breeze of thousands of bows thrust into the air. Robbie bowed to the woodsmen as they began their long departure out of the cave.

Rune stood at the top of the wooden stair with Una, and watched him high in the air on the top of the lodge. "Oh, he is such a show off, really Una look at him, he loves it." Una tittered and nodded her head.

"He has a very powerful presence Rune; just look at all those woodsmen hanging on his every word. There are not many men with that sort of power."

Rune smiled. "He is as sexy as hell when he gets all lordly, don't you think?"

Una patted Rune on the shoulder. "He is a little too young for me, but if I was not over a thousand, I might have gone for him." Rune started to giggle with Una.

"Come on here they all come, it will be a busy day moving this lot into the trees." They turned and went back to the bar, where Jade smiled at them. She held an apple in her hand.

"You know those saplings we passed on the way in here a few nights ago, you should see em now, they are twenty feet high and covered in fruit." She took a huge bite and smiled as she chewed.

Each of the troops came through the door and the commander handed Rune a slip of paper, she read their destination, and then waved her hand across the shimmering window. The troops marched through, and then the next lot arrived. She spent most of the day locating all of the troops, and finally the last one went through towards late afternoon, and she flopped into a chair and gasped at the red-faced Una. Jade appeared with Crystal and cold drinks.

Robbie came in from the cellar dressed in all violet woodsman attire, and Rune smiled. "Wow you look very sexy, I love violet." He beamed at her

"Calm down darling we are about to give the Dark One a real worry, although I must admit, Maggs has done a wonderful job, it's very comfy."

The group all arrived behind him and Jett kept winking at him, and then giggling. Robbie looked at Rune and handed her a piece of paper. "Open the window here, and grab your bow."

Mother handed Rune a quiver filled with violet arrows. She looked at them and then back at Robbie.

"What's going on Rob, this is just short of the main gates?" He took her hands in his and then kissed her softly.

"Trust me Runestone Sapphire?" She closed her eyes and for a moment she felt like her toes would curl up, Robbie leaned back and her eyes had burned violet. She took a deep breath and gasped.

"Whatever you just did, save it for later. Wow Rob you have my heart racing." He smiled.

Rune opened the window, and they all stepped through. Robbie looked down on the wide road lined with thick trees. "Ok Rune open another window on the other side of the road." She waved her hand, and the window shimmered. Robbie turned to his dad.

"You know what to do, wait for the violets?" Robert Lox nodded and pulled Robbie into a hug.

"Masks on." He barked as half the team followed him into the window. Almost instantly, he appeared in the trees on the other side and waved. Rune closed the window as Robbie faced his group.

"Alright you all know what to do? Rowan, please get as close as you can, we have ten minutes." Rowan nodded as the group put on their violet masks, and faded into the trees and Robbie turned to Rune. "Rune we are going to introduce ourselves, I want you to touch the floor and fill all of that road right up to the gates with violets, can you do that?" She smiled and nodded. "I will then step out."

"No!" She grabbed his arm. "Robbie he is up there I feel him." Her eyes were filled with fear, and the colour ran from her face. Robbie gently opened her hand and lifted it. He kissed it softly.

"Do you love me...? Do you trust me Runestone?" She saw the flashes of blue in his eyes.

"Rob your eyes." She looked surprised. He smiled and raised his arm, and the white bangle glinted blue.

"Rune, the last gift she gave you was my protection." Rune spoke softly as she began to smile.

"Gwendolyn, you are her heir, she has protected you, which was how Iona found you." Robbie nodded and drew out a long violet-feathered arrow. He handed her a violet mask. Robbie pulled his mask over his face and slipped up his violet hood.

Rune looked at him and giggled. "Wow you should wear that in bed." She started to laugh, as she pulled her mask on, and pulled up her hood. Robbie took her hand and led her slowly through the trees to the side of the road.

"Ok Rune as soon as the violets hit the gates, load your bow and shoot anything that looks like a threat."

Lord William stormed up on to the ramparts. "What the hell is going on? Who has stopped the men leaving? Get those gates open now; a few lousy weeds will not stop my plans. Do as you were ordered or you will taste the black blade." Lord William Knox, turned his cold black eyes out over the gate, he looked down at the road through the trees. The officers all looked at him in fear, they were not happy with a whole forest growing in one night. This was a power of the Violet Bowman they had not heard of before, and it terrified them.

Violets ran down the road like the torrents of a stream freshly broken from the dam. They ran in wide ripples, and William Knox looked down and was unsettled. He hated the colour purple; it was the colour of that woodland witch. The officers froze as they saw the river of violets heading their way, one panicked and pointed.

"See... see My Lord, it is his work, he has come back from the spirit world to claim our souls, we are doomed."

The cold voice of Mordred drooled out of his mouth. "You were doomed the moment you spoke; your soul is mine not his." Mordred gripped the man in one hand, and with an almighty twist he snapped his neck, and the man hung like a rag doll in the hand of the Dark Lord. Mordred dropped him off the wall, and watched as the violets covered his body. The torrent of flowers lapped like water against the stonewall, Mordred watched fascinated. He looked up as some of the men cried out with fear, and his eyes met with the figure in violet, that had appeared out of nowhere. Robbie raised his bow. Mordred could feel the power in him and all around him.

His voice was cold and cruel and everyone shuddered as he spoke, except Robbie. "Well bowman, you certainly look the part, get off my land before I slice you into confetti." Robbie fired, and the arrow hit the wood of the flagpole by Mordred's head. A long shank of blonde hair was pinned with the end of the arrow. The violet tip vibrated in the wood.

Mordred had a slight glimmer of fear in his eyes, and looked back at the pole, then back towards the road, and Robbie's raised second arrow. "KILL HIM!" His voice was loud and terrible, and eight archers ran to the wall and raised their bows. From nowhere violet arrows swished, and the archer's reeled backwards dead on the floor, long violet tipped arrows stood from their chests. The wild-eyed officers looked at the solitary figure in the middle of the violet road.

Hooded with a violet face, the figure aimed the bow. He stood as if frozen, his dark and menacing eyes burned bright within the violet. One soldier was panicked and shook violently. "Why hasn't he spoken or moved?" His eyes were wide with terror as he stared down at the lone figure in all violet.

Mordred looked either side at the soldiers lined along the walls. "WELL... WHAT ARE YOU WAITING FOR? I SAID KILL HIM."

They lifted their bows, and the violet arrows rained in upon them. They shot backwards off the wall, as the power of the arrows lifted them off their feet, and they fell, already dead off the high wall. The violet hooded figure stood silent unmoving holding the bow loaded and ready to fire.

Fear now slipped slowly across the dark eyes of the Lord of the city. Mordred could now see the fear that had been instilled in the men around him was failing, as the fear of the silent Violet Bowman was greater. A huge rage was growing inside him and he spun on General Jarrod. "OPEN THE GATES, AND SEND OUT YOUR MEN, KILL HIM OR YOU WILL DIE NOW."

Mordred drew out the black blade of Dunnottar and held it high in the air, as he shook with rage. Robbie fired.

His arrow struck the tip of the blade, and there was a resounding scream inside Mordred's head. The black blade glowed bright purple and a voice echoed into his brain, as the sword vibrated in pain in his hand. He shook with fear. "Hear me Mordred spawn of the black witch; for I am Runestone, and bringer of life and the daughter of death, violet is my colour, and you well know what that may bring. Your soul will be mine as my bowman draws you from the sword, and you will die by my hand and never return. Leave this land now and you will live long enough to face me in your nightmares."

Mordred snapped his hands to his head, the ring of the black blade echoing all over the insides of the castle. He screamed in pain and for just one second above all the wails and pain another voice screamed louder. "ROBBIE HELP ME!"

Robbie's heart almost stopped, as the voice of Billy drowned his ears, Rune gasped and looked over at Robbie, and she saw the anguish in his eyes. Robbie released his third arrow. Mordred waved about wildly, the screams of pain in his head, and the long violet arrow struck and splintered Mordred's hand, and the sword fell to the floor with a resounding crash. It sliced through the hard floor, and the whole of the stone observation deck collapsed behind the gates. The officers darted backwards to safety pulling each other out of harm's way in panic, not one hand was extended to Mordred, who fell screaming, and was covered in stone.

As the dust cleared a hand with a long violet arrow through it stuck out of the pile. The General swallowed deeply, and looked at the silent figure. Robbie slid back his hood and pulled off his mask, and he stared at the General high on the wall. The General breathed just one word.

"Loxley." Robbie's voice was calm and clear.

"You are on my woodland, leave now and you all will be spared. If you remain you have been warned, you will face the wrath of the hooded man of Loxley." He turned and walked into the trees, as dark clouds rose from the black rock. The Dark One swooped screaming out of the air, snatched Mordred, and his sword from the floor. She rose into the air her malicious face burning with hate. Flashes of lightening radiated from her, striking innocent men who screamed as they fell dead on the floor.

The fear swept over the soldiers who cowered in her presence, Mordred hung moaning in her arms, and her head whipped round as she looked down the road leading out of the castle. On to the sea of bright violets, Rune stepped out from the trees and raised her bow. The Dark One screamed with rage, and blasted the violets into the air. The arrow whooshed through the flowers and there was an almighty scream. The dark clouds exploded into the air, leaving a blast like a hurricane scattering debris across the whole of the gates, and she flew to her castle, wailing through the air.

General Jarrod looked up from the floor at the long dark smouldering lock of black hair hanging from the flagpole. It slowly faded to bright white, as the colour drained out of it. It crumbled to dust and blew across the gate yard. He turned to Captain Gregory who was very white and trembled behind him.

"Oh lad, we are in trouble, we are caught between two very powerful forces, and both of them are pissed off women." He rose up, and looked at the empty road. "I am not sure which one scares me the most."

Rose looked very pale as Robbie and Rune walked up to her beside a large beech tree. He smiled at her. "Cheer up we just found her weakness." Rose looked stunned.

"No offence My Lord, but how the hell did all that show you her weakness? We were just trying to stay in control we were so frightened."

"Trust me Rose, if you look in the right places, you will always find the right answers." He smiled at her and patted her shoulder, and walked down the line to find Rowan, and a wet legged Jade.

Rose gave Rune a weak smile. "He is starting to sound like the Green Lord."

Rune gave her a sweet smile. "Ignore him, he is just showing off again," she pulled on her arm, and lifted her off the floor. "Robbie just realised that the Dark One had made a big mistake, Mordred is afraid of me, and Billy who is trapped in their somewhere, knows what I can do, and he is using that fear to fight Mordred. The Dark One never expected that, I felt her fear for the first time ever, we have gained a few feet."

"What now Runestone?" Rose looked at her with total respect.

"Well Rose, you attack anything not woodsmen trying to leave. The word is now out that the violet bowmen was really the true hooded man, I feel our Specialists will be back on the roof tonight, and tomorrow we look for a way into the dark castle, I have a few ideas, which I want to run past Rob. Set your blockade and get a good night's sleep, we will be busy from now on."

The word was out as the soldiers talked rapidly. It was now hard to work out who was the most frightening. The Violet Bowman had touched the heart with the fear of every childhood, which in turn had resurfaced in the adults. The biggest fear now was that the stories of the hooded man scared all the adults, especially when groups talked of the men left to die in agony having been brutally butchered first. The hooded man had taken on and killed Mason Knox. What chance did a soldier have against him?

The horror stories told by Cutters of Robbie were enough to scare just about anyone, but they had also heard many things about his companions. He had a man of iron who looked like a pirate, who would tackle and kill any man, even if he was a good five feet taller. Then there was the spinning girl in black; with a sword so sharp it would cut you in half before you knew. She laughed, and screamed, and could kill a hundred men alone in less than an hour.

Many shuddered as the survivors had talked of the bow woman who could set fire to forty men with one arrow. On the other hand, there was the woman in white who would freeze you, and then break you into a million pieces.

There was also the story of the mad man and his little spiky haired girl, who both fought with two swords so fast you could not see the blades to fight them. But the two stories that brought real fear to the hearts of the soldiers, was the one about the green eyes that followed you, and opened your throat. It brought deep fear to the soldiers knowing that you could not see the owner of the eyes. They came from nowhere with no warning, and if you saw them, the chances were, you were already dead.

The little girl in grey was by far the most frightening. Two soldiers from Canterbury had visited the city three months earlier, they talked of a tiny little girl who had red eyes and wore glasses because she was blind. They shuddered as they had told how she smiled and asked them to play with her, when they laughed; she wagged her finger and called them naughty. Everyone in the room had laughed until they saw the fear in the men's eyes.

The two men talked with terror as they told how she had looked up, and a light brighter than the sun had leapt from her face, and sixty men in front of her had been burned to dust within seconds. The whole room had fallen silent and swallowed hard. The story of Ruby was doing the rounds again.

Soldiers were ordered into action to repair the gates, and scouting parties were almost forced outside to go into the trees and search for woodsmen. None made it more than a few feet past the gates. Groups bringing in supplies were ambushed, and their carts pulled off the road into the deep woods. The city of stone was surrounded, and now sat quietly waiting, unsure of what the Dark One could do to save them. Throughout the rest of the afternoon and evening, any soldier not exercising extreme care was hit with an arrow. They fell screaming from the walls.

The confrontation of the bowman against Mordred, and the strange girl with a bow that shot at the Dark One had well and truly placed the seeds of doubt in the minds of everyone. Robbie had gambled, and it had paid off. In his mind, knowledge was power, and now the enemy could see that the Dark One could be faced and fought. He had also proved that his men could face them, and to the group of Specialists that was a mighty hurdle to climb over.

Robbie had achieved it with a little success. The group now believed they had a chance, and so he could now focus on the job at hand. Planning the assault of the dark castle was a priority, but now he had wreaked havoc outside the city, he planned a night of fear inside the city walls.

The group sat in the warehouse laughing and joking, as he walked in with Rune and Rose, their chuckles died and fell silent. His bravery on the violet road had won him even more respect, and he looked up and smiled at the group.

"You all played a very important role today, thank you. Alright tonight we have more fun and games lined up." Everyone smiled excitedly. "Rune has a few things for you to do, and as for me? Well tonight, we go up in green and in high visibility. I want every guard taking out, use your skills and create as much havoc as possible. Maddy bring your own bow, you too Crystal. I want the Dark One screaming with rage by morning, her little boy has a poorly hand, let's give her the headache to match."

The whole group nodded as Rune walked around handing out small paper bags. "These are seeds, wherever you hit scatter a few. Throw them thinly they grow fast, and if you drop any at your feet run like mad. These are the same strain as those at the House of Good Hope, if you want to know about the speed they grow, I am quite sure Martin will tell you." She smiled at him as the others giggled.

Robbie nodded. "Ok, it's getting nice and dark so finish your drinks; we leave in half an hour." He stood up and made his way across the room towards Rune. John stood up. "Excuse me Boss, but... well we all want to say... you know... That was really brave what you and our lady did today, you are always telling us what a good job we have done... well we want you to know, we think you both are the best and we love you for it."

John blushed, as Martin clapped his hands. "Here, here." Everyone nodded and agreed.

Rune felt the tears in her eyes. "Thank you, all of you, we both think the world of all of you, and we are very proud of you. It means a lot to me that you think that." She gave a soft sob. Martin slapped the teary eyed John on the back.

"We said thank em, not bloody upset them." Everybody laughed as Rune gave a giggle as she wiped the tears from her eyes.

Robbie pulled her close. "Thanks everyone... we are a team, only as strong as the next man, and you guys are the strongest." Robbie gave her a soft kiss. "Are you ready?" She lifted her cloak, as Robbie turned to Rose. "Welcome aboard, are you up for a little hooded action?" Rose smiled and pulled her cloak round her shoulders. Robbie turned to the group. "Alright Jett, lead us up and out." She beamed a big smile.

"Oh goodie, it's play time, let's go guys. Hoods up and let's hustle."

Jett shot up the ladder closely followed by Jade and Rafe; the assault of the city was starting to happen. It was Robbie's hope to break down the city, and get the woodsmen in control, at which point the dark castle would be isolated, tonight would be the third in a row with no sleep for the soldiers, but this time they faced Loxley and the fear brought with stealth and surprise.

They gathered on the roof in the dark and sat in a large circle around the violet arrow from the first night, Robbie crouched in the middle. "Ok they are already scared of the violet bowman, now they know we are here, they should be more worried, there are lots of rumours flying around about the various skills of us all... Let's give them the full works; anything goes as long as the job is done. Jett you are off the leash, you too Pebbles, go play girls."

Jett spun up off her boot, and smiled down at them all, she winked at Blades. "Hey girl, you going to join me and Rafe?" Blades smiled.

Robbie stood up. "You have three hours, wreak havoc, see you all back here, and remember... Stay sharp and watch each other's backs. Ruby Maddy and Crystal stay close to me and Rune, we have a few ideas." Rose watched as within seconds the group had gone without a sound, shadows floated across the roofs in every direction.

Robbie led his party south; his first targets were the barrack houses. It was not long before Jett's whoops could be heard, and wild screams came out of the darkness. Rose looked across, and Robbie smiled.

"That little display of sword fighting the other day was just fun, when you see her in action, she really is very scary, I am always glad I don't have to face her." Rose swallowed deeply; she was not use to the levels of fighting the Loxley group were.

Robbie slid up against the low wall and peeped over. Rune rolled over and had a peep. "They are very nervous I can feel it."

"They have not had the best of days really." He winked at her and she smiled.

Rose sat back in the dark, and watched as Robbie flicked his wrist and gave hand signals; Crystal and Maddy slipped out of the shadows and took up position. Rune peered over the wall, and Rose watched as she patted the floor with her fingers,

Robbie relayed the signals back, Ruby giggled at the side of Rose. She slipped her glasses into her pocket and whispered. "This will be interesting."

Maddy leapt up from the wall with her long white bow. The arrow ignited as it left the string and Rose jumped not expecting to see flames. Soldiers screamed, and ran in every direction as the flash of light hit the main gate, and they instantly burst into flames. Maddy was already down behind the wall.

Crystal popped up a few feet further down from her, and the barrack house was her target. The burning gate had raised the alarm, and soldiers ran down the stairs to the main doors. Her silver arrow exploded out of her bow, and as the door opened, it shot inside. The whole building suddenly filled with a thick white frost, as ice formed and entombed the whole lot. Rose shuddered at the chilling consequences for anyone inside.

Ruby jumped up, ran forwards and jumped on the ledge. "Hey boys, you want to play with me?"

There were terrified screams as the guards looked up and saw the little frowning blind girl in grey, her pale skin and white hair shone in the moonlight, and her red eyes flickered. They fled screaming as light flooded the compound. Rose stood up in disbelief as she saw the effects of Ruby's eyes.

The ground was littered with black scorch marks, as Ruby jumped off the wall. "What's next Robyn in the Hood?" He gave her a smile, as she beamed up at him. "They were boring, they never want to play." Ruby gave a sinister grin.

"Let's go look at the castle, we want to see what protection it has Flash."

Rose looked at Rune. "Flash?"

Rune nodded. "We all have nicknames, that is hers. If you are lucky Harry might find you one." She turned and followed Robbie over the roof.

Jett and Blades spun side by side. Most of the soldiers were afraid of them, but had little choice but try to defend themselves, Rafe went at one man, who swung a brutal punch and caught him on the chin, he saw flashes before his eyes as he dropped his sword, and skidded across the floor. The large soldier came pounding down on him; Jett saw him undefended and began to spin his way.

Rafe growled with anger at the man as he rubbed his chin. As the man lunged, he rolled, and pounced upwards sinking his teeth into the side of the man's face. The man screamed in pain and dropped his sword. Rafe rolled over on top of him in anger, and pulled back hard. Jett stopped and screwed up her face. "Urgh! Honey that can't taste nice, you can wash your mouth before you kiss me again."

Rafe spat the large chunk of flesh out of his mouth and picked up his sword he screamed at the soldier rolling in pain. "I DO NOT LIKE BEING HIT, IF I HAVE A BLACK EYE IN THE MORNING, I WILL GET RUNE TO BRING YOU BACK TO LIFE, AND KILL YOU AGAIN, OK?" He whipped his sword across the man in temper and he rolled over dead, he turned and looked at Jett, he had rage in his eyes, and blood down his chin. "Did you see that, he hit me?"

"Rafe honey calm down, these are soldiers, they have no manners, they were dragged up."

Rafe swung his sword into its sheath. "That's the bloody problem with today, no one cares how their kids are brought up, there's no bloody respect in these cities."

She smiled. "Howl for me wolf man." Rafe started to laugh.

"Wait until the moon comes out from the clouds, come on, Blades needs a lift." They shot into the dark in the direction of Blades laughter, and the soldier's screams.

A group of soldiers huddled together down a dark alley; they were deep in the shadows holding their breath. The smell of fear was all around them as they thought they could hide safely until first light in the dark. Two bright green eyes came round the corner, and peered into the dark at them. The one pushed into the far corner, looked up and then back down at the others. "Oh bugger... Bye guys." Two lifted their heads and whispered. "What do you mean bugger and bye?"

The soft quiet voice crept into their ears. "He means me." They looked up into the two green eyes and screamed.

Jade came round the corner laughing towards Rowan. "I am getting soft with all this baby talk, I left one. He did a poo in his pants, I hadn't the heart he was so embarrassed." She giggled. "He will stay there all night smelling, that's worse than death."

The arrows came out of the dark and the guards fell from the walls, Robbie stopped and pulled up his bow, John and Martin were with Fish moving towards them, taking out the guards as they came. Robbie gave a little whistle and they stopped. A whistle came back out of the dark, and Robbie leaned forwards into the light.

John smiled and pointed to the wall ahead. Robbie signalled and moved forwards into the light. He crept up, and leaned over the wall. Twelve guards patrolled below them. The others slipped up as he gave his hand signals. They sat on the top of the wall, and dangled their legs over and looked down. "Hey guys where is your boss tonight?" They looked up, and then fell down. Robbie looked out across the black bridge. Soldiers lined both sides all the way along from the mainland to the castle. "Ever hear of the walls of Jericho?"

They all shook their heads. "It was in a book given to me by Sister Mary. It was really interesting, the castle was unbeatable, so they stacked wood up against it and set fire to it, when the stone was good and hot, they cooled it really fast with water.

The stone cracked and the castle fell down. I thought it was a really good story, nearly as good as one I read about a Samaritan."

Rose looked at him. "So, what is your point?"

"The point Rose is I want that bridge gone. I want to make sure all the eggs are in one basket when your people take over the city tomorrow."

"What do you mean my people? No offence Robbie but this place has thousands of soldiers."

Robbie shook his head. "Not by morning it won't, the gates are open, and fear is rife. No by tomorrow, the only soldiers we will need to worry about will be there across the water. I want that bridge down tonight to keep them there. Maddy, can you hit the bridge just short of the cliff on this side?"

Maddy leaned over the wall a little. "That's not a big problem from this high up."

"Good, put a few arrows in the road on either side, and get that floor good and hot for me."

Maddy loaded her bow and took aim. The arrow hit the concrete bridge and burst into bright orange flames; she loaded a second arrow as the soldiers fled backwards away from the roaring inferno. The second arrow hit on the other side and flames roared into the air. She smiled as she leaned back. Robbie held his hands out and rubbed them. "You can almost feel the heat from here." He smiled. "Give it a few minutes and then Crystal, give it a good freeze."

Crystal looked at her arrows and pulled a long sliver one from her quiver. She fitted it to the string, as men ran up and down the black bridge, she fired with amazing pace. The long silver arrow hit the centre of the bridge, and the ice formed very quickly. The tall flames dropped and hissed across the width of the bridge. They could hear the creaks and groans from the floor and then suddenly there was an ear-spitting crack and a whole section of the bridge crumbled and fell away from the cliff and into the sea. The water bubbled as the ice melted quickly.

Robbie took a bag out of his pocket. "That will do, now let's sow the seeds of misfortune and head home to bed, a good cup of chamomile tea and we will sleep like babies." They headed back across the rooftops scattering the seeds as they went and soon the whole group were gathered around the violet arrow in the roof of the General Store.

When everyone was back, they slipped down the wall, and into the cave below the store. Robbie looked round satisfied with the nights work. "Ok everyone, get some sleep, we will see our handy work in the morning." They all made their way back to the lodge happily joking and said their goodnights as they entered their rooms.

Rune slid up next to Robbie and curled round him. It had been a very long day and he enjoyed the feeling of her close to him, he closed his eyes and slid back on the pillow. "Well that's the easy bit done with; tomorrow we work on the hard bit." He looked down at her bright white face and her long eyelashes and smiled.

Rune was fast asleep; Robbie softly stroked her long red silky hair. "Good night my darling, sleep well."

The city was dark and silent, flames still crackled by the gate, and the walls of the barrack room dripped. The walls were quiet with the odd silent cry, as a soldier lay hidden and weeping. Some soldiers staggered without weapons, dazed and confused down the road, out of the city.

The woodsmen in the trees let them leave. They had only heard the screams and seen the flashes of light, but they knew that the Specialists were at work. The respect in the air for the men of Loxley was high, the joy of seeing a city defeated pumped through the veins of every Scotsman.

Strange noises rose from the city, and the few brave workers in dusty grey who looked out of their windows saw something very strange indeed. Plant life grew everywhere. Flowers and climbers sprung from the paths and the walls. The walkways covered themselves with lush green grass, and ivy with honeysuckle and Jasmine, covered the large dark walls of the city.

The soldiers were dead or gone, and whispered voices spread down the long alleyways, as silent grey clad figures walked out into the night air. Small groups of men gathered in the open and whispered hurriedly. It was not long before grey clad figures could be seen walking out of the city, and were gathered by their kinsmen into the trees.

Rose sat exhausted at her desk. Sinclair handed her a coffee. "I have never seen anything like it, they move like the breeze and they don't make a sound. They laugh and joke as they destroy everything in front of them. I am telling you these are not normal people; they scare me more than she does." She stared at the cup. "Have you seen the speed of him when he shoots, and Rune and Rowan? They just rose out of the floor like ghosts in a flash, and whoosh. By the time his arrows had hit, he had another in the bow and was hitting someone else. He fired six to my two."

Sinclair rubbed the back of her shoulders, and she moaned with delight. "Oh god today has been scary, I am not up for all this, they work on levels I will never reach."

He smiled as he rubbed her shoulders softly. "Come on you are tired, get some sleep." He kissed the top of her head and smiled.

CHAPTER EIGHT

RUNE'S GARDEN AND DESTINY RISES

It was a late start, as Robbie came up on to the roof with Rune. Sinclair stood with Rose; she had tears in her eyes, as Robbie came to her side and put his arm around her shoulder. "Now that is what I call a city." Rose turned weeping, and put her head onto his shoulder, Robbie smiled and pulled his arm round and gently patted her. "You have your people free Rose, once we know it really is clear, you can bring your woodsmen in and we will look at the castle."

"I have no words to thank you all. I have spent most of my life helping these people. You come along in a day and just take it back for me."

Rune smiled as she pulled Rose into a big hug, "Rose what you have done just to keep them alive all this time is an incredible achievement. Look at the city you have built under the crystal. Neither Robbie nor I would have even thought it was possible. We have a few extra friends that come in handy in a bind that's all, and we thought you could use them." Rose laughed from deep within Runes embrace.

"They are a little more than handy Runestone," she giggled, and Rune pulled her back and wiped the tears from her eyes.

"No more tears now, look at my garden in Scotland, isn't it pretty?"

Robbie stood at the top of the roof, his hair blew in the breeze, and he looked out with wonder. Every path and road was carpeted in a lush green lawn, and down the sides grew thick masses of bright blue Geraniums, and bright purple Asters. Rudbeckia grew tall in deep yellows, and the cool whites of wood anemones littered the floors. Thrift and carnations of hundreds of colours, bobbed their bright frilly flowers in the soft breeze, and every roof was covered in mosses and heather, and had an abundance of wild bilberry spreading in thick black-berried domes.

In the open courtyards, trees had grown up, and gave restful places of shade, and protection from the sea breeze. The walls were covered in green of all colours and shades, many bright coloured flowers of clematis and honeysuckle hung and the sweet smell of Jasmine was everywhere.

Wherever you looked, there were roses. Thousands of them in all colours and strong with perfume, from neat little shrubs, to thick bushy climbers. Rune walked

Rose to the edge and looked at the breath taking display. "I thought a rose garden for a Rose Queen would be nice. This place will always be the garden of Rose Macintosh, the saviour of her people." Rose was at a loss for words, the kindness of these two unusual people was so overwhelming all she could do was cry.

The group wandered the city checking that all was indeed clear. Jade waved from the top of the gate, in amongst two thick bushy Alder trees, and Robbie loaded his bow. "Give the order Rose, and your people will own their city again." Rune touched Robbie's arrow tip, and it glowed bright violet. Rose nodded, and he raised the bow into the air and fired straight up. A violet streak shot into the air as it whistled loudly, and then with a mighty explosion the arrow burst into a huge ball of violet. Flower petals poured from the sky like soft rain, and the woodsmen had their signal, and began to move out of the trees and into the city.

Skip laughed as he danced with Treen in his arms, and smiled with delight as the soft violet petals fell like snow from the sky and decorated their shoulders and hair. The old barrack house had gone, in the night it had crumbled and fallen to dust, and in its place was a giant fountain of white marble. In the centre, was a statue of a hooded bowman holding his bow aloft in salute to all those who entered through the burned out gates. Water sprinkled out over the stones, and trickled gently down to the cool pool below.

The Specialists all gathered, and sat around it as the first woodsman walked in and saw the garden of wonder and glory that had been a city. They all bowed to the group as they passed and the group nodded. Every woodsman looked up at the statue and smiled, they would never forget that the hooded man stood high on the lodge balcony and addressed them. Robbie looked up, and Rune smiled as she put her arms round him, and rested her head on his shoulder from behind. "You like it?"

He nodded. "It is very beautiful... I just thought I was taller."

Rune's eyes glowed violet, and the statue creaked and groaned. It grew several inches and Robbie smiled, she giggled into his neck. "I was working in the dark you know?"

John and Jett giggled as they looked up at the bowman in bronze. "Hey Robbie, can we all have one around the gardens, we can call it the hooded park, and I can have one made out of black marble and fill the whole place with yellow. Jett Amber corner, how cool would that be?"

He smiled. "That is not me, that is all of us and anyone who slips up a hood and fights for the weak. You are all in that symbol of hope."

Jett looked up and giggled with Jade. She rubbed John's proud belly. "You will need some more bronze Rune if John is in there. I am sure he grows by the minute." John beamed a huge smile as everyone giggled and laughed at her bright dark eyes filled with mischief.

The long stream of woodsmen filed in and took up their position of defence. Robbie walked along the observation area with Rowan. "I want the crew up here permanently, get Skip to organise a headquarters in one of the buildings, and put everyone into the lodgings around us. I want to be able to see that castle every moment that we plan. We have achieved nothing, except being more frightening than the last bunch. The real job is still at hand; we have to prize her out of that castle. Rowan my friend no one knows yet, but York and Loxley are in danger. All those troops you saw were heading south as Mordred builds a huge force to overcome us. War is coming and we must prepare."

Rowan nodded. "I knew when I saw them it had to be us. It never ends, does it?" Rowan looked out across the water at the tall dark tower. "God, I hate that place."

Robbie patted his shoulder. "We have done much, but we still have a long road, we will end this my friend have no fear. I will leave for Loxley shortly with dad, I need him home where he can watch out for the people there, and prepare for our return. I will take a few with me, but we will be seconds away, Jade can talk freely to Rune above ground. If she moves call me, she will be mad as hell, and I have no trust of her at all. She will try to retaliate; we must now prepare." Robbie pulled Rowan into a hug, "I will see you soon my friend."

The group got busy moving all of their things up from the caves under the city, and sorting out their new headquarters. It was a very long morning's work before Skip had an observation and planning room, and all of them had quarters set up all along the viewing area.

The large map was gone and now information on the black castle was being pulled together from any eyewitness report. Mother and Smokes now doubled Skip and Treen, with Una and Maddy helping out. Harry went out with Fish and Jett round the houses of the city and collected supplies. Robbie now wanted his independence from the rest of the woodsmen. He wanted to focus on just the castle and the target of the Dark One. Angus seemed to have become a part of the group, and Rose and Sinclair spent more of their time with the Loxley Specialists, so much so, that Maggs and Judith set them up a small house at the end of the block. The viewing area was now command central and from the large window, Robbie stood and watched the dark castle.

Maggs and Blades set up a kitchen, and she was happier now she could do the cooking, Scottish recipes were not to Maggs taste, and she had Judith and Blades bobbing about with Harry collecting the foods she preferred. All in all, it seemed like a happier affair, and the group laughed and joked as they rested and watched, waiting for Rowan and Robbie to give them their orders.

Rowan had been seen for some time now as Robbie's second, but his authority now could be seen, Rowan commanded the respect of the entire group, he was even-handed and fair. The day slowly passed as Robbie sat waiting with his father, and when Rune was ready, she stood by the door of the headquarters and opened her window. Robert Lox and Melanie stepped through with Bear and Skip holding Treen's hand, followed by Robbie and Rune. They came out at the postal office, and Rags squealed with delight. She threw her arms around Rune and hugged her. "I was really worried bout ya all, why dint you write?"

Rune smiled as she hugged Rags, we were too far away, and there is no post where we have been."

"Wot no postie's? Tell me where, and I will put it on my map." She smiled at Robbie. "Hey big guy I missed you, wot no kiss for old Rags here?" Robbie started to laugh and bent down; he grabbed her and gave her a huge kiss. Rags was lost for words just for a moment, as Rune laughed at the look of shock on her face.

"Phew Rob baby... That's two on lips." She seemed flustered, as she smiled at Rune. "Corr you are so lucky to get that all the time, he is definitely going to have to tell Bobby his secret."

Alice squealed with delight as she came out of the door and saw Bear. She looked funny as she tried to run with her extended belly. Robbie smiled as Bear lifted her gently into his muscular arms, and held her tight. She beamed at Rune. "Thanks for watching him for me."

Robbie patted Bear on the shoulder. "We have not got long, enjoy your time." He walked to the kitchen door where Jess held her husband tight, and sobbed into his broad shoulders. "Hey Jessie love, now don't cry baby I am back and safe." Robbie thought it best to leave them alone for a while.

The rest of the group made their way down Hawthorn Lane to the Village Hall, and the main hall filled with the large map, and bustle of many people running about coordinating the whole country.

Fuse burst into laughter and hugged everyone as he greeted them with a lot of relief and a great deal of joy. Skip wasted no time going over the map and he talked to many of the head organisers around it. Treen seemed to be barking out orders, and bringing a lot of the women to her station as she viewed what was on her desk, and began telling everyone what she needed doing. Robbie watched, and within seconds it was as if they had not been away.

He looked at the map with Rune on his arm, as the woodsmen were placed, they turned from blue to green dots. Robbie was amazed to see how large the woodland population had grown. Most of the west coast was now a sea of green that stretched across the York moors. The east coast was as always, thick with red. The walled city from the south of Birmingham, down to the south coast was red. Detail was now being added, and Robbie looked at the little pins that labelled factories, and a power plant and what looked like endless hospitals and orphanages. Robbie now saw that Knox had been breeding children for well over twenty years. Devon and Cornwall were littered with them, and a cold tingle ran down his spine as he saw the vast number. Rune bent over and looked at the map. "If he has a thousand children in each of those, he will have an army of hundreds of thousands." She looked shocked as she stood up and looked at Robbie.

"He has planned this for a long time Rune; remember for twenty years no one has known what has happened behind his walls, Mason was breeding a country full of people, his kind of people."

The map showed the long lines of soldiers moving slowly towards York. Mordred had also been busy, black dots now marked the army on the move. Seventy thousand soldiers had been moved from Scotland and Newcastle, and they all were heading south towards York.

Groups of woodsmen had been set in wait, and it looked like the plan of Fuse was to slow them by attacking them constantly. Robbie looked at the green lines leading over from the west and now a thick green buffer was being formed around York.

Henry smiled down, as the slender figure in all pale blue, rode into the yard through the inner gate. She looked up and smiled, her slate grey eyes flashing under her battered straw hat. He patted David on the shoulder. "You got company." David turned and looked down. The huge smile, and the brightness of his eyes said it all, in a flash, he was off the observation deck and sliding down the ladder. Henry smiled as he whisked her into his arms, and she hugged and kissed him.

"I only have until sun set." David looked up at Henry who peered over at him.

"Go on I got you covered, you covered me enough times." He smiled. "Hi Mel love, he has been a right misery." Melanie smiled as David pulled on her hand, and they ran off together down the lane, past the barrack houses to his small cottage.

Henry looked at the soldiers who had turned, and were watching with smiles on their faces. "You lot.... Eyes front." The heads of the soldiers snapped forward over the wall to the road out of Loxley. Henry smiled to himself. "Bless em they deserve each other."

Rune giggled as she sat on the front of Robbie's horse, and he kissed her neck, as he rode down the Sacred Wood Road, toward the woods to the Mere. They came on to the glade and the small garden of colour looked beautiful set amongst the trees, and the wooden house. The sunlight sparkled across the mere, and she slipped down into his arms. She laughed and squealed, as he tickled her and kissed her up the steps to the glass doors. He pressed her up against the glass as she giggled. Her bright blue eyes danced in her pale white face, and her hair sparkled radiantly as the sun hit it. She was so beautiful and he loved her. He pulled her close as she put her arms chuckling round him. She was slightly out of breath from her laughing; he gave her a long and loving kiss. "You have no idea how much I love you." She smiled and kissed the end of his nose.

"Oh no, I am a sorceress, I know all your secrets." She chuckled and then looked at him very seriously.

"Please be careful Rob. You are the life in my heart, don't leave me." She pushed her arms round him, and he squeezed her tight, he held her, the soft scent of Jasmine and honeysuckle all around him.

"I won't leave you again Rune. Not ever, I promise."

Being home again felt great, Rune scampered around the bedroom as she got dressed in clean clothes and then jumped on the bed. "Come on we have work to do, I can't believe I fell for that kiss, I have so much to do, and only half the time." He snatched her back in his arms and kissed her. "Oh god Robbie please... Oh wow, whatever Gwendolyn put in that bangle I am truly grateful but... Oh god Robbie." Her eyes burned bright violet. "No. No, no, no!" She jumped off the bed and giggled. "Robbie, we have to get ready, I have to visit my table."

He jumped up, and she squealed, and ran out of the room. He heard her run down the stairs laughing. He laughed as he slid on his clean clothes. Slowly he made his way to the kitchen, and wandered around the house as he pulled things he would need together. Rune shouted up from the cellar. "Robbie throw my pants down, it's freezing down here." He chuckled as he wandered back to the room.

Rune sat at her table, and she waved her palms across the smooth surface. Violet flashes flickered from her hands, and the swirling mist began to form on the table. Her eyes glowed deep purple as the image began to form. Robbie wandered in, her green pants over his shoulder and he stood and watched as the mist cleared and the picture of a tall dark brown cube of crystal appeared. Rune watched through violet eyes, and Robbie lowered into the seat as he watched Morgan le Fey walk laughing round the trapped old wizard. Rune lifted her head. "Sound."

Robbie jumped as the cold quiet deathly voice of the Dark One slid off the walls.

"You have no choice Merlin; you think I worry they are up there watching from the cliff top? They will not come here and endanger dear old granddaddy."

Merlin turned his head in the crystal. "Listen to me Morgan. You cannot win; thousands of years of corrupting men's minds, and you are still no closer to your goals. When will you realise that Arthur was a true man? I did not control him; he chose his own path as the first true king. It was not I that ruled with a puppet king; he ruled freely as a man of honour, you have never understood this. You will never be more than a student of the craft Morgan; you have not the understanding to rule."

She spun round, and faced the old wizard, and screamed at him. "STUDENT!

YOU OLD FOOL, I AM THE ONE WITH YOU AS A PRISONER, AND YOU CALL ME STUDENT? I HAVE RULED FOR A THOUSAND YEARS, I TOOK THE FORM FROM EVE, I CAUGHT GWENDOLYN AND DESTROYED HER. I HAD OPAL IN MY HAND AND TORTURED HER, AND ONCE AGAIN I HAVE YOU." Her eyes burned evil and black in her white pallid face; her thin lips twitched as she stared with hatred at the old wizard.

Merlin's voice was quiet. "And you have learned nothing. You are blind to the power, and cannot see what is right before you. You will never rule Morgan; there are others who have more power."

"What, the flower girl?" She screamed with laughter, and she staggered as she walked. Rune's arm shot out across the table.

"Go on do it." Robbie looked confused, as Rune smiled, and her eyes burned with the deepest purple he had ever seen. She waited ready her arm poised as he watched the howling Morgan le Fey walk around the crystal pillar.

"You really think those two foolish children are a match for me? They have been lucky. I have been busy, and had things of greater importance to do, but do not worry old man I am clearing time on my calendar, and soon they will be dealt with."

Morgan stepped onto the red five-pointed star on the floor of the dungeon, and her foot sunk into the surface. She screamed, and Rune grabbed. "Seal!"

Robbie jumped back as the table glowed violet around the foot sticking up out of the table. "Got you witch." Rune's voice was loud, and filled with hate. His heart pounded with shock as he looked at the screaming figure in the violet mist, as she heaved on her leg caught in the circle of Victor Thornson. The foot wiggled madly sticking out of the table. Rune let go and sat back smiling. "Not bad for a flower girl."

Morgan le Fey screamed at the top of her voice. "Release me witch, or I shall kill him now." Rune leaned forward over the table, and Robbie gasped with shock as the pale violet figure of Rune rose out of the circle in the pictures above the table of Rune. The leg wriggled madly. The violet figure of Rune stood in the centre of the red star in the dungeons of Dunnottar. She smiled at her grandfather, and then looked into the eyes of the Dark One. Panic rose inside Robbie, as he looked at the sitting Rune, her eyes flaring bright purple, and then back at the pictures where she stood in the castle. Sweat ran down his face and his chest heaved as his heart thundered.

Rune looked with hatred at the Dark One. "Flower girls can be quite tricky at times witch. Release him or you too will share his fate, I have a much nicer box for you." She clicked her fingers.

Robbie watched as a brown crystal cylindrical tube appeared round the foot on the table. It rose into the air, and then slowly it began to sink into the surface of the table. He saw it rise on the other side as the Dark One fought to get free.

"RELEASE ME YOU BITCH OR DIE." Morgan waved her arms, and Robbie jumped as flames burst out of her hands, Rune waved a hand, and a violet wall appeared, the flame bounced back on Le Fey.

"You have no power witch; you are on my soil now." The tube continued to rise inch by inch, pulling the struggling Dark One into it. Her eyes widened with fear as Rune stood and watched smiling. "We won't be long now Grandfather, just got some rubbish to remove, and then I will be with you."

Le Fey screamed as the tall crystal container rose past her chest. "YOU WILL NOT HOLD ME, THEY COULD NOT BEFORE, I KNOW THE INCANTATION OF LIFE, DEATH AND REBIRTH, I WILL SOON ESCAPE YOU WILL SEE FLOWER GIRL."

Rune smiled. "I use deeper magic than that old thing witch, the true lines of Celts wrote far greater magic than your old hat books of trickery, I serve the white line and the circles, you are no match for the powers of time itself."

Robbie's heart was thumping behind his shirt, he leaned closer to the table and his fingers sunk in slightly, as he gripped the edge, violet ripples ran across the surface, he snapped his hands back out in fright. The cylinder was almost level with Rune's table and le Fey was screaming at the top of her voice, as she thrashed around inside the brown crystal clear tube that surrounded her. Rune stood and watched smiling.

He had no idea how she was doing what she did, but it scared him on levels he had never thought possible. The power of Rune was now at it fullest, and for the first time he realised that the old lady he had seen so many times in white, was nothing compared to Runestone. He trembled as he watched, and the violet intensified in Rune's eyes, as she turned to her grandfather, she pointed a finger and a bright violet beam shot out at the end of it and hit the top corner of the crystal containing her grandfather.

The cube vibrated and then rocked gently. Robbie watched as it moved slightly on the floor, Rune was pulling it towards the circle; it groaned and creaked as it slid on the concrete. His eyes fixed on the floor, and felt a pulse of joy each time it moved a little. He gripped the edge of the table in nervous suspense. "Come on sweetheart you can do it.... Oh hell Rune, hurry."

It moved another inch, and he bobbed desperately, his eyes glued to the point of the floor where it scraped along. He closed his eyes and breathed deeply, he had been holding his breath for so long, he thought he would pass out. It moved another inch, and he leaned right over the table, he was gasping for air as the sweat ran down his head. The Dark One pounded at the side of Rune, her wild eyes screaming and silent behind the thick sealed tube; she cursed and screamed silent charms and incantations to no avail. Rune had caught the Dark One, and Robbie could not believe it, he looked at her sat at the table. She was almost invisible, in the cloud of violet light that surrounded her.

He shuffled on the floor, and twitched as he watched her. "OH RUNE MY DARLING, COME ON WE ARE ALMOST THERE, JUST ANOTHER FOUR INCHES AND HE WILL BE IN THE CIRCLE." He looked back at the cube and laughed out loud with joy; it was almost there as it scraped across the floor.

The dungeon flooded with bright light, as the door at the top of the stairs flew open, Robbie screamed as the figure in black drew a long black sword, and jumped over the rail from the top step. He crossed the room and swung the sword high at Rune. It was a defensive reaction, and Robbie's hand dropped to his side, and with speed unknown; he drew the bright gleaming sword of Destiny. His arm plunged through the table and Mordred faltered as the gleaming sword came up through the floor followed by Robbie's white bangled arm, and crossed into the path of his black blade.

There was a shower of sparks as they clashed, and the room filled with heavenly singing voices, Mordred screamed in fear and recoiled away, smashing into the tall crystal tube. The black blade bit deep into the crystal, and there was a blinding flash. Robbie hit the wall of the cellar with terrific force, and the wind was knocked out of him, he gasped and panted on the floor trying to get the words of fear out and breathe.

"Ru....ne .... Rune ta...lk...to m...e." He gasped in the dark, and tried to crawl fighting the suffocation inside him. "Rune... Rune..." He drew a long deep breath. "RUUUUUUUNE?"

Violet light lit the room, and she knelt and pulled him close. He collapsed gasping for breath as she held him close. He shook with fear, and dropped the sword still sweaty in his hand, as he grabbed her and pulled her to the floor. "Oh Rune, I thought I had lost you." She lifted him up against the wall, and kissed his hot sweaty face; her hand pushed into his chest and glowed. His breathing came more easily and he panted as he breathed more slowly. "You scared the hell out of me sweetheart."

She smiled and leaned forward and kissed him. "You saved me My Darling from Mordred."

Robbie flopped his head back on the wall, and drew a long breath. "I am so going to kill that bastard. No one threatens my wife." She giggled and pulled him close.

"Another minute and I would have had her. Still, she knows not to mess with me now. I have more power than even I realised. Robbie my table is so cool." He smiled at her as she looked back at the swirling violet, just in time to see Mordred being screamed at by his irate mother as she pushed him up the stairs. "She has put a binding curse around the circle; I cannot pull him through now. I can only remove it from her side... Poor grandfather."

Robbie grabbed her arm. "I will get you in there, have no fear, we will get him back."

Rowan stood tense by the rail with Jade and Una. Screams wailed from below in the hidden depths of the dark castle. Jade shuddered, and gripped Rowan's arm. "I don't like this; I would much rather see what was happening. My imagination is too vivid for guess work."

Rowan pulled her close, and Una looked down as her violet eyes flickered. "Close your fear Jade and feel her. Rune is in there."

"What?" The anger was swift to rise inside Rowan. Una touched his arm.

"It is her essence; she is using the table. Those screams are the fear of the Dark One. Rune has her cornered and she is screaming for her life."

Jade leaned over the rail and her eyes turned pale green. "She will need power; we must send it."

Una touched Jade on the shoulder. "Gone are the days when Rune needed to channel us through her Jade. Rune is the centre of the circle, and sat at her own table now, she is power. The forces of nature and knowledge are hers to command. Relax and feel her, feel the true power of Runestone Sapphire. She is now awesome." Rowan watched nervously as the dark clouds in the sky swirled around the tall black tower of the castle. Lightening shot out as the screams howled from the sinister depths of the castle of fear. They were high on the cliffs, and yet they were loud and clear, he shuddered at the thought of whatever was happening.

"Is she alright Una?" He was very worried. She was alone in there and unprotected.

"Rowan fear not, those are the screams of the Dark One, believe me when I say that the greatest power in that castle today is Runestone."

Jade looked back frightened from under her long curly fringe. "Are you sure Una? I feel her, but I am afraid."

"She is in control of the fight, and whatever she is doing it is draining the power of the Dark One, I feel less dark and more white, I think she has caught her."

Rowan looked round his face was pale. "Who has caught who?" Una smiled.

"I cannot be sure Rowan, but if I am right, Rune has caught and contained the Dark One, her presence is fading. I am a protector of the light, I feel darkness stronger than any, it is my task to keep dark out and light in. I am sensing less and less dark and more white. Rowan, Rune has found a way to contain the Dark One. I have no idea how; I just feel the Dark One is being imprisoned."

Rowan stared down, the clouds were thick and deep now, and the top of the castle was barely visible. It was as if the darkness of the sky was being slowly sucked in through the windows. The sea was smashing up over the bridge, and the guards had run down to the gates, as the huge violent waves whipped over the bridge, and swept the men off into the pounding sea. The lightening exploded into the sky and every one ducked as it bounced off the cliffs leaving dark scorch marks. "Oh, wow she is pissed off." Jade peered round from behind Rowan.

Una's eyes burned bright purple. "There is another coming, I feel his anger."

Rowan stepped forward and gripped the rail. "It's Mordred and she is alone; we must help her."

Una touched Rowan's shoulder; her head moved from side to side as if she was trying to look for something hidden. "She is not alone, but it cannot be, she has gone to the other realm." Una opened her eyes and stared at the castle. "Mother?"

The flash was blinding, and the wails deafening, the earth shook and they stumbled. Rowan snatched Jade from the rail as his eyes went blind. He threw her with all of his might backwards, as he staggered, and then felt the ground hit his back. The wail lifted into the air as the earth shook violently. He rolled over and clawed his way towards the wall. The floor shuddered still, and he rolled over blinded, "Jade... Jade where are you?" She crawled up on to him and clung to his neck.

"I am here, I can't see Rowan I am blind." Rowan pulled her close and held her tight, as he felt the dust and debris fall onto his face.

"Me too sweetheart, it will be alright do not be scared, Una where are you, are you safe?"

There was a loud cough, and Una sat up from a pile of dust, she spat the dirt out of her mouth. "I am fine, just covered in plants and dirt, are you two alright, that was one hell of a flash, I can't believe Robbie used it."

Rowan's head moved as he saw dark shapes in the bright yellow spots before his eyes. "What's Robbie used Una; I don't understand?"

Una crouched in front of Rowan, and looked at his eyes. Jade was huddled tightly into his chest. "Keep your eyes open, and when I say close them, keep them shut for at least ten minutes, alright?" Una put her face close to Rowan's, and holding his eyes with her finger she drew her violet eyes level with his. Her eyes glowed, and Rowan felt the heat in his own eyes, as the violet light spilled into them. "Jade close your eyes, and connect with me, might as well do you both at the same time."

It was a very strange sensation, as both Jade and Rowan could see Rowan's eyes in their heads. "Hey Honey that is really cool, can you make his eyes permanently violet Una? It's dead sexy."

Una giggled. "Sorry Jade, it will last for just a day or so. Make the most of it. All right close your eyes and sit back against the wall, keep your heads down and wait until I tell you to open them." She pulled their hoods right over their heads to shade their faces.

"Una what did Robbie use?"

"Oh yeah sorry Rowan, Robbie pulled Destiny, he must have protected Rune with it, the flash was the Black Blade hitting a more powerful sword. That will have upset old Mordred, that's twice now Robbie has angered him."

Rowan held his face down under his hood. "What can you sense, are they safe?"

"I feel the Dark One, she has escaped Rune, there is just her and Mordred, and Rune has gone back to Loxley. They are fine, phew we almost had her."

Jade moved slightly. "Did you say your mother was there?"

"I felt her power, it was not her it was Robbie, when the swords clashed, Destiny pulled some of my mother's power out of the Black Blade, Destiny is even stronger and the Black Blade is weaker, Robbie has somehow inherited some of my mother's power. You know, I have felt it in him before, ever since that night at the table with Gwinne. It is strange I must talk to Rune."

Jade crawled up Rowan and slid her face into his neck. "Rowan honey, I am sorry, I have done it again."

Rowan pulled her close. "I know sweetheart my legs are wet." He held her tight. "When I can see, I will find you a nappy." She started to giggle.

"I am sorry, I just can't control it when she is about."

"Jade darling you know I love you. The night before we go into the castle, do not drink."

"Yes sweetheart."

Robbie came up the steps to the living room with Rune, his hair was wet with the sweat, and he was very white. Rune held him close. "I almost had her Rob; I will not get a chance like that again."

He flopped down in the chair he felt exhausted. "You were incredible Rune that was very brave, I am not sure I could have faced her like that."

She curled around him on his lap. "I felt you touch the table, knowing you were there helped me. You have some of the power of Gwendolyn in your blood, and the bracelet is intensifying it. It is even stronger now; Robbie I think your sword can draw the white power from the black blade. You hold the sword and you are her heir, I think her power is drawn to the bracelet. One day that will be Iona's, she will be the new white circle, and I think the bracelet knows, does that sound mad?"

He lay his head back and laughed. "You have relatives who walk through walls, and talk to birds, or turn invisible, Rune how can you call anything mad?" She started to giggle, and he felt her shake on his lap. He looked down at her bright blue eyes that danced, and sparkled. "I need a bath, I stink of sweat, do you want to wash my hair?" She nodded as she smiled, and slipped off his lap.

David pulled Melanie close. "Please be careful." She kissed him softly as Henry held her horse, and smiled happily.

"I am with Robbie." She turned and walked to the horse. "Thanks Henry."

"Mel that's why I worry, he is not exactly in the safest place on earth."

"Dave please stop worrying, I will be fine, tell him Henry." Henry beamed at her and turned to David.

"She will be fine won't she lads?" All the bowmen on the wall laughed, and shouted. "Yes Sir." Melanie smiled as she slid on her straw hat.

"See... I will be back soon, keep your head down and be careful." She turned the horse slowly to the open gate and shouted. "Look after him for me boys." David smiled as the bowmen shouted back.

"Yes My Lady, we will." She kicked the horse, and laughing she made her way waving up the road to the village. Her blue cloak flowed in the breeze behind her, Henry slapped David on the back.

"She is a mighty fine woman Dave."

He nodded. "I tell you Henry, it took long enough, but I really am very much in love with her." Henry smiled at his best friend, he was very happy for him.

"That makes me very happy to hear Dave, she really is very nice, she loves you too it shows."

"You think so?"

"Trust me I am a keeper of the watch; I spot stuff quicker than any."

Rune sat with Alice, who hugged and kissed her. Bear beamed as Alice exploded with excitement. "We will be mums together, I am so excited, I bet Rob is thrilled?"

Rune beamed with delight. "Look he is about to tell Jess, he made Robert promise not to say anything." Rune watched from the Postal Office steps, as he walked up the steps to the greenhouse and gave his mum a hug.

"Hey mum, see I told you, I am back again." She pulled him close.

"Oh Robbie, you look tired, don't let them work you so hard, delegate more. Oh, your hair smells wonderful."

He laughed. "It's Rune shampoo, she washes it for me, it helps me relax." She smiled. "Mum... I know you are sort of the expert... and you never miss anything, but there is really something important you should know."

Jess looked worried. "No one is hurt, are they?"

"No mum." He smiled at her. "Will you stop worrying about everyone? Mum sometime around June, July next year I will be a dad and you a granny."

Jess's eyes opened wider and her jaw dropped. "I missed it, that's not possible, are you sure? I can spot a pregnant girl at a thousand yards."

"I am sure... it's twins, one of each, are you happy for me?"

She flung her arms round him and wept. "Oh Robbie, I am over the moon." She stepped back smiling with tears in her eyes she looked him in the eye. "This is what you want, isn't it?"

"Mum... How can you ask that? You know how much I love Rune."

"Robbie dear I am a mother, and mothers always check. Oh, let me see her. Come on, I am so excited I haven't knitted in years."

Rune stood up, as Jess came smiling over. "Hi Jess."

Jess threw her arms around Rune and almost squeezed her to death. "Oh Runestone, darling you have made me so happy. My boy will have heirs, and Robert will love being a granddad. Oh, I am so happy for you both, you will have to get married, it will not be right for the Lord of Loxley to have children out of wedlock." Robbie gave a grunt.

"Mum I have already asked her, please don't embarrass us like this, she said yes over a month ago."

Jess smiled. "Sorry Runestone. Robbie, we lead this community by example, we have always upheld the traditions of the woodsmen."

Robbie slid his arm around Rune. "We have a job to do, and when we return, you can help plan the wedding, alright?"

She pulled them both close and hugged them. "Oh, I am sorry, I am so happy for you both, you will see Runestone when you have yours, you will fuss just like me. It is what we do Rob because we love you."

Skip and Treen came up the side of the house with Mel, Bear got up and kissed Alice, they came up as Jess hugged Rune. "Take care of my boy and my grandchildren." She beamed with delight.

"I will Jess, you can depend on it."

She turned to Robbie. "Oh Rob, look after yourself, and protect that girl at all costs, I know it's still very early, but watch her closely." She kissed his cheek.

"I will mum you know it. Watch out for dad for me." She smiled as Rune opened the window, and the group stepped through. Robbie had barely made it two feet when he was dragged into a hug. Jade clung to him like a limpet.

"Hey Pebbles, it's nice to see you too."

"What the hell were you doing going in there alone?" She looked up with tears in her bright green eyes. "You scared Rowan and me to death."

Rune touched her sister on the shoulder. "Jade we had a rare chance to catch her, we almost had her as well, if we had been successful, all of you would have been spared the task, I was the one who went after her, Robbie came through to protect me."

Jade hugged Rune. "I was really scared; I could hear the screams up here." Rune looked up at Rowan and Una, who both nodded.

"That is not possible, unless she was projecting; was there dark clouds and lightening?"

Una nodded. "Yes, we had quite a storm, why is that important?"

Rune walked to the viewing rail, and looked down on the castle. "Yes, it is very important, you heard her scream from this point, and it was loud as if you were there beside her?"

Una looked confused. "Yes Rune, it was deafening."

Rune stamped the floor hard, Robbie looked at her. "What does this all mean Rune?" She turned and looked at Rowan and Jade stood just behind Robbie and Una.

"What it means is she is not here and never has been, it means she has a table, and she is somewhere else watching her precious children. I wondered why it took her so long to get here and help Mordred, I expected her sooner, she would have had to travel from wherever she was to help him."

Robbie looked stunned. "So, where the hell is she, if there is just him in there?"

Rune looked at Una. "It is funny there has been no sign of Mac since we freed Alice, Mac will be easier to find, where ever he is, you can bet your last bit she won't be too far away."

Jade looked out across the water at the castle as darkness fell, it looked more sinister than ever. "But Rune, if she is not there, that is a good thing isn't it? That just means we have to get Mordred out of the way to free Granddad."

Rune looked disappointed as she slid into Robbie's arms. "I wanted both rats in one basket, we will have to deal with them one at a time, this could go on forever, and if we go in, she can pop up just about anywhere. If it gets too hot, she will fade and pop up in another place. This will make the job harder for all of us. Oh Rob I am sorry, if I had known it was just her essence there today, I could have killed her forever. I missed the best chance we have ever had to clear the world of that witch forever." She buried her head in his shoulder, and he pulled her close. Robbie stood on top of the cliff looking down on the dark evil castle that filled the island of Dunnottar, his hair lifted gently in the breeze, as his eyes hardened; he stroked her long silken hair, as he watched out over the sea. He knew where she was, he had often wondered about it himself.

"She is still in Cornwall; she has never left her family seat. I always wondered why he had built such a big fortress there, when he had a wall around the whole country. He was keeping her safe, we just missed her."

Rune looked up at Robbie, he made perfect sense. There were two large buildings at Tintagel, one for Mason, and the really big one on the headland, which was her home, they had both missed it. He looked down and kissed her softly.

"We will take care of Mordred, and then we will find her and rattle her out of her cage. I will give you the honour of killing her." She looked up into his dark brown eyes and she smiled and nodded softly.

CHAPTER NINE

TALISMAN'S OF THE VIOLET CIRCLE

It was just before dawn, and the solitary figure of a bowman stood high on the top of what had once been a house, but was now a tall mound of green leaves and flowers. From the top of the cliff, the figure watched through the night. The guards looked up and felt reassured to see the hooded figure, his cloak flapping in the breeze, and his bow across his shoulder. They would turn and wink to each other, knowing the Lord Loxley was watching with them. They turned back and watched from their places scattered all over the face of the rocks, ready for the attack when it came.

The sea crashed endlessly into the island, its waves smashing against the rock face, and whipping the water into bright white foam that rushed back to the swirling water, before being lifted, thrown and smashed against the rocks once more. It felt sinister in the shadow of the dark and brooding island of Dunnottar. The rocks were rough and sharp, covered in the crystal, which jutted out like knives and spears, it was the deathly beginning to the walls of black smooth shining stone, which lifted from the cold threatening waves to the top of the island, and the symbol of fear to a nation.

The dark walls were high, and decorated with horrible and ugly frightening faces of gargoyles and beasts of destruction. It loomed black and fearsome out of the sea, rising with barbed and spiky ledges that protected the top of the walls from attack. The atmosphere around it was of death and despair. A tall central tower climbed up from the centre, smooth and dark to its summit, which widened out with hundreds of long shards of pointed spear like stone. This was what the woodsmen called the 'Nest of Death'.

On top of the nest, the tower was sculpted into a huge black and vile looking raven, its beak screamed open at the coastline, and in the dark throat were two tall arched leaded windows, behind which burned red light making the mouth look like it was filled with blood. The base of the beak was her balcony, and below it on the spikes of the nest, hung the last uneaten remains of those who had displeased her. The eyes of the raven were cold as pale blue light flowed out, everyone who had been questioned, told of the room where she hid and worked her devious evil magic. This was the room of fear and devastation; this was the lair of the Dark One.

There had been silence all day and night since Rune had visited through her table. Now the air hung with the foreboding of the fear, and apprehension before the revenge began. The lonesome hooded figure was plain enough to see, and he knew if she was there, she would be watching him, stood tall, proud and unafraid of her. Robbie was the symbol of hope to the world of the woodsmen, never more so on that long night where his vigil warmed the hearts, and lifted the courage of the men, who sat in small groups by the thousand, waiting to start the fight of their lives.

Rowan looked out from the viewing rail, across the cliff top towards Robbie. His slate grey eyes burned brightly under his hood, as they scanned the darkness watching the cliffs down to the black bridge. His eyes lifted back to the figure on top of the cliff in front of the Dark Tower. "You watch him as he watches out for all of us My Lord." The quiet voice of Rose slipped through the dark. Rowan blinked as he felt the warm cup touch his hand. He moved slightly as he smiled and took it.

"He is a man like no other, and I watch for him yes. I love him as my lord, but also my brother."

Rose smiled under her hood. "I have seen much this last week, and I am sure he is like no other man. The Lord Loxley and his Lady are truly exceptional. I have learned more in two days than I have in two years. He has more than command and respect from his men; I see he has their devotion."

Rowan turned to Rose and their eyes met in the gloom. "My Lady, I have spent less than a year in his inner circle, and I always thought that I was a man of courtesy, honour and integrity, for that is the way I was raised by my father. I am nothing compared to him. To be by his side day and night, and learn from him as he carries a burden that would crush most men, is an experience that has changed me forever. I am a better man for knowing him."

"He favours you highly Rowan of Loxley, I see the bond that has been forged between you."

"I care not for his favour My Lady. If he respects me for who I have become, that is indeed a gift worthy of any man, and a tribute I will carry with honour." Rowan turned back and looked to the south cliff, and the figure of the man who for him was the symbol of what all men should be.

The first rays of the sun broke the edge of the sea, and pale light bounced across the water to the base of the cliff. The lines on his face showed as the light brushed up his hood, and the darkness below his bright shining eyes showed the concern he carried for the fate of his people. A slender figure walked up behind him, and rested her head on his shoulder, his cloak parted as his hand slid out and slipped around her pulling her close. "I woke and I missed you."

"I could not sleep and came out to do my watch. They will do something today Rune, I feel it, be on your guard. We will be the first targets."

"I am ready. Let them come they will not pass us easily."

"What the hell is he doing stood up there all bloody night? Why does he just stand and stare, why hasn't he attacked us? I am ready for him now." The dark eyes of hate and malice looked out through the tall arched windows, and burned venom across the bay to the figure stood holding the dark slender shape of Rune by his side. The Dark Lord of Dunnottar was anxious and frustrated; he wanted the fight to start.

"Calm yourself; he has had his taste of glory, now we shall give him back a little of his own medicine." She fawned over her son in a sickening way, as she stroked his hair in an incestuous manner. Hesketh felt sickened to his stomach, as the Dark One soothed her son by the window.

"I shall go to my room and prepare, I have a few tricks of my own for the flower girl, you go and get ready, and when the gates open your men shall ride through to victory." She kissed his cheek in a fashion not becoming a mother, and Hesketh felt the need to retch.

Mordred contained within the body of Billy smiled an evil and ghastly smile. "I love you mother."

She gave what looked like a smile, but it seemed forced around her withered lips of black. "That's my boy, now go and we will have his head on our bridge before the day is out." Mordred turned with new malice in his eyes, and headed towards the door. Hesketh pulled open the door, and he brushed past without any notice of the servant at all.

Rune looked to the tower and the raven of black as the sunlight lifted bright in the sky behind it. "She is there, I feel her, and we need to prepare." They turned together, and left the rooftop, and headed back to the command post. The war of Dunnottar was about to begin.

The sun was up, and everyone had finished eating their breakfast. It was a moment of calm as they talked and joked. They drank coffee and tea as they checked their weapons, and Rune came out of her room with a bag of violet velvet in her hand. "Can the members of the table of Runestone form a large circle as you would be seated at it please?" The group looked up at her bright smiling face. "It's alright it is nothing sinister." Robbie started to laugh at the others who had for a moment looked worried. They stood in their places and Judy beamed as Robbie winked when he saw her take her rightful place within the circle.

Rune made spaces where Gwinne, Amethyst and Scarlet would normally sit, and ensured everyone was an even distance apart. She looked at the others stood watching. "I want all of you to come inside my circle and form another circle... Rose, Sinclair and Angus, you are part of this please would you enter."

The others came in and formed a smaller circle. Rune smiled, as she joined the circle in her place, and looked at Maddy with a grin. "Looks a little like Carnac doesn't it?" Maddy gave one of her rare smiles.

Rune raised her hands and her eyes began to glow. "White light, white circle green life we summon your power into my violet circle." Her eyes glowed as the others gasped, and below them the large circle of white appeared on the floor. A bright sapphire blue twenty-pointed star appeared within it. A silver star came up through the centre and touched at the feet of the inner circle. In the very centre a circle of violet glowed containing a large silver runic 'R'.

"Welcome to the violet circle my friends. Today you will bind with me as your centre, and I will cloak you with protection. You will no longer feel the dark touch of fear from the witch across the water; let your hearts be free of her."

Rune stepped into the circle, and walked to Jett. She faced her and smiled. Rune kissed Jett on the cheek, and drew from her bag a Talisman pendant. "This will guide and protect you my sister." Jett's eyes burned blue as Rune pressed it into her hand. The Talisman was round and contained a white circle with the sapphire star of Rune on it. In the centre was the sword of Excalibur in bright gleaming gold.

"Rune this is beautiful." She turned it over in her hand as she smiled, and showed Jett the other side. It was deep violet with the silver runic 'R'.

"Wear it for I love you sister." A tear welled in Jett's eye.

"I love you too Rune." Rune smiled and moved on to Jasper.

"For you my seer and converser of spirits, I give lilac, the symbol of death and rebirth, be protected my brother." She kissed his cheek and he smiled as he looked at his hand with blue flickering eyes.

Rune kissed Ruby who giggled. "My little Flash whom I have seen grow with such joy, you have the sun, for you radiate the warmth and happiness it brings." Ruby looked down and gasped at the beauty of the Taliesin. She threw her arms around Rune and hugged her.

"I love you Rune." Robbie smiled as he watched the joy in Rune's face.

"I love you too Ruby." Rune looked at Judy who stood looking happy.

"My new student and member of this table, you have a hidden deadly sting, so my little hornet." She drew the pendant out of the bag. "You wear the bumble bee, which brings life to all flowers of my garden, but should not be angered for fear of her sting." She hugged Judy who had tears in her eyes, and Rune moved on.

"Skip my dear friend, you have become such a man of great value and worth, long gone is the frightened young lord from the woods. You have helped my Rob so much, you have the scales, for you have dealt justice evenly to all." Skip looked down.

"My dearest Lady you honour me beyond worth."

Rune kissed his cheek, and crossed the vacant space where Gwinne would usually sit. "Dear Gwinne is not here, but she has her gift of the heart."

Rune looked at Maddy. "You carry the heaviest burden with such grace my sweet sister." Maddy looked down at the floor with sorrow, and Rune lifted her face. One day you will be free to return to your circle and be happy." She pressed the pendant with a single teardrop on it into her hand and Maddy's eyes glowed purple.

Steph smiled as Rune stepped in front of her. "Mother to me, and mother to all, I love you Mother, your knowledge has and will play a great role for us soon." She pressed the pendant with a golden book into her hand as her eyes burned violet. Steph gave her daughter a hug.

"I am so proud of you sweetheart."

Rune stopped at the gap that was her own and smiled, she stepped across and faced Crystal. "Take off your gloves I am centre of all powers, have no fear of touching me. Be free to feel a human form, for you have the coldness of isolation and it should not be so, from the moment you place this on your neck, you will have the freedom to choose. Your isolation of others will end today Crystal." Crystal burst into tears and hugged Rune with bare hands, and Rune smiled as she hugged her.

"I will not have any around me lonely, especially one who has so much love inside her." She pressed the pendant of the icicle into her hand. "Be cold only in need my sweet sister."

Rune stood before Robbie and she smiled as her eyes twinkled brightly. "My Darling, we have joy between us that nothing will ever destroy." He smiled as she drew from her bag the pendant. He looked down at the strange symbol. It looked like a capital 'C' with a tail leading from the top and what looked like a capital 'L' sticking out of the bottom. "I am Runestone the creator of all runes. This will soon be a new rune in the world. It is the joining of white lines with the white circle, and the circle of green life. For around you these things have all happened. You have created this, to read it will be just one word 'Iona' for through you the Queen of Fae will once more walk on this earth. I love you Robbie, you are the life of my realm." He felt a surge of love and joy as he looked at the strange little symbol, and smiling she passed on to Sapphire.

"I have carried my message through you many times my sister. You should have been placed as a centre also, and I know of the sadness you felt. Take this butterfly, for it is the centre of my words and the bearer of my news, carry my power with you always and know you are close to my heart." Sapphire felt the tears and hugged Rune.

"I could not do what you do, I love you Rune and will do so always." Rune moved on to Jacques.

"To be loved so deeply by my sweetest and dearest of friends Alice, tells me much of the proud man before me. You are truly a friend of huge value, and I thank you for the defence of your lord." She pressed the golden bear Talisman into his shovel like hand. "A bear has great courage, but also great heart," she stretched up on to her toes and kissed the broad smile of Bear.

Rune crossed the gap of Scarlet. "My dear sister has her shield." She turned to Melanie who smiled. "Little birds talk to me too my sweet sister, I see flowers bloom at our gates, I am happy for he is a man who is so worthy, and yet so forgotten at times." She pressed the pendant with a golden eagle into her hand and her eyes flowed in bright blue.

"Amethyst works in other realms, the fish has reached her."

Jade looked upset as Rune stood before her. "Oh, sister if only you could have had this sooner, I love you so dearly my sister, and I cannot tell you of the happiness I have in my heart for the one I love above all others." Jade gasped a loud sob under her fringe. She threw her arms around Rune and wept.

"I know what you have done for me sister, I can never give back what was taken." Rune held her close.

"That balance has been restored, and I would make that choice freely again for the love of my kin. Take this and be safer my little chameleon." Rune kissed Jade softly and wiped her eyes with her finger. "I love you Jade." Jade sobbed as she looked up and Rune smiled. "I hope we need no more buckets now." Jade gasped a big smile and clutched the pendant tight. Rune looked at Rowan.

"My brother, my friend, ever watchful is your eye on my road. I have felt calmness knowing you stand by the side of your lord. You have been a rock beside him and I owe you more than any for the devotion you have shown the man that I love. Take the hand that binds friendship and guides in an even and fair manner." Rowan bowed to Rune.

"My Lady of the Woods, I am, and always will be your servant, I serve both of the lords who are kin to you, and you honour me beyond words. I have love in my heart through your kin and your realm; it is I who should honour you."

Rune nodded. "You have honoured me greatly My Lord of Loxley." She paused for a moment as she realised for the first time that Rowan had recognised her by the same title as he gave Opal. The honour of his words touched her deeply, and knowing he felt the same respect for Rune, as he had her grandmother was something she had not expected. She moved to Una.

"I cannot give a greater gift than that of Arthur Pendragon, but like your staff I can give a holly leaf, for it like yourself is the power of protection, it will work well with your gifts."

Una looked at Rune as her violet eyes burned. "I have a gift from a lady the equal of My Lord Kings wife Guinevere; it will be a treasure of my line My Lady Runestone Sapphire and Lady of the Green Realm." Una pulled her close and kissed her.

She moved finally to Citrine. "My sister, you have lost the bitterness of the lemon and found the sweet taste of the orange." Treen smiled as she glanced at the smiling Skip. "The soul can be seen through the eyes, and you have the gift of persuasion through those eyes. This is the eye for you to see always." Bright orange erupted into Treen's eyes as Rune turned and walked into the inner circle.

Rune looked up at Big John and tears filled her eyes. "I find it hard to find words for a man so worthy of this group. You have protected me, and my kin beyond the measure of duty. I have come to love you as family, for you have stood tall and proud and fought with such honour for my lord."

John looked down with tears forming in his eyes. "The pride is mine to serve such a worthy couple, my life is yours my fairest of all ladies, take it when you need." She gave a small sob as she pressed the Talisman with a single golden violet into his hand.

Martin spoke before she could. "John here is right My Lady. We would lay down our lives to protect such a noble line and consider it an honour, you honour us greatly." She gave him the same golden violet and he pulled it around his neck with pride.

Rafe smiled as she handed him his. "Captain Rafe, you have earned a new name." Rune gave a soft giggle. "I believe the Lady Jett Amber feels we must name you and as tradition decrees, Harry has approved it, you will be known here on in as 'Wolfie', it appears you fight with sharper teeth than your blade."

The group all laughed, as Rafe looked across at Jett and winked. He bowed to Rune. "If My Lady agrees, then so will I." Rune nodded and looked up at her father. She handed him the pendant of the violet.

"I have spent so much time alone without you; I cannot tell you the joy you have brought back to my life. I love you so much Daddy." Smokes pulled her close and gave her a huge hug.

"I love you too princess, I am so proud of what you have achieved, and I too have the joy of my children every day."

Blades beamed a big smile as her eyes danced with delight, as she lifted the pendant over her neck. "Thanks Rune, I love all of you." Rune pulled her into a hug.

"For one so young you have seen a great deal, we are all in awe of your skills." Everyone nodded and mumbled agreement.

Keith gave a smile as she looked at him. "You are still new to our group but you have proved your worth every day. You are a true man of Loxley and My Lord is proud to see you here today." Keith bowed to Rune.

"I am a true man in the service of the highest lord and lady in this land."

Rune looked up at Fish as she handed him the violet pendant. "Your family has honoured me above all others James Ashford. The sacrifice of your brother Anthony will never leave my heart. I should honour you more than this token for your loss." Fish bowed and kissed her gently on the cheek.

"I have a home and friends, who are the high lord and lady of my home. You can pay a man no higher honour my dearest Lady Loxley, my brother did not die in vain." Rune put her head down as she felt the twinge of pain in her heart. Fish placed his finger on her chin and softly lifted it back to meet his gaze. The tear ran from her eyes. "My brother loved his lord and lady, for they were kind and honourable. Do not look down My Lady. There is not a person here who would not gladly give their lives to protect one so fair and beautiful." Everyone murmured in agreement. She nodded as he smiled at her.

Maggs rattled as she threw her arms around Rune. Robbie smiled unsure quite where Maggs would hang the pendant she had so many on. It had always amazed him how she stood upright under the weight. Harry stood tall and proud and Rune smiled as she handed him the necklace of a single violet flower. Her fondness for Harry showed in her face. "I am not sure it will keep green evils at bay, but it will the Dark One, I hope with your glasses this will do the trick, and double the power. You are very special Harry, please keep yourself safe for Maggs."

"Hey Rune baby girl, this is like totally cosmic. I love you chicken you know that yeah?" Rune grinned and nodded. He smiled a huge smile. "Hey girl you got my number... cool."

Rune looked up at Rose. "The violets are for those in Loxley. Yet you have become part of our circle, the three here are for you Sinclair and Angus. They are our tokens of love and protection, when we leave, you will be watched by my great grandfather." Rose looked down at the three pendants, they contained as the others did the wheel of Runestone, and each had a golden rose on them to signify the garden they had fought for so long to save. The garden of Runestone filled with flowers would be theirs forever to watch and protect.

Rune now took her place in the circle, and smiled at everyone who wore their pendants. She slid her own over her head and the golden rune in the centre of it glowed. Violet light streamed out of it, and connected with all the others, a large circle of purple surrounded them all, and everyone's eyes glowed lilac. "Hear me for I am the centre of the wheel of Runestone Sapphire, power of the green lord and servant of the white lines of time, bind with me and join me, for you are all loved and protected from the darkness. I bring life to the world and through you; I shall honour and protect it. Be at peace as our minds join as one, and we fight the cause of life. We are now united as one in the violet circle."

Everyone felt a cool feeling wash over them, and their hearts lifted and lightened, the warmth of the love of Rune flowed into them, and they felt joy. The light faded and the circle on the floor gradually soaked into the stone and was gone. Rune bowed to them all, and they bowed back and broke apart, the violet circle was complete. Rune turned to Robbie, she felt very emotional, everyone had paid both of them such high compliments that she was not sure what to say or feel. She had been deeply touched, and it was nice just to feel his arms slide round her and pull her close. She rested her head on his shoulder.

"I have done all I can do now to keep them safe; she will not freeze their minds with fear like she might the others. I can feel her building her powers; she is looking for something to beat us. She will not attack until later when she thinks she is stronger. She fears your sword."

Robbie kissed the top of her head and held her tight; he looked across at the tower. It still looked evil and sinister in the full light of day. "When she comes, we will fight her and any of the others that are contained in that place of misery."

She nuzzled into his neck. "Come and sleep, you have been up all night. Please have some rest before it all starts; you look exhausted Rob." He smiled and nodded knowing better than to argue, and she guided him back to their room, where he slid under the blankets and closed his eyes. He had not realised how tired he was as he relaxed in the soft bed. Rune stood by the window and watched out across the bay.

It was just gone noon, when Robbie woke up, the long golden red hair of Rune was cast across the bed as she slept, curled around him. He could see the large shape of John silhouetted behind the curtain outside as he stood watch. He smiled and looked at the pale white face of Runestone, her long white freckled arm stretched round him and he softly stroked it, she moaned in her sleep and pulled him tight. He lay and watched just enjoying the moment knowing that soon he would have to face the dark forces that lay past his door. He looked down at the bright blue sleepy eyes that stared up, and watched him. "Hey beautiful." She smiled and squeezed him tight.

"Hi gorgeous." She moved slowly up to his face and he pulled her close as she kissed him.

"You slept well; I thought it was supposed to be me who was tired?"

"I miss you when you are on watch; I don't sleep well on my own anymore." She kissed his chest. "You have spoilt me too much; I am used to my man beside me."

"I am hungry, I wonder if we missed dinner?" She slid up and kissed him.

"Maggs will have something when we get up, just hold me for a while Rob. It will get harder today, and I want this time alone with you."

He pulled her into a tight hug. "Rune we will be fine."

"I know, I just worry about you. It will always be you they go for, I have so little time alone with you, just stay with me a while longer." She lay her head down on his shoulder and he slid his arm under the sheet, she giggled as he softly tickled her. The sound of her laughter always brought joy to his heart.

It was midafternoon, and Robbie sat with Rune, his shirt flapping open and his boots by his side. He ate a large plate of stew that Maggs had saved especially. Rowan came stretching out of his room and smiled. He too had been up most of the night, and Jade had insisted on him going back to bed, although it had been some time before she had let him sleep. He came out into the sun and sat beside Robbie. "All still quiet then? I expected something sooner."

Maggs wandered up, as Jade staggered yawning to the door wearing Rowan's long shirt, she beamed at Maggs who handed her a plate. "Cheers Maggs I am starving."

"I think some pants my dear lady might be in order." Jade looked down at her bare legs.

"It's alright Maggs I just put some new knickers on." She giggled as Rune smiled. Maggs handed a plate to Rowan who nodded with a smile and yawned. He spooned the hot stew up and started to eat.

Robbie looked across the bay. "Look for dark clouds and we will know when she is coming, I want to be lower down when she does. If I can draw her below the cliffs, everyone up here will be safe, the five swords should now stay together, we must not separate."

Rowan nodded. "That pleases me, I will be happier at your side than elsewhere. The bridge is smashed how will we cross it?"

"She will repair it before she attacks." They both looked at Rune, and she smiled as Jade flopped beside her.

"She will need to get her guards out, she will repair the bridge, and they will stream out. Mordred will be hidden safe directing the battle. We cannot step on the bridge it is a trap. We will have to go under."

Robbie looked at Rune, and then at Rowan. "Crystal will provide a bridge of white."

Rune leaned back. "We need dust to coat the bridge, I will take her down shortly and see what we have, and I want to be invisible when we go in. Jade you will need your white marble."

She looked at Rune. "Why, what will it do?"

"Opal told you it will help you get through when there is no other way. Your marble is our key to Dunnottar, I have thought a lot about it since she gave it to you. I think she saw this day coming."

Jade nodded and smiled. "I love my marble, I was going to put it on a chain, I keep it in a velvet pouch in my pocket. I hold it when I think of her."

Rune took her sister's hand. "I think of her often, I miss her as well, she will be with us today in our hearts, and it will help us."

Jade gave a big grin. "I hope so."

They finished the meal, and Robbie called the team together. They all gathered round in a wide circle. "I wish I could tell you that I had a blue print of this one, I don't. I think soon she will attack, and her forces will spill out over the bridge, we have upset our black opponent and be under no illusions, her anger will show. We will try to deflect her and push her away, at which point we will go under the bridge and enter the castle. I have no idea of what we face in there, so be careful. I want all of you to take your time and keep a good watch on each other, we will move slowly around the place, until we find what we seek. Right let's prepare, take extra arrows, use up the violets, and then load with white."

The group jumped into action and pulled together their equipment, Jade scampered off and arrived a little while later, fully dressed and armed to the teeth, she had collected quite a few weapons together cleaning up after fights, and Robbie noticed the extra daggers in her boots. She carried her own sword, and a short close quarter's sword on her belt, her bow with extra arrows was slung across her back.

The group headed off round the road that twisted down through the cutting to the base of the bridge, Robbie looked up at the walls of the carved out cutting, at the masses of bowmen all sat protected behind large boulders ready to pick off any who entered. The long road ran through to the base of the cliff, and the start of the dark bridge. A huge statue of a dragon with a raven sat on it, and suppressing it was at the end of the bridge. It was vile, black and ugly, and the dragon wore a submissive look on its face. Robbie wondered if it was meant to be the Pendragon or Mason she was keeping in place.

The black bridge was wide with tall pillars down each side, wires were attached across from pillar to pillar, and the group gazed in horror, as they saw the endless rows of woodsmen's severed heads, hanging by their hair. Anger rose quickly inside Robbie, Rose shed a tear, as she knew some of the faces.

Jaz looked sadly at the heads as he walked with Harry. "I hear their tears and the screams of fear, as they lie between worlds. They moan with such sadness." Harry jumped away from him as if he was infectious.

"Hey man cut it out with that freaky shit, whoa you are not cosmic man, you don't talk to em dude, it jangles your vibes and chomps on your karma. Talk to the living it aint cosmic speaking to them." Harry lifted the pendant Rune had given him and kissed it; he slid on his glasses and smiled. "Hey man, I am mellow; my karma is cosmic and fully together man. Look dude how peaceful it can be, you gotta think cosmic man."

Jaz smiled. "They like you Harry, they say you are funny, but they watch you with interest."

Harry danced on the spot, and waved his hands about making loud shushing noises. "What you doing dude, you don't talk to em, get like real peaceful and stop hassling all our vibes man, I done bad things for Robbie man, they want to send me to the land of uncosmic monsters' man."

Jaz looked very seriously at him. "Harry, you know of that place?"

Harry swallowed very nervously and shook his head. Jaz spoke with a very soft frightened voice, "I have been there, it is a very freaky place full of people who died by your swords." Harry's eyes opened very wide as he shook with suppressed terror.

"Whoa man that aint cosmic." He grabbed his pendant and kissed it over, and over. Harry turned and ran up the line close to Rune. He nervously looked back at Jaz, who laughed with his head down as he walked.

Una smiled behind him. "You are as wicked as Jade, Jasper." She laughed as his shoulders shook. "Poor Harry he has such a hard time with all of you, the poor man has enough on his plate with his wild thoughts." John and Martin laughed in front of Jasper, which just made it all the more funny, Jasper looked up and Harry snapped his head forwards.

Robbie brought the group on to the long carved out front, at the start of the broken black bridge; he looked down at the water lapping up onto the shale beach. "Alright spread out and take cover, on my command we all slip under the bridge, and you all follow me quickly."

He turned to Rune. "I need powdered crystal under there, can you do it?" Rune smiled as her eyes glowed, and dust came out of the cliff face. It floated through the air in a sparkling mist and swept under the bridge where it formed a large sparkling pile on the beach. Crystal knew what to do, and slipped down with Mel to prepare. The rest scattered all along the front, they were now at the first line of defence. The whole of the front of the cliffs were filled with bowmen, who all sat waiting ready for it to begin.

Just to the right of the long black bridge was a carved out shelter. Robbie pulled Rune inside, followed by Jade and Rowan, Jett and Rafe waited just outside behind a large stonewall. Bear and Skip sat a few feet up and talked quietly, Rune's eyes flickered behind Robbie who stood by the open front of the shelter, he saw the dark clouds on the horizon and gripped his bow.

"Watch carefully now, when that bridge repairs, all hell will break lose. He walked out of the shelter and signalled to Rose, who now covered the whole left side of the bridge. Sinclair stood to his right and nodded as his men slipped forward to the sea wall.

Crystal and Mel looked out across the water to the rough rock of the island; it shimmered slightly with the Cairngorm crystal mixed with it. The black bridge above their heads was very wide and supported on long high archways. The sunlight burned brightly through the hole created by the section that had been blasted out, and Crystal leaned forward and looked up at the wires with the heads hanging below. "She is a vile woman, what I would not give to hang her head up there to frighten the birds away."

Mel shuddered as she looked up. "I have no understanding of that Criss; I find it hard to understand how anyone could do something so evil."

"Give me a blade and a good swing at her shoulders, and I will teach you." There was a rumbling sound deep under the bridge, and they both jumped back to the edge of the pile of powdered crystal. The sea began to bubble and the large pile of black rock that was strewn in the water began to vibrate. Mel gripped Crystal's arm. "It is starting."

The black rocks shook in the sea, and then began to roll towards each other. Small pieces jumped out of the water and stuck to the larger ones, slowly before their eyes they watched the bridge rebuild itself, and rise into the gap above them. The light dimmed with the crunch, as the rock seemed to glue itself back and glowed red for a moment.

Rune touched Robbie's arm. "I see it My Darling, get ready." He jerked as she swung him round, and pulled him into a heavy and passionate kiss.

"I love you Robert of Loxley." He smiled and kissed the tip of her nose.

"You are my life; you are why I will live." She beamed a huge smile as he pulled her round, and the large section of the bridge flew up from the sea into place.

Robbie and Rune slipped their bows off their shoulders.

"Here we go people let's stay alert, and be ready, hell is coming for tea, give her plenty for after's. Maddy let that white bow of yours do its thing, give me arrows at their gate." Maddy raised her bow and took aim. The long arrow whistled right across the bridge, and buried itself deep in the wood. She winked at Robbie.

"This one is a Carnac special."

Robbie watched through his telescope as the large gate opened. Giant muscular warriors in black leather walked forward. Maddy's eyes flared blue, and the arrow exploded spraying fire in every direction, the warriors screamed in pain as they burned and ran down the bridge throwing themselves into the water, the sea hissed wildly as they hit it. Mel jumped as the flaming bodies hurled themselves in to the sea, Crystal went to work, her eyes turned white as she focused her powers, and a breeze blew up under the bridge, she plunged her hand into the huge mound of glowing sparkling Cairngorm Crystal dust, and it was whipped up with snow and blown across the whole underside of the bridge.

Mel looked up at the white shimmering ceiling that was the underside of the black bridge, now she fully understood what Robbie had wanted to do, she realised that from above the Dark One, would not see them, and they would be hidden by the deep frozen layer that coated the bridge. She breathed a sigh of relief as Crystal smiled. "Under here Mel, we are as invisible as Jade." She smiled, as her eyes became their normal black circle with a black dot in the centre. Una and Hornet slid down the bank with Harry and Jaz. Blades dropped down with Keith and Saff. The five swords stood together around Robbie, Jade loaded her bow ready, and the rest of the group slid over the wall and under the bridge.

Rose screamed her orders, as her bowmen stood up all along the wall; they lifted their bows and took aim. Sinclair followed suit, and Robbie patted him on the back. "Keep that bridge busy for as long as you can, we will find her in the castle." They slipped over the wall and down under the bridge, Robbie was the last one to drop, and as he came under the ice covered underside of the bridge, he pulled Rune and Jade by his side. "Alright Crystal, let's cross."

Crystal crouched down at the edge of the water, and lowered her hand down as her eyes turned white. The sea crackled and shimmered, and water rose into the air and froze solid. A long white tube crossed under the bridge to the rocks on the other side. She smiled at Robbie. "It's harder with sea water; it has a lot of salt in it."

Robbie smiled at her. "You are really a little wonder; do you know that?" Her cheeks, showed a little blue, Crystal was blushing.

Robbie took the lead, and they followed him down the tunnel of ice. It felt odd as they ran, because it was not at all slippery; he looked down at the coating of soft silver seabed sand and understood. It was bright white inside and it dazzled the eyes as the tunnel shimmered and sparkled, he could see the wall of rock coming closer and he looked at Jade. "I think a marble about now would be nice."

Jade pulled the cloth bag from her pocket as she ran, and slipped the marble into her hand, they slowed their pace, as she raised her arm and threw it. The marble hit the rock face and disappeared, the rock glowed white and an archway appeared. Robbie walked up and peered in; he shook his head slowly as Rune looked round. "Opal really was wonderful." Rune smiled at him.

"I think so." She clicked her fingers, and a ball of light appeared in the centre of a large crystal cave. "I thought so." Rune slipped in and looked up at the ceiling high above them. Most of the island was hollow and the group stepped in, and gazed around at another cave as big and as beautiful as the one containing the small wooden city.

Jade laughed as she picked up her white marble. "This is way cooler than I thought, I can use it again." Jett looked closely at it.

"Wow that is cosmic."

"And totally like radical." Harry's voice echoed around the cave.

Rune's eyes glowed as she walked along under the ceiling of the cave looking up, Robbie watched carefully, screams echoed from outside, and dull splashes rebounded down the tube of ice. He understood why Crystal had made a tube;

no one could climb on it and come after them, as they would have been able to with a bridge. Rune looked up at the ceiling and smiled. Robbie watched as she raised her arms and her eyes exploded with violet light, slowly the ground below her began to rise. A spiral staircase of stone lifted her into the air. "Jade come with me." Jade ran and jumped onto the steps as they twisted around rising higher into the air. She wobbled as she ran to catch up with Rune at the top, Rune walked down six steps, and the top step met the ceiling of the cave, and the steps ground to a halt.

Jade flicked the white marble into the air, and it went straight through the roof. A large hole appeared shimmering white, and the marble dropped back into her hand. She chuckled. The stone stair moved up into the ten feet of thick grey rock. It twisted with Rune on the top step, and she rose out of the floor, into the far corner of the room, with a huge dark cube of crystal in it. Rune's eyes flared purple and the room filled with violet; she scanned around and saw the red dome over the star on the floor. The cube glowed red surrounded by a protective field placed there by the Dark One.

She looked down at Jade's green eyes peering up at her. "Stand on the top step and let no one pass until I tell you." Jade nodded, and Rune stepped off into the room. Rune raised her arms and violet mist spun around the room. "Nowled ant lif, Circlee ant leens, releesay te thy wuds, wot nite byndeth." Her voice sounded old, and lost in the realms of time, it bounced round the room as her eyes blasted purple light everywhere. The light stopped as quickly as it had started, and Rune smiled at Jade. "You can come in now." Jade looked at Rune.

"You can be as weird as Harry at times sis, you know that?" Rune giggled.

"It is a language older than the world; it sounds odd but it has deep power." Jade looked at her.

"Knowledge and life, Circle and lines, release to the woods, what darkness binds. I understood you Rune; I just got freaked by the weird voice." Rune stared at her.

"You understood? Jade that is amazing, there are very few who have the gift of the old tongues of the past."

Jade looked at the floor. "Your son will know it." Rune slipped her arms round her.

"All life from me will my sweet sister. I have told you that life with its gifts has been restored, I am pleased you have some of the gifts of my children, they will protect you... come on we have to help grandfather." Jade looked up and smiled, and Rune bent and kissed her on the tip of her nose, Jade giggled as the others started to come up through the hole in the floor.

Robbie looked around the room he was familiar with already, Una and Mel recognised it immediately. Mel looked at the door at the top of the stairs, where

Martin and John were heading to keep watch. Robbie looked at the solid cube with the dull figure of Merlin hanging inside it.

Rune touched the crystal. "He is weak, I need him protected, help me get him in the circle."

Her eyes glowed as Robbie had seen before, and he signalled Harry and Jaz with Bear to help him, the cube vibrated as they heaved with all their might. The cube moved closer to the circle. Another push as Rune's eyes blazed, and it moved faster and further. "One more big push lads." Robbie forced against the block, and it slid into the centre of the star, they slid to the floor and breathed a sigh of relief.

Rafe watched through a nick in the side door. Huge men in leather sleeveless tunics lined up with big axes, and long silver swords. "Hey Bear look what we got to play with."

Bear pushed his eye to the nick in the door and smiled. "Will it be your teeth or your blade my friend?"

"He will use neither, I will deal with these, you are needed in here." Maddy peered through the nick, and then stood back from the door. "Move behind me and help Runestone, there will be some sadness around me for a moment."

Maddy stood quite still as her eyes began to glow blue, two blue tears hit the floor and the group jumped back as they saw sad faces grow out of them. They rose in the air and began to swirl around her, as more tears ran down her face and fell on the floor. It was heart breaking to watch the sadness and hurt pour out of her, as Maddy finally expelled all she had absorbed and sobbed.

Harry closed his eyes and kissed his pendant. Treen wiped her eyes, as did Una. The sadness inside Maddy would have driven anyone to despair, and it spun around her head, before it flowed through the nick in the door. A long stream of pain drifted across the assembled masses in the yard, which all looked instantly unhappy. The last tears dropped to the floor, and Maddy lifted her head and smiled, as the last of the strange clouds of pain flowed through the door. Una walked over and embraced her. "How you hold in such misery defies me, be happy for a while my sweet sister." Maddy pulled Una close, and she had the most beautiful of smiles on her face. The soldiers became very despondent; their arms flopped to the ground as they dragged their feet. The commander barked an order and they looked up with sad and lonely eyes. He looked at them in rage. "Come on you bunch of lazy gits, pick your feet up." Five of the soldiers burst into tears and sat down crying. Jett giggled as she watched through the door.

"Wow Maddy that is so awesome, you should see them crying like babies because their boss called them names." She giggled as Jade pushed her eye up under Jett and watched chuckling.

The circle around the large pillar glowed purple, and the light began to spin around it, Rune raised her arms as flashes of electric blue sparked and jumped out. Everyone stepped back and jumped away as they bounced off the floor. The voice of Rune was terrible and loud, and they all trembled as they felt the room fill with an awesome and terrifying power, the circle of light around the pillar of crystal spun faster.

"Leens nay timeth, Circlee nay Nowling. Clar nite afore my, Broth for wot ist owning, Rocketh nigh, rocketh Wyte. Sen for yon filleth un thy lif."

There was a blinding flash, and Robbie jumped forwards to help her catch the limp figure of her grandfather, as he flopped to the floor. Rune gasped as the tears ran down her face, and Robbie supported the old wizard. He was pale and drawn, the bones showed through his face, and he looked his age of over a thousand for the first time since Robbie had met him. Rune lay over him and wept. Jade fell to her knees as all his daughters and granddaughters looked down with tears in their eyes. Rune looked up violet tears dropping on to the old wizard's face. "That witch has stolen his essence, I want it back." Sapphire knelt down and took his hand.

"Rune I am stronger than some of the others, grandfather will die soon, if it can restore him, take some of my life and give it to him." Jade nodded.

"Mine too," the murmur went round the circle of the family, and Robbie looked into her eyes. "I too am of Gwendolyn's line, use mine as well." His white bracelet burned bright blue. "She knows Rune and she is also asking." Rune nodded and smiled at her family.

"We are a true circle, thank you my sisters and brothers." Rune held her hands above her grandfather. Jade's eyes exploded green, and a beam of bright green flowed out of her and into Rune. Blue came out of Saff's eyes, and white out of Crystals. Melanie flowed light blue, and Una strong violet, Ruby emitted a bright beam of red, and Maddy and Treen both flowed a pale golden yellow. Jasper released a deep beam of burgundy followed by the deepest blue from Jett. A thick golden beam flowed from Steph, and then from nowhere the brightest and purest white light appeared.

Judith stood silent as the light streamed from her eyes, and into Rune. Robbie smiled as his eyes flickered, and he turned to Rune. "I love you Runestone." Thick lilac light streamed from him with sparkling flashes of bright blue, it hit Rune and she shuddered such was the force. The light flowed through her and into the still weak body of Merlin. He trembled in Robbie's arms as the light coursed around his body. Slowly the colour in his face deepened, and the thin skin seemed to thicken and darken. He drew a long drawn out deep breath, and he coughed. The beams broke and he slowly sat up and smiled at Rune.

She gave him a smile with tears in her eyes, and pulled him into a hug. "Oh, Grandfather I thought I had lost you." He raised a weak arm and patted her on the back.

"Takes a lot to kill an old badger like me." She squeezed him tight as Jade threw her arms around him. All the others smiled and breathed a deep sigh of relief. Rune slid back and looked at Treen.

"Will you and Mel stay with him? Keep him in the circle and you will be safe." Treen nodded, and pulled her grandfather close. Rune stood up and pressed a finger to the tall empty crystal cube. She gave a loud scream of anger and the cube exploded into dust and blew round the room, everyone jumped and covered their eyes. She turned and looked at them all.

"I am sorry, she has pissed me off for the last time." The group spat crystal dust out of their mouths and brushed their shoulders, Harry stared around at the sparkling room.

"Whoa baby girl, that is like so happenin and cosmic. Man this whole room is like totally beautiful, it's like happy vibes everywhere." He waved his hands and watched the dust twinkle in the air. Jasper smiled and Jade started to giggle, as she shook her head and the air around her flashed and sparkled. Robbie lifted Merlin on to a chair in the centre of the five-pointed Star. Treen and Mel sat close and held his hand as he smiled.

"Runestone, her room at the top has many jars, one will shine gold. You will find the lines of time inside. Do not open anything in that room, there are powers in there that will burn you alive and destroy this place."

Rune nodded looking pale. "Alright Grandfather, sit tight and I will get it for you."

Rose stood in the midst of her men, barking out her orders as a hail of arrows flew on to the bridge, she held high her sword and screamed, as yet another volley of arrows thickened the sky. The warriors of the dark tower were big and very strong. They drove down the bridge in their hundreds, taking twenty arrows each to finally fall. She wiped the sweat from her brow. "Bloody hell these are tough buggers." The young captain smiled at her.

"They have no made our side yet My Lady."

She nodded and smiled. "I feel My Lord Robert in my men today, let's hope he is safe in that dark hole." She turned and dropped her arm; another volley of arrows hit the left side of the bridge, and bodies rolled over into the sea.

A dark cloud rose from the top of the tower, and moved towards the shore; bright red bursts of lightening shot out of it, and exploded on the road in front of the sea wall. Woodsmen were blown backwards on to the cliff, and slid down it broken; Rose looked up as the cloud came towards her.

Her necklace burned bright violet, and light exploded out of it. She staggered back in surprise. Rune appeared in a violet haze; she stood on the front of the shore and pointed a flattened palm to the cloud. Golden light flowed at the cloud, and there was an ear splitting scream. Rune's voice echoed loudly around the whole bay. The warriors on the bridge slowed as they saw the violet figure of Rune pushing their lady of dark back. "Get back in your hole witch, I will have words with you shortly." The cloud burst into flame and was gone, Rune turned and smiled at Rose, and then faded away. Rose looked at the shocked captain and shrugged.

"She did say they were Specialists."

Rune pulled Robbie close. "Leave them here, let me go." His eyes were fierce.

"We go as one or you stay here, I will not discuss this Rune. You have my children with you, Destiny will be beside you, and it will be my hand that wields it." She nodded.

"Alright Rob, we go together, but please stay close to me."

"Consider me your shadow... Is everyone ready? Right, you all know what to do? This is just another forest, keep close, stay tight and let's go with stealth. Martin open the door, we hunt for darkness."

Martin heaved on the door, and he slid out quietly with John at his side. Robbie kissed Rune on the cheek. "Come Mrs Loxley, let's reunite your family." Robbie dropped his bow off his arm, and pulled a long violet tipped arrow on to the string. "The last march of the Violet Bowmen my Specialists let's move it out."

CHAPTER TEN

A MAZE OF CONFUSION AND STEPS

The corridor was long and dimly lit; two grey walls led either side of the door. John and Martin separated, and made their way down the corridor to cover both sides. Martin slid with his back to the wall, and his bow raised, the corridor veered off to the right, and he slowly moved down watching the path in front. His breath seemed to smoke out of his mouth, as it got cooler towards the bottom. He peered round at yet another corridor, which seemed to lead downwards on a slight incline.

John made his way to the top of the other side of the corridor. He popped his head round the corner fast, and looked left and then right. Silver glinted, and he pulled back, and waited for a few seconds and then looked again.

A shiny suit of armour stood at the bottom of the long corridor, and several doors seemed to line it. Again, it was a dim and dull corridor; the feeling of bleakness from outside, was a theme that had been continued inside. Robbie looked left and right, as John and Martin signalled back, Robbie read the signs, and looked at Rune. "Which way do you think? I think east and then north to get to the tower."

Her eye's flickered lilac. "I am not sure, she is in here, but there are a lot of things in here that are confusing. I suppose we should follow John; I don't like the feeling from down there."

Rune looked down the corridor in the direction of Martin, as Una stepped out of the door. She looked in the direction of Martin and frowned. "Stay away from down there, only Jaz can talk to them."

Harry looked at Una with a worried look, he slid his glasses back on quickly, and kissed his pendant, Harry started to walk towards John very quickly. Rune smiled at Robbie. "Follow Harry, that way aint cosmic."

Robbie started to giggle, turned and whistled quietly to Martin. He shuddered in the cold, and came back up towards them. Robbie turned, and ran quietly up the corridor towards John and Harry. Harry with his purple mirrored glasses on, leaned around the corner and jumped back, he looked at Robbie. "Hey man! It's like split time."

Robbie looked at him. "Why?" Harry was off, as John gave a quick peep round.

"Bugger, run lads... and lasses." He turned, and shot off down the corridor. The growl of four tigers with handlers came down the corridor, it was not actually a noise, Robbie had ever heard, but somehow, he knew it was enough to follow Harry and John. Rune looked up the corridor as Robbie sprinted down.

"Don't ask just run." The group needed no more persuasion, and turned and followed Harry and John as they sprinted past. They all flew down the long corridor at high speed and straight round the bend, the corridor dropped away sharply, and the temperature fell. It was becoming darker as John peered ahead, he came panting up to a set of smooth dark double doors and stopped. John leaned on the wall and gasped for air as the others came running up. Robbie leaned against the wall and breathed deeply. "Just what exactly made that noise?"

He lowered his head down and drew the air in, John looked up at him. "Not too sure what they call them... They are like enormous cats with stripes, they eat people."

Harry nodded wildly. "Uncosmic monsters' man."

Smokes laughed. "No Harry just tigers, probably Bengal if they were really big. Not something you would wrestle, unless of course you are Bear, and one is enough, not several."

Robbie nodded. "Ok, we avoid the tigers for now. We are here so we may as well continue; it is pretty much the direction I wanted to go. We will just have to look for a way up." Rowan leaned in through the double doors, and Jade slipped through the gap. Robbie saw her fade as her leg went into what looked like a very dark room. He moved up to Rowan and waited, and after a few seconds a faint tap came on the door, and Rowan opened it enough to let everyone pass, Robbie went first followed by Rune.

The room was dark and felt very cold, it seemed tall, although at first it was hard to say, Robbie moved forward and felt the small cool hand of Rune enter his, he gave it a gentle squeeze as he moved forward. Dark figures loomed motionless on either side. "Hey Flash, what can you see?" Rune's eyes glowed as Robbie looked back for her. Rune gasped quietly.

"You do not really want to ask Rob."

"Why, what is it?"

Jasper's voice echoed in the dark. "They say they died in horrible ways, they are telling me that she has tortured many more, and will bring their bodies back to fight in the war. They say you cannot kill what is already dead."

"Hey man what is it with you? Cut the freaky vibes and don't talk to em, you're jangling all our vibes man."

"Harry, they say they know of you?"

"Whoa man this is totally like not cosmic, hey Robbie man lets like split from here, I would rather fight the uncosmic monsters now. They chew on your legs man and not your karma."

"Harry keep your glasses on we are here now, Rune can you see any way out of here?" Flashes of violet lit up some of the grotesquely disfigured faces, and Robbie felt the group jump as they saw them, stifled gasps came out of the dark, followed by squeals and moans from Harry. Robbie held on to Rune who was now guiding him through, he had someone else's hand on his shoulder he was not sure who it was, Rune squeezed his hand and pulled him, he felt a tug and followed in her direction, straining as he saw odd shapes in the darkness all around him.

Rune stopped and he stopped. "What is it?"

Her bright purple eyes turned to him. "A door, wait while I check." A white line of light appeared as she pushed the door open a nick and looked through. "There are two guards up ahead, either side of the corridor. The rest of it looks clear, do you want to risk bows?"

"Yeah, I want out of here it gives me the creeps." Robbie slid down his bow and pulled an arrow from the quiver; he fitted it to the string, and came up beside Rune. "You right, me left, on three... One... two... Three." The doors burst open, and Robbie and Rune stepped out and fired, the door swung back behind them and the two guards fell dead.

Rune turned and kissed his cheek. "Not too shabby." He smiled and pulled open the door; Saff and Keith came through and ran up the corridor, the others followed. Robbie looked back through the door. "Harry...Jett...Wolfie...Jaz... Blades, hey guys over here." No sound came back; he looked at Rune "Where the hell are they? I mean they were with us just seconds ago." Rune walked back, and stepped into the room, she raised her arm and white light shot into the air,

Robbie gasped and jumped back in shock. Row upon row of white limp bodies hung suspended from rails, they had arrow wounds and gashes on them, Robbie realised some of these were the dead from clashes with woodsmen, one in particular wore a look he would never forget.

He knew the face of the man that Rune had killed by showing him everything evil he had ever done in his life. His contorted face of fear looked down at him with dead eyes; Robbie shuddered, as Rune turned round. "They are not here, they must have gone back or found another way out, what do you want to do?"

He felt uncertain. "Are they alive, can you feel them?"

She turned and looked into the room. "I can feel Jett, but I am being blocked, she cannot hear me."

"Ok Rune, we will have to trust to luck, Jaz is very cool and Jett is no slouch, we can come back later and look for them if they have not shown up, we must find a way up." She nodded and came back through the door. Robbie shuddered as he had a last look at the dead.

The corridors seemed to be becoming dimmer; the others all waited standing by the doors, and keeping watch as Robbie and Rune walked back up. "We have lost five, everyone please keep close, and stay together. We will search later if we do not find them before."

"Hey man I told you not to do that uncosmic funky stuff, now we lost the others. We are like totally in an uncosmic place. Whoa man my vibes is beginning to jangle."

Jett peered round at the room filled with statues of serpents, dragons and other strange beasts, she did not recognise. She tapped the bronze teeth of a half snake, half woman statue, using her silver knife, it pinged loudly and everyone turned and looked at her. "Sorry... wow you lot are freaked, come on and chill out, this place is kinda cool." She walked slowly along the hideous statues marvelling at them, she stopped and stared at a really ugly one. "Hey you know these are so realistic, I would love this one in my house that would freak the visitors out, hey honey what you think? Shall we get this one later?"

Rafe looked up as the ugly statue grabbed Jett by the throat. She lunged back, as Rafe drew his sword, and began to run up the room. The guard pulled his knife as Jett's eyes exploded with blue, the guard froze and began to shake violently, he dropped Jett and she fell to the floor gasping for air, but still holding her eyes on him. Two more stepped out from the line of statues, and Blades bounced into the air and landed by Jett, her blades flashed, and a severed arm hit the floor as a squeal of pain, blasted into the air. Wolfie hit the second, and with the speed of lightening, he sliced off the head and the body hit the floor, as the head disappeared behind a statue of a giant hideous lion.

Jett's eyes flared, as the ugly guard shook, his eyes and ears and mouth bled. Wolfie lifted Jett off the floor and her eyes flashed back to normal, the guard slumped to the floor. He pulled his arms round her and held her. He was trembling. "Wow honey, you really scared me then." He put his head onto hers, and just held her, as Blades her golden blades glinting, looked carefully round the other statues. He smiled at her. "Let's stick to normal stuff, I will get you a sword rack instead."

"Wow Wolf man, you really love me don't you?" He smiled and kissed her softly.

"Stay wild, and I will love you forever." A tear welled in Jett's eye.

"God Rafe, I never realised. Wow you really do."

Jaz came up fast. "Let's move this place is not safe." Harry ran wide eyed behind him, eyeing each statue as he passed. Strange moaning noises came from behind the rows of statues. He held the pendant of Rune's in his teeth, and kissed it repeatedly as he ran.

The long corridor led to a large hall, two wide wooden doors stood open into the hall, across it was a set of ornate carved mahogany stairs. All seemed quiet as

Robbie looked through at the room. "It is very quiet, somehow I just expected loads of guards."

Rowan looked back down the corridor, and signalled to Martin and John. He followed Robbie into the room as the doors swung silently shut behind him. Robbie walked cautiously across the hall, and looked around. The large carved staircase led up to a balcony that skirted the whole of the hall. Its dark wood gleamed in the light from the huge chandelier of crystal that hung from the centre of the ceiling. Tapestries of old coats of arms hung from the grey walls, their bright designs of serpents and ravens seemed somehow out of place. Armour stood on stands from many generations of knights. The hearth was huge with a roaring fire burning in it, and a long wooden table of oak ran down the centre of the room, with heavy silver candle stands, and ornate bowls of gold filled with fruit. The group walked round their bows ready as they looked in some surprise at the quality of the place. Rune looked at Robbie. "Quite a sense of style, there is no way she did this, she must have got someone in to do it." He smiled.

The doors burst open behind them, and John came flying through. "RUN!" Robbie pulled his face. "Not tigers again?" John headed on to the stairs.

"Big Buggers with swords, bloody loads of em." Martin came flying through the door and ran up to John.

"Takes about ten arrows to kill one.... We are going to need more arrows, or longer swords."

"On the stairs quick." Robbie pulled an arrow, and fitted it to his bow as he backed across the room; Keith and Saff took up positions with John and Martin at the top of the stairs, as the others ran up. Robbie, Rune and Rowan walked slowly backwards up one step at a time as the doors burst open, and a band of warriors about eight feet tall dressed in black leather came through leering with evil, and waving some very long heavy swords.

Rune gasped. "Wow boys those are really big ones." She stepped back with Robbie and Rowan, as they hit the first warrior who staggered. Flash climbed up on to the balcony rail, and folded her glasses up, and slipped them into her pocket.

"Hi guys, you want to play with me?" The warriors looked up and smiled at the little girl. Flash smiled and waved at them. "Oh I like big boys they can be so much fun." Robbie pushed the others back quickly, as one of the large warriors stopped, smiled and waved at Ruby. "I like him, he is cute." She smiled and blew him a kiss. John looked at Martin.

"These guys are not too bright, are they?" Martin shrugged.

"To be honest John, I was so busy running, it never occurred to stop for a chat?" Ruby giggled as she waved again. The warriors made for the stairs and she frowned. They stopped and looked at her, as Robbie reached the top step and backed away. Ruby wagged her tiny white finger.

"You don't play on the stairs it is dangerous." One of the warriors looked at the other one, who stared blankly back at him. He gave a smile and lifted a heavy booted foot onto the step. The room filled with light, and Robbie and the group covered their eyes. The smell of burnt flesh and wood seeped into their nostrils. Ruby jumped onto the floor and walked over to them. "They were very naughty."

Rune leaned over the rail and looked down. The table was ash, and so were the warriors, the walls were black and thin wisps of smoke rose off the tops of the tapestries. "Looks like she will be redecorating at some point soon." She turned and walked into the corridor at the side. "This way I think... oops no, I think not." Rune turned back, as more soldiers came running down the long corridor, she hurried back round the wall and pulled her bow, Rowan and Robbie released their arrows, Bear pulled his sword and his axe.

Fish shot over to the other side with Keith and Saff, He looked down one of the other corridors and then glanced over the rail of the balcony. "Err guys we have guests on both sides and down stairs." He fired up the corridor, as Rowan and Jade crossed to meet him. Mother and Smokes took up their positions on the stairs, and fired into the crowd, now crossing the floor of ash below. Crystal loaded her silver bow and fired. Frost shot into the crowd and they screamed with the pain as it burned at them.

Robbie and Rune backed round another corner as they fired. Una and Ruby ran with Hornet in front of them, as soldiers appeared, and Una spun her staff of holly. Ruby broke her stick apart and entered the throng spinning wildly; they cleared the path through for Robbie, Rune and Hornet, who now fired at the advancing soldiers.

John backed slowly down the hall with Martin, as Skip and Bear waded in to the soldiers with their swords, Maddy raised her long white bow. "Hey guys time to move, it's about to heat up." They looked back and saw the white bow of Gwendolyn, no more words were needed, as Bear swung his huge blade round releasing Skip, and then turned and ducked as the arrow of flame flew past him into the crowd. Bear fled towards them as flames burst out in every direction. The whole group turned and ran, as the fire followed them down the corridor. Screams wailed behind them. Skip grabbed Maddy by the hood and swung her in through an open door, and as the others followed through, he slammed it shut and heard the screaming masses pass. The door grew hot and he pulled his hands off fast.

The ice crackled as the figure went rigid, and Crystal smiled. "It's snow joke fighting these."

Smokes gave a laugh. "Oh Crystal, that is sad." He smiled and looked up. "Where are the others?" The top of the balcony was littered with bodies, none of which they recognised. Each corridor was the same; a long line of death ran down each of the four.

Mother leant on the wall and wiped her brow. "She is trying to break us down into small groups, it makes us easy to overcome, I cannot get Rune we are being blocked." She looked round at the others. "It's up or down, what do you reckon?"

Smokes looked around. "This was the corridor Rune wanted, but none of us made it, we might as well continue as we intended, the others must have gone on with Robbie." Crystal nodded.

Rune walked slowly watching the corridor behind them. "Rob, we have lost the others, what do we do. Should we go back?" He sat low with his back to the wall, and wiped his hands of the blood from the dead. He picked up his long golden sword, and with a rag he had ripped off the jacket of a soldier, he cleaned the blade. The sword gleamed bright on his face as he looked up.

"The way I see it, she somehow seems to know where we are. This is her place, so that is not really a surprise, we have come here to do a job, and I think all of us know that. We have to go on, and then all we can do is hope that the others either meet us or find a way out, we have no other choice Rune if you want to regain the essence of your grandfather."

Una nodded as Robbie spoke, Hornet looked a little scared. Flash smiled. "Robbie is right Rune, we must do what we can and hope it is enough." Rune looked at him sat low, she knew he was worried about the others, but she also felt his determination to move forward and find the Dark One. Una looked at the five corridors in front of them.

"This place is like a maze, how the hell, does anyone find their way round it?"

Rune looked around thinking, her eyes narrowed as she scanned the walls and floor, power left traces; the Dark One had tracked Una and Mel. There must be traces of her power around, Robbie stood up and watched as Rune stared at the floor her eyes sparkling with lilac. He knew a tracker when he saw one and he grinned. "The way of the woodsman has always been our guide, we are forgetting the skills we have, good thinking Rune." Una looked confused as Rune smiled. She pointed to the bland blue grey carpet.

"She has been this way Rob; I see her traces."

He leaned down and gave her a soft kiss. "Lead on beautiful." Rune walked to the second corridor, and then turned into it, Robbie picked up his bow and loaded an arrow. Slowly by her side, he followed with the others.

Bear pulled the door open, and looked through the gap at the blackened and sooty walls. He opened it a little more and looked from left to right. "Ok, it's all clear." He stepped out onto the black smoking carpet. "Phew that stinks."

Maddy slid out and looked down the corridor, her eyes flashed blue as she swung her head from side to side. The others looked at her and waited. She looked back at them. "I feel the others but they seem distant and cloudy. I have no idea which way they have gone."

Skip looked around. "Robbie will continue with Rune, he will head for the tower, we must head upwards. The way I see it, eventually we will all end up in the tower, so if he needs us we will be there. I am sure the others will head that way." Bear agreed, and they turned and began to head back towards the burned and charred balcony, where they could choose a direction to head upwards.

Rowan slid around the corner. There were yet more guards all along the passage. He pulled back into the wall, and whispered. "This must be the right way; there is a guard every ten feet."

Jade looked up at him. "Shall I cause a distraction?" Saff placed her hand on her shoulder.

"Let's just think a minute Pebbles. I have been thinking about my powers, they are strong Rune told me."

Jade looked confused. "Meaning what?"

"Meaning I should have become the centre of my circle, which gives me similar powers to Rune."

Rowan now seemed confused. "Saff, Rune has powers beyond everyone. What are you getting at?"

She smiled. "Rune in the past would share powers by channelling. I know I can channel because I have done it before when Rune channelled protections through me. I could share some of Pebbles powers, and become invisible, which means we could work as a double act, and she would not have to keep going alone."

Rowan smiled at her. "That I like the sound of, I must admit sweetheart I would be happier if you had company down there." Jade smiled at him; she could see the relief in his eyes.

"Ok, let's give it a try and see what happens."

Jade stood still, and her eyes flared bright green, her legs began to fade and match the carpet. Saff stared at Jade and her eyes turned a deep bright blue. Jade was just a head and shoulders, as Saff saw her legs start to fade. "Oh, it tickles."

Jade gave a giggle as she went completely; she reached up and kissed Rowan. He jumped with surprise, she giggled. Saff looked down at nothing but walls and carpets. She looked at Keith. "What do you think?" Her bright blue eyes hovered in front of him.

"I think Rowan and me will worry until we know you are both safe."

"We will be fine won't we Pebbles. Right how do you want to do this?"

Jade gave a giggle. "Well, we should start at the far end and work back, if anyone runs it will be this way, and the guys can deal with them."

"Ok, you lead and I will follow, I will take the left and you take the right." Rowan watched carefully as they slipped off, he could not see them, but he knew Jade well enough to know she would have a little fun. Halfway up the long corridor, a guard jumped as his sword belt undid and fell to the floor with a crash, Rowan smiled, they were almost there. Two green eyes hovered in the air; a blue pair appeared on the opposite side.

"You Ok Saff?"

Saff nodded, and then realised she was invisible. "Oh... Yes fine."

"Right, we go one guard at a time. I like to talk to them, give em the willies as it were; you can do what you want."

"Ok, I will learn from you... are you ready, let's go then?" The two guards stood facing each other, they looked bored stood against the wall, they stared into space and their minds wandered. A deep voice croaked into the soldier's ear and he jumped back to reality.

"I think I really fancy you." His eyes snapped across at the other guard.

"I am not like that, what makes you say that?" The guard opposite came out of his dream, and looked at the irate guard in front of him.

"What did you say?" The first guard glared at him.

"Another word from you and you will feel my sword, you're disgusting."

"It wasn't him it was me; I think you are both really cute." Saff covered her mouth as the two guards turned, and looked down at the third guard who was watching from five feet away.

They looked at each other, and then back at the third guard who smiled at them. The second guard pulled a disgusted face. "You are sick you are."

The first guard smiled. "You tell him mate."

The third guard stared at the two of them, as a pair of green eyes and a pair of blue appeared in the air at their sides. He raised a shaking hand, pointed and screamed, the first two laughed. "Oomph" They slid down the wall, red streaks on the paintwork, as the third guard fled in fear; all the other guards looked in shock as the panicked guard ran past screaming hysterically. Jade giggled at the side of Saff.

"I love being naughty." Saff gave a giggle and walked beside her as they made their way to the next two who looked around confused. The guard turned to look back and his gaze met two green eyes.

"Boo!" The knife went in as he jumped, the guard opposite slipped to the floor. Lower down the remaining guards could see their colleagues slipping to the floor dead, and began to walk backwards slowly. A terrifying scream came out of nowhere, and the two at the front fell dead, the rest bolted down the corridor towards Rowan, Keith and Fish. Jade grabbed Saff and pulled her into a doorway. "Let the boy's fire, and don't get in their way." They stood with their backs to the door and Saff giggled.

"This is fun; I can see how you wind up Harry so much."

"Harry is afraid of the dead, he thinks I am the green evils come back to get him, its great fun." She gave a soft giggle as Rowan stepped over the body and walked towards the laughter.

"I thought stealth was meant to mean quiet?"

"Sorry sweetheart." She grabbed him and kissed him, Saff laughed as she saw Rowan puckered up and kissing the air, Jade faded back into view, and smiled at him her eyes twinkling under her fringe with delight. He nodded and laughed at her. She winked.

Jett stood still at the bottom of the stone stairs and listened quietly, as Harry looked nervously around in the dim light. "That was definitely screams, what do you think Harry?"

"Hey man, this place is like freaksville, I want to scream like forever."

Jett closed her eyes as they flickered blue. *"Rune, Jade anyone Hear me?"*

"I hear you Jett Amber of Caerleon, welcome to my home witch." Jett flattened quickly to the wall, as her eyes flashed open and she gasped for breath. Harry jumped with the sudden movement, and grabbed his pendant and started to kiss it.

"Hey baby girl what you like doing jumping like that? You jangled my vibes and rattled my karma man."

Jett stared at Harry with blue flickering frightened eyes; Harry gulped and started to tremble. "Harry I just had the Dark One in my head." She looked pale and scared.

Harry began to murmur and put his fingers in his ears. "Oh whoa man this is like not happenin, I am going to get karma chomped for certain, I knew I should not have done those things for Robbie man. This is like cosmic pay back; I gonna lose all my cosmic funky abilities."

Jaz slipped past him with Wolfie and they looked at Jett who was breathing deeply, she put her hand on Jaz's shoulder. "Do not talk to Rune, The Dark One is listening." Jaz nodded and looked up at the roof.

"I felt her inside you, have no fear she has gone." Jett breathed a sigh of relief. Harry looked up at the roof, to see what Jaz was looking at. He snapped his eyes shut, and continued to mutter under his breath.

At the top of the third flight of stairs, and down yet another long corridor Crystal stopped and leaned against the wall. She let out a long sigh, and looked out of the window on to a small stone balcony. "My legs are killing me. This place is all stairs and corridors; I have no idea where the hell we are." Mother slid down the wall to the floor.

"This is hopeless Pete; I think we are going round in circles. It is all starting to look the same to me." He leaned on the window and stared out across the bay.

"We are making some progress, look how high up we are?" Smokes watched as the woodsmen in the cliffs opposite, fired volley after volley at the advancing troops who had now made it off the end of the bridge, and were pushing forward against the defence's of the woodsmen. "They are having one hell of a hard time out there."

Crystal slid off the wall and looked out of the window. The black army of the Raven was swarming on to the bridge, and pounding in against Rose and Sinclair's woodsmen. "They need a lift, open the window." Crystal slid her bow off her shoulder as Smokes pulled down on the handle, the wind howled into the corridor as the glass doors opened out, she stepped out and looked down. Far below the generals screamed their orders at the men spilling onto the long black bridge. Crystal brought a long silver arrow out of her quiver; her pale eyes peered down in the afternoon sunlight.

Far down below in the thick of the fight, Rose had a bad cut on her face, and Angus was bloodied all over from dragging his wounded men back behind the line of defence. "FIRE," she screamed, as her sword went down and a thick volley shot through the air. The mass of black stumbled and fell only to disappear under the feet of the hoard that surged forward. "Angus there are too many we will have to fall back." She looked across the chaos at Sinclair, as the mass pushed them both back into the wide cutting, and arrows rained down from above. Sinclair had his silver sword and cleaved at any that came through the ranks.

A glint of silver caught her eye over the bay and for a moment she saw a figure in all white stood against the wall of the black tower, hope rose inside her. The silver flashed into the mass of black, and the screams raged from inside as she saw the ice rise like a wall in front of her men. "BACK! TO ME NOW, FALL BACK!" She screamed, as her woodsmen came backwards in a surge, to avoid being caught in the white wall before them. Rose smiled and gasped. "Oh, thank you Crystal."

The woodsmen moved slowly backwards, looking up at the wall of white in front of them, all of them breathed a sigh of relief as they had time to recoup their energy, and wait for the next attack. Rose knew it would not last for long, but it gave her the time to think and regroup. She pulled back to the halfway point up the cutting. "Get those carts over here quickly, I want a barricade and bring us more arrows."

Crystal smiled, as she loaded her second arrow, and she aimed for the centre of the bridge. The arrow was swift with great pace, it buried deep into the concrete, and frost sprayed into the air and over the soldiers advancing in black. They stopped in mid track, and as others bumped into them, the soldiers exploded into millions of tiny fragments. The black tide on the bridge came to a halt, she loaded again, this time her target was the wall above the gates with the generals. The white figure was easy to see against the black walls and as she turned and pointed her bow, they began to flee. The arrow chased them across the top of the ramparts, and as it hit, a wall of ice crunched into the sky, the generals that were caught, and vanished as the ice, turned white and glistened in the sun. She leaned back and smiled. "That will slow them down for a while." She looked at Smokes who was looking above him. He looked back at her, and she looked up at the long spikes jutting out of the tower very high above them. "Smokes you are mad, but at least we would be going in the right direction." Mother stuck her head out and looked up.

"Bugger off Pete, that way would be suicide."

He kept looking up. "Coming inside was certainty of death. I just feel Robbie and Rune will make it, I love those kids, I do not want them alone with her. If this way is more dangerous but faster, I will risk it for them." He looked at Mother. "She risked everything for me love. I owe her that much." Steph looked at her husband and she knew he was right. Robbie and Rune had planned and executed Tintagel, they had been the last ones out, and had almost not got out of the cave. She remembered how he had stood on deck of the yacht watching the cave mouth watching the tide pound in. Pete had almost lost hope, and he had been filled with despair thinking his two daughters had died in his rescue. Steph knew he would not fail them now.

"What you got in mind?"

He looked up and smiled. "If Crystal here, can give us a ladder like Liverpool, we can climb up, and try and work from the top down, give her a surprise she will not forget." Crystal looked up and loaded her bow. She took aim and fired between the large spikes that stuck out all around, what the woodsmen named the nest of the raven. The arrow hit stone and stuck, it glowed white as Crystal's eyes clouded, and became all white. Thin strands of ice whipped out like ropes. A thick net formed under the spikes, and then ran down the wall towards them, as a ladder formed out of clear white ice. It came running fast towards them and stopped a foot off the floor of the balcony.

Crystal pulled her white snowflake pendant over her head, and she smiled as she pushed it into Pete's forehead. "This will make you light enough to climb the ladder and not feel the cold. The drawback is that the wind will also be able to blow you off, please hold on as tight as you can." She turned and pushed the pendant into Mothers head. "Ok let's get up there."

Pete grabbed the first rung of the ladder and pulled on the ice, he lifted his leg and began the long climb of over four hundred feet to the nest. Mother followed and Crystal closed the glass doors and sprung nimbly onto the bottom of the ladder behind them.

Mel held her dad who smiled, colour was starting to come back into his face and she pulled him close. "Oh dad, you knew she had crossed into the other realm, you should have known it was a trap."

He gave a long sigh; "I know, I was so foolish, you have to understand the pain I have felt. I lost your mother and that hurt me so deeply Melanie, your mother was beauty and warmth beyond the lines of time. When I lost her, I suffered endless years of pain and loneliness, I wandered the forgotten realms caught in the age of sleep looking for ways out. Seven hundred years of pain passed me by. It was there I met Opal, and we fought together to free ourselves. She was nature and young and beautiful, she was very like Runestone is now. There are times I look at Runestone and it reminds me so much of Opal. She has the same loving warmth and gentleness as her grandmother, I never thought I would meet any one who could help me overcome the pain of Gwendolyn. Losing Opal as well has left me as I once was, and when I saw her, I thought she had found a way back. How could I not go to her?"

Melanie gave a soft nod. "I felt like that with Tor. I have lived so long in the stones knowing he died an old man alone having never found me. Jasper is so like him." She gave a soft laugh. "Do you remember how he would ride round the farm, with this silly old hat on? He loved it so much when he wasn't at court? He barely had any time with Sapphire; I wish he had known what had happened."

Her eyes filled with tears as she looked down at her father. "She will pay for what she has done; I will not forget the day she came. It is funny, I saw his hat and just grabbed it, and now it is all I have left of him. When we came out a thousand years had passed, and he was dust and gone forever. That is why I went to Callanish; he is buried below the circle there, it helped me feel close to him again. It's silly I know but I have spent years talking to him to make up for the life he was robbed of."

Merlin lifted his white hand and stroked the tears from her eyes. "You will have happiness again, and do not think he has not seen his children. He knows of them, and watches from the other realm. Jasper has spoken with him many times my Darling. Tor knows how you loved him; he listened through Jasper many times when you spoke to the children of their father."

Melanie gave a sob. "I want him to forgive me the pain I caused him. He spent a whole life looking for me."

"Oh, my sweet daughter, do you not see? He found you in the end, please forgive yourself for something you could not control. She took you so young, you would never have been able to fight her and win, and that was why we joined the two circles." The door to the yard burst open and Treen jumped. Four large brutal looking men walked in; Mel looked up with fear in her eyes. The star on the floor glowed white, and a twenty-pointed blue star came through the floor and glowed over the red one. Mel and Treen's pendant began to shimmer violet. The three chairs sunk down into the floor as the soldiers stared in surprise. One pulled out his sword, and a violet figure appeared before him with a sword of flames, she swung the blade and the soldier jumped back in surprise as the violet figure lowered her hood and stared at him.

"Leave here and you will live, if you stay I will show you horrors you have not dreamed could come true." Her eyes glowed bright purple, and the soldier dropped his sword and clutched his head as he screamed. The others turned and ran.

Mel looked at the table of Runestone in the cellar as the dim light glowed bright. "We are safe Dad, we are back in Loxley, this is Rune's table, she has sent us back to wait, come on I will get you to bed."

The violet figure rose out of the table and smiled. "Hear me for I am Runestone and your centre. You must remain in the house for you are protected, Treen please remain at my table and wait for the others, I have other work with Robbie and will return last." Treen nodded and Rune faded back into the table. Melanie helped her father slide off the table, and guided him up the stairs. Merlin suddenly seemed to fill with happy curiosity.

"I have heard much of this house; it's the talk of the other realms you know? Hearne let everyone put an idea or two in, I even suggested a hidden office for Robbie, you know how he likes to hide away at times? I thought he would like it."

The growls came from round the next corner. Robbie pressed flat against the wall. "I just knew it would be me who found them again." She smiled and winked at him, as her eyes began to burn with deep violet light. Rune walked out into the centre of the corridor, the handlers stopped, and moved their hands to the clips on the chains. She smiled at them. "Wow boy's you certainly have some big pussies to play with." Rune waved a hand, and the eyes of the tigers turned violet. "I hope you boys washed for dinner; cats seldom eat rotten meat." The men looked doubtful as they unclipped the chains.

The tigers roared and jumped at Rune. They landed by her side and sat looking fierce and threatening, they were huge, with black and golden striped faces, their fangs showed long and white. She slid her arms sideways and scratched the ears of the two sat closest. The tigers purred with affection. "Run boys, it's time for feeding." The handlers looked on with fear in their eyes; they turned and fled screaming down the corridor. They ran as fast as they could, Rune smiled at the purring large cats. "Go on babies, play with the soldiers." The tigers leapt forward with happy growls, and ran down the long corridor. Rune came up close to Robbie and slid her arms around him. "Robbie sweetheart." He looked at her smiling face and bright blue eyes. "Can I keep one, I promise I will walk it and feed it every day, they are really soft when you house train them."

He smiled, as horrific screams came down the corridor, and growls and roars mingled with the screams and pleas for help. "It's your birthday in October, let me have a think about it." She gave him a huge smile and kissed him.

"That really big one is a real softie; we could call him Furry Face." Una looked round the corner and shuddered as Furry Face tore the soldiers apart.

Jade sat at the top of the stairs panting as Rowan dragged his feet up the last forty steps towards her. She wiped the sweat from under her fringe. "Phew... one thousand, six hundred and ninety two steps." She beamed a huge smile, as he came up the last few and flopped beside her. He lay back on the cold stone floor and gave a long moan, she looked down at him smiling. "You need building up; when we get home you can rest up and have a long break. We will sit in bed, talk, eat and have loads of sex." Rowan moaned, and she giggled and leaned over and kissed him.

Fish dragged his feet up the last few steps and collapsed by the wall. "Why don't people just live in houses on the floor? Who hell wants to carry their fire wood up here?" He slid down the wall, and gave a long sigh of relief. Saff walked in bare feet and trotted up the steps smiling. She perched on the second step and smiled at Keith with his bow on his shoulder, as he walked red faced up the last few.

"Just exactly who was it that suggested we take this as a short cut?" He fell to his knees and moaned, as he rubbed the back of his calf muscles. "You know, somehow I thought we would run in and while we had a good scrap with her men, Robbie and Rune would just grab the old witch, and give her the beating of her life and toss her out the window. Being lost in this tomb was not on my game plan."

Rowan sat up and wiped his face. "The higher we are the closer I think we will be to Robbie and Rune. They must be closer to us now. I just hope the others are fine."

Bear moved quickly down the corridor with Skip, as the sound of rattling steel came from both sides of the adjoining corridors. Maddy heaved on the door at the end, it burst open and John skidded to a halt as he almost fell over the balcony rail. Martin nimbly jumped aside as Bear and Skip came through. Maddy turned and fired at the large group of evil looking guards in black uniforms, which had followed them round the corner, and were closing in fast. The flames exploded and roared down the corridor engulfing the guards; Bear grabbed the door and heaved it shut as flames shot through the sides scorching the wall. They all stood panting on the balcony, huddled together looking out across the bay at the army of black that massed at the foot of an ice wall. John turned to Bear. "Looks like Crystal is still about." Martin looked down the castle wall.

"She is closer than you think." Smokes came up the side of the balcony and smiled at Maddy.

"Rose could still use a lift."

Maddy looked down as the swarming masses of black were hacking their way through the wall of ice. More soldiers made their way down the black bridge. Maddy looked at her arrows and lifted a pure white one out, she looked at it with great reverence, and she gave one of her rare smiles. "This is a very special one; I have always wanted to use one of these." Maddy loaded her long white bow and took aim at the centre of the bridge. "I would cover your eyes, just in case."

Mother gasped, as she appeared sweating on the white ladder. John helped heave her on to the rapidly filling balcony.

Maddy released the arrow, and her eyes began to shine bright blue as she guided it. It tore through the air like a bullet with a blue smoky trail spiralling behind it. The arrow hit the centre of the bridge and there was a blinding flash of white light. A huge red dragon of flames danced up into the air on the bridge, and blasted the wall of the castle with a torrent of red flame, the guards hardly blinked and they were dust. The dragon turned and looked at the shoreline where soldiers were running for their lives screaming with fear, as the dragon gave one long sweep from left to right, and the inferno blasted across the bridge and along the water's edge. Soldiers exploded into instant ash as the red flames touched.

Maddy leaned back on the wall with a gasp. "Wow mum, you knew how to make your weapons." She watched as the dragon reared up on the bridge and dispersed in a flash of white flame. The bridge stood quiet and empty, and the front of the shoreline was filled with a lake of water from the melted ice wall, and thousands of shocked looking woodsmen. Rose sat back and rubbed her face with her hands. Her face was red from the heat, as was all her men's. They had suddenly been given suntans as the force of the inferno had crossed the front of the cutting, melting the ice instantly. Crystal appeared on the ladder. "It is up or across." Smokes looked up at the tower.

"It is still the most direct route, I say up." He climbed back on to the ladder and began to climb; Mother gave a huge sigh and followed. Crystal touched each of them with her snowflake, and they all joined the ladder and began the long climb up the tower to the nest of the raven.

Rowan slipped back behind the door, as four large tigers prowled out across the hall and sniffed around. He watched through the crack in the door as dark shadows moved on the wall. He pulled his bow ready, as he aimed through the gap. The shadows on the wall grew larger, and he pulled back the string. The figure appeared and called to the tigers, Rowan breathed a long and happy sigh, as he saw the bright smiling face of Rune as the biggest of tigers padded towards her, and nuzzled on her leg. She crouched down and gave him a scratch under his chin; the tiger lifted his head and made soft growling noises of pleasure. "You are such a good boy, and oh such a big baby." The tiger rolled over on to its back, and Rune scratched its large spotty tummy.

Rowan stepped out from behind the door and smiled, three tigers instantly turned and growled at him, he froze where he stood as Robbie came round the corner, Rune looked up and gave a happy smile. "Girls he's a friend, let him pass." The tigers sat back on the floor and bowed their heads. Jade, came running out, across to Rune.

"Oh wow, can I have one Rowan, they are so cool?" Rowan gave a help me look at Robbie who smiled at him, he leaned over and whispered.

"I told Rune I would think about it." Jade crouched down and scratched Furry Face's belly, as he rolled around and purred very loudly, she giggled and talked to him.

Rowan looked at the large square room; it was as bland as the rest of the castle with grey plain walls, and grey carpet. The only ways into it came from the corridor that Robbie and his party had come from, and the stairs that he and his party had just climbed up. Saff and Keith seemed to be thinking the same as him, as they nervously looked about, Una and Hornet stood alert by the door to the stairs, Una looked back at Rowan.

"If we just came from up there and you have come this way, we have hit a dead end, what do we do now?"

Rune stood up and looked around the room; it was just four empty walls with a dim looking ceiling and grey carpet. Rowan watched as she walked along the edge of the wall looking very closely at it. It was as if she was inspecting every brushstroke on the paintwork, her eyes began to flicker, and she stopped and stared for a moment before turning to the rest of the room. Her eyes sparkled as she gave them all a bright smile. "It's this way." She turned and walked straight through the wall. Robbie shuddered.

"I have told her about that, she promised never to do it, that's twice now." Rune's head came back through the wall and he jumped back. She smiled.

"Hi gorgeous." Her arm came through and she held it out to him. "Honestly Rob it is fine, you will see, although we will have to leave the babies, you need one of my Talisman's to pass." Robbie looked back at the tigers, somehow that did not worry him too much. She took hold of Robbie's hand and pulled; he walked slowly forward and passed straight through the wall, and onto the base of a very grand stairway. Rune smiled at him. "See, it's a wall, and not a wall, it's designed to throw us off the track that's all."

He looked back at the wall as Rowan and Jade slipped through followed by Saff and Keith. Una came through holding Hornet and Flash by the hand, and then a puzzled looking Fish passed through. They all stared at the high staircase that rose up several floors, they were heavy and very ornate dark carved wood, they were, covered with red plush carpet and they gave an impression of majesty. Intricate golden brackets came out of the wall and held flickering candles to light the pale grey stonework. At the top of each flight of stairs on the top of the rail was a carved raven, with eyes of rubies that glinted in an evil and sinister way. The room felt cold, and Robbie could feel the hairs on the back of his neck prickle. "Something is not right." He stared up through the centre of the winding stair and his eyes met with the cold black eyes surrounded by blonde curly hair that stared down at him. "Mordred." Rune's eyes flared violet.

"Oh man this is heavy." Harry looked through the door out on to the yard. Jaz stood by his shoulder, and peered at the rows of guards all sat quite still waiting for orders.

"Harry it's fine they are dead."

Harry jumped back from the door. "Whoa dude that aint too cosmic, say what you mean and talk fast, those dudes is ready for war man."

Jaz looked at Jett and Wolfie. "This is what that lot down there in cold storage were waiting for; she has somehow been able to get corpses to fight."

Harry snapped his eyes shut and squeaked, as he murmured with his fingers in his ears. Jett smiled. "Harry don't do dead coming to life, he does life going to dead." She gave a giggle as she pressed her eye to the gap in the door, and looked out at the soldiers all blue in the face, with black lips that sat silently waiting for their orders. "Hey Jaz can you talk to these guys and make them see things our way, I am sure they would much rather fight for us." Wolfie nodded and leaned into the gap.

"They are armed to the teeth and unable to feel pain, it's your ultimate army, we could use a few of them on our side."

He looked up at Jaz, who did seem to be considering the point he shrugged his shoulders. "I suppose it would be worth a try."

Jaz pulled on the door and it opened slowly, Harry grabbed his arm. "Hey man you aint going out there? Oh whoa that is like totally none cosmic dude, these beasts will chomp on your karma, and you will like be spirit toast man."

Jaz touched Harry's hand. "Harry it is fine, I am just going to have a quick chat and see if they will help us instead." Harry lurched back and shook violently.

"Man, you are more twisted than Robbie, what you sayin dude, that aint right, it aint cosmic. No man, you have lost your vibes and gone none cosmic. I am like totally out of here."

Jett grabbed Harry hard. "Listen to me Harry, if you move so much as a hair, I will get Jaz to wake up all the none cosmic monsters down in the basement, and have them come up here and hold you until we are done. You getting my vibe dude?"

"Hey peace chicken, I get your uncosmic hassling vibe, you aint too cosmic at the moment either, chill for a mo and let the mellowness flow."

Jett's eyes blazed. "Harry I know you don't like this, none of us do. We have come around in a circle, and we need to get back across this yard to the cellar to Rune's circle, and that man is right across there." Jett pointed past the door and across the yard of corpse fighters, to the large building that housed the castle and the tall tower.

Harry swallowed hard. "Please baby girl, don't make me do this, Robbie messed my karma for weeks with this kinda freaky stuff, an I am starting to feel real weird."

Wolfie smiled and whispered to Jaz. "Wow if he is starting to feel weird now it's a good job he aint gone crazy."

Jaz smiled as he slipped out of the door, and Harry slammed his back into the wall and put his hands over his face. Jett started to laugh. "If he can't see them, he thinks they can't see him." Both of them giggled as they watched Jaz sneak into the middle of the group. He crouched low and his eyes seemed to flicker a very pale silvery blue. The dead soldier in front of him lurched and slowly lifted his head. Harry screamed and fainted. Jett started to giggle with Wolfie as they saw the white faced and very freaked out looking Harry on the ground by their feet. Wolfie looked at Jett. "Poor sod, I was more freaked out when they were alive." She giggled as she watched Jaz. Harry moaned on the floor.

Harry slid up the wall, and rubbed his face as Jaz slipped in through the door. "We have a problem... She has promised to bring them back to life if they fight for her. I tried to convince them that she was lying, and Rune was the only one with the powers of life, but she has all their souls in a big jar somewhere, and they cannot leave here without them, they also hate Harry, he killed most of them with Blades."

Harry slid back down to the floor as he fainted again, Jett looked round. "Hey where is Blades anyhow?" She peered back down the passage into the darkness. "Blades where are you girl?"

Soft stifled sniffles came out of the dark; Jaz peered down and walked back. Blades, was curled up in a corner with tears in her eyes hiding. Jaz crouched down to her. "Hey come on sweetheart it's alright to be scared at times. Come on, we are just as scared but you will be safe with us I promise, I won't let anyone hurt you." Blades pulled her arms around Jaz as he lifted her up, she looked really frightened, and with Harry out cold again, she had no one to reassure her. Jaz came back up the passage to the door. Wolfie lifted her into his arms.

"Hey Blades, it's alright, I hate them as much as you." He looked at Jaz. "We will have to run for it, and hope we get across before she gets them working. Can you carry Harry?" Jaz looked at the silent figure on the floor and nodded.

Jett helped Jaz lift a very heavy Harry on to his shoulder, and then she leaned on the door. "I will lead, it's a straight line so just run like hell, Wolfie babe stay right behind me with Blades." Jett drew out her sword, and it glowed in the dark as small rainbows glinted off the walls. She kicked the door as hard as she could, and it flew open, they raced out into the gap between the long lines. The yard was at least a thousand meters long. It was going to be a long run.

Wolfie flew behind her holding Blades hand, followed by Jaz, they were about a hundred meters in, when Jett saw the first twitch, and she swung her blade and sliced off the head and carried on. Behind them, others were rising off the floor, they turned to follow them and there was suddenly a very high, pitched scream. Harry had woken up. "Oh whoa... Hey man run like faster!" The sound of drawing blades rung out above Jaz, and he knew Harry was preparing to fight, he breathed a sigh of relief and tried to pick up his pace, Jett sliced her way through as two in front tried to stand, Jaz saw the head roll across between his legs.

Harry swung his blades and whimpered. "Oh man they don't die like they should, I knew it man, they are uncosmic monsters and after our vibes." Jaz felt the lurch as Harry swung madly, and sliced as fast as he could. "Man, these dudes have no vibes they is empty inside, this is so not happenin, and not at all intensely cosmic."

Jett hit the heavy cellar door as Harry sliced and screamed, the wood exploded open and she saw the circle and threw herself sprawling into it. Wolfie followed with Blades and pulled her down pushing her face into his chest, as he clutched her tightly in the circle. Jaz staggered as one of the follower's grabbed Harry's head. He screamed wildly, and Jett sprang out of the circle and with a spin of her heels, she exploded into the mass of the dead. Jaz fell quickly into the circle with the sprawling Harry and Jett leapt across, and vaulted through the curtain of violet light that sprung up around them. The floor melted, as they all fell through into Rune's table in Loxley. They landed in a heap, and rolled off the table onto the floor.

Treen jumped with surprise, as they seemed to fall through the ceiling, hit the table and crash on to the floor, Jett jumped right back up not realising where she was with her sword gleaming, and seeing Treen, she smiled and let out a long sigh. "Whoa girl that was totally the meaning of freaky."

Blades appeared nervously from under the table and smiled at Treen. Wolfie sprang up and looked around, as Jaz staggered to his feet. Harry stayed on the floor. Jett slapped his back and grabbed the back of his collar and heaved. "Hey Harry we are in Loxley and safe."

Harry bobbed up from under the table and Treen screamed and then fell backwards, Harry stood up and Wolfie jumped back. "Whoa, Urgh!"

Harry turned as Jett burst into laughter. "Hey man like what's with the laughter vibes." Blades started to giggle as Jaz lifted Treen off the floor. Jett pointed at Harry.

"Hey Harry I totally love your cosmic earmuffs." She held her sides as Harry lifted his hands and felt his ears. Two severed hands still gripped his ears tightly.

Harry pulled hard and they snapped off with a squelch, he pulled them round and looked at them. He gave a terrified high pitched scream, and then fainted. Jett rolled on the floor kicking and holding her sides as she screamed with laughter next to Harry, even Jaz started to giggle with Wolfie.

Treen slowly came round as Mel ran down the steps, she threw her arms round Jaz, as Wolfie lifted the gasping Jett of the floor. He turned and pulled Blades close. "You did fine Blades, even your messed up dad did his bit." He gave her a huge hug. "Come on let's get your dad a drink, and wake him up, you are going to be busy calming him down."

Rune looked up at the figure of Mordred and grabbed Robbie by the arm, as he went for the first step. "Wait it's a trap."

CHAPTER ELEVEN

THE RAVEN'S BELLY

Rune pulled him back off the step; her eyes were going wild with violet to lilac flashes. "Please Rob do not go after him it is a trap, I feel many souls in a great deal of pain."

Robbie looked up at the dark malicious eyes that burned with hate. He was about four floors up, and leaning over the rail. Robbie looked back at Rowan and then to Rune, he could see her concern but he pulled his hand free. "Rune they are both up there, which is why I am here, whatever they have in mind, I must defeat it and them. This is my destiny."

Rowan walked up to his side. "It might be your destiny, but you will not go alone." Jade, and Una stepped on to the first step and waited for him, Rune nodded, and she took his hand.

"Come on then, let's go and face whatever it is, but please all of you keep a very careful watch out." She like him worried about all of them, but he knew that none of them would wait, he gave her hand a squeeze and she smiled. Fish and Keith ran up the first flight of the steps with their bows ready and panned around, it was clear; Saff and Hornet passed, and went to the top of the next flight and stood guard. Robbie walked and watched the face of Mordred who was watching him, a cruel smile on his lips.

They came to the first level, and all was clear. It unnerved Robbie, he expected to be attacked and it had not happened, Mordred moved, and Robbie slowed. He watched as Mordred heaved a large glass bottle on to the rail, he gave an almighty push and the large glass bottle wobbled, Robbie grabbed Rune and flung her, as the bottle began its decent, he lunged at Rowan and the group sprawled towards the wall as the huge glass bottled hurtled past them and hit the stairs just below them. "Robbie what the...?"

There was a thundering crash and moans and wails rose into the air. Mordred hung over the rail and wailed with laughter. "If you want to fight, you may as well have an even match bow boy." Robbie got up from the floor and lifted Rune. He turned and looked at where the bottle had passed, Smoky figures rose into the air as he walked with Rune slowly forward. He stepped back, and pulled her back from the rail as the figures wove through the rails in the balcony towards him.

One stretched and writhed, and then rose from the floor and began to take a form slowly, Rowan stood and watched in horror, as the smoky figure became Robbie. It was his perfect match in every way, his dark brown hair, and long cloak, his belt and sword with a sapphire acorn clasp. The copy of Robbie smiled and Rune saw the difference. "Rob the eyes are dead." She stepped back as the copy of Robbie drew its sword, and began to advance. Robbie swept his hand round and pushed her behind him.

He pulled the golden sword of destiny out and prepared for combat. Sapphire stepped back faced with two Keith's and one Sapphire on the balcony. She drew her sword and prepared to fight herself, Keith grinned at the two copies of himself moving towards him, he winked. "Wow you guys are really handsome you know that?" He lunged and made the first strike; the copy of himself cut up quick and blocked the shot.

The copy of Rune rose up at the side of Robbie, her black eyes stared at him and then turned to Rune, and he blocked himself and lunged back. Rune looked at her copy as it walked towards her. "Oh please girl you have no idea." Her eyes burned bright purple and the copy of Rune screamed and grabbed her head,

Robbie found it disturbing as he watched the copy of Rune writhe in agony. Four more Rune's walked onto the top of the steps.

Robbie winked back at the real Rune. "Finally, I get my absolute fantasy, and they are all evil Rune. I have no luck." He spun the gleaming sword of destiny, and the head lifted off the copy of Robbie. The body flopped and became smoke. He felt his own neck and swallowed deeply. "Finally, something worse than shaving."

Rowan was fighting three of himself, and Jade laughed wildly, as she let her three copies get really close and then simply faded out of sight, the copies all looked at each other confused and then bent double as the real Jade's sword swiped unseen through the air. Flash spun against four of herself, and Hornet fought off two of herself. Una with bright violet eyes now had a glowing circle round her, as six tried to pass the barrier of light but could not. She raised her holly staff and spun with a huge speed, the light seemed to part as her staff came through and it hit the copies sending them flying in every direction.

Robbie watched as more smoky figures came up the stairs, and began to form into copies of him, he dropped his bow off his shoulder and loaded an arrow, as they became solid he fired. The arrow shot right through the head of the first and stuck in the second, he pulled his sword and sliced at the first, swinging round and cutting deep into the third. Fish ran up on the rail, and ran along it. "Hey Flash give me a lift." Eight copies of Fish ran along the rail behind him, Flash broke her stick apart, and while still dealing severe blows to her other smoky selves, she hit and battered the legs of the Fish copies running along. Fish swung his sword and sliced through two of Ruby's copies. She beamed brightly. "I love you Fish."

He spun on another copy of himself. "Hey Flash baby, you are beautiful." His sword sliced through the figure and it disappeared. Rune watched as another seven copies of herself came towards her, she pulled out her sword and it burst into flames, she smiled as the copies pulled theirs and they were just gold.

"You got to admit girls, mine is way cooler." She gave them a sweet smile and spun in a blur. Seven arms blurred around the flame of knowledge; Robbie leaned back having killed his last copy for the moment. He watched the violet blur and really could not tell which was, and which was not Rune, he loaded his bow and waited, she spun out of the blur and stood waiting with her flaming sword. He fired in quick succession, as she caught her breath, Rune after Rune fell dead. She came over and slid her arm around him.

"Hi gorgeous." she smiled.

"Hi sweetheart." Rune gave him a sweet smile, and stuck the knife into him, his eyes widened as he fell to the floor and turned into smoke. Robbie walked up the steps and smiled as he saw the smoke rise from the floor.

"Hey beautiful." He dropped the glowing blade back into his sheath, and picked his bow up off the floor, Rune looked at his eyes and nodded as she slid her arms around. She felt the knife at her throat he looked at her. "I said hey beautiful." She smiled at him.

"Kiss me gorgeous." He smiled and pulled the knife away and kissed her softly.

The smoky cloud came over the balcony and formed into half a Rune and half a Robbie, he turned as he kissed her, and saw the distress as the smoke formed from one to the other. It was confused, and he pulled her closer and hugged her tight. It was Rune then Robbie, it became Robbie with red hair, and then Rune with half red, and half brown hair. It writhed as it tried to form into one being. A white face with contorted features looked at him; it had one brown eye and one bright blue, Robbie pulled out his sword and sliced through the air taking off its head. It fell to the floor; he looked at Rune in a concerned way. She frowned at him. "What?"

"Please tell me none of our kids will turn out like any of those." She gave him a huge smile.

"They will all be as beautiful as you, not at all like a Smoggart."

Jade looked at the ten Rowan's in front of her as they advanced towards her, she thought for a second and then gave a devilish smile. "Sweetheart what do I like to do the most in bed?"

One Rowan looked very embarrassed. "God Jade, I am not telling these that, it is private."

She gave a huge grin and with lightning speed, she unleashed all her knives. The very red looking Rowan smiled and she slid up close. "I knew that would always be our little secret." He beamed at her.

"I promised I would take that to the grave didn't I?" She kissed him, and gave him a huge smile and her eyes danced under her long blonde fringe.

"Just wait till we get home."

Hornet stood surrounded by twelve copies of herself, her eyes shone brightly and she began to swing from side to side, the copies, all leaned with her, and back again. She did it a little faster, and then a little faster. As they went down, she pulled her long hatpin from her boot, and all the others went for their boots and found them empty. She was fast and furious, and poked the eyes of all her copies, which made them squeal and thrashed in pain. They bumped into each other and staggered in blind agony. She moved free of them and left them stumbling into each other. Four fell over the balcony rail as she headed towards Robbie; he leaned against the wall with Rune. "Hornet over here and stand really close it confuses them." She stood in between Robbie and Rune as another drifted over towards them.

Robbie and Rune laughed, as it made strange mixes of the three of them, some of them looked very funny indeed. Rune flashed her eyes, and smiled as it wailed loudly and fled. Una and Jade came over and closed in close against the wall,

Rowan was stood close to one of Flash and it stretched and shrunk. Flash screamed with laughter as a three-foot Rowan with bright white hair stared confused at them both. "Rowan you look funny." He giggled, and pulled her closer, the smoky figure became half Rowan and stretched with a really elongated face to become Flash. She giggled wildly. "Rowan this is fun." She slid in front, and watched Rowan's chin stretch and form a white beard. "Rowan you look like Merlin," she howled with laughter. He bent down and it grew two heads, Flash almost collapsed with laughter. The smoky figure bent and twisted, it grew and shrank and then it just burst into a cloud and drifted away. Flash came giggling across the balcony. "Robbie that was fun."

Fish walked slowly down the steps towards them; he flopped down, a long cut up his arm. "That was so weird, I cannot even begin to describe it. I think I just committed suicide about twenty five times."

Rune bent down and looked at his arm. "That is nasty, here let me stitch it, she pulled out her small sewing kit and placed it on the floor, Robbie shoved the blade of destiny through Fish, and he dropped the knife and burst into smoke. Rune fell back with a gasp, and stared up at Robbie. He pulled on the sword, which had gone right through into the wall, and looked up, as she turned to see Fish stagger on to the top step clutching his side. He had a bad slice on his side and he was bleeding quite badly, Rune turned and ran to him. She stopped and looked at him closely. "Why did we not cross the bridge at the river?"

He sat on the step and smiled. "It's Ok Rune it's me, there was no bridge to cross, we almost drowned." She smiled, and knelt down slipping her knife back into her belt.

She gasped as she looked at the wound. "This is bad Fish, I need you with

Alice." She leaned forward and lifted his pendant; and gave it a soft squeeze and a round white circle appeared on the floor below him. "Tell the others we are fine and I shall see them soon." Fish slid through the floor and was gone.

He rose out of the table and Mel leaned over him. "Jaz go and get Alice, this is bad. Harry help me get him upstairs." Harry lifted Fish carefully off the table, and walked up stairs with him. Mel looked at the table. "Please be careful Rune."

Keith appeared covered in blood, and yet he was fine, none of it was his, well in a way it was his, it was the blood of his copies. He had lost his temper and thrashed wildly at them slicing them into many bits. Sapphire looked exhausted as she slid down the wall next to the rest of them. "Who ever said be true to yourself, was an idiot, I have just faced myself two dozen times and won."

The group leant back against the wall out of sight of the top of the stairs. The reality was plain it was not going to be easy getting higher up. Sheltered under the balcony Robbie tried to think, as the others caught their breath, Rowan stood beside him.

"What now, is it worth trying to rush him with a volley of arrows?"

Robbie looked at the ceiling knowing that Mordred had the advantage of height. "He will expect that, I think we should take it easy, and see what else he has in mind. We are one down, he probably hoped for more." Robbie slid along the wall towards the bottom of the stairs; he kept out of sight knowing that there had to be more to come. Slowly he stepped forward, and looked up at the polished wooden balcony rail. Mordred was gone; he fitted an arrow to his bowstring, and stepped out as he looked around. It was clear and he moved a little further, slowly he walked up the stairs, as Rowan stepped out and covered him. Rune and Jade followed; his eyes never left the flights of stairs.

Outside on the tall wall of the black tower, Smokes slipped between the long stone shards that stuck out from the sides of the tower. He pushed on them, as he raised his legs, and put them on the top of the long shafts of black stone. He stood up and breathed a sigh of relief, and looked around. The raven's nest was not that pretty a place, long white bones littered the insides and rags of old woodsman's cloaks flapped in the breeze, from the victims that had been cast down, and impaled on the spikes inside. Steph struggled as she wriggled through the gap; he took her hand and pulled her through. She looked about the nest. "Oh very homely." Smokes smiled as he helped Crystal. One by one, the group slid through the gaps, and wove and twisted into the large formation of spiked stone shafts that made up the Raven's nest.

Bear and John had quite a squeeze, and after the exertion of pulling them through, and making the long climb, they all sat exhausted and breathing fast.

Maddy looked through the gaps between the stone spikes; it was a very long way down. She looked across and saw she was almost level with the top of the high cliff on which the city sat. She leaned back against the wall. "So, what now?" She looked at the balcony in the beak still very high up above her. "That is not going to be an easy climb." Smokes slid down beside her.

"We won't be climbing that far up. Robbie leant me his scope yesterday. There is a small wooden door just under the wing on the other side, I assume that is how they come out and check the dead."

Maddy looked at the others and then back towards Smokes. "We need to get in and find Robbie and the others, I sense danger, we must not leave him alone to do this fight." He nodded and looked at the others who still looked tired. Smokes stood up and walked carefully around the nest, it was smooth stone, and slippery with bones everywhere, and he wobbled several times before he disappeared from the sight of the others, and walked carefully to the side he knew had a door.

The wooden door was about four feet square and heavily built with thick iron straps bolted across it. There was no way of getting hold of it; all the edges were smooth and fitted well into the frame. It locked from the inside, which was of course the whole point. The Dark One would not want anyone she had thrown out to die being able to easily escape. It was not long before Skip and Bear appeared; they looked at the airtight door and Bear stroked back his thick blonde curly hair as it blew across his shoulders in the lifting wind. "I can smash it in, but you will lose your surprise factor, they will hear it all the way to the top."

Skip looked up at the black balcony stretching out from the beak of the raven. "I do not really see we have much of a choice, I do not fancy climbing into her balcony. I am all for surprising her; I just do not fancy her surprising me."

Smokes patted Bear on the back. "Try to lever it, and if that fails, smash the bloody thing down."

Bear slipped his silver axe out of his belt; it glinted in the sunlight as he pushed it hard into the gap where the lock was bolted on the other side. Bear heaved on the axe blade, his thick muscles fattening with the weight he applied, there was a faint crack and he pulled with all his might. The wood seemed to bend, and then with a resounding splintering, it cracked, and the door came away from the frame. Bear red in the face from his efforts gasped as he smiled and the door swung open. "I assume they took axes off this lot before tossing them down, right let's go find Robbie and that old hag, I will watch, you help the ladies in."

Bear pulled himself in through the door, into a dark and musty smelling passageway. He glanced from either side to ensure all was clear, and then leaned on the wall twirling his axe, his dark eyes shining in the darkness.

Crystal was the first one through, followed by Maddy, they moved swiftly and quietly up the corridor to scout ahead. The others followed, and Smokes pulled the splintered door back into place and wedged it with a slither of wood. He slipped out beside Bear into the dark corridor. "I suppose we should look for a way up and hope to hell we find Robbie and Rune." Bear patted his back.

"We will, you can pretty much depend on it my friend, wherever she pops up, Rune and Robbie will be." They wandered into the darkness of the passage towards the shuffling sounds of the others.

Robbie moved very slowly at the top of the stairs, Rune guided him around as he pointed his bow upwards, looking all the time at the rails high up. Shadows moved on the walls high above him, and his eyes scanned the rails carefully, as the others followed. Rowan shadowed Robbie from the other end of the line. Keith and Saff moved as one unit checking the way ahead, and covering the corridors as they slowly rose up past the second floor towards the third.

There was a slight movement, which caught Robbie's eye; it moved quickly along the top balcony and he saw a slight glint of red, he swung his bow across the balcony following the shadow. "Back," he barked his order, as the group moved swiftly under the cover of the lower balcony. He pulled back hard on the string, as the red cloth came into view, his arrow left the bow at an alarming speed, and Rowan's shot off in the opposite direction.

There was a scream above him, and a squeal behind, Robbie saw the small figure dressed in red slide onto the rails and crumple on to the floor. Robbie stared into the dead eyes of a small dwarf like person; their head was pressed hard against the bars, wedged watching down. Rune put her hand on his arm and gently pulled him backwards under the cover. "What was that Rune?" She pulled him close.

"That was a dwarf. A little man, it is not a child Rob, he is fully grown, he is just not as tall as the rest of us." He had never seen one before and had no idea. His reaction had been like lightening, he was acting on impulse and he breathed a sigh of relief. For one heart stopping minute, he had thought he had killed a child. He placed his head on her shoulder just for a moment and enjoyed her arms around him.

Rowan looked over at him. "Watch the little people, I have heard of them before, they blow their arrows down pipes at you, they like to use poison." Robbie nodded and pulled back from Rune. He walked slowly forward along the wall and then slid out into view, there was a flash of red, and he stepped back quickly. Eight long fine darts impacted into the floor and everyone jumped back, Robbie looked across at Rune.

"Just where exactly are they?" Her eyes glowed violet and she focused for a moment.

"You have three evenly spaced directly above us, and five opposite on the balcony, they are lay down which will make them harder to see and hit." Her eyes came back to normal and she looked worried. He gave her a broad smile and fitted his arrow to his bow.

"Rowan cover me, but do not follow, I have something they will not expect, and Pebbles keep your knives handy." They both nodded, as Robbie backed up to the wall. Rune pulled her hands to her mouth and took a deep breath. Robbie flew out from under the balcony, and on to the staircase, holding his bow tightly he extended his left arm and silently hoped. The darts hit the floor behind him, as he ran and as he reached the top step, his thought was proven right, he spun round to aim and a large silver shield appeared on his arm as the darts impacted. Three large golden dragons appeared on the shield and raising their heads, fire exploded out of them. The whole of the balcony was engulfed in flame as the shield of Morbihan protected him. Rune danced with excitement, she had completely forgotten about the ring, everyone else looked stunned. They ran up the stairs and took cover behind him, but there was no need, the sight of three Pendragon's coming alive on a silver shield and breathing fire was enough. They had fled without a trace.

Robbie lowered his arm and the shield disappeared as Jade bobbed excitedly. "Wow that is the coolest ring ever." She grabbed his hand and examined it. "Oh, this is good, wow Rob, this ring is really old, it was a gifted hand that made this." Una smiled at her.

"Thank you Pebbles, my mum made it, she was good, wasn't she?" Jade gave her a beaming smile as she let go of Robbie's hand.

Robbie scanned the stairs and balconies. "Ok, let's keep sharp, they might not be here now, but they will be lurking somewhere. Let's get up as quickly as possible." He raised his bow and began to walk slowly round to the next staircase. Violet light spilled out of Rune's eyes as she walked beside him. He knew she was sensing if any of the dwarfs were about. Evenly spaced, the rest of the group followed as they made their way to the top landing. Robbie stepped slowly off the top step and onto the long corridor, his bow was raised and the silver arrow tip glinted in the candlelight. Rune's bow was raised at his side as they walked together down the corridor towards two large brown wooden doors.

They somehow seemed out of place. These were the sort of heavy doors you would expect to find on the top steps to a castle entrance, they did remind him somewhat of Caerleon. Everywhere was silent, and his ears strained for the slightest noise, he could feel his heart beat as he breathed slowly, his eyes fixed on the two large heavy doors. Two large black rings of steel hung side by side against the wood, ready to be twisted and pulled to open the doors. Rune stopped and lowered her bow; her eyes flickered as she moved her head from side to side. "I have no knowledge of what is behind here; she is blocking me and protecting whatever is here."

Robbie gave her a wary glance. "How do you mean, whatever is in there?"

She gave him a soft smile and raised her eyebrows.

"This is her place; it will not be unprotected."

He looked back at the others, as he leaned forward and took the two large steel rings in each of his hands. "Are we all ready for this?" Rowan nodded, and all the others tensed as they gripped their weapons. Robbie turned to Rune and winked. "Let's go beautiful." She smiled and her eyes twinkled, as he slowly brought down pressure on the steel rings and they turned. He leaned forward as the two doors moved and they began to swing inwards, with a good push he let go, and the doors glided back; they looked into the room of what looked like a dungeon. Rune leaned forward and peered round the large room.

"Now this is more like it. Dim, gloomy and grotty, you can tell she did the decorating here." Holding her bow up she took a step forward with Robbie. Rowan and Pebbles slipped either side and watched. The room was very large and round. It looked like the whole inside of the top of the tower was built on this one room. The walls were grey and clammy, and the air smelt damp and musty. The floor was the same heavy grey slabs as the walls, and it unevenly made its way across to a stone set of steps, with a carved rail that led upwards to an overhanging dark balcony.

The walls hung with heavy iron shackles, and implements that looked strange and twisted, and Robbie assumed these would be her toys of torture. Large ugly stone figures like gargoyles stood round the edges with huge stone clubs, and stared menacingly at them, the air was cooler than that of the corridors.

Una edged forward across the floor her staff of holly held tight, Flash shadowed her, the long white pole glinting in the dim light cast by the slow flickering candles. Saff ran swiftly with Keith to the base of the stone steps her bow ready, Robbie and Rune flanked by Rowan and Pebbles moved carefully into the chamber. Robbie's eyes wandered the walls and up the stairs to the balcony, where the statue of a large golden raven sat with eyes as black as hate. Rowan turned slowly round, full circle making sure that every aspect of the dungeon was covered, Rune's eyes flickered lilac. "I feel them Rob, but they are all over the place, I cannot pinpoint any one location."

"I think we should move upwards; they have to be somewhere around here." Keith and Saff stepped on to the stairs. Pebbles screamed, and Rowan flew across the room and landed in an unconscious heap on the floor. Robbie spun round as Pebbles dashed across towards Rowan; he grabbed Rune and pulled, as the giant club of the stone gargoyle swung past just missing her.

Una and Flash stepped across Rowan and Pebbles to protect them, Robbie stared in panic as two more of the stone monsters began to move, he knew a sword was no match for stone, Keith's arrow bounced off the gargoyle in front of him. "We got trouble Robbie; these guys will not die quite so easily."

Keith pulled Saff back a few more steps as Pebbles wept across Rowan's bleeding head. Robbie stepped back, and the huge stone creature moved towards him. He pushed Rune behind him he could feel her fear. "They want me; move up the stairs, they will leave Rowan as long as they can attack me."

He slowly pushed her back and felt her small hand slip into his; he gave it a gentle squeeze his eyes never leaving the stone figure. His mind began to race, stone, what will destroy stone, his sword and bow were useless, and his knife was for one specific task. "Any ideas?" He felt Rune tense behind him as her feet went up the first step behind Keith and Saff, who now stood guard at the top of the steps.

The three huge figures with contorted twisted ugly faces slid across the floor towards them, they backed slowly up the steps away from them. The dark eyes buried deep under the heavy eyelids of the lopsided face burned with malice, there was a very Mordred look about them, and Robbie realised that somewhere above him they were being controlled. He glanced over the rail at Flash. "Hey Flash I need a little help here, this guy has sight, how about showing him your sunnier side?"

Una slammed her staff on to the side of the stair, and Flash beaming with a huge smile came running up and over the rail on to the steps. "Hey Robbie, pull up your hood this will be a bright one."

Little Ruby with her bright white hair stood eight steps up, as Robbie and Rune backed up behind her. She looked so tiny stood alone in front of the huge stone creature and his two pals. "You boys are huge, are you going to play with me?" She gave them a sweet smile and a little giggle. The ugly stone figures stopped. Robbie knew that if Mordred could see through the eyes, he would not understand what was going on. Ruby looked at the ugly faces in front of her, as the first one seemed unsure about lifting his foot on to the step. Ruby wagged a warning finger. "You boys cannot come and play with me and Robin Hood, you have to stay here and be good." She slipped her glasses off her face into her hand, and looked up at them with red eyes. The leg was stating to lift, but went down again. Ruby smiled and gave a little chuckle. "Good boys."

Rowan moaned on the floor as Pebbles held him close, Hornet watched at her side nervously. Una seemed uncertain, and still held her staff at the ready, her violet eyes flickered as she sensed the evil contained within the stone monster at the foot of the steps, she felt the force build and turned to the others behind her. "Cover your eyes quickly." The stone leg lifted and came down with a resounding thud on the first step.

"Oh boys, don't be naughty." Her eyes began to sparkle as she raised a finger and wagged it. "I warned you, if you're naughty I will get cross." The huge gargoyle pulled on the rail and he lifted his other leg.

"BAD BOYS!" The room filled with the blinding light. High above them in the tower, a terrific wail screamed out, the gargoyle brought his arms up to his face and staggered. Una pounced and grabbed Rowan's hood, and pulled with all her might,

Hornet helped as he slid backwards out of the grasp of Pebbles, she looked up in a daze and saw the now blind giant of stone thrash wildly with his club.

Robbie grabbed Flash from behind and yanked her up the steps. The club came crashing down and the steps exploded, where she had just been standing. Splinters of stone shot off in every direction as the now blinded group of three lashed out at everything. The handrails shattered into tiny pieces, and rained all over Una and her group, who were now huddled against the wall near the door, protecting themselves. Two of the stone gargoyles swung in their blind rage, and hit each other, their clubs smashed and fragments of each other fell to the ground, one of them keeled over and fell with a heavy thud smashing in to large chunks that writhed and squirmed on the floor. Una shuddered, even though she knew it was stone, she still felt that there was some form of life in it, and it disturbed her greatly.

Robbie stood with his arm round Rune, and watched as the last of the stairs collapsed, Una was lifting Rowan with Pebbles and they dragged him through the door. His head was bleeding badly but he was moving, Rune lifted her pendant and gave it a gentle squeeze.

They slid backward quickly pulling the slowly reviving Rowan down the corridor towards the stairs, a violet light appeared around them, and Una sensed Rune's presence. The white circle appeared on the floor and she stopped and held Pebbles hand, she took the trembling hand of Hornet in hers. "Our time here is done and Rune knows that." Slowly they began to sink as a cool feeling flowed over them. Melanie gasped as they all rose out of the table in Rune's cellar. Jaz slid Rowan into his hands, as Mel hugged Una and then Hornet.

"Oh, I am so glad you are alright." She held Hornet so tight she almost squeezed the poor girl to death. Una looked around at Treen and Blades.

"How many are here; do we know if the others are safe?" Blades lip seemed to tremble.

"Maggs is still at the camp, we do not know if she is safe." Una knelt and pulled her into a hug.

"Rune has protected everyone; if she gets in trouble, she will bring her straight back here." Blades nodded and gave a weak smile, Una looked at the stairs where Rowan was coming too, as Jaz carried him off for Alice to look after him, Jade stayed close, a look of worry on her face. Una looked back at the table and breathed a long sigh. There really was nothing she could do but wait and hope, she flopped down into the chair, and watched Treen, who stared at the centre of the table. Una knew that Treen was worried about Skip, her arrival had not helped because now Treen knew that Robbie and his group had lost track of them. Her eyes carried the strain, and she sat frozen waiting for news.

Rune stood at the top of the crumbled stairs watching as the blind gargoyle smashed and thrashed around the room below, Robbie stood with Keith and Saff as he watched the wide corridor that led down to what looked like another hall with a rising stair that seemed to be far more elegant. The gargoyle below stumbled and crashed into the large glass window, it splintered, and he fell down the tall black tower smashing through the shards that formed the nest and on to the rocks below. Rune turned and smiled at Robbie, as she slid her arm into his. She gazed down the hallway at yet another set of steps. "Oh, why can't people just live on two floors like the rest of us?"

Robbie pulled her close and chuckled. "Come on then, let's head upwards."

The group was starting to get considerably smaller and Robbie was now becoming more and more cautious. He was still aware that somewhere about was a small group of very small and deadly assassins, with his bow loaded he followed Keith and Saff. Rune walked at his side and Flash with her pole walked in the middle of all of them. The air was growing cooler as they came once again to the end of the corridor and looked round the inside of the hall like room. The floor was decorated with large cheque tiles in black and white, and the mahogany red wooden stair curled up to the landing above. Thick rich red carpet lined the stairs and the cold walls were painted in a dull bleak shade of pale matt grey. Rune stepped forward and put her hand on Keith shoulder, Saff had already seen and felt the highly decorated runic archway that led into the hallway and she stopped, she looked across at Rune as Robbie and Flash stopped beside them. The blue in her eyes seemed to flicker slightly. "I feel her." Rune nodded back and turned to Robbie.

"She is right above this archway. It will tell her when we pass, be on your highest guard." She stretched up and kissed him softly on the cheek, her blue eyes sparkled with her love and he smiled at her.

"I will take care, I promise."

John stared down at the shuddering rock of the broken gargoyle. It vibrated with life and quivered at his feet. It jumped slightly and he stepped back and shuddered. Martin looked down at its hideous and disfigured stone face. "Ouch, he has took a pasting, Robbie cannot be too far away."

Skip surveyed the wall with the crumbled stone staircase. Crystal read his mind and fitted an arrow to her bow, the steel arrow shot into the top of the wall as Skip stepped back. Ice formed and began to unfold as it slipped down the wall, and bright glowing white steps formed in the ice, and sparkled like a staircase of diamond. She bent down and touched one of the large moving pieces of stone. The chunk of rock froze instantly; Crystal raised her leg and stamped down hard, the rock exploded into dust as her eyes turned all white. A breeze with a flutter of snowflakes rose in the room, and the dust lifted, and spread across the steps, Skip was very impressed. "You know, you really are a very remarkable young woman." Crystal gave him a smile, as her eyes became the clear circles out lined in black. Maddy gave her a big grin as she passed, and headed on to the stair with her white bow loaded and ready. Bear looked at the ice as he put his first leg on to it.

"It will hold." Crystal patted his back as he gave a sigh of relief, smiled, and raised his second leg on to the next step. John and Martin chuckled as they followed, and ran up the stairs. Steph looked out of the broken window and across the bay, it looked like Rose was inching forward and beginning to regain the control in front of the bridge.

Rune stepped forward and raised her hand, and a violet light filled the archway, she gave a nervous look back. "I am not sure this will work; I suggest you run to the stairs and up them as quickly as possible." They all looked nervously across the empty hall way, and then back at each other. Keith slipped his hand into Saff's and she gave him a weak smile.

"You Ready?" He looked back at Robbie as Rune slid her hand into his. He slid his hand down and took Flash's small pale hand in his. He nodded to Keith. The violet light flashed and shimmered for a moment as they erupted out of it. The group ran as fast as they could. Bolts of lightning shot from above and hit the floor by the archway leaving smoking and smouldering holes in the tiles. Robbie glanced up and saw the lines of soldiers drawing their swords. They hit the bottom of the stairs at a fast pace, before he saw the trap. It was too late, and as the soldiers piled out in to the hall behind him, his hand slipped to his belt and he released Rune's hand. Flash spun round as Keith drew his sword, Saff and Rune raised their bows and prepared to fire. Robbie spun fast the white gleam of his blade high in the air, he swung and lunged at the first guard, the guard behind dropped down pierced with Rune's arrow. Flash jumped off the stair breaking her pole apart as Robbie's blade crashed down on the second soldier.

Saff released her arrow, and a soldier screamed as he fell off the balcony into the mass below, Rune's eyes blazed as she brought a twister into the midst of the crowd flowing out into the hall. It lifted men in black and threw them hard into the walls; she backed up the stair to get a better view as she controlled the wind that attacked anyone breaking out towards Robbie, who was fighting with ferocity to stay on top of the throng.

Flash spun in the middle of the crowd like a top, her pole broke apart, and she hurtled with horrific speed, and figures flew back as her white sticks blurred. Keith waded in into the black shirts and disappeared, Rune spun and her eyes blazed as the wooden handrails burst into life and ivy ran out of it grabbing and snaring the soldiers around Keith and dragging them back. Soldiers disappeared under the rapidly growing leaves.

Robbie staggered back on to the stairs, the crashing blows ringing on the sword of Destiny. Rune felt fear as she saw him struggle, and drew her sword of Knowledge, which ignited into flame as she rushed back down the steps to help him fend off the masses. There was a scream and Flash crashed into the side of the stairs, and slipped to the floor, the mass of streaming soldiers pressed up on to Robbie and Rune. A small mop of bright white hair could just be seen through the gaps in the rails, and Rune turned her face and bright glowing eyes at the soldier clambering forwards. She gritted her teeth, and the light flooded out as the soldiers whipped into the air and crashed against the wall. Moaning and groaning, they slid down to the floor.

She flew across the wide step, and grabbed the shoulder of Flash's jacket. Rune let out a loud and painful gasp as she pulled with all her might, and Flash rose up the rail, hanging limp. Robbie kicked hard as he swung his blade hard, and the soldiers recoiled under his force. He leaned over and snatched Flash, with one massive pull, as his sword swung back round, she came over the rail and into Rune's arms.

"GET HER OUT OF HERE!" Robbie bellowed, but his voice was drowning in the clash of steel as he stepped up onto another step. Rune hurriedly grabbed the pendant and pressed it, the white circle appeared on the floor and Flash began to sink into it.

Mel watched with Jett as the table glowed, and Flash began to rise. Jett jumped instantly on to the table and sunk down below Flash, as Mel stretched over to pull Flash to Harry. Jett disappeared and sprung out of the floor on the stairs.

The sword of truth glinted rainbows, as Jett burst into the air and over the rail with a scream like a wild banshee. Robbie jumped back as Jett sailed high into the air, and landed with the grace of a cat with a wide beaming smile, the light flashed in every direction, as the sword of truth swung round at an alarming speed.

Rune beamed at Robbie, as she swung down hard on the soldiers trying to climb up on to the stair over the rail. Jett spun like a deadly ballerina; her blade twisting and lunging as the soldiers fell back against her well practiced fighting skills. Still more soldiers poured from above and below. Jett winked as she flew past Robbie taking the legs out from under five guards. "Hey Robbie, you miss me?"

"I was thinking of you, glad you popped in for a little exercise."

Keith was now lost in the crowd as he battled hard against the group. Saff was loading and shooting arrows with huge speed and pace trying her best to protect him. The crowd of soldiers was still growing, Robbie and Rune were now side, by side thrashing out at anything that stepped towards them. "I love you beautiful; but I think we are really in trouble."

She lunged forward, stabbing a soldier and lifting her boot, she thrust him backwards. "I love you too gorgeous, we are not finished yet."

Jett was backed into a corner, and her eyes began to flicker blue, rainbows danced reflected from the blade. Her eyes flared as ten soldiers in front of her clutched their heads and fell to their knees, they screamed in agony, and the men behind them stepped back as Jett's eyes burned a bright deadly blue. "Hey guys what's up, all the noise given you a headache?" She looked up and the blue light splashed across the soldiers behind the screaming front row, they all jumped back as the light crossed their tunics.

Robbie was growing tired, sweat dripped from his nose as he swung the golden blade that shone white in the air above him. More soldiers dropped and others scrambled up on to the dead that fell before him. He pushed Rune back up another step. Saff's back touched his as Keith appeared at the top of the stairs, badly cut and covered in blood. He pushed two in front of Saff over the rail, and down in to the masses of soldiers now climbing the stair rails. Spinning round he sliced through two soldiers, and backed to Saff's side. They were all now surrounded, and Robbie knew he would not hold them off for long. The stair rails burst into leaf, and brambles shot along the top of them. Soldiers screamed as they gripped the rails, and found long barbed spikes puncturing into their palms. They let go fast, and dropped down onto the others climbing below, who slipped and fell backwards.

Rune pointed a hand at the top of the stairs, as a burst of strong wind lifted the soldiers into the air and flung them backwards violently. Rune looked afraid, she twisted and hit out at a soldier, her glowing hand burnt his skin. "Oh, Rob there are too many I cannot keep this up." The soldiers swarmed back up the stairs, as Robbie fought harder. Three men went rigid and turned white, Robbie crashed his sword onto them and they exploded into a thousand frozen pieces. Four men fell dead above Saff with violet coloured arrows sticking out of their chests, and Rune beamed as John winked from the far archway.

The shining silver axe, and bright golden sword of Bear, swept through the throng towards Jett, and Skip hacked his way into the startled soldiers as he pushed into the crowd. Smokes and Steph fired arrows from just inside the archway. Soldiers dropped around the group on the stairs, and Skip waded up towards Robbie and Rune. "Thought you needed a lift, there seemed to be one or two more than expected." Robbie smiled as he stepped down to the side of Skip.

"You have no idea how happy we are to see you, for a moment there I was worried." Skip's dark brown eyes twinkled as he smiled. Four more soldiers froze on the spot and exploded as Skip swung into them. A hail of arrows shot up the stairs and muffled grunts and moans seeped out of the soldiers who crumpled to the floor.

Bear patted Robbie on the shoulder as he bolted up the stairs to help Keith, blood dripped from the blade of his silver axe, Robbie slumped against the wall and wiped his brow as more soldiers wailed in pain and fell in the hall. The first five steps of the stairway were now a trampled ramp of the dead, and as Rune slipped beside him on the step, he stared at the wide open eyes of all of the slain. Rune slid her arm across his shoulder and pulled him close. His hand trembled, it had been round his sword and locked for so long, Robbie dropped his head on her shoulder, and closed his eyes for a moment. He felt utterly spent and exhausted. "Hey gorgeous." She kissed the side of his head. "We made it Rob, I wasn't sure for a minute, but we have got this far."

He slumped lower on to the step. The task of finding Mordred and the Dark One was still ahead of him, and he felt like he could already do no more. His arms ached as they flopped by his side, Rune pushed her hand into his back and it started to glow.

Robbie felt the warm feeling rise inside him and lifted his head to hers, her soft warm lips met his and he basked in the pleasure of knowing he had lived, and she was still there. Just for a moment, he had lost hope and fear had overcome him, the fear of losing her, and losing his children. Feeling her now against him and her lips of warmth on his seemed to bring him back to life.

He pulled slowly away, and saw the two bright sapphire blue eyes staring back at him; her red hair sparkled with golden streaks. She gave him a huge smile, and he smiled back at her. "Hey beautiful."

"Hi gorgeous, feel better now?" She stroked back the damp hair from his fringe and gazed into his deep brown eyes. Robbie nodded as she kissed his forehead.

"I am fine, please be careful this is getting harder and harder." John and Martin pushed past with their bows loaded, and Robbie got to his feet, the bottom hall was a mass of dead, and Jett staggered through to the step and smiled at Robbie and Rune. "Wow you guys certainly know how to party, I am exhausted."

Rune gave her a smile and slid an arm round her. "You took a big risk coming back, but thanks Jett, we really needed the extra hands." She pulled her into a close one armed hug.

Robbie looked up at the top of the stair where the fight continued, Bear and Skip with their bright golden swords had waded into the mass of soldiers. Bear was a terrifying sight, and many staggered back in his wake. His long golden heavy sword flashed in one hand as his axe came down with thunderous blows in the other. Martin and John crouched at the top of the stairs with Saff and Maddy, she had borrowed Keith's bow, as hers was a little too explosive for close quarters shooting; Keith backed Bear and Skip with his sword. Steph and Smokes had now moved along the corridor and were using a combination of bows and swords depending on their combatant. Robbie had not seen Steph with a sword, and was very surprised at her ability, she had a look of a very blonde Scarlet, and he could really see now how alike they were as sisters. He picked up his sword and looked at the other two. "Are we ready?"

Jett gave him a huge smile. "Let's sort this lot out Robbie, I have to get back to my wolf man, he promised to howl for me."

Rune started to giggle as she nodded her head. "You are incorrigible Jett; do you know that?"

Jett beamed, raised her sword and headed up the steps in front of her. Robbie lifted up the sword of Destiny and shouldered his bow; he leaned over and kissed the smiling Rune on the cheek. "Right here we go again, keep behind me." She kissed him back, and raised the golden sword of knowledge. Together they headed up the stairs, and passed Martin and John, there was now at least twenty feet of floor littered with the dead, as the soldiers of the Raven's tower were pushed back by the brutal onslaught of Bear, Skip and Keith. Arrows hit with precision as soldiers either side of the main group fell dead.

Robbie came up beside Keith and Steph, and waded into the mass with his sword. The group now formed a line of swords, as Jett whooped into them and as a wall of fine blades; they hacked and cut their way down the hallway that turned slightly to the right as it rose on a soft slope.

None of them had realised, but they were now in the heart of the black raven. The corridor rose up and broke into a wide hall, with the tall winding stair up to the lair of the Dark One. Mordred now dressed in black armour, stood and watched as his men backed into the hall below him, the noise of the fight echoed around the large stone hall, as Robbie and his group pushed the struggling and pain screaming soldiers back.

Bear was a tower of terror, as he screamed at the soldiers, frightening them before dropping his axe and sword with heavy violent crashing blows, his torn shirt showed the blood soaked chest, and rippling muscles of his arms as they twisted and spun. Jett was her usual self, as the room expanded and she spun into the space, her sword glinting and flashing as it cut through the air and into the soldiers with surgical precision. Her screams and whoops of delight and joy, sent the soldiers who were not used to such a wild looking woman with a lethal blade seeming to be enjoying herself, staggering backwards.

The soldiers were dropping like flies as the pace eased, many staggered back and some ran away down the side passages. Robbie looked up for the first time as he came into the hall and he saw Mordred stood watching, he dropped back and Keith and Steph closed the gap. John and Martin followed pulling used arrows out of the dead, and reloading their quivers.

He could see the start of the stairway up, and Robbie ducked behind Bear and Smokes, and with a few fine cuts of the sword, he saw his chance. He leapt up on a fallen body, and cleared the gap on to the stair, his eyes met with Mordred's as he walked slowly up. The black eyes gazed from under the black steel helmet, and the long curly white locks of hair hung down his back. He was filled with malice and evil, as he sneered at the Bowman who calmly walked up towards him. Robbie felt the calmness on him as he breathed and relaxed, he shook his free hand to loosen it, and slowly he composed himself. His heart still pounded in his chest, this was not going to be easy and he knew it. "You do not belong here Mordred; your time has been and gone." His dark brown eyes burned above his blooded cheeks, and his long hair fell lank with sweat. Mordred gave a sneering sort of grunt for a laugh; he was not unlike his mother.

"Well wood chopper, I took a king in that time, you are hardly worthy of the fight, but my blade needs sport." The dark blade of Dunnottar glinted very slightly as he raised it up, his cold malicious voice slipping across the floor towards Robbie like a rotten snake.

Robbie lifted the gleaming sword of Destiny up and for a moment, Mordred seemed to shudder. Robbie smiled. "You have met my swords brother I believe?" He turned the handle and the name was revealed to Mordred, it had an impact. "You have a black sword, it is hardly the spear you pushed through Arthur, and you will have to come much closer to kill me."

"I fear no blade in the hand of a woodcutter; I am the killer of men of quality." His eyes did not leave the gleaming blade of Robbie's sword, and the air around it seemed to be filled with the voices of a small and gentle people. Robbie stopped face to face with the son of the Dark One encased within the armour plated suit, and Billy's body. Below him, the sound of the battle continued, and yet loud as it was, in Robbie's ears it seemed miles away. His whole body and attention now focused on the black armour and black eyes of Mordred.

Robbie's hand hung limp and relaxed, the moonstone handle of the sword and dagger both seemed to shimmer as if knowing their time was coming. Robbie raised Destiny before him, and to his surprise two claw like blades slid out just above the hilt. He knew instantly that the sword was preparing for its own destiny; the claws would trap the sword and allow him to get close enough to use the dagger on the blade. Mordred raised the defiled black blade, and licked his lips ready for the taste of blood.

Robbie and Mordred faced each other high on the balcony, as the group pushed forward below. The soldiers were spilling backwards into the corridors, Smokes now led the way, his bow on his shoulder, his long red hair hanging damp around his shoulders, he fought with determination and aggression. His bright blue eyes shone from his blood splattered face, he looked menacing, as he glared at the men before him, his long silver sword matching the glint in his eyes. He showed no fear, and it unnerved those who stood before him, they backed away as the figure of a man who once was stockier, and yet still had the power confronted them. Steph covered his rear with a bow, and Crystal using Rune's bow took out any Steph could not cover. They worked as a team and pushed hard and aggressively into the now depleting mass.

Two large doors burst open under the balcony, and the soldiers ran. Bear swung round startled at the sudden reaction of the soldiers, and confronted the dark and oppressive figure of a large black feather clad Raven. The blast of blue lightening hit him and he was blown off his feet, he felt his back hit the wall and the saw the plaster dust before his eyes as everything went black. Crystal spun and her arrow sped off, as did Steph's they never made their mark, as they burst into flame and the blast of fiery vapour was carried back with the force of a hurricane, throwing them both into the air. Steph felt the pain in her arm as she rolled on the floor, and faced the still figure of Crystal. Her eyes blurred as her head pounded and she slipped into darkness, Smokes spun dodging her blast of blue, and as he side stepped and brought up his sword, she twisted like a snake and snatched him by the neck, like a striking cobra. He felt the air run out of his throat as the pressure increased, and she lifted him into the air, her cold voice ran down her arm like a worm, and slipped into his ear.

"Don't flatter yourself woodsman." He stared into the hate that was the two dark cold orbs of her eyes set in a face so white it carried the coldness of winter, her thin lips parted with what looked like a pallid smile, and he felt fear like he had never known as the coldness seeped through his body.

"PUT HIM DOWN WITCH!"

The last words Smokes heard as everything went blank. Rune stood alone, her bright red hair shining like an autumn sun, and her bright blue eyes blazing fierce, and radiating the force of life and power that she now was. She stood small and slender, dressed in the green of her woodsman, splattered with the blood and sweat of her enemies, yet defiant in front of Morgan le Fey. Rune clicked her fingers and the Dark One recoiled in the sudden pain that ran through her hand. She let go as if burned, as the violet light shone from the pendant of Smokes. A white circle appeared on the floor and Smokes slipped through it. The Dark One stared with hate at Rune as Crystal and Steph slipped away from her followed by Bear. John and Martin stood resolute behind Rune, with Maddy; Skip lay bleeding on the floor behind them.

The Dark One turned to face her, and glanced at her white hand with black finger nails, as she rubbed the fingers together feeling the last of the burning sensation as it eased away. Her eyes rose back to the young figure of Rune, her eyes flashed red with her irritation. "So, Flower Girl you think you have come of age, do you? You will need more than just party tricks in my house."

The three wounded figures rose out of the table, and Harry grabbed Smokes and pulled his unconscious body across the table towards him. Una helped lift the others off, and Steph gathering her wits after the heavy fall, quickly followed up the stairs behind Harry. They gently lifted Crystal and carried her up to the bedrooms. Alice waddled up and down the corridor from room, to room checking on everyone, Rowan and Bear were now awake, although in pain and heavily bandaged. Alice had become very upset at the sight of Bear, and was only just starting to settle down. Jess had arrived to help, and she sat with Crystal who had taken quite a bad bash to the head. Alice attended to the broken arm of Steph, as she sat with Smokes who moaned and groaned, large red finger marks burned brightly on his neck.

Blades shuttled about with trays of drinks and piles of bandages, as she kept Alice supplied, Treen sat down at the table of Runestone and waited. Steph stroked Smokes fringe back, she looked very pale as she spoke to Jess and Alice. "The last thing I remember Rune was stood facing the Dark One, and Robbie was up the stairs fighting with Mordred."

Jess looked terrified. "They faced them?" Her hands came to her mouth as she stared a look of horror on her face. She glanced at Alice who sat with her hands on her large tummy looking pale and very frightened. "Oh god I hope they will be alright; I cannot believe Rune would face her in her own castle."

Steph looked lost in thought. "She is stronger than she has ever been; I just hope it is enough." All of them looked at each other, there was nothing else that could be said, Robbie and Rune were now facing the first part of their destiny, and all of them knew that the outcome was uncertain. They would have to sit and wait and tolerate the long hard minutes as they slipped by until they knew the final outcome.

CHAPTER TWELVE

STRONG TEA AND ESSENCE

Maggs fussed as she wandered round the wounded, slipping hot cups into their hands. "There you go my sweet, you drink up it will do you good, it strengthens your vibes." Her herbal tea was one of her most famous recipes; somehow it had the effect of lifting the spirit and soul, whilst relaxing the legs. The soldiers sipping it smiled in a dazed sort of way, and yet as they tried to stand their legs seemed numb and they just slipped back on to the floor. Her beads and chains rattled with her bracelets, and her body seemed to shimmer as the sun shone its early autumnal rays on her. She smiled with her overly large teeth and gave a horsy gasp as she poured her tea.

If the truth were known, she was filled with fear. Harry, Blades and Lucy were somewhere in the tower, and she looked across each time she stood up. It had been an hour since something very large had fallen from the window level with the south wing of the Raven, and she had looked across her heart pounding. Her eyes strained against the sun; she had thought just for a moment she had seen a faint glimmer of blonde hair. The whole of the group, and the people she loved most were somewhere over there, and she felt a strong sense of unease rising inside her. Maggs remembered the time when she was so much younger, when she had heard of the attack on the road south, and how Mason Knox had captured a bike rider and killed the other one.

It was still a painful memory of a bitter time in her life, the time when she had thought that Harry was dead. The pictures of the market in Southampton came to mind when a traveller had talked about the fight of a man with two swords, and the capture of a red haired man. It had haunted her dreams for years, as she had tried to contact the spirit world and find her beloved Harry. Now once again she had to endure the pain of waiting and not knowing, Maggs smiled as the soldier gratefully accepted a cup off her. "There we are darling, this is groovy stuff, it will clean your aura and make you feel chilled and happenin." She looked across at the dark tower across the water, was that flashes of violet she saw?

Rose slid an arm around her shoulder. "Don't worry Maggs pet, he will be fine, Robbie and Rune are watching him." Maggs nodded, and tried to hide the tears that had suddenly risen in her eyes, Rose rubbed her shoulder. "Maybe you should take a break and have some tea yourself." She smiled weakly and nodded, she was tired and a rest seemed a nice idea. The two women sat quietly on the edge of the lookout platform, both lost in thought, each of them knew of the risks and dangers that were held behind those dark sinister walls, and both of them feared the outcome.

The breeze was strengthening, and as she stared into space, with pictures of Harry in her thoughts, her long mass of feather and bead strewn curls lifted, and Maggs blinked the tears from her eyes, and they ran down her cheeks, and dripped into the masses of silver and gold chains around her neck. Rose gently pulled her round to her shoulder, and Maggs pushed her face deep into Rose and cried with her fear.

Robbie was tired, his hand ached around the hilt of the sword, and his wrist shook slightly. His eyes never left the black blade as Mordred prepared for combat. The evil dark eyes shone brightly under the blonde fringe, as he surveyed the blood and sweat streaked face of Robbie. He sensed his tiredness, and his confidence grew, as he smelt victory. Robbie waited knowing he would see the flicker in the eyes of the enemy before he moved. He tensed his arm and prepared, it could not be much longer now as he saw the stature of a confident man start to rise before him.

He blinked and moved fast, Robbie was ready and swung the sword up to meet the black blade. The two blades crashed together with an almighty force, and sparks shot through the air, the ring of the metal was deafening, as the opposing swords bit down hard on each other, Robbie could almost hear the cries of pain from both swords. Mordred was stronger than Robbie had realised and he felt the painful jolt to his elbow, it burned hot with the impact and he bit hard, gritting his teeth, as he forced the sword of Destiny up and back on the black blade. Mordred whipped his blade back and laughed. "You are no match for me, killing you will not even feel like sport." Destiny came round with anger and speed, Mordred stepped back and parried the blow, Robbie watched happily as he saw the impact surprised Mordred.

"I am not yet warmed up dark boy." The smile was forced, as he hid his own pain and yet it had the desired effect, as he saw the startled look on Mordred's face. Destiny exploded white light as he pulled back with speed, and launched another crashing blow on the Dark One's son. Mordred staggered under the weight and stepped back a few feet, he smiled an arrogant smile.

"Maybe this will be fun after all, leaf lover." He swung wide and heavy as Robbie twisted his sword round, the black blade bounced on to his sword and flicked upward. Robbie felt the searing pain as the blade sliced into his left shoulder. He twisted backwards defending against another crashing blow, as Mordred stepped forward, and began to crash and batter his wounded opponent, a sense of victory in his mind. Robbie swung and defended, but each crashing blow shook his whole body. Mordred licked his lips as if tasting the woodsman's blood, and laughed wildly as he stepped forward raining down the thunderous blows. Robbie staggered further back towards the top of the stairs, and the corridor that led to the lair of the Dark One. The bones in his hands seemed to vibrate together, and the swords screamed and sparked with each murderous meeting, Robbie felt a sense of panic rising inside him.

The Dark One looked into Rune's bright blue eyes with utter hatred. Rune calmly smiled sweetly. She felt strong and relaxed, and knew that the power of Opal was rising inside her, the whites of her eyes began to flicker with lilac, and Morgan knew her true power was rising. In her mind she chanted the incantations of the black book, knowing the calm child before her had untold power. She still knew she had learned her art over a thousand years, and no other had ever gone deeper into the ways of the black lines as she had. "You cannot defeat me Flower Girl, the white lines are no match for the black. Your grandfather could not defeat me, and he is stronger, what makes you think such a girl who has not fully matured can even face me and win?" She sniggered, and raised a white hand of black talon like nails to her mouth as a young girl might. Rune gave a soft smile.

"Unlike you witch, I have the love of my family, his power is mine and so is that of my mother's line. I am not afraid of you witch, I am here before you am I not?" Her face sharpened and a little anger rose within her. The Dark One noted the change.

"Maybe your unborn will favour me more, Flower Girl." She gave a flick of her wrist, and Rune felt the searing pain in her stomach, she gasped and she bent forward and clutched her stomach. Tears filled her eyes with the agony of her tortured children, she whispered quietly as she gasped, and anger and love mixed together, and the full force of Rune surfaced.

"IONA... NO...! YOU WILL NOT HAVE HIS CHILD!" Rune's eyes exploded with deep purple light as she raised herself up, and the bolt of bright purple light that shot from her, crossed the room to the laughing and unexpecting Dark One, as Rune screamed. The ball hit Morgan full on, a terrible scream of agony rose in the air, as she somersaulted back through the doors, and crashed twenty feet up the room in a pile of murderous screaming hate. Black feathers floated down from the air all around, as Rune stepped forward her eyes burning with power of immense strength. "How dare you touch what is pure and beautiful with your foul and decrepit mind." Rune's voice contained a coldness and loathing so deep that even John and Martin who stood amazed with Maddy, shuddered with fear. Rune walked slowly to the dark figure sprawled on the floor.

The whole room filled with the evil screams of hate, and a blinding red flash exploded, and Rune came crashing backwards through the doors and slid on the stone floor back towards John who jumped to protect her.

The screams of wild madness rose into the air, and John was lifted ten feet in the air and smashed against the wall, Martin was on his feet with his bow, as Maddy tried to grab him and missed. His arrow shot straight through the open door, and with a flash of blue, it swerved in mid-air and came back out at high speed. Maddy screamed and dived for Martin, as it flashed through the air and Martin swung round a look of shock in his eyes, as he fell to his knees and collapsed. His face hit the floor at the side of a startled Rune and their eyes met, she saw the light in them dim, and she knew he was gone. Maddy gasped and loaded her bow with three arrows; they exploded in flames as she screamed on top of her voice "GWENDOLYN, MOTHER OF THE WHITE CIRCLE HEAR ME AND HELP ME!"

Blue light exploded out of Robbie's white bracelet as flames erupted from under the stairs, the heat licked up round the banister rails and Mordred jumped back, Robbie seized his moment as his knees had given in, and he staggered back to his feet, new power in his arm that clenched tightly to the sword of destiny.

Anger coursed into him as he swiped and hammered blow after blow on top of the staggering, and utterly surprised looking Mordred. Robbie watched the heavy vibration, rhythmically dance down Mordred's arms, as he moved with speed and fought with all of his last dying strength in his tired and aching arms, as he cascaded pounding heavy blows that even Bear would be in awe of.

Rune sat up as the smoke billowed out of the room, and Maddy crawled weeping to Martin, John moaned his bloodied face to the wall, his legs were twisted and broken. Rune looked with sadness to Martin's dead body and raised her hand, she clicked her fingers and John began to slide into the floor, Skip lowered through and Maddy begged. "Please Rune no, do not send me back let me stay and help."

Rune turned with tears in her eyes. "Take Martin back and look after him, he has a family." Maddy nodded her tears streaking in the dirt and grime of the fight on her cheeks; she slid off her quiver, and pushed it across the floor with her white bow, towards Rune.

"Let my mother help you my true sister, may the lines of time and the circle of white protect you." Maddy sank weeping with Martin into the floor through the glowing white circle on the stone floor.

Treen screamed as she lunged at Skip, and pulled him crying into her arms, Harry came hurtling down the stairs and froze as the body of Martin and Maddy came up through the liquid surface of Rune's table. John slipped to the floor and cried with Martin cradled lovingly in his arms. He stroked his soft short curly brown hair as he wept, the limp slender frame of Quiet Martin resting on his lap. Harry knelt with Una at the side of the heavily bleeding John, as he looked up with pain in his eyes. He shook as the emotion cascaded out of him.

"I loved him like my brother Harry; he was my friend always beside me. What will I do without him?" He lowered his head and wept long gasping bitter sobs. The tears ran down Harry's face and Una gasped loud sobs. Harry put a large hand on John's shoulder.

"Hey man he loved you as much you know, you were like the truest of buds. Come on man, let's like clean him up and make him his best." John howled into the chest of his best friend. He lifted his sobbing head as the others watched with pain in their faces.

"Help me take him up Harry, I want too. Let's do right for him like we did young Eric."

"Yeah man, you do like you did for Eric." Harry gently patted John on the shoulder.

Jaz lifted Big John up, as Wolfie stood with Martin cradled like a child in his arms. John swallowed deeply and nodded to Harry. "This man was one of the truest Loxley ever had."

"Totally man." Harry stood up with pride, and slapped his hand in salute to Martin. Jaz helping John staggered to the stairs, as Wolfie sadly carried their friend up and out of the cellar. Treen, held Skip tight and hugged him, Skip smiled in her arms.

"Now come on sweetheart it's not as bad as it looks." A large pool of blood surrounded him and Treen on the floor, and stained her dusky orange skirt. She pulled him even closer and wept on his shoulder.

Rune stepped into the charred and burned, smoky room. The smell of singed feathers filled her nose; she slowly scanned around what was left of the furniture, and the smouldering carpet. Shafts of white light streaked across from the small window in the smoke. The Dark One was not there.

Sweat dripped off Robbie's head and chin, as he continued to pound the sword of Mordred, he gripped the hilt of Destiny with both hands, as he swiped and twisted the sword in his hands. Mordred squealed as Robbie brought the sword round, and sliced deep into his arm, Destiny cut through his armour like a scythe through fresh grass. He kicked out wildly at Robbie's feet, and Robbie stumbled and crashed forward rolling over Mordred and across the floor onto the top of the stairs. His hand hit the rail and pain coursed into him as the back of his knuckle broke. Destiny slid free, the golden sword rattled out of his hand and clunked down the flight of stairs, flashes of white glinted in Robbie's pain filled eyes, as he pulled his hand up to his chest with it burning in agony. Mordred scrambled to his feet unsteadily, and seeing the undefended Robbie, he swung the black sword at him. Robbie's hand came up in a single reactive second, and as the black blade crashed down, a shield exploded on to his arm, and three golden Pendragon's absorbed the blow and wailed in pain, as Mordred lurched back with fear in his eyes. The memory of Arthur, and the fear he felt in his final moments shook him to the core, and he staggered backwards afraid of the symbol of his father and true king of Britain. Robbie moaned under the shield and sat up as he watched Mordred step backwards shaking a finger at him with fear.

"That's not yours, you cannot use it, it is his, I saw it on his horse. Who are you? You cannot be him; it is not possible I killed him. The spear? I watched and laughed." He looked with fear into the clear brown eyes of Robbie, who now felt renewed strength flow into him. "THAT IS NOT YOURS; YOU HAVE NOT THE RIGHT TO USE THAT ON ME!" Mordred screamed with fear like a small child before his strict father, Robbie pulled his painful hand on the rail, and lifted himself up biting down hard with the pain. He rose unsteadily to his feet and looked Mordred in the eyes.

"This is mine son of evil, he knew you would come back, and he left it for me." Robbie nodded slowly as he walked forward, the shield now held up right in front of him. Mordred shook more violently, the black blade loose in his hand as it swung to his side, his eyes watching the shield in total terror. "Your father, the High King of the Britain's, he hated you Mordred and he wanted you dead, he pushed Excalibur into you and took your life." Mordred placed his hand on his stomach as if he was reliving the memory, his lip trembled and he looked up with one black eye and one blue.

"OH GOD SAVE ME FROM THIS PLEASE."

It was hard to tell who screamed the loudest. Was it Mordred in fear of his father's shield? Or was it Billy trapped in an internal hell trying to get free from the prison of the Dark Ones son? The flicker of blue in the right eye was a memory from Robbie's past, and he staggered wearily forward towards the now mixed personalities of what was Billy, and was now Mordred. Robbie shook his long wet hair from his face.

"Billy fight him, come on Billy for the first time in your life repay the love of your mother of Loxley." Mordred shuddered, as the internal conflict seemed to have hit a resounding note. Robbie saw the conflict in the two eyes. "She loved and raised you Billy, repay her and help her other son, your brother of the woods." Mordred shuddered as he shook his head, Robbie knew that Billy was doing his best to come back, and force through the magic to free himself of the evil contained within him. Robbie smiled. "That sounds like a plan to me Smooth Billy." Mordred screamed and brought his hands to his ears.

"NO... I WILL NOT LET YOU WIN; I WILL NOT GO BACK I SHOULD HAVE BEEN KING AND I WILL BE AGAIN, LEAVE ME!!!"

Robbie began to laugh a quiet laugh, as he watched the tortured Mordred and stepped closer; his own eyes now looking right into the blue eye of Billy's. "Come on Billy boy, get rid of him, Alice needs you... Your child will be born soon, you will be the father of a son of Loxley, I am lord and can grant you a pardon." The blue eye filled with a tear, and Mordred screamed in agony, as the love of a child and Alice surfaced.

"YOU WILL NOT DEFEAT ME, I AM THE KILLER OF A KING, YOU CAN NOT COME BACK, YOU ARE MINE FOREVER."

Robbie gritted his teeth as he came closer, his hand slipping to his belt behind his shield, where the moonstone on the dagger shone brightly sensing its purpose. "Come on Billy what you waiting for? Be the man of Loxley we made you, and fight him. Prove to your lord you are worthy, show your mother and brother the love you really felt before this scum polluted you." Robbie's eyes filled with his anger and they shone darkly for the blue eye of Billy's to see clearly. "I KNOW YOU LOVE ME AS A BROTHER, NOW FOR THE SAKE OF HEARNE YOUR MASTER, PROVE IT WOODSMAN!" The fierceness in Robbie's eyes burned brightly as he screamed at his brother locked deep under the layers of evil. Mordred fought hard to contain Billy, but he fought a power greater than he had ever known.

He fought truth, the truth that Billy was no longer a Knox. He had been raised as a man of Loxley and he had been proud of it. A woman, who had given her home and her love to him without question, had loved him unconditionally. He had lived side by side with the man now before him, and he had without doubt loved him as his brother. Billy felt hope, and it was defeating Mordred. The hope of being free and loving his child, and Alice rose inside Mordred. The love of Robbie his brother, the love of the woman who wore her hair in a bun, and spoke with the softest and most caring of voices. The woman, who took him in her arms one night in the snow, and nursed him to health, and gave him a home. A home of love where he could look into the kindest hazel eyes he had ever known, and see nothing but the love they had held for him.

Mordred screamed a wail so loud that Robbie jumped back. Mordred lifted the sword and ran at Robbie, the dagger came out glowing in his hand, and as the sword blade crashed down, the hilt of the dagger kissed into the black blade. White light filled the hall, and screams wailed into the air of a woman and man locked in a verbal battle. Robbie's arm shook with the force, as the dagger fought to pull the evil from the sword made by Victor Thornson, the last great sword maker of the great circle of swords men.

Robbie felt the sudden impact on his legs, and before he realised what had happened, he was falling backwards, the step hit his head and his eyes filled with white light, he rolled and crashed down the steps, the floor and ceiling bouncing in his eyes at high speed, and the ceiling shook violently as he stopped.

Robbie's head spun and his eyes blurred, he tried to move but the pain in his arms and legs was too much, his head lolled round and his vision shook for a moment, and as it cleared, he saw a dark shape of a middle aged man lift the armour clad Mordred on the top step to his feet. With his arm around him, he steadied him. Voices swirled in Robbie's mind as he heard the weakened voice of Mordred.

"Hesketh we must kill him." Robbie's eyes vibrated and his head spun and blackness took him. Hesketh dragged the limp weakened figure of Mordred up the corridor, as Mordred raised a weak arm still holding the black blade and pointed it back to the stairway. "Hesketh I must go back and kill him." His eyes caught a glimpse of the sword; it was dull and darkened as if burned.

"It's alright Master Knox, we can finish him again. There is great danger we must leave here; your mother wants you back in safety. Leave the woodcutter he will be back." Mordred was too weak to fight and staggered along led by the butler through the dark lair of the black Raven.

Robbie lay crumpled at the bottom of the stair, the golden sword lay three feet away, and the golden knife was just by his hand. The shield was now once again his ring, his eyes were closed, and blood was running down his forehead, and he did not move. Jett gasped as she came round the corner weary and tired her face splattered with blood and sweat. "NO!"

She flew across the hall tears filling her eyes, and collapsed by his side. She pulled him into a hug and held him tight, he moaned and she laughed with relief. Robbie raised his arm around Jett's back to hug her. The shield clattered loudly, and she jumped and twisted back, as the vile looking small men in red tunics raised their pipes to blow. She reacted without thinking spreading herself across the limp body of Robbie. Violet arrows hit them and they shot backwards out of sight, Jett turned and smiled. "Hey... Cheers guys."

Saff ran across the hall and dropped to her knees as Keith looking slightly worse for wear held his bow up and watched the balcony. Saff stroked Robbie's face and he opened his eyes. "Rune?" She looked up at Jett who hunched.

"I had eighteen down there, a real tough bunch of buggers I can tell you, I haven't seen her. I came back and found him like this a minute before you did."

Saff looked down at Robbie. He seemed to be drifting in and out of consciousness; she took his pendant and gave it a soft squeeze. "Take him back Jett, we will find her." Saff stood up and stepped back as the white circle appeared on the floor, Destiny slithered across the floor to his hand, and Jett reached for the dagger. She jumped back as a face appeared in the moonstone on the handle.

"Do not touch the knife with your bare skin, it must know only the hand of the bowman." Jett grinned as she recognised Gwendolyn's voice. She took her cloak, and lifted the dagger, and slid it into the sheath on Robbie's belt.

"See you Grandma Gwen." Robbie and Jett slid through the floor and disappeared. Saff slid her arm round Keith.

"Where now?"

He shrugged. "I suppose the higher we go, the nearer we get. Rune is after the Dark One; she has to be at the top... I hate bloody stairs." Saff smiled, and gave him a soft kiss on the cheek. She picked up her bow and turned with him, she gave a long sigh.

"Up we go then." Together they walked slowly and cautiously up the stairs, and peered round the corner.

Morgan le Fey scurried around her room. It was a small compacted little room with two blue stained glass round windows. A small heavy old wooden table sat in the centre, on which rested a large leather bound, and very old parchment book. The whole of the room was filled with bottles of shimmering liquids, and dried fungal looking ingredients. Strange tools and silver objects hung in rows on the edges of the shelves, these were her devices of extraction, for her many and varied ingredients.

She scurried as if agitated and in a rush, she slid the large book under her arm and collected a small rack with a handle, in which many shimmering bottles sparkled. "I will show her." She cursed under her breath. Collecting all her things, she swiftly stepped onto the black metal spiral stair, and began to descend backwards. The bottles rattled and chinked as she wove round to the ground of her rooms. Morgan turned and caught her breath.

"Going somewhere witch?" Rune stood by the doors with her back pressed against it. "You have something of my grandfather's I believe?" Her blue eyes covered the wooden rack in her hand, and they flicked back to stare deeply into le Fey's.

"Your friend was lucky not to burn herself, and you for that matter. No worry I can finish the job." Morgan slowly crouched, as she placed the rack on the floor, and then slid out the large book and placed it on a small table beside the base of the spiral stair.

Rune looked at the heavy book, with its black leather binding and golden edged pages, it was very old, and she knew from the descriptions she had been given, just which book it was. "You still have not learnt have you child? You cannot defeat me; I am busy and am growing weary of your interference."

Rune leaned away from the door; she was prepared and expected something any moment. "Tell me Morgan, why wait all this time? You could have taken the world any time in the past when man was weaker, why now?"

Morgan looked impatient; her dark eyes scowled at Rune. "What, I have to teach you as well? What does it matter to you when I do anything? You could never understand the complex nature of the magic I have woven."

Rune took another careful step forward. "I don't know, my grandfather is after all Merlin, enlighten me." Her slender frame moved gently forward, her bright blue eyes never leaving the cold stare of Morgan le Fey. "You like I, were once a student of the white lines, why change?"

Morgan shook her head in amazement. "You have no understanding of the power I can control; it will burn you to a cinder if you even tried to look at it. Life is no power compared to that of knowledge... Knowing it all is everything, you think I give a dam about the power of life?" She looked like an irritated parent whose child had asked too many questions.

"Yet you must have studied life to have lived so long? Without the power of life, you could not have lived long enough to finish your study... Was that why you needed Gwendolyn and Opal?" Morgan sniffed arrogantly.

"They were tools of the trade girl; have you no idea of the magic that rules the universe?"

Rune smiled at her. "A life for a life, the charm of bonding and the charm of breaking, I know of the charms that you seek. Only the ruler of life can read those runes, Gwendolyn and Opal would never have translated them correctly for you. That is why your son is still trapped by a sword, you do not have them Morgan. Only I and the Green Lord can use them."

Morgan flicked her wrist, almost dismissively, at the sound of his name. "That bunch of old sticks, what use is he with his riddles and his talking in circles?" She seemed almost interested in being able to have a discussion with someone from her own profession. She gave Rune a curious look. "You have an interest in these matters? Why would the flower girl want to turn against her old father of logs, and side with me?"

Rune's eyes sparkled as she smiled at the dark witch. "I am interested in what it is that has held your mind for so long. Time is hard to endure for any of us." She took a few more steps forward towards her.

Morgan looked unsure at Rune. "You care what entertains me for a thousand years?" She sneered with her white drawn face, and her eyes burned with distrust. "You have power enough for your life, why are you so concerned about mine?" Rune shrugged as if losing interest and her eyes met the Dark Ones.

"You keep telling me of your true powers, and yet I have not seen them, I have matched you several times; it seems odd to me that with such extreme power, you fail to use it. Why is that?"

Morgan seemed to rise as she swelled with pride from the flattery of Rune. "The powers of the dark lines can consume easily if not followed correctly, you have little knowledge of this child, it is dangerous and takes time. The charms must be spoken correctly and fluently, it takes many life times to learn." Rune seemed fascinated and nodded as she walked forward and gave a smile.

"I see…Yes… the language of the old Runes, of course they can be tricky, I have heard my grandfather say that, I once heard him say the runes of the taking spell and I practiced it, but could never get the words to come out right…what was it he told me?" Rune looked at the ceiling as if trying to remember. "Nowled nay destraught, draw be mitt hanta… nowled nay craf devow mitt…" Rune frowned as if trying to remember. The Dark One looked delighted, and tried to encourage her. Rune shook her head, and the Dark One sighed.

"It's POW." Her eyes widened as she realised she had just completed the ancient runic charm, Rune smiled at her.

"All that power, which of us is the fool now old woman? Caught by the same trick you played on all the others." Morgan screamed as blue light exploded out of her, and her powers were drawn back to the lines of time, Rune lifted an empty bottle from the rack and looked at it. The dark crystal coating sparkled, as she pulled the cork and held it into the air, the blue light was sucked into the bottle with a long terrified painful wail and Rune pushed in the cork and waved her glowing purple hand over the top. It crystallised instantly and the Dark One was caught and imprisoned.

She gave a little giggle as she dropped it into her pocket, and lifted a jar with golden sparkling essence out of the rack. She gave it a huge smile. "Hi Grandfather, soon have you back." She slid the bottle into her other pocket, and then lifted a bottle of white shimmering liquid out, and inspected it carefully. Rune stared and nodded at the bottle as she slid it into the top pocket of her tunic; she hummed as she lifted the black book, and walked back to the doors. She picked up the white bow and its matching quiver and slung them over her shoulder.

Saff and Keith came warily along the corridor as Rune stepped out of the door; she gave them a big grin. "All is clear now."

They looked at each other bemused as Rune walked down the corridor towards them. "We have little time this place will soon fall; the magic used to build it will fail shortly as will many of the tall walls. I need to find a window. I have to get back across to Rose, but first to Robbie, is he alright?"

Saff nodded. "He is quite bashed about but he will be fine, Rune is she dead…? Have you killed her?"

Rune looked at the two of them both looking very surprised indeed, as they stood and stared at her. Her bright eyes twinkled. "She is not dead, but she has been contained for a while. She has escaped before and she will again, she knows some old magic, for now we are safe." She gave Saff a smile. "Is my Robbie really alright? I felt him go back."

Saff nodded. "He was thrown down the stairs, but I think he has nothing too serious wrong with him."

"Good let's hurry there is much to prepare, York is in big danger."

At the bottom of the steps where the gargoyle had fallen through the broken window, Rune waved her hand across in front of her, and a ring of violets ran up one side and across the top and down again. The curtain of light shimmered and she stepped into it followed by Saff and Keith. They gasped as they walked right into the yard of the house of good hope. Alley stood smiling, her lilac blouse blowing about her tight brown leather trousers. "You took your time I've been waiting ages." Rune gave her a big hug.

"It has been harder than we expected, are you ready? We have quite a few injured." Alley lifted her bag, slipped on her black brimmed hat, and stepped forward as Rune waved her hand back across the shimmering curtain, and then walked though into the landing of her house in Loxley.

Alice jumped with surprise, as Rune appeared just in front of her. "I can see why Robbie does not like that, you made me jump."

"Where is he? Is he all right? I need to see him." Alice smiled and touched her arm.

"Rune he is fine, a little bashed about and very tired, he is asleep in his bedroom." She smiled and kissed Alice on the cheek.

"Thanks." She ran down the landing, and in through the door and gasped as she saw him. His head was bandaged, and it looked like he had several stitches in his head. His right hand was bandaged and splinted, and a tight bandage bound his broken ribs. A line of stitches ran across his left shoulder, his eyes were closed and both blackened, and he seemed to mumble very quietly. She slipped carefully on to the bed and leaned forward gently kissing him.

Robbie jerked slightly as he felt her lips, and gave a soft smile. "Hey beautiful"

Her bright blue eyes danced as she broke into a huge smile and he opened his eyes and looked at her. "Hi gorgeous." She kissed him gently on the lips and he strained with slight pain. Rune pushed her hand on to his stomach as she kissed him, and it glowed, bright purple. She pulled away and stroked the side of his hair off the bandage. "I wish you would be more careful; you worry me so much at times... You must sleep now and I will be back in a while, I have a few things to finish." Robbie gripped her arm.

"Not the Dark One." She gave him a smile, and pulled the bottle from her jacket and held it up.

"She is not dead, just a decrepit old wreck in Cornwall, I have her essence here, she will probably get free like she did last time, but for now we have her right where we want her... Ok have a sleep and I will be back soon, I want to see Rose and get Maggs back, Harry is missing her."

Rune handed the jar with the golden shimmering liquid to Una. "You know what to do?" She slipped out the dark glass bottle. "He will know what to do with this one; I will be back as quickly as I can. Alley will help Alice, just keep everyone here you are still all protected." Una nodded as Rune turned and hurried down the stairs, Jess jumped up with Robert Lox as she came down.

"Runestone, where did you come from?"

Rune gave her a quick hug. "Jess I want you to come with me, I will need your help." Jess looked confused but nodded in agreement. Robert winked at her. Rune turned to him. "He is in his bed if you want to sit with him a while?" Robert beamed a big smile.

"Aye, I do." Rune reached up and gave him a small kiss on the cheek.

"Go on Dad, look after your boy." Robert beamed, and she chuckled. Rune took Jess by the hand and waving her arm she opened the window and stepped out on to the viewing platform, Jess gasped as she saw the Raven tower above the dark castle.

"Is that it? Is that where you went?" There was a jangle and rattling sound followed by shrieks and wails, a mass of bushy blonde hair and beads and feathers ran into Rune, and squeezed her tight as Maggs mumbled wept words from somewhere under all the hair. Rune pulled her close and gave her a huge hug.

"They are all fine and waiting for you, the window is still open so hurry. He is there, your big baby pops and he is missing you so hurry." Maggs gave her a huge kiss and then swept through the veil of purple; they just had time to hear the shrieks of Harry as he ran down from the kitchen before Rune closed the window.

Rune walked over to the smiling Rose who was sat with a very dirty faced Grace. "Well girl, I got to hand it to you, they sent everything they had at us, and we fought a fight worthy of our people, they are stuck on the island, and will not be coming off for a while."

Rune gave Rose a big hug. "We have her under control, Mordred got away, Rob is fine he just got knocked around a lot.... Rose this is Jessie Lox, she is Rob's mother."

Rose gave her a warm smile, and she stepped forward and embraced Jessie. "Your son is a very brave laddie, we all owe him such a great deal, I cannot tell you of the difference he has made in just a week. He will be honoured here forever." Jess seemed much overcome, and she smiled as Rose spoke words of such quality about her son.

There was a deep rumbling sound behind them, and all of them turned and looked out across the wide bay and down to the island. The tall tower of black stone with its enormous black raven like top shook violently. Rune looked as the masses of woodsmen gathered along the edge of the shore in front of the black bridge. They waved their bows and swords, and cheered as the top of the tower fell inwards, and Stone rained down from the sky and crashed on the rocks below, smashing into the water to be beaten down by the rough sea. It fell inwards smashing through the roof of the other buildings and behind the high walls of the black fortress. A thick black acrid smoke rose up into the sky; it fanned out over the cliffs and drifted south blotting out the sun as it passed. The dust swept out over the bay and billowed across the water like a fog. It swirled like smoke in the breeze, as it gently blew along the black bridge, and the woodsmen danced and revelled in the moment. Rune gave a soft smile and turned away from the edge of the cliff top.

The old figure with long white thin hair, dressed in all white with a long pale blue cloak stood watching. He nodded softly to himself as he saw the tower fall, and he lifted his head and then gave a soft bow to Rune as she walked towards him. "My Lady of the Woods, again I am honoured." Rune pulled the old man close into an embrace.

"My Lord of the Isle, your line has done well. We have achieved half of the goal we set out to do."

Gwynfor smiled at her. "It was told he would clear this place; we both know that his meeting with her will happen at another place." Rune slipped his arm into hers and walked slowly with the frail old man towards Jess.

"My Lord this is Lady Jessica Lox... Jessie this is Gwynfor Lyle Osborn and Lord of the isle of Fae"

Jessie bowed and took his hand. "I am honoured to meet you, My Lord." The old man smiled as he took her hand.

"It seems my line has the gift of choosing exceptional women, I have heard much of you and your husband My Lady. Your son is indeed the true descendant of my grandson." Jessie looked very confused, and she looked to Rune for guidance.

"Gwynfor had a daughter, she was the mother of the first Robin Hood, and this Jess is your oldest living relative." The old man gave a wrinkled grin and his eyes twinkled with delight, he stepped forward and took her arm enjoying the surprise in her eyes.

"Come my dear, we have much to discuss, I see your son has learned surprise from his mother."

Rune stood with Rose as the old man walked slowly with Jess and spoke with her; Rose gave a soft sigh. "What now for Robert and yourself?"

"He will need to recover, and then the call to York, you have much to do here Rose, but we will return, and will be visitors often."

"I am sure with this victory; the men would like to see the hooded man and his Specialists walk amongst them again. I am sure they would like to thank him."

"They will Rose, he will return when he is well, we have many injured, and I think all of them would not want to miss their return here." Rose smiled as she looked out across a sea that was no longer hindered by the site of the ugly castle. Rune turned and took her hands in hers. "Until we meet my friend, take care of your people my Queen of the Scots." She leaned forward and kissed her cheek.

Rose gave her a slight bow. "Until we meet my friend and Lady of the Woods. Go with speed and stay safe." Rune turned, and waving her hand a violet curtain appeared in front of Jess and Gwynfor. They were so busy talking they just walked straight through, and Rune chuckled as she followed.

Gwinne was already hugging Gwynfor when Rune came through, and he beamed with delight as he stood once again on the isle of his people, she broke apart, and came over to Rune and pulled her into a tight hug. "My dear Runestone, how happy I am to see you." Her bright blue eyes shone with delight, and her robes of dazzling white flapped with the wind as she hugged her. "Come inside we have much to discuss."

Rune slipped out the white shimmering liquid contained with the bottle. "This is the last of Gwendolyn, it should be returned to her people and her home isle." She handed the bottle to Gwinne, who looked down at it and understood that Rune had only a short time.

"It should be done in early evening; it is a great thing you have done for the people of Fae Runestone. You have shown them great honour by this. Most would have taken it for themselves."

Rune gave a small smile and looked round at the coastline of silver sand. "One day this will be the isle of my daughter, she will want the true queen of the fairies here with her. Gwendolyn was born here; it is fitting she returns to the land of her people." Gwinne slipped a hand around Rune, and walked her across the wide green lawn and back to the tall carved Celtic cross. They passed and crossed the small lawn and entered in through the door talking and laughing.

Jess spent the rest of the afternoon talking to the old man, who reminded her so much of her own husbands father. They walked and talked, and Jess laughed and smiled as the old man told his stories and cracked jokes with her. Rune watched happy knowing that the past history of a whole line of Loxley was being passed on from its oldest member to its most studious. One day Jess would tell the stories to Iona, and the chain of knowledge would remain intact.

Amethyst appeared later to find the small crowd gathering by the cross. She had spent the whole day in the sea, and her hair hung damp and curled as her violet eyes peered out from underneath it. As the sun started to wane across the early evening sky, Rune whispered a silent incantation of return, and then drew the stopper from the bottle. White and pale blue light swept out and swirled into the sky, Rune watched with tears in her eyes as she felt a joy and happiness she had not known pass through her. The white mist swirled and then stretching out above them it fell like glittering snow on to the land.

A whispered voice echoed like a voice from the past in her ears. *"Hear me Runestone, for you have bestowed a great blessing on the people of the violet isle. Your daughter will prosper under us; you have secured her future and saved her people. Know you will have high honour here always."*

Golden light rose from the floor to meet the shimmering dust and fragments of light that fell to the floor, and as they met a blue haze formed and soaked back into the ground. The group stood silent for a while with bowed heads, and then slowly they stirred back to life, all had been in some way touched by the power of Gwendolyn. Gwynfor wiped tears from his eyes as he felt the love of a sister long since lost to him, Rune had honoured his family and its lines, returning the queen stirred deeply within him, as he knew that soon his time would come to an end as the new queen came forth. He felt a joy that a life of such age would be over, and he could pass into the other realm and join with all his family at last.

Rune turned, she had to leave and return to the life of the hooded realm and Robbie. Gwynfor smiled at her. "Have no fear; my time is not done yet. We will meet again My Lady of the Woods. I will await the coming of the queen."

Rune gave him a hug and kissed him softly. "Robbie will want more time alone I would think, he will be pleased to know you will meet once again... Goodbye Gwynfor until we meet." Rune turned to Gwinne, and they embraced.

"Take care of my daughters Runestone, and hurry back to us." Amethyst turned smiling and picked her small grey bag off the grass.

"This is going to be cool I can't wait to meet everyone." She gave her mum a big hug. "I will see you soon, don't worry about me mum I am with Crystal." Gwinne kissed her daughter who turned with a huge smile to Jess and Rune. "Ok I am ready." Rune waved her arm across the air in front of her, and a veil of shimmering violet appeared. Jess hugged Gwinne, and turned to the opening. Rune waved and stepped through followed by Amethyst and Jess. Gwinne watched the veil of light fade and then took Gwynfor by the arm.

"I think a nice cup of something is in order." Gwynfor gave her a cheeky grin and slowly as the light began to fade, they headed across the grass to the house and the small warm kitchen.

The breeze blew across the island of Iona and the grass leaned over and rippled. The sea gently lapped onto the white sandy beaches, an in the hills around the rocks tiny shimmering lights flickered and glowed in the dark. Two figures rose from the well of youth, and walked to meet their lord returned. The sparkling lights hovered in the darkening air, and it was known that the spirit of the queen of Fae had returned to the land of buried kings and saints. Iona was now about to start its long preparations, for the time of the violet Isle was about to begin again. The new Queen would come and her name would be that of the violet stone. Iona the queen and island would become one.

CHAPTER THIRTEEN

SECRET UNDERSTANDINGS

Robbie stirred, and opened his eyes, it was dark, and through the window he could see the clear sky covered with stars, his arm throbbed, and his ribs hurt when he moved. He felt the warmth of Rune beside him and looked down on the long golden and red hair shimmering in the moonlight. Her face looked almost like plaster in the moonlight, she looked a lot paler than usual, and he softly stroked the loose strands of hair from her face. She moved gently beside him and slid a pale arm across his chest as she snuggled towards him. He tried to move closer but it was a very painful affair, and he relaxed back into the pillows and breathed with difficulty. He smiled as he watched her sleep beside him, and he felt a great relief to be back at home again with Rune. She was beautiful, kind and loving, she had become over the year everything to him, and now he lay in the dark and watched her, the mother of children yet to come. Robbie lay there and recounted his moments with Mordred, his insides showed very mixed feelings as he fought with hate and love.

Billy had betrayed him in ways he could not even comprehend, and yet as he had stood there looking into one blue eye in a face he knew so well, he had felt the love of his brother, and wanted desperately for Billy to force Mordred out and come back to him. His mind seemed to whirl with endless thoughts of the past, and what could be in the future. How long he lay thinking he had no idea as at some point he slipped from this world into the world of dreams, where Billy had come out and fought with Mordred using Excalibur. Pictures flooded his sleepy mind of Rune and Iona running through the glade laughing, and happiness seemed all around him as Rune ran up and kissed him, her bright blue eyes close to his. He opened his eyes and there before him was the sapphire blue eyes he loved so much, she smiled and her eyes twinkled. Her voice was soft and quiet. "Hi gorgeous."

"Hey beautiful." She slid up and kissed him gently, he was very tender, and he felt the slice in his shoulder burn as he moved, she curled very carefully round him.

"You took too big a risk Rob; he is a lot more powerful than you thought." He looked at her white concerned face lay beside him, her dusky freckles, pale on her almost porcelain skin. "Billy was good with a sword and very strong, Mordred would have had the use of those skills, you took him for granted, and you are very lucky he did not kill you."

"It wasn't him; it was his servant who crept up on me from behind that did the damage, Mordred was losing to Billy." Rune lifted her head and looked at him strangely.

"Billy!" Robbie nodded painfully.

"Billy tried to push Mordred out, I was encouraging Billy, and it was defeating him, when someone hit me from behind and I fell down the stairs... Honestly I was fine." He lifted a heavily bandaged hand and stroked her face softly, she leaned her head on to it and he knew that although she was trying to hide it, she had been frightened at the sight of him all cut, stitched and bandaged. He took a deep breath as his chest tightened, the bandages were very tight and he found it difficult to breathe easily. He gave her a soft smile. "It's nice being home alone again." She giggled.

"We are hardly alone; our house looks like a war zone. All the bedrooms are full and the chairs; we have the stitched and bandaged everywhere." Her smile faded as she realised that he was the only one who had not yet been told.

Robbie looked at her carefully as her eyes fell away to the bed and back, he watched the sadness creep over her face slowly and he did not need to ask why, it was a face he had seen only twice before. "Who?" It was a long quiet drawn out question, for which he did not really want an answer. The tears welled in Rune's eyes as she looked mournfully at him. It confirmed his thoughts, and he prepared for the loss of another member of his team. She swallowed as she tried to find her voice.

"Martin." It could not have been worse; he closed his eyes and bit his lip as he leaned back into the pillow. The picture of his happy smiling proud wife, and his two beautiful small girls came to his mind as he swallowed down hard. "I am sorry Robbie, he tried to take on the Dark One to protect all of us with an arrow, she turned it back on him, and I had no time to stop it." She pushed her face into the bed at the side of him, and he felt the soft vibration next to him as she wept.

He laid his hand on her head and stroked her hair, "I will have to go and see his wife and daughters." He tried to sit up and fell back with the pain moaning. Rune raised her sad face with wet eyes.

"Rowan has gone with Jade, I got up earlier while you were sleeping, and he wanted her to know as soon as possible, he knew you were not up to it, so he said he would do it... He left about an hour ago."

It was in a way a relief, but in others it was not, Robbie was the leader and the Lord of Loxley. It should have been his job to see her, although at the moment it did seem a little difficult. His whole body ached with pain and his arms were stiff and heavy. "I want him to be given the funeral of a true Loxley hero. He was one of our best, and he should be praised for his defence of this realm. I will miss him; he was a good woodsman and a true friend." Rune snuggled closer to him, and he held her as close as was not painful. They lay together silently for some time lost in thought, Robbie listened to her breathing softly beside him, and closed his eyes and lay back on the bed trying to find a way of relaxing that was not painful.

He must have dozed off because he woke with a jolt. Rune had slid over his arm and on to his right shoulder, she was fast asleep, her arm gently resting on his stomach, he turned his head to see Steph with her arm in a sling watching, she gave him a soft smile. "How long have we been asleep?" He kept his voice low to avoid waking Rune.

"A few hours... How are you feeling?"

He breathed hard. "In pain." Her smile widened to a grin.

"There is a lot of it about, that lot out there are a right bunch of babies, and you should hear Bear moaning about his headache, I think he has given me one just listening to him."

"Are they badly hurt? I have no idea what happened to everyone yet." His voice trailed a little. "Rune has told me of Martin."

Steph nodded sadly. "He was a nice bloke, I used to talk to him a lot, I really liked him. I will miss our chats in the dark woods on watch, discussing the finer points of the old sciences."

"Sciences?"

"Oh yeah... Martin loved science; he knew a great deal; he would talk to dad for hours about it. Read just about every book in the stockade on science."

"I never knew, I knew he was well educated, you could tell by his manner and the way he formed his words. He was a nice guy with a very nice family, I feel so sorry for them."

"Rowan came back a while ago; Beth is up there now with them. Poor love she really loved him; it will be hard for her without him. Mind you, Rowan looked wretched it's not something I would want to do."

Robbie looked down at the floor near the wall opposite. "It should have been me; I am the Lord; I should have spared him the task." Rune gave a little murmur, and slid her hand up on to Robbie's shoulder. He gasped and gritted his teeth as she brushed the red angry looking stitches.

Steph nodded as she gave a little chuckle. "She always was a fidget as a small girl; she has grown up so much this year already. I hardly recognised her at Dunnottar. Her command and authority was total, you do know don't you that she slipped off alone to face the Dark One?"

Robbie looked at her, and then back to Steph. "No, I didn't, I thought she had others around her, she told me Martin died protecting her and the others."

Steph nodded. "Maddy saw that happen, she then sent everyone back leaving herself alone. That was when she went after the Dark One and faced her in her own rooms. Keith and Saff found her coming out. Robbie that was very brave, she must have some power to not fear the Dark One like that."

"Rune fears her, and she does not underestimate her. She knew before we entered the tower that the Dark One was not there. It was her essence that was there, the Dark One is in Tintagel."

Steph stared at him in wonder. "How is that possible...? You mean she was there the night we were, and she got away?" Robbie nodded slowly.

"It looks that way, Rune was not up to full power, and she had no way of knowing. Even if she had known, Rune could not have faced her back then." Steph silently nodded as she watched her daughter sleeping in Robbie's arms.

"Will it ever end? It could be Jade or Rowan, maybe even Pete or me next. I worry so much about it all Robbie." He looked up from Rune and leaned back as he sighed.

"There really is no answer; I am too deep in it all now. I am slowly losing people I care about, and I have no idea when it will all stop... I want it too; all I want is to live here in peace with Rune."

"You will not be happy to see Fuse then, he is down stairs waiting for either you or Skip to surface, and somehow I think he will be waiting for some time, Treen has not left Skip for a second since he got here... Right, I know you are safe and well so I will head back to Pete and see how he is feeling. His colour is a lot better now." Steph leaned over and gave Rune a soft kiss; she patted Robbie on the arm and smiled as she left. He lay quiet on the pillows his mind once again filled with the struggle he faced, it was never looking like it would get any easier. His mind once again drifted on into sleep without him realising.

Rune giggled as she laced up his shirt. Robbie felt it rub on his stitches and winced. "I am sorry but all your open fronted ones are being washed. When I have a minute, I will make you some more... There we go you look fine." He looked in the mirror at his odd shape from all the bandages under his top. He hated getting dressed up; Rune pulled a matching green sling round his neck and lifted his arm. He looked like a sight, and frowned; she knelt down, and gave him a huge smile. "You are looking beautiful, and very like the lord you are." He rose up from the bed and gasped as his ribs hurt.

"Affairs of state, what the hell am I doing? I am a woodsman. At least it is here and not in the village, I could not cope with a crowd today. Is Martin's widow here yet?"

"No not yet, Beth is bringing her later." Robbie nodded. He felt very tired and in a lot of pain, Alice had given him a hot cup of a yellow earthy smelling tea to help ease the pain, but as yet it was not having much effect. Rune held his arm as he came down the stairs into the living area. She smiled sweetly holding on to his good arm, Skip remained sat down bandages and stitches all over him, as the others rose from their seats. Fuse came forward and introduced the group.

"Lord Loxley this is Lee Sherman of Settle, I believe his son Keith you already know? This is the new Ambassador from York, this is Elliot Selby."

Robbie nodded and took each of them by the hand. "Welcome to Loxley Gentlemen, I do hope you will excuse my lateness, we are not long returned, and have had men to care for." Rune smiled. "Have you met the Lady Runestone?" They both nodded to her.

Lee nodded and smiled. "My Lord it is nice to be home, I see you have received the place that your grandfather meant for you. It is a very lovely setting; he would be delighted to see it used in such a manner."

"It is nice to see the men of this land return, especially one who was a dear friend of my late grandfather... Please gentlemen sit down and be at ease while we talk, York has been on my mind for several days now." Selby smiled as he sat down, and waited for Robbie to address him. He was a man of medium build, and dressed very smartly in all black, his dark eyes surveyed the wounded lord as he moved in his seat to get comfortable. Robbie looked at the tanned face with a black neatly clipped beard, and well groomed hair. "Tell me Ambassador, how are things at York? I hope that the good trade you built up has not suffered with all of the activities of Knox."

He leaned forward in his chair and clasped his hands. "Trade so far is unaffected, but supplies from the north are almost at a standstill. Knox has a large army heading south, and we fear that York will be its first target, I have come here with our supporter to ask Loxley for aid My Lord."

Robbie smiled as he leaned back in his chair. "There is no doubt that Loxley will aid you Ambassador, I am just returned from Scotland where I saw the host that is preparing its march south. I need a little time with my advisor here, who will give me all the facts that I require, but I can assure you Ambassador that wherever the Knox Empire rises, Loxley will send aid."

Selby smiled and relaxed a little. "We have repaired the stone wall around us, but you must understand My Lord, we are not fighters, we are diplomats and well versed in commerce."

"Lord Jacques has given me a very detailed view of York, and I have been meaning to visit, but it has been a very busy time. Be at peace in the knowledge that our eyes are well and truly focused on York and the wide stretch of moor that falls before it. I believe Master Sherman has been very busy in that particular field?" Robbie looked up and noticed the cart with Beth sat on it pulling on to the edge of the glade. "Gents I must ask you to excuse me, I have lost a man in these past days, and I must attend to his widow...Fuse please extend every courtesy to our guests, and I will meet you all tomorrow at the village hall, we will have a good look at York and see what we can do. Thank you for your time."

Robbie struggled to his feet, the pain obvious as Rune helped him, he shook hands with both men, and then made his way to the glass doors, and out to the steps. Hanna Reef dressed in all black came across the grass of the glade. Robbie felt the bitter pain rise inside him; as yet again the responsibility of another man's death rested heavily upon his shoulders. Rune gave his arm a squeeze as she sensed the pain inside him.

He stepped forward on to the path and walked to the small gate, he swung it open Rune at his side, as Hanna looking upset and forlorn came across the grass guided by Beth. She looked up at Robbie with tears in her pale brown eyes, her shoulder length dark hair shining. Her face was very pale and withdrawn, and her eyes were red from the many hours of grief she had to endure. Robbie found it hard to speak.

"My dear Lady...I cannot express the sadness and loss I feel, which I know is by no means comparable to yours." Hanna raised her hand with a lace edged hankie and exploded into tears, she stepped forward and Robbie pulled his arm around her as she embraced him. Tears filled Rune's eyes as she watched Robbie with great care hold her while she wept. He spoke softly to her of the bravery, and the decency of her husband, and assured her that she would be well cared for and her husband honoured.

To Robbie though it seemed to have no meaning, how could it when he knew that she would live out the rest of her days, parted from the man she loved so much? It tore at his insides, as he felt useless holding this poor woman in his arms. Rune touched his shoulder and he turned with tears in his own eyes to look at her.

No words needed to be spoken; he knew she felt as he did, and that she understood the feelings inside him. Beth stood at Hanna's side and wept bucketful's, dabbing her tears on a large white hankie. Rune gently slid Hanna from Robbie, and pulling her close, she guided her into the kitchen. Beth followed leaving Robbie alone.

Robbie stood for a long time as the sun passed above him, down by the edge of the mere. His heart was heavy, and he felt an even greater burden than ever before. He stared at the still water reflecting the sun high above, he was lost in thought as the tall figure of Rowan came up by his side and laid an arm across his shoulder.

"You have not the power to protect us all Robbie, no matter how much you want to spare life, we will lose some. We all make the choice, including you whenever we face their armies, there is not a man here who has not accepted death in service of those who cannot defend themselves."

"I cannot imagine a world without my father in it; you have suffered the same fate as those children... How do you continue with such a hole in your life?"

Rowan breathed deeply and gave a long sigh. "I imagine him."

Robbie turned to him and looked at him. "Is that what you do when you sit alone?"

Rowan nodded. "It has been hard for me to lose the man I looked up to, I left home in the morning, and by nightfall he had gone forever. It is the strangest of things to happen my friend, the emptiness you feel inside knowing you will not see him again is terrible. I still wake in the night in hope he will be there when I get up, I felt like a huge piece of who I was, and who I will be, has been torn out of me with great force, and it is a wound I have feared would never heal."

Robbie was quiet as he listened carefully to Rowan. "Has it...you know...healed?"

Rowan looked at Robbie and he saw the haunted look on his face. "It could only heal if he came back, I know he never will. I sit alone and close my eyes and I can see his face, and in my mind, I talk to him. I tell him how much I am missing him and how hard it is without him. He tells me he is there and he gives me advice, which I know is my heart talking to me. Inside my heart, he will always be alive and so the wound slowly repairs and the pain lessens a little. It will never fully heal, and I will never let it, for while I carry the wound I can never forget him. He will be beside me all my life and guide me. That is how I cope with it my friend, I cannot speak for others, it helps me to remember every detail of his life, and replay them in my mind. If I forget him, he will die forever and I will not let that happen. I have no idea how, but it has given me the strength to fight forward and survive."

Two tears ran down from Robbie's eyes as he felt the overwhelming sense of privilege in knowing Rowan had shared a deep and well hidden secret, somehow he knew it was the only time he would ever reveal this. Robbie lifted his arm and pulled Rowan close. "Thank you, my friend, you have honoured me." Rowan patted Robbie's shoulder in appreciation and gathered himself, as he turned and looked across the mere and dried his eyes. The two men stood tall and proud as they watched the still Mere, and the trees reflected in the water on the opposite side of the bank.

The day drew by slowly, and Robbie spent the rest of it sat in a chair on his bedroom balcony lost in thought. The loss of another comrade weighed heavy on the group, they all seemed to be quieter and more in thought than normal, melancholy drifted in the air, as the group began to recover from their injuries and their grief. Robbie thought of Rowan and his father, and he felt the deep pangs of loss as he thought of his experience with Mordred.

He had called out to a lost brother. A brother who has caused him great pain, and yet in his hour of need, Robbie had taken his side and shown the loyalty of his kin. He had wanted so badly for Billy to appear and he knew that if he had won and Mordred had been thrown out, Robbie knew he would have embraced his brother and not killed him. Billy was in every way the enemy, but he was also a brother and a man of Loxley in Robbie's eyes. His mind filled with confusion and for the first time in his life, Robbie found a problem he could not discuss with Alice.

Sleeping that night was difficult, Rune had placed her hands gently on his ribs and tried to ease the pain, it had worked for a while, but now he felt the pain return. He moved from side to side trying to get comfortable in the dark. Rune turned over and looked at him. "Sorry... I just cannot seem to settle, what with the pain every time I breathe and the thought of Martin's funeral... I am not going to sleep, it's useless." She gave a comforting smile and then waved her hand across him, he felt the warmth wash over him, and a strange painless relaxed feeling pass through him, and soon his eyes fluttered and he slipped into a deep and restful sleep.

Robbie woke to the sound of birds singing outside in the trees, autumn was approaching and the birds were gathering for their winter flights south. Rune was already up and sat brushing her hair at the table; she spotted him watching in the mirror and smiled at him. "Hi gorgeous."

He smiled. "Hey beautiful." He leaned forward and felt a small twinge of pain, it seemed a lot less than the previous day, and he found he could actually sit up without wanting to yell aloud. Her hair sparkled as the brush passed through it; somehow it seemed brighter against the black velvet top she wore. Robbie noticed the clothes laid out on the small chair in emerald green, and felt his stomach jolt. He was not looking forward to the funeral of Martin at all.

The long black cloth draped cart sat in the yard at the farm. The polished casket of Martin sat on the top surrounded by violets and chrysanthemums. John and Harry dressed in long black robes hitched the horses with long black plumes on their heads, and pulled them round ready. Robert Lox in his Wolfhead robes stood up front, as a line of the fellowship prepared the way, and fell in behind the cart ready. Robbie stood holding the weeping Rune, as she sniffled into her hankie. He watched Hanna and her two four year old daughters guided by Beth and Jess, come out behind the back of the cart and stand weeping as they prepared for the journey to the burial ground.

John and Harry took the reins of the horses, and the procession began at a slow pace. Down Hawthorn lane and into the Village Street the procession slowly trooped, everyone came to their gates and bowed their heads in respect for the fallen man of Loxley, Hanna walked with her daughters held in each hand, and Robbie felt her sorrow and his insides twisted.

The procession passed down the road past all the new wooden houses, and across the front of the gates past the barracks. Bowmen lined the walls in salute to their fallen comrade, and slowly they approached the side gate and entered the woodland of sacred rowan trees outside the walls. Woodsmen stood along the whole of the route to guard the procession and offer their respects, outside the wall was not a safe place, but the burial ground was in a sheltered and peaceful part of the wood, just below a small stone circle.

Robbie was pleased to see that his father commanded the service, and his mind wandered as they slid Martin off the cart, and carried him to the freshly dug grave. He stood with his head bowed feeling completely helpless and knowing he alone carried the guilt of another man's life. He watched the group who were his friends, and saw the pain on their faces, Big John was distraught, as was Steph who wept into Smokes, and Fish hung his head low as memories of his brother surfaced. Beth howled, and Rags kept very quiet and looked the saddest Robbie had ever seen her.

The whole group stared at the casket as it lowered into the hole, knowing that once again their endeavours had ended in loss. The service ended and he was not even aware that people were leaving; he stood silent and still staring at the mound of earth, which now contained his friend and comrade. Rune gave him a little tug, and he looked up at her red eyes. "You must not carry the blame Rob." She had told him before and it had not meant anything to him then.

"I am Lord of Loxley, I am responsible for everyone, I handpicked Martin to join us, he did not volunteer for this, Hanna is a widow because of the choice's I made Rune, and that is my responsibility."

It was a long quiet walk back through the woodland to the side gate, Rowan and Jade shadowed him, and Jett and Rafe walked up front. He turned on the road inside the stockade, and took the short cut up to the Village Hall, he did not feel much like talking but he had an ambassador to meet.

Robbie looked at the table in the busy hall and examined the map carefully, the tall black wall curved down the country from Aberdeen to the top of the Yorkshire moors where it turned and ran to the coast at Scarborough. From the black wall to the edges of York was a thirty-mile gap of trees and wild moor. It was a long front line to defend; especially considering the amount of soldiers that the Knox Empire had now brought together behind the high walls. The odds were stacked very heavily against York, and Robbie looked at the placement of the woodsmen around them, there would be little chance of attack until the black army came forth, and out of their walled protection.

The grey haired figure of Fuse came up at his side and looked at the map with him; Robbie looked at the warm friendly face and the pale blue watery eyes of a man who had served him with great dedication. Robbie patted his back. "My friend we have a very difficult job on our hands, this one will be fierce, it is very open country there will be few places to hide out there." Fuse nodded in agreement.

"I have read of many such battles, and all of them have been hard fought and cost many lives, he will create a lot of death on those fields. I really fear for York."

Robbie heard doubt in the voice of Fuse for the first time in a long time. "I think we should evacuate York and bring all the innocent lives back here, if what I saw at Dunnottar is just a small part of the army, we will be heavily outnumbered."

Fuse took off his half moon glasses, and polished them on his shirt. "I have advised the ambassador that York should consider it, we have space in Old Sheffield, and around Bradford, there is a lot of woodland below Hull, their people could relocate quickly and return if we are successful, they say they are not adapted to woodland life and their people would suffer. I think they are foolish not to listen to us, My Lord you must convince them."

Robbie sighed. "I will do what I can." Fuse turned to walk away and Robbie called him back. "Fuse." He turned and looked at him. "I don't suppose there is a way we can get behind these walls is there, you know... have a look at what's coming?"

Fuse considered his point for a second. "Lee Sherman is probably the only one who could tell you, he has contact with a man inside near Scarborough." Robbie smiled.

"Thanks, I will ask him."

Lee was sat outside on the fence, smoking a long clay pipe and watching the bowmen on the range with Keith and Saff, he nodded to Robbie as he approached. "My Lord do you smoke?" He gave a sharp cough.

"No thanks... I am not sure you should either." Robbie gave him a pat on the back as he coughed even harder. The smell from the pipe was quite pungent. "You should see Joe, he grows that stuff, and it smells a lot nicer than that does." Lee gave one final big cough and sat back up.

"This is wild hemp not tobacco, I have not seen real tobacco in about 20 years, if this Joe fellow has some, I would love to acquire some, this stuff is awful but you do get used to it after a while, it just has the odd habit of sneaking up on you."

Robbie looked at the pipe with distaste. "I came to see the ambassador but he appears to be somewhere else, I wanted to try and convince him he should evacuate York of all the women and children."

"He won't do it, god knows I have tried to convince him for weeks, they are a strange lot up in York, they love their wall and their markets, but they will not see reason. The only reason they still have a city is that we all planned their protection... Pride Young Robbie... It was the downfall of mankind, and yet they have not learned a bloody thing. They think like Knox does bricks and stone, I remember life before the red death, I prefer my life now, less hate and greed and more standing together." He turned and looked at Robbie. "You have done your grandfather proud Robbie lad, you have so much of him inside you, I am not sure you realise it, he would have been so proud of you for fighting for the innocent."

Robbie smiled. "I do not really remember him; he died when I was very young, you knew him well didn't you?"

"He was a lot older than me, but he was my best friend. I loved him dearly. Aye he was a good apple and that is for sure, hell of a man like your dad. I tell you Robbie when old Jake shouted, all of Loxley paid attention, he had true authority and yet I never once saw him abuse it. He was fair and just and also the kindest person I have ever known. I could tell you tales of him behind the scenes of Loxley that would make you weep." Robbie liked hearing about his grandfather, he had only really heard his mum talk, and he could see how much she had loved him. He felt a bond with Lee, knowing how much he had loved the old master of Loxley somehow it made him feel closer.

"Lee, I need to get into the city above York to have a look round, I need to do it alone. Can you get me in; I know you have a contact in there?"

Lee looked up at Robbie with mild surprise. "That is no mean feat young Robbie, not alone though. If you mean to go in you will have to take me along, I cannot let you go unaided. I understand you have lost a man; I know of the pain of leadership. Count me in and yes I will get you inside, but I cannot give my word that we will get out again."

Robbie nodded. "I know the risks, that's why I want to leave the others behind. I want to leave at dawn in two days, can you arrange it." Lee nodded as Robbie leaned off the fence.

"Make it three, there is much to arrange." The agreement was made, and Robbie walked up the roadway towards Hawthorn Lane and the Lox Farm.

Everyone had gathered back at the farm, where food and drinks had been supplied in the orchard. The group wandered around and talked, Robbie slipped quietly into the barn and pulled out his horse. He walked it round to the cottages, and then mounted up and rode off for home. Rune looked up from Alice and saw him, as he slipped up the lane. She smiled as she knew that he could not face them, his pain and loss she had felt in him all day, and she knew a walk in the woods would be his way of releasing his pain and coming to terms with things, she walked slowly to the gate and slipped through and headed to the barn. Jess gave a small smile as she saw Rune slip quietly away to her son.

Robbie grabbed extra arrows, and walked into the woods at the back of the house; he knew the paths by heart and wove quickly through to the tall stockade wall, where a small side gate was hidden. He laid the arrows down and buried them in loose leaves to hide them, and then turned and walked back into the trees towards the house. Rune sat on the seat by the steps as he came round the corner; he was surprised to see her but gave her a smile. "Hey beautiful, I thought you were at the farm?"

She stood up and slipped her arms around him. "I missed you; I knew you would try to avoid it, and when I saw the ambassador go into the post cabin, I knew you had finished and would slip past at some point. Robbie, you have to stop shouldering all the pain of these people, it was their choice to go." She pulled him into a soft kiss; he spun down and whisked her up into his arms. Rune gave a surprised scream. He felt the pain in his chest but wanted her close, and giggling he carried her into the house and up the stairs.

It was late evening when he woke, he felt warmth surging through him and he opened his eyes. Rune was sat across his lap her eyes glowing violet, her hands slowly moved across his ribs. She giggled as she noticed he was awake and leaned forward to kiss him. "You caught me...how does that feel?" He smiled as he lifted his arms and pulled her closer; the pain was more of a dull ache.

"That is so much better; can I take these bandages off and see if I can breathe better?" She sat up and looked for the two silver pins that held them together. She took out the pins, and pulled him into the sitting position. Slowly Rune undid the bandages and he felt the tension ease round his middle. He took a long deep breath, it hurt a little but he could live with that, he lay back and breathed freely as she rubbed the black bruised patterned skin from the bandaging on his chest. The house seemed quiet as he lay with Rune in his arms, Crystal and Amethyst would be back soon with Una, but all the others would return to their own places, and take their time to recover. Robbie enjoyed the quietness, and enjoyed the warmth of Rune curled on him. His sleep was deep and happy.

Robbie woke the following morning alone in bed, he felt strong and healthy although he still ached and his stitches did give a twinge as he slowly dressed. His shirt flapped as he came down the stairs and looked around the empty house. The door by the stairs was ajar and he knew that Rune was down at her table; so he wandered out into the front garden where he saw Una up the side of the house cutting fresh flowers for the kitchen table. Crystal was nowhere to be seen, and as he looked out across the glade, he could see ripples in the mere where Amethyst swam.

Robbie wandered into the trees, and enjoyed the light shade as the sun came through the now yellowing leaves above him. He walked with his hands in his pockets, his feet sinking into the deep damp brown leaves that had signalled the start of the autumn, and shed early. The air was damp and earthy, he breathed deeply, it had felt like a long time since he had wandered alone. His hair blew back in the breeze that softly cooled his face, and he felt a strong sense of life all around him. He had been so busy and involved for such a time that in many ways he felt like he had forgotten the importance of what he was trying to do.

Deep in the oldest part of the forest, he sat on an old fallen tree and buried himself in thought. The last birds of the year called above him, as the sun broke through in wider shafts where more leaves had fallen and created large gaps in the canopy. The grass seemed to be greener as more light cast down on to the floor, and Robbie felt that strong sense of belonging he had always felt reunited him with the world that he loved so much. His mind drifted as he felt the power and freedom of nature, here was his dream and for a moment, he understood how he had lost sight of it.

A firm hand gripped his shoulder as the white mist swirled around him, and Robbie turned and looked into the old wise eyes of Lord Hearne. He jumped to his feet and bowed. "My Lord, I am sorry I was lost in thought." The Green Lord gave a soft smile. His bark like face creased with more lines, and looked like the aged bark of the oak.

"I find this part of my realm an ideal place for thought my young Bowman; you will find peace and ease of mind here."

"I had forgotten my love of the woods for a while, and I needed to find it again."

Hearne creaked as he bent and slowly lowered himself to the old tree, he patted it for Robbie to sit by his side. "You have faced trials and have more to come; it is good you seek comfort and advice from the green world. I have felt the troubles inside you, as has my daughter of life. You rest for a few days before facing again the world of snakes, yet I read the doubt you hold." Hearne lifted his long dark twig like fingers to Robbie's shoulder and gave it a gentle squeeze. "You must let your instinct guide you; you have a strong heart, it will always point you in the right direction young Bowman. Share the trust that my daughter of life has in it and you will find the right path. I will say only this to you, take the one who will not be separated from you, his hand has always been steady beside you."

Robbie looked in disbelief at the Green Lord. "You know of my plans?"

Hearne gave a soft chuckle that sounded like the water of a stream as it chattered across the small smooth stones. "Very little can be hidden from me young Bowman. I think you show wisdom, your men need rest but the job cannot wait, stealth in small numbers I feel will bring a reward. My daughter of life will not take kindly to this young Bowman, she will fear for you."

Robbie nodded. "I understand My Lord, but I will not have her walk in that realm, she would be in danger the moment she entered, and she now holds the future of two lines. The risk must be mine and mine alone; I can walk unseen when I need to."

"I will watch over your companions my Bowman; they will heal faster under my gaze. The lives you have lost have taken some of their spirit, but it will heal and return before they are needed. Your woodland family has good heart, do not blame yourself for the choices they make, they have all faced and made the same choice as you have. Each man must follow his own destiny, and many are interwoven in the fabric of this place."

Robbie felt a little of unease within him lessen. "I am glad to have spoken with you My Lord; I feel more at ease knowing that you have seen what has been, and understood it better than I."

"You are still a sapling in the eyes of the woodland, and yet I see the making of a mighty oak. Once before I sat with a young sapling in doubt and I guided him to the path of knowledge, you favour him greatly for you were chosen for that reason, but know this my young Bowman, he too had the same doubts and yet he overcame them, and began the process that you will one day finish."

Robbie felt a strange sense of surprise; he had never for a moment considered that the first hooded man would have had doubts. Robin Hood in his mind was a man of action, a man certain of himself and filled with the confidence of a born leader. Somehow, it made him feel better and at ease knowing that he shared the same doubts as the legend of old. He smiled to himself as the old man got up, his legs creaking and groaning like the old trees in the wind. "I see my young Bowman you have good food for your thoughts, knowing is enough to open your path. I will be wherever you need me."

Robbie looked up and smiled at the old Lord. "Thank you, My Lord, you have given me much assurance, it has helped." Hearne smiled.

"You have time yet, spend it with my daughter of life, I feel she will comfort you and aid your recovery. Enjoy this time there is much to come. Goodbye my young sapling, we will talk again, have no fear." Robbie watched as the white mist rolled out from the trees and engulfed the Lord Hearne, it rolled back and Robbie was alone in the midmorning sunlight surrounded by trees. He felt more light hearted, and the anguish he had suffered walking into the woodland seemed to have subsided. He turned smiling on the path, and thinking of Rune, he headed back through the old wood towards the mere and the home he now shared with the love of his life. He chuckled to himself as he walked enjoying the feel of autumn all around him.

Rune stood dressed in pale lilac at the edge of the mere and watched the pale sun in the sky across the water; her long red hair flowed down past her waist, and shimmered as it fluttered in the soft breeze. He came up behind her and slipped his arms round her placing his head on her shoulder. He softly kissed the side of her neck and she giggled as it tickled. "Oh Robbie... you give me goose bumps when you do that." She rubbed her arms to push them back, and slid round to face him, her bright blue eyes shone like stars and she smiled. "You have been with my father of the woods; I feel him around you." The Lord Hearne did have that electric charge all around him and Robbie still felt it in the air, he gave her a smile and kissed her.

"He came to see me and we talked, I feel better for it. He has a way of putting things, that at first seem confusing but when you think about them, you fully understand him.... I am glad he came; everything now is clearer to me."

"I felt him from here and I was glad to know he was there for you, I worry about you Rob, you take so much upon yourself, can you not share the load with some of the others." She gently pushed his hair from his face as he watched her face and saw the concern in her eyes.

"I am fine, I will talk to Rowan and see what can be done, let's not talk about it, I have you in my arms alone by the mere, and it is all that I need at the moment."

She giggled as he pulled her close and hugged her and kissed her and with his arm around her, they walked into the trees and set off around the edge of the mere.

Rowan and Pebbles sat quietly with Crystal, and Amethyst at the front of the house, Una came out with a tray of hot drinks and an iced tea for Crystal, Amethyst watched and smiled as Rune ran laughing out of the trees chased by Robbie. He caught her in his arms, and twisted her into the air and caught her as she squealed with delight and he pulled her close and kissed her.

"Oh, I wish I could find someone as perfect for me, look at them they seem so incredibly happy, Rune looks so radiant whenever they are together, they are so lucky to have each other."

Pebbles curled up more on Rowan's knee. "Speak for yourself; I have the man of my dreams right here." Rowan smiled as she reached up and kissed him.

Amethyst watched almost in envy, Robbie and Rune walked giggling hand in hand up the grass to the small gate at the end of the garden.

The rest of the afternoon was spent sat out in the garden laughing and joking. Robbie and Rowan set up a table outdoors in the watery sunshine, and the table was laid with food, and they all sat together and shared a meal, Rune's eyes glinted across the table as she spoke and Robbie enjoyed watching the small group laugh and joke together. His spirits seemed to lift and the last couple of days of depression seemed to melt away. The women talked together, as Robbie walked at the edge of the mere with Rowan, he told him of his plans with Lee to get inside the walls, and see what the troop activity would be. "I realise Rowan this will be dangerous, and I also want it a secret from Rune, she will want to come and I cannot risk her now. I am telling you because someone will need to know what is happening, if it goes wrong, I will need someone with Rune."

Rowan looked at him as he stopped walking. "You cannot leave me here, my place is beside you Robbie, and we will stand a better chance together. Lee is good, but he is no spring chick, I would rather your back up be me."

Robbie smiled. "I cannot ask you to come it will be very dangerous. If we get caught Rowan they will show us no mercy, you have a wife to care for."

"I am coming, together I think we will find a way out, the only problem will be Jade, if she finds out, she too will come and then Rune will know, and before you know it we will be back up to twenty."

Robbie gave a long sigh as he faced the water. "Then no one must know, we will leave at dawn the day after tomorrow, we will go through the back gate behind my house, and head north to York. Lee has a contact that will get us inside the walls."

Rowan nodded at Robbie. "We will be fine; it is better we go in as just three it will give the advantage of flexibility." They walked back up the long grass glade to the gate; Rune looked up and smiled as they came through laughing and Jade gave them a huge beaming smile. Robbie sat back at the table and talked until late with the others, as the darkness fell and Rowan and Jade headed home, he slipped his arm around Rune and they headed happily up the stairs to bed.

She slid round him in the dark, and he pulled her close, her bright eyes stared at him in the dark. "I love you Robbie." She crawled on to him and held him as close as she could. He wondered if she had an idea about his plans, but he knew she could not directly know, maybe she felt his pangs of guilt. He did not like the idea of not telling her, but what choice did he have? Rune would be insistent on coming and he could not risk her.

He pulled her into his arms and kissed her, she smelled of Jasmine and honeysuckle, with cherry shampoo. He breathed in her scent as he looked at her with her shimmering red and gold hair strewn across the pillows, her soft skin pressed close, she was everything to him, and he knew now he had to do everything he could to protect her, she was Nature and the dream of saving her was his mission and life's task.

The glade was silent and the moonlight fluttered across the still water, foxes prowled in the dark and the owls swooped silently, as they hunted small mice on the forest floor. High in the branches of the tall trees outside the house and above the windows of Robbie and Rune's room, two tiny bright lights danced in the trees and watched the world of the woodsman as silent guardians. Iona the queen was already being guarded in secret.

CHAPTER FOURTEEN

DARKNESS RISING

The room was tall, long and wide. Large arched windows allowed the dull light to force its way through the oppressive gloom of the room. The flickering of the flames in the large ornately carved stone fireplace only broke the cold grey of the stone. Most of the room was empty apart from the far end where an array of tables and shelves littered the corners and walls. A long wooden table with large tarnished silver candle sticks ran across the width of the room, it was filled with bottles and jars containing strange coloured liquids and preserved parts of animals.

Flasks bubbled and sizzled over the small burners and long coiled tubes of glass fed liquid from one mix to another. Behind the walls of strange objects and bubbling sounds, the tense angry mutterings floated into the air. The small huddled figure with thin white straggly hair fumbled with her books, and read quickly as she added the ingredients to her next batch of foul concoction.

The missing fingers on her right hand impeded her work. She cursed as she fumbled the powder on the spoon, as she shook it above the glass flask; wild angry muttering rose into the air above the bubbling potions as her anger rose again, for the hundredth time that day.

Down the centre of the room lay a row of long tables and on the middle table, encased in a long glass box lay a figure bathed in a golden light. He was tall and well built, his long grey curly hair carefully laid out neatly, and his pale face glowed white, with closed eyes. The Body of Mason Knox looked as if it was just sleeping entombed in the glass case, his goatee beard neatly combed, and he wore his best suit of black, his arms lay folded across his chest, as he lay in state.

The erratic cold laughter of the old hag filled the room, and bounced across the walls as a black toothed smile crossed her lips, and she mumbled between chuckles a strange and old runic language. The potion in front of her glowed a vivid red and silver sparks shot out of the beaker, as she stirred in her final ingredient.

"So, my little woodland flower, you dare to challenge me?" Her voice echoed around the room in a cold and chilling tone. "You will not cheat me again; my own book has more power than the one you hold... You think in a thousand years of life I did not have time to improve on what was done before me?"

Her long grey straw like hair flowed in the air as she turned, and then scuttled up the room to the large fireplace, where two old wooden chairs dressed in red velvet, and showing the years of wear, stood solitary. Across the back of one, a long black cloak made of the feathers of ravens hung shining black, with the hint of reflective blue.

She held the glass with both hands as she ran up the room, and smiling a black toothed grin she sat in the chair and faced the roaring fire. Her black eyes sparkled as she felt the delight of her work, and she lifted the glass to her thin pale lips and began to drink greedily. Without taking a breath, she gulped the brown liquid down and gave a large satisfied gasp, as she finished the liquid. "Now my dear flower I will sleep and awaken returned and stronger than you ever expected, the days of the leaf lover are over."

The old hag lifted the cloak from the back of the chair, and pulled it around her, she snuggled back into the chair and gave a cold chuckle as she closed her eyes and rested. Two days it had taken to brew the strange liquid, but now she was ready to come back and fight. First, the sleep of renewing, she needed to conserve her strength until the process was complete.

Robbie sat in the moonlight and stroked her soft white tummy as she slept, he knew it was only the start, but just knowing that there inside her was his first child with her brother was enough. He gently ran his hand across, as if he felt that they would know he was there and waiting for them. Rune's eyes exploded in violet light as they snapped open, and she sat bolt upright in bed. Robbie jumped back in surprise snatching his hand back. Her head turned and she looked at him as the violet light faded. "She is back."

"Hearne, Rune you scared the life out of me... Who is?"

Rune relaxed a little. "It was as I had feared, she has copied the book, and she has drawn her essence back to her. The Dark One has awoken again and she feels stronger." Her hand slid across the bed to his and he gave it a small squeeze.

"We knew she would, I just wish we could have had a little longer than two days. The time will come when she is destroyed forever, you will see." He smiled, and he pulled her into his arms and held her tight. Rune stared out of the window at the stars.

"When will this end Rob?"

He stroked the long red hair softly down her white back, as he held her warm body against him. "I am not sure Rune; all I do know is it will be you and I side by side that does it." Somehow his voice seemed to carry the smallest hint of hope, and it was enough to give her a sense of ending to it all. Rune wanted the life she had dreamed of and yet whenever it came close, another turn in their fate took them further away. She pushed herself closer to him and he drew her deeper into his arms, she rested her head on the front of his shoulder below the angry looking stitches, and closed her eyes. Robbie sat in the moonlight holding her close as she slipped into sleep, he gently rocked her, and for the moment, she felt safe in the world. She was Nature and a force of power and destruction that many feared, and yet she too felt the need to feel comfort. Wrapped in his arms alone in the night under the moon, Runestone felt protected. Guarded by the hooded man, his arms were the walls she could shelter behind, and his heart was the life force that beat back the fear. His touch was everything that pushed her boundary of fear back into the darkness.

The two doors burst open, and light streamed in down the long room, highlighting the cracks in the grey stone floor. The black clad figure with long flowing curly blonde hair paced down the side of the room. His voice rang with his arrogant impatience. "Mother." The dark black feathered cloaked figure rose from the chair behind the fire, her black eyes shining from her powder white face, malice dampened her lips as she smiled. He slowed his pace at the sight of her, and his voice softened. "Oh... Mother I see you have been cooking again?"

She gave him a withered smile, as she examined her hands with a full set of fingers, which had the long black talon like nails of a vulture. "Mordred darling, see I told you not to worry, the flower girl has not the wit to defeat me, I have powers she will never understand."

"You look wonderful Mother." He smiled at her as she pulled him into a cold embrace. "Have you finished the potion for me yet, this idiot is driving me crazy talking about the love of a family all the time, he is growing stronger somehow, and I cannot think straight." Morgan looked at the eye of her grandson, it was still bright and blue and she could see the persona of another looking back at her, she gave a cold grin at the eye seeing the hate inside it cast back at her.

"Mason prized you so highly Billy, you could have had it all but you turned woodsman on us. I warned him, but Mason would not listen. I told him not to underestimate the love of a woman; he should have seen it in that wife of his. He treated her like dirt, and yet she loved him all the more, and you Billy, you fell for the mother of a leaf lover, how could you turn on your own blood for them?"

She turned from the face of Billy with one black pupil of Mordred, and one soft blue eye of Billy's, and she strolled back to her table of bubbling containers and coloured bottles. She stopped at the old dusty full-length mirror and looked upon herself. She looked more slender and almost Rune like, with her long black flowing hair that now touched the back of her waist. Morgan le Fey slid her hands down over her flat stomach and on to her thighs and smiled, she turned from left to right an approving look in her eye, as she looked at the outline of her firm rounded breasts. "Do you think my breasts should be bigger?"

Mordred looked unconcerned. "I have no idea, the flower girls are about that size, and she seems happy enough. What the hell does it matter? I cannot even understand why you want to even have her shape."

"She is feminine and very elegant, we sorcerers must look our best, I know you hate her, but you cannot tell me you do not think she is pretty. The girl has definite style, and we must keep up with the trends Mordred." She smiled as she viewed the firm buttocks at the back of her dress. "You would not refuse if I could catch her." The Dark One stopped and gave a faint smile. "Would you like that? I know how you enjoy the thrill of rape. Should I catch her and let you tear her up?"

He considered the point and smiled. "That would be good sport I must admit, but I doubt she would have enough fight to entertain me, I like them screaming and biting." Morgan shrugged and walked across to her table, where she busied herself with the mixtures and potions. Mordred strode round the room walking up and down the table; he peered through the glass at the body of Mason lay almost as if sleeping.

Smoke and vapour issued from the table as Morgan flicked through the pages of her book, she added small amounts of coloured powders to the flask that hissed and spat sparks. She seemed to carry a face of delight as she worked, and Mordred noticed how she would occasionally look across at the mirror and catch a glimpse of herself. He walked over to the roaring flames in the hearth and warmed himself, his hands behind his back; he rocked impatiently as he waited for her to finish her work. The time seemed to pass slowly, and he sat in the red chair and dozed with boredom. He hated the coast and preferred to be inland amongst his army. Here there was so little to do, he preferred the life of organisation that allowed him to focus his rage and instill fear on all those around him. Finally, she came round the back of the chair with a frothing beaker of sickly green liquid, she handed it to him as he looked up. "Drink it quickly and stay sat down, he will struggle for a moment."

He already felt the turmoil inside him, as he lifted his hand to the glass; his fingers snapped shut, and Mordred clenched his teeth as he fought internally to regain the power of his hand. The fingers slowly and reluctantly opened, as his face reddened with the pressure. He focused all he had on drawing the beaker to his lips, as Billy summoned the power lost somewhere inside him to prevent Mordred from drinking. Mordred was powerful, and Billy fought without hope, for all of his time as a prisoner inside his body, Mordred had forced more and more control. The glass met his lips and the liquid flowed into his mouth, he gasped as the first of the hot burning liquid flowed into him, and as he finished the beaker, he fell back into the chair and shook violently as if in a fit.

Morgan watched her first born son wrestle with that of her disappointing grandson, she smiled as she saw the bright blue eye begin to darken, and she knew that although Billy had put up a good fight, he was never going to win against her own flesh. Mordred slowly shook less and the darkness returned to his eye, he now looked up with two dark malicious eyes, as the arrogance of his smile crossed his lips. "It seems my nephew has decided to sleep, how long will this last?"

Morgan studied his face carefully. "I cannot be sure, but it will be quite some time before he comes to the surface. I must say he had more of Mason in him than I realised, no normal man could have resisted that long... Still, he is out of the way for now, and we can get back to business, how goes it at York?"

Mordred stood up and stretched his limbs making sure he really did have full control. "My people there assure me they will not be any problems; York is not taking the good advice of Loxley. You were right about the Philips boys; they do not have the skills of their father. The one who could cause us problems is wrapped up with Loxley, so we can undermine them with ease."

"What level are the soldiers at now, do we have enough to move on them? I do not want to wait much longer."

Mordred patted his mother's hand. "Mac is doing very well; he seems to enjoy leading more than babysitting. Be patient it has been a long march from Scotland, they are arriving day by day, and they are being rested. I must say those hormones you gave us to inject them with have had a wonderful effect on them; we will have a force so powerful none will stop us. It's a shame about the castle; I had another ten thousand in there almost ready."

There was the trace of a small glint in her eye as she turned back and walked to the mirror to view herself. "I have not finished there yet, do not concern yourself, I still have plans for Dunnottar." She turned and ran her hands over her breasts, and down to her lower stomach. "You know with a body like this I could have any man I wanted... I think I will, find me a soldier with good looks, and good staying power, it's been a long time since I enjoyed the life of a woman."

"Really Mother, I thought Hesketh had been caring for you?"

"What that old flannel, I wore him out years ago. No, I want something young and vibrant." She giggled almost girl like, yet somehow the coldness of her voice killed the effect. Mordred walked back up the long room past the glass box containing his brother, and gave it one last smirk as he headed towards the door.

"I will send word of York to you, don't forget Lance wants to see you this week, he has problems in London." He pulled open the door and swept through it, and he left her alone to continue viewing herself in the mirror.

"No Robbie push it the other way it's not straight." He leaned on the thick metal post with Rowan, as they pushed hard under the strain. Rune beamed with delight at the side of Jade, as the two boys pushed with all their might to get the thick pole straight in the hole. Robbie felt the twinge in his shoulder, and slackened a little.

"Right Wolfie hammer the pins in." He swung the sledgehammer high above his head, and it came down with huge force, the steel sparked as it connected and the metal rod shot deep into the earth, Jaz on the other side hammered his pin hard, and the pole wobbled for a moment. Robbie and Rowan now very red in the face, moved out of the way, as Wolfie and Jaz moved on to the next two long pins. They smashed them hard into the solid earth and Rune's eyes flickered, as she helped the soil in a pile at the side, slide slowly into the hole and fill it. Robbie and Rowan stepped back and collapsed on the grass as they looked up at the tree of chimes. It was the biggest sculpture Jade had ever done, and they marvelled at the large shining tree filled with various shaped disks and long poles that began to swing in the breeze and play a gentle peaceful tune.

Rune slipped her arm across her sister's shoulders. "Oh Jade, it is so beautiful, it is your best work yet."

This was to be the centerpiece of Jade's new garden, and it was without doubt her best work. All her free time since her wedding day, had been spent in her workshop constructing the huge oak tree of steel, and making all the golden chimes and tuning them to perfection. It now stood in what would become a small courtyard surrounded by small benches, and it was meant to be a place where all her guests could gather and relax. The soft sun was reflected all over the floor in small star like patterns, and it did bring a feeling of harmony and tranquillity.

Robbie walked round underneath it and gazed with a smile up at the wonder of her work. Rowan slipped his arm round Jade, who was filled with pride and excitement, as they all stood in quiet reflective thought as they viewed it, and felt the calmness of it around them.

"HEY GUYS DRINKS." The silence shattered as Jett came out carrying a tray of tall glasses. She gave a huge smile as she saw the tree of chimes. "OH WOW!" She drowned out every note, as she came up the small path and passed the tray round. "Jade girl that is the coolest thing I have ever seen. Oh, Harry and Maggs are going to love this." Jade beamed with satisfaction, she knew Jett well enough to know her wild forms of compliment, and she was very happy.

"It should play the music of all the seasons as they progress." She slid her arm around Rune. "It is inspired by nature and all the things of hers that I love." Rune filled up as Jade gave her a squeeze.

"Thanks sis, it is so beautiful, it is hard to find words that are as wonderful."

Robbie slid his arms round her from behind and rested his head on her shoulder; he felt a great deal of happiness and enjoyed seeing the joy in Rune's eyes. Jade spent the rest of the morning walking round the large plot of land, as she showed Rune and Jett what she wanted to do with her garden. Rowan sat on a small log with his back to the wall of the house and talked with the other men. Wolfie leaned quietly forward.

"What is that Lee Sherman up to Robbie? I saw him packing supplies on to three horses this morning and leading them up to the old wood behind the house... You are not thinking of taking a trip, are you?"

Robbie and Rowan sat forward surprised at Wolfie's observation. Robbie looked slowly round. "I have a small task to do for the Lord Hearne, and he is going to help me, why are you watching Lee? He is a man of Loxley?"

Wolfie nodded. "So was that Billy bloke from what I have heard. I am in the employ of My Lord; it is my business to know what goes on around the man I protect."

Robbie raised his hand. "Alright Wolfie, I have a task, but no one knows of it, Rowan and myself will fulfil this task. You must understand neither Rune nor Pebbles know of this, you cannot come with us; it has to be stealth in the smallest of numbers. If you must watch everything in this area, watch Rune and Pebbles whilst we are away and protect them at all costs."

He looked unsure, but he sat back and looked at Jaz. "I suppose if it is for the Green Lord we must accept your answer, I will watch your families you have no fear of that, when do you go?"

Robbie breathed a sigh of relief. "The day after tomorrow at dawn." He nodded and sat back and watched Jett as she walked at the side of Rune laughing.

Rose and Sinclair walked down the long path from the observation deck with Angus, towards the deep cutting that led to the black bridge, and the large statue of the dragon with a raven sitting on its face. "What kind of strange noise?" Rose looked concerned as she walked by the side of Angus.

"I am not sure how to describe them; they sound like moans and groans as if someone is in pain." Sinclair shrugged.

"We know there were still troops in there, only the tower fell in. Maybe there are wounded trying to get out." Rose did not feel too sure; the fact that parts of the castle remained gave her cause for concern. The woodsmen who guarded the defeated castle now felt very nervous. All had been quiet since the Specialists had left, and then suddenly a few hours ago strange moaning noises had begun to rise from inside the black walls.

Rose and her group came down through the cutting in sight of the black bridge. It still carried the same cold unearthly feeling as it spanned out across the rough sea, to the island and the walls of shining black stone. The tall tower was gone, and the large building at the edge of the walls was crumbled, and smashed. Parts of the roof hung in midair where large chunks of stone had crashed through leaving huge holes and splintered roofing beams. It looked the same picture of devastation; it had two days earlier, when Rune had left with Maggs and her group for Iona. Rose stared out across the black bridge, it was stark and empty, and yet none would step onto it, as a sinister air seemed to brood around it. Even without the heads that had hung from the wires suspended above the bridge it still felt evil.

"I want the guard doubled, and all men placed on standby. Have extra barriers set in place and bring down more arrows... I hate this place, and while there is a chip of that black stone here, I want it watched." Angus nodded to Rose, and turned barking his orders to the captains along the front line. The woodsmen sprang into action and men scurried in every direction. Rose shivered and Sinclair slid his arm round her and pulled her close.

"What is it you feel?" She shook her head.

"I cannot really explain it, but I do not want anything in there coming out here, if it does, I want it dead before it reaches the shore. Let's just hope the lad is better and has a look before anything happens." She turned to Sinclair with a worried look on her face. "Promise me... if anything moves get the hell out of here, I could not bear my life without you, please Sinclair, promise you will?"

He pulled her in to a tight hug. "Hey those are not the words of the lassie I know, come on Rosie, whatever happens we will keep here side by side. You know that."

"I am frightened of this place, there is evil here the world has not seen before I just know it, oh god I wish Runestone was here." Sinclair held her tight, as his eyes lifted and he saw the cold rock before him, nothing had changed and yet now he felt a small amount of fear grow back inside him. In all the years he had known and watched Rose fight for her people, he had never once watched her show fear in the face of the enemy, let alone admit to it. That was more frightening to him than anything the dark castle could contain.

It had been a long day and Robbie yawned as he walked with Rune through the trees, the late evening sun was sinking and the clouds were rolling in dark and brooding, Rune was happy and giggled as he twirled her around the trees to avoid bumping into them. Her hair lifted into the air as she spun round laughing and becoming quite dizzy. She staggered giggling into his arms, and he laughed at her as she wobbled around almost pulling him off balance. He felt very light hearted as he watched her bright eyes flowing with life twinkle at him, her cheek bones white reflecting the last of the sun, and small flashes of fire reflecting off her eyelashes. He pulled her close as she staggered and tripped, and giggled wildly as she staggered to one side. She slid her arms around him and swayed as she walked. "Oh Robbie, I love being home and in the woods, and I love having the time to be alone just you and me."

"I know I love it too." She gave him a huge smile as she looked up at him. She was so beautiful, and he loved her so much and yet he felt a small pang inside him, he knew that she would be so devastated when he slipped off with Rowan and Lee.

They came out of the trees, and on to the grass, she jumped up onto his back, and he grabbed her legs and ran across the grass, jumping like a bronco. She screamed with delight as he jumped in through the gate, and let her slide slowly down on to the floor. He turned to her smiling bright face and he cupped it gently in his hands. Softly he kissed her. "Remember this moment forever, you are my life Runestone Sapphire."

Her giggle died down as she slipped her arms round him. "Oh Robbie... You are mine; I could not live without you by my side." It was an intense moment and he held her close and breathed the smell of fresh cherries in her hair, as if it would be his last. She slipped back and she looked up at him. "Take me upstairs make love to me, and hold me all night." Hand in hand, they walked up the path and in through the doors, the others sat in the kitchen and they waved as the two of them waved back, and went upstairs to their room. Una smiled at the sight of them, they looked so happy arm in arm as they climbed the stairs, she thought of the pain that Rune had suffered at the loss of a life, and was glad now to see the pain had gone.

It was late morning and Robbie stood by the window next to Rune's drawing board in the office, he turned and looked at Rowan, who was sat at the desk with the ambassador for York. "You just do not understand, do you? Ambassador it is very easy to grasp, there could be as many as one hundred thousand troops behind that wall. The force of them will crush York, even if I put men of Loxley at your disposal. We will still not have enough to keep them all out. Parts of your city will fall."

The ambassador had refused to hear Robbie's advice for over an hour now, he stroked his beard and nodded his head. "We have spent years rebuilding the walls; if you let us have enough men to double the guard, we can hold them off and keep everyone safe."

Rowan gave a long sigh and looked at the pig headed ambassador. "You must listen to Lord Loxley Ambassador, is he not confirming what Lee has told you already. You must evacuate while there is still time."

"We cannot undo what has taken so long to build; can you two not see that? York is the only enclosed city that still has the rules and government of the old ways. It is a shining example of how the rest of you can rebuild. York cannot and will not fall."

Robbie turned back to the window, and leaned his face against the cold frame as the rain pounded onto it. "Ambassador the reason you are being singled out is for exactly that reason. Holding on to the old ways is why they will throw everything at you. The Knox Empire want to dominate, if they crush York, it will be a massive blow to the rest of us. You have no understanding of what they are capable of. I do, I have seen it hanging from trees, and I tell you now, it still haunts my dreams.

You must evacuate now while the knowledge of your city still lives."

"Lord Loxley please, I understand your concerns, but democracy must be kept intact if we are ever to bring this country back. The rule of Westminster dates back hundreds of years, we are the last bastion of that time and we have to keep those who have protected it safe in the city."

Robbie banged his head on the window softly. "Westminster is a crumbled old building covered in weeds, your way of doing things is dead Ambassador. The red death did not spare your precious politicians; it ate them alive like the rest of us. The way of the future has to be different; we can never go back to that way of life. Why will you not listen to what I say?"

"I can never accept that Lord Loxley." Robbie turned and looked him in the eyes. He had a sad look on his face.

"Then you too will die when Mordred opens his gate, but only after a whole city has been raped, tortured and butchered by the Cutters. I will do everything I can to prevent it, but I cannot give you my word York will survive, I have seen what he fights with and how many there are. If he just sends what he has in Scotland I will have the fight of my life, if he has more Ambassador, we are all doomed." Robbie walked down the room to the staircase. "I am Sorry Ambassador, I have a lot to attend to, please enjoy the hospitality of Loxley until your return, now I must set in place what protection I can, I have orders to despatch." The ambassador stood up and shook Robbie by the hand.

"We appreciate all you have and will do; you will see My Lord we will come through this." He smiled as he turned and walked down the stairs; Robbie looked down and watched him leave with sadness.

"I hope so Ambassador, I really do." He looked at Rowan who sat watching him. Rowan shrugged.

"I am a man of the trees; I think he is mad. Amongst trees we all have a fighting chance, you won't get me behind his walls, I want to live." Robbie smiled.

"Well, my dear friend we have another impossible task to face, they are foolish, I fear for York." He walked slowly back up the room to the large rain streaked window, and looked out across the mere. The surface of it was dulled as the raindrops danced and skipped into it, the wind blew the heavy drops in sheets across the surface to the trees on the far side. He watched the large dark clouds that billowed across the skies of Loxley. The ambassador ran down the path and across the grass to a waiting carriage. He briskly jumped in, the driver wrapped in his cloak cracked the whip, and the carriage pulled away. Robbie spoke almost to himself than to Rowan. "If York falls, Loxley will be alone in the north, we could lose everything we hold dear."

Rowan's hand gently squeezed his shoulder. "We will do all we can, Loxley will not fall easily Robbie, wait until we have seen what is in store for them first, come on let's organise the instructions for Skip and Fuse. Never underestimate the power that sits beside you Robbie."

Robbie turned and looked at the man who had become so much more than a friend. "I will not risk Rune, not even for Loxley, and I might add neither should you risk Jade. I know she has the power to defeat the Dark One, but if I can find a way to do it myself I will. Rune carries my children Rowan; she will be in danger every moment she does. I will not let the Dark One take the life she holds, and she will try."

"I speak of more than just Runestone. Her family also have immense shared power, and you have the power of the swords alongside you. We will not be defeated easily, and we will all fight to the last man if we have to, believe me Loxley is safe enough for now."

"I hope so my friend, I am not keen to leave here with her unguarded." Rowan smiled at him.

"She is hardly unguarded, I feel Rafe and Jaz have their eyes and an ear on everything, Rafe has impressed me greatly, he shows the qualities of leadership and a good captain. You should put more trust in our flesh tearing wild man; he has a quality that does command respect."

Robbie started to laugh. "Or the people he addresses are afraid he will bite them."

"You may have a point but remember Robbie, there will come a time when you must begin to split the group and single out the leaders, Rafe will be one of them, and I also think Smokes."

"I agree, but now is not the time; I want them all to rest and recover." He stared back out into the rain. "Scotland was hard, but our biggest challenge is coming. If they attack as I think they will, we will lose many woodsmen, I want the whole of our team of so called Specialists to be sent out with other groups, I want their skills bringing back up to scratch, we have all been out of the trees too long."

The stairs creaked as Rune came up with two hot coffees, both of them turned to her, as she looked round the rail and spotted them. "I see the Ambassador had a short stay; I take it he does not agree with you?"

Robbie took the hot cup out of her hand. "The man is a fool; pride and arrogance have clouded his judgement." He sipped his drink as Rune stared into his eyes.

"York will come to its senses Rob, you will see."

"But will it come in time? They cannot waste precious time Rune, there are thousands of innocent lives in there we can save."

She touched his arm, as she felt the frustration in him. "Talk to Bear, he will have more influence, even better, send him to York." She turned as she stepped on to the stairs. "They are his brothers, if he cannot work them round none of you can." She gave him a big smile and headed back down the stairs to the landing. Rowan grinned and shrugged his shoulders.

Rune came out through the door as Alley came smiling up the corridor. "Let's see how he is today then." She turned the handle and stepped into the room with two single beds. Rune followed her in smiling. Merlin looked older than he ever had, his face was heavily lined and his beard seemed whiter and longer. His eyes stared up at them as he smiled weakly. Alley sat on the bed and gave him a big smile. "Hey granddad, you look a lot better." She lifted his arm and took his pulse, as Rune sat beside him and softly stroked back his long white hair from his face.

"Hi... how do you feel now? We needed you a little stronger, and then we can return you to how you should be." She gave him a big smile and she saw the glint of love in his quiet eyes. "I love you grandfather and I miss you."

Alley stood up and looked at Rune. "This is as good as it gets, you know the magic what do you think?" Rune looked down at his white face.

"Are you ready for this? It will take a lot of your strength but it will do you good, and after some more rest you will be fully restored." Her eyes shone bright blue, and he saw the love of his granddaughter. Merlin nodded and closed his eyes, Rune looked up at Alley. "Bring the jar." Alley nodded and turned to the small cupboard at the other end of the room. She walked over and opened the door. There on the shelf was the bottle filled with a swirling golden liquid light. She very carefully lifted it, and cradling it in her hands; she carried it back to Rune. Rune stood at the side of the bed and muttered in a strange language under her breath, she passed her hand over the jar and the contents began to glow and spin inside. Rune waved a hand that glowed for a moment, and her eyes began to flicker as violet light flashed from them to the jar, the cork in the top began to slowly lift as it pushed itself up out of the container.

The cork fell to the floor and a stream of golden light flowed up into the air, and swirled round the room coming to a halt above Merlin stretched out on the bed. It hung over him like a shimmering cloud, Rune gave another incantation under her breath and the cloud began to vibrate, almost as if snowing, small particles began to fall and land on Merlin. As each small particle hit him, it glowed brightly and soaked into him, and disappeared from sight.

Alley was fascinated and gave a wide smile at Rune as she watched, the cloud descended as the flow of particles became faster, and faster. The cloud slowly disappeared and Merlin drew a long breath, he lay quite still with his eyes closed. Rune leaned over him smiling. "Is that better grandfather?" Merlin's eyes snapped open.

He opened his mouth and let out a terrifying scream, Rune jumped back, and Alley staggered away with shock as she lifted her hands to her ears. His eyes wide with fear, and still screaming he clutched his stomach, Rune looked on in horror as the faint black wisp of smoke oozed out of him, and rose in the air. Merlin shook violently and began to thrash about on the bed, Alley screamed with fear. Rune waved her hand and violet exploded around the bed, as the door burst open and Robbie with Rowan came rushing in with their swords drawn. The smoke formed into the screaming and laughing figure of Morgan le Fey, her eyes burned and danced with pleasure. "You think I would let you have him so easily Flower Girl? Do you think I am so stupid as to just hand him back on a plate? You fools, his essence is still mine, and I will not give it back to you easily, call yourself a force of Power? YOU ARE A BEGGINER STUDENT!" She threw back her evil head, and laughed and cackled waving her arms madly in joy. Robbie raised his sword and went to strike her.

Rune threw herself at him and caught him straight in the front of his chest, pushing his arms back out of the way. "NO YOU WILL KILL HIM." Robbie recoiled with the impact, and staggered backward still staring at the wildly laughing Dark One. She spun in the air, and gathered the limp body of Merlin up into her arms, and with a blinding flash, all of them were blown off their feet, and the room was empty. Merlin and the Dark One were gone.

Robbie coughed as he sat up with Rune held firmly in his arms. Destiny stood up right in front of the bed, the blade stuck deep in the wooden floor. He looked at the weeping Rune and lifted her face. "Are you alright, she has not hurt you?" Rune nodded as the tears ran down her face, he pulled her into his arms and held her tight as he looked at Rowan and then Alley. Alley smiled and sat up and leaned on the floor.

"She is one ugly bitch." She wiped her hair back from her eyes and smiled almost Jade like. Rowan got to his feet and offered her a hand, Alley grabbed hold and he pulled her up. Robbie rocked Rune as she cried into his shoulder.

"I should have known, it was all too easy... Oh Rob I should have expected her to lay a trap, she knew I was there." He rocked her in his arms and gently whispered in her ear.

"Rune listen to me, she has lived for a thousand years, she has learned many tricks, it is not your fault, you cannot blame yourself." He pulled her away from his shoulder and lifted her wet face with red tear filled eyes. "She is pure evil, now you know what to expect, next time you meet her, finish the bitch off." Rune gave a small giggle and he pulled her back into his arms, and held her close as he kissed the top of her head. Crystal and Una came running down the corridor, Rowan put his hand up to stop them and gently pulled the door closed. Robbie held her tight as he sat with her on the floor.

Morgan le Fey laughed as she walked around the large glass box on her long table. Merlin lay still staring upwards; his eyes in a fixed dull stare. "She is not as bright as you thought, is she? You called me student. Not quite as arrogant now are you Lord of the Lines of time?" Her eyes danced with her delight, as she paced up and down the glass box. "My son will be so much happier to have you for company, maybe we could bring you both together and then like my first son, I will have the love of two again." She laughed hysterically, and waving her arms, she walked down to the table at the bottom. "You can be guest of honour at my little party Merlin, just you watch now as the daughter of a king goes to war and wipes out all the leaf lovers in this land. You can watch and learn as I undo what your precious little flower girl has done."

She grabbed a flask of red dust, and walked to the side of the table next to Merlin in his glass box. She cast it on to the floor, and it swirled round on the stone, the floor began to vibrate and she smiled with her thin black lips, as a round stone table began to rise from the floor. Slowly it twisted out of the earth, grinding and rumbling until it reached the level of her waist and stopped. "Seems like the flower girl, I have a table of my own too. Shall we see who now wields the balance of power, five points against my seven?" She waved her hand across the table, and it shimmered like flowing liquid, slowly the flowing surface formed a pattern and there in the centre of the table was a bright red seven-pointed outlined star of black, set on an all black table with a thick golden edge to it. She leaned over and crooned on her table.

Morgan waved her hand, and dark vapour rose into the air above the table, it swirled and then formed a picture of an island with a dark broken castle of black stone. She gave a soft cackle as she went to work and began to talk hurried words under her breath, her eyes fixed on the pictures. "It is time to show the guards on my doorstep who they are really messing with."

Sinclair walked over to the small cave like shelter dug out of the rock face where Rose sat staring out at the dark castle. He handed her the cup, and she nodded as she gratefully took it. All day the temperature had been falling and she shivered, as the warmth seemed to flow into her from the cup. He sat down beside her and lifted the cup to his lips; water dropped in a big drip on the floor just outside the shelter. Rose watched as more large drops appeared and made large damp circles on the dry stones outside. Sinclair leaned forward and looked up at the sky, he put his cup on the floor.

"Well to be honest I would have said that today we would not have had rain." It began in earnest, and the downpour began as the rain intensified and beat the floor, Rose shivered again, and he pulled his hand over her and round her shoulders, pulling her closer to him. Lightening forked across the sky, as the rain grew heavier, a few moments later the loud crack and rumble of the thunder began. Rose stared at the cup of coffee on the floor in front of Sinclair. Small ripples crossed the surface of the dark coffee. Rose blinked as the cup vibrated and moved a few millimeter's. She held her breath and it moved a little more. Rose gripped Sinclair tightly by the hand, and he looked down at her and followed her eyes to the cup. It slid an inch on the floor and shook more violently.

Large tears formed in the eyes of Rose as she slowly turned and looked at Sinclair. Her voice was barely a whisper. "I have loved you since the moment I first met you, you have made my life complete."

He smiled at her, and watched as the blue flame erupted out of the floor and engulfed her, Rose was flung out of the shelter and lay smoking, and dead on the floor in the rain, her face pale and her eyes staring fearfully at the castle. Sinclair opened his mouth to scream, and he felt the heat. No sound passed his lips, as he lay dead by the side of the woman he loved. Bodies fell from the cliffs all around the front line of Dunnottar.

The tall tower slowly rose into the sky as the blue lightening engulfed it, and the dark clouds swirled in the rain. The ugly looking raven of stone with cold blue glowing eyes stared at the coast and the cloaked mountain of dead. In the beak of the bird on her balcony the Dark One screamed with laughter, and mocked the falling burned bodies of the woodsmen of Scotland. The castle of Dunnottar brooding and dark was back, and grown bigger, engulfed in dark cloud with the sun blotted out, the gates slowly creaked open and the long line of corpses dressed to kill slowly moved forward under the cloud and over the black bridge. Morgan looked down on her army of lost souls. "Go my warriors into the wilds and bring darkness and death to every corner of the green world. Go my beautiful callers of death, and let the darkness of Dunnottar be known to all."

The rain bashed down and slapped on the stones and the ghostly figures of death and destruction illuminated briefly in the flashes of lightening, they were gruesome and horribly disfigured, armed with fear they marched to meet with their leader and general. Mordred waited at York.

CHAPTER FIFTEEN

STEALTH AND LONELINESS

Rune had taken the loss of her grandfather back to the Dark One badly, it had taken some time to pacify her, and slowly she had calmed down. Robbie breathed a sigh of relief as he came up the steps from her table room. Rune sat and tried to find where her grandfather was, she stared at the table as images appeared and disappeared, the Dark One had shrouded herself, and Rune found it impossible to find him. She sat back feeling exhausted as the violet mist swirled across the top of the twenty pointed sapphire blue star of Runestone. Una came down the steps and smiled at her. "How are you feeling?" Rune gave a weak smile.

"Like a fool... I should have known better. I had him here safe, and I let her slip right in here and take him." Una sat down beside her and pulled her in to a hug.

"She did not come under the veil, even she does not have the power to do that, she left a trace of herself inside him, which was the only way she could get in here undetected; it was also how she helped hide my mother. You know I have the power of protection Runestone, you know I sense darkness quicker than others? I felt no trace before, during or after she entered here, she came in disguised as part of your grandfather. None of us saw it, so you are not a fool."

Rune gave a small smile. "Thanks Una." She patted Rune on the arm.

"It's what aunties are for, now come on let's see that wonderful smile that a certain young woodsman can put on your face." Rune gave a little giggle and her face brightened; Una gave her a warm smile back. "Wow he really does love you." Rune pulled Una into a tight hug.

"I am so glad you came here."

"Me too."

Robbie sat on the balcony lost in thought; he leaned back in his chair and rested his boots on the rail. His unfocused eyes stared out into the heavy rain, as his mind wandered. York was swirling around inside him, there was a huge expanse of open woodland and scrub in front of the black wall, and then the wind ravaged, wide open moors. How could he hide his men to allow them to face the oncoming opposition? He knew, he would be grossly outnumbered, and his men would be cut down quickly. He leaned back on the chair and rubbed his eyes; a glint of blue caught his eye and he looked up at the side of the glass door. Rune stood smiling at him; he slipped his feet off the rail and righted his chair. "Hey beautiful." She came out and slid on to his knee, she put her arms round his neck and gave him a soft kiss.

"Hi gorgeous." Her eyes sparkled bright and blue, and her hair shone with the light behind it. He pulled her close, and she curled around on his lap. He held her tight and felt the warmth of her body passing through into his; he closed his eyes as he leaned on to her head and softly kissed her. She was still upset and feeling insecure and he knew that he could only hold her until she felt safe again. She nuzzled into him and he smiled. The rain continued to bounce down through the rest of the day, and Robbie sat contented with Rune in his arms and his eyes closed. Nothing needed to be said he just sat and held her tight, and waited for her to speak to him. He knew at some point it would come, and so silently he waited enjoying each passing moment alone and close to her. His mind drifted as he felt her warmth around him and slowly with his eyes closed, he seemed to relax and float within himself. How long he had been like that he was not sure; he awoke abruptly with Rune's scream. "OH NO...?"

He jumped as he felt her move, and his eyes opened as his heart began to beat quickly sensing Rune's distress. Rune stood in the centre of the balcony, the rain pouring down behind her. Her eyes were bright violet and she looked horrified. He stood up and took her by the shoulders. "Rune...What is it...? Rune will you talk to me?"

Her voice was quiet and unearthly. "Take me to my table." Robbie stared at her for a moment, and then sprang into action, he whisked her up into his arms and turned and ran. Violet light streamed out of her face as he ran to the top of the stairs, Crystal, Una and Amethyst looked up as he came thundering down them, and twisted round the bottom towards the door under the stair. The look on his face was enough, and they jumped up from their seats and followed him. Robbie slipped Rune into her seat and she raised her hands to the cool surface of the table of Runestone. The others fell into their seats, and watched as Robbie stepped back and took his own seat. The violet mist swirled and he looked up to see the pictures clearing, as a violet Rune appeared in what looked like a dug out shelter in the cliffs at Dunnottar.

The rain thundered off the rock floor as Rune looked down and wept. She lifted the soaking wet body of Rose into her arms, and cried long gasping bitter tearful sobs. The white face hung limp as Rune lifted it to her and clutched Rose to her heart. She kissed her on the forehead, and then slid her fingers over her eyes to close them. Robbie felt the chill run down his spine, as he watched Rune with Rose. He knew what was coming before he saw it. Rune turned and looked out across the bay, and there on the island the black castle stood looking bigger and darker than ever before. The paths all across the front of the cliffs were littered with the dead. Small gasps came from the others as they watched, and he saw Una rise slightly in her seat, as she stared at the pictures.

The black bridge was filled with row upon row of hideously mutilated soldiers, as they marched out and into the deep cutting that led to the gates and down the coast to England. It was a host that had been created with the single task of defeating its enemy, and Robbie knew whom that enemy was. It was him, Rune laid Sinclair and Rose side by side, and then pressed the talisman pendants round their necks. White circles appeared on the floor, and slowly the two bodies sunk into the ground and were gone. She walked slowly along the front of the high cliff wall towards the black bridge. The army of the dead flowed out across it, she glowed brighter and brighter, as she headed toward the entrance to the front of the bridge, the soldiers slowed and halted as Rune raised her arms. She was small and slender; her hair blew and flapped soaking wet behind her as she stood with her arms outstretched either side. Her voice was loud and carried all around the island.

"HEAR ME, FOR I AM THE RUNESTONE ON WHICH ALL HAS BEEN WRITTEN, I AM THE SERVANT OF THE WHITE CIRCLES OF KNOWLEDGE AND LIFE, AND THE WHITE LINES OF TIME, YOUR TIME HERE IS DONE, AND YOU CAN NOT PASS INTO THIS REALM. RETURN TO THE OTHER SIDE, OR KNOW THE PAIN OF DEATH RETURNED ON YOU IN THE REALM OF DARK PASSAGE.

The floor began to vibrate, and Rune exploded in blue light that shot from the floor and engulfed her. It blew like a fountain of fire into the air for five hundred feet, and the soldiers stepped back afraid of the flames. Robbie jumped from his seat and lurched towards the table. "No Rune... No!" Una and Crystal seized him and pulled him back away from the table, as his eyes fixed on the pictures. The flame fell and Rune stood with her arms out unharmed and smiling. Robbie let out a long gasp and fell back into his chair. Una and Crystal stood either side, and watched as Rune lifted her head.

The soldiers now moved slightly backwards as Rune smiled. "Is that it Le Fey, is that all you can do? Her eyes burned brightly as she opened her mouth and screamed. The sound was deafening, even in the room of Rune's table they all covered their ears, as the wail of pain flowed out of her, and the whole area began to shake and rumble.

The floor trembled and shook violently, and the deep cutting behind her began to shake as small rocks toppled from the top down into the bottom. The soldiers in the cutting were hit and smashed as larger rocks fell, and the whole of one side started to move as Rune's scream of the pains in life continued. The deep cutting filled with dust as both sides collapsed and fell inwards sealing the way through with a wall of glistening stone and crystal rubble. Her eyes flared at the soldiers as she spoke.

"Return now to the other realm, or suffer for eternity." Violet light bathed them and they seemed to stagger and become more aware of themselves. Some of them dropped on the spot as white light left them, and flowed into the sky. Rune took a step forward towards them, and the grotesque figures showed fear. "I am Runestone, wielder of the green circle, and giver of life. I command you in the name of my father and creator to return to the other realm, or I shall reveal the white lines and banish you to the realm of ever living death."

There was a scream in the top of the tower, but it was too late. Rune exploded with white light and engulfed the whole island, screams and hideous wails lifted into the air through the blinding white light, the dark clouds parted above the castle, and a stream of white blasted down into the light below. Screams shot into the air as the inner souls of the soldiers who had disobeyed her were torn from their rotting bodies and dragged to a place of such fear none would ever speak of it. The column of light flowed into the sky and then the clouds rolled in and darkness was all around.

Through the heavy darkness, a small violet light sparkled. Robbie sat clutching the table, and staring with tears of fear in his eyes at the pictures, the faint silhouette of a slender young women glowing in pale violet turned and walked away from the bridge, which was covered in the torn rotting bodies of the army of the dead, she faded away into the cliff. The pictures on the table faded and the violet light swirled around on the surface, he looked sideways to Rune who sat straight and still, light flowing out of her eyes, he saw the tears run down her face as the two bodies rose gently up through the violet light on to the table. Una came round and patted Robbie on the shoulder. "Leave her a moment Robbie; help me with Rose and Sinclair."

Between them, they carried the two lifeless figures upstairs. Robbie looked at Una not sure if he should ask, her face was solemn. She understood, and looked him in the eyes. "Rune has just done something no living person would want. She will feel the pain of her actions; the realm she spoke of is never mentioned in our world Robbie. It is an evil place where the soul is torn and tortured forever, many left in time to pass over and be free of the clutches of the Dark One, those that did not, have entered a place so vile we have no words in this or any other language to describe it. She is the power of good and for her to use that place will not have been easy, do not speak of it to her unless she mentions it."

He looked, and felt frightened as he nodded to Una, they walked slowly back down the steps to the table where Rune sat pale and looking exhausted. She was drying the tears from her face as he walked in. He gave her a smile and she stood up, and came over and slipped her arms round him. He held her tight and felt her trembling in his arms. She buried her head in his shoulder and he stroked her hair. Small stifled sobs rose from his chest. He held her very tightly.

Crystal rode to the farm, as Robbie put Rune to bed. The power she had used had been a force that none could easily endure. She was tired and exhausted and as he pulled the sheets over, she was already asleep. Rowan and Jade appeared followed shortly by Robert in his cart; Harry helped him unload the two coffins for Rose and Sinclair. Robert and Harry took them to the burial site just down from the stone circle, and Robert Lox spoke kind words over them and asked Hearne to protect them. Robbie stood out on the steps and watched through the rain, Una came out and stood by his side. "She will be fine with me; do not worry when you leave."

"What?" He spun round and looked at her violet eyes. She smiled and put her arm on his shoulder.

"Robbie, I see things in ways others do not, it is part of my power. I see the concern in your heart, I see the fear of leaving her unprotected, you do not always have to say the words, I sense more from silence, than I ever would words. It has been there inside you since the funeral; just make sure that whatever it is, you get back safely. One squeeze of that pendant and Rune will be by your side, and we will not be too far away, I am sure."

Robbie breathed a sigh of relief as he looked down at the white flat pendant with a blue star and golden symbol of Iona on it. "Thanks Una, I am worried about leaving her, but many lives lie on what I have to do. I have to go unseen for this task, and I cannot take the others, Rowan will come with me alone."

Una nodded. "His heart is heavy; I did think it would be impossible to separate you two. Have no fear I will watch Jade as well." Robbie smiled.

"You and Steph make a good team between you." She gave a laugh.

"Stephanie loves you both as I do, both of us will always be around if you are in need, now go and be with Rune tonight, show her your love and make her feel special."

"Thanks Una." She smiled as he walked into the house and went upstairs to the bedroom. Rune was asleep her hair spread across the pillow, he slid in beside her and pulled her close, she gave a little whimper and snuggled into him. Robbie lay awake and held her into the early hours of the morning. He slipped carefully out of the bed, and in the darkness; he dressed and collected his things. Robbie looked down at her pale white face as it shone in the moonlight; she looked so peaceful and calm. Her small slender frame hardly seemed to leave a lump in the bed, he felt his resolve breaking and turned to the door. He had to do this alone and protect her, he knew it would be hard being separated, but it was also important to rest and strengthen all of them for what he knew would be the fight of their lives.

As quiet as a leaf, he crept downstairs, and opened the cupboard door where he stored his travelling things. He lifted out the bag that was always packed ready, with his blanket roll and cooking equipment; he slipped his telescope into his pocket with his compass, and lifted his best rowan bow and quiver filled with white tipped arrows. Robbie rolled up his heavy black hooded cloak and tied it in a roll, he knew once inside the city, a Loxley crest would be the worst thing to wear. Black walls and dark nights would at least provide him with cover, and with his black cloak; he knew he would soon merge into the background. Robbie took one last look up at the window where he knew that Rune was sleeping. A glint of light caught his eye, and he turned and looked up into the top of the tall trees. Just for a moment, he thought that he had seen two faint lights. He smiled to himself and then blew a kiss up to the window where he knew she was asleep, and he turned into the trees and faded from sight.

Nothing stirred in the woods as he moved with lightning speed dodging the trunks and weaving along the path, it was cold and his breath streamed in white vapour out of his mouth. The clouds swept across the sky, and the moon appeared for a few moments lighting the way through the thinning canopy of the trees.

Rowan stood by the gate in the tall wall; he peered into the dark waiting, his bag on the ground at his side and his bow in his hand. Robbie slipped up at his side through the dark. "Boo!"

Rowan jumped. "Bloody hell." Robbie grinned as he patted his shoulder and Rowan shook his head.

"Just for a moment I thought it was Jade." Robbie laughed as he pulled on the lever, and the small door swung open into the woods beyond. Rowan snatched up his bag and they slipped through Robbie's own private gate and into Loxley woods. Lee Sherman sat cross legged on the ground, his back to a tall oak. The horses were tied up fifty feet further down, and grazed quietly; he rose to his feet with a smile as the two of them appeared from the undergrowth, and tapped his pipe into his hand. Robbie threw him a small bag.

"My dad dropped this off last night, its Joe's; you will find it smells a lot nicer." Lee opened the bag and took a deep breath, as the look of sheer delight crossed his face. The smell of real tobacco was nectar to his old nose.

There was no time for talk, Robbie knew Rune could sit at the table and track him, he wanted to be as far away as possible before she woke up and discovered he was missing. They sprung on to their horses and sped into the trees, skirting the glade of Opal and heading in the direction of Three Step Rock. The sky was starting to pale, and he knew with the dawn, the light would reveal them; he wanted to get as far from Loxley as possible. As they headed into the trees a dark figure slipped from behind a wide beech tree, he put his hand to his mouth and gave a shrill call whistle. Far down the track figures in dark clothing moved.

Robbie broke the cover of the trees at first light, and headed onto the riverbank, the ground was soft and the horses picked up speed, with their hoods up, they rode with pace, the dark clouds in the sky looked brooding and dull.

Robbie looked over to Lee. "How long will this take?"

He leaned forward on the horse. "We must ride all day with few breaks, we should enter the walls at midnight tonight, we can only move in there under cover of darkness." Robbie looked back at Rowan and winked, he smiled back as they rode faster along the grass covered path.

It was late when Rune woke; she had been very tired, and had slept throughout the night in a very deep sleep, she smiled as she sat at her dressing table. For the whole night she had been aware of him there at her side, she somehow had known he was awake and watching. She braided her hair and clipped it back with her butterfly hairpin. She slid on a purple velvet waistcoat to match with her lilac top and skirt, and made her way down to the kitchen. Amethyst sat at the table eating toast as Rune poured a coffee and yawned, Amethyst pushed the plate piled with toast towards her as she sat down; Rune took a slice and put it on her plate. "Have you seen Rob this morning?"

She swallowed and nodded. "I think he might have gone to that big meeting in the village, there is a lot of talk about York. Skip has groups of men all over the place down there; Saff was saying Keith and Rafe have been called back to their commands. They will captain some of the men going to York."

Rune buttered her toast. "Rob won't be happy; they are part of his Specialists. I can't see him allowing them inside the city, he wants all his people outside, I know Rowan has refused to go behind the walls."

Una walked in and headed for the coffee pot. "Good morning." The two others nodded chewing their toast; Una sat down and cradled her cup in her hands, as she sipped. Her violet eyes watched Rune carefully. "What you got in mind for today girls?" Amethyst stretched her long tanned muscular body.

"I am going to go for a run round Loxley and see the whole place in a day, I don't fancy swimming if it rains. I also hear that the guy they call Fish has been teaching the long bow while he recovers, I like the sound of him and have wanted to meet him for a while.

Rune gave her a big smile. "I like Fish, he is a really nice man. You will get on with him with no problems, he is very calm and easy to talk to, and he has made me laugh many times on the road."

Amethyst smiled as she stood up wearing her usual very tight fitting crop top with skin hugging pants in dark green. "Well, I will see you both tonight, have fun I know I will." She smiled as she left the room and Una with Rune to finish their breakfast.

By mid afternoon Lee had stopped for a break near a watering pool, deep in the woods somewhere south of Scarborough, Robbie was not exactly sure where, as Lee was doing the navigating. He crouched down at the water's edge and filled his canteen; he looked round at the dense forest, covered in hues of yellow and red. The earth was damp and musty, the air was fresh in his lungs and the sun was pale when it appeared from behind the darkened clouds. There was a stillness in the air as the season prepared for the long sleep of winter, and yet Robbie felt a deep sense of life and calm inside him. He looked up at Lee who was preparing a quick meal. "How close are we?"

Lee stirred the chunks of chicken mixed with various vegetables in a quick stir-fry fashion. "We still have a few hours of fast riding to get there. There is a woodland settlement not far from the walls; we should meet up with a group there who can help. They are a type of woodland bandit who prey on the Knox supply routes, they have men inside and out. They do not follow any man of Loxley, but they will support any enemy of Knox. I have used their information many times; they can help in many ways for a price."

Rowan sat back on a log and watched the trail. "And what price will this little expedition cost us; we carry no gold."

Lee gave a smile, as the food steamed and sizzled in the pan. "They have no use of gold they buy very little; these are bandits they take what they want. Loxley will have something they need, all we have to do is find a way to keep them happy, and that should be easy enough."

Rowan did not look so sure, but Robbie nodded. "I think we will be fine, although when we meet them, I think we should play down the Lord Loxley bit, I will remain Robbie, I do not want to broadcast my presence, this trip is supposed to be about stealth."

Lee handed him a plate and fork. "I think it would be wise to enter only as woodsmen on a fact finding mission, there will be guards all over. I have a friend who lives close by; he knows of your group, and will provide shelter for the horses... Come lets finish up our food and make way, we are still against the clock."

They hurried the meal, and soon Robbie found himself back on his horse, and weaving through the dense new growth of the woodlands that expanded across what was once farmland. From what he could tell from his compass they were working in a straight diagonal across the country towards what once was called Filey, he followed the lead of his grandfather's oldest friend, and put his hope on getting in and out quickly.

Rune smiled, as she removed the roll of sage green fabric off her loom. Una helped her lift it, and place it on the shelves with the other greens, sage green had come into vogue, and the demand for clothing in the colour had increased. Steph and Smoke's had been overrun with orders, and now back at home Rune was working flat out to catch up. Back at the cottage Melanie had joined in, and now sat at Rune's old loom weaving fabrics, Saff now found employment with Steph sewing on the foot driven machine as she followed Rune's patterns and made up all the clothes that had been cut out, yet never sewn.

Alley was now helping with Alice, although she had meant to head straight back to the house of Good Hope. Alice was looking very pregnant with only a few months left to go and she lifted her feet to rest them, as Alley helped in the now busy surgery. With the influx of thousands of new people, the surgery had become a much bigger operation than it was when Leenard had run it.

Una marvelled as she watched fascinated, as Rune restrung the loom with violet cotton, she worked quickly and with great skill, her hands moving like lightening, as she ensured every fine thread was correctly threaded and ready to run. She looked out through the window at the sun in the sky. "Robbie is late; I didn't think it would take all day." Una looked down for a moment. She had kept her talking all day in hope she could distract Rune, now the time was fast approaching when she knew that Rune would discover he had left her to complete his dangerous task.

Rune glanced over at Una, and a look of concern crossed her face. "What is it Una...? Are you alright, are you not feeling well?" Una looked up with her violet eyes, straight into the bright blue eyes filled with life of Rune. Rune smiled at her.

"Rune... Robbie will not be back tonight; he might be some time." Rune stopped with the violet threads hung limp in her hand.

"What do you mean he might be some time?" A look of fear came across her face, Una stood up and crossed the room to her, and she took Rune's hands in hers as Rune began to look distressed. "Where is he Una?"

"He has been given a secret task to do, and he left this morning with Rowan. He could not risk taking the group, as he needs to move unseen where he is." The threads snapped as Rune pulled too hard.

"Where has he gone?" Tears started to rise into her eyes, she knew without having to ask, and fear rose quickly inside her. Una pulled her close.

"He will not risk his children, and asked me to watch over you... Rune, Robbie has entered the black city above York." Her eyes flared as she gasped, she pushed herself out of Una arms.

"NO... WHAT IS HE PLAYING AT? HE HAS NO PROTECTION THERE." Tears streamed down her face as Una snatched her back into her arms.

"Rune he is using all the skills of the hooded man to evade detection, you must let him do this." Rune trembled as she tried to focus on him, her eyes moved erratically as she tried to connect her mind to his. Una squeezed her tightly. "The Lord Hearne has placed a protection on him, you will not sense him Rune, he has been hidden even from you. The black city is too dangerous for you now; the Lord Hearne wants you safe for the moment."

Rune gasped as she slumped into Una and wept. "He is alone and without me, he promised he would not leave me."

"He has no choice Runestone. York is disobeying the will of the woodland realm, he is the woodland lord, and must now try to find a way of saving his realm, and York has endangered it. There is no other way to know what is coming;

Robbie now has the lives of many thousands in his hands."

Rune pulled back a defiant look in her eyes. "I am Runestone Lady of Loxley and companion and partner of the hooded man; if I cannot be with him, I will help him." She gritted her teeth and the power showed as her eyes flickered. Her voice dropped. "I am frightened for him Una, please help me protect him?" Una pulled her close, as she felt the hurt, and pain and loss inside her.

"What can we do that will help him Runestone?"

Rune squeezed her tight, and then drew away, and with a flick of her wrist a shimmering window appeared. "We will convince York. We need Jade, Bear and Crystal. I want to speak to the ambassador."

Una smiled and nodded at her. "He is at the village hall with Skip."

One hour later Bear sat with the ambassador and Skip, Bear rubbed his face with frustration. "Elliot, Loxley is right, can you not see that? You talk like my father but you do not listen. If you really want to protect the work we have done at home, you must scatter it to the wind. York must be emptied so that the knowledge is spread where they won't find it. If you all stay together and the city falls, everything my father achieved will be gone forever. Can my brothers not see that?"

"Jacques you are younger than your brothers, leave them to handle the policy of York, they have worked for years at your father's side, and understand the work he did. You now belong here as the fighter you are."

The front doors of the hall burst open and Rune came in, flanked by Crystal, Jade and Una. Rune looked angry, and was tooled up in her green woodsman attire for war; round her shoulders she wore the heavy velvet violet cloak with the Loxley crest in gold on it. Skip smiled and it dropped from his lips as he saw the anger in her eyes. Rune raised a hand and clicked her fingers; a violet archway appeared in the air close to Bear. The ambassador rose in his chair looking a little unsettled. "Lady Runestone it is a pleasure to see you again."

"It's Lady Loxley Ambassador, we have business of a pressing nature and I must ask you to accompany me to York... Would you please join us Bear, it is very important you talk with your brothers?" Rune stared at the ambassador, her blue eyes burned brightly in her pale face, and she showed the force that was contained within her.

The ambassador raised himself with arrogance. "I must say Lady Runestone that your timing is not very convenient, I am already having a discussion with your associate which is of great importance." Skip took a step back from the side of

Elliot.

Rune now glared at him "It's over... and my name is LOXLEY!" She snapped her fingers and the ambassador gave a high pitched squeal, as he rose into the air, and was flung through the shimmering window. Rune smiled at Bear, as the others came up behind her. "Will you help Jacques? Robbie is in great danger because of York."

Bear rose from his seat and took Rune by the hand. "I would be honoured to escort the Lady of My Lord of Loxley." He bowed and kissed her hand. Jade giggled behind them, and Rune softened, and gave him a very bright smile. The doors burst open and Alice waddled up the centre of the room.

"I am coming too, I want to see Mickey's home, he has told me loads about it." She caught up with him, and slipped her arm into his. "I am also so bored sat at home doing nothing, Rune you need my counsel." Rune gave a giggle.

"Alright then... Shall we?" She slipped her arm into Bears other arm, and together they stepped through the window and into the main hall of the famous Assembly Rooms at York.

Elliot Selby laid flat on his back on the floor in front of a silent audience that viewed the window of violet with fear. Bear came through smiling with Rune and Alice, Crystal, Jade and Una followed. The captive audience looked stunned, at the sight of Bear with a very pregnant and beaming companion, and a slender girl dressed as a woodsman with a long rich violet cloak.

Elliot sat up and pointed a long gold ringed finger at Bear. "You have no right to treat me this way, I have served your father for years, how could you let her humiliate me like this?" Rune clicked her fingers and his voice faded. He clasped his hand to his mouth, and tried to scream, no sound emitted.

"Mickie." Bear turned and smiled, as the large form of his elder brother came forward smiling, He dragged him into a huge embrace and gave a rousing and hearty slap on the back. "Welcome home brother. I have missed you so much. You have been making quite a stir with your new friends, the gossip about you is simply all over the place; I am so pleased you are back with us."

"Sebastian, I have missed you, how is Brett? I am so sorry I could not get back with my father, I wanted so much to be here."

Sebastian hugged him hard. He was as big as Bear, with long dark hair and a manicured moustache and beard; he looked very much like the drawings of the musketeers Alice had seen in her books. Bear broke apart a huge smile on his face. "Brother we must talk alone, there is much evil around and we are all in danger. This is the Lady Runestone of Loxley, she is the companion of the hooded man, you must listen carefully to her, we may not have much time."

Sebastian turned and gave a regal bow to Rune. "My Lady you honour us greatly, please excuse me my manners I have not seen my brother in some time, and was quite carried away by the moment."

Rune nodded and smiled. "My Lord, I understand the love of family, you have no need to apologise, I am sure I would have acted the same if it was my sister, however I have come here on matters of extreme importance, of which your ambassador has little grasp. I must speak with you as soon as is possible." Elliot sat holding his mouth, his face red with anger, Sebastian gave him a glance, and then turned back to face Rune with a slight smile.

The stature of Rune was impressive, for she was small in the company of the men of York, mutterings quietly whispered around the room of tall columns and high windows. Bear introduced each member of the group, as Rune approached Elliot on the floor. She offered him a hand, he looked up in doubt, and then feeling he was safe amongst friends, he took it and she helped him to his feet. He dusted down his coat and pants.

"I am sorry Ambassador, but you must understand the danger you have put Lord Loxley in because of your arrogance, I will try to restrain myself and ensure your safety, if you would be good enough to act like a diplomat and not like a fool."

Bear and Sebastian approached Rune, Sebastian offered his arm to Rune who gave a sweet smile and took it. "My Lady Loxley, if you would care, I would greatly appreciate it if you would join me with your party at our dining table, I trust you have not eaten yet?"

"Thank you, My Lord, your hospitality would be very much appreciated, I would be delighted to dine with you." The gathered crowd of diplomats all bowed as Sebastian guided Rune out of the room. As the doors closed behind them, the sound of hurried voices could be heard as everyone turned to each other and discussed the extraordinary events.

It was dark as they sat in the trees looking down at the old farm cottage below them. The lights burned dim in the windows, Robbie scoured the dark looking for any signs of activity. He pulled down the scope, and looked across at Lee. "It seems quiet, but in this darkness, there could be a hundred men down there and we would not spot them." Rowan moved uneasily in his saddle. Lee scratched the white stubble on his chin, which seemed to reflect the moonlight.

"You seldom get people in these parts, since the dark prince took over there have been fewer raids, he stays behind the walls and trains his men to fight. Even then, they are still noisy and stupid; I think if there were any of them down there, we would have heard them by now. We are not expected by any other than my old friend Alfie. He is more loyal than you think; he is only alive because your grandfather saved his life, which is a powerful debt to repay in the world of old woodsmen."

Robbie looked over to Rowan, he could see his keen eyes watching through the dark, Rowan nodded, and Robbie looked back over to Lee. "Ok let's get down there."

The three of them kicked their horse's forward, and headed in a straight line for the farm cottage, they jumped a few limestone walls, and crossed the fields as they headed towards the pale light in the window. The hooves of the horses clattered on the cobbles of the yard, as Lee led them into the farm, and around to the back of the house. He dropped down from his horse, and opened the old wooden doors of the barn that creaked and groaned on rusty worn hinges.

Robbie and Rowan dismounted, and followed Lee in with the horses. They pulled the horses in, and unsaddled them in the stalls; Lee dropped his saddle on the door of the stall, and walked to the large doors, and pulled them closed. He struck a match and lit the lamp; he pulled the long match out of the lamp, and lit his pipe. The tobacco glowed red in the dim light as a large puff of white smoke floated into the air. He winked.

"Gentlemen, meet Alfie, my youngest brother." Robbie and Rowan spun round, and there sat on the stalls was a slightly younger version of Lee. He looked almost identical; except for the fact he still had the remains of brown streaked through his hair. Lee walked up the barn as Alfie slipped off the door, and they greeted each other with a hug. "Alf this is Robbie and Rowan, they need our help."

Alfie looked Robbie close in the eyes, as he gripped his hand in a tight hold and shook it. "You got your old pa in yer eyes, there's a lot a Jess there too. Those hairs are yer dad, his was scruffy when I taught him too."

Robbie smiled as he shook Alfie by the hand. "I am pleased to meet you; I had no idea Lee had a brother."

"He nearly didn't, your old grandfather saved me from falling off the high escarpment, I am glad to help any of his kin, I owe him a life. We better get a move on, we are on foot now, and need to move fast if we are to get you in by midnight... grab your kit."

Robbie and Rowan slipped off their Loxley cloaks, rolled them up and hid them in the saddles. Robbie swung his black hooded cloak over his shoulders, and picked up his bow and quiver. He slid his sword backward a bit to hide it from full view. Lee watched, and tore a small piece of rag off and old sack, he handed it to Robbie.

"Bind the hilt, it will keep it dull, and out of sight of prying eyes." He gave a piece to Rowan who wrapped it around the hilt of the sword of honour. He picked up his bow and nodded. Alfie swung the door open, and they slipped out into the dark courtyard. He led them round the back of the old barn, and they slipped silently in to the trees, and headed north into the dense forest that would lead them to the bandit camp. An old owl hooted at them as they passed by, its orb like eyes followed them as they moved without a sound in the trees.

Sebastian sat at the head of a very long table, Rune sat to his side facing Bear with Alice at his side, Jade, Crystal and Una tucked in as Elliot scowled at them, the day's indignities had been just a little too much for him. Around the table footmen dressed in black served from large silver serving dishes, it was clear that Sebastian, unlike Bear, appreciated the finer things in life. He sat almost erect, in his fine silken clothes, and adjusted his posture, and placement of his lace edged napkin. He gave a courteous nod to the servant and the food was placed in abundance on the table. Considering this was a meal that expected no guests, Rune was quite taken by the volume and the quality of the service.

Sebastian cut a large slice off his steak, as he looked up at Rune. "So Lady Runestone, your intended is in great danger due to my lack of ability to defend my own people. I have heard many things about him; I must admit I would like to know more of the situation I have apparently created."

Rune rested her fork on the side of her plate, as she lifted her wine glass and sipped. "At this moment in time, he is so concerned that York will fall that he has taken it upon himself to enter the black city."

Sebastian lowered his fork, and looked at her in amazement. "Surely you jest? No one would enter that city if they wanted to live."

Rune's bright blue eyes showed the concern she felt for Robbie. "I want you to understand me clearly, I want no confusion here. Lord Loxley is the only man alive that I respect and admire, for I have powers that can defeat any man." Elliot shrunk back in his chair. "He is the single most important thing in my life, and it has concerned me that he has chosen to enter that land, because your ambassador chose to ignore the best advice he will ever be given. He is risking his own life to find out what awaits York on the other side of that awful wall. If anything happens to him, I will hold York responsible, although I doubt there will be a York left. Am I clear enough for you, My Lord?"

Sebastian looked at his brother; Bear nodded with a very solemn look on his face. "My dear Lady I had no idea... I admit it was I who gave the order that we would not empty the city. Please accept my deepest apology, for if I had known of his plan, I would have offered my services in his stead."

Jade placed a hand on her sisters, Rowan was with him, and she too felt the same fear. Bear leaned forward to his brother. "Seb, you must consider getting the women and children away, I have seen some of the army that is heading our way and it is vast."

Sebastian gave a long exhausted sigh, as he dabbed at his mouth with his napkin. "This is a walled city just like Loxley, are you telling me that you will evacuate most of Loxley if they come for you? You will not, Loxley will stand behind its walls and fight."

Rune nodded. "In some respects, My Lord you are right, but our defence of Loxley will not be sat on top of the wall hurling things down. The men of Loxley are very skilled in what they do, we will have half of our forces outside the wall to fight, and those within on their absolute worst day, will still be far superior to your best. Our life has been war, I mean no disrespect, but your people are used to haggling for goods, not beating off the dark forces Cutters. It took seventeen men of Loxley, to bring down Tintagel, how many of your men could achieve the same?"

Sebastian seemed uncomfortable with her remarks, his face narrowed, and he looked into her resolute blue eyes. "Your Lord has promised us aid, is he now going back on his word?" Rune now felt more anger grow inside her, her voice although still soft, sharpened a little.

"Lord Loxley has never broken his word, neither has he turned his back on those being threatened by the dark forces. He is currently risking his life for your city; how dare you even suggest he would turn his back." Her eyes flared violet, and Sebastian knew he had crossed the line, he held up the palm of his hands.

"Please... please I honestly meant no offence my good lady; I will happily withdraw the comment, and fully apologise to you Lady Loxley. Everyone in the free realm is aware of his deeds in aid to others, please you must forgive me my temper."

Rune calmed down, and her eyes faded back to their usual shade of lilac around the bright Sapphire blue pupils. Elliot looked very white and trembled slightly. Una nudged him. "For Hearne's sake man, grow a spine."

Bear gave a short laugh, and looked back to his brother. "Loxley will place as many of its men in front of York as possible. It is our hope that we will stem the tide, but I can tell you this brother, they will be outnumbered by at least fifty to one. York will suffer before the end, but Loxley will pay the higher price. If York falls, it will be Loxley men that fall with her, that will leave Loxley unable to protect itself, and Loxley will fall as a result. I suggest you think very carefully my brother, before you make your final decision."

Rune rose gracefully from her seat and bowed. "My Lord thank you for providing us with the chance to speak, and also for the hospitality you have shown to us. It was gratefully appreciated." Rune placed a blue butterfly made of a strange blue metal on the table beside Sebastian's plate. "When you have decided what path, you will take give this a gentle squeeze, and I shall return to hear your decision, until then My Lord, I will bid you farewell." Rune turned, and waved her hand across the air in front of her, and the shimmering violet light of her archway appeared. She walked through as the others rose out of their seats. Sebastian looked up at Crystal and smiled.

"Will I see you again fair lady of the winter?"

Crystal smiled. "If you make the right choice you will live, and it will enhance your chances, make the wrong one and no you won't." She gave him a broad smile, and walked through the archway and disappeared. Bear hugged his brother.

"Please think of what Rune has told you, she speaks sense you must see that? I will see you soon as I return to defend York." Bear turned, and taking Alice by the hand he stepped through the violet archway, and it faded away, and Sebastian looked at Elliot.

"Nice people, tough negotiators I like that, they would do well in business. No idea about defence though, I think we need to review the wall guards, call in the captains."

Rune looked up at Bear. "Thank you, Jacques, I could see in his heart and he will not change his mind, I fear your bother has much to learn before he understands the world outside his walls. It is your home and it may well fall; please remember you have a life here as well as there. Do not be as foolish as your brother, and stay when all hope is lost, promise me you will use the pendant and come back to us, Alice could not stand to lose you. Neither could Robbie or myself."

Bear placed a large hand on the side of her face. "You are the finest woman I have ever known Runestone of Loxley, if you truly ask this of me with your open heart, I cannot refuse you." She lifted her hand to his and squeezed it.

"I do Jacques; you are very special to all of us."

"Then My Lady I will honour your request with a promise to obey you as I would my friend and lord." She smiled at him and felt a wave of relief come over her. She had felt the anxiety in Alice all night, and now relaxed knowing he would return to her.

Robbie slid down in the bushes with Rowan. Lee looked into the dark with Alfie. It was pitch black, and there were no signs of life anywhere, Alfie gave a shrill little whistle and a knife appeared at his neck. The large dark clad man with a thick beard grinned down on him. A long golden dagger slipped up to his chin, he swallowed deeply as the soft voice spoke in his ear. "It appears we are becoming quite crowded for such large woodland. I would suggest you remove your blade from my friend's throat, you will make a far bigger puddle on the floor than he will." The large man swallowed hard, as he slid his hand down and dropped the knife. Robbie smiled. "Good, now why don't we sit and talk about killing the dark forces rather than each other?"

Lee gave a smile as he looked up at the satisfied look on Robbie's face. Robbie removed his dagger and slipped back into the bushes. The large man turned, and jumped to see no one there, he looked back at Lee and Alfie who shrugged. He looked nervous and sat down fast, Robbie appeared opposite him with Rowan, and the large man jumped again with surprise. Lee stood up and offered his hand to the stranger. "I am Lee Sherman, and I have need of your help, this is Robbie and Rowan, we are on business from Loxley at our lord's command, we need entry into the black city, can your people help?"

The large rough bearded man looked up surprised at Lee, he was shabbily dressed in patched clothes, and his odour was more than noticeable across the campfire. "I am Bevis, but everyone round here calls me Ox. You ask a great favour for strangers, I know of your lord, and what he wants to achieve, you should go back and tell him he hasn't a chance."

Rowan leaned forward. "We must see for ourselves Ox, can you help us or should we just sneak over the wall ourselves, as you have seen we pride ourselves on stealth."

Ox nodded as he thought. "There is a way in but it will cost you." Robbie looked through the dark at Ox.

"What is your price Ox?"

Ox scratched at the heavy thatch of his beard, and splinters of wood fell into the fire and ignited in small flashes. "We robbed a cart a year ago; it had a barrel of Loxley ale on it, and some bottles of red wine. The price will be twenty barrels, and fifty bottles. If your lord will give his word to pay up, I will take you inside and place you with a friend who knows of Alfie Sherman here."

Robbie almost felt relief; he had thought they would have wanted far more for such a dangerous task. He looked around at the others and then back to Ox. "I can speak for Lord Loxley; you will have his word if I shake your hand." Robbie offered his hand to Ox who smiled. He took Robbie by the hand and gave it a good shake.

"Good that's the business end done, now on to the task, follow me and go quietly; we will not have much time." Ox got up from his seat and picked up his knife. He smiled to himself as he headed into the trees in the dark followed by Lee and the others.

Rowan watched the large man carefully; he did not trust anyone this far from his hometown. They moved very quickly for about an hour, when Ox slowed. They stood on the edge of the woodland and looked out across two hundred yards of barren and scorched earth. A small stream ran out of the wall and down towards the trees. Ox pointed to it. "There where the water comes out is a grate, it looks secure but we have fitted false bolts on it. Give it a tug and it will open. Follow the tunnel up to the street inside, as you come out of the grate on the other side, you will see a row of ten houses. Second on the left from the far end, go into the back yard, and tap on the door twice. Tell them Elizabeth sent you, you will be well hidden."

Robbie thanked Ox. "When we return, I will find you and arrange your delivery.

"Thank you, My Lord." Robbie looked stunned.

"Why do you call me lord?" Ox patted him on the back.

"I am a bandit, not an idiot, do you think rags can hide a sword of such value to me. Only the hooded man could sneak up and put a knife to my throat, I almost did this for free knowing of the stories and free meals I will get out of tonight." Robbie gave a small laugh.

"Loxley will not forget this Ox, just do me a favour, keep your story a secret until I am out of there, gossip can move faster than even the hooded man." He pulled up his hood and winked at Ox.

"Good luck My Lord, be on your guard at all times, that place gives folk the willies."

Robbie nodded, and then sped off across the open ground in the dark, he moved swiftly and quietly towards the grate. Lee hugged his brother and then followed. Rowan went last having had a good slap on the back from Ox.

Rune sat alone at her table and looked at the violet mist, she muttered strange words under her breath, and wrote a charm to let her under Hearne's veil. The violet mist swirled and began to clear. She felt a jolt as she saw Robbie run through the dark to the wall, he stopped with his back flat against the cold stone, as he waited for the others to catch up.

"Hi gorgeous." He stiffened.

"Hey Beautiful where are you?"

"I am home at my table, and lonely without you."

"I am sorry Rune, this is not a safe place for you, I had to do this one alone."

"You are not alone, I am here... Oh please be careful Rob, I don't want to be alone like this forever."

"I have you in my heart to guide me, I will be safe."

"When you enter, I will not be able to see you, use your pendant and I will help you."

"Please Rune, I will be fine, you focus on keeping my two children healthy, protect Loxley for me."

"I love you, Robbie."

"I love you too Runestone Sapphire."

He ducked down, as Rowan ran up and jumped into the tunnel, Robbie turned and entered the tunnel behind him under the black wall; the pictures on Rune's table went blank. She sat and stared at the violet as it swirled. He was in the black city, and out of her reach; she lowered her head and put her hands to her face, and quietly she wept with her fear.

CHAPTER SIXTEEN

THE BLACK CITY CHURCH

Rune lay in the dark and stared at the windows. The clouds drifted across the sky of the mere hiding the moon, she stretched out her arm and he was not there. She turned on her side and looked at the empty pillow, she felt afraid and alone, knowing he was miles away and hidden from her, her stomach was in knots with worry. She rolled back, and looked at the ceiling and closed her eyes. "Hi gorgeous." There was nothing, her eyes filled with tears, and she rolled over and buried her face in the pillow. Rune sobbed quietly alone.

Lee tapped quietly on the door, as Robbie and Rowan pressed their backs against the wall. The whole city had guards everywhere, and sneaking up to the house at the end of the row had taken ages. The door creaked open a jar, a thin line of light spilled onto the yard, and drew a white line on the grey floor as it headed to the small back gate. "Elizabeth sent us." The door closed, and Robbie could hear the soft muttering going on behind it. The light went out, and the door slipped open, Lee, Rowan and Robbie slipped inside quietly.

The room was very dark; there was a dull glow from a candle in a deep red jar, in what looked like the far corner of the room. Robbie felt the presence of others and slid his hand to his dagger, a voice came from somewhere to his left. "Name yourself." Lee's voice spoke out in front of him.

"I am Lee Sherman, and I am accompanied by two bowmen of Loxley, their names are Robbie and Rowan. We are here at the command of the hooded man, to seek information on the army of the Dark One. The hooded man wishes to send aid to York and needs to know what he is faced with."

Robbie could hear others, somewhere in front of him breathing. Feet shuffled to his far right, and he tensed, he felt Rowan close by his shoulder, and his hand firmly gripped the hilt of his dagger. The voice in the darkness spoke again. "The name Sherman is known to us."

"He is my youngest brother." Lee seemed to have moved further away from Robbie, and he wondered if Lee wasn't like himself, preparing for attack.

A match struck, and the face of a man around forty lit up. He had short brown hair and deep green eyes; he was unshaven and looked tired. "I am Malcolm Prosper; I was a woodsman here many years ago before the walls came. You have no worry; all here are loyal to Loxley." He lit the oil lamp on the table at his side, and the room brightened bringing into view three women. "This is my wife and two daughters, for now I will not give you their names; they are best kept out of this. Times here are difficult, and many live with such fear that they would tell just to protect what little they have, in here secrets are best kept exactly that."

He put out his hand and Lee took it and gave it a shake. "It is good to find loyalty to Loxley within such high walls. I am sure that Lord Loxley will be very grateful to know he has support in dark corners." Malcolm offered his hand to Rowan who shook it, and then to Robbie. He looked him in the eyes, and his gaze lingered for a minute as Robbie nodded to him, Robbie released his hand, and stepped back allowing Lee to continue.

Malcolm offered them a seat. "Please sit and have something to eat, we will have to make a few arrangements for you." He waved to one of his daughters, who up until now had sat quietly with her mother and sister. She got up and walked across the room to a small stove; she threw in some wood, and pulled a large pan over the flame. Robbie sat quietly with Rowan, and watched as Malcolm gathered some things together, and then pulling on a long black coat and a thick woolly hat, he slipped out of the door. The other two women just acted as if they were not there, they picked up their sewing and got on with it. Robbie found it all a little surreal and sat staring at the table.

The young woman stood by the pan and would occasionally glance back at them, Lee pulled out his pipe and asked Malcolm's wife if it would be all right, she gave him a nod, and he lit the pipe and sat puffing grey clouds of smoke in the air. The room was dull, but it was quite large considering.

It seemed to be the whole of the bottom floor of the house. Heavy black curtains hung front and back keeping the light in, and prying eyes out. The kitchen was mainly a sink area and a stove, with a small table at the side of it. It ran under the back window along the wall, and a long settee ran along the sidewall, on which the two other women sat. Most of the room was empty, apart from an old chair by the small fireplace, and a rickety old bookcase with a few old and well-worn novels.

Robbie and Rowan sat at the large pine table in the middle of the room, it had six chairs round it, and it appeared to Robbie, it was the focal point of the whole house. The large brass oil lamp sat in the centre of it, and lit the whole room, it had the essentials, but to Robbie it lacked personality. He thought of his own home, and how Rune often left her clothes hanging from the end of the bedpost or under her chair, she had pictures of him, and Loxley on the walls, and the rug with a large coat of arms in front of their fire. It was obvious by the vase's full of cut flowers all over the house, and the shawls scattered over everything that Rune lived there. This place seemed to have nothing, if everyone left you would have no idea anyone had ever lived here.

Malcolm's daughter sliced bread, and cooked what looked like a stew, he watched her with her tight plait of black hair, and her white apron over her dull greyish looking clothes, just like the house they all dressed as drab. She turned with two bowls and placed them on the table with a smile. Robbie gave her a smile back and nodded. She seemed to appreciate it and turned quickly to the sink to wash the pan. The stew was hot, and quite spicy, he had not realised how hungry he was, as he tore at the bread, and dipped it in to the steaming stew.

They ate in silence; Rowan gave a slight grin as if reading his thoughts. It was not the happiest household he had ever entered. The pan washing was finished, and it was dried and put back, as Rowan and Robbie finished their meal, the young woman whisked their plates and bowls off the table and washed them. She wiped the table with a cloth and then sat down between Robbie and Rowan. She gave them a smile. "I am Meg." Robbie seized a chance to talk.

"Rob and this is Rowan. Thanks for the meal it was really good of you."

"Are you as good with a bow as he is... you know, the hooded man?" She nodded to the two long bows leaning against the table. Her bright green eyes sparkled. Rowan gave a slight smile as he looked at Robbie.

"There is no other man in the country who shoots better than the hooded man, we have skill, but his is beyond ability." She nodded and gave a big smile; she seemed very excited about meeting someone who knew of the hooded man.

"They say he is married to the Violet Witch, is she really as terrifying as everyone says? I find it hard to believe that the hooded man would marry anyone as evil and horrible as they say.... He is my hero." Rowan gave Robbie a huge smile, and his eyes twinkled. Somehow, he knew Rowan would now sit back and enjoy the spectacle. Robbie leaned forward and noticed that Meg's mother and sister had stopped sewing, and were listening intently. Robbie took a breath.

"If you see Lady Runestone Sapphire, for that is her full name, you will understand that the dark forces have painted her as evil for the purpose of frightening you all against her. She is the Lady of Loxley and the hooded man. They call her the violet witch because she frightens them, she is a sorceress like the Dark One, and she is very powerful, she has to be to match her enemy." He smiled to himself, as he saw the full attention, he was receiving from everyone. "As for evil or witch, you have my word she is neither. Lady Runestone is very elegant and immensely beautiful." Meg's eyes widened as Robbie softly spoke.

"When you talk to her, she listens to every word you say and has great understanding. Her eyes are the most beautiful sapphire blue, and the whites of her eyes have a faint tinge of lilac. They are filled with the life and love of her realm and her people, she is softly spoken and very gentle, and she is quick to smile and can bring great joy to people with just a few words of comfort. She is natural around everyone, and I know of no one in Loxley that does not love her."

"Oh wow." Meg placed her elbows on the table and rested her smiling face in her hands. "She sounds amazing; they say she can fight with great skill."

Robbie leaned back in his chair as pictures of Rune floated through his mind; he missed her and wanted to feel her close. "She is without doubt the most amazing woman I have ever met, she has a skill with a bow to almost match the hooded man, and she has a sword of great power that ignites and burns with the power of knowledge when she fights. There are few who can match her with a sword. Do not listen to the poison you hear in this place, she fights for the good of us all, and they hate her for it."

Meg beamed with delight, as her thoughts drifted, her mother smiled at Robbie. "I have told her this many times, maybe now she will listen. You honour your Lady of Loxley greatly."

"She honours all of us in her protection of the woodland realm." Meg's mother smiled and nodded, her eyes lingered on him for a moment, and then they dropped to her sewing.

Talking of Rune brought a strain to his heart and a twist to his stomach, her last words echoed in his thoughts and he missed her. This was the first time in a long time she had not been by his side and it felt strange. Rowan understood the thoughts of Robbie and sat quiet, as he thought of Jade alone in his house without him. The time seemed to slowly drag by, as Meg lost in her thoughts smiled at the lamp. Lee seemed to doze, his pipe hanging from his lip.

Robbie jumped as the door suddenly opened, and Malcolm reappeared. He slipped in with a smile and closed the door quickly behind him; Lee stirred in the chair, as he pulled the pipe from his mouth and yawned. Malcolm looked around at everyone and then to Lee. "We have a safe house for you that should help you get what you need, gather your things and we will leave. We have to move fast before the sun comes up, there has been a disturbance over by the gate, and there are guards everywhere. We must leave now and quickly."

Malcolm seemed very agitated, they quickly gathered their bags and bows, and pulling his dark cloak around him, Robbie followed Malcolm out of the door into the small yard. The air was cooling compared to the warmth indoors; Robbie looked round through the darkness. Lee and Rowan followed as they passed through the gate, and ran quietly down the long alley behind the houses. Somewhere in the distance, Robbie could hear a bell chiming as if in warning. His mind wandered as to who would cause such a problem, everyone within the walls seemed to live in fear, and he got the very distinct impression that the bandits would never attack the city, they like him, used stealth.

Malcolm flattened himself against the wall and peered round the corner. Robbie slipped an arrow into his bow and looked back at Rowan and Lee. They too had loaded their bows, and he smiled at Rowan, who he knew was not worried about being attacked, but more about protecting his lord.

Malcolm turned to Robbie. "We need to cross here, but it is floodlit, and there are many soldiers watching the whole camp. If we get spotted, there is a church. You head down the alley to the end, and then turn left. Follow the street to the top and turn right into the last alleyway, at the end of that alley slip over the wall and you will be in the churchyard. Use the side door it will be open, the priest will help you, he is called Warren."

Robbie nodded and Malcolm smiled. He looked down at the arrow fitted into the bow. "Nice bracelet, nice ring too, them rags don't really hide the sword with your cloak open; I feel honoured to serve you, My Lord." He winked at Robbie, and then with a sudden burst, he headed across the wide roadway and into the alley opposite. Robbie glanced around the corner; it was clear. He ran with all his might across the road and slipped into the darkness of the alley. He pressed his back against the wall, and slid up his hood. Robbie watched up the street facing Malcolm, who watched down the street. Robbie signalled the two to come together, he gave the all clear and they shot out into the light. A figure in black appeared on the roof and lifted a crossbow as Rowan and Lee hit the centre of the road. It took Malcolm long enough to just blink, and Robbie had brought up his bow aimed and fired at the guard.

He looked round the corner and saw the guard on the roof clutch at his throat and then stumble to the floor, he looked back and Robbie had his second arrow fitted, and was aiming at the roof. Malcolm gave him a big smile. "They aint kidding about you are they?"

Robbie winked and nodded up the alley where Lee and Rowan now moved swiftly and quietly in the dark. Malcolm turned and followed; they kept against the walls in the shadows, and made their way up to the top of the long corridor of dank grey concrete. Rowan and Lee both stood at the end in the shadows, they watched the brightly lit road.

Robbie slid up at Rowan's side. Rowan nodded down the street, and Robbie leaned forward to see the nine guards all stood in a group talking. It looked like one was giving orders to the others; they were about one hundred yards up the street. Robbie gave a smile, he drew a violet arrow out of Rowan's quiver, he winked at Rowan. "Let's see if rumours really do get around fast." Rowan slipped back, as Robbie loaded his bow and flattened himself against the wall. He slipped a second violet arrow out and passed it to Lee. Robbie lifted the bow and took aim.

The Sergeant bellowed at the men. "You keep bloody well alert, you hear me? It is not possible for anything to get into this city, but if they have, we will bloody well get them. I don't want them passing under the noses of men on my sec..." The violet tipped arrow passed right through his throat, and his men all jumped back and screamed with shock, they turned and looked down the street. The black cloaked figure of a bowman stood with another violet arrow loaded, his voice was eerie in the late night cold.

"You will all come with me tonight, for I know where you sleep." Shivers ran down the young soldier's spines as he released the second arrow. Rumours did move faster than even Robbie had expected, two of the men pointed and screamed as the arrow hit the tallest soldier in front of them. They dropped their crossbows, turned, and ran.

The others looked at the two dead, and then back at the two running soldiers, they seemed torn as to what exactly to do, the violet bowman had not even twitched, and yet from nowhere a third arrow took out another soldier. It was enough, they all turned and without a word, they ran down the street away from the spirit of the dead bowman who stole your soul, and came for you in the night. Robbie ran swiftly up the street, followed by Rowan, Lee and Malcolm. He reached the three dead soldiers and pulled out his arrows.

As Lee and Rowan stood guard, Robbie quickly wiped the arrows on the cloaks of the guards, and then taking three crossbow arrows from one of the dropped quivers, he inserted the smaller arrows into the wounds of the dead. "That will confuse em." He winked at Lee and Rowan, and then at a good pace, they all headed for the alley to the back of the church.

The church stood silent under the passing dark clouds. It was smooth polished black stone, built very similar to the churches of old, yet somehow it just did not seem to fit in with the rest of the long rows of grey squared off stone buildings that surrounded it. Robbie had never imagined Mason as a religious man, and found it odd to find it in the middle of what he saw as concrete hell.

The four dark figures slipped quietly over the low wall and on to the grass, Robbie was surprised to see so many graves in what looked like a relatively new church. He looked up at a cross in front of him at the date that read 2037.

Remembering where he was, told him enough to know that like in Scotland people were brutalised for fun in these cities. Malcolm led the way as they wound their way through the graves to the wooden side door. Robbie, Rowan and Lee sheltered behind tall gravestones in the dark as Malcolm knocked gently on the door. The bolts drew back on the other side, and the door opened a small fraction, a pair of dark eyes looked through the small gap. They blinked, and then the door swung open and Malcolm stepped inside, a few seconds later Malcolm's face reappeared and he signalled. The three of them dashed out from behind the graves, and in through the door into the very small vestry.

Robbie turned round and looked into the almost black eyes of Farther Warren. He was a man of medium build, with very short jet-black hair and a very pale face. He looked drawn and yet his eyes seemed to burn with life. He offered a hand and

Robbie took it. "I am Father Warren, welcome to the Black City, it is not the best place in this world to be, but you will be safe here, the dark army fear the church."

Robbie nodded to the priest. "I am Rob, this is Rowan and Lee, we are very grateful for your kind offer of shelter, we have important work to do to help save many lives. Loxley has all of its hope on our shoulders."

Father Warren offered a hand toward the door that led into the main church. "If you would care to follow me, I see you have the light of the Pagan faiths inside you, fear not my lord accepts men of all faiths here, we are descended of Cille."

Robbie seemed surprised. "You know of the faith on Iona?" He smiled.

"The Violet Isle is the home of our church here for we serve all, and all are welcome." Robbie felt a wave of relief; he was suspicious of the church.

Canterbury was not exactly the best confidence builder. He had spent a lot of time talking to Rune about Iona and its strange little Abbey, which seemed to celebrate both Earth and Christian faiths. Knowing that this church was based in that faith seemed to relax him, he had been a little tense at the thought of the church being his protector.

Robbie followed the Father out into the small church. The white walls glowed in the candle light, he looked up at the large golden crucifix hanging in front of the altar, which was draped in green and had a heavy stone cross on it, which he recognised. Only a short time ago he had stood by the original, and watched the ancestors of Fae come forth and present themselves to Rune and himself. The long wooden rail that crossed the front of the altar was heavily carved with acorns and oak leaves. Symbols of the sun and moon were all over the place, he felt very much at home.

The others walked around looking up and down the isle of twenty rows of pews, and the balcony at the back that seemed to stand above the large double brass hinged doors that led out to the front of the church. Robbie passed the main altar and looked at the small altar set back behind the pulpit. His thoughts turned to Sian, as he looked at the statue of the woman in pale blue holding the child in her arms. He knew this to be Mary with the Christ, and yet to him he saw his much loved Sister Mary. He felt comfort as he felt some how she knew he was here and she was with him, it was a strange feeling, and yet her presence felt like it was all around him. Father Warren watched him, with curiosity in his eyes. "You know of Mary?"

Robbie was still lost in thought. "Yes, she was very special to us... I mean the person who told me of this statue was also called Mary. She too cared for many children, this statue always helps me feel close to her, she was a great help at a troubled time, I miss her."

Father Warren smiled. "I hope you find comfort here then, let me show you where you will rest." Father Warren led them down the centre of the church below the balcony; he turned right at the front doors and went through a small doorway.

It took them down a wooden staircase to a small living space. This was where Father Warren lived his solitary life. There was a small stove and an old battered table, a few comfortable chairs and many bookcases. In the corner was a very old heavy oak desk. It was filled with papers and books lay open scattered on the floor and across the top of the desk.

From the centre of the room ran a short corridor with four other doors off it. Father Warren opened the first door. "You can wash in here, the door opposite is my room, and the two at the bottom are empty, there are two beds in each room, please make yourselves as comfortable as possible. It will be a long night there has been some trouble, and there will be guards all over for most of the night. I have work to do, so if you do not mind, I will bid you goodnight, and we shall talk in the morning."

Father Warren walked Malcolm out, and returned about ten minutes later and sat at his desk, Robbie and Rowan took one of the rooms and let Lee with his pipe have the other. Rowan sat on the bed in the very sparse room. Robbie dropped his bag and laid his bow with two arrows at the side of it, along the floor at the side of his bed. He lay back and rested, Rowan sat with his back to the wall. "What do you think, can we trust him?"

Robbie opened his eyes and turned his head to Rowan. The small candle flickered on the old cabinet besides the bed. "I have no trust of the Christian church, but this man has beliefs I have only seen in Sister Mary, I think we can trust him. I will still keep my bow and sword close, just in case."

Rowan gave a smile and nodded. "I have thought the same my friend"

Robbie closed his eyes and drifted. 'I miss you Rune.'

Rune sat bolt upright in bed. The moonlight poured in through the windows. *"Robbie is that you?"* Her eyes burned bright violet.

"Rune I can feel you, how is that possible?"

Rune burst into tears as she sat alone in bed miles away in Loxley. *"Oh Robbie, I don't care I miss you."*

"Hey beautiful, I miss you too, please don't get upset, my heart is with you."

"Where are you Robbie, the Black City is supposed to be shrouded, you should not be able to reach me."

"I am in a church; the Father here is from Iona and follows the same faith as Sister Mary"

Rune sat on the bed in their room in Loxley, *"You are under the roof of Colum Cille, and you are of the line of Gwendolyn. That explains it, remember sanctuary?"*

"What about it?"

The violet figure of Rune came through the wall, Robbie jumped on the bed as

Rowan tensed. Rune gave him a big bright smile as he stood up. She slid her arms around him and held him close. Robbie touched her as he felt her warmth; she felt solid which was strange considering she had just passed through concrete. "That's three times now you have done that." She looked up and smiled at him.

"I can go back to bed if you don't like it." He pulled her closer.

"No, this time I think I can overlook it."

Rowan smiled as he watched her in his friends' arms, he longed for his precious little Pebbles, yet drew some comfort as Robbie and Rune sat close on the bed. She kissed him softly and he felt his world return to normal. "Do not ever leave me alone without saying again, I cannot handle the separation Rob, you should have told me. I would have understood."

He looked her in the eyes. "You would have come; I know you Rune. Look here you are, even though you know it is dangerous."

"Not here it isn't, this place is protected in ways she will never know. This is the home of Iona; it is her soil below our feet. This place is sacred and the Dark One has no power within these walls, you will be safe inside here and that gives me comfort, as it will Jade."

Rowan looked up at Rune, who was now looking at him. "She will know you are safe soon; she is at my house and is very upset you left her."

Rowan looked at the floor. "I will not risk her here; she is too important." He looked sad and very miserable as he looked up. "Tell her I miss her."

Rune smiled. "Tell her yourself." Rowan's eyes flickered, violet, as Rune reached across the gap between the beds and touched his knee.

Jade lay alone and quiet in bed. She stared at the door filled with misery, it shimmered for moment and she blinked. The violet light grew out of the door, and Rowan looking very surprised stepped into the room. Jade bounced out of the bed and flew into his arms. He felt her warmth as he pulled her close as she sobbed into his arms. "Jade I am alright, Rune is with Robbie, I have no idea how she did this, but I miss you and she has sent me here for a short time." He held her tight as she shook in his arms. Jade slipped back and looked up at him. She brushed back her fringe, and her eyes narrowed.

"Don't you ever pull a stunt like this on me again, I mean it Rowan, you have scared the life out of me and broke my heart, you should be ashamed of yourself, and you can tell that Robbie that he too is in for it when he gets back here. I mean it Rowan, do this again and you will be sleeping in the workshop. I am your wife; he is not married to you. If he needs you, he tells me, do you understand?"

Rowan felt awful, he looked down at her angry green eyes. "I am sorry sweetheart, I should have told you."

She gave him a smile and her eyes danced. "Good... Kiss me." Rowan bowed down and she hung from his neck as he embraced her. Holding her in his arms was enough to quell the pain of his separation; she looked up at his sorry eyes. "It's kinda odd you being all purple and shiny, I find it sexy though." She gave him a soft giggle.

Rune slid her head on to his shoulder as he held her close. He felt the calmness flow over him that radiated from her. She snuggled closer. "Be very careful Rob, there are great dangers here, that we know little of. The Dark One still has powers we have not seen; you must not drop your guard at all. The table cannot tell me anything of what will pass behind these walls. I am blocked from here, as she is in Loxley. Keep Rowan close to you and protect each other."

Robbie lay down and she curled into him, it was the early hours of the morning and he felt exhausted. He held her close and breathed a deep sigh of contentment; he closed his eyes and enjoyed the feeling of her beside him. His sleep was deep and peaceful knowing she was close.

The sun was rising when Rune slipped carefully off the bed and kissed him softly on the head. "Sleep well my love." She turned to Rowan who now had normal eyes and smiled. "Stay close to him for me." Rowan nodded.

"I will, you know you do not have to ask." Rune turned to face the wall. "Rune?"

She turned and looked back at Rowan who was sat on the edge of the bed. "What is it Rowan?"

"Nothing, I just wanted to say thanks, I miss her." She gave him a smile, and turned back to the wall and passed through, the violet shimmer faded and the walls danced in the light of the flickering candle.

It was late morning, when Robbie woke, his arm automatically slipped to his side for Rune, she was not there and he sat up and looked round. He yawned as Rowan smiled. "Good morning, you slept well My Lord."

Robbie scratched his head and swung his feet off the bed, he was still fully dressed. "What time is it?"

"It's just past eleven, there is a service going on upstairs, Warren thinks we are better staying down here out of sight until it is over."

Robbie stretched his arms. "Please tell me there is coffee." Rowan gave him a grin as he got up off the bed.

"Come on there is plenty, although I will warn you, Mason sells inferior beans." Robbie rose aching to his feet, and slipped on his boots; he followed Rowan up the little passage to the stove.

Life in the Black City seemed so different to Robbie, he was not used to being surrounded by so many different types of industry. The small area of housing within the city was surrounded with factories producing everything to feed the growth of the cities. People filed out of their homes, and up the streets as horns announced it was time for a new work shift to start. He watched from the small window next to the bell above the church. Within twenty minutes of the mass exodus to work, he saw the black smoke belching from the chimneys. The air coming through the window felt oppressive, and tasted bad in his mouth.

In the distance above the roofline of the factories and grey houses, Robbie saw the inner wall. This was the wall that separated the workers from the soldiers. From the little he had learned from Warren; he knew that behind there was where the soldiers were housed. Somewhere over that tall hard wall, was also the palace that had been built for Mordred. Robbie knew that as he looked out, he was there hiding in the dark and planning the downfall of York. His eyes wandered the high walls, from here; it was difficult to see with any detail a weakness that could be exploited, never the less he looked. The information he needed would be over that wall, and he had to find a way of being able to observe in the daylight

From what Father Warren had told Lee, it seemed that from the high outer wall that ran down the country, the whole of the land inside had been broken into sectors. Each sector was enclosed by walls of fifty feet high, on which the guards patrolled and watched. Each sector was designated to a certain type of industry, here the workers worked on making bricks and stone.

Two walls ran up the centre of the whole complex that ran north, and between them was the long road that ran to Scotland. The workers rarely were allowed to cross the road into the eastern sectors, as on the other side now lay the vast farms that grew food for the cities, and they edged right up to the sea. On the inner walls large flights of steps led up to the high wall that ran from west to east, all of the troops gained access through the large archways at the top. These led back to the barrack houses behind the high dividing walls. Knox had made it very difficult for the workers and their families to get anywhere near the soldiers.

Father Warren had planned to take them out to the market place. He had told Lee how people came from all over to trade, and it was a place where many different kinds of people could be found. Blending in would be easier, and at least it was close enough to the wall to see if there was any way to get in. He had supplied two sets of brown robes that once belonged to a Monk who lodged at the church. They were a little baggy, but they covered Robbie and Rowan's woodsmen attire. He hung carved Celtic crosses round their necks and pulled up their hoods.

Lee with his scruffy white hair and chin of unshaven white growth, with an old patched cloak looked every bit the part of one of the bandits; Father Warren tied a thick headband of black silk round his forehead. It was a tribal trademark of the bandits, and he knew that no soldier would try to remove his long bow. The bandits had some sway in the city, in the early days; there had been a few groups, who had worked for the Cutters. Ox had exploited this, and used it as a way of passing goods to and from the city; the guards knew a black headband was untouchable.

The long bow was a banned weapon in the cities. Therefore, for Robbie and Rowan they slid their bows down the insides of two long bamboo poles. These now served as staffs to walk with, and helped with Farther Warren's cover story of travelling Celtic Christian Monks. Robbie tied his quiver to his waist and slid it round the back out of sight under the long black cloak. When they were finally ready to leave, he unbolted the doors, and they stepped out into the street filling with women and children all heading for market. Lee trailed behind them, as no bandit would ever be seen in the company of the priesthood. It also provided Lee with the opportunity to hang back, and watch in case he was needed.

Everyone walked on the left side of the road. This way the soldiers could control the flow of people in each direction easily. Farther Warren warned them not to look at the guard's faces, it appeared that this got them angry and they lashed out. Rowan and Robbie walked either side of the Father, their long poles tapping the ground dimly as they walked.

Robbie watched the silent masses, as they quietly made their way up the street. It was odd how well behaved the children were, as they walked with their heads down holding the hands of their parents. He thought of market day at Loxley where the children ran wild screaming and laughing, as they played whilst their parents bought their goods. The market was bigger than Robbie had at first expected. Hathersage had always been the biggest he had known with around fifty stalls. This market was vast, and he marvelled at the huge number of stalls. There had to be at least two hundred, all lined out in a huge square. People of the city mixed with Bandits, and with a few woodsmen. It seemed that quite a few of the city dwellers lived here only by force and refused to give up their woodsman identities.

Mason had been very shrewd and cashed in on the travelling trade to York, and by creating a massive trade area within the confines of what was in all intents and purposes, a captive audience of workers, he had managed to draw a very large population together for the market days. The stalls were crammed with breads and foods, preserves, clothes, rugs and furniture. There did seem to be a thriving market for clothes from the old era, as second hand stalls selling the old designer labels seemed to outnumber just about everything. Ten stalls in a long row at the end seemed to be selling re-labelled old tins of food. They had bright red labels that clearly stated they were a Knox reclaimed product. Two of the stalls sold new tins of food, Robbie looked at the piles of canned fish, and meats, Knox had got new factories set up that were now canning fresh foods.

People poured into the market from every direction, and the noise of haggling and debate filled the air. Many different smells wafted into the air from the many stalls selling cooked foods, Robbie stayed close to Rowan, and once buried deep within the crowd he started to look up surveying the walls of the city, and the main wall that separated this part of the city from the military barracks. Just at the back of the market were two huge heavy gates, they were set in a large stone archway in the large high dividing wall. Robbie knew behind them was the death of York, he looked round at the rest of the square.

Long ramparts ran along the tops of the walls. There was no visible signs of how the soldiers who walked in red raven and dragon crested shirts along the top, actually got up there. Robbie traced the ramparts back to the huge dividing wall, where a series of archways led back into the barracks. Rowan stood by the side of Robbie. He slid back his hood slightly and his slate grey eyes creased against the pale sun, as he watched the men high up. "That is quite a climb; we will not find it easy getting up there."

"There must be a way my friend, give me a little more time and I will find it." He smiled at Rowan from under his hood, his dark eyes narrowed as he followed the walls slowly back along towards the church. He looked right past at one point, and then he spotted what he wanted. He tapped Rowan on the shoulder, and Rowan turned to look in the same direction. Robbie whispered as an old couple squeezed past them. "The power lines to the floodlights, you see them?"

Rowan spotted the three rows of heavy cables that ran from the floor up the wall. They were black and heavy and bolted to small metal brackets; each line was at least an inch thick and would without doubt hold a man's weight. Rowan gave a slight smile of relief, he knew that Robbie would want to move fast, and then he could leave the city that unnerved him and return home to Jade. He leaned into Robbie. "When do you want to try it?"

"Tonight, as soon as it is dark, although it will not be that dark, not with all the lights they have here."

"Maybe they need to have a power cut; it's a pity Harry isn't here that is his field of speciality."

"You worry too much, if they have bulbs and we have arrows, then the lights can go off for a while." Robbie gave him a grin. "Come on I am hungry, let's find something in this lot that is edible."

After much squeezing through the crowds, they managed to find a source of hot food, and returned to a rustic looking wooden bench, where they could sit and eat, whilst still watching for missed opportunities. Robbie bit deep into his large dripping burger, he chewed as he sat watching the guards. "Not that bad, what did he call it?" Rowan swallowed hard.

"I am sure he said cow burger."

Robbie nodded. "Cow burger, well I suppose the meat is the cow, is this weird bread the burger?"

Rowan shrugged. "It must be, it is sort of odd, isn't it?"

Lee leaned against the tall flood light tower a few feet away. "Watch your backs; there is a guard who is curious about you over to your right."

Rowan leaned forward and let his hood slide over the top of his face. Robbie scanned from the side of his eyes, and spotted the guard watching; he turned and smiled at the guard. Robbie got up and walked through the two women talking towards him. Rowan felt a panic rise inside him. "Robbie what the hell...?"

He got up quickly and scuttled behind him. Robbie walked right up to the guard, who seemed a little surprised, and viewed the long pole in Robbie's hand with a certain curiosity. Robbie held out his palm and smiled a very broad grin.

"Greetings my brother, I notice your interest, are you aware your lord is all around you waiting to embrace and love you?"

The guard was instantly uncomfortable, and stepped back a little. "I got Christian already Brother." He fast became very nervous of Robbie who continued to smile at him, as his eyes fixed on the carved wooden cross on his chest.

"Knowing the lord is within you is joy my brother, maybe you would like to join us tonight and pray, we have room for everyone who has been embraced by their lord." The guard staggered back and raised a hand.

"No offence brother, but I got guard duty all night on the south wall." He backed further away. Robbie continued to smile.

"Maybe some other night then? Our mission will be here for some time, bring your friends and rejoice with us."

The guard turned away. "Yeah, brother I will." He walked quickly into the crowd as Robbie followed him with his eyes a large smile on his face. Rowan looked really angry.

"Robbie that was stupid, what the hell were you doing?"

Robbie gave a little chuckle. "Is he watching us now?"

Rowan looked up as he saw the back of the guard heading into the thick of the crowd. "Ok, so he is gone." He gave a little laugh. "You scare the hell out of me at times... what if he had attacked you?"

Robbie turned and looked at Rowan. "I think if we had not confronted him, he may have rumbled us. Talk like a churchman and they are freaked out, look what they do for a living Rowan...? Do you really think men like that want to get into a conversation about what their god really thinks of them?"

Rowan understood the point, his heart rate started to slow down again, Robbie had acted as fast as he could without using a weapon, a fight out here would be suicide, he was right to use their faith rather than a sword. He nodded at Robbie. "Can we head back now; I hate this place?"

Robbie gave a little chuckle. "Tolerance my dear Brother Rowan, tolerance, we shall feel leaves above us soon enough." Rowan started to giggle as he followed Robbie through the crowd. Lee stayed in view at a safe distance. The rest of the day seemed to drag, but not long after they returned to the church, Robbie sat in the high window watching the guards, and working out where all the lights were situated, and what advantage points he could use.

As with Scotland he quickly worked out the fastest route would be by rooftop.

This time though he would have to watch out for the high walls, the guards were much heavier in this city, and he knew it could be a long slow night. He leaned back on his chair and felt her head touch his, he jumped and her soft giggle danced through his ears. Robbie turned and saw the violet image of his smiling and beloved Rune. "Hi gorgeous."

"Hey beautiful... I missed you." She leaned closer and kissed him softly.

"Me too." He swung round and she slipped on to his lap, and wrapped her arms around him. His thoughts had been with her all day, and now he felt the calmness she brought fill him up. "I am glad you are here; this place is awful. How they can live in these boxes without trees, plant life and the freedom to roam beats me."

She hugged him tight. "I felt you trying to decide what to do; I wondered if I could help."

"I need to find a way across the roof without being seen from the walls." He looked out of the window at the long wall that ran down the side of the city, about 2000 yards from the edge of the church boundary. The whole length of it was swarming with guards in black with bright red ravens on their chests.

Rune leaned across and looked out of the window. "You need a diversion, which should be easy enough. What time?"

Robbie viewed her suspiciously. "I do not want you out in those woods, they are full of bandits Rune, it's not safe."

She gave him a big grin. "Alfie introduced me to a few, they are quite sweet when you prove that Lord Hearne is a family member. Even big men fear him, they think Crystal is wild, and of course Jade gave them quite a fright with her green evils. You worry about the guards in here; me and the boys will give you a chance to have them look away for a while." She gave him a very sweet smile and kissed him. "I am Lady Loxley you know? Do not go thinking just you have the power of that name. Although considering my condition, I do think you should hurry up and put a ring on my finger. To be honest Rob it looks a little odd that I am going to have the children of a lord who has not married me yet."

Robbie looked at her in disbelief. "You and the boys... Rune they are robbers and cut throats."

"Don't let that fool you, they are softies at heart, us girls have had a right laugh, even Maddy is grinning around them, they are so polite and attentive, I tell you Rob I could get use to that sort of treatment."

Robbie looked scandalised. "What do you mean, I treat you alright?" She gave him a grin and kissed him softly.

"Right, I have to go and sort things, wait till sundown, and we will provide a little entertainment for the guards." She slipped off his lap and twisted to the wall.

"Hey hang on; I do treat you alright... Rune wait, you know I love you, and actually I have asked you to marry me." But giggling, she had slipped through the stonework and was gone. Robbie scowled out of the window. "I spoil her bloody

rotten, what's she bloody well on about?" He turned to the empty stone wall.
"Bloody rotten, do you hear me?"

Darkness slowly crept over. It had felt like an age since Rune had once again
passed through a wall. In full woodsmen gear, and black cloaks with their hoods
up they waited for the darkness to thicken. Robbie nodded to Rowan, and he
slipped the door open and peered out. Like shadows, they slipped across the
graveyard, and over the wall. They scaled the drainpipes quickly, and within
minutes they were sat on the roof in the shadows. Robbie signalled, and Lee
scurried along the wall in the thick line of shadow, and took up his position.
Rowan and Robbie waited with their bows loaded. Lee watched the guards pass
by and then nodded out of the shadow. As the guard fell on one side of the roof,
two hooded figures sprang into the air, and the lights across the way exploded as
the arrows hit the bulbs. The entire section of the church area across the rooftops
suddenly was plunged into total darkness. There was a slight ripple in the darkness
as the hooded figures passed by. Three more guards lay silent and dead.

Outside the large heavy wooden gates, set in a reinforced concrete archway,
an old canvass covered cart trundled down the road from the trees. It creaked and
groaned along the rough uneven concrete road, and came to a shuddering halt
outside the gates. A hatch in the large wooden door opened, and a fat red face
poked out. "Sod off... we only open in daylight."

The tanned slender figure of a barely dressed woman slipped off the cart, she
flicked her long blonde hair back from her shoulders, and smiled with teeth so
white they sparkled in the dark. She moved with the grace of a gazelle, and her
violet eyes held captive the red faced guard. Her voice was soft and seductive,
which made his legs tremble as it oozed around his body, waking every cell of his
manhood and making it very alert. "Well, hey there."

He drooled. "I seem to be a little late; I have business with your Captains." She
gave a sexy wink and smiled, he knew he wanted to open the gates and lie on the
floor so she could wipe her feet clean on him. Her wide violet eyes danced and
sparkled; he was almost hypnotized by them. Her gaze and soft voice seeped into
him. "You wouldn't be a Captain would you soldier?" His eyes dropped down,
and slowly rose back up her, admiring and wanting the soft toned shapely, bronzed
body, right up to those hypnotizing violet eyes. He gave a hard swallow and lied.

"I will be in a month." She gave a delicate chuckle, and she lifted a soft hand and
stroked his cheek through the hatch, her touch was almost enough to cause his
shaking legs to fail.

"Oh... I am not sure I could wait that long; I need attention tonight if you know
what I mean?" He felt his knees shake faster. Two green eyes slipped under the

horses, and unfastened the harness. "Although I do think I am tempted to wait, should I stay here tonight, and then you can have me in there in the morning?"

The guard swallowed deeply. "Oh God." She gave him a smile, as she pushed her face close to the little window, and he felt her sweet flowery breath blow across his face.

"Bugger it." His hands shook on his key ring as he shut the little window, and fumbled at the lock, the door gave a resounding click, and he hurriedly pulled back the heavy retaining block, pushed open the gate, and excitedly stepped out to meet the vision of female wonder.

The two horses sped away from the cart and the gates, as the guard looked up and an arrow of flame hurtled out of the darkness towards the cart. He had just enough time to spot the barrels of gun powder. "Shit!"

Robbie peered over the wall edge, as the flash illuminated thirty blocks of houses. Wood, stone and meat, rained out of the sky as the sound of the explosion echoed and reverberated around the high stone walls, Robbie ducked and covered his head as debris rained down on them.

Pebbles and Amethyst came riding up to Maddy and Rune, who stood at the side of Ox and forty bandits, Jade squealed with laughter as she slipped down off the horse and ran round to Amethyst, the bandits all seemed misty eyed as they too paid her a great deal of attention. "Oh wow Amy that was so cool, I wanted to laugh my ass off, oh Rune you should have seen the guard, it was so funny." Rune smiled and looked anxiously back at the city, where flames billowed throwing the darkness back thousands of feet, and illuminating the inner front section of the city. Where once a large gate had hung, there was nothing left of the cart or gates, except a large burned and charred hole in the floor. "Be careful my love." Her quiet words heard only by Maddy.

Maddy raised her long white bow, and sighted the arrow, pulling hard on the string, another arrow, whisked into the mass of soldiers pouring out of the gates to defend the city. From so far away, the screams could be heard as soldier touched soldier, spreading the fire into the city and over the other troops. The men backed off fast, and ran backwards avoiding their comrades who were engulfed. Robbie sped up the cables in the dark, Rowan was not far behind, and he pulled with all his might, his feet pushing against the smooth wall. As he approached the top, a hooded figure leaned over the top of the wall and clenched him tightly by the wrist. "If you go for that dagger, lord or not I will bite your nose off." Robbie almost fell back with the shock, as his eyes met with those of Rafe.

"Wolfie how the hell did you get here?" He pulled hard, and Robbie flew up and on to the top of the wall, Harry leaned over to help Rowan. Rafe smiled at Robbie.

"You are bloody hard to track, do you lot leave any foot prints? I almost lost you twice, it's a good job we had Blades, she was the one who found you in the dark." Rowan and Lee both looked as surprised as Robbie; Blades chuckled, as Jett dropped her hood.

"Hate to break up the party guys, but Keith and Saff are up there alone, and all hell is breaking lose at the gates." Robbie looked at Jett's bright face.

"Don't worry about that, it's just Rune and Crystal, and some of the girls playing."

Jett beamed. "Thought cousin Pebbles would have had something to do with it, shall we move then?" She winked at Robbie, and brushed past as she headed along the wall. Guards lay dead all along the two hundred yards that led to the arched entrance to the barrack compound. Robbie shrugged at Rowan, and turned and followed Jett.

They passed like shadows in the dark, running down to the entrance, Saff and Keith stood hooded with their bows loaded. Robbie came up as the others took a defensive stance, any guard that appeared fell quickly. Rafe winked at Robbie from across the doorway.

"We had a bit a trouble getting in the other night, Harry dropped the grate, it made one hell of a racket. Thanks for the violet bowman bit, it really got us out of a scrape."

Robbie remembered the bells ringing, and Malcolm rushing them to the church, he was now starting to understand the picture. They had been followed out of Loxley, he was quite impressed with Rafe and Blades, he ruffled her spiky hair. "That was a good piece of work young lady." She gave him a beaming smile.

"Martin was one of the best, he taught me well. We always used you as a way of learning. I owe him a lot." Robbie nodded at her, and he saw the slight sadness on her dimly lit face.

"I miss him too, he was the finest tracker in Loxley, I am glad you learned from the best." Blades gave a radiant smile. Rowan looked at the archway and the closed door; he glanced over to Robbie and nodded. Robbie gave him the nod back and seizing the handle, he turned it and stood back as the door swung open. Arrows whistled into the guardroom, and screams and wails rang into the night.

There was a glint of steel, and a flash of spectrum on the walls as Harry, Blades and Jett shot into the room. Robbie leaned against the wall next to Rafe. "So, you have been hiding here all along?"

"Well, we have not exactly been hiding; the first night in we had to knobble a few guards, so we nicked their gear, and then stood up here all the time watching you and Rowan act like monks. Each time they sent out a relief we just whacked em and sent em over the wall."

Robbie frowned. "You do realise you all acted against my orders?" Rafe shrugged.

"We figured you would see the funny side and let us all off." He gave Robbie a big smile and winked. Robbie gave him a shrewd look.

"Why do I think you planned all this?" Rafe shrugged.

"It's funny really cause, I seem to remember my Gov saying something about how we are all Specialists, and we always work as a team, I wasn't aware any one person could make that kind of a decision, except for the Gov of course... Sorry Gov my lady wants a quick chat." Rafe pulled out his sword, and ran into the room where Robbie heard him in the midst of the fight. "Hey sweetie that was a nice bit of slicing, if you're a good girlie later I could bite." Jett laughed wildly as she spun on her heels, and her sword came swiftly round into the steel of the guard commander.

Moments later, Harry stepped out wiping his blades down on an old piece of black and red cloak. "Hey man it's like cosmic and funky in there now, give em a second and the place will sing with totally cosmic vibes man." Robbie patted Harry on the shoulder, and walked into the guardhouse, the floor was littered with bodies; Rafe and Keith had several by the feet and dragged them out, as Harry and Lee lifted them up and slung them over the high wall. Robbie stood at the window and gazed down on the barracks and the black palace of Mordred; even he was not prepared for what he saw. "Oh hell its worse."

CHAPTER SEVENTEEN

DARKNESS VIEWED ON HIGH

Bobby Thorn walked into the stables, it was late, and he looked exhausted. John Lox looked up from his big chair, where he sat working on a sword blade. "Bob lad you are late, I think Rags expected you back hours ago." He gave a weak smile as he pulled on the horse's reins.

"Laddie here threw a shoe; I have walked miles with him." He flopped down on the straw bale near the door; John gave a smile, and got up out of his chair. He came down the barn and laid the sword on the bench at the side of Bobby. John pulled up at the side of the horse and raised its leg to look.

"Oh, that's not too bad I will have a new shoe on him in no time, there is a pot over there, make a brew and I will get on with it."

John set to work, he had a wide range of shoes already made that just needed to be finished for the final fittings, and he picked a shoe and threw it into the coals. Bobby sat back and rested as he waited for John to fit the shoe, his eyes wandered on to the blade that was lay on the table at the side. The sword was the large silver one of Big John's. Since he had two broken legs, and was stuck in a chair all the time, he had sent it up for repair. There were one or two chips in the blade and John had been filing them out before sharpening the blade. Bobby picked up the file and looked at it.

"Would it not be better to use a rougher file and then work down to a finer one?"

John looked up from the horse's foot he was cleaning ready for the shoe. "That is my best file; it is the way my dad taught me to do it, I run em off on the grinding wheel, then finish em by hand... It has worked for years so I just carry on as I know. Why do you know about swords?"

Bobby shrugged. "When I was a small boy my mum and me stayed with my granddad, he was a sword maker; he let me file the edges before he gave them their last real sharpening." Bobby twisted the file in his hands as he spoke. John looked up at his bright eyes and a look of sadness on his face.

"Do I know of him? I know of a lot of sword makers, maybe I have met him."

Bobby gave a smile. "Probably not, he lived a long way from here across the water, we spent a whole day on a yacht when we came back over here. I wish we had stayed, mum got killed just after that." Bobby looked a lot sadder, as his thoughts drifted to his mum. John could see how much he missed her. Bobby looked up at him; he had a haunted look in his eyes.

"They came in the night looking for granddad, she told them he was not there but they killed her anyhow. I climbed out of the window and ran; it is why I only ever use half my name. I think it is a lot safer."

John straightened up as he watched Bobby. "Half of your name, why what is your full name?"

Bobby looked a little worried; he fingered the file in his hand nervously, as he looked at John. "You promise you won't tell?" John put down the rasp he had been using on the hoof, and crouched in front of Bobby, he put out a large hand and rested it on his knee.

"Bob lad, you know you are safe here under our protection? What is it lad that has got you so scared? I promise I will protect you."

Bobby bit his lip as if trying to decide, he looked up into the caring eyes of John Lox. "It's Thornson... Bobby... well Robert Thornson, my granddad, well actually he was my great granddad, was called Victor."

John looked at him in complete disbelief. "Bloody hell lad, no wonder you are scared, grandson of one the greatest sword makers ever?" John sat flat on the floor, and stared at Bobby as he realised the fear the young boy must have hidden inside him all this time.

Victor was hunted day and night by the Dark One until she had found him, and then forced him to make the Black Blade of Dunnottar, which had been used to siphon Mordred into Billy Knox. John wiped his forehead of sweat. "Listen here lad, you are on my land now. You have my word you will be safe, none will know of this, although I think you should tell Robbie, he is the lord of this land, and he should know whom he guards. He will take care of you Bob lad, I know Robbie, he will protect you at all costs."

He nodded looking pale at John. "Thanks John, I have wanted to tell, but I was scared. Rags does not even know, there was only Sister Mary who knew, and she is gone now. She told me to tell Lord Loxley as well."

John got to his feet. "She was right, he should know Bob lad, if you are afraid, I can have a word, but only if you want me to. I will not break my promise to you." He put his hand on Bobby's small shoulder. Bobby looked up at him and smiled.

"Would you John...? I get a bit nervous, he is really nice, but he is sort of famous." John gave a hearty laugh.

"Aye he is a bit, but don't you worry lad I will have a word on the quiet for you... Right, I think we were making a brew were we not?" Bobby gave him a big smile and slipped off the straw bale and wandered over to the small stove at the side of the furnace, he slid the bright orange coffee pot onto the top of the stove and grabbed two cups. John pulled the glowing horseshoe out of the coals and banged it with his large hammer to make the final adjustments. Holding it in the tongs, he walked over to the horse and pushed it on to the hoof, smoke rose from the base of the hoof, and John pulled it away and steeped the shoe in a vat of water. It fizzed and hissed.

He held the shoe in place, and pulled over his small tin of shoe tacks, he hammered the first one in. John looked up at Bobby making the coffee and smiled. "I don't think you should be riding all over the place and putting yourself at risk Bob lad."

Bobby turned with the cups. "But that's what I do, I am a postal rider?"

"Oh no you aint lad, if you have one drop of your great granddads blood in you, then you are a sword maker. You belong in here at my side, tell Rags I have offered you an apprenticeship, and you will be working for me from now on. I can keep a proper eye on you then." John gave him a wink and smiled at him.

Bobby seemed to fill up with joy and his face glowed with the sudden happiness inside him, as he handed a steaming cup to John. "Thanks John, I really would love to work in here with you."

"It's a deal then, you start first thing in the morning, you cannot be worse than my last apprentice, he was always buggering off when I needed him." John stretched out his large hand, and with a big smile, Bobby placed his small hand into it and shook it, the deal was done. It was an hour later when a tired but happy Bobby walked in through the door of the little cabin, Rags leapt out of the chair and threw her arms around him.

"Oh Bobby, I was scared out me knickers I was. I thought they had gone and got you I did."

It felt nice to know that he had someone who cared so much for him. He pulled her close and gave her a kiss. Bobby looked at the red eyes and knew she would never admit she had been crying. "I am fine, my horse threw a shoe and I had to walk him."

Rags squeezed him hard. "I don't want you out there anymore; it's just too dangerous, I want you here I do, where I can watch out for you."

He started to laugh, as he rocked her in his arms, she looked at him. "John just offered me a sword making apprenticeship, I start in the morning." Her brown eyes sparkled, as the smile broke out across her face; He stroked the strawberry blonde hair back from her face. She was special. "I don't suppose there is anything to eat, I am starving?"

Robbie looked out across a vast concrete plain. Miles upon miles of levelled land housed a huge city of tents, all of them bearing the red raven and dragon crests of the Knox Empire... The amassed army of the black city was huge.

Soldiers in massive blocks marched up and down parading under the floodlights. A large area of grass was home to row upon row of archery ranges, large groups fought with swords and poles under instruction from their trainers. There was building after building to house the horses. Robbie felt the cold chill of real fear sweep over him, as he noticed the long lines of polished brass cannons. Rowan stood silent at his side, his face carried a look of utter shock, Robbie raised his hand, and squeezed his shoulder. "We have our hands full this time my friend." There was nothing Rowan could think of to say that would express what he felt.

The two friends stood high at the window in the black wall, looking down on what had been gathered for one purpose and one purpose only. The complete and utter destruction of the woodland world, Mordred had planned on a bigger and greater scale than Mason ever had. Robbie took out his telescope and put it to his eye, he scanned the row upon row of tents, the soldiers looked so young, they had to be barely fourteen years old. Robbie had heard many stories since his journey from Caerleon about the orphanages of Mason Knox; he now began to understand the pure evil of the man he had killed. "This is an army that has been bred for just one purpose, look at them Rowan, these are just young boys."

He passed the scope over to him, and Rowan looked down at the soldiers training. It was hard to really understand, Rowan had seen the doubts in Robbie who was seventeen and he understood them himself, now faced with the reality of having to fight such young boys, he felt a strange sense of unease. To him they were children, would he really be able to face, fight and kill children? The cold truth was that Mason had bred them, for the one purpose of overwhelming the enemy with numbers. "These will be the first wave, they will try to overwhelm us with their army of children to wear us down, and then they will follow with the power, we must find out what their true power holds Robbie." He turned and saw the same lost look in Robbie's eyes as he had.

"If this is just the first wave my friend, then I really do fear for York. These are his weakest and yet they are well armed, if fear drives them, we should not underestimate their valour."

Rowan stared out across the troops as they practised. "Maybe we should not underestimate the fear, we have after all used it ourselves to great effect, if we can find a way to strike fear into the hearts of these children. I would rather scare a child who runs away, than kill them my friend. This does not sit well with me."

Robbie felt his tenseness, and he too understood, this would feel wrong whatever they did, but he was clear that he knew defending York, also meant the survival of Loxley, Robbie could not be detracted now from his goal. "I need to get further in while we still have some darkness."

Harry patted Robbie on the shoulder as Rafe and Jett came up by their side. "Hey man whatever non cosmic freaks he has, as long as they like breathe, I can totally mangle their vibes." He nodded, and Robbie smiled as he saw Harry's very serious face reflected in the glass in front of him. He looked at Rafe and Jett.

"We need to know absolutely everything they have, we are about to face the biggest challenge ever. York must not fall; if it does Loxley will be next." He saw their grim faces reflected back at him as they stood in the guardroom, looking through the large glass window at the barracks.

Saff leant in through the door that overlooked the market. "I don't want to worry you guy's but there is about thirty guards coming down the far side of the wall. Are we in or out of here?"

Robbie spun round. "We are in; get inside and bar the door, Harry give em a lift. Rowan, Jett, Wolfie, Lee, let's get out on those ramparts and find a way up to the top end. I want to look at that palace, Wolfie we could use less lights."

He looked down at the panel in front of him. There were rows and rows of switches, all silver and shiny. He looked up at Jett and smiled. "Don't suppose you know how to work one of these?" Jett leaned over and shrugged; she glanced back up at Rafe, and then smiled. Jett took two steps back and raised her sword; Harry spun round and saw Jett with her sword raised ready to crash down.

"Whoa girl Noooooooooooooooo..." There was a blinding flash, Jett lifted into the air, as Harry lurched across the room, he caught her and they both slammed into the wall. Everything went dark.

Robbie looked around in the dark, he was temporally blinded by the flash; two eyes flickered blue near the floor. "Wow Harry that made my elbows go all wiggly, what was it?"

"Whoa girl you just got your karma like totally electrocuted."

"Cool, it made me tickle all over, and I mean all over Harry. It was awesome."

"Hey girl, you could have been killed, that aint cosmic stuff in them wires; it can like fry your vibes to toast. You are one lucky dudet." Blades offered a hand in the dark, as Harry lit his lighter, the room had been filled with smoke and every now and again, the light panel flickered and sparked. Rafe pulled Jett close, she giggled but her eyes kept flaring in a pale blue, he looked at her as another pulse emitted out of the whites of her eyes, she seemed fine and he turned to Harry, who stood up and dusted his black pants down. Keith slid two spears across the door to wedge it shut, and headed across to Robbie who now stood with Rowan at the other door. "I am not sure that will hold forever, but it will at least give us a head start." Robbie nodded as he looked back along the top of the wall.

"Everyone Ok? Alright let's get a move on, I want speed and accuracy, we will have to take out the guards as we go, let's keep them on top of the wall. The last thing we need is bodies falling all over the place, especially with that lot down there; I would prefer them not aiming up at us."

The group gathered their weapons together, and slipped up their hoods ready. Loud bangs and crashes resounded on the door to the market ramparts. Harry pulled the door to the barrack ramparts open, and they dashed out with bows loaded.

The first guards were fifty feet up the rampart peering through the dark at them, Robbie and Rowan let fly, as Keith and Saff came forward in front of them. They took the lead as Robbie reloaded beside Rowan. Blades and Jett followed, as Rafe and Harry with Lee barred the door the best they could. The group moved quickly and quietly.

It was pitch black, the wall could just be seen and they kept close to it. Far down below everyone seemed to be scuttling about trying to find their way. Torches flared up in amongst the tents, as the young soldiers looked around for guidance.

Keith and Saff fired, and slipped back behind Robbie and Rowan, as they leapfrogged along the wall taking out the guards as they met them. The wall seemed to go on and on, Rowan and Robbie breathed deeply as they finally saw the black palace and the next large wall silhouetted behind it. The group, were now tightly bunched, Harry kept his eyes back to try and see the guardroom in the distance, and work out if the soldiers were through yet. No alarm had been sounded, and so Robbie thought for a moment they would be safe. He looked ahead and saw the wall behind the palace. There was either another barracks for older soldiers or another part of the city, either way he would find out what the dark army had to offer.

The second part of the city had lights on, and he slowed a little to catch his breath, and ensure that they still remained hidden as more of the wall came into view from the palace which was still lit up. He gave his hand signals and everyone slipped up against the wall in single file, the pace was slower as they crept quietly along. The Black Palace loomed up and rose higher than the walls, light blazed inside the rooms, and he could see the detail of the building, it was like nothing he had ever seen before.

The Palace was enormous, and to Robbie it appeared as if it had been built in layers. The bottom was very wide and tall, it seemed surrounded by pillars that rose to a sloping roof, out of which grew another layer of the building. That too had a sloping roof, which was decorated with sharp spikes and strange contorted head like stone faces. The next level was similar, and as he looked up at the rest of the building, he could see each level slowly became smaller. It was almost pyramid like with the distinct sloping almost curved roof extending out at each level. The very top of the palace seemed like a large box with the sloping roof, and a heavy set of spikes that ran along the top of the apex, at each end was a curled dragon looking up into the sky as if waiting to strike at its prey. A long clawed leg was raised in defence, and their eyes burned in a deep vivid red, Robbie shuddered. Was this Mordred making clear to his mother that he would also fight her for the ultimate seat of power? It was a chilling thought, and Robbie actually felt he would prefer the Dark One on the seat of power before her son.

The sloping roof came to within twenty feet of the high wall. Robbie looked down on the walkways that led from the rooms around the building. Nothing stirred as the group sneaked past, soldiers of a bigger stature moved around on the floor far below. They passed the palace, and then they were on to the final stage of the wall that brought them to the guardroom, and the second inner wall. Robbie, stopped still hidden in the shadows, Rowan slipped up close. "We would be better to rush it, if they see us; it will give them less time to prepare." Robbie nodded as the others huddled close.

"Ok, Keith and Saff hold back and cover with the bows." They nodded. "Harry, Jett, Rafe and Blades, stay close to Rowan and myself. We will shoot as we move; Blades keep your crossbow handy just in case. Stay close to Lee." She gave him a smile and nodded. "Rowan and I will take either side of the door, Harry I want the door down in one move, step back, and Rowan and I will send twins in, swords follow." He took a deep breath. "I want this fast and as clean as possible, stay sharp."

They all caught their breath and prepared, as Robbie pulled two arrows out of his quiver, he cut away the feathers on one side of each of the flights. With the arrows fitted, he gave the signal, and then ran into the light as fast as his legs would go. Robbie and Rowan slammed into the wall on either side of the door, Harry hit the door at a fast pace and the wood splintered, then exploded inwards. Robbie spun with Rowan into the gap and fired, there were dull screams as the arrows connected, and as Robbie rolled back on the wall, Harry, Jett and Rafe entered. He took a deep breath and looked up.

Across the gap on the highest level of the palace, Mac walked out on to a balcony above him. He stood and took a deep breath looking up at the sky; he wore the red crested uniform of an enemy officer. Robbie felt the rage explode inside him; his arrow was out and fitted as he brought his bow up and aimed. At that moment, Mac looked down, and his deep brown eyes connected with Robbie's.

Robbie saw the colour drain from his face, as he recognised the hooded figure with the bright burning eyes of life and hatred below it. Mac jumped backwards, and fell into the doors as the arrow ripped through the top of his hair and sunk deep into the wooden doorframe. The arrow shaft vibrated above him, as the red line ran down his nose and dripped on the floor.

Robbie cursed, and stamped his foot. He pulled another arrow into his string, and lifted the bow and aimed at the balcony where Mac now lay almost face down on the floor out of sight. Robbie strained his eyes down the arrow as he swept the balcony looking for movement between the rails. He got the slightest glint of something metal, the arrow whipped through the air at huge pace. The squeal was more fright than pain; whatever the arrow hit it just grazed the target. Robbie felt a tinge of happiness rise inside him, knowing that he had brought fear to Mac, and at the same time given him something to remember when they met again. Robbie knew that time would come.

Saff patted his shoulder as she passed looking back up at the balcony. "Better luck next time Gov." She slipped inside the now cleared guardroom followed by Keith. Rowan's arm appeared around the doorframe, and pulled on Robbie's hood. He felt the tug, and felt himself dragged backwards into the guardroom. Harry winked as he watched the rampart, his bow now off his shoulder and loaded.

Robbie looked around the room. "Are we secure?" Rowan nodded as he looked down from the window, Rafe looked out.

"Bugger?" Robbie came across the room, but he already knew before he looked. His biggest fear became very real; Rune had taken care of many of the dead at Dunnottar, Robbie remembered the columns of soldiers that left before they attacked; he now looked out on thousands of dead soldiers, all reanimated and sat quietly in long rows waiting.

Harry strained, as he looked over at them from the doorway. "Hey man what is it, come on dude what's Bugger?"

Jett looked back from beside Blades who looked a little white. "Hey Harry man, you want to stay there and not look down here."

Harry gave a deep swallow. "It's like them isn't it? Oh whoa, I knew it, I done bad things and I am going to go to the land of uncosmic monsters man."

Jett smiled. "Harry man, you don't need to travel, we just arrived." She looked out on the army of the dead.

Harry made funny little squeaking sounds, as his legs seemed to tremble. "I knew it man; I always knew not to mess with em. My karma will be sucked clean out, and I will be like a totally hollow Harry man. My vibes will be gone forever and be stretched and pulled by uncosmic beings and radical mind benders."

Keith patted him on the shoulder. "Hey Harry relax man, chill out dude you are unravelling man. I will get Jaz to put a good word in for you man." Keith gave him a smile as Harry shook his head and moaned.

"He's done that dude, they hate me man, I chomped them into unhappy vibes land, they don't see me as cosmic man, they will chomp my karma first chance they get."

Robbie had seen enough. He looked at Rowan. "We have what we came for, now we know what we face, we can plan ahead, I think we should get the hell out of here." Rowan smiled.

"Are we thinking adventurous, or just get the hell out fast?" Robbie gave him a broad smile.

"I am the hooded man you know; I have a reputation to uphold. I know how much you like a good end to the day." He patted Rowan on the shoulder, and pointed out the window. "Am I right or is that a very large hut next to the palace with explosives in it?"

Rowan crossed the room and looked down with a keen interest at the long wooden building with bright hazard signs either side of the door. "I do believe you are right Gov." He smiled at Robbie. Harry gave a moan.

"Hey man we have like dudes all over the place here, it aint looking cosmic."

Robbie peered round the door; along the wall soldiers were now running with their crossbows at the ready. Keith and Saff stood either side of the door with their bows raised. Harry loaded his arrow and took a stance. Blades slipped on to the floor, and raised her crossbow as she knelt below the large frame of her dad.

Rowan tore at the hem of his cloak, and bound strips round the end of his arrows; he looked across the room at Harry. "Harry I need your lighter and your little bottle of tonic off Joe."

Harry looked back surprised as Robbie gave a smile. "Hey man it's my nerve medicine, it keeps my vibes unjangled."

Rowan laughed, as he tied the strips on to the arrowheads. "Harry it is 200% proof, that won't unjangle anything, and if we do not use something to burn these arrow heads, we may not be around long enough to have vibes, jangled or unjangled. Give me the tonic."

Harry looked miserable as he slipped the small bottle out from his jacket, and threw it across to Rowan.

He bit the lid and twisted the bottle; the top came off in his mouth. Rowan spat it on to the floor. "Phew!" Robbie was stood at least five feet away, and the smell hit hard. Rowan blinked and shook his head, as he poured the clear liquid on to the arrow tips. "Bloody hell Harry, how the hell do you walk with this stuff inside you?"

Rowan handed six arrows to Robbie. "Hold your breath when you shoot, I think breathing the fumes could be hazardous." Robbie took hold of the arrows, Keith and Saff fired at the first of the guards to come in range. Robbie looked at Jett.

"We need rope, there are flag poles on the roof can you get up there?" Jett nodded as Rafe took her hand. He pulled her to the door as the four bowmen sent a volley into the guards. The soldiers were now holding back just out of range, not entirely sure what to do. "Lee, keep the wall clear." He climbed up, and knelt down as he took aim.

Jett and Rafe slipped through the door and ran in front of the window. Rafe clasped his hands together, and Jett stepped on as he rose sharply throwing her high into the air, and on to the flat roof of the guardhouse, she pulled out her sword and swiped with all her might. The blade shone brightly as it connected with the first flagpole, and with a thunderous crack and a deep grunt from Jett, the pole wobbled and toppled over.

Robbie and Rowan paced onto the rampart and aimed at the building below. Guards were now appearing on the stairs of the palace, and Rafe loaded his bow and took aim, the first guard through the palace door, took an arrow in the chest, and was thrown back inside on top of the others. Rowan clicked the lighter and lit the end of Robbie's arrow. Flames exploded everywhere, and he fired quickly as he felt his eyebrows singe. Robbie blinked as Rowan laughed. The arrow hit the door of the powder store; Rowan leaned over the rail as he watched it burn.

"Bugger lighting them Robbie, just hit that door." Robbie fired his second arrow as Rowan took aim. The arrow hit the centre of the door and instantly exploded into flames. One of the soldiers, who ran at it with a bucket, fell backwards as the flames roared back at him. Rowan's arrow hit and flared up brightly. Soldiers were now spilling out on to the balconies of the palace just below them, Robbie loaded an arrow, and at arm's length he lit it. The arrow flared, and he turned to the balcony and fired at one of the soldiers. It hit him as he tried to run, and he was engulfed as the tonic soaked rag caught on his clothes. The soldiers recoiled and panicked; Rowan sent a second unlit arrow at the balcony as the door on the powder store began to burn. Robbie ran back into the guardroom and snatched the half-full bottle of tonic off the table. He ran back out and with everything he had, he launched the bottle into the air towards the door.

It had the desired effect; the bottle hit the door, smashed, and flames exploded in every direction like a bomb going off. The whole building was engulfed in flames. Soldiers now ran away from the building, as they saw how quickly the flames took hold. Spilled buckets of water rolled on an empty area of paving. Robbie loaded his last fire arrow, and aimed at the balcony where flames were starting to spread, he fired right into the centre of a group of soldiers, Rafe took one as the group spread wide, and Rowan took another. More flames exploded into the throng of screaming soldiers. Jett slid down off the roof pulling the ropes together, and running them quickly through her hands as she coiled them and tied on the other ropes.

"Hey Robbie, this is the best I can do, I just hope it is long enough?"

Robbie loaded his bow and winked at her. "It better had be, you are going first." She looked up from tying a knot.

"Why me?"

"I need Rune, get down and as far from the wall as possible, she is out there somewhere, get her here fast for me." He fired at the soldiers. Jett tied the rope to the rail, and threw the other end to Lee; he dropped it over the wall. She climbed up the wall, and in a flash, she was gone slipping down the rope on the other side towards the ground. The rope ran out fifteen feet short, and she dangled, and then dropped onto the dry dusty floor. Lee looked down and smiled, and then fired at the guards.

Jett set off at a fast pace, as she ran towards the trees across the wide expanse of burned land. Her eyes flared blue as she ran, and as she looked up across to the trees, she saw a violet light appear twenty feet in front. She gave a smile as she ran into Rune's arms.

"Robbie and the team are on the wall where those flames are, we have a rope but someone is going to have to stay and defend the rope." Rune looked across the ground and her eyes flared. She stared at the wall and waved her arm, a violet

curtain shimmered at her side and Maddy stepped through with her long white bow. Crystal followed and looked across to the wall. She knelt down and touched the ground as her eyes turned pure white. Ice ran across the black ground

towards the wall, it rose steadily up into the air as it approached the black city. The ice would only reach within a foot of the wall; the protection from the Dark One prevented it going any further, Rafe laughed as he stood on top of the wall. He jumped across on to the ice. "Hey Blades, come on your next, it's time for a slide home."

Harry grabbed the back of her tunic with one hand, and lifted her up into the air. He sat her on the top of the wall, she pounced like a cat across the gap, and Robbie heard her scream with delight, as she shot off at high speed down the slide towards Rune. Robbie climbed on top of the wall. "Rafe give me your arrows and go." Rafe slung his quiver across at Robbie who caught it, and with a wolf like howl he shot off down the slide. Robbie loaded two arrows and fired at the guards. "Saff, Harry, Lee your next, get a move on."

Harry climbed on to the wall and shuddered. "Whoa man this is uncosmicly high, I like don't do birdie stuff." Robbie pressed his foot into Harry's back, and with a huge push Harry screamed like a baby as he fell across the gap on to the ice, and hurtled head first down the slide. Saff was up on the wall, and with a scream of delight, she followed. Rowan climbed up and covered Keith as he climbed up. Robbie and Rowan fired two arrows each together. Lee jumped and in a second he was gone Keith turned.

"You two go, you are more important to York, I will cover." Robbie nodded.

"Alright Keith." Robbie grabbed the back of Keith's hood and pulled him hard; Keith went sprawling across the gap and hit the ice. Before he could right himself, he shot off at high speed down to the others. Robbie smiled at Rowan.

"Adventurous endings are for us two, are you ready on three?"

They loaded two arrows each and took aim; Robbie took a deep breath as six guards crept forwards. "One ... Two... Three." Rowan fired, and Robbie pushed him with all his might, Rowan lunged out to grab Robbie and missed, he fell arms waving back on to the slide as Robbie fired his shot.

Rowan yelled insults as he shot backwards, Robbie loaded his bow, and his

pendant began to glow violet. He fired as a volley of arrows came at him, and turning, he jumped. The arrows shot upwards into the sky as the ice turned violet, and he slid at high speed down the slide. The powder store ignited.

Flames and bits of wood and stone shot into the air, and the slide wobbled as the earth shook, Robbie felt the heat as the whole area illuminated and he saw her for the briefest second, her hair shimmering autumnal golden red in the fire light. He shot off the end of the slide with a bump, and Maddy stepped over and rested her bow on to the slide and fired three arrows at once up the slide.

The soldiers climbing on to the wall saw three lines of flame coming up out of the dark towards them and turned, jumping madly out of the way. The arrows rocketed off the ice and under the power of Gwendolyn; they pierced through the protection of the Dark One and fired down into the courtyard below. The troops of the palace ran around as flames engulfed the whole yard, and the soldiers barely had time to understand what was happening, before the inferno blanket engulfed them.

Rune pulled him close and kissed him. She wrapped herself around him and he held her tight. "Hey beautiful, nice work." She nuzzled into his neck and he felt the slight tremble in her. "Hey I am fine."

"You really scared me. I hate being afraid like that." He turned and kissed her cheek.

"I promise, it will never happen again, I am sorry Rune. Come on let's go home."

A rough hand gripped Robbie firmly. It pulled the three arrows that were embedded in his spare quiver from Rafe. "You're goin nowhere, we have a celebration planned." Robbie turned, and looked at the large rough face of Ox. Rune gave a grin as she pulled away from Robbie.

"I told the boys you would drop in for a bit, they are really excited about it." Her eyes sparkled with delight as she gave him her sweetest smile. He nodded and shook his head.

"Lead the way Ox." Ox gave a beaming smile, and stepped through the curtain of light.

The head guardsman slammed into the wall. "YOU DO NOT KNOW? HALF OF LOXLEY RUNNING WILD ACROSS THE WALLS, AND YOU DO NOT KNOW HOW THEY GOT IN...? IT IS YOUR JOB TO KNOW. ARE YOU GOING TO TELL LORD KNOX WHEN HE GETS HERE?" Mac was bright red in the face, as the anger coursed through him. The watch guard shook with fear as Mac advanced for the fourth time.

"Please sir, you have to understand they just slipped out of the dark like shadows, we had no lights." He held his palms up in front of him as Mac came closer.

Mac seized him roughly by the throat as his temples throbbed with anger, his teeth bared as he flung the guard back across to the other side of the room. "OF COURSE THERE WAS NO LIGHTS; IT WAS LOXLEY WHO SMASHED THEM. HE IS THE VIOLET BOWMAN YOU FOOL. I SHOULD HAVE KNOWN ABOUT THIS LAST NIGHT." The guard lay bleeding his arm twisted from the power of the impact on the wall, he lay watching from the floor as

Mac screamed at him, Mac whipped out his sword of black steel, and with a whip like action, the guard jumped on the floor, and slithered back. Mac viewed the dead head of the watch with contempt. He spun on his two Lieutenants and glared at them.

"WELL DON'T JUST STAND THERE... GET THAT MESS CLEANED UP." Mac stormed out of the room, and the door slammed behind him, shaking the room and making the two soldiers jump, one looked at the other one and gave a long gasp.

"Bloody hell Jeff, I thought we would get it then, poor Frank it wasn't his fault. He was right you know? They came out of nowhere like ghosts." He grabbed Frank's dead legs as the other soldier grabbed his shoulders. Frank was lifted up, and half dragged, half carried out of the room.

Jade sat on Rowan's lap and screamed with laughter. "Oh, Robbie it was so funny, he said bugger it, and started unlocking the door, we legged it, and the next thing you knew boom. He certainly got a bang, that's for sure." Rune giggled as Jade almost fell off Rowan's lap laughing hysterically. Amethyst gave a huge smile as all the others laughed with Jade.

The 'Boys,' as Rune called them, were a band of large and very rough looking bandits, they were all the size and measure of John Lox, and they had a strange odour of sweat, alcohol and damp woodland. Robbie watched them in their oddments of patched clothing, and armed heavily with just about any weapon they could sling on their backs or tuck in their belts. Ox was the leader and he was no fool, he had managed to keep them all safe and alive by raiding the supply trucks of the Knox army. They reminded Robbie very much of his Specialists, they were very adept at woods skills, and very efficient in what they did.

Most of the time the Knox supply wagons had not even noticed they had been robbed. They were indeed a very slick outfit, and Robbie could not help but feel that they could be put to better use. Rune sat close as they all joked and laughed around the campfire. It had been a long day, and Robbie stretched and yawned. He leaned back against Rune, and she slid her arms round him and held him close. Lee talked quietly with his brother and Keith; it seemed like a long time since they had seen each other, and Alfie was delighted to find that Keith was his nephew. He rattled on about the old days and brought Keith up to speed with every aspect of the Sherman family tree.

Rowan stared at the fire; it was not hard for Robbie to work out what was wrong. Rowan now had the same understanding as Robbie; he knew that York would be stretched to its limits, if it were going to survive the sort of attack that they both now expected. Mordred's army was even bigger than even Robbie had thought; the numbers they now faced had grown tenfold.

Rune sensed his apprehension. "What is it?" He looked up at her bright eyes, dancing in the moonlight; her eyelashes seemed to sparkle in reds and golds from the light of the fire. He gave her a soft smile; he loved the way she always knew when to ask the right questions.

"I will have to go to York, I have now seen what they have, Rune they must evacuate or they will all die, we face more than just soldiers. I saw at least two hundred cannons; bows will be no match for their weaponry. I must convince them, because if I don't." He gave a pause. "I cannot send men of Loxley to be slaughtered, and they will be, and Loxley will fall. I will not risk the future of Loxley on the pig headed arrogance of an ambassador, as soon as we get back I will see Skip and Bear, and then we go to York."

Rowan sat up and leaned forward. "Robbie you have given your word to supply aid to York, if you withdraw it now you will lose a lot of credibility. I am not sure you should risk that; it holds the woodsman's world together."

He looked across at Rowan. "York will have aid, but before they get it, they will give me a little something. I want the lives of all the women and children, without it, not one arrow will go their way. I will not slaughter good men in a war they cannot win, especially for an ideal that died with the red death. The will of Lord Loxley will be heard in York, and they will bend to my view, without us York is dead."

Ox burped as he pulled a bottle from his mouth. "I hate York, there are no trees, it's impossible to hide, I say let them fall, they have always held themselves higher than the rest of us. Think they are something special that lot." He put down the bottle and fell backward fast asleep. Rowan started to laugh.

"Words from the wise Robbie."

Robbie chuckled and looked up at Rune. "It's almost midnight, let's go home to bed."

She leaned down and kissed him. "Alright gorgeous." Robbie slid up off the floor and he looked at the other bandits.

"Stay in this place and I will send the agreed payment to you in the morning, if I have more paid work would you all be interested?" A tall thin Bandit known as Woody nervously nodded. Robbie smiled. "I will be in touch, thank you for the aid you gave to my people; the Lord of Loxley is in your debt." Robbie gave a brief bow, as Rune waved her hand and the shimmering violet curtain appeared. He stepped through into the glade and the small gate to his garden. It was close to midnight.

Maggs sat with Judith on the steps of the house, she stood up as Robbie appeared and he smiled. "Maggs how wonderful of you to visit, he is safe and will be here in a moment." She gave a beaming smile and came rattling a tune down the path; Harry stepped through and into her arms.

"Hey baby cakes, oh whoa I missed you." She pulled him down to her short level and smothered him in kisses.

"Oh, my big brave Harry Pops, I missed you, I hate it when you go, and it leaves my vibes all uncosmic. It's not at all groovy." Blades stood smiling and found herself snatched rather embarrassedly into Maggs arms; she received as many kisses as Harry.

Jett and Rafe headed through the woods with Rowan and Jade, as everyone waved goodnight. The rest trooped into the house for the night, Robbie quietly made his way up to bed and sat on the edge aching. Rune slid over behind him and rubbed his tired shoulders, she noticed the three red marks where the tips of the arrows that had hit Rafe's empty quiver, had slightly cut him.

Robbie had been lucky to escape; the extra quiver had saved his life. She knew he had gone last to protect his group, and it worried her that he was taking more and more risks in defence of his men. She gathered his hair up and kissed his shoulders softly. "You are taking too many risks; we all need you alive Rob. I need you alive, please promise me you will never put yourself in danger like that again?" She poked the cuts on his back and he jumped. "Those could have been fatal if they had passed through the quiver, stop telling your men to stay sharp, and then ignoring your own advice."

He leaned forward as she massaged his back. "I am sorry, but there was no other way of finding out. Now I have seen what they have, I almost wish I had not gone. Although I did find something out that could be useful."

She leaned over his shoulder and looked at him, he smiled and kissed he quickly, she looked at him. "Well... what did you find out?" Robbie gave her a big grin.

"Rune there is a lot of people captive behind that wall loyal to Loxley. I always thought that those behind the walls were all men of Knox but they are not. The hooded man commands men inside as well as out, we may have a chance of causing quite a bit of trouble in there before all of this is over, and I have just the man to get inside."

Rune gave him a beaming smile. "That is great who?"

He kissed her again. "You."

"What?"

"Rune you can pass information through the church, and do it safely and undetected. There is a man in there called Malcolm, he is very loyal and so are his family. They could help us cause a little disruption for the guards. We already know they fear the Violet Bowman, and there are many very young soldiers in there. I think we could have the making of trouble for Mordred, and Mac." He turned on the bed and pulled her into his arms; she curled around him as he stroked back her long red hair, and kissed her softly on the neck. Rune felt the goose bumps rise on her arms and gave a soft giggle, she pulled on the blankets and they slid underneath, she felt happy and relieved to have him back where he was safe. He was in her arms. "Hey beautiful"

"Oh God... Robbie!!!"

Robbie banged on the table, and the room went quiet. The village hall filled with all of the officials, stood and stared. Robbie's eyes glared at the ambassador for York. "WHO THE BLOODY HELL DO YOU THINK YOU ARE? YOU WILL ADDRESS ME AS MY LORD. I AM NOT ASKING YORK TO EVACUATE THE WOMEN AND CHILDREN I AM TELLING YOU THAT YOU WILL!"

The ambassador blinked. "But My Lord, the Duke has made it quite clear." Robbie's eyes flared with the anger; Robert Lox laid a hand on his shoulder.

"Easy lad." The doors at the bottom of the hall opened, and Bear walked in, Robbie breathed a sigh of relief. "Finally, a man of York who will listen to reason... Bear will you tell this envoy of your city what exactly Mordred has in mind for him, because he has not the capacity to understand a word I am saying."

The ambassador spun round to see the impressive figure of Bear in a long sweeping dark blue cloak with the golden seal of York embroidered on it. Bear walked with great authority, the golden sword of courage gleaming in its sheath. Elliot began his mutterings and then stopped as the deep violet clad figure of Rune came through the door smiling with Alice. He gave a wary look at her, and then looked back at Bear. "Jacques I have tried a dozen times to tell Lord Loxley that what he asks is too much, we have not the facilities to move such a large number safely."

Robbie looked across to his friend and shook his head. "I have seen what is coming, listen to me my friend. The soldiers are greater than we expected, and he will have at least two hundred cannons pointing right at those walls your ambassador is so fond of. Jacques, York is going to fall even if I put every man in Loxley there to defend it."

Robbie saw the understanding between Bear and himself. Bear nodded at Robbie. "I will go to my brothers and try to convince them."

"What? How can you side with him? He is not a man of York, you wear the colours of your house, but you are no true man of its people." Elliot looked outraged. He swallowed deeply and whimpered, as the long golden sword of Bear came up from the scabbard and met his throat.

Bear glared at him. "I side with a man of high honour; I side with a man who pleads for the lives of my people. York is stone, it can be rebuilt, if my people die, they will not be replaced as easily. My Lord Loxley, I will travel to York and consult with my brothers. Elliot you will remain here, if you leave, I will kill you myself."

He swung the blade back into its sheath as Robbie stepped forward. "I will come with you we must make haste, there will be a great deal to do, and your brothers are proving more than a little stubborn. I give you my word I will do everything to protect your city, York will not fall easily."

Bear smiled and pulled Robbie into a hug. "My dear friend, the day of our meeting was the turning point of my life. I am honoured by you."

Skip coughed. "Before you two go running off again, might I have a word?" Skip stood as always flanked by Fuse and Treen, both of them held large rolls of paper in their hands. "I took the liberty of drawing up a plan of evacuation. You would be surprised at how much empty space there is in Lancashire and Saddleworth, with a little preparation we could start moving people very quickly. I did take the liberty of assembling one hundred carts for the job."

Bear gave a roar of a laugh. "Skip you never cease to amaze me with your efficiency, thank you my friend I will take all the advice and help I can get."

Rune slid her arm into Robbie's. "We should take a show of Loxley, and bring the Specialists in on the task; we will need a mighty argument to convince the powers of York we mean business. I know you hate it Robbie, but I think a little dressing for the occasion would benefit." Bear smiled at the look on Robbie's face as Rune beamed a radiant smile, Robbie nodded he knew that now was the time to pull out all the stops, even if it meant awkward clothes.

CHAPTER EIGHTEEN

NEW RECRUITS

The drizzle was fine, as the captain of the guards walked along the top of the walls above the gates. He looked out across the crumbled stone and small trees that had sprung back up since the last clearing of the undergrowth. In the distance, either side of the long road he could just make out the tree line of the green wilderness that led south.

What had been masses of thriving towns, and farmland when he was a boy, was now a thick uncontrolled dense wild land of trees and shrubs, that grew out of the tumbled bricks of what had become a forest of decay. The road was clear all the way down to the trees, now the visiting traders had left for the week; he wiped the fine rain from his face and watched with his men across the dim landscape, under the partially obscured pale sunlight. His men leaned on the wall staring out for the fourth hour running, and they were cold, wet and bored. Some of them had closed their eyes in hope of resting, and providing the relief they needed from the now tedious life they lived.

The violet shimmering light was not at first noticed. The many figures on horseback, cloaked in fine long cloaks with golden coats of arms, soon caught the attention of the captain who ran to the top of the gates and watched the convoy make its way slowly towards them up the road. The captain's shout soon had everyone wide-awake. "READY YOUR ARMS. HALT THERE WHO APPROACHES THE GATES OF YORK?"

Rafe road forward at speed towards the gates, he pulled on his reins as his horse slipped on the wet stone floor. "Open the gates in the name of Lord Robert of Loxley, 51st Earl of Huntingdon and hooded man. He leads the delegation of the woodland world, and must have immediate discussion with Sebastian of York."

The captain looked down at the golden coat of arms of New Avon on the long emerald green cloak of Rafe. "Why does a man of Avon carry messages for Loxley?"

Rafe controlled his horse as it moved from side to side in a restless state. "I am a member of Lord Loxley's Specialists, and form part of his guard as well as others duties, he is accompanied by many dignitaries from across this land, I strongly advise you open your gates Captain, otherwise you may find yourself on the receiving end of a very upset lord. He is in no mood to be messed with so hurry." The captain looked across at the young lieutenant who seemed eager to obey, he gave him a nod and the signal was given, the large metal clad gates of York, began to slowly swing open as Robbie and his party approached. Rafe sat to one side, and allowed the group to pass through; he took up his place at the side of Jett and rode into York with the rest of the party.

Sebastian sat in the high chair at the long table with his advisors, Brett his brother, had just returned from the north and had brought word of the hooded man's encounters with the black city. The talk was sweeping the woodland, and he had talked quickly as he filled his mouth with food and ate hungrily. Sebastian appeared bored and snorted at the way Brett marvelled at the deeds of Robbie and his group. "I do think we should find another subject my dear brother, after all, he is not the only one who has managed to defy that Knox fellow and his group of ruffians." Many round the table gave an agreeable nod and Sebastian seemed happy to see he had equal support amongst his own.

Brett tossed his chicken leg on to his plate and sat back with his large glass of claret. "That may be so Seb, but even you must see, that he is a strong force against the dark army, it would be foolish not to cooperate with him."

Sebastian threw his napkin onto the table looking agitated. "Brett you really need to see the bigger picture, I mean the man is good at bashing things off walls, but really, do you think he has the skill to understand commerce and government? I do think not my dear brother; the man is just another ruffian, with his gang. Believe me, we need a little assistance, but at the end of the day, it will be our skills as civilised diplomats that saves this country." Sebastian lifted his glass and sat back, he felt confident it would be his vision that would rule the day for York.

At the very far end of the long hall, the door opened, and a small man in a black coat and tails ran quickly up the hall to the long table. Sebastian looked up at him. "Yes, Watkins what is it?" The small man bent into a bow.

"Begging your pardon My Lord, but there is a very large party arrived from Loxley, they look like they are important dignitaries from all over the country." Sebastian seemed uninterested and waved his hand at the servant in a dismissive manner.

"Alright Watkins tell them to wait in the other chamber, and I will see them when I have finished my meal. I have no wish to be bothered whilst I am digesting." The little man scuttled off down the long hall, to the highly polished doors and slipped back through. Sebastian looked at the gathered group of his advisers.

"Oh, I do hope that frightfully odd woman isn't back with her demands, what was she called Broomstone." Everyone started to giggle, as Sebastian pulled a face. The doors at the far end of the room burst open and everyone jumped. Bear stared up the room at his brothers.

"YOU HAVE GONE TOO FAR SEB. You will see these people now." Bear stood to one side of the door and announced each member as they entered the room. The whole group gathered at the table stared in disbelief as Bear brought each pair in through the doors, and announced them by the full titles.

"Lord Brandon Duke of Gloucester, accompanied by Lady Citrine Du Luc of Morbihan. Lady Sapphire Tor of Callanish, accompanied by Keith Sherman of Loxley. Lady Jett Amber Bedivere, Ambassador of Caerleon, accompanied by Captain Rafe of New Avon. Lady Stephanie and Lord Peter Lane of Avon. Lady Amethyst and Lady Crystal Rimmer of Glastonbury. Lady Ruby Bedivere of Caerleon, accompanied by Lady Judith Hargreaves of Tintagel. Lord Harold and his Daughter Katherine of Loxley. Lady Madeleine Du Luc of Carnac, Lady Una Rimmer of Castleriss Derwent. Lady Melanie Tor Rimmer of Callanish, accompanied by her son Lord Jasper. Lee Sherman, Woodsmen leader of Settle and Loxley. Captain James Ashford of Northwich. Lady Alice of Loxley accompanied by Vice chancellor Simmons of Gloucester. Lord and Lady Rowan and Jade Opal of Loxley." Bear took a deep breath and boomed down the room. "LADY RUNESTONE SAPPHIRE LOXLEY, LORD ROBERT OF LOXLEY 51ST EARL OF HUNTINGDON AND HOODED MAN RETURNED."

The group stood and lined either side of the hall as Rune dressed in bright flowing violet, and wearing her Loxley tiara walked smiling at the side of Robbie. Her long flowing cloak of the deepest violet shone with the golden oak leaves that she had embroidered around it edges. On her right shoulder she had, a deep green oak tree over which had been embroidered with the Loxley wolf head in gold. Her bright golden sword glistened at her side. Her long flowing red hair sparkled in the bright light.

Robbie walked proud besides her, in his best deep emerald green, his cloak flowed to the floor, his golden coat of arms of Loxley shimmering as he moved. He looked angry and his eyes seemed to burn. Everyone knew he was restraining himself. Robbie stopped in front of the table with the beaming Runestone. They looked every bit as impressive as their entrance had suggested. Rune gave a curtsy as Robbie bowed to Sebastian. "My Lord of York, I am happy to finally meet you, I am sorry that we may have inconvenienced you, but time is not on our side and we must speak immediately."

Sebastian dropped his chicken leg on to his plate. "Your people do have a habit of appearing at meal times, won't you join us?" Rowan stepped forward grasping the hilt of his sword, and Robbie slid out his hand and stopped him. The slate grey eyes of Rowan burned deeply with dislike at Sebastian. Jade pulled him back by the hand. Robbie smiled at Sebastian. "I am afraid My Lord we have already eaten, my associates felt last time there was a distinct lack of flavour in the food of

York."

Sebastian rose quickly from the table, throwing down his napkin. "I will not be insulted by you at my own table, how dare you sir, waltz into my chambers like you own the place, and then have the nerve to insult my cook, who I may add, is renown throughout the entire region as being the best." Brett leaned back in his chair and smiled at Bear. He had worked out very quickly that Bear had given Robbie a thorough briefing before he left.

Robbie watched coldly as Sebastian finished his outburst. "Considering your life and that of your people lie in the hands of my people my dear Lord of York, I would consider having your tantrums later. I have important business here, and have not the time to worry about the hurt feelings of your cook. I will say this to you just the once, and if you do not listen, I can promise you York will fall long before the black army arrives. Am I making myself quite clear?"

Everyone at the table looked at Robbie with a worried look; they all turned to the face of Sebastian who still looked defiant. "I am not now or ever going to empty this city, we will stay here and defend from the walls." Brett watched very carefully as Robbie's face did not alter or move.

"Is that your final word my dear Lord of York?"

"It most certainly is." Sebastian folded his arms, and sat smugly in his seat.

Robbie looked round the table at all of the faces. Brett was the only one smiling. Robbie stared into the eyes of Sebastian. "Captain Rafe, Captain Ashford?" The two captains stepped forward; Robbie's eyes remained fixed on Sebastian. "Take our good lord outside and shoot him."

"Yes, My Lord." Rafe and Fish walked forward as Sebastian let out a gasp of shock.

"What...? You cannot...? I am the Lord of York; This is outrageous, you cannot just walk in here and order my death?" His eyes grew wide with fear as Rafe smiling, very casually walked up.

"Come on My Lord, don't fret, my mate Fish is really good at his job, you won't feel a thing." Sebastian leapt out of his seat, and staggered away from Rafe, a look of terror on his face. The whole group separated and surrounded the table, their hands on the hilts of their swords, as Sebastian stared in horror. Robbie looked at him coldly.

"My responsibility is to the free realm of England, I will do whatever it takes to spare the lives of your people, if that means your death, then so be it. Who is going to stop me? None of these gents have moved." Robbie looked at the table filled with white frightened faces.

Rafe grabbed Sebastian's arm. "Come on now sir, don't make more trouble for yourself." Fish took his other arm. Sebastian stared at the table of silent white faces his eyes widened with fear and shock. He opened his mouth but no words formed. Rune raised an arm and clicked her fingers. Sebastian fell to the floor fast asleep.

Robbie grinned at Brett.

"Bear said you wouldn't fall for it. Nice to meet you My Lord, don't worry he will sleep for about twelve hours." He held out his hand. "Robert of Loxley and this delightfully beautiful woman is my dearest Lady Runestone."

The whole table gasped in relief as Brett started to laugh. His deeply brown eyes twinkled and his very long blonde hair flowed and swayed down his shoulders. He took Robbie's hand in a firm grip. "My brother Mickie has told me much about you Lord Loxley, he was right about your nerves of steel, Seb is not a match for many he is highly skilled with a sword."

"So are we." Jett smiled as she glanced over at the sleeping mound of Sebastian on the floor.

Brett took the hand of Rune and kissed it, "My Lady Runestone, I was told of your great beauty, but I fear my friends did not emphasise the point enough."

Rune gave a wide smile. "I see you have the same good manners of your brother Mickie My Lord, it will be nice to converse with another member of the family with his good sense."

Brett laughed. "Indeed, My Lady, I feel I will listen very intently to your lord from now on, I intend to live a long and happy life." He bowed to her. "Would you all please join us at the table? I am sure our cook can find something less bland for you all."

Brett pulled out a chair and offered it to Rune, she nodded and smiled, as she sat down and he adjusted the seat to her. Robbie sat beside her as the others all filled in the gaps. Wine flowed and more food was brought to the table, Brett spent a great deal of time with his brother as they had a lot of catching up to do. Robbie smiled at the advisors and introduced the guests sat either side of them, Rowan sat beside Rune and watched carefully.

Brett turned to Robbie, and with Bear chipping in they began to talk and negotiate, the advisors listened carefully as Robbie recounted his story inside the black city. When he started to give the numbers of the forces they faced, the expression on their faces changed and they began to look more and more concerned.

Rune sipped her wine, and ate her meal; as she listened to Robbie negotiate the conditions of removing all the women and children. He sipped a glass of iced water as he spoke, and finally he sat back and watched as Brett looked round the table at his advisors, who all suddenly seemed to be more inclined to the ideas of the hooded man. Brett looked back at Robbie. "Your plan makes sense, but won't it just leave the city wide open so the black army can just walk in?"

Robbie smiled at Rune as she looked back at him, his eyes crossed back to Brett. "That is precisely my point." He leaned forward in his chair. "Look they have a lot of cannons, if they have to use them then York will just be a pile of rubble. If you leave an empty city then yes, they will occupy it and they may do some damage, but my point is this, if it keeps the city intact, we will have a place we can win back as we did in Gloucester. If you let them use all of their force, there will not be a city to fight for anymore. My way leaves us an open option to return, with your people hidden and protected in our world, you will be able to return and rebuild the systems you have now. Under your brothers command York will die forever." He lifted his glass and took a long drink.

Brett seemed to understand. "I know what you say is good sense My Lord, I can see what you are saying. If I let this city fall to the dark army, realistically what are our chances of winning it back?" Bear patted the sad looking brother on the shoulder. Robbie put his glass down on the table.

"I have found that fear is the tool used to motivate the black army. It is a good tool and works very well; we have played with it against them and had some very good results. The thing is that fear often becomes replaced with complacency, believe me if we bide our time, it will set in. We wait and then when it does, we strike fast and quiet in the dark and hand you the keys back to your city." He smiled at Brett.

Brett was filled with doubts, his father had spent most of his life working for York, and Brett did not want to be the one to lose it all forever. Bear put his arm around his brother. "He is right and you know it, I know you feel the same way as dad, but think of it this way, we are just lending it to them until we can weaken them enough to destroy them. A true king will come to this realm one day, and York will be around to put him on the throne."

Brett nodded. "Ok, what do we do?" Rune gave a huge smile at Robbie as he sat forward in his chair.

"If you do not mind at this point, I will excuse myself and my good lady, and leave you in the most capable hands of the good Duke of Gloucester and his very able vice chancellor. They can tell you more about the evacuation than I can. I would like with your permission to have a wander around this city I have heard so much about." He stood up from his chair, and Rune rose beside him, Robbie and Rune bowed to the assembled table, and Robbie walked down the hall with her, followed by Rowan and Jade. Jett and Rafe accompanied them.

Robbie walked quietly along the walls of the city with his arm around Rune; she could sense the slight relief he now felt knowing York would cooperate. The soldiers all nodded as he passed, the golden coat of arms did give away his identity, yet Rune smiled as he would occasionally stop and talk to one of the soldiers. They bowed with honour as he asked their names, and complimented them for fighting for their people. The captain stood at his post on watch, down the road, a long row of carts were all pulled off on to the rough land waiting for the signal to start moving people out. He saluted to Robbie and Rune as they walked up. Robbie gave him a smile. "Good evening Captain, all quiet I hope?"

The captain was surprised that Robbie was so natural with him. "Yes, My Lord, it is very quiet."

"Good, have you met the Lady Runestone?"

"Err no My Lord... It's nice to meet you, My Lady."

"It's nice to meet you too Captain." Rune smiled at the surprise in his face, and she loved the way Robbie always seemed to welcome everyone and always introduce her. She giggled as she squeezed close to his arm. Robbie turned and looked out across the vast cleared land to the trees.

"You see Rune; to the south we have a chance. I can use the trees as cover for our men, on this side we can slow them down long enough to cause them trouble, and actually have a chance of reducing their numbers. Our people fight in the trees, without them, we are just too exposed. The north is barren for miles, it's just open empty moor."

She could see the concern in his face. Rune knew how worried he was about the high cost of life, this would be one occasion where the battle would be vast, and she knew he could not be at every point to ensure the safety of everyone. She stared out at the trees and the cleared land that provided an open space for defence.

"You know Robbie, grandfather could give you a little help like he did in Scotland, he did create a forest over night with a little help from Mother Nature?" Robbie chuckled.

"Mother Nature. I like the sound of that, Runestone Sapphire the mother of all nature." His eyes seemed to sparkle as he said it, and she knew where his thoughts had gone. Rune pulled him close.

"You will have to be patient Rob; she is growing as fast as she can." He gave her a loving smile.

"I know, it's just that I see those pictures of her in my mind, and I want her here now. I want to hold her up and look into those violet eyes, and just absorb every moment I can with her, does that sound daft?"

Rune slid in close. "No, it sounds wonderful, I am so excited as well you know? She will be beautiful like her father and loved so much. I love you, Robbie." He looked down at her bright sapphire blue eyes, and that wonderful pale smiling face that radiated all the love and joy in his life, and he bent down to kiss her.

The light flashed across her face and there was a scream. Robbie looked up, towards Rowan and Jade, who stood with Rafe and Jett. All four of them had their bows raised, and looked at him with relief in their eyes. Rune jumped as she looked down at the captain of the guard with four long white arrows sticking out of him, the long silver dagger still clutched tight in his hand.

Rune gasped as she saw the long gash in Robbie's cloak as it flapped, she seized it quickly with shaking hands, and pulled it back to inspect him, his shirt was cut and there was blood, Rune gasped and fought the tears of panic rising quickly from coming to her eyes, as she franticly pulled at his shirt.

"Oh... Robbie. No... Oh please not now." She pulled furiously, tearing the cloth apart, the panic rising quickly inside her. She gulped for air, as Robbie moved back against the wall, and she tore wildly at his shirt until it came away and revealed a long red line across his side, where the blood flowed out and ran down to his boots. "Oh Hearne no... Please Hearne no!"

She fell to her knees, as she looked closer, and cried in relief as she saw the skin was sliced, but it was not a deep cut. Robbie looked at the thin cut, as she wept clinging to the torn fragments of his shirt. He knelt down and pulled her sobbing into his arms. "Hey Rune come on I am fine." She pushed her head in to his shoulder and shook with the fear. He held her close, and kissed her softly as the tears of anguish flowed out of her.

"I thought he had stabbed you; I should have seen it coming, Oh Robbie I thought I would lose you." Tears poured on to his shoulder, as she wept trembling with her subsiding panic as she squeezed him tightly. Rowan and Rafe both dragged the lifeless body of the captain to one side; Rafe removed the silver dagger from the hand, and threw it to Jade. Jade looked closely at it as she turned it over in her hands.

"Nice well tooled weapon, you don't buy these on a captain's wages." She spun it in her hand, and then slipped it into her belt. Rowan turned to Robbie, he looked angry and his face was sterner than Robbie had ever seen it.

"That is enough; I do not really care what you think. I want you out of here, and now, Rune get him home. Rafe you take Jett and do not let him out of your sight. I will finish up here and then I will let Jade know, and she can get you to open a window. Now go, God knows how many more spies there are in this place. Their defences are so full of holes I could sneak half of Loxley in here." Rowan's eyes, burned with anger, but also with fear. Robbie stood up holding Rune tightly; he lifted an arm and pulled Rowan close.

"Calm down my friend I am fine. Please Rowan, you are scaring Rune more." Rowan threw his arms around Robbie and gave him a tight hug.

"When will you listen to me? You are the lord of this land; you must take more care and be on your guard. I have no wish to lose my lord and greatest friend." Robbie patted him on the back. Hearing the panic in Rowan's voice was enough.

"I will do as you ask, to see fear in you as I do now has made me more aware. I will go home with Rune and wait for your safe return. Please be calm now, I am fine." Rowan released him and nodded at him. Robbie held the weeping Rune into his arms and she waved her hand. The shimmering archway appeared and they walked on to the top of the stairs in the wooden house at Loxley. Rafe and Jett came through as Rowan's voice still barked orders on the other side.

"Right, I will brew, Wolfie baby you see that the house is secure. Rune come on now we are all safe, that cut needs seeing too. Take Robbie into your room, and clean it up before it gets infected, I will bring you both a good cup when it is done.

Come on now, let's hustle."

Rune gave a soft smile as he looked down at her. "You, Ok?"

She nodded her eyes red and swollen from her tears. "I am fine now, Jett's right, I need to see to that wound, come on."

It was a deep scratch, nothing more, and he sat on the bed, as she cleaned it to make sure. She smeared some of Alice's paste on it and covered it with a strip of fine silk. He sat in the chair by the window with Rune curled on his lap, and his mind wandered.

It had been a very precious moment between them, and he had not seen it coming, Robbie realised more than ever, how dangerous things were becoming. Earlier that night he had spoken of complacency, and yet he too had suffered the very same. Right at the moment when he had seen a glimpse of what his future could be, he had let down his guard and almost suffered a fatal injury. He stroked her long red hair and looked down at her. She felt his movement and her eyes moved upwards to his. "I am sorry Rune; you have been right. I have taken too many risks; I never want to see fear in your eyes like that again. I promise I will be more careful in future."

She curled closer and snuggled into him; he pulled her close and held her until she fell asleep. As midnight approached, he lifted her carefully on to the bed, and pulling the blankets over, he left her to sleep. Robbie came down the stairs and saw Rafe and Jett sat side by side on the steps to the house, they talked quietly as they watched the Mere. Robbie sat quietly in the chair.

"I am only a Captain; I do not have a lot of money Jett. You are a lady of standing use to life in a castle with all that offers; I can only give you a small house in Loxley."

"Wolfie I keep telling you, I don't care. Yes, I live in a big huge castle with servants and a million rooms, but it is empty, cold and lonely, I would love to live here with you. This is my family here; I have Rune and Jade and all my cousins. I do not need servants, look how great it is when we get up in the night and cook for each other. I even washed your pants for you."

"I know you shrunk them, god they are tight."

"Yeah, but I tell you, they look great on you." She giggled and he put his arm round her.

"I tell you what, after York I will speak to Robbie about number six in the village, if I do extra shifts on duty, I will have enough for the rent and some furniture. I will transfer to Loxley as a captain here then I won't get called back to New Avon, and we will see what we can do alright?"

"Yeah cool. I love you wolf man, go on howl for me."

"Well, I can't do it loud, Robbie and Rune are sleeping, but I can do a quiet one... Ow Ooooh!" She gave a giggle.

"Wow you are cool." He chuckled as she beamed a bright smile at him.

Robbie tiptoed back up the stairs trying not to laugh. Rune must have woken and got undressed and back into bed, her clothes were strewn on the floor. He slid back the blankets and slid into the bed. He pulled her close and felt the warmth of her soft delicate body against his. Suddenly he felt exhausted, and closed his eyes. Pictures drifted of a little girl with brown wavy hair and bright violet eyes running laughing up the mere. Light twinkled in the trees above her.

Sebastian woke with a start. He looked around wildly, and saw Rowan pouring a coffee. "Where am I? What time is it? Who the hell are you, and why are you drinking my coffee?"

Rowan glanced at him. "You are at home, it's eleven in the morning, I am Rowan of Loxley the hooded man's second in command. I am drinking your coffee because I am thirsty, and I have a sword which you don't." He turned to Sebastian. "And remember I am the one who would have killed you, just for the disrespect you showed to my lord. He let you live; I feel it was a mistake. Any more questions?"

Sebastian sat up and rubbed his eyes. "Sorry, I am not at my best in the morning."

"You weren't at your best last night either, here." Rowan handed him a coffee. Sebastian nodded.

"Thank you, Rowan." Rowan smiled to himself, as he poured another cup.

"I hope I am not going to have any trouble from you, your brothers have a greater understanding of the peril you are all in, and are preparing the way. I do not want you thinking you are still in charge here because you aren't. York is now under the protection of Loxley, and it will remain so until the black army has been dealt with. After that you can fight all you like with your brothers, until such time you can either help or stay out of the way it's up to you?" Rowan sat on a chair and lifted his feet up on to the table. He closed his eyes for a moment.

Sebastian sipped his coffee. "I don't suppose I have much of a choice?"

Rowan opened one eye, and looked at him. "You have a choice, just don't make the wrong one, I am not as forgiving as Lord Loxley." He closed his eye, and left Sebastian to think about it.

Rune slid up on top of him and smiled as she looked down at him. He opened his eyes and saw her smiling. "Hey beautiful."

"Hi gorgeous." She giggled. "How is your side?"

"It's fine, you saw it, just a bad scratch that's all." She gave another little giggle.

"Oh goodie." He started to laugh.

Robbie came down the stairs quite some time later, he stretched as Rafe and

Jett came in through the door yawning and looking tired. Rafe patted his shoulder. "We are going to get some sleep; you have five bowmen out there to watch."

Robbie pulled Rafe back. "I need Rowan back here later; I want you to replace him in command at York. Obviously, you will need a higher rank than Captain, I will get Rune to sew you a commander's crest on your cloak, leave it here. The new rank comes with a pay rise, and you will have to move post. I know how proud you are of New Avon, but you must have the authority of Loxley. Find a house here to be a man of Loxley; you must live within the stockade... Congratulations Commander Rafe, you have served me well, I hope my gesture is agreeable to you?"

Rafe looked stunned. "Robbie, My Lord... I am lost for words; you know you have my service and loyalty. I am honoured; I will not let you down."

"Right, go on and get some sleep." Jett ran down the stairs and kissed Robbie on the cheek, she gave a huge giggle.

"Thanks Robbie, I love you, you're the best ever."

He smiled at the happiness on her face, she squealed with delight as she raced up the stairs after Rafe. Rune came down smiling. "What's got Jett so happy?"

"I just made the Wolf man a commander, he will have to live here now." Rune gave him a soft kiss.

"How did you know?" He winked.

"I am the Lord of Loxley you know? I have a good sense of what my subjects want."

"You overheard them talking then?" He pinched her and she squealed, and ran screaming to the kitchen as he followed her laughing. She giggled as he cornered her by the table.

Skip and Bear watched as the first carts rolled into the city. Just after sunrise, soldiers went to every house, and the word was spread to abandon the city. All women and children under the age of eighteen were to pack one bag each, and head to the town centre. Carts were gathered from every corner of York, and those who owned their own were allowed to take extra as long as they accommodated others in their carts. By ten o'clock, the first carts had been allocated a town, and were starting their long journey out of York. It was going to be a long process, but Skip was filled with his usual enthusiasm, and smiled as the first carts left.

By midafternoon a long line of carts stretched from the gates to far inside the trees, and Rowan began to breathe a sigh of relief. Rafe arrived with his new Loxley cloak and took over command with Jett at his side. Rowan and Jade returned with some of the others to Loxley, as Robbie began to plan for the attack.

He now took over at the village hall with his father, and he began to prepare for the attack on York. His mind drifted back to the conversation with Rune shortly before the assassin had tried to attack him. His mind turned to the power of nature and the power of the Lord Hearne. Slowly he began to develop a strategy that would not defeat his enemy, but it would make it hard for them to attack him openly. More and more his mind turned to delay tactics that would divide the large host, so he could pick them off without losing his own men.

Robbie spoke with his dad and Rowan for hours sat at his desk in the hall, he was sure that if he could draw the attack out over a longer period; he could wear down his enemy. He needed the best at stealth he could get, and turned to his own Specialists. He also began to think more and more about the tactics of the bandits. They had a way of attacking, without being spotted, and Robbie needed knowledge. In his mind the more knowledge he had, the better the chances of York surviving. This would be a long battle and it would be fought and won or lost on the use of knowledge of the other side, and some good defensive planning. Robbie felt the faint light of hope start to grow inside him. The odds were overwhelming, and yet somehow, he felt with a little extra planning and a great deal of luck mixed with stealth, he may just overcome his biggest hurdle to date.

Father Warren looked back at the doors as they closed with a dim thud, he heard the bolt draw across, and rose from the altar rail, and turned to meet his guests. Malcolm walked quickly with Meg up the centre of the aisle towards the Father, who smiled. "What is this new news Father? We came as quickly as we could." Father Warren took Malcolm by the shoulder and turned him around to face the doors.

"I have a guest coming shortly that will answer your questions; you have done much to help this community, Malcolm." He paused and looked him in the eyes. "Now will come our hardest time, are you prepared to aid your people in their fight for freedom?"

"You know I am Father; I will give my life to bring these people back to the trees."

Father Warren nodded and smiled at Meg. "You especially I think will enjoy the company of my guest." He looked up as the violet mist swirled into the church. "Right on time." Malcolm took Meg's hand as the mist swirled in the air and began to take the form of a figure, it was an elegant and slender figure, it pulsed as the violet light burned brightly in the dim church, and slowly the figure became solid as Rune wearing a gentle smile walked towards them.

"Fear not friends, for I am Runestone, daughter of the line of your Green Lord and creator of all, I bring news from the hooded man and aid to your cause." Meg's eyes sparkled with delight as she watched entranced. Excitement pulsed through her, Robbie had been right this was no violet witch, Meg thought she was beautiful and marvelled at her.

Rune came to a halt before them, and Malcolm seemed lost for words.

"Greetings Father of Colum Cille, I am pleased to see you again. Greetings

Malcolm, and thank you, you gave aid to my hooded man and I am forever in your debt." Rune looked into the eyes of Meg. "I bring you a special greeting my daughter of the trees, for I see you have your father's line of the woods deep inside you. Am I the violet witch they speak of?"

Meg trembled. "No, My Lady, you are beautiful, the hooded man was right, and now I can see why he loves you so."

Rune gave her a big smile. "There is much beauty left in this world, I see it all around us. Do not let those with black tongues corrupt your thoughts, you will see one day the true beauty of the world, when we bring down this world of grey and black." Rune looked to the father and Malcolm. "My hooded man wishes to know if you are ready to stand and fight for the cause of freedom, and to help restore the true heirs to this kingdom?"

Malcolm nodded. "We are restricted in here My Lady, but we will do what we can, what has our Lord of Loxley in mind?" She saw the pride in his eyes and the faith in his heart, and Rune knew that Robbie was right in his choice of a leader to the resistance movement.

"My Lord speaks highly of you Malcolm; he wishes to know if you will bring destruction and chaos to this city? He plans to confront the Black Army in war; he will need help inside these walls. Your task will be to coordinate the attacks inside, and pass back information to him at Loxley. He wishes you to gather your men and prepare, he has a contact outside these walls that will aid you with weapons and explosives. Will you take on this role in the name of the woodland realm?"

Malcolm swelled with pride. "I will My Lady, tell our lord we are here and preparing."

Rune gave him a smile. "This house is protected by the powers of the people of Fae. I have placed extra protection inside, no man who is not true to the cause will be able to enter without feeling pain, watch for those who would undermine you. Speak only of your tasks within these walls, and I shall protect you all... My time here is done I will return to you at this time tomorrow, gather your people and prepare."

Rune turned to Meg. "Hold out your hand child of my realm." Meg lifted her hand and opened her palm. Rune gave a smile and touched Meg's palm carefully. "In this lies hope for your people, treasure it." A small violet grew in Meg's hand and burst into bloom. Meg gave a huge smile as she looked at the flower.

"It is beautiful My Lady."

"It is but one of many beautiful things in my realm, this is the first of many flowers that will one day grow here, care for it, and let it bring life and hope to the hearts of your people." Rune turned and began to walk down the aisle. "Farewell my friends, we will meet again tomorrow." Her voice faded, as she broke apart into the violet mist and faded from sight. Meg watched as two more flowers uncurled their petals and gave a burst of bright violet.

"Oh, dad she is wonderful." Malcolm put his arm on his daughter's shoulder.

"Aye. she is something alright, clever man that Robert of Loxley."

Rune opened her eyes and smiled at Robbie. "It is done, they will prepare."

Robbie smiled at Jade and Rowan. "Ok. now we start to give Mordred his first taste of woodland anger, and we shall show him what dangers a beast of burden can be. I think Rowan my friend; we should go hunting for a nice large Ox." Jade giggled as Rune stood up from her table, she slipped her arms around him.

"I think an Ox hunting party usually carries a team of at least four, does it not? I am looking forward to seeing the boys again." She gave him a very sweet smile. "I will go and change." Rune skipped on to the steps in joyful mood and disappeared. Robbie looked at Rowan and knew it was pointless to comment. He knew that from now on being alone was not something he would have much of outside of Loxley. He wandered upstairs and lifted his bow; he checked the string tension and put extra arrows in his quiver. Robbie reached for his sage green cloak, and picked up his extra knife.

Autumn was now showing its full colour in the trees. The floor of the glade was decorated with yellows, red and rusty browns from the leaves that had blown across it in the night. The air was cool and damp, and Robbie felt stillness to the whole feel of the glade, winter was waiting in the corners ready to wave her hand of sleep over the natural world, and he felt a deep sense of calm around the place. How nice it would be to just curl up and rest with Rune for three months he thought, as he walked slowly down to the edge of the water. His mind drifted in a restful way as he looked out at the few birds that remained, a slight twittering beside him caught his attention, and he turned to see the first Robin of winter with his large fat red chest singing on an old stump. He gave a smile to his namesake.

"Hey little guy, wrap up well the cold is coming." The little bird seemed to cock his head as if listening, and then flapped his wings and began to chirp. The bird knew that the man before him was no threat, and Robbie watched as the little red-breasted fellow sang to him.

Rune watched from a few feet behind him and smiled, the small bird saw her and bowed. Robbie noticed and turned to her. Rune was dressed in all green with her bright shining sword, her hair moved in the breeze and shimmered. Her eyes were bright with life as she came closer. "It appears my little friend here knows his mistress when he sees her?"

"He is part of my realm and he knows this. All life in the world is my domain Rob. He will tell the rest of this realm about his meeting with me, and they will be happy to know that here close by, their lady of life is watching over them. As I am you, my love." She slid her arms around him.

"Oh, Rune it is so peaceful today, I could sit for hours and just enjoy what surrounds me, I feel so busy at times I barely have time to walk in the woods."

"Then maybe you should make time. Never forget this is your realm as well, do not lose sight of what you fight for. Your dream must be the one to conquer all Rob, forget it at peril. This is the beginning of the age of dreams, and only one dream can win, and it must be yours."

He looked down at her and gave her a shrewd look. "You sound more like Opal every day."

She gave a soft giggle. "Good, I loved my grandmother, and to be like her would be wonderful. She was Nature in my eyes, and so to be seen as she was, would be a compliment beyond even my dreams."

Robbie watched as she lifted her arms out wide and spun round, her head back and her hair lifting into a wide arc around her. "How do you do it?" She stopped and smiled at him.

"Do what?"

"That...? I look at you and I see the girl I love; you are sweet and beautiful. You are my Runestone, the girl I have loved so much longer than I have known her." She looked at him with her bright sapphire blue eyes that seemed to sparkle with love and compassion and the joys of life. "With a snap of the fingers, you have all of this power. You brought down half a mountain, devastated a forest, killed a man by looking into his eyes and letting him see himself through the eyes of life. Hell Rune, a bird just bowed to you... How can you be all that, and yet still be my Runestone?"

She threw back her head and laughed, Rune spun very fast, and bright violet light exploded from her, snowflakes fell around him, and small violets burst into bloom on the floor round his feet, she yelled into the air on the top of her voice as she spun. "I am life, I am the world that brings joy and goodness, and food to the life I have given. I rejoice in my gifts for I am the power of Nature."

She suddenly stopped on the spot, and looked right at him. The power she held inside could be seen in her eyes. "But I am a woman also. I am a woman who has gifts beyond my powers, for I have the love of a man I would die for. I rejoice at the life he put inside me and grows, for without it I would be just a woman with gifts more than most. I love you Robbie, and what I feel in my heart for you; I give freely to the world around me. Without you I am nothing."

The honesty and sincerity of her stood before him, suddenly looking vulnerable impacted on him. She was small, slender and elegant; he had loved her for most of his life, and never more than in that one single moment.

"I have not the words to describe how much I love you Rune. This language is not enough to fully explain how I feel." Her face broke into a huge smile as she leapt into his arms, and he pulled her close and held her for an age. Her heart beat fast inside her, and he felt it as he held her close. Jade wandered down with a smile.

"You guys just make it look so easy; we are all jealous as hell. Go on tell me your secret?"

Rune gave a chuckle, as she slipped out of his arms and turned to Jade. "Oh, don't give me that sister, I have seen you and Rowan alone in the woods, you know full well what to do. The man glows in your presence, any one would think he was the one with the powers."

Jade giggled. "He does sort of, doesn't he?" Robbie pulled his arm around his two favourite women, and walked slowly up the glade back to the house. The others were waiting to move off to the woods in search of Ox and his men.

One hour later the group slipped into the trees, in the deep woods five miles south of the black city. Keith and Saff took point and crouched in the trees, Jade and Rowan swung out left as Blades and Hornet went right. Rune squatted in the grass and sensed the surroundings as Robbie waited. "Half a mile to the left of centre, there are a couple of groups." Robbie nodded and gave the hand signals. The group moved off slowly through the thinning trees, they passed like shadows in amongst the trunks, the birds and rabbits hardly noticed they were there.

For ten minutes, they moved with speed, but as the woodland got deeper, they found themselves slowing as the trees became thicker. The group tightened and they made their way through slowly and quietly. Keith's hand shot up and the group went to ground. Robbie made his way forward to the side of Keith. "What is it?" He peered into the dense lines of birch trunks. Keith raised a finger, and Robbie followed the direction. At first, he saw nothing, but then a slight moment caught his eye. A flash of red fabric on black appeared for a moment, and then sunk into the large ferns. Robbie looked back at Rune whose eyes were already coloured violet. "Where is Ox?"

She crawled close to his ear. "There is a group sat camped just up ahead in the trees. Another group is creeping round them; I think Ox is about to be ambushed."

Signals passed quickly across the wood from Robbie to the others, Rowan and Jade signalled back and melted into the trees. Blades sent her response and soon there was no sign of Hornet or herself. Keith and Saff, moved off to follow Blades, and Robbie and Rune pushed forwards. The signals were clear and precise, hold off attack until the enemy strike.

He pulled an arrow from his quiver and winked at Rune. She had already fitted her first and was ready, he smiled as he looked at her, and remembered that very first day in the woods with her. It now seemed like such a long time ago. Rune had changed a great deal; she understood all his signs, and now reacted with instinct. She slipped in and out of sight with such ease, and she had become a bow-woman of exceptional skill.

Ox gave a loud roaring belch as he dropped the large pork bone on to the fire. He rubbed his stomach and lifted the bottle of red wine. He drank heavily from it and then sat back, a look of contentment on his face. The others all had their heads down eating and drinking, two were already asleep. It had been a long night, and a long walk back from the attack of the convoy.

Ox settled back and began to daydream as he rested against the stump of an old felled oak. He smiled as he felt the strains in his legs melt away. His eyes wandered the trees and watched as the soldier in a black vest jumped up with a crossbow, and then jerked forward into the camp with a long white feathered arrow sticking out of his back. It took a moment to register. Woody and Todd were already up with their swords out, although there seemed to be little to do, as black vested soldiers fell dead into their camp, Ox gave a big laugh as the hooded figure walked up through the trees. The hood fell and long bright red hair fell down from the shoulders, as Rune shook her head. She gave a big smile. "Hi boys... Did you miss me?"

Hooded figures came out of the trees; Robbie dropped his hood as he looked around.

"Keith, Blades. We are two short on your side." They turned and melted back in amongst the woods, Robbie winked at Ox. "I hope you left enough for us, we are starving, missed breakfast I've been so busy." Two squeals came from deep in the woods, as Robbie walked into the clearing and pulled a chunk of meat off the roasted boar, he bit deep and chewed. "Oh now that is food with flavour."

Ox sat down with a big smile next to Rune. "Is he always so casual about things?"

Rune nodded, as she smiled at him. "Not always, but we do work in ways that surprise other people."

Robbie pushed his knife with the pork on the end towards her. "Taste this it is wonderful." Rune took a bite as Robbie gave a grin at Ox. "You should watch your back my friend, it appears our old friends have taken an interest in you."

"You saved our lives My Lord; we owe you a great debt of gratitude."

Robbie swallowed and gave Ox a smile. "I believe that is the way of the woodsmen. A favour for a favour, do you not agree? Please call me Robbie; out here I am the hooded man."

"I understand the code, what worries me is what kind of favour you want in return. No offence, but you do sort of live on the edge a little." Rune gave a giggle as she sliced meat on to a plate, and passed it to Rowan and Jade. Robbie took a large mouthful of wine to wash down his food; he passed the bottle to Ox who was waiting for a response.

"I am working with people inside the city; let's just say we do not intend to let our old friend in black have things his own way. I need someone close to pass them supplies, and help them if needs be. I also want to create havoc around the outside of the city walls. I just think some guys could have a lot of fun at the same time as helping my friends inside. You all seemed to enjoy blowing the gates up."

Ox smiled and nodded. "It was a fun evening, what exactly have you in mind?"

"York appears to have quite a large supply of explosives, now with an imminent attack on the horizon and an enemy armed with cannons, it does seem to make more sense to remove it. My idea is simply this, you smuggle explosives to my friends inside the city and take some for yourselves. You already raid the supply carts and get away with it, why not light a fuse as you leave. You take what you need, and ensure the black army get nothing."

Ox furrowed his brow as he thought about it. "That's all you want us to do?"

Robbie sat forward and looked at all the bandits sat around. "That is it... are you in or out?" It was now the turn of Ox to evaluate the thoughts of his men.

"Can I speak alone with my men before we decide?"

Robbie stood up and looked around. "I think that would be a wise decision, I would not ask any man to risk his life in my service if he wished not to. I will walk in these wonderful woods for a while; give me a whistle when you have reached your decision." Robbie offered his arm to Rune, who took it with a beaming smile. He shouldered his bow. "My Lady Runestone... After you?"

They walked out into the trees quietly talking; Rowan looked at him. "What do you think, can we trust them?" Rune answered before Robbie could.

"These are woodsmen Rowan. They have been forced into the life they live; I have spent much, more time around them than you, and believe me, they are true to the woodsman's code. They may not show it, but they are true to Loxley. If they join us, you will not need to worry about them, I would worry about any who oppose us. There are few who will have an argument with these boys believe me."

"They are very skilled with their weapons believe me." Jade seemed very impressed. "Their wood skills are some of the best I have seen outside of Loxley, every one of them Robbie would fit into the Specialists no problems. That Todd is like a shadow in the trees." Jade smiled, and her eyes twinkled under her thick curly fringe, Rowan gave her a smile. Her faith was enough to convince him, wood skills was something Jade took very seriously.

It was about ten minutes before a long whistle came through the trees; Robbie turned with the group, and walked back towards the camp. The outlaws stood close together, they were rough and unshaven with their patched clothes and old weapons. They all stood in a line looking serious, as Ox slid his hands into his pockets and gave Robbie a serious look. "We have a few demands, and if you can agree, we are in." The group smiled with black teeth, and in some cases no teeth. Robbie looked at Rune, who gave him a big smile. He turned back to Ox.

"Ok, what are your demands?"

Ox shuffled his feet. "We all need new boots." He looked embarrassedly at the floor. "We need better weapons ... and err... well...we did sort of wonder... If we could have a Loxley woodsmen cloak each, you know... all of us." Robbie gave a big bright smile at Ox, who looked up and grinned back as Robbie offered his hand. "Gentlemen welcome to the woodsmen of Loxley, if you would like to join my good lady and myself, we can return to Loxley now and kit you out. You're in, it's a deal." Ox snatched his hand with a nod, and he looked at his men who all shook their heads in agreement, he gave a big smile as Rune opened a window. Robbie waved a hand to Ox and invited him to walk through with Rune. He gave a long whistle, and Blades and Hornet came out of the trees with Keith and Saff. The whole group walked through, and stood in the glade in front of Robbie's house. Rune stood at her gate and opened it. "Gentlemen welcome to our home, please come inside."

Ox hesitated and looked at the woods to the side of the house. "If it does not offend my kind lady, we do sort of stink; it helps in the woods you know? We would mess up your nice home here; we will be comfy in the trees there."

She smiled. "If you are happy with that so am I. We shall set the tables on the garden lawn later if you would dine with us, in the meantime Jade and myself will measure you all for boots and cloaks, I am sure that we have whatever weapons you may require stored here already. Robbie does seem to have built up quite a collection."

Ox gave a nod. "You are very kind Lady Loxley thank you." They headed into the trees as Robbie came up the path towards her.

"Aren't they sweet Rob? They are so rough looking and yet polite. I find them very endearing."

"You call me for having fans; I think most of your club is now sat in our woods." She giggled at him.

"You did well Rob, these guy's will cause havoc, and it could be just what we need."

Robbie gave a sigh as Rowan rested an arm on his shoulder. "I hope so, every little thing we can do to frighten them will work our way, and we still have a long way to go yet."

Rowan shrugged. "I am not so sure Robbie; I feel more hope now than I did stood on that wall looking down at his army, using all the skills of our fathers has kept them alive, maybe it will us."

Rune slipped her arm round his waist. "Come on we have new recruits to kit out, and then we have a meal to prepare, you and Rowan can make a start on the vegetables, whilst Jade and I take their measurements. Once they are sorted, we will have a meal together, it's going to be cool tonight I think a big hot stew will be ideal." She smiled as she led the way in, Rowan and Robbie headed for the kitchen, and Rune with Jade went to get their measures.

CHAPTER NINETEEN

USING STEALTH

At the top of the light coloured town house on the balcony, stood the pale thin figure of a dark haired woman. Her soft blue eyes seemed to hold the coldness of the morning, as she looked out across the river at the burned and broken remains of the old palace of Westminster. Barges and boats passed noisily up the river, carrying scrap iron to the furnaces that burned day and night, in the new metal complex that had been built two miles further upstream. She shivered lifting her pale white hands off the white metal rail.

Dana Knox had managed to elevate her position from close personal secretary, to wife of what had been seen as the most powerful man in Britain. She had been by his side day and night for twelve years, and now she was a widow. For a moment, the hooded man had destroyed her hopes and dreams, but now she found as the Step Mother to the new heir and future mother of another heir, she had been given a position of power she had never thought possible. Lance had been heart broken and filled with fear at the loss of his father, Dana had quickly filled the void and given him the strength and support he had needed. Under her guidance, Lance had assumed control of all of London, and now things had begun to move again as she pushed him from behind, and showed him the ways of his father.

Dana had been the only one who really knew the full plans of Mason. For twelve years, she had been a single witness to him, as he worked endlessly to gain control, and set up the infrastructure that would eventually lead to a return to the ways of Modern Man. Behind the scenes, she had shared his bed and given him comfort, away from a wife whose hysterical outbursts, endless tears and cries for affection had driven Mason mad. He hated the weakness of Zandra Hargreaves, and soon found comfort in the arms of a strong and ambitious woman.

Dana was cool, controlled and ruthless in her desire to get to the top of the new world, he admired and respected the coldness at which she would carry out his orders. Dana had helped him reform and control the orphanages and hospitals, to help him build his new population and armies. From the balcony where Mason had first brought her ten years earlier, she now stared into the light of a new day, it was almost four months since she had lost him to Robbie, and she had worked harder than ever to keep Lance in control. Under her guidance he had changed, and began the transformation from frightened young boy to the pale imitation of Mason he was now becoming.

Dana rested her hands on her stomach, she was five months pregnant and only now could the faint bump in her stomach be noticeable. Already she had plans for the child, the dark figure of Morgan le Fey had seemed to have taken a strong liking to Dana, and she had helped her to understand the truth of what was inside her. Dana carried the future of the line of le Fey in the form of a female child, a child that would have gifts of the old times, and help her control and rule with far more authority than she even had with Lance.

Her cool blue eyes rested on her stomach, and she gave a slight smile. She held the future, and she now held power beyond her wildest dreams. Her body contained the future sorceress that would bring devastation to any that tried to stop her. Her dark hair blew up round her shoulders and she stroked it back as she smiled, the long black car moved into the driveway far below, and she watched the black suited, blonde figure step out. He looked up and smiled as he spotted her and waved. Dana lifted a hand and turned as the young man headed in past the guards.

She walked in through the patio doors and lifted her long black cloak off the back of the chair, pulling it round her shoulders; she walked to the door and waited for the gentle tap that would signal his arrival. Dana and Lance would be touring the factories, and then heading to see the board at the hospital. Today they would see just how many they had for the army, as the rooms were cleared for the new arrivals, and the boys would enter the academy of war ready to strike from the south.

The tap softly came, and she opened the door to the taller looking Lance, who was now dressed in all black as his father always had. He smiled and pulled her into a warm hug. "Mother."

"Lance darling, you look wonderful." She gazed at him on the edge of his seventeenth birthday. "You look so like your father." She kissed his cheek as he offered his arm, and she stepped out into the hall. "Now remember what I said, this lot can be tricky, you must not show them any weakness, from the moment we arrive you show them you are the son of the greatest man ever to rule this land. Lance honey, you are now the Governor of England, show them and do not compromise. Your father hated this lot, but he was no fool, they do their jobs well but he never gave them an inch."

"Yes Mother."

Robbie stood by the bedroom window and looked out at the Mere and the woods. "Do you think the boys will be alright out there? It's throwing it down"

Rune sat in the bed and smiled. "Rob, they have lived in the woods for years, they will be fine. Come back to bed I am getting cold without you." Her eyes twinkled as he turned away from the windows. She lifted the sheets and he slipped under and pulled her close. The heat radiated out of her soft skin and he held her tight. "Oh Rob, your feet are freezing." She giggled as he slid them up her leg and she pushed them away. "No..." Rune squealed with laughter as he lifted his legs and pushed on to her. She rolled around under the sheet fighting him off, and then giggling she collapsed and he leaned over her.

Robbie looked down at her pale happy smiling face; her eyes sparkled up at him, as his hair fell forward surrounding her face. "Hey beautiful." She gave a giggle.

The captain gave a salute and stood upright. "Commander." Rafe walked up on the platform, and looked out across the road at the last of the day's carts as they disappeared into the darkness, all that could be seen was the glint of spear tips of the soldiers of York, who gave an escort to the outer edges of the city, where the guides of Loxley took over.

"That's the last for today Captain, you can close the gates and seal this place for the night, it's been a long day, I will be in my quarters if you need me."

"Yes sir." The captain turned to the young Lieutenant. "Close it down and bring on the night guard." Rafe walked slowly along the top of the wall toward the small rooms he had been given, just down from the gates. The faint candlelight burned in the window and he smiled as he approached the small black door. He felt happy inside, his new command and position had elevated him, and he now was a man who could see his own future. He opened his door and stepped in, undoing the clasp on his cloak, he walked through the small living space and into the bedroom. Jett beamed at him from under the blankets. "Hey baby." Her eyes glistened and sparkled, and he smiled as he sat on the bed and pushed off his boots. Jett slipped up behind him and rubbed his shoulders.

He swung his arm round and grabbed her, pulling her round in front of him, she felt good in his arms as she slid her arms round his neck. She gave him a warm smile and kissed him. "You... Ok?"

Rafe looked into the eyes of Jett Amber. Two pools of dark black surrounded by a faint pale lilac looked back at him. "Are you sure this is what you want? It's not exactly much is it?" Jett pushed herself closer and squeezed him tightly.

"Please Wolfie... don't do this, you have no idea how happy I am; forget the castle and all of its grandeur. Honestly, I would live in a tent, as long as I knew you would be there by my side. I was so lonely there; you have no idea how hard it was to live so isolated and away from anything that could matter. Mum and dad were so busy with the war, Ruby and me just rattled around for weeks doing nothing.

Believe me, I have found something so great I will never let go, I love you Wolf man, don't you see that it is the only thing that matters?"

He gave her a smile, he loved her more than he had ever said, and yet he knew the life she had lived was better than anything she would ever have with him. He stroked her long soft black hair back from her face, for all her toughness and wild behaviour, he saw a gentle and very beautiful woman. He smiled at her and her eyes twinkled. "Bite me baby." She gave a wild giggle.

Rafe seized her quickly and lifted her into the air, Jett screamed wildly as he threw her on to the bed and pounced, he pushed his face into her stomach and made to bite her, as she thrashed wildly and screamed with laughter. Rafe sat up and tore off his shirt, he threw back his head and as loud as he could he wailed. "Ow ... Ooooh!!!"

He looked down at her laughing hysterically and smiled. Her eyes caught his and he saw the happiness in her. "Yeah, wolf man... attack me I am yours."

The soldiers looked back from the wall to the small rooms below, they gave a smile at each other as the laughter rose from the small rooms into the air outside, their new Commander was not like the others that was for sure. He already had quite a reputation, and yet the men of York in just one day had warmed to him. Rafe had been stern and reorganised everyone, and yet in his manner they had detected a little of the manner of the hooded man. He had pointed out their weakness and instead of screaming as the other commanders had, he had talked to them and explained why they should do as he told them. He had finished with a comment of, "that is how it will be done from now on, it is what I expect, so stick to it and we will all be fine. Piss me off, and you will know about it and regret it for the rest of your lives."

Somehow, they knew he meant it, and yet they felt that his even-handed approach was enough, and they knew they would follow his lead without question. Robbie had taken a bold step in giving Rafe the command; it was a decision he would never regret. The next few days were very busy, Rafe established himself as he got to know all of the workings of the guards of York. With Jett at his side, the two of them walked all the walls and looked for weak points, he changed the guard rotations, and brought more men to the weakest points. Jett was the daughter of a warrior, military life was in her blood, she had learned much as she sat bored at Caerleon, and now she found an authority besides Rafe, she had never known she had. The two of them were an ideal partnership and her eye for spotting a weakness in the defences was swift. In their first seven days in York, they improved its security a hundred fold.

The endless evacuation continued, Bear with Skip and Fuse could be seen in the town working with the officials to continue the endless stream of carts. By the end of the second day, some of the first carts to leave returned to take more, and so the long lines in and out of the city of York continued.

Robbie with Rowan and his father worked in the village hall. They brought in all the scouts from the moors, and they pooled all the information to build up a very detailed picture of the moor. There were vast areas that were open to invasion, and could not easily be defended, the moors were wild and open, there simply was nowhere to hide any number of troops. Lee had returned to his brother with the bandits, and now took on the role of organising the rebellion inside the walls. He had been delighted when Robbie had asked him to oversee the whole operation, and felt he was back in the fold, as he once was with Robbie's grandfather.

Ox in new boots and cloak seemed to have filled with a sense of purpose, and now led with skill, as he organised his bandits into groups to cause as much chaos as possible. Robbie had the start of a plan to bring havoc to the army of Knox, and through stealth and woodcraft; he employed the skills of his people to their best. The future of Loxley lay in his hands alone as he commanded the woodland realm from the centre of the stockade. It was very noticeable how much he had changed, and how now he had the stature and command often given to that of his father.

He would finish each evening and then go up to the farm with his father. Robbie would walk round the greenhouses with his mum, and sit by the stove and talk to her. He had missed being around her, and it was nice to spend time sitting and talking with her, about his hopes and dreams for his children and his love of Rune. Jess would sit and quietly listen, her hazel eyes filled with warmth and the love of her son, she saw how he was growing up into the man that would lead Loxley, and could not help notice those small traits that reminded her so much of his grandfather. She would smile as he sounded like Robert Lox. Being around his father, he had learned more than he realised, but she spotted it, as he spoke using similar phases.

As the light fell, he would ride home and be greeted at the gate by the slender figure with the long flowing red hair, and the bright dancing eyes and he would bask in her arms having missed her so badly during the day. Coming home was always the best part of his day, and he felt a happiness and contentment that he had not felt before. Gone were the days of sitting in the large greenhouse back at the farm, and trying to work out what he wanted to do with his life.

Robbie sat in his house as the wind howled outside, and stared into the fire in the hearth. Rune was asleep curled up on his knee, and his mind drifted back to those days earlier in the year. He smiled as those first archery lessons with Rune came to mind, he would never have dreamed he would have the life he had now. How strange it all felt as he remembered the strange ceremony where he had been made lord, and he had not wanted it. It had been thrust on to him, and he had done all he could not to panic and run. It felt like it had been years ago, he had left with his party to go to Kirklees, and inside he had been riddled with self-doubt and worry. He had painted a brave face on and struggled with every decision he had made in hope he had got it right.

It was odd now to see himself, he was Lord of Loxley and almost a father. He led almost half the country and spent his day fighting to protect them. The place he had wanted to leave so badly had now become the centre of his world, and he felt more at home than ever before. He softly stroked Rune's hair as she slept curled in a tight little ball, and he looked down at her peaceful pale face. The threat to Loxley was greater than ever, and he now faced the hard task of protecting it. York could easily fall and he knew that all that would stand between him and the black army, would be a thick band of trees, under which he would have to fight to the death to defend his home, and Rune.

The flames flickered in the hearth as he sat lost in his thoughts, the red and yellow light lighting the face of a young man with an older man's destiny, Rune murmured in her sleep and moved slightly. He gave a smile as he gently lifted her into his arms and carried her up the stairs; he placed her carefully on the bed and slid off her boots and skirt, and drew the thick warm blankets over her. Robbie curled round her and felt the exhaustion of his day, she rolled over and curled around him and he slipped his arm round the soft slender figure of the woman he loved. His eyes closed as he let out a long tired sigh, tomorrow was another day.

Lee Sherman crouched in the dark with his fellow rebels; it was almost time as he waited for the hour to strike. Malcolm grinned in the gloom as the first chime of midnight struck. Lee nodded and the group prepared pulling the long dynamite loaded arrows into their strings. The Bandits were set and ready outside the city, four roughly made catapults stood just inside the trees, and the tall sturdy bandits gripped the handles tight and prepared for the run to the wall. Dark shadows passed quickly across the rooftops of the houses of the city, the thirty men and women who made up the rebel army, moved swiftly and got into position. Violet tipped arrows now had become the colour of rebellion and as the clock tower hit the last stroke of midnight, a long row of bows lifted into the air.

The fuses lit as Meg ran along with a smouldering piece of charcoal, and everyone waited for Lee to give the command. He pulled back on the string and nodded. Thirty highly explosive arrows lifted into the air and sailed over the tall wall into the soldier's compound. There were terrified screams, as arrows fizzing violently, hit the first rows of tents and hit some of the soldiers.

As the first arrow exploded throwing cloth and wood into the air, the bandits charged across the wide open space towards the wall. The guards stood high up on the walls, no longer looked outwards, as the debris from below showered them, and the catapults with much larger explosives packed on to them, were rammed down hard as the spikes on their feet bit hard into the floor, and the fuses were lit. Thirty bandits stood with bows pointed high waiting for a soldier to appear as the first four highly explosive loads of dynamite were lit, and then hurled high into the air and over the wall. Soldiers ran around in chaos as arrows rained over the wall and explosions blew across the tented area. Flashes of light lit the sky and the deafening roar instilled panic all over the camp.

The first of the bandit's explosives landed, and a young soldier stared as he saw the violet coloured ball with a fizzing fuse, his scream of fear was wiped from the world with the horrendous explosion that opened a crater twenty feet wide, and blew everything within one hundred feet away. The flash was as bright as the sun, and was followed with three more spaced two hundred feet apart. The large walls shook, and the loud bangs of the explosions echoed off the walls contained within the barracks. Soldiers crawled in pain bleeding across what was left of the grass; the whole area was a scene of fear, panic and total devastation.

Soldiers flooded into the market square as they looked to the rooftops for the bowmen of rebellion, Lee gave the signal and rebels fell back into the shadows out of sight... He watched the walls as more soldiers ran through the arches onto the high lookouts above them. He caught Meg by the arm. "Give me the charcoal and run like hell." He pulled the long arrow out of his quiver and fitted it to his string.

"No, you aim and I will light, it will be faster." Lee cut the fuse short and lifted his bow, Meg slipped the hot coal held in small metal tongs on to the fuse, and Lee released the arrow at great pace. They ducked behind the low wall, as a soldier appeared and Meg slid her bow off her shoulder. They were trapped, and could not continue without being seen. Lee winked and she smiled as they huddled together, and loaded their bows, and took aim as others scrambled on to the roof. Meg released first and took out the first soldier; she grabbed the tongs and pushed it on the short fuse of Lee's arrow. She dropped to the floor at his feet as he let the arrow go. Lee bent over her to protect her.

The soldiers screamed as the fizzing arrow hit the lead man and he was lifted off his feet and thrown into them. They franticly scrambled and struggled to get free, as they fought to get away. Five dived off the high roof, as the light lit the whole of the market square, and the wide storage building shook. Brick, stone and parts of soldiers rained out of the sky, pelting down hard on the two woodland rebels.

Lee was up on his feet as the building shuddered, he pulled Meg up by the hood and almost threw her forward, they ran like the wind and jumped the gap onto the next roof, voices shouted from below as they landed with a thud and staggered forwards. Lee pushed Meg in the back to keep her running, and slipped another arrow out of his quiver. He cut the fuse short as he ran, and pulled his matches from his pocket. They flew sprawling across the next alleyway and landed better on the roof on the other side. He was gasping for breath as he fitted the arrow and turned. "Run girl, run like hell." He struck the match and lit the fuse as he drew air into his old lungs.

Meg turned and sprinted across the top of the roof; Lee leaned over the wall and whistled to the soldiers who were moving along the road in the direction of Meg.

They stopped and looked back, spotting the old woodsman gasping for breath at the top of the high rooftop. They turned and sprinted up the street lifting their crossbows towards him, as they gathered at the foot of the wall Lee swung the bow out and pulled on the string the smoke rose from the arrow and the fuse, as he released the string and then fell backwards on to the rooftop. He jumped up and struggled forward, as the explosion shook the whole building. The wall fell away and he gasped and clawed his way across the roof, away from the parts of the roof that were now slipping into the street, and covering the soldiers in rubble.

"I am too old for this kinda shit," he groaned as he fought his way across the top of the lop sided building. A small white hand took his and pulled hard, he looked up into Meg's green eyes she smiled.

"You aint that old yet." Lee chuckled as she heaved him back to his feet, and they set off again in the direction of the church. Meg held his hand tightly as they jumped the last alleyway and the tall roof of the church loomed up in front of them. Lee took one last look back as Meg slid down the drainpipe. The sky was orange lit by the fires inside the barracks, black smoke rose in columns into the sky, and soldiers ran up and down the walls in panic as loud bells rang out all over the city. Captain's in long black cloaks screamed at the soldiers, who ran blindly around, trying to put out the fires.

He gave a smile and nodded his head. It was a good start; the black army now knew it faced the entire woodsman world, and even those behind the walls now had a voice and its name was chaos. He slipped onto the pipe and slid down in the darkness, he turned to face Meg as she lowered her hood and smiled. "Thanks Lee." She stood on her tiptoes and kissed his cheek.

"What for?" Her eyes sparkled as she gave him a knowing smile.

"You have brought us all hope and leadership, you are the symbol of our hooded man in the city, I have dreamed of this moment for years. Someone should thank you; I wanted it to be me."

He gave her a smile, she was so young and yet in many ways she reminded him a lot of Rune, her youth, her gentleness and her courage. "Come on let's get inside and have a drink, I am buggered, I haven't run like that in years." She gave a soft chuckle as he lifted her over the wall, and they ran through the gravestones toward the small side door. Meg gave the knock, and it quietly opened as they both moved like shadows and entered. The door closed without a sound, and the city all around echoed with alarm bells and the calls of the officers as their men now swarmed the streets. The black city had tasted the long arm of Robert of Loxley, and it had shaken it to the foundations.

Once again, the colour violet crossed the desk of Mac, this time in the form of a half burned arrow. It was the colour he hated the most, as it stood now for hope. He knew it was the new battled standard of his enemy, and he slammed his fist down on the violet scorched feather. The violet arrow no longer stood for a bowman of legend used to frighten small children; it now stood for Runestone, the hooded man, and the hope of his enemy. He hated it and his temper now rose quickly at the sight of it, for it also had one more meaning, which he would never admit out loud.

Violet also stood for fear, his fear, for whenever he came across it, he knew somewhere in the shadows was a bowman, and that bowman was waiting for him. He was not violet he was green, sage green. Mac had the scar on his head and the scar on his hip to remind him that Robert Lord of Loxley was biding his time. He knew that sooner, or later, they would meet, and fear rose inside him, as he knew that Robbie would be a force of power that he was doubtful of whether he could win against. It now prayed on his mind, and he felt his insides twist.

Robbie was no ordinary man, and Mac was not going to underestimate him for one moment. Robbie fought for a cause, he was fuelled by his idealism, and Mac knew that it was a driving force that just kept him going. Robbie would never stop until he had won, Mac had never thought that the woodsmen could even have a chance against such a massive force, and yet he now saw the fear in the eyes of his men at the mention of the hooded man or his Specialists.

He now understood the true power of fear and it lay in stealth, never knowing when or how he would be attacked, placed an uncertainty in the minds of his soldiers that kept them always on the edge of panic. No matter how hard or evil Mordred had been to instill fear into his men, without being seen, the hooded man had brought a bigger and more frightening form of fear to the hearts of the black army. Tonight, he saw it truly for the first time, he saw doubt and panic run through the city, and it had greatly unnerved him.

Lee sat and panted on one of the pews. Meg gave him a hot coffee, and he nodded taking a huge swig. "Thanks Meg love." He sat back and breathed hard. Malcolm sat down at his side, he was happy and felt for the first time in a long time he had actually done something positive, instead of complain about how hard life was in the city.

He looked at Father Warren. "When will she be here?"

The father looked at his watch. "I think a little while longer, we have some time yet." Malcolm turned to Lee who was now getting his breath as he drank the hot coffee. "How long will you stay with us? It has helped having a man of Loxley here." Lee raised an arm and patted Malcolm on the shoulder.

"I am here for as long as it takes, Rune will bring new plans, and I will slip off to see my brother and the men in the woods, and then I will be back and on hand until we see this whole thing through. Robbie wants a man of Loxley with you too."

Meg smiled at her dad. "Dad worries a lot, Lee; he thought the hooded man had forgotten us. I knew he would not do that."

"He is a busy man believe me, I have seen the workload he carries, and quite frankly I am glad to be here. There is little of the country he has not seen this year, he has taken his time but believe me, I know him, and he will not desert you. As long as there is just one man who calls from the walls for his help, he will answer."

Malcolm spoke softly. "I knew you know...? That night when you came to my house, I knew it was him the moment I saw him, I looked at him, and as young as he is I felt the power inside him. I watched him shoot that guard and I blinked, and he had another arrow in the string and pointing up, I knew it was him and I thanked him."

"It was he who owed you the favour; he was the one who you gave shelter and protection to. He told me that knowing you and your family were here gave him great hope, he is with you at all times, and his spirit surrounds everyone who wants to fight for justice, that is what the hooded man is my good friend. He is justice for us all; your faith in him has honoured him."

Farther Warren nodded as the violet light appeared at the bottom of the church, they all looked back and stood up, and Meg beamed a smile, as the slender figure appeared, bathed in violet light. She gave a big smile as she walked up the aisle of the church. "Greetings my woods folk, I come with the compliments of Lord Loxley, and my grandfather." Rune gave Lee a huge smile as he stepped forward, and she embraced him. "Hello my good friend, I am pleased to see you are well, although I sense the pipe is taking its toll on your legs."

Lee gave a little chuckle. "I am honoured that My Lady of the Woods would notice a poor old man like me."

She smiled and looked at him. "I would always recognise one who has such loyalty to my hooded man and his family, you are one with all the Lox line my friend."

Lee nodded into a short bow. "You honour me greatly My Lady." Rune gave a little chuckle and slid her arm into Lee's. "Tell me of your nights work, I have spoken to the men of the woods, and they are safe and well. They seemed pleased with what they saw, but you must have more detail."

"For a first strike it went very well. It is hard to see what damage we have done, but I think by the flames and smoke, as well as the panic we instilled, we could say it was a big success. We placed at least ninety explosives from our side into their barracks, and we made sure we scattered them. I have no idea what the woodsmen sent over the wall, but it made a hell of an impact, it blew all of us off our feet that is when we decided to call it a night, by then the guards were pouring out of everywhere."

Meg stepped forward and smiled at Rune. "Lee was a true hero, he hung around and cleared off the guards that were following us, and he blew up the high ramparts to keep them from hitting us. He is the bravest man here."

Rune smiled sweetly and gave his arm a squeeze. "He is a man of Loxley; he has the courage of ten men." Lee coughed a laugh

"And the lungs of a boy."

Rune opened her arm and she drew Meg to her side, as she walked up to Father Warren. "I believe my young daughter you played your part tonight."

"My dad had always taught us the ways of the woodland, even if we cannot go into the woods, I have practiced with my sister at home, and we have a secret range in the attic. Dad built the houses we live in, and all of our row are true to the lord hooded man, we take it in turns to practice."

Rune looked to Malcolm. "You have done well for your lord my woodsman, he will know of your efforts to keep the code we all live by alive, I am touched by your loyalty, and I am sure that when all this is done the hooded man will want to show his gratitude to you." She smiled at Meg. "You will run in green woodland one day; I will make sure of it."

Father Warren bowed as Rune turned to him. "My Lady, again you honour my church."

"This place is sacred and honours us all my dear Father, in here lie the spirits and memories of a long time past, as does the work you do below, how are you coming with your history of this faith. The line of the hooded man feels it is very important."

"I have struggled, My Lady as it is hard to get the books I require, but I am moving slowly forward."

"Father your work is important to many, it will be very relevant when the new king comes, prepare me a list for my mother Stephanie is the guardian of her father's books. You must have heard of the historian Rimmer?"

Father Warren's eyes widened. "He is your grandfather; I was not even aware he had survived the red death."

She smiled. "It will take more than a virus to kill my grandfather believe me, he has many books that will help you in your work, I will see that you get them."

Father Warren looked astounded and bowed yet again, Rune turned with Meg and Lee still on her arms. "I will have to leave soon, but will return have no fear, you are no longer alone behind these walls. I will let my lord know of what was achieved here, if you have any more news, Ox will be at the grate in the wall, at nine o'clock tomorrow evening, pass it to him I will see him at ten." She slid her arms out of the arms of Lee and Meg and she turned to Lee. "Please take care of yourself, you mean much to the family Lox." She pressed her hand into his chest, and the palm glowed in a bright violet. Lee found his breathing ease a little. He lifted his hand and touched hers.

"I am old, even you cannot cure the wear of time my sweet lady, I am thankful for your concern." He squeezed her hand and she smiled, she felt the disease that now grew inside him, and she felt his acceptance of it after a long life. He was dying and he knew it, and she too knew that he would die as he had lived and this would be his last fight.

His eyes met hers and he saw the sadness, he squeezed her hand tight and whispered. "I have done well to get this far, let me go out as a true man of Loxley, and honour the family that has always honoured me. I will be happy to be back at his side in the other realm; no one will know of how much I have missed my good friend."

She nodded and a tear ran from her eye. "I will keep your secret although it saddens my heart."

Lee bowed. "Thank you, my good lady of the woods."

Rune turned and walked towards the doors as they all watched. "Good bye my loyal friends, we will meet again soon." She faded into light and was gone, and the church seemed quiet and almost lonesome without her.

Rune opened her eyes, and smiled at the two dark eyes looking down at her. "Hi gorgeous."

He leaned down and kissed her softly. "Hey beautiful." She lifted her arms and pulled him closer and he curled around her.

"They have done well tonight, Mordred has had a very busy time, no one can see inside the barracks, but they must have had many casualties."

Robbie looked saddened; she gave him a curious look. "Are you not happy?"

"I just wish they were not so young; I saw them Rune, and they were scared little boys dressed as men. I wish there was some other way without having to kill them."

She gave him a squeeze. "If what I have heard tonight is right, maybe you have found a way, they now know and have some idea of what they face. They know the woodsmen can strike out of nowhere, I wonder how many will desert when they are out of the walls."

He watched her bright blue eyes as she spoke. "If they do, I will make sure they are spared, we can take them and hide them, and I would rather spare them than kill them." She leaned forward and kissed him.

"What's that for?" She gave him a smile.

"For being a true Lord of Loxley." She giggled, as he looked confused.

The next morning Robbie was up bright, and early, he left Rune sprawled across the bed her white arms stretched out side-to-side, and her red hair all over the sheets. He came down the stairs to find Una sat on the large chair by the fire, watching the rain streak down the windows.

She smiled and yawned. "There is a fresh pot of coffee in there, help yourself."

She dropped her feet off the chair opposite on to the rug, and sipped her cup. Robbie returned and sat down with his drink.

"What you up to today?" She stared at the window blankly.

"I will probably help Rune again, she has been busy on her loom, with more people in the stockade the business is booming, and she is cutting out patterns today." Una looked at Robbie and he felt a question coming.

"What?" She smiled.

"Its October 12th, Samhain is not far off. That is also Rune's birthday, I just wondered if you had anything in mind."

Robbie smiled as he leaned forward. "I have thought of a big party or something to surprise her. What do you think?"

Una seemed to pick her words carefully. "Have you thought about... you know.... marrying her?"

Robbie seemed surprised and sat back a little. "Well, I have asked her and she has said yes, but it's been so busy I have not really had time to set a date." He felt guilt rise inside him. "Has she said anything? She is not upset is she Una? I would hate her to think I won't, I will." Robbie looked very distressed, and Una laughed and raised her hands.

"Rune has said nothing honestly, it was just an idea I had. I saw her wedding dress yesterday."

"She has a wedding dress? I had no idea."

"She is still making it, but it is almost finished, she sneaks it out when you are away at the village for the day and then hides it before you get home... Robbie she is pregnant."

He felt offended. "I know, as I said it has been so busy recently, I just have not had the time."

"Oh, calm down Robbie, I am not having a go at you. Look in order to do this you will need to have everyone back here, Keith and Saff are leading the scouts on the moors and Lee is in the black city, Rafe and Jett are in York with Bear, Skip and Treen. Samhain is the celebration of the end of the woodland year, and the start of a new one, it is her birthday, and it could also be the end of her old life and the start of her new one. I know she would love it Robbie, it would be the nicest thing you could ever do. That dress will not fit her in a month or two, do it now while it does."

"I must admit Una, I know she will want everyone back in time for the festival, and with a war looming, it could be the last time we are all together for some time." He gave her a big smile. "It would be a great surprise, wouldn't it? How the hell could I pull it off without her knowing?"

"Oh, that is so easy you would not believe, just tell Steph and Jess, and believe me with those two working alongside me, we will have it all sown up without a hint of her knowing... What do you say are you in?"

He had to admit he loved the idea; he knew how happy it would make her and it would also make him very happy as well. Robbie gave a huge smile and nodded. "Ok let's do it, I will let Steph and my mum know today, you come into the village later and we will discuss it, all four of us.... What about Jade should we tell her?"

"We will need Jade in on it, she will be a great diversion for us, Jade can tie Rune up for hours without it looking suspicious, we will also need to prepare everything somewhere else, and her house is the closest to the sacred oak, we will not be able to do anything here she will spot it."

Una chuckled at the look on Robbie's face. "Can you tell her Una? I am not sure I could handle the excitement." Una leaned forward and patted his knee.

"Robbie relax, everything will be fine, just leave it to us women, we are professionals at this sort of stuff." Una sat back and laughed at him. "No really Robbie, this will be so nice and so special for her, honestly, I feel almost jealous."

Robbie smiled, and then looked worried. "You are sure about this aren't you...? I mean, it might just be too much and she might not turn up... Oh I would hate that."

"Robbie believe me she will be there, I promise you."

He did a quick calculation in his head and looked at her a little calmer. "Ok it's the twelfth day today so we have 18 days to prepare, then it will be the thirty first and her special day. You know it is not very long, is that enough time for a wedding?"

She gave him a bright smile. "Robbie it will be more than enough, don't worry about it, we have plenty of time." Una had that way of giving him reassurance, and he felt his insides that had suddenly started to squirm calm a little. He headed into the rain, and mounted his horse and rode for the village hall as fast as he could; he clattered through the farm, and on to Hawthorn Lane, his mind a whirl. He felt a great happiness inside him, the rain was hard and lashed at his face, and he smiled as he rode on through to the track down to the village hall.

The stable boy took his horse as he arrived, and he gave him a huge grin as he passed inside through the doors to the busy room of planning. Rowan looked up as Robbie walked past to the door to the back room, which was now his full time office, Robbie nodded to Rowan who understood, and got up and followed him into the back room. He sat at his desk and told Rowan of his plans for the secret wedding; Robbie sat back and watched his friend carefully. Rowan gave him a smile.

"My dearest friend, I think it is a wonderful idea, Jade will go bonkers when she hears."

Robbie breathed a sigh of relief. "You are sure she will go for this? You don't think it will pressure her and freak her out?" Rowan laughed at him.

"Robbie relax, remember me on my wedding day, I was just as nervous, it is quite normal to feel jittery, just keep it hidden around Rune, remember she is fast to pick up on things."

He felt more nervous again as he nodded. "Oh Hearne, I am not going to survive this Rowan, look at me, I have not even seen her yet and I am becoming uravelled, hell I am Lord bloody Loxley, I have fought evil brutal men and faced Knox and Mordred as well as the Dark One. Why the hell does this scare me more than anything I have ever faced?"

He looked desperately at Rowan for answers. Rowan leaned forward and smiled. "This is pay back for my wedding day." He began to laugh. "Oh Robbie, my friend it is as clear as the nose on your face... This frightens you the most because very simply Robbie, Rune matters more to you than anything else in the world, hell she is your world."

He sat back in his large chair as the words of his friend sunk in. "Yes... you are right... she means everything to me, I guess I really want this to go perfectly for her, I know how important it will be to her, and I do not want to let her down."

"You won't, you never have, and you never will. Robbie in her eyes you can do no wrong, believe me it will be the best day of her life... Now come on we have a campaign to plan, I need you sane for a few hours." He gave a giggle as he got up and headed for the door, he looked back and saw Robbie staring at the wall with a smile on his face. Rowan nodded to himself and left him with his thoughts.

Keith Sherman now wore the cloak of a Loxley Captain; he stood in the heather at the top of the wild moor, and looked down on the thin line of woodland that stood before the black walls of the city of Knox. Saff now in all green with the eagle of Callanish on her cloak stood by his side and looked with him; she remembered the sight from inside and gave a shudder knowing what was waiting behind the walls. The group of sixty woodsmen all sat in the grass and looked out, they had no idea what lay there in wait for them, but still they felt the cold chill of the place deep inside them. "There is about two miles of trees before it breaks into this heather, it will not be easy to attack there, we have no chance of escape." Keith's eyes narrowed as he scanned the horizon and took account of every twig, leaf and branch as he panned round.

The long thin woodland led down for about ten miles before it opened out into thick dense woodland of several miles wide. He pointed, and Saff looked in the direction. "Now there we could use the cover to our advantage, mark it on the map, if we can get some of their men under those trees, we could take them apart and they would not know what hit them." Saff quickly marked the points down on the map with her pencil, as Keith walked along the top of the ridge and looked out to the west. There were large areas of pine forest that had been planted in the days of old modern man as part of a forestry program. They were wide and dense and although he knew there would be little cover, as very little grows under the pines, he knew it would be dark and gloomy enough to conceal many men. Saff made a note of the exact location and pencilled in the pines.

Keith walked back to his horse. "Alright we fall back and see what we face, I would think that the black army will try to avoid trees, they will not temp fate, so let's see if we cannot work out their route first, and then maybe we will find a weakness to exploit."

He lifted Saff to her horse and sprang up on to his own saddle, she smiled as they turned and began to walk slowly across the vast moor towards York. The horses spread into a long line to represent a large invading army, everyone sat ready waiting for Captain Keith Sherman to give them the order, and he smiled at Saff as she sat watching with large blue eyes and he lifted his arm and waved the group forward.

The long line of green cloaked woodsmen rode across the moor in the direction of York, Saff charted every group of trees and swamp line they came across in great detail, Keith sat alert on his horse and watched every angle; he knew Robbie would want the best survey they could provide. It was a long way to the edge of a high rise in the moors and Keith pulled up his horse and called his men to a halt. York lay in the distance amongst the scattered small remnants of trees that grew in small groups; he turned his horse and looked back from where they had just come. Miles of moors stretched back to the black city, which was a small tiny dot on the distant horizon. He turned and looked across at Sapphire.

"This is it; this is the place... From here, we can see everything; this is where Lord Loxley will direct the battle from." He turned to the other woodsmen and waved his arm, they grouped in towards him to hear his words. "Gentlemen this is the place. I want a camp setting up here right on top of this spot, I need two riders to head to your city and see Commander Rafe, I need the supplies to build our first out post bringing here as quickly as possible." Two riders nudged their horse's forwards. "Good men... Ok Peters and Slater off you go, the rest of you dismount, I want a fire going and the start of a camp. Today we begin the first watch for Loxley, if York falls, Loxley will be next so keep sharp and let's watch everything."

Sapphire slid down into his arms, and stood and looked back over the heather and scrub to the black city. "I hate that place, I hated being there... Do you think we will be able to stop them?" Keith slid his arm round her and pulled her close.

"I really have no idea; you saw what is behind those walls. Robbie and Rune are a force to be reckoned with; I will put my faith in them. You know Saff they have never once let us down; he will lay down his life before he does."

She turned to him and gave him a soft kiss on the cheek. "I love the way you admire him, from the day I first met you, I have seen a loyalty and faith in you for your lord that no other can rival. It is one of the reasons I love you so much."

Keith gave a smile and looked into the wind and across to the black city. "I would lay down my life for him Saff. I cannot describe it, but there is something about him, as young as he is that is more than most men. He is my lord and the hooded man, but more than that I think he is the most honourable man I have ever met; I respect him above all others. If I am a tenth of the man he is now, I will die happy knowing I died a man of value."

His eyes scanned the wild landscape of rough looking thick twiggy heather and long pale harsh grass. The wind howled lifting his cloak, as it swept with power across the wide open plain, this was a hostile environment that was bleak and harsh. This was the worst place on earth to fight, and Keith knew that it would be the biggest challenge any man of Loxley would ever face. But face it they would, he knew in his heart this was the last defence of the green realm, and a way of life. On these wild moors the fate of the woodland realm would be decided once and for all.

CHAPTER TWENTY

SAHMAIN AND SURPRISES

Life at Loxley seemed to go on no matter what was happening in the rest of the country. Bobby Thorn now worked beside John Lox in the large barn, and very quickly picked up the skills of sword making, John thought he was a natural. Rags was happier knowing he was no longer in danger, something Lucy was pleased about as she had been upset to hear her sister cry at times when Bobby was late. Rags worked long hours as she brought on new riders to cope with the growing demands of the Postal Service. Riders now covered the entire woodland realm, as she ensured all of the commands of Loxley got through.

Maggs had the school up and running, and Melanie in between weaving, covered as a second teacher, teaching history and math's. Robert Lox had put a great deal of time into converting the cottages into the school, and it was fitted out in every minor detail to ensure that every facility required by the children was met. Jess had an educational background, and she ensured her husband did Loxley proud. Harry wandered around the school having fun with the kids and doing odd jobs. One or two of the parents seemed concerned at first that their children had started using words like 'Funky and Cosmic,' but just put it down to the other children from outside the stockade.

Alley decided to stay in Loxley longer helping Alice, and tending the wounds of the Specialists, Fish who had also been given the rank of captain still had problems, and he visited a lot, it seemed odd that on the days he came to the surgery, Amethyst seemed to be helping out with the nursing duties. Not something he complained about as her smile always set him at ease. Melissa and Jasper were now officially dating, and Agatha seemed delighted with the young new lord, she had found out his history, and was over the moon to discover that Jasper was actually the next Lord of Callanish. She had wasted no time popping next door to inform Alice and Anne Kirk in the bakery shop.

Ruben Stein, at number eight on the village row, took on two new apprentices in his leather shop. He found that the increase in people to the stockade, had almost doubled his business, and he spent most of his days inside the back rooms making and repairing shoes, as well as doing much of the saddle work for the army.

Number six, was invaded by Una and Maddy who gave it a thorough clean out and painted it ready for Rafe and Jett. They had not been seen for a week as they were on duty in York, Robbie had quietly purchased some furniture, from Ian Hall at the furniture shop, and had it delivered and installed, so when they returned there was little to buy. Jade made a plaque for the wall that read

'Commander Rafe and Lady Jett Amber.' Agatha Patterdale was scandalised to find they were not married yet. Rune made no comment.

Hidden behind the scenes, was the undercurrent of planning that was led by Steph and Jess. Una was the go between with Jade and the four of them slipped about quietly arranging. A hidden excitement grew around the town, and at one point when Jade giggled in front of Rune, she had quickly jumped on the story of how happy she was that Judy and Blades were opening the bookshop again the following day. Hargreaves books had a new sign, and a fresh coat of paint. Robert Lox had taken time with Harry to help get it ready with the girls. Blades had great fun with Judy as they sorted out the large piles of old books, and reorganised the whole shop, which now had a bright and happy feel to it. Gone was the old stale musty smell, and the tatty old bookcases. There were even a few comfortable chairs to sit and read by the window.

Judy found large piles of educational books, and she donated them to Maggs at the new school, who stared with wide eyes of tears, and rattled several tunes with her jewellery. She swept Judy into her arms and kissed her muttering. "Sweet child, oh darling, how wonderfully cosmic your vibes are." Judy smiled with embarrassment as Jess and Steph tittered.

Rune weaved her fabrics, and made new patterns for Robbie, and after he had worn the clothes for about a week, she would produce more in other colours to sell in the shop. Rowan became more involved in the military and spent a lot of time working with the troops. His ability to speak clearly and simply was a big benefit, as he taught archery and sword skills. Ruby, was changing and growing up, although as small as she was, she started to teach defence with the pole. There were a few recruits, that made the mistake of thinking her child like speech and partially blind vision was reason to ridicule her. The bruises they suffered as a result, taught them the full meaning of respect.

Melanie now spent most of her spare time down by the gates when not working, with David Williams. She stayed at his cottage most nights and it seemed like she had moved in, although no one seemed to actually ask. Rags delivered her mail to David's house, which was sort of a clue, and everyone just seemed happy to see them walking and laughing arm in arm round the fields together.

Market days were busier than ever, as more traders came to set up and sell their goods at the three day a week markets. Maggs still had a stall, which Blades would stand selling all of her shawls and odd jewels, Harry stood beside her selling ale for Joe, and spent the market days grinning and falling over with a very cosmic sparkle in his eye.

Jess and Beth slowed the pace as they prepared the winter crops. Chutney and pickle production was a high priority in one of the greenhouses, and Jess had brought in ten of the new residents to help out. Martins widow Hanna was now the manager of the preserves section, and had become a very close friend of Jess. Big John was frustrated, as he could not walk for the long splints on his legs. Robert made him a chair with thick rimmed steel wheels, and he now spent his day trundling up the farm lanes shouting at the staff and getting them organised.

Robbie moved between York and his office in the village hall. A guard always accompanied him, most of the time it was Rowan and Bear, and the evacuation continued. He would arrive home tired and exhausted, kiss Rune, and spend happy hours alone with her in his bedroom, or on the high balcony watching the Mere as the seasons moved slowly onward. The trees were almost bare, and the garden below had been cut back so the cyclamen could cover the beds in bright pinks and purples. He found it strange to see that the violets continued to grow in the garden; they never faded, and always brought a happy smile to his face. The days of October slipped idly by, and the village now prepared for the last day of the month and the festival of the ending of the woodland year. Samhain was almost upon them, and the celebrations around the village were underway, as the whole village knew of the secret that had been planned by the Sacred Oak.

The twenty ninth of October slipped past quietly, and the day before his wedding arrived with a bad attack of nerves, as Robbie woke curled up next to Rune. He lay quietly on the pillow and watched her sleeping; it was just after dawn and the sun glistened off the frost on the rails of the balcony. She was breathing softly curled in a tight ball beside him, and he enjoyed just lying and watching. Her long eyelashes twitched, as she had soft dreams and her hair seemed to glow in the pale light. Her freckles seemed paler against her skin that now had a slight rosy glow about it.

Alley had given her a tonic to build her up and give her extra strength, and Robbie had to admit that it had given her a look of radiance that just highlighted her beauty more. She gave a slight murmur and twitched, he pulled her close and she instinctively curled around him. She slid her head on his chest and gave a slight smile. "I know you are watching, stop it."

Robbie gave a slight giggle as she opened her eyes. "Hey beautiful." She stretched as she smiled and her eyes sparkled. She reached up and kissed him.

"Hi gorgeous... What time is it?"

"A little after dawn."

"Good you are still mine for a few hours." She looked at him and he knew she was going to ask something. "Do you have to go in today? I have hardly seen you for two weeks... Let's stay in bed like we use to all day." She giggled as she kissed him.

"What about the festival...? I have to collect everyone and bring them back for the big meal in the hall tonight... I thought you wanted everyone back here for your birthday?"

She looked downhearted. "I do... it's just... I want you, just for a while. I miss you Robbie."

Robbie pulled her close, and she slid her head into his neck. "I tell you what, I will take the morning off and we can stay here together alone. But I will have to go to York later and collect all the others, Jett is missing everyone, and Keith has spent so much time in that tent on the moors he has forgotten what a bed feels like... I will go and make you breakfast in bed and then my dear Lady Loxley you are mine for the morning." She gave him a big smile. "What would my beautiful Lady like...? I think we have some bacon and eggs." Rune suddenly went pale as he watched her. "Are you alright Rune?" She shook her head.

"No." Rune pounced out of bed and flew out of the room down the corridor her hand clasped tightly over her mouth. Robbie rolled out of bed, and slipped on his robe, he grabbed hers, and followed her down the hall.

Una smiled as she popped her head out of her room. "Morning sickness, I wondered when she would start." Robbie suddenly understood, and he smiled as he passed to the bathroom. Rune crouched shivering over the bowl. He knelt down beside her and covered her with the robe, and pulled her into his arms.

"You Ok?"

Rune gagged and gasped. "No I feel awful." Her voice was weak and he could not help but smile, as he felt sorry for her. "Oh God Rob please tell me this will not happen every day?" She turned and vomited again.

It was an hour later when a pale looking Rune sat back in bed nibbling a piece of toast feebly. "You feeling better?" She nodded as she lifted her cup and sipped her black coffee.

"That was horrible, I will have to talk to my grandfather, no woman should have to put up with that every day." He gave a giggle and she slapped him. "It's not funny, you know how I hate being sick." Robbie smiled as she cast him a bright blue glance with her eyes; he sipped his coffee and kept his head down. She gave a giggle.

The morning moved slowly and he was grateful, Rune lay in his arms and they laughed, talked and dreamed of the future, he slid his hand on her tummy and felt the hardness of it; she giggled as he stroked it, and lay back happy and contented.

"Wow it feels hard Rune."

"Well I am only thin, and there are two in there growing." He laughed as he slid back up to her. "It's a month and ten days."

"I know... I hadn't realised you were counting."

He kissed her softly. "I have a calendar in the desk draw; you will be due around June twenty second I think."

She pulled him tight and giggled, "you are funny at times, I can't believe you are crossing each day off."

"Of course I am, these are my children, I will be ready every second of the day until they come." He looked into her happy bright eyes. "It will be great, won't it?"

She gave him a big smile. "Oh Rob, it will be so wonderful, I am so happy, we will be a real family like your dad and Jess, and my mum and dad. Daddy Lox, it sounds so great, I cannot wait to say, oh yes Lord Loxley is my husband, and these are our children." She giggled.

Robbie seemed to drift as his mind wandered. "Our children," his voice was quiet and almost as lost as his thoughts. "Iona and Hal," she curled round him, and let him enjoy his dream. Violet eyes danced in his thoughts, as warm and cosy surrounded by Rune he slid into dreams and sleep.

It was late afternoon when they both appeared at the top of the stairs laughing and joking, Robbie walked down with his arm round Rune, and they prepared to visit York. Arrangements had been made to all meet up in the assembly room's as Keith and Saff had arrived the night before, and they had been replaced on the watch post. The blue butterfly Rune had left with Sebastian was now in the hands of the captain of the watch, who had been instructed to press it if any sign of the black army was spotted. Groups of troops were, now dispersed all along the borders of York, as over ten thousand woodsmen, had been shipped in behind the hill of the watch post to defend the city. York again was busier than ever, as all the women and children were finally out, and woodsmen trooped in from all over the region. York was now one big military camp, as they prepared for the winter and for a battle of their lives.

Rafe headed up the main street to the assembly hall with Jett, his long green cloak and golden Loxley crest glittered in the cold light of the afternoon. "It will be nice to go back for a bit, I have missed it."

Jett gave a happy smile. "I miss Ruby and Jade, it's fun here winding up the soldiers, but I seek the talents of professional fun raisers. It will be nice to see Rune; I am really excited, are you?"

Rafe squeezed her arm. "I hope your mum is happy, I don't fancy having to fence with her, I have seen her fight."

"Mum will be cool, relax Wolfie, I told you she is very happy about us."

He gave a sigh. "I know, I am just nervous." He gripped the large handle, and swung the doors open; they walked into the warm entrance to the Assembly. The group were gathered talking and Saff gave them both a hug as they entered. "Isn't it exciting, I am amazed Robbie has been able to pull this off?"

Jett Laughed. "He hasn't yet, but I must admit it's one hell of a surprise. Are you sure Rune will be able to make it...? If Rafe pulled this on me, I tell you I would faint."

The shimmering violet light appeared in the middle of the room, and the slender figure of Rune stepped out holding Robbie's hand, Jett squealed and pounced as she threw her arms round Rune, Bear seized Robbie and pulled him into a hug, there was laughs and smiles all around. Brett shook his hand warmly and as Rune turned, she came face to face with a sheepish looking Sebastian. He bowed to her.

"My Lady of the woods, I am pleased to see you are well."

She gave a slight curtsy. "My Lord Phillips, you are looking well yourself, I am pleased to see you."

"I owe you my deepest apology My Lady, and would hope we could start again on better terms." Robbie watched, as Rune looked up at the humbled face of Sebastian. She gave him a wide smile.

"Lord Sebastian, we all face a common enemy, and we must stand together and face our destiny. If you stand with Lord Robert, you have nothing to worry about. I hold no malice towards you; in fact, I am pleased to see you here beside your brothers. I would very much like it if we could be friends instead of enemies."

Sebastian gave a broad smile, and lifted Rune's hand, and kissed it as he bowed. "My Lady is as gracious as everyone has commented, and I am pleased that we can begin as new."

Robbie slipped his arm round Rune's waist. "Lord Sebastian, I hear you have been busy in the cause of your city." He extended a hand, and Sebastian took it and shook.

"I have Lord Loxley; I have learned much from my time with your Commander Rafe, we have revised the whole defence of the city, and fortified a great deal more of the wall."

Robbie smiled at him, he could see that Sebastian was trying hard to undo his stupidity, and he respected him for it. "I think My Lord we should be less formal, please call me Robbie. Will you be joining us at the feast, I feel it fast approaching meal time at Loxley."

Sebastian laughed a deep booming laugh. "If you could find me just a little something bland, I am sure I would be delighted to join you." Rune gave a giggle as Robbie laughed with Sebastian.

The village hall had been cleared of most of the desks, and around the large map in the middle of the room; tables had been lined out in a huge square, and the banquet tables groaned under the weight of the candles, crystal and food. It was a feast to beat all feasts and Robbie smiled, as he looked at all the happy faces of his family and friends gathered together.

The meal had been a big tradition in the Lox household for many decades, the Lox family led the celebrations of the end of the woodsman's year, and usually they were so busy with their formal duties as community leaders that they seldom had a chance as a family to enjoy the time. Robbie's grandfather had introduced the eve of Samhain feast so he could share the event as a family man. It was a tradition that stuck and now on the day of October 30th, the whole of the Lox family gathered together.

Robbie slid the chair in behind Rune, and took his seat as the others all moved to their places. Scarlet blew him a kiss as she waved from across to his left. Rune slid her hand into his and he turned and smiled at her. "I feel the happiness of your company around you." Her eyes were bright and sparkled at him.

"This is what it is all about Rune. This is what I fight for, family and friends and the community in which we all live together as one." Jess touched his hand from his other side and gave it a squeeze. He felt happy and relaxed in the company of his closest circle, everyone was dressed in their best. Even Rowan was starting to get use to his clothes of state, and looked a little less uncomfortable. Robbie was pleased to see Hanna and her two daughters sat at the far end of the table, she sat next to Big John, who had been lowered into his chair, and beamed a big smile at his friends gathered around. John had taken to keeping an eye on Hanna, and had spent much time with her helping her adjust to her new life.

Jett laughed down the table and raised her glass. "Hey John how is your thirst?" Everyone laughed as he rubbed his belly and his eyes twinkled.

"I think I feel it rising inside me, you still think you can match me my skinny opponent?"

Jade and Rune giggled as Jett laughed out loud. "Remember Caerleon? I matched you drop for drop, you get those legs mended, and I will show you who can drink."

Everyone laughed as Robert Lox stood up and tapped his glass. The room settled down, as the large figure of the community leader smiled happily around him.

"My friends and family, it is the eve of Samhain, and we are gathered here to say thank you to the world we live in, as it comes to the end of another woodland year. It has always been my place to give thanks, but tonight we sit under a new leader of the realm of the woods, and I think it is time for me to bow down, and hand the mantle of the realm to my son. Please raise your glasses and toast Lord Robert of Loxley."

He raised his glass high as the others followed his lead, and with deafening voices, they toasted him. Rune winked as she held her glass up to him. "My Lord Robert." It was one of those moments, that caught him off guard, and he smiled at her as her eyes sparkled back with delight. He looked at all the happy smiling faces of the people he cared for as they saluted him.

Robbie rose from the table and bowed to them; Rune held his hand as he lifted his glass. "My friends and my family. You honour me. I am but one man who is surrounded with such support of quality, I am proud to lead you." He nodded his head as he slowly looked at every face. "But for me, it is a greater honour to know you." He raised his glass and saluted them all and drank.

Beth sniffled in her hankie. "Oh Robbie my love that is so sweet." Everyone giggled as she blew hard into her hankie, and wiped her eyes. The grouped settled, as he remained standing and watched them all.

"Tomorrow will as always be a holiday, as we celebrate the eve of Samhain, the end of our year and the season of light. Make it a good one because never before in the history of Loxley has it been more relevant. It is the eve when we thank the natural world for all it has given us over the year, and begin the harvest to gather in for the winter, and prepare for the coming darkness of winter. We face more than the darkness of winter this year, as we gather the apples and bring the animals down from the high pastures. This year we will be facing a time of great trial, I stand here before you surrounded by love and kinsmanship. Enjoy your evening, and remember it well, for in the hard times that may come to this land, it is what we have here in this room that will bring us through. We are of Loxley and proud to be so and yet since last year, I see many new faces at my table, and some I am saddened to say are missing." Robbie looked at Hanna and her daughters and nodded. Fish looked up and smiled at him. "Remember my friends, and embrace those who are new amongst us, show them your love and support, for we need each other more than ever before." He lifted his glass and drank and the whole of the gathered party smiled and joined him.

Rune kissed his cheek as he sat down. "That was nice Rob... A little less energetic than Scotland." She started to laugh and Rowan and Jade both began to giggle, Robbie gave her a smile and kissed her.

The volume rose as everyone tucked into the meal, and soon the room was filled with the chink of cutlery on plates, and the happy sounds of fun conversation. Jess leaned over and kissed his cheek. "You are so like your father; I am so very proud of you."

"I have missed you Mum; I have been so busy these last few weeks."

She smiled at him. "Yes, I had got quite used to our little walks and chats, I have missed you too Robbie. We are all so busy and have the quiet of winter coming, you must come and mope round the greenhouse for me, or it will not feel like winter." Rune gave a giggle, and Jess's eyes twinkled. "Oh Rune, he can be a real misery in the snow, I hope you are ready for it." She chuckled. "You should come once a week for a meal with the family, I know Beth would love it and so would Alice."

"We would like that Jess, I think sometimes Rob and I get so wrapped up at the Mere, we forget there is another world outside. I would love to see more of you all."

Jess gave a big smile. "Alright let's say every Sunday evening we will meet at the farm and have a meal together, it will be the celebration of the Lox household, I will even invite Harry." She winked at Rune. "If that doesn't liven the night up nothing will." She gave a quiet laugh as she cut her pork and ate it.

The night passed through the main course and into the next, and soon with the flowing of wine and the good food, everyone sat back and relaxed. Robbie tapped his glass and Rune rose from her seat. She looked nervous, as she looked round to give the blessing, a job normally done by Jess.

"My good friends, soon we will part from this meal, and head home into the darkness, it is almost midnight and the eve of Samhain is upon us. Tomorrow night our world and the realm of the other world will be the closest they can be in our year, and we will feel closer to those of our lines of the past than on any other eve. The spirits will pass amongst us, and guide us into the new year of my realm. Go home in peace and give praise to our guides and our lord and creator, may the blessing of our high Lord Hearne be with you all in the year to come, may he guide you and protect you. Honour him and give thanks. Hearne protect all of us."

The whole room bowed their heads and spoke as one. "Hearne protect us."

Rune gave a smile to see the honour bestowed on her family line. Steph gave her a smile and nodded; Rune gave a grin and sat down. The room was silent for a second, and then the noise level began to rise, as everyone slid back their chairs and wandered the room talking and hugging each other. Robert Lox banged the large gong as midnight rang through the hall and the eve of Samhain begun in earnest. Now the doors were unlocked and everyone walked out into the last day of the woodland year, and the day's holiday began.

Una and Crystal sat in the carriage as Robbie and Rune came out of the hall with Rowan and Jade. Skip wandered up and patted Robbie on the arm. "I am sorry Robbie but we have just had news that I think you need to hear." He looked at Rune who had stopped and looked back. "I am sorry Rune; could I steal him back off you? It really is important otherwise I would not ask."

Rune looked disappointed but she understood. "Alright, will you be very long?"

"I am not sure really Rune, we have quite a lot to look at." Robbie gave her a kiss on her cheek as he walked her to the carriage.

"You get home and warm the bed, I will be back as quick as possible." He turned her round and kissed her softly. She smiled as he pulled her close. "Happy birthday my darling." Her eyes lit up with a brightness he had never seen. She had forgotten it was past midnight and she was a year older.

"I love you, Rob." He kissed her again.

"I will rush and see you soon." He pulled a small shining blue box from his pocket and slipped it into her hand. "This will be enough until I get home, there will be more." She giggled excitedly as she looked down at the small blue box, and then threw her arms round him and gave him a long slow kiss. He laughed as she sprang into the carriage and waved as he closed the door, and the carriage moved off. Robbie watched as it headed up the track and off onto Hawthorn Lane, he turned quickly.

"Skip that was wonderful, right people we have a lot to do, let's get busy."

The room was filled with busy staff that rushed to clear away the remains of the meal, Jess directed operations inside the hall. She stood by the doors as the tables were cleared. "Alright everybody, let's get busy, we have little time and a lot to do, tomorrow night there will be the wedding feast of the century here, so let's make this place look like our Lord Hearne himself decorated it."

"It will."

Jess fell to her knees as the long twiggy hand of the high lord touched her shoulder. "My Lord I am honoured." There was silence in the room as Hearne bent low and stepped in through the door. Everyone bowed in silence. Robbie gave a bright smile and walked to his lord.

"My Lord we are honoured you would visit here." He bowed.

Hearne gave a chuckle, as he looked around the village hall. "I knew many of the trees that volunteered themselves to the making of this place. Marion was a wonderful woman and filled with such love for her hooded man, she built this in his memory."

His legs groaned as he walked into the centre of the hall, a smile on his lined bark like face, his robes softly swaying and giving the sound of the slightest breeze through the leaves of high summer. He put his arm around Robbie and gestured to Jess. Nervously she rose and came over towards him; he placed his arm round her and pulled her to his side. "You have a boy of high value Lady of Lox; I feel the same love in my daughter as I did once in Marion the flower of the past. I would ask that you allow me to bring to this room the truth of their love for this special day, for it is a mighty union that will be forged under the oak of our fathers tomorrow."

Jess was stunned. "My Lord you are the creator of all things, you can do as you please, this is your realm." He gave a chuckle like the sound of a happily bubbling brook.

"I am lord and yet my respect for you My Lady is such; I feel it is right I should ask." Robert Lox beamed a big smile; it was not often Jess was at a loss for words. The high compliment from a lord of such high standing was more than she could comprehend.

Robbie smiled at his mother. "My Lord, I feel that your contribution would be greatly appreciated by your daughter of the woods, and we would welcome your part in our day. It would honour us."

"Leave this place and return before your feast, I will bring gifts of our world and others to your table to celebrate. Fear not and sleep well my children, your lord will be around you at all times on this day."

Robert bowed to his Lord Hearne, and took the hand of Jess; everyone gave their respects and left the High Lord alone. Robbie stopped at the door and looked back at the old twig like man, clothed in his robes of the natural life that surrounded him. "Runestone will be happy knowing you have done this for her, it will make it a more special day, and I thank you My Lord."

"Your love of my daughter does you great justice My Bowman, you have honoured me in your love of her, I will not forget it. Runestone Sapphire daughter of Opal, and the true force of Nature is very special to me young bowman. Go and prepare for your time with her is precious, war is coming, but not for a short while." He gave a bow to Robbie. Robbie walked out into the cold darkness and Rowan stood waiting silently. Together they walked up the track towards the lane and the farm, it was cold and dark and yet he felt warmth inside him.

Una smiled as she watched Rune holding the small blue box in her palm, as she looked down at it smiling. The carriage rocked from side to side as it headed up past Harry's cottage. "Aren't you going to open it?"

Rune looked up at her. "I am afraid to." Una smiled.

"How can you be afraid to open a small box, which contains such a power of love from the man of your dreams?"

"I feel the power within, he has had Hearne make this for me, this will be the truest token of his love he will ever give me, and I am frightened of it. There is a force here stronger than me."

Una leaned forward in her seat. "Then you should open it and rejoice for your power will be enhanced by the love he holds. You should not fear the purity of what lies between a man and a woman. That box can only contain the power of good."

Rune's hands trembled, as Jade and Crystal leaned in to see what the box contained. She clasped the box tight in her shaking fingers, and gently opened it. The carriage filled with blue light as everyone gasped, and Rune shook as the tears welled into her eyes.

The box contained a small ring of platinum, on which was set a single large sapphire of immense quality. It was cut into a twenty-pointed star, and the light flowed in and radiated out of it. In the centre was a single heart shape diamond that drew the blue of the sapphire into its core, and reflected it out in every direction.

She gasped with the wonder of the ring that was the most beautiful and most precious thing she had ever seen. Two violets sprung on her lap, as the tears dropped and she looked up at Una. Una's violet eyes glistened as she smiled. "The sun has less power than the love of your man."

Bright blue danced on the faces of the group, and Jade was lost for words, it was a jewel beyond measure, and she felt like a beginner to her craft. Her words were quiet. "Rune that is work like I could never copy, that is the finest piece I have ever seen. Wow... Robbie loves you more than even we realised... Put it on."

"I can't I am shaking too much." Crystal took the ring gently from the box, and lifted a small note out from underneath it, she handed it to Rune, as Rune slid some of her rings down her finger. Una placed a hand on her fingers.

"A ring of such love can only be worn on one finger." Rune looked down at her hands. One finger was bare. It had always been left for the golden band of her wedding day she looked up at Una.

"That is my wedding finger, his golden band will be the only ring I wear on it."

Una clutched her hands warmly. "That is the finger that shows all who loves you, when your band comes you should wear them together." Crystal and Jade both nodded and as Rune lifted her hand, Una slid on the ring and pushed it down to the base of her finger. It was a perfect fit, and Rune smiled as she looked down and knew it was the only finger that the ring would ever fit.

The coach drew to a halt as they reached the edge of the wood, Jade and Crystal jumped out, and waved as they ran through the dark to Jade's house. The sculpted tree in the garden played soft chimes through the darkness, as the coach moved on to the woodland track that led to the wooden house in the glade.

The time seemed to drag past, and finally Rune sat alone in bed and looked at her ring, as it lit up the whole room in the moonlight with fine shafts of blue light. She happily leaned back into the pillows and she thought of him.

"Hey beautiful."

"Robbie where are you?"

"I am still stuck here but I miss you... Have you opened your present?"

"Oh, Robbie it is so beautiful, I cried when I saw it."

"It's not that bad." She gave a soft chuckle.

"I love you so much Robbie, I want you here with me."

"I wanted something to show you how beautiful your eyes are to me, it's close but not quite as wonderful... I will be some time; get some sleep and I will wake you when I get home. Goodnight beautiful."

"Goodnight Gorgeous, I love you." Rune lay on her side and looked at the ring; the small folded note lay on the table at the side of the bed, next to the ornate oil lamp. She had been so excited she had forgotten to read it; she laughed as she slid across the bed and turned up the lamp to read. Rune unfolded the small piece of paper and read the neat small writing of Robbie.

My Darling Runestone Sapphire.

I give to you the light of my heart, caught by the moon in a stone of your name. You have brightened my days and lightened my dreams. I am lost in the dark when I am not with you. I hold to my promise and will give you another ring soon, and we will never be parted in this world or the next.

Happy birthday I love you.   Robbie, xx

She lay back on the pillows with tears in her eyes, and held the letter close to her heart. She lay awake for a long time thinking of him, and then slipped into dreams of the man that she loved. The ring sparkled like her eyes around the room all night. Robbie arrived at Rowan's house in the dark; Jade jumped up and gave him a squeeze.

"Rob that was some ring, oh wow you should have seen her face. She was blown away totally, man you are smooth. She has no idea at all, I am so excited I cannot wait to be there in the morning when she wakes and mum tells her."

Her bright green eyes danced around under her long curly fringe, as she shrieked and laughed as she flew around the house checking everything was ready for the following day. Robbie was tired and collapsed on the chair by the fire.

Rowan handed him a drink, and he took it sliding back into the cosy cushions. Rowan gave him a big grin. "How's the stomach?"

Robbie seemed pale as he looked up at him. "Squirming."

Rowan patted his shoulder. "Good, that means your mortal." He started to laugh and Crystal giggled as she looked at Robbie feeling a little sorry for him.

Rune's wedding day had become the biggest kept secret Loxley had ever known. Building Jade's house had been hard, but this had been a nightmare for Jess and Steph. The whole of the glade around the Sacred Oak had been screened off with green fabric to hide the tree and the decorations that had been put up. A canvas sheet roof had been woven into the branches to ensure that no rain would spoil the celebration.

Rags and Lucy were bridesmaids, and Jett and Jade maids of honour with Alice. They had to have dresses fitted and made without Rune seeing when she popped to the shop with extra stock. Sapphire had made Robbie a new set of clothes in a deep royal blue, but had been sent off to the moors before she could finish. Steph and Beth had done his final fittings.

The Kirk sisters had been sworn to secrecy, which was not easy as they loved nothing more than a good gossip. They had set up another room in the house to work in secret on the wedding cake.

Maggs and Blades with Judy, had worked on the decoration of the sacred oak, and Joe had worked hard with Harry hiding extra supplies of Ale at the farm for the big celebration. Mel and Treen had worked in secret in the back room of Rags house writing all of the invites out in their finest hand writing, Rags had personally delivered each one, and threatened everyone what would happen if they let it slip to Rune.

By far the hardest Job had been Una's. Her task had been to keep Rune busy and out of the way, there had been more than one occasion where Rune had wanted to visit somewhere Una knew preparations had been underway, and she had employed all her skills of gentle persuasion to steer Rune away somewhere else. Steph felt brain dead as she had been heavily involved with all of the preparations, but had also been used to block Rune as the family talked using their minds, to make changes and fine tune the plans. The nearer to the day it got, the more frantic everyone felt, and now as the sun rose on the thirty first day of October Rune hit seventeen, and they all took a breath after a sleepless night and prepared for the announcement to Rune herself.

Una was waiting as Jess and Steph slipped quietly into the house. Luckily, Rune had been awake until late and was now sound asleep, the small piece of paper with Robbie's words of love was still clutched tightly in her hand. Crystal had stayed at Jade and Rowan's house because her room now held all the clothes for the bridesmaids. There had been panic as garments flew from all over Loxley, as Rune had left the day before for York. They hung in rows around the room, carefully protected in silken bags.

The women sat at Rune's kitchen table, and prepared as Jade and Jett slipped quietly in through the back door. One final drink of coffee, and a long deep breath and the women gathered at the bottom of the stairs. Steph took a deep breath and smiled at Jess. "Are we all ready?" Jess looked more nervous than ever.

"It's all finally done, let's wake the bride and be ready for tears." Like a small army, they walked up the stairs as if ready for war, the most organised women in the north of England. All of them looked terrified.

Rune was fast asleep as Steph squeezed in through the door. She sat on the bed and smiled at her daughter asleep. She placed the hot mug of coffee down on the mat on the small table next to the blue box. The ring sparkled and she caught her breath, everyone had known of the ring, but Robbie had shown it to no one, he wanted Rune to be the first to see it. Steph stroked the long red hair back from her daughters face and Rune opened her eyes. "Hi sweetheart, happy birthday."

Rune blinked, sat up, and rubbed her eyes. "Mum... What are you doing here?" Rune looked around the room. "Is Robbie here?"

"He had to work all night sweetheart, he asked me to tell you he loved you, and to look under the bed."

Rune had lifted the coffee to her mouth and stopped. "What?"

Steph smiled. "Look under the bed... I think he has hidden one of your gifts there."

Steph took the cup off her daughter who suddenly broke into an excited smile; she dived over and bent round to look below her, Steph giggled as Rune's bare bum lifted into the air. Under the bed was a large blue box, with a pale lilac envelope on it. Excited little chuckles came out from below, as Rune stretched and pulled the box towards her. She lifted it on to the bed, her eyes dancing with excitement, through a crack in the door all holding their breath, the others equally excitedly watched.

Rune slipped the envelope on to the pillow, and carefully opened the box. She gasped with delight as she parted the fine blue silk, and lifted out a diamond and sapphire tiara, this was Jade's finest ever work.

Rune stared lost for words in wonder, as she looked at the fine woven gold oak leaves, and intricate butterflies covered with diamonds and sapphires.

"Oh mum look," was all she could gasp as she turned to look at her lost for more words. Steph handed her the Lilac envelope. Rune placed the tiara carefully down as the others behind the door braced themselves. Rune slid open the envelope, and pulled out the paper with the official Loxley coat of arms on it. She unfolded it and read Robbie's neat handwriting.

My dearest Runestone,

Happy birthday my darling, and happy Samhain. Today my love, you have reached the age of seventeen, and it is also the end of another year, and the start of a new one.

At midday as the sun sits at its highest, I will be waiting stood by the sacred oak. Runestone my darling today is a new start for everything in your life. Be quick my love, and wear your wedding gown, for this day will end with you being Mrs Runestone Sapphire Loxley, and you will start this new year as I promised. You will be my wife.

I love you so hurry. I am nervous.

Robbie, xx

Rune stared at the letter and then read it again, Steph smiled as she saw the look of sheer surprise on Rune's face. "Is everything alright darling?"

Rune looked up at her mum, as the colour drained from her face. "Oh God Mum, help me?"

The door burst open as Jade, Jett, Crystal, Una and Jess came in. "Surprise, happy birthday."

Rune suddenly looked terrified. "You all know?"

Steph touched Rune's arm. "Everything is organised and ready; all you have to do is make yourself look beautiful."

Rune looked back down at the letter. "Oh God, I am going to be sick."

She flew off the bed, and ran naked down the hall into the bathroom.

Jett gave a huge smile as she looked at the others. "I thought that went really well, congratulations girls we pulled it off."

CHAPTER TWENTY ONE

THE JOINING OF LINES

Robbie sat up in bed as Jaz smiled, and handed him a drink. "She knows."
Robbie felt his stomach twist as he took the coffee of him. "How did she take it?"

"She is being sick." Jaz started to laugh, as the colour drained from Robbie's face.

"Oh hell I have freaked her out... what if she won't marry me?" He visibly began to unravel in front of Jaz. Jaz patted his shoulder.

"Robbie she is pregnant... and in shock, it's not every day you get up and get told to put a wedding dress on you will be married by tea time." He chuckled. "Come on Rob she will be there, she loves you."

He nodded uncertainly as he sipped his coffee. Jaz opened the door. "Breakfast will be ready in ten, ok."

He sat in bed alone sipping his coffee as his stomach did somersaults and twisted, he had faced the Dark One and fought Mason Knox to the death. On both occasions, he had felt a sense of calm and destiny, now on his wedding day where he would finally marry the girl he had loved for as long as he could remember, he felt terror. Ice cold, knee trembling, and wrist shaking terror.

The cup rattled on his teeth, and he pulled it away. He gave a sigh, and felt the strength running out of his body. "Come on Rob pull yourself together, it's a ceremony with a ring... Oh hell the rings, what have I done with them?" He cursed to himself as he dived out of bed, and looked through the pockets of his pants. He checked his waistcoat. "Oh no I have dropped them."

Rowan looked up as Robbie in his green woodsman pants came tumbling down the stairs. His eyes were wide and his face was pale. "Rowan the rings."

Rowan stirred the eggs in the pan calmly. "I have them... Good job as well, look at you. Relax Robbie this is just another adventure, Rune will be there and everything will go well, so calm down will you... Here now you are up eat this. Mel will be here shortly with Maddy to help." Robbie breathed a long sigh and walked nervously his legs shaking to the table. Rowan gave a chuckle.

Rune sat up and Steph pulled her close. "It's alright sweetheart, it is just the morning sickness. It will pass." She looked over at the bowl as Rune trembled in her arms. "You are too small to have much more inside you." Rune twisted and was sick again. "Maybe not?"

Una gave a soft titter at Steph, as she watched from the doorway and passed Rune's robe in to her. Rune gasped as she sat back up. "Oh god I hate this." Steph wiped her face with a damp cloth, and Rune clung to her mother. "Thanks mum; I don't know what I would do without you."

Steph gave a smile. "I have always been here for you, and I always will be, even when you are Mrs Runestone Loxley."

Rune looked up and her eyes widened, they shone with intense blue, and flickered a little purple. "Oh God Robbie...? He is waiting." She leapt in the air, and hurtled through the door.

"Rune your robe." Steph held up the pale lilac robe, but she had gone at high speed down the hallway. Rune tore into her room and picked up the letter off the bed, she read, and read it again just to be sure, as Steph with Una walked toward Jess at the top of the stairs. She turned from the letter and looked through the open door.

"I AM GETTING MARRIED TODAY." She flew back out of her room, and ran back up the hall into her mother's happy smiling arms. "Mum he wants to marry me today." She flung her arms around her, and Steph felt the tears in her eyes as she squeezed her daughter, and pulled the robe round her.

"I know sweetheart, he loves you." Rune slid back to look at her mother, her eyes shone as they had never shone before, and she turned to Jess.

"I really love him Jess, are you happy for him?" Jess passed the plate of toast over to Una, and pulled Rune into a hug.

"Oh Runestone, he is so happy with you, how could I not be happy, I love you both so much." Tears welled in Una's eyes as she bit into a piece of toast, Jett looked at Jade.

"This could be the longest morning of our lives, how many hankie's you got?" Jade pulled about two dozen out of her pocket, and smiled at Jett.

"Just enough I think." Jett beamed a smile.

"Cool."

Sickness turned to happiness, which very quickly turned to panic. Rune let go of Jess a look of fear on her face. "Oh God."

Jess looked worried. "What Rune?"

She struggled for her first words. "He is going to marry me... Today... At noon...

My hair, my nails, my dress, oh god I won't have enough time, I have to look the best I ever have or I will let him down." Rune started to unravel as Una pulled an arm around her from behind.

"Rune please be calm, it is all taken care of, and that's why we are here. Now please settle down and have something to eat, just relax it will all be fine."

Jade looked at Jett and smiled. "Famous last words eh?" Jett giggled.

"Were you as mad as this on your wedding day, I don't remember?"

Jade smiled. "I was way worse than this at first, I peed myself twice I was that scared."

Steph looked at Jade. "Please Jade, you are not helping." Rune had turned a strange shade of white and green. She blinked and looked at her Mum.

"My hair." She shot out of Una's grip, and flew past Jade and Jett back into her room and the door banged shut. Jett squealed with laughter.

"This is going to be the wildest day ever."

Una raised a pointed finger at the two girls, "I mean it you two lay off her, the poor girl is panicked enough, you will have enough on your plates getting ready yourselves." Jett and Jade put their heads down peeked at each other; and they both started laughing. Jess placed an arm round each of their shoulders.

"Come on you two troubles, I have the happy task of getting you ready." She looked at Steph who was smiling. "How come I got the short straw?" The two girls chuckled under their fringes.

The morning was busy Rags, Lucy and Alice arrived shortly after with Beth and Smokes. Sapphire arrived with arms filled with flowers, which she placed in the cool kitchen. Rune's door opened and closed, as Una and Steph wandered back and forth. Alice brewed one of her calming teas for Rune. Maggs had sent one, but Alice thought it would be better if Rune had the use of her legs, and poured it down the sink.

Bear arrived later, which cheered up Smokes, who felt he was locked in a house full of mad women, which was for the moment not entirely wrong. Bear looked very regal in a silk white shirt and new black pants, he wore a long waistcoat of gold under his heavy long dark blue jacket, and he looked more like a pirate than ever before, this was a pirate with flare. Smokes had really gone to a huge effort, he wore a long black coat with the Loxley coat of arms on it, and a deep black silk shirt to match with his trousers, he had a belt of golden violet flowers in honour of his daughter, and his heavy sword had been polished to perfection.

Robbie stood at the foot of the stairs and Maddy gave a rare large smile. "Oh Robbie you look so handsome... Oh Melanie look at him." She clasped her hands together and beamed with delight, as Mel came out of the kitchen. He stood in all deep blue with new black boots; his cloak was heavy and deep violet, and carried the golden crest of a tree, overlaid with a wolf head. His belt was heavy and silver, and had woven honeysuckle and Jasmine interwoven round oak leaves. Round his neck over his shirt hung the Talisman of Rune, with the symbol of Iona on it. He looked like a lord of great stature, with his long brown hair brushed and hanging neatly down his back.

Mel swept up and kissed him on the cheek. "Oh Robbie, Rune will have her breath taken away when she sees you." He gave a nervous smile.

"I hope so." Rowan came down the stairs smiling; he was dressed identical except he wore a blue cloak to match. He lifted an arm and patted Robbie on the shoulder.

"You look truly like the Lord of Loxley, good luck my friend. Enjoy your day, I can think of no other who deserves the happiness today will bring." Maddy started to weep, as did Mel.

Rowan slipped a hankie out of his pocket. "My good Lady Madeline, I appear to be a wife short today, would you do me the honour of taking my arm, and walking with me to the sacred site?" Maddy gave a slight giggle, and took the hankie and wiped her eyes.

"My Lord Rowan you honour me, I would be delighted." She slipped her arm into Rowan's, as Jaz in all burgundy with the golden crest of a Callanish eagle on his cloak, opened the back door that led them out into the woods. Melanie gave Robbie a smile.

"You look wonderful, I am so happy for you Robbie, I can think of no other who deserves to be as happy, as I know both of you will be." She gave a short sniffle and dabbed at her eyes, and smiled as she offered her arm. "Are you ready my Lord of Loxley?" She slipped her arm into his, and together they followed Rowan and Maddy into the trees. Jaz closed the door and came after them.

Jess flew down the stairs in her long white and blue robes; she gave a big smile as she saw Smokes. "Oh Pete, she is beautiful, she will be ready soon, I have to get to the tree and prepare for the service, I will see you all soon."

Jess lifted her hood and whisked out of the door, as Alice appeared at the top of the stairs. Bear watched unmoving as she smiled shyly when she noticed his attention. Her hair, was braided back, and filled with soft violet flowers, she wore a long gown of lilac and a cloak of violet. She was seven months pregnant, and found it hard to walk fast, but to Bear she was a vision to behold and he pulled her softly into his arms and kissed her.

Jett and Jade followed, they too were dressed in violet of the softest hues, their hair was braided with flowers, and both had long cloaks of violet. Jade had the golden coat of arms of Loxley, but Jett wore her own colours of Caerleon, with a proud lion of deep red set on a golden five-pointed star. Smokes opened his arms and greeted them both. "Oh girls you look so beautiful." Jett gave a smile.

"Cheers Uncle Pete, I hope it is not to softie for Rafe." Smokes gave a smile.

"Believe me you will bowl him over." She gave a huge smile.

Steph came down with the bridesmaids dressed in lavender with long flowing frilly dresses. It was hard to believe that the tough talking tomboy Rags was actually under all that fabric. "Not bad eh... do you reckon Bobby will recognise me? You never know he might see I am actually a girl. Maybe I got a chance of getting his kit off in this." She beamed a big smile, and Steph laughed at her as she came down the stairs in a long flowing blue velvet dress, her golden oak leaf belt now had the star of Runestone's table on it in a deep sapphire blue.

Smokes pulled her into his arms. "You look absolutely beautiful baby." He kissed her and looked up at the stairs and his heart nearly stopped. "Oh princess."

Rune stood looking pale and nervous. Her long white lace dress flowed to the floor, and it was covered in the smallest most delicate pale lilac embroidered flowers. It fitted her to the waist and flowed in layers of fabric, and shone in the light it was so white. Her hair was braided, and Una had worked fine violet ribbons into it, so her braids had the softest of violet streaks in them that shone out from her shimmering red and golden hair. From her shoulders ran a long cloak of the deepest violet, and she carried the emblem of a golden oak tree under which was a leaf and two acorns. The tiara of sapphire and diamond butterflies sparkled, and cast light all around her and matched with her eyes that danced with happiness. The ring on her finger sparkled with bright blue and she looked like she was bathed in a mist of shimmering white and blue light. She swallowed nervously. "I am ready daddy."

Smokes felt the tears in his eyes; Steph fought back her own tears as she watched her husband look at his youngest daughter with love and pride. "Oh Runestone, you look like a fairy tale princess."

She gave a big smile as she walked down the stairs and into his arms. She wiped the tears from his eyes. "I always thought someone else would give me away, oh Daddy I am so happy it will be you." A tear ran down her face.

He wiped it clear. "Hey no tears, I would have got out to be here, I was never going to let anyone but me give either of my princess's to their husbands." Jade slid her arms round her father. He pulled her close as he looked at the others. "Look at me; I have two of the most beautiful women in Loxley as my daughters. I am a man blessed beyond my dreams." Rune and Jade leaned over and gave him a kiss on the cheek. He took a deep breath and then looked back at the others. "We have a lord waiting for us; shall we make him a man as happy as I am?"

Robbie stood in the trees as Maddy and Mel walked into the glade of the Sacred Oak with Jaz. Melissa broke into a smile and ran to him. David Williams stood with Henry and his family as they prepared to be seated, Mel ran over into his bright smiling arms.

Robbie suddenly felt very nervous, as his stomach gave a sharp twist. "Oh hell, Rowan there are hundreds." Rowan smiled and patted his back.

"You two are the star attraction, what did you think, there would just be a few dozen like at mine?"

Robbie nodded looking very pale. "I did actually." He looked out at the wide circle of seats and most of Loxley seemed to be there.

Harry was easy to spot with Maggs at his side, in a very bright pink tie died top and skirt, her violet and lilac shawls hanging from her shoulders. Everyone was dressed in their best, this was the occasion of the year in Loxley, and it looked like Steph and the crew had been very busy preparing at the clothes shop. The chairs ran round in rows, and there were so many that John and Robert Lox had built a small stage round the base of the tree, so that Robbie and Rune would be on a platform where all could see them.

The tree was draped in violet net, to hide the green sheeting that would keep out the rain, Robbie knew that would not happen with Rune as the bride, one flick of her fingers and it would be golden sunshine. All of the seats and the trunk of the tree had been decorated in violet flowers interwoven with the whites of Jasmine. An archway of oak had been built to conduct the service, golden acorns hung down woven with willow and holly. Rowan berries rich and red had been tied in large bunches, to mark the fruits of nature and the power of protection. Maggs had done an incredible job, and he had to admit it looked wonderful. Rowan squeezed his shoulder. "It's time Robbie."

He took a long deep breath and walked out from the trees with Rowan at his side, everyone turned to look as he approached. There were gasps from the women and nods of approval from the men, as Jess turned on the platform and smiled. Robert Lox gave his boy a big hug.

"My Lad, married... and you look like the lord of this land you are my boy. I love you son." He patted him hard on the back and stepped back. Jess gave him a smile.

"Oh Rob you look so handsome... Just wait until she gets here, she will feel a flutter in her heart... Mind you so will you, oh Rob she is beautiful, I have never seen anyone more radiant."

He breathed deeply and looked at Rowan. "She is definitely coming then? Well that's a good start."

Rowan shook his head and laughed. "Robbie how could you ever have doubted? She is Runestone and ..."

Robbie could no longer hear him as he looked down the aisle between the seats where the vision of a fairy queen stood waiting with her father. She glowed in a pale light of sparkling blue and white, and he felt his breath leave him as he looked at her. "Oh wow." His voice was almost a whisper, but Rowan heard it and turned to look.

His eyes were locked on hers, and she smiled as her eyes danced and sparkled in the brightest of sapphire blue. The sun came out above her, and she shimmered as if surrounded by a thousand twinkling fairies. The guests had gone completely quiet, and Robbie felt like time had stopped as he looked in wonder at Runestone Sapphire, the power and wonder of Nature.

Jade and Jett stepped out with Alice in front of them and walked slowly towards him with large bunches of flowers, the petals fell on the floor as the bridesmaids with posy's of white and soft lilac followed. Rune walked behind with Smokes his head held high with pride, Beth wailed into a hankie and all the other women seemed to follow suit, as Rune appeared. Robbie felt Rowan grip his shoulder.

"Oh Rob she is beautiful." He slowly nodded unable to take his eyes off her, Jade winked at him as she got closer and he smiled. The maids of honour cast the last of their petals and stepped aside, and Rags and Lucy came close.

Robbie hardly recognised her, and he gave a big grin, she winked and whispered. "No more snogging now you are married, Bobby gets jealous."

Rune came up to his side and gave a soft giggle. "Hi gorgeous." Her smile was radiant and he was overwhelmed.

"Rune you are beautiful." Smokes kissed her on the cheek and stepped back, Rowan slid an arm round Robbie and pulled him round to face the steps at the base of the platform. Jess stood with tears in her eyes and smiling down at them.

"Children of the woodland realm, come to me below this most Sacred Oak of our woodland realm." Robbie lifted his arm and Rune took it, together they stepped on the three wooden steps and climbed slowly up to the top of the platform. There were gasps as everyone got to see them together, as Jess turned them to face each other and she placed their hands together.

His deep brown eyes looked from the frail slender hands covered with rings, and one in particular that sparkled like a star in the heavens, up into her bright blue eyes that seemed to sparkle more. He gave her a smile, and her cheekbones lifted as she smiled, and her eyes spoke words of joy and love to him.

Jess wiped another tear from her eyes, and raised her arms in the air, her long white sleeves hung down and she spoke loud and clear to everyone. "I am here on the eve of the festival to mark the ending of light and the coming of the dark months, and yet before me I see a light that shines brighter than any I have known." She glanced at Rune and smiled.

"People of the woodland realm, I stand under the watchful eyes of our lord of the forest and of all creation, to bind together a lord of this realm with the daughter of the lord of creation. Through me our High Lord will join your union and celebrate the meeting of creator and life." She looked at her son and future daughter in law. "In the eyes of this world and time you are children of the woodlands. Will you love each other, and care for each other, and live as one in this realm of green lands?"

Rune gave a smile as she looked in his eyes. "I will." Robbie grinned at her, and looked at his mother.

"Yes mum, I will." Rune started to giggle, as the crowd tittered. Jess gave a huge smile and tried hard not to laugh.

"We all clearly see the deep love that you hold, and we feel the commitment you have brought here today. I bring you together now as seed and life, and may your happiness grow to full bloom through all of the seasons of life." Jess slid a long silk violet ribbon out of her robes, and she loosely wrapped it round their ring hands as she spoke. "Take the rings of life that bring you ever back to each other and share them. Wear them as tokens of your love, and a symbol of your life together. May the circle of love hold you close and bind your destiny together from this realm into the next?"

Rowan stepped up to the platform with a small green cushion, and handed Robbie the ring. He stepped back down, as Robbie lifted the ring to Rune's finger.

"I give to you as the symbol of my love the greatest heirloom of my house, this is the ring of Marion of Blidworth, it was placed on her finger by the first hooded man. Runestone Sapphire, I know the love they held still holds today, and through this ring I hope in a thousand years my love for you will still hold true. You are my life and all I ever hope to be."

Rune looked stunned as he slid the old golden band onto her finger and it glowed with a faint light of blue, the power of Gwendolyn was strong in the ring of the hooded man. He smiled as she saw the band of gold next to the sapphire stone of Runestone. Her eyes filled with tears as she smiled at him.

"I have no words to express this Robbie." He lifted a hand and wiped the tears from her eyes as violets sprang up on the platform below. "I need no words when I see clearly before me the love you hold."

Rune swallowed hard, as Smokes lifted the golden band carved with the finest of Oak leaves up to her. Rune took the ring and placed it at the tip of his finger.

"You are My Lord, and I am your Lady, we both carry lines of power. As I stand here before you, in front of my family, and all the woodland realm of my grandfather's. I am a woman only, I am a woman who knows that she loves you, I am lost without you, as you are the light of my world and the warmth in my heart. In this world and the next, I will be by your side always. I love you Robbie with all of who I am." She slid the ring down his finger, as Jess stood above them tears streaming down her face.

Jess wiped her eyes on the hankie, and looked out at the assembled gathering.

Most of them were in tears, John gave a huge sniff, and shared Hanna's hankie. Harry swallowed deeply a huge smile below his glistening eyes. Maggs sniffled as she raised a handful of multi coloured hankies to her eyes. Beth wailed as John beamed a huge smile. Alice and Anne Kirk held hands as tears ran down their cheeks.

Jess raised her arms high in the air. "Lord Robert of Loxley, and Runestone Sapphire daughter of the woodland realm have vowed their love before you. Take them into your hearts and into your lives as one. Hear me My Lord, and grant them life, love and seeds of the future." Jett and Jade sprinkled petals across them as Jess put her hands down onto their shoulders.

"My children, and children of the woods you are now one. Go in peace and live in this realm together." She pulled on the ribbon, and it slowly unwound from their hands. Jess handed it to Rune who gave her a huge smile, Jess nodded.

"Welcome to my family my daughter, congratulations you are now man and wife."

Rune exploded with happiness as Robbie snatched her into his arms and kissed her, everyone rose from their seats and cheered, and threw petals and rice in the air. Jade leapt up on the platform as Robbie parted from Rune, and she wailed into her sister's arms. Robbie turned to his mum who pulled him close.

"Oh Robbie, you are a married man now. I am so happy for you two." Jess burst into tears as she hugged him and Rune slid her arms round them both. They broke apart and Robert Lox stood before his son and dragged him into a big hug.

"You take care of her now Rob, she is special, there is a lot of Jess in that lass." Jess gave a giggle as she remembered her own day many years before when she had married Robert. She understood the compliment. Roberts strong bear like arms folded gently round Rune. "I am proud to have you as a daughter; you are very special to all of us Runestone. Good luck my love, and enjoy every moment you have as I have with my Jess."

Rune looked up at the smiling face of Robert Lox. "I hope we are as happy as you and Jess have been, I have always admired the love between you." He beamed a smiled and sniffed hard.

Holding hands, they were almost dragged off the platform by Rowan, Steph, and Smokes, who hugged them both for an age, and Jett cried as she hugged her two greatest friends. Alice wailed as Bear comforted her, and Beth was on her twentieth hankie. Maddy and Una hugged Mel as they wailed, and Rafe stood proud as they approached him.

"You two people have honoured me in so many ways I wish I could repay you. All I can do is tell you that I would lay down my life to protect what you have, for what I see in you two has made me stronger and better as a person. I wish you both my deepest best wishes and happiness for all of your life together."

Rune gave him a hug, and Robbie pulled him close. "Commander and friend, your words have repaid us ten times over, for they are honest and true. But do not lay your life down too quickly, we wish many years of your company." He patted Rafe on the back and as he broke Rafe nodded.

"I am proud to serve you My Lord and Lady."

Two seats decorated with flowers were brought forward to carry them, and just as they were about to sit down, the whole crowd went silent, everyone bowed to one knee in wonder. At the edge of the forest, the Lord Hearne stood and watched; a mist swirled around him and drew back as the trees leaned over to be close to him. Rune's face lit up as she saw him, and grabbing Robbie's hand she turned and ran across the glade of the Sacred Oak towards him. Everyone watched in wonder as Rune flew into his outstretched arms and he hugged her as a father would his child. "Oh, my father of all creation you came to my wedding, I am happier than I ever could have thought possible." Her eyes exploded with violet as he pulled her close.

"I could not miss a chance to congratulate my loveliest leaf of my woodland, for you little flower are the brightest bloom in my realm." He looked up at Robbie who bowed. "You have grown little sapling; I see a bowman who has no doubt in this decision."

"I chose the life I have many years ago My Lord. Today it has come true for me, your daughter of the woods has honoured and blessed my life."

"My children I wish you to kneel before me, for I wish to offer you a blessing of old to match the ring that my daughter wears." Rune slipped out of his arms and took Robbie's hand. They both knelt down on the floor.

Jess stood with her husband, Steph, and Smokes and she gasped as she watched Robbie and Rune kneel before Hearne. She gripped her husband's arm tightly. "I don't believe it?" Everyone looked at her as she watched stunned; Robert turned and looked at her.

"What?"

"Lord Hearne himself is going to bless their union, it has only ever happened twice in this world before. Arthur and Guinevere were the first, Marion and Robert of Loxley the second. This is incredible."

Hearne raised his hands high and everyone bowed. "Hear me my children of my realm, hear the words of your Lord and Creator. I stand before you in this place on the last day of light, to bring praise and blessings to the line of Loxley as it unites with the realm of my world. See my children before me, and know they will now carry the mark of their lord. Praise them for the purity of their love in their hearts, and bless them, for in them is the fruit of the land and the future of your world. As lord and creator, I bring together the power of the green circle and the strength of the white circle. They will be joined here on out with the binding of the white lines of time, know these children of mine for they are blessed, and will write the future for all of us."

Jess fell to her knees, as white light flowed out from the trees, and was mixed with a pale green light. It swirled around Robbie and Rune and then violet light erupted from the eyes of Hearne, and mixed with it, as it spun round the couple at high speed. Then suddenly Robbie and Rune's head fell back and the light flowed into their eyes and was gone. Jess crouched on the floor and stared in shock,

Robert knelt down as the Lord Hearne turned and walked into the forest.

"You alright Jess love...? What is it? You look like you have just seen a ghost." Jess spoke quietly so only Robert could hear.

"I have Rob... I have just remembered something that was told me by your dad, God Rob; your dad must have had mystical powers. Everything has just suddenly fallen into place." Robert looked worried and lifted her to her feet.

"What did my old dad say?" Jess slid close to him.

"Rob your dad once told me that every so many generations the power of the Green Lord is renewed, he was convinced that the hooded man when he passed from this realm entered into the Green Lord, and took on his role and knowledge. He could not be certain; he was convinced a child conceived in the sight of the sacred oak would one day have powers beyond the early realm." She looked into the questioning eyes of her husband. "Robert don't you see...? Robbie was created the night we sneaked off and came here. That is the reason your dad left Robbie this place alone. Robert I just think the Great Green Lord Hearne has just named our son as his successor... Don't you see? Rune will live for ten life times like Opal did. He has just made sure they stay together forever."

Robert suddenly understood what his wife was saying. "Bloody hell Jess, are you sure?" He looked to where Robbie and Rune had got up from their knees, and stood away from all the others kissing each other. Jess knew that Rune had worked it out and so had her son.

"Look at them Rob, they know, she is telling him." Robert watched as Robbie suddenly pulled her into his arms, Rune flung her arms wildly round him and she shrieked with laughter. It was obvious to Jess, that Rune's biggest fear had been removed; Rune would live all of her life times with Robbie. Robert Lox stared in disbelief as the two of them came happily scampering over to the others and took their places in the chairs.

The band broke into tune and the people celebrated as they made their way laughing and joking out of the glade of the sacred oak, and down the lane towards the farm and the village hall. Jess stood holding her husband's hand as they walked slowly. "They are so lucky to have such a long time together."

Robert lifted his big arm round her shoulder. "What you talking about girl, we got the rest of eternity together; you won't get away from this old badger easily. I told you a million times Jessie. I loved you from the moment you first slapped me in that bar."

Jessie burst into laughter. "You will never let me forget that will you? I had no idea it was Harry who pinched my bum, you were right behind me, how was I to know?"

Robert rubbed his cheek softly. "It still smarts now in the cold." Jess roared with laughter and staggered as she walked down the lane.

"You are an old fraud, you know that Robert Lox? Still smarts... What a baby you can be."

Robert stopped and pulled her close. "Best thing Harry ever did for me that... I loved you like mad but could not seem to tell you. I still love you like mad Jessie love, I have been the happiest man in this realm with you."

She slid into his arms. "Oh Rob, you have made me so happy too... I love you more with every moment that has passed." She stretched up and went to kiss him.

"Watch the cheek now, it's still smarting." Jess exploded with laughter, and she kissed him. Laughing and joking like two teenagers, they ran down the lane hand in hand to catch up with the rest of the party.

Rune and Robbie stood lost for words as they entered the village hall. Most of the guests were seated, as the tables ran round the outer edge of the walls. The large square of tables from the previous night had been increased in size, and now at least two hundred guests sat and waited the arrival of the happy couple, and the families. What had taken Rune and Robbie's breath away, was the decoration. The tables were filled with every kind of flower in bloom known. The whole room was filled with strong vibrant colour and filled with a heavenly scent. From the beams hung large, fragrant bunches of lavender and lilac, entwined with honeysuckle and jasmine. Grapes hung in fat juicy bunches, Oak leaves and acorns were mixed in vases with rowan berries and rose hips, the whole place looked like a paradise of nature.

Rune clapped her hands with delight as she walked beside Robbie up the room led by Blades to their seats. "Oh Rob look, I feel the presence of my grandfather of the woods all around me." He took the back of her chair as she moved in front of the table.

"If I may Mrs Loxley?" She stopped and turned back to see his smile. A wide beaming smile broke out across her face.

"Oh god I am aren't I?" She twisted and pulled him into a kiss. "You will never regret this."

He held her close. "I have a wife who is beautiful and wonderful and is life herself. How could I ever even consider regret...? Now Mrs Loxley may I seat you so we may begin our feast?"

She bit her lip and smiled. "Yes, my wonderful husband you may seat me." She kissed the tip of his nose and slid happily into the seat. Rowan gave a laugh as he watched and nudged Jade.

"They are worse than we were." She beamed a smile at him.

"I have made you happy haven't I Rowan?"

Rowan smiled and stroked her cheek. "Oh Jade, look at you, how could any man be with you and not be happy. You are my world, we are the same as Robbie and Rune, and our happiness will never fade."

She smiled at him. "I do love you, and I have been happier than I ever thought possible Rowan."

"I know sweetheart, me too." He leaned over and gave her a soft kiss.

Jess and Robert were the last ones in, and came in quite breathless. Judy showed them to their seats and then headed back to her own. The food flowed and everyone tucked into the meal. For the second night in a row, Robbie felt he could eat no more as he leaned back in his chair. The chatter bounced all over the room and Rune giggled with Jess at her side as Jess told the story of Harry's wandering hand, and Roberts slapped face. He leaned over and moaned how it still hurt as he rubbed it tenderly.

Rune shrieked with laughter, as he smiled and Jess raised a fist to punch him. Robbie watched everyone enjoying themselves, and felt happy just watching the laughter of Rune. Deep inside he found a place, which was complete contentment, for most of his life he had struggled with the restlessness inside him, and now surrounded by his family, friends and this one very special person, it all seemed to be irrelevant. Happiness came from what he always had and yet had somehow not noticed. Steph touched his arm and he came out of his thoughts, she smiled at him. "Thank you, Robbie."

He leaned over to her. "What for Steph?"

"You have made my daughter happier than I ever thought possible, you overcame your fear, and you chose her above all others. Oh, Robbie for years she would watch you afraid to talk to you, I told her a million times to get in your way and strike up a conversation. The day you came to share those cakes with my father, you changed her life forever. I was terrified Melissa would get to you first, whenever you went into that cheese shop, I used to hide my face, and hope she was too busy in the back. You know Jade once promised to beat her up and make her permanently ugly...? You know Rune always said you knew in your heart she was yours, and she was right you stayed faithful to her belief, I am so happy for you both and I am relieved you finally found each other." Rune gave a giggle as he smiled and looked at her laughing with his dad.

"There was and will only ever be Rune, when I first saw her watching through the gate of your yard at the age of six I knew it then, and that was the day I fell in love with her." Steph gave his hand a soft squeeze as Robert Lox stood up and banged on his glass.

"Ladies and Gentlemen, I believe we have feasted to excess, and are now sufficiently drunk or sedated enough to hear the speeches." Everyone laughed and sat back in their seats, Robert waited for silence.

"Earlier this year I sat with pride as I watched my son be made Lord of Loxley, it was a bit of a shock to him, because no one had told him. He was just a young lad and yet he shouldered the burden of a man and walked into the unknown on behalf of his people. It was a very brave thing that would have shrivelled the heart of most men." He looked round the room as many of the men folk nodded in agreement with him.

"I must admit I was worried for him; I am his dad and I love him... what put my mind at ease more than anything else was the wisdom he showed in picking his team. Most men would have chosen an army and rode with banners and trumpets to the gates of Mason Knox, my son didn't, instead he chose a close group of friends and a slender young woman who he knew had faith and loyalty enough to follow his lead. I told him just before he left how I thought that young Runestone had a lot of my Jess in her. It was the highest compliment I could pay her." Jess put her head down and blushed, and Rune put her hand on hers.

"You all know how clever my Jess is, you all know how kind and gentle and loving she is... well I said it then, and I will say it again. Rune here, has done for my son, what my Jess has for me. Hearne love her because he went down south, and gave em a good taste of the north, and he did it because Rune was at his side. Tonight I am the happiest man in the north, because I now got both the best women in Loxley in my family." Everyone burst into laughter as Robert raised a glass and shouted above the noise. "Lord Robert and Lady Runestone Loxley."

Glasses waved in the air and the noise from the toast was deafening. Robert sat down with a beaming smile and Smokes rose up and waited for the noise to calm down. His bright blue eyes shone with happiness, as he calmly began to talk.

"I have sat in a prison for over ten years not knowing if I would ever see my family again. I have now had the honour of being beside my daughters at both of their weddings. I have the joy of seeing them every day, when I thought, they were lost to me forever. My new son is only young, and yet despite the overwhelming odds, he planned the most daring raid ever, and he brought his team of Specialists over the walls of Tintagel and he rescued me."

The tables rattled as Big John, and Harry banged their applause, and everyone smiling clapped at such an achievement. Rune beamed as she took Robbie's hand in hers. Pete gave a broad smile and waited for the applause to quieten.

"I will never forget the night the door burst open and my wife fell on the floor beside me. I looked up from her embrace believing I was dreaming, and I saw the slender figure of a boy with a man's heart, he called to Rune and suddenly I realised that this young man was about to give me the life I had lost back again. How can a man repay such a debt? Robert of Loxley is an extraordinary man who has courage and honour beyond all of us. Today my daughter became his wife and I cried with joy to see it happen before me. He gave that to me, he planned it because it mattered to my daughters. It mattered to Runestone, and for her he risked everything so she could have a father again. I am proud to call such an honourable man son. Please join me and thank him as he starts his own life with my daughter, raise your glasses to Robert and Runestone Lox."

Rune swept from the chair to her father's arms as all the room toasted their health. Robbie watched as Jade got up and cried on her dad's shoulder, Steph smiled at him as she dried her eyes, and Smokes hugged both his daughters as everyone applauded.

Rune leaned over and kissed him as she slid back into her chair, Harry banged on the table. "Hey man let the groom speak, hey Robbie dude, let's have a speech." Others joined in, and Rune giggled as he looked at her.

"Just remember, this is my wedding day, be sweet Robbie." Her eyes sparkled as he rose up and everyone cheered, Robbie took a long drink of his iced water. He leaned on the table and took a deep breath. "There is no one from Scotland here is there?" All the Specialists started to laugh, and banged on the tables. Robbie gave a big smile and looked at the huge crowd of people.

"I am lost for words and humbled greatly by the compliments of my two parents, I suppose a son and daughter want very much to earn their parents respect, I have tried and I know my wife has." Rune gave a smile, and lifted her hand and slipped it into his.

"My father is very right; I am the one who picked the team we all know today as the Specialists. They have become my second family and I love them dearly; I have also felt the pain of losing some of them and they are dearly missed here this afternoon, Eric, Hog and Martin all held my wife in high esteem, and I hope they are watching as the spirits of those we love draw nearer tonight." Robbie gave a look to Fish, John and Hanna. They all gave a soft smile and acknowledged his gesture.

"I chose to take a girl with me who I have to confess I have watched for a life time, and both of my parents are right. At a time when I felt lacking in confidence and doubtful, it was Runestone who gave me the strength and the willpower to dig deeper and continue. It is much the same today, as I plan our next big hurdle in defence of our realm. She is my courage and my strength, and it is her who gives me the power to force my way forward when everything looks bleak. Rune has inspired me to levels I never thought I could achieve, so when all of you talk of the hooded man remember this. My Specialists are also the hooded man, but more than anything else, behind my hood is the love of a very wonderful woman. I ask all of you to welcome and salute the first Lady of Loxley. Runestone Sapphire

Lane Loxley."

Robbie raised his glass and bowed to Rune as she blushed at the table and giggled. The whole room stood to their feet and bowed to her; they toasted her and sat down. Everyone cheered as she turned and slid her face into his neck, Robbie held her tight. "It is true Rune; you have always been there at my side."

"Oh Robbie I want to cry, please tell me no one is looking at me." He gave a small laugh.

"It's alright you can look now." She slowly drew back and he smiled at her. The light bounced from her tiara all over her face and she looked wonderful.

"Can we go home soon? I want us to be alone." He smiled.

"I will get the carriage ready and then we can leave." She nodded and he turned to Rowan and gave him a nod, Rowan raised his hand and a woodsman on guard by the doors nodded and slipped out.

Jess rose from her seat as the room all turned to her, she carried a smile of delight and her hazel eyes shone. "The happy couple will soon depart for their time together, let us seal the joy of this wedding feast, and bring in the cake."

There were gasps as the door to Robbie's office opened and a tall cake of five tiers was carried into the room. It was huge and white and decorated with pale lilac violets. It was placed on the table in front of Robbie and Rune who both smiled at the two hooded figures stood on the top. They were set side by side with their bows held high, Rune giggled as she saw that they were a perfect likeness.

Rune looked across to Alice and Anne Kirk and she smiled and mouthed thank you, she brought her hand to her heart and the two old ladies grinned with tear filled eyes at her pleasure. The whole room smiled at the delight of the couple. "Oh Robbie it is beautiful, do we really have to cut it?"

The room gave a soft giggle. He held her hand gently. "You are my destiny Runestone Sapphire, and so it will be Destiny that binds us." Rune giggled as he drew the bright gleaming sword of Destiny from it sheath. The blade shone with the light of a thousand stars, as he pulled her hands gently on to the hilt with his. Together they lifted the sword and cut a deep slice into the cake, the whole room cheered as she threw her arms round him and hugged him. Never had two people looked so happy

Robbie lifted her long violet cloak on to her shoulders, and she pinned it with the oak leaf clasp, Jess and Steph pulled her into a hug as Robbie shook the hand of Smokes and then embraced him. Steph hugged him and kissed his cheek. Jess almost squeezed the life out of him. "Enjoy your time away, I know it's not long but relax and sleep late, you look so tired Rob, both of you do."

"We will mum I promise... thanks for today, you made it more special conducting the service for us."

Her eyes filled with tears. "I felt a huge honour Robbie to be able to join two very special people, I love you Robbie."

"I love you to mum."

Robert pulled him into a bear like hug. "I am proud to have you as my son, go and enjoy yourself with that wonderful wife of yours." He slapped his back and Rune took his hand and they walked slowly toward the doors, everyone stood in a long row and wished them well as they walked. Una, Mel and Maddy hugged them as they passed, as did Crystal and Sapphire. Rags beamed as she hugged Rune.

Robbie crouched down. "Hey Rags where is Bobby?" She giggled.

"He is over there, why?" Robbie dragged her quickly off her feet and gave her a huge kiss. He put her down as her legs swung limp in the air and he smiled. "That's your last, I am a married man now."

Rune gasped with laughter at the surprise, and dreamy state that crossed Rags face. "Wow Robbie baby, that's one hell of a goodbye, I feel faint, God Rune if I had purple eyes and secret powers I tell you, I would give you a run for your money. Robbie you have got to show Bobby how to do that, I can't breathe."

Robbie gave her a hug. "Watch Loxley for me while I am gone."

"You got it lusty lips." She winked at Rune. "Hey girl, you got some good times coming I can tell you." Rune chuckled with laughter as she hugged Rags and finally, they made their way to the door. Rune turned to all the smiling faces of the community of Loxley.

"Thank you everyone, it must have been the biggest kept secret in Loxley." They all giggled. "You have all overwhelmed me with your love. All of you have made this the happiest day of my life, I will never forget it."

"You are the first Lady of Loxley, and we all love you My Lady. It was our biggest honour and pleasure." Rune looked down at the bright eyes of Big John in his wheel chair as everyone nodded and smiled. Rafe patted him on the shoulder. Tears welled in her eyes and she walked forward, and bent down and kissed his cheek.

"Thank you, John, I have no words." He beamed a smile as Robbie nodded to him and took Rune by the arm; they turned to the doors and stepped through. A huge cheer rose in the air as they walked down the path of the village hall, petals flew into the air and Rune smiled with joy and giggled on Robbie's arm. The whole of Loxley seemed to have turned out as they got into the large black carriage. Rowan and Jade climbed on the back and Jett and Rafe walked down one side as Sapphire and Keith walked down the other.

The carriage made its way very slowly, through the hordes of people who yelled their best wishes, and Rune laughed and giggled at the masses of people who all said such wonderful things to them as they passed. It was obvious through the hearts of the people how much they were loved, and it touched Rune deeply. In years to come, she talked often of that day when the entire town of Loxley turned out to wish her well and show her their love. The cart was almost filled with flowers by the time they reached the farm, and Robbie pulled her close and she curled into him, as the carriage made its way down Sacred Oak Road, and into the glade of Robbie's Mere.

He lifted her into his arms and swung open the gate as she laughed and giggled. Her eyes danced with delight as he carried her over the threshold of their home and he set her down and pulled her into a close hug. "Welcome home Mrs Loxley."

Rune stood by the window of the bedroom and light passed in reflecting in every direction, she looked at herself in her wedding gown in the mirror and smiled, she had woken almost twelve hours ago in her bed as Runestone Rimmer Lane, and now she would leave for two days on Iona as Mrs Runestone Sapphire Lox, the first Lady of Loxley, and wife of the hooded man. It had been the best birthday ever.

Robbie organised Rowan and everyone, as he prepared to leave for two days, Rowan raised his hands. "Robbie, I have been stood at your side all year, please trust in me, just go and enjoy yourself. Sleep late, eat toast and be with your wife will you, you are driving me nuts." He gave him a smile

Robbie nodded, he put his arms round Rowan and gave him a big hug. "You are my rock you know that brother?" Jade squealed with delight.

"Oh, wow yeah I forgot, me and Rune are sisters, you two are brothers now, oh wow how cool is that? Hey Robbie you are my brother as well, this is so cosmic Harry will be thrilled." Her smile beamed out below her long shaggy fringe and he chuckled.

Rune came down in all violet with her small bag and slid her arms around him. "Give me a minute will you Rob... Jade will you come with me?"

Rune led Jade down to her table and sat in her seat. "Jade you have powers in you that have passed from me. The life for a life gave you gifts, I want you to watch from my table while I am away, and if anything happens you must let me know."

Jade looked scared. "I am not sure about this Rune; you have powers beyond all of us." Rune smiled.

"You are of my line with the same blood, my table will help you, and it will protect you... see come here and sit in my seat." Rune got up, and Jade slipped into Rune's place. Rune waved her hand across the surface of the table and violet sparks shimmered. "This is Jade Opal and sister of your owner, recognise her and help her, she is of the line of Runestone and will seek to watch." The table glowed a bright vivid violet. "See it has recognised you... tell it to picture Iona."

Jade looked nervous, she held her hands over the surface as she had seen Rune do a million times. "Show me Iona." The violet mist rose out of the table and swirled into the air. The picture of a carved stone cross came into view, and Jade saw Gwinne waiting beside it. "Oh wow Rune, look it is doing it." Rune smiled at her

"Remember Jade it will only show you the present, the table will not show the future or the past, I have instructed my table to show you and you alone what is happening, if there is an attack you will know first, if you are not at the table, it will call you."

She looked really worried. "What do you mean it will call me?"

"If I am not in the room, I hear my own voice telling me to come to the table. It could be my voice you hear or your own. Either way if a voice in your head tells you come here, then do so alright?" Jade nodded and Rune smiled at her. "Enjoy yourself and learn about your powers, just behave." Rune kissed her on the head and left Jade alone watching Iona and Gwinne.

Crystal and Amethyst stood in the room with Saff and Keith. Despite all of Robbie's protests, Rowan had insisted on him having a guard. He assured Robbie they would be discreet and stay well away, but Rowan would not risk leaving him out of sight for too long. Robbie was not going to win, and so he backed down. Rowan gave him a huge hug. "Go and enjoy yourself." He patted him on the back.

Rune opened the window and they all passed through into the courtyard of the Abbey and the large stone cross, Gwinne swept into Rune's arms and screamed with delight as she saw her two daughters, it was a happy moment for everyone.

Robbie and Rune were given their own room out of the way. The abbey still had a few monks who had survived the Red Death, and continued the traditions of a life lived for hundreds of years. They kept themselves very separate although they did recognise and talk with Gwinne.

The room was small and yet still very cosy; it reminded Robbie greatly of the small room at Sister Mary's house of good hope. He liked the seclusion, and it was not long before they curled up together and lay arm in arm. He stroked back her long red hair. "You had a nice birthday?" She snuggled close to him.

"I have had the best day of my life. I cannot believe you managed to hide all that from me. Oh Robbie it was a wonderful surprise, I will never forget this day, no matter how long I live."

"Good." He kissed her head and she snuggled down closer, the evening passed slowly as Robbie and Rune who both now felt exhausted slept and dozed and made love into the night. It was very late the next morning when they woke.

Gwinne sat with Sapphire and Keith, and watched as they walked hand in hand along the edge of the water at the bottom of the long hill. The sea was bright blue and the sun shone down from high in the sky. She smiled as she watched Robbie splash Rune and she ran screaming along the beach as he chased her, and caught her laughing wildly in his arms. The happiness and love between them radiated out from them, and Gwinne thought of Rayne and the fun they had before they had been separated, Robbie had reminded her very much of him, and there had been many nights when she sat alone and thought of her greatest love and the father of her two children. Sapphire leaned forward. "I don't mean to pry but who is Rayne?"

Gwinne blinked and smiled. "I am sorry, I have spent so much time alone I sometimes forget to block. Rayne was my husband and is the father of my children. His sister Eleanor was my best friend, which is how I met him. Robbie reminds me very much of him, when I see how he treats Rune, I see a little of the way Rayne was with me. I miss him a lot at times like this."

"What happened to him?"

Gwinne gave a sigh. "He was called back to his people, I was not allowed to go with him, it is the rule of his people, he is part of one of the lines of Fae, his line is of the moon."

Saff straightened in her chair. "The line of the moon is Vivian Lady of the lake, was Rayne her son?"

Gwinne nodded. "I am the guardian of the lake until the next true sister is born, one from Crystal or Amethyst will be the true heir of Vivian, and the line of Rhiannon will be restored. I hope that when the new Queen of Fae is born, it will be Rayne that is sent to welcome her. That is why I chose to come here to Iona."

Sapphire understood and slid back in her chair as Robbie and Rune stood in the sun and kissed as the blue water lapped on to the shore by their feet. She smiled a bright smile and gave a long happy sigh. "It is nice to be alone together, I love this small island it is so peaceful and quiet." He slid his arm round her as they walked on the silver sand.

"We will be back when Iona comes, but I must admit I will miss this place when we have to return."

"Let's not think about it Robbie, this could be our only true time alone for some time, hold me in your arms and tell me again how you love me, that was the greatest letter I have ever read."

Robbie pulled her close and looked deeply into her bright shining blue eyes. "Hey beautiful, do you know how deeply my love runs for you?"

She gave a long giggle and her eyes danced with happiness. "No, please tell me?"

CHAPTER TWENTY TWO

SECRETS AND STONES

Robbie and Rune left Loxley feeling happy, and the whole town felt a surge of hope, as they lit the bonfires and celebrated the end of the woodsman year. On the market ground a huge bonfire was lit, and people gathered to sing and dance and celebrate. It was a long night of laughter and joy, bobbing for apples and eating hot pies, as they all gathered before the large fire and warmed themselves. The following day marked the start of the preparations for winter, and the stockade would become a hive of activities.

Harry and Maggs with Robert and John Lox led the celebrations, Joe stood by his cart as his special recipe ale flowed. The Specialist's walked with pride in amongst the town folk as they were recognised and praised by the whole community. Jett, Jade, Blades, and Judy, staggered around, wearing happy smiles as they swayed. The trouble twins with their apprentices, had much mischief in mind. It was a long night of happiness that ended with Jett and Jade hanging like rags, as they giggled on the shoulders of Rowan and Rafe. Robert stood with his arm around Jess a proud man, this was the night, he always thought of his dad, and he knew that tonight he would look down on his son with pride. The night slowed as they all headed home in the dark and prepared for the coming of winter.

Jess had many families helping up at the farm, as all the remaining apples in her vast orchard were picked and packed for the winter months. The ash from the bonfires all over the stockade, were collected up and sprinkled into the fields for next year's crops, and vital repairs began on the houses to ensure all was sealed and safe for the winter. The next fifteen weeks would see gales, rain and eventually snow; it could be bleak this far up north.

Jett and Rafe had a few days leave and so they headed for number six, Jett burst with delight when she saw everything Robbie had bought for her home, and after a frantic four hours of running around with Jade organising her new house, she collapsed on the bed in her room next to Rafe and cried with happiness.

Steph finally cleared Rune's bedroom, and boxed the few things left there, and took them to the house at the Mere. Crystal's things were moved into Rune's old room at Steph's and Maddy who now seemed to be alone in Leenard's house got Una back. Mel was spending most of her time at David's house and Saff was there most of the time, as Keith lived with him.

Ruby had a great life living with Jess. She had Rags just across the way and Alice next door. Blades and Judy who were her two best friends lived just up from the farm, and they now formed a very elite group who would all sit around Rags cabin, and laugh and joke and have fun. Jasper moved into Jade's old flat behind her old workshop, which was very quiet and secluded, and it was not uncommon to see Melissa slip out in the early hours of the morning. Scarlet and Philip had decided to stay for a while, and they stayed as guests in the large hotel that had been built at the side of the Village Hall. There were many members of the woodland community now fulfilling their official roles that came and went to Loxley.

The talk around the bar at night was one of war and defending the realm. Skip and Fuse spent all day in the hall discussing the plans and in order to have a break in the evening, Skip rented one of the cottages just down from the farm. Treen spent most of her time there, and Fuse enjoyed being taken care of. He had given his whole life to the care of the line of the duke, and now he found that such was the bond with the young duke since he had been saved by Robbie and his

Specialists, that Skip would no longer tolerate him acting like a servant. Skip looked to Fuse as the father figure he had always been, and he treated him as such. It had been hard for Fuse to accept at first, but with long hours of working together over the past months, he had found that it had become easier.

He still found it odd on some mornings to walk into the kitchen and find Treen cooking breakfast, with Skip wearing an apron and washing the pots. Fuse had become a very well liked and very respected member of the Loxley community. He ran the village hall operations room, which now had a large staff of many of the soldier's wives. He treated everyone with a courteous manner, and they all had grown very fond of him. It was not unusual to find a freshly baked cake, or a bag of biscuits on his desk in a morning.

Rowan was Robbie's number two, and he had become one of the most respected figures in the stockade. He was often seen at the side of Robert Lox, and the two of them had become very firm friends. Jade was treated with the highest respect in the village, which in many ways still amused her. Gone were the days when she was scowled at by the women for being a tomboy. Jade still walked around in her uniform armed to the teeth, her long curly hair often seen bobbing around under her wide brimmed hat. Alley would be seen sat laughing with Jade in her own hat; they looked almost like twin sisters. There were many new children in the town, and it was not uncommon in the playgrounds to see groups of girls argue about who got to be Jade Opal when they played.

By far the biggest change in the town was the increased presence of soldiers, and the much tighter security. The barracks had increased in size, and two of the large lower fields had been set up as tented accommodation, for those units preparing for the front lines. A constant stream of troops from other areas arrived and left depending on where they were stationed, as Loxley became the centre of the war to save the green realm.

For Robbie life had changed completely, and for the first time in what felt like years, he finally had a few precious days away from it all, but even then, there were still moments where his thoughts turned to his current campaign, especially when he walked along the beach with Gwynfor, while Rune took a long bath on the first afternoon of his honeymoon.

The sand was almost white, and contrasted perfectly next to the bright blue water, as he walked slowly along at the side of the ancient Celt. Gwynfor had talked of love and happiness, but he felt now was the time to move to more pressing matters. The old man gave a cheeky smile, as he stopped and watched the fishing boats returning in the distance. "I feel the tension within you has lessened a little since we last spoke, I see you have given much of what we discussed great thought, I am happy Robbie that you are starting to realise why certain events have come about." Robbie gave a small laugh.

"I am not sure that I understand everything, I find a lot of things connected to the lines of the past confusing, but I have given a lot of thought to many things... I think I still find it strange that I am related to Una and her sisters, not to mention Sapphire and her cousins." Gwynfor turned and gave a slight nod of understanding.

"There are many generations from my daughter to your parents, I understand that from my sister there are really only two, it is easy to find it confusing, but you must ignore the generations and look to the passage of power young Robbie, for therein lies the key to understanding all things. It is true to move into your future you must understand the past and learn from it, but it is more important to see where the lines of power have worked their magic." Robbie felt the conversation slipping away again; the powers and conditions of those powers with Rune's family were a constant source of confusion. He gave a long sigh.

"That is exactly what throws me, I just seem to understand, and then you or Rune, or one of the others makes a comment about it, and I am lost again."

Gwynfor gave a happy little chuckle.

"I am afraid it will never get any easier, magic weaves its own path, each person directs their energy in whatever direction they chose." Gwynfor leaned on his stick and lowered himself to the tufted edge of the white sand, and sat on the grass. He patted it at his side for Robbie to sit. "All you need to do is look at the lines of the female, and not just in my line, but also in that of the Dark One... It's all really very simple... Your line is that of Fae or as we call it, the White Circle. It may be many generations away, but the blood in your veins still carries some of the powers of my line, and it is that very fact, which has blended with your union to that of Green Circle, and I may add combined in a way no one foresaw, and created a new line of power. The Violet Line." Robbie turned to Gwynfor looking a little exasperated.

"You see that is my point... You talk of circles and lines and it gets so confusing, isn't power just power?" Gwynfor gave a little shrug.

"In many ways yes... But it is the intent by those who wield it, now that is the key. Let me put it this way to clear the way you understand me, because all of the power on this earth today, has its starting point at one source." Robbie understood.

"You mean the White Lines?" Gwynfor gave a large smile; he could see that Robbie had spoken with Rune about it.

"The White Line of power was shared by each of the Ruling Council, but like all things in life, each member used their power with a different intention, and so the gifts of Knowledge, Life and Creation were released into those things which each of the members created. The Lord Albanlin was the head of the council and his was the purest form of the power, hence today it is named after him. Alba means white, in the old tongues, and Lin is the ancient word from the first language that means line. His intention was one of study, and at first played no role in this world, it was Eve who gave life to all that Hearne created, yet Hearne restricted that life with death, and so the first circle was formed."

It was simple enough to follow, and Robbie did wonder why it was that all the others couldn't speak in such a simple and clear manner about their gifts, somehow the Old Celt made it so much easier.

"Gwendolyn was Fae, and studied the powers of her people, didn't she?" Gwynfor looked at the sea for a few seconds and smiled.

"My sister was very clever; I sometimes wonder if others have really understood the way she used her gifts." He patted Robbie on the knee. "Eve was also very smart, when the Fae were created it was the powers of the three that made them unique, but it was Eve alone who made the circle of white, when she chose to guide the hidden powers to increase with each passing of the queens of the Fae. I feel you will find that your daughter when she comes will have gifts beyond the powers of my sister." His face suddenly became very serious. "I must warn you though, much of what she learned was stolen by the Dark One, I know others do not take me seriously at times, but heed my words young Robbie, for I still think that little Morgan has learned more than she has shown."

The look on his face was enough to see, he was afraid of what the Dark One could do, Robbie felt a cold chill run down his spine. "You think she can increase her powers, as your sister did?" He gave a serious shake of his head.

"I do... It has given me much to think about, she learned a great deal from

Merlin, and we will never really know how much of my sister she stole before the end. Listen to me young Robbie... You must never underestimate her, when she found a way to enhance her own life, and she brought back that vile soul of her son, I knew she had taken a far greater proportion of my sisters' powers than the others were willing to admit, never forget she is born of a mortal line, and yet she still lives and grows in power." He paused for a second as if thinking then turned and looked Robbie straight in the eyes. "A mortal cannot possess the powers of Fae, and yet she has managed to survive for a thousand years, there are still many questions about her true line of origin, Merlin proved it to contain a great deal of Saxon, but I have often wondered what else has been mixed with it?"

Robbie found himself putting the pieces together quickly, as his mind took careful consideration of what Gwynfor had told him. He was not sure at first, but decided to voice his thoughts. "You think she is Fae, but how could that be possible?" At first, he thought Gwynfor had not heard his question, as the Old Celt stared at the horizon lost in thought. His words at first were quiet, almost as if he was voicing his thoughts to himself.

"Fellowship and Earth...Fae... Fellowship means many things, the sharing of mutual things for example, such as knowledge, harmony and activities." He blinked, and seemed to slip back to the moment, and Robbie, gave a slight smile. "In the early days, many of our people were very innocent, they shared much in the pursuit of harmony, and travelled widely from our roots in the Isle of Erin. I have to say my young Robbie, I have wondered many times how far they travelled, and into which lines they mingled. In the ancient days, Celts and Saxons were the largest numbers of all the tribes of man; I would think there are many Saxons with a line of Fae deep within them, I believe hers to be one of them, because only then could she have taken the power from my sister and defeated her. The others do not agree, but I am convinced she is born of a small part of the White Circle."

It was a sobering thought that stayed in his mind all that night and much of the following day. Robbie knew it made perfect sense, but he also knew that the other members of the council could never admit it was true, because although he had little knowledge of all the workings of the power and magic, he knew to understand, that if Morgan le Fey had the power of the Fae, and had been taught to harness the White Lines, they all knew she was attracting extra power from the Merle and the dark power to corrupt it, which gave her the advantage of wielding a power that no one could predict or gauge with any accuracy. Only time would show the truth of what she had done, and Robbie suddenly understood why Gwynfor had taken the time to explain it. Rune had found the way to discovering the Violet Lines, which was a power no one had seen coming, and if she could create such a strong new line of power for good, it made perfect sense that Morgan le Fey could do the same for a power of darkness. It was a very frightening thought, because none would know the outcome until the final moment when

Rune and the Dark One met for the final confrontation.

Long after Rune fell asleep, he lay in the dark and thought about everything Gwynfor had told him. Tomorrow would be his final day on the small island and then he would have to return to Loxley, Rune was so happy and he decided that he would not mention it for now, he thought it best to enjoy what little time he had alone with her, but when he returned, he knew he would have to talk to someone about it, and the only person he could think of would be Steph.

Robbie gave a long sigh as he stretched in bed. The sunlight washed in through the windows as he felt Rune move by his side. She pulled on the blankets and snuggled into him. "Oh, hold me it's cold." He gave a smile, and turned on his side and pulled her towards him. He gathered the blankets around them, and held her soft warm body next to his. The two days they had been alone together had been bliss, they had laughed and walked and talked. Rune was so happy and filled with fun, apart from his conversation with Gwynfor; he had felt like he was living another life. It was November the third and that evening they would head back to Loxley, and Robbie knew that eventually a battle would begin to save York. "Don't think about it." She giggled as he moved.

"How do you know?" Rune rolled over and her bright blue eyes met his.

"Easy, you tense at the thought of a war." She pulled herself close as she giggled at him. Rune lay with her head on the pillow looking at him. "Hi gorgeous."

"Hey beautiful... happy?"

"Never more so." He leaned forward and kissed the tip of her nose. "What shall we do today?"

She kissed him softly. "I don't care as long as it is just us." She slid up her hand and stroked the long hair from his face. The blue of the sapphire on her ring sparkled and she looked at the fine golden band that rested next to it. Rune moved her hand from side to side and smiled. "This finger has been empty for so long, oh Robbie I still cannot believe you have given me her ring. Do you realise it is over seven hundred years old?"

He took her small delicate hand in his and kissed it. "I have the two greatest treasures of my house together, that is what I am happy about." She gave a grin as her eyes moved across the band.

"Gwendolyn made this; I felt it when you slipped it on to my finger. It was this ring that joined all the lines of our houses, the lines have now become one. Rob we are the start of a new line of power, Iona will be as strong as Opal and Gwendolyn put together. She will be a huge force in this world."

"She will be as beautiful and as powerful as her mother. She will be cute and run wild round the glade with her brother, and they will be loved and adored by us." Rune gave a giggle.

"I am so excited Robbie. I am the power of life, and I have life growing inside me, finally I have become what I was destined to be. I will bring life to the world I love." She pulled closer and slipped her arms round him, and he held her tight and enjoyed her happiness.

It was midday when Rune walked out on the long grassland. Saff stood alone watching the sea her arms folded in against the breeze. Her long auburn hair blew behind her and she narrowed her deep blue eyes, and stared across the rough water. Her sapphire blue cloak flapped round her, she seemed lost in thought as Rune walked up by her side and enjoyed the wildness of the breeze on her face. She looked at Sapphire and smiled, Sapphire seemed to come out of her dream. "Your words at the wedding had a big impact on me Rune." She turned and looked at her. "You have tremendous power, and yet you stood before the man you loved and declared to him you were nothing more than a woman."

Rune smiled and slid her arm around her. "I think at the end of the day my dear cousin we are just women. I have powers, but what would be the point when without Robbie, I would not have the will to live. As powerful as I know I can be, I need his love to sustain me."

Saff looked out at the water. "It is my father's birthday today." She lifted a finger and pointed slightly off north to the east of it. "He lies there on Callanish in the stones." She gave a sigh. "I hardly remember him; I was only a very small child when we were taken." She turned and her deep blue eyes met Rune's. "Do you think it is strange to miss someone you hardly even knew?"

Rune gave a soft smile and lifted her hand to Saff's cheek. "I would say you knew him a little more than that, he was your father... Sapphire he loved you from the moment you came to this realm, and that kind of love leaves a mark you will never forget. You may not have all the pictures in your mind, but you do have the feelings in your heart." She looked at the lost look on her face. "Would you like to visit him today? I will take you there if you wish? I have always wanted to walk in the stones that your mother holds such a high regard for."

Tears welled in Sapphires eyes. "It is your honeymoon; I could not be so selfish as to ask." Rune pulled her close into a hug.

"Well let's just say I offered. Rob and I have walked round this island enough times now. A change of scenery will do both of us good. But we will need a guard." Sapphire wept on Rune's shoulder, and Rune held her close for a moment. "Come on now no more tears, you have to look your best for him."

Saff dried her eyes and nodded as she smiled. "Thank you Runestone. It will mean a great deal to me." Rune stretched up and gave her a soft kiss on the cheek.

"I know it will, and it will be special to Rob and I, just knowing that."

The tall waiting stones stood proud and grey, looming out of the mist as it swirled around them. The eagles screeched high in the sky as they swooped in and out, of the white vapour that lay across the island. The wind came up off the sea and howled over the land singing to the stones of old. They felt her long before she arrived, they knew she was coming and they stood tall awaiting her.

The violet shimmering light bathed the stones that glinted with it. The window opened, and the slender figure dressed in the deepest of violets with her long cloak stepped out, she had one they knew already with her. Rune looked around into the mists as Robbie slid his hand around her.

"Can you feel it Robbie...? Can you feel the strength of the ancient ones here? This place holds powers we still are not sure about." Her eyes flickered with violet as she looked around the ancient site. The wild wind howled, and Robbie felt a presence within the stones that in many ways unnerved him. He felt as if Hearne was beside him, as the same sort of electricity filled the air around him. He looked at the straw coloured grass that lay flattened by the constant force of the wind, and watched as Rune moved through the swirling mist towards the centre of the stone circle. He walked slowly as Keith and Sapphire followed her.

Rune stood in the centre of the circle and raised her hands. Her eyes flickered with violet light and she smiled. "Oh, this place is wonderful." She slowly spun round, and the mist seemed to follow her. It drew in towards her and then spinning around her, it lifted into the air and the wind stopped. Robbie gave a little shudder, the clouds parted and the sun broke through, burning down on to them. Rune beamed at Sapphire.

"Oh, cousin I had no idea this place was so special," she slowly turned round and looked down each of the long avenues of stones, which led out from the central circle. "Moon and death, sun and life, it is all here, stars to guide us and tell of our past present and future, this place is a calendar and temple of the earth, why has Melanie not told me more of this place?"

Rune gave Robbie a huge smile as he walked over to her. "Oh Rob I feel alive and flowing with power beyond my body, here I am one with everything, can you feel the life in the air all around us?" He smiled at the joy she was getting from the place. He watched as Sapphire knelt on the centre of the circle, and placed a small posy of heather, Keith knelt down and helped her force a stick into the ground to wedge the posy and stop it from blowing away.

Sapphire stared at the floor in the centre of the large circle. "Happy birthday Father." Keith placed a hand round her as she tried to force back the tears. Rune watched and was saddened.

"Sapphire, Keith, take my hand." Rune stretched out her hands and both of them looked nervous as she smiled at them. They stood together and walked to the outer edge of the circle of stones. "You too Rob." Rune lined them together, and made them join hands. "Stay here till I say you can move." She smiled sweetly as Robbie gave her a what are you up to sort of look. Rune stood once again at the very centre of the circle and began to speak in a language no one understood.

Robbie looked round as the moon appeared in the sky and slipped towards the sun.

The light faded as Rune's eyes intensified with violet, the sun was now slowly being eclipsed as the moon passed over, and Rune spoke words rapidly as the violet began to flow out of her eyes. She leaned her head back, as her arms stretched back as far as she could move them, and she spoke to the sun and the moon as they met.

"I am light, and my father is the darkness, I am life and my father is the creator of all and the bringer of death, hear me and obey me, for I am the guardian of the white lines and white circle. See me as you look together, for I am here in the green circle of life and I command you bring forth what I seek in your time together. Hear me and obey me for I am the Runestone and the queen of all stones in this land. It is on me that the truth shall be written, and through me the truth shall be understood. Share your time together and bring forth what I seek one last time."

Robbie jumped as violet lightning struck the stones, and a wall of violet light exploded out of the earth. A circle of white light that flickered with violet flashes surrounded the whole circle. The air grew still as the last rays of the sun faded and darkness fell. Rune glowed in a circle of violet light. "Sapphire come to me we have only the time until the sun appears... Sapphire he is here, come to your father."

Robbie looked in complete disbelief as the tall figure of a knight stepped out from one of the stones, Sapphire burst into tears as she ran across the circle, and into his outstretched arms. The mighty figure of Tor, Lord of Callanish, gently pulled his daughter close to him. Rune closed her eyes.

"Melanie hear me, Jasper hear me, for I am Runestone centre of your circle. Join me now for you have a guest of high honour."

Two violet figures grew out of the earth as Rune focused her powers, Robbie watched as Mel, and Jaz ran to Tor, and he embraced them with the weeping Sapphire. Jaz looked over to Rune and she needed no words. Rune gave him a smile and nodded to him. "I cannot give you long; I can only hold the moon for a short time, for I am not of that line." The violet light flowed out of her eyes and into the air. Keith was on his knees as he watched unable to comprehend the power of Rune. Robbie crouched by his side and patted him on the back. He understood the surprise as pictures of Kirklees Priory, and his first encounters with the power of her line came to mind.

"She is quite a girl, isn't she?" Keith looked lost for words as Robbie chuckled.

"Robbie that is Tor, a knight of the round table? Your wife just brought him back to life and she is holding the moon across the sun." Robbie gave a chuckle at the look of surprise mixed with fear on Keith's face.

"I will warn you now." Keith's head moved slowly round to his.

"What?" His face was pale and he looked like he had just seen a ghost, which technically he had.

"Keith my friend… never ever play her at chess." Robbie started to laugh, as Keith gave a slight smile, his face changed and he began to chuckle.

"How can you be so calm about all this Robbie?"

Robbie smiled. "I know her… and I love her Keith. Look what she has just done, so that Saff can have one good memory of her father. That is the true power of my Runestone."

Keith watched as Sapphire embraced her father and mother at the same time in her memory. He smiled at the happiness on her face, Rune stood still and the light flowed out of her, and a small beam of light fell to the earth.

"Hurry my children, our time is leaving." Melanie gave Tor a hug and kissed him, he pulled Jasper into a heavy embrace, and Robbie saw for the first time how alike he was to his father. Tor held his daughter close and whispered words of love to her. They stepped back as he started to fade, and the light of the day grew stronger. Robbie looked up as the moon slid away from the sun and the light streamed down to the stones, Melanie and Jasper gave Rune a hug and they sank into the ground. The circle of light dropped back to the earth, and the light in Rune's eyes faded to normal. She looked across at him and her bright blue eyes twinkled, Sapphire pulled her into a hug; tears still ran from her eyes.

"Oh thank you Rune, you have no idea how much that has meant to me." Rune held her tight and she hugged her.

"Rest your heart cousin, for now you have the memory of a father who loves you." Robbie walked with a very quiet Keith over to Rune, Saff slipped into Keith's arms, and Rune came forward smiling. He pulled her close.

"You did a nice thing Runestone."

"She once saved your life, I owed her that." Robbie nodded and rested his head on hers.

"I love you, you know that?" Rune's eyes twinkled up at him.

"Take me back and prove it." She gave a soft giggle as he pulled her into his arms and looked at the stones standing high in the air like guards on watch. Robbie knew they had been here for thousands of years, he could not imagine what they had seen in their span of time, they had felt power from endless ages, and he knew they would stand here alone for another thousand life times. This was something even the line of Knox could not destroy.

The four of them walked around the impressive site of the Callanish stones as Saff laughed and giggled, as she talked of her early life with Jaz and her mum in the stones. They visited the small house where they had lived, and watched from the gate as the waves crashed up on the rocks. By late afternoon Rune opened her window and they stepped back on to the island of Iona. Saff hugged Rune and Robbie, and both of them saw a happiness in her they had never seen before.

Sunset on Iona was glorious. Gwinne watched as the two figures stood arm in arm, were silhouetted as the sun glowing in deep red slipped into the sea. They watched together and spoke quietly to each other; both of them knew their time of peace was over. War loomed over York, and Robbie had to return now to take command of the operation.

Rune felt happy, she had spent the last three days completely alone with him, and they had laughed, talked and planned a future together as they had lay in bed alone in their quiet secluded room.

A deeper closeness had grown between them, and now she felt as if they truly were one. Gwinne smiled to see the two very relaxed and happy people as they walked hand in hand up the long grassy slope towards her. Rune squealed as Robbie pinched her from behind and Gwinne laughed aloud, as she ran giggling and he chased her. Rune ran right into Gwinne's arms. "Oh I am so happy, thanks for letting us stay here with you."

"Runestone this is the Isle of your daughter; you have a place of high honour here."

"Come back with us Gwinne, come and see Loxley and Scarlet. She yearns to see you, and mum would love to see you again. Come back for a few days and live in my house with me, I would love you to."

Gwinne laughed. "Rune I would love to, but there is still much to do, and Gwynfor will need to be cared for." Rune pulled back and smiled.

"Do not try to fool me Gwinne Harmony, Gwynfor has Isolde and Filomena to care for him, they do not spend all of their time in my trees."

Gwinne looked surprised. "You know of them?

"I am the lady of the woods; do you not think I cannot sense life when it enters my realm? Of course, I know. We are honoured that Gwynfor feels he should protect us, but they can take a few days off and give you some time with your family. You spend too much time alone thinking of Rayne. You need your sisters, if only for a short time."

Gwinne smiled at Rune. "Your powers are strong My Lady of the Woods, you can see what others cannot." She gave her a loving smile. "Alright give me an hour and I will return with you for a few days,... I have missed Steph and Scarlet."

Rune giggled and pulled her into a huge hug. "Oh you will love Loxley, and the Mere, oh Gwinne the mere is so beautiful." Her eyes danced as she released Gwinne, and Robbie slipped her back into his arms and held her close.

Rowan sat on the steps of the house and looked down at the mere, the sun had fallen and the moon painted its weak silvery lines across the breeze kissed surface of the water. "He is late."

Jade giggled with Jett by the fire. "Sweetheart it's his honeymoon, let him enjoy it, they have only had a few days, God we were in bed longer than that on ours." Jett winked and Jade chuckled. Rafe walked down from the kitchen to the doors. He stepped on to the top of the steps and passed a hot cup down to Rowan. Rowan's slate grey eyes watched for any sign as he lifted the cup to his lips.

There was a faint flicker of light, and then the window appeared right in front of the gates. Crystal and Amethyst appeared first laughing, followed by Keith and Saff. Rune came through giggling with Robbie and Gwinne followed.

Rune turned to the house and showed Gwinne, as the window behind them disappeared. "Welcome to our home of Robbie's Mere."

Gwinne looked round in the moonlight. "Oh Rune this is so beautiful."

"AUNTIE GWINNE!" Jade and Jett raced past Rowan knocking him sideways, as the girls bounded down the path to the gate and into Gwinne's arms. Gwinne smiled with delight at the welcome of the two excited girls as they hugged her.

"Oh, my little nieces, look how much you have grown." Rune stepped back as the trouble twins took over, and excitedly picked up her bags and talked non-stop all the way into the house and up the stairs. Gwinne was carried along smiling as the girls told her all about Loxley and the house and Robbie's Mere.

Rune watched happily as Rowan raised his mug in salute. Robbie opened the gate and swept Rune up in the air, she squealed as he carried her up the path and into the house. Crystal and Amethyst followed along laughing. Rowan looked down at Keith.

"They were safe at all times?" Keith nodded.

"We did our job, but Iona is safe. Glad you did not make me sit in the bedroom, I felt like a right gooseberry, you know Rowan some things are sacred, he is my lord and I respect him. He is also a man and you forgot that." Keith stomped into the house and Rowan gave a smile as Saff came up the steps.

"I am sorry, but we cannot risk him or Rune ever." Saff nodded

"We kept them in sight at all times Rowan, Keith felt he was prying in on something deeply personal; I understand why you sent him. You knew he would keep a respectful distance, because you know how much he respects Robbie, I will explain it to him."

"Keith is a good person Sapphire, I trust his judgement, and yes I knew him more than most would have been discreet, but I also knew he had the best skills at distance. I knew they were safe at all times with Keith on guard, he has the eyes of a hawk, and it is a gift."

Sapphire smiled. "You sound like Robbie at times Rowan." He gave a big smile and saluted her with his mug.

"That my good Lady Sapphire is a compliment I will accept with honour."

Sapphire walked past and into the house, she followed Keith into the kitchen and sat down with him. Rafe stood smiling at Rowan.

It was nice to be home and Robbie sat on the stairs with Rune at his side as everyone gathered in the living room. The fire roared in the hearth, and round the room happy voices chattered, Scarlet and Steph had arrived, and it was a happy moment as the three sisters reunited.

Everyone sat and listened, as Jade told her story of the graveyard and Harry, Gwinne screamed with laughter as Jade reach the part where her head disappeared, and poor old Harry had a break down, and crawled under the bushes as the green evils watched him. Rune giggled beside him, as Gwinne wiped her eyes, it was a very happy end to the days of rest, and as the night progressed and their guests all pulled on their cloaks; Robbie felt tired and wanted nothing more than to curl around Rune and sleep.

He lay back in his familiar bed and she slipped under the covers, her warm body curled round as he closed his eyes and drifted. The sounds of the sea on the silver beaches lapped through his mind and he floated off into sleep.

CHAPTER TWENTY THREE

A TRUE HERO

Ox gave the signal, and Harry and Blades came out of the trees with Woody and Todd. They each carried a large pack on their back, as they crossed the wide stretch of dark earth to the grate in the wall. They flattened up against the wall and slid down the packs. Ox opened the grate and Blades shot in like a cat, Todd followed. She now knew the tunnel better than any, and she flew up to the grate on the other side of the wall with ease. Blades watched through the bars at the top, waiting for the signal.

Harry and Blades had volunteered for the duty to help run supplies into Lee. Blades especially wanted to do it as her first encounter with the city had affected her. Seeing how people had been forced to live had made her mad and so when the chance came to help, she was the first to ask for the job. Harry could not let his daughter go alone and he too stepped forward and took her hand.

Harry and Ox seemed to hit it off, and they formed a good working partnership. Todd was the youngest and soon warmed to Blades, as he loved the weapons she carried. Todd was a walking arsenal, and so it had not been long before he offered her advice on her weaponry. Blades had arrived a few nights later to find Todd had made her a new harness. He was a skilled leather worker, and he fitted the harness to her and showed her how the new one worked better. Her crossed swords were a little higher, and she found she could pull them a lot faster. Instead of one crossbow, she now had two new redesigned ones. They were made from the last of some scrap alloy he had left, and they were lightweight, so she had better balance when using her swords.

He loved the name Blades, and was inspired to fit some small spring loaded catches to her crossbows; he stood back and told her to slide her thumb over them and squeeze them. Blades gasped with delight as two five-inch blades shot out of the end of the crossbows. The crossbows were attached to a small spring loaded chain, as he had seen her drop her crossbow when she pulled her long blades.

She was thrilled when she dropped them, and the chain pulled them back to their holsters, as her two long shiny blades rose into the air. He was scruffy and a little on the quiet side, and yet with tools he could fashion anything. Todd and

Blades now found common ground, and they formed a good working partnership. The following night Blades had appeared with a spare Samurai sword; Todd was overwhelmed as she handed it to him. It was a mighty gift and he was knocked out as she smiled at his delight.

Todd tapped her on the shoulder, as he saw Lee slip out of the shadows. Lee gave the all clear and as a fast as a cat she shot out across the street and took cover. Blades handed the first sack of violet arrows to Meg and winked. Todd raced across the street with a long bundle of bows. Blades looked up at Lee. "A gift from Robbie, they are rowan wood and the best you can use." She shot back across the square, dodging the lights, and clambered back into the hole in the wall, where Harry heaved a bag up to her. Todd signalled from the alley across the road, and they both ran crossing in the middle, as he jumped in through the hole and she headed into the alleyway.

Blades dropped the sack of arrows on the floor and turned to watch. A guard moved on the wall high above the street. Blades signalled to Todd to wait, they melted into the shadows, the guard walked slowly on, and she leaned forward as she watched him disappear high above her. She leaned into the light and nodded, the grate opened and Todd flew across the street, Harry pulled the grate to, as Blades filled in Lee on the next plan of action. She pulled a roll of papers out of her tunic and handed them to him.

"These are posters, Robbie wants them putting up wherever the soldiers go. They are encouraging the young ones to desert. Robbie has promised them protection if they run away from the army when they are let out." Lee nodded.

"Does he think it will work?" Blades Shrugged.

"If it does, it will be less for us to deal with, I suppose it is worth a try." Harry was getting impatient, he did not like her being in the city too long, and he gave a soft whistle. "I got to go Lee, take care; Rune is back tonight so you will all see her soon. Give our best to the father, and keep smiling Meg."

Blades winked, and with Todd, she sped back to the wall, Harry swung open the grate and Ox pulled his legs so he shot down the tunnel. Blades jumped in followed by Todd and they both slid down and out of the city. Hoods up and cloaks unrolled they slipped quietly across the open space unseen by human eyes and back into the trees.

Woody tripped and fell head first over a root into the nettles; he gave a squeal as they stung. Ox snatched a large handful of Dock out of the floor and shook his head; he pushed them into Woody's hand as he resurfaced a look of pain on his face.

A permanent window now ran from the gate behind Robbie's house to the barn at Alfie's used by the bandits. Rune had thought it was a better idea as it allowed fast passage from the secret gate behind Robbie's Mere to the woodland three miles south of the black city. Like her table, there was a protection placed on it, and no one who meant harm to Loxley could pass through it. Harry and Blades now made regular trips out, and on one or two occasions, Mel and Una had ventured out with them.

The passageway as it was known, was also a good way for the bandits to sneak into Loxley woods and relax, they would sit at Badgers Bank knowing they were miles from their enemies and rest up for a while. They had become very valuable to Loxley, as they had already blown up forty convoys of supplies for the army of Knox.

Harry kept Fuse up to date on the bandits; Rune kept him up to date on the rebels in the city, and Robbie now had a chance to fine tune the operation to maximum effect. Steph had produced an abundance of black hooded cloaks and now all the rebels of the city had the right clothes to fight in at night.

Every night in the city, the troops called a curfew and clamped everything down, yet each night they were struck and more soldiers died. Mac was going insane as he tried everything to curtail the activity of the rebels, the problem was becoming so bad now that Mordred ordered him to spend all of his time on sorting it out. More explosions and violet tipped arrows killed guards, and they were now so worried that they volunteered for the front line, which was looking a safer duty by the day.

Lee's reports came back with Rune and Robbie smiled. He had only been back in Loxley for two days, but in a short space of time, he could see that stealth was the best weapon he had. The greatest thing was it was working; morale amongst the troops in the black city was visibly weak. A feeling of hope rose amongst those who toiled in the city, and rumour fuelled those few moments out of earshot of the guards, when the workers could talk. The biggest was that the hooded man now lived in the city, and would free them all from the oppression of Mordred and Mac.

The small church in the centre of the sprawling mass of the city was the centre of the rebellion, each night the woodsmen gathered in secret, armed themselves, and then headed out into the darkness. It was a shining symbol of hope, and yet the Farther was not sure for how much longer it could continue.

Lee sat and leaned over the table, he breathed with difficulty as he coughed hard, Father Warren watched him shudder and wretch. "You should not be here Lee, you are ill... Look at you, how can you expect to go on like this?" He looked at the old woodsman with concern in his eyes. Lee raised a hand.

"Father please... I am an old man; there is no cure for age and a hard life. What ails me is death is waiting in the shadows." He looked up and smiled at the priest. "I stood at the side of old Jake Lox and I built his town with him. We were not like Mason Knox, we used no magic or machines, we used our bare hands and our muscle. I have lived a life worth living and there are few who will know the love and friendship I have known. I will not last this war Father, you know it and I know it." Lee heaved a huge cough, and gripped the edge of the table in spasms. Father Warren poured him a glass of water and handed it to him, Lee drunk quickly as he gasped for air.

"Please Lee let me take you to a carer who could give you something to help."

Lee gave one huge cough and put down the cup. "Father there is no point, what I have has no cure, it didn't in the days of old modern man, so I am sure as hell there is no cure now." He stood up from the chair and picked up his cloak. "I will die as I have lived, a fighter, fighting for something I believe in. I am the last of the old breed of Loxley; there will be few old bulls like Jake and me, in the new world, I will die as I have always wanted to." He gave a wink to the father. "In the service of my lord."

He threw his cloak over his shoulder and walked to the stairs. Lee came up into the church and walked down the aisle to the altar, he looked up at the large golden cross with the figure of Christ and he laughed. "Sorry pal you cannot have me, my bones are Hearne's."

He coughed as he turned to walk to the side door, what he needed was some air. The church doors at the bottom burst open and light flooded into the church, the pale face of Meg ran into the bottom of the church with tears in her eyes. "Oh Lee, please we need help."

He saw the fear and heard the pain in her voice; he whipped round and ran to her. "Meg love, what the hell has happened?" She collapsed into his arms, as Father Warren came round by the main door at the bottom of the church.

Meg sobbed. "It's the market place, they have gathered everyone together who was there, and pulled every third person out of the line. My mum and dad are there." Meg looked up with bright green tear filled eyes. "They have given one hour to hand over the leader of the rebels or they will kill everyone." Meg wailed into Lee's arms.

Father Warren looked down in utter disbelief. "They cannot do that it is barbaric." Lee lifted Meg and pushed her on to the Father as she sobbed.

"Really father... You never read any books on the Nazi's." Lee turned and walked back to the end of the church, and made his way downstairs to his room. He opened his pack and pulled a long green cloak of Loxley out. "No more pissing about Lee, it's time to show these bastards who is boss." He swung the cloak round his shoulders and lifted his bow and quiver.

Robbie walked down the stairs fastening his belt as Rune swept past him; he looked at Rowan and Jade. "Rune what is it?" She had already gone down the steps to the table. Jade looked at Rowan.

"See what I mean it tells you to get there fast." Robbie walked round to the steps and followed Rune down. Rowan and Jade came behind.

Rune sat in her seat; her eyes were flowing with purple light as pictures appeared in front of her. Robbie watched Mac as he looked down from the top of the wall and people were dragged out of the lines and thrown on the floor. Rune looked up. "Sound."

The room filled with the terrified screams of the city folk, as they stared at their relatives pinned to the floor with a soldier above them brandishing a sword. The crowds were pushed back by the soldiers as they jostled forward weeping, and trying to see if their loved ones were in those chosen to die.

Mac walked with a cocky arrogant stride across the top of the wall, he turned and looked down at the screaming masses, in the large square before the market gates and the market stalls. He held up a microphone and his voice bellowed loud into the crowd. "SILENCE!"

Everyone in the market square looked up at the figure of fear. Mac glared down in his temper at the frightened masses, he felt a wave of happiness at the fear he saw in their eyes. "I have had enough of your ingratitude. We feed and clothe you; we give you jobs and pay, AND HOW DO YOU REPAY US?" His face turned red with anger. "You shoot bombs at us, and creep around in the night shooting my soldiers; you call yourself the rebellion and put up posters telling my men to desert." He waved a piece of paper high above his head. "IT WILL STOP NOW."

Robbie looked across at Jade. "Call all the Specialists." Her eyes glowed green as Robbie looked back to the pictures of Mac on the top of the wall. Mac paced as he looked with contempt at the people below him, he raised the microphone. "You will surrender your so called rebellion leaders to me here within one hour, or all of your citizens chosen here will die. Is that clear?"

Wails of fear for the lives of those contained by the soldiers, rose into the air, as the soldiers began to beat and push back the crowd, leaving those chosen to be dragged to their feet and tied to posts of the market stalls. Mac felt the power hanging in the air as he watched the scene of terror and smiled.

"RUNE we are leaving come on." Robbie turned and flew up the stairs; Rune was up in a flash and ran behind him.

"Robbie what are we going to do, just hold on a moment, we cannot just run into the dark city."

He turned and she saw the fire in his eyes. "They want the leader and they will get one, no innocent will die in my place while my heart pumps blood. Her power only runs to within a foot of that wall; open me a door in front of the grate. You have great power Rune, but in this, you will not stop me."

Rune nodded. "You will not be alone, I know that city like the back of my hand, I have planned every attack with Lee. We go together Robbie, you promised me on my wedding day. No matter what we stay together."

He looked into her bright blue eyes and he nodded. "I promised and I will not break it, stay close by my side." She nodded and waved her hand, out in the glade a window opened and Jett and Rafe came through. Harry Blades Judy and Melanie came next, as the Specialists gathered on the grass. Robbie came down the steps in all green, with his cloak of Loxley flowing behind him, he looked at his team.

"We have big trouble in the black city, there are over a hundred woodsmen about to be put to death, and I aim to bring them out. This will have to be fast, furious and lethal as hell, are you in?"

They all nodded. "Yes Gov." Rune gave a giggle and even Robbie smiled, Harry gave a bigger smile and innocently shrugged.

"Hey man it's like tradition you know, you like need a happening and cosmic name like the rest of us, it kinda boosts our karma man, gives everyone happening vibes. It's like Keith here man, the Wolf man tells me he has the talents of a Hawk, he sees for miles and strikes from distance, that is cosmic and happening, he is the Hawk man now dudes."

"Thanks Harry, at least it's not chicken."

"Whoa dude, I told you chicken is cosmic and totally cool and radical, hey man chicken is sweet."

Robbie gave a chuckle as he turned to Rowan. "Break out the boxed arrows." Rowan gave a smile, and signalled to Fish and Hawk, who gave a huge grin as they ran up the path to get them. The striker arrows were passed quickly round to everyone, as Rune handed them all fuse lighters, Skip winked as he took his off Rune. Everyone dropped the explosive arrows into their quivers; Robbie slipped a second quiver on to his shoulder, he looked at the group.

"We will appear in front of the wall at a grate, it is wide enough for two people but we go in single file, the market is straight ahead. We use the rooftops and shoot anything we see in black with a red raven or dragon on it. These new arrows have a better point they are specials of John's. They will sink into concrete and brick so aim for the middle of your target, don't forget to duck. Jade, Jett, the chains are off, hit them hard and show them the true power of the woodland." The whole group gave a grin, and he turned and walked to the window Rune had opened. Jett beamed as she winked at Blades.

"It's party time girls." Rune clicked her fingers and Robbie walked through.

Mac stared down as he walked slowly across the top of the wall, there was a scream and three guards fell dead from a rooftop, a hooded figure in green rose up from behind the wall and aimed an arrow at Mac.

Mac froze on the spot, as the voice called up. "If one of your men shoots, you fall with me Mac."

The large gathered crowd fell silent and stood still, as they saw the green hooded figure standing on the roof behind them. Eyes were drawn from the hooded figure to the group in black above the gates, where Mac stood looking a little nervous.

Mac waved a hand. "Hold your fire." He stared with fear at the bowman.

"What's on your mind Loxley?" Lee's eyes burned with glee under his hood, Mac thought he was Robbie and he was afraid.

"Let them go, this is between you and me Mac." He pulled harder on the bowstring; the light glinted off the sharp steel point of the arrow.

The officer stood behind Mac whispered. "Do not listen to him sir, no long bow can make that shot, he is too far away, I have men coming behind him. Keep hold of the prisoners, he will not live long enough to see them reach their homes."

Mac peered down at the lonesome figure. "Where are the rest of his men, he is never alone? That Rowan for one thing is always by his side."

The officer moved closer to Mac. "Give the order to shoot and step back, you will be protected."

Mac gave a smile. "Tell me Loxley, what makes you think your arrow will reach me? No bowman is that good."

Lee felt his chest tighten as he pulled on the string. "You were not in Loxley long enough to see what we can do Mac, have no worry this one carries your name, now release everyone, I am growing tired of your dull conversation." He gave a small cough and swallowed hard.

Mac raised his arm as if about to give the order, he twisted his arm and pointed to Lee as all his guards aimed at him. "KILL HIM!"

Mac stepped back as Lee released his arrow, the officer stepped in front of Mac and pushed him to the wall. Mac watched as the officer's eyes widened, he fell to his knees with the violet tipped arrow sticking out of his back.

As he slumped, he saw the hooded figure step back as arrows pierced him in ten different places, Meg screamed as she ran along the roof to Lee, a mighty explosion went off behind her, and Mac froze with fear as he saw high on the tallest roof two figures both aiming at him, Robbie released first, and then Rune followed.

Behind the two figures fixed in his gaze, rubble and stone lifted into the air, as the sky flashed white and blue. The roar of the explosions exploded in his ears, as the arrows came thundering towards him.

His eyes opened wider, as the scream formed in his throat, his eyes fixed on the bright eyes of Robbie as they stared at him with hate. The scream did not come, he had no time to move, he felt the burning pain in his throat and the liquid flow into his mouth. The second arrow hit and he felt it shudder into his chest. Mac felt weakness flow into him as he stared at the only figure not wearing a hood. Robbie watched as Mac slid to the floor on his knees.

Mac heard the gargle in his throat as he tried to raise a hand to the woman stood below Robbie and Rune. She stood with a bow raised, and a long holly pole resting under her arm, and her violet eyes stared across as he struggled and gasped for one word. He coughed as the blood splattered out of his mouth. "Mother." Mac fell forward on to the rampart as flames burst up all over the city.

Robbie dropped quickly down and ran across the rooftop, he leapt across the gap and came to a sliding halt, dropping to his knees, he looked down as Meg cried over Lee; Robbie eased her back and looked into the eyes of Lee Sherman. Lee gave a smile. "My Lord."

Robbie shook his head. "Why Lee, why do something so dangerous, I was coming you must have known I would not leave you?" Tears formed in his eyes as he looked at the last of his grandfather's generation.

Lee raised a hand and Robbie took it, he coughed and spluttered. Robbie gave it a squeeze as Lee fought against the pain to talk. "I am proud to have served... Three generations of true men... I will sit with Jake... now and rest."

Robbie smiled. "I was proud to know a true man of Loxley Lee Sherman, you were true to your word and your lord, but you were true to me my friend. Go and rest with my grandfather, and be with good company for eternity." He smiled as his eyes flickered. Robbie lowered his head as Lee Sherman died, and Rune came to his side and lifted him gently up.

"Rob we must move fast, leave him for now, we will take him back and give him a true send off fit for a royal man of Loxley."

Robbie stood up and wiped his eyes. "Stay with him Meg, I want to travel back with him." Robbie viewed the market where Hawk and Saff were herding all of the people out down the street to the blown up gates.

On the roof at his right Crystal and Maddy fired shots at the walls, large areas of ice and fire swept across taking out the high guards. Mel and Una now fired explosive arrows over the walls. Rowan moved with precision alongside Jade as they singled out and took out guards hiding and shooting at the group of sword fighters who crossed the market square with a deadly rage.

Harry and Jett seemed to fight with an aggression far exceeding their usual level; Jett's screams, could be heard high above the explosions, as she thundered into the mass of terrified soldiers. Her shining blades rose high into the air and glinted as the sun caught it, then it flashed round with huge speed. Her screams were deafening and the power of her blade lifted soldiers off their feet and into the air, as she violently cut through them.

Blades spun with her swords flashing like lightening, her temper flared through her bright blue eyes, and all before her fled in horror. She squealed and grunted as she cut a path through the heavy line of terrified troops, who tried simply to block her yet failed and died before her.

Flash yelled at the men as she swirled with elegance and her pole was almost invisible, a circle piled up around her as the soldiers fell. Their bones were battered and broken, never had the Specialists fought with such aggression and force, as they did in the market square at that moment. Even Skip fought with a force unknown as the large numbers of soldiers hesitated with fear. Bear screamed with rage as his axe sliced through the heads of those in front of him, followed by his gleaming golden sword. He swung and sheared a path through the lines; his force and power were overwhelming as he left a trail of screaming wounded and severed limbs.

Robbie looked back as he loaded an arrow and lit the fuse. "Let's wreak havoc." He fired into the factories as he walked back and loaded his bow; Rune stayed by his side never more than a foot away as Robbie fired and took stock of the situation. The market was almost clear of the citizens, and littered with hundreds of the dead as his swords team devastated the army of the black city.

Robbie signalled a tactical withdrawal using explosive arrows. Under the cover of the bows, the group moved fast across the market and clambered back up the walls on to the rooftops. Sheathing their swords, they loaded their bows, and looked to their leader as he stood on the edge of the wall with Rune by his side and his hood up. The fuse burned as Robbie lifted his bow and began the final stage of the devastation, the Specialists lifted their bows behind him and explosives rained into, and down from the sky.

Smoke blew across the city as most of it burned, the factories of the Knox industry erupted into flames, as more arrows shot high into the air, the group moved across the rooftops guarding the citizens as they moved to the gates. All along the road black hooded figures appeared with bows and shot at the guards, Robbie had over a hundred black hooded figures under his control as he walked slowly back to the gates.

He looked down from the roof and into the eyes of Malcolm. "Take your people into the trees, we will meet you three miles south by an old farm. We will give you the time you need." Malcolm nodded as he saw Meg beside Rune, she held Lee's bow and she fired at the guards as they came through the top gates by the market and moved slowly down towards them.

The workers of the black city fled through the gates and ran down the long road to where Ox stood proud with his men to shepherd them into the woods and away to safety. Todd, and Woody, with his long crooked staff, led them deep into the trees. They turned to head for Alfie's place, where the gateway to the wood of Loxley was open and waiting ready for more refugees to enter the realm of Loxley.

Maddy pulled a long arrow out of her quiver and smiled as she slipped it into her Bow. "This one is for Rose and Scotland." Rune gave a smile as Maddy heaved back on the string, and the arrow rocketed off her long white bow. Rune watched as it hit the wall just above the large gates to the military barracks. There was an almighty explosion and fire sprayed into the air, it burned with the heat of the sun, and Rune covered her eyes, Maddy turned to Crystal. "Put a real big one in the centre and everyone else load up it's show time." She smiled as Robbie winked at her.

The whole group formed a long line across four lines of buildings, they all slipped explosive arrows into their strings, Maddy turned to Robbie and winked, he raised his bow. "Can I give the order Gov? Just this once?" Robbie winked at her.

"For a smile of such love, I will allow you this one." Her face lit up and she gave the most wonderful radiant smile. Maddy turned to Crystal

"Hit it girl." Crystal released the arrow, which shot into the mass of flames and hit the wall, which was now glowing red in the heat. The ice arrow exploded in a blizzard of snow and the wall groaned, as the ice ran rapidly along it quenching the intense heat with speed. The wall fizzed and hissed as the ice expanded; cracks appeared and ran in long jagged lines across the wall.

Maddy raised her arm and yelled on the top of her voice. "GET READY!" The wall fractured as the bows all aimed high. It moved slightly and wobbled. The central section of the massive wall lurched backwards and fell into the barrack compound, soldiers screamed and fled back.

"NOW!" Maddy's arm dropped like a stone, as the huge hundred-foot, wall slipped over into the compound of the barracks. Stone and brick fell like rain and the soldiers covered their heads as they were smashed into the floor by the hundreds and buried under the falling rubble. A huge cloud of dust chased those who had managed to get clear, and they coughed and sputtered unaware of what was to come.

Twenty six fizzing arrows shot into the air in a straight line, they cleared the rubble and rained down on the fleeing dust hidden soldiers. Robbie's was deep inside the compound with Rune's and Rowan's not far behind. It was like a chain reaction as explosion after explosion lit up the sky, Robbie gave the signal and the Specialists withdrew, there was no one left to see them leave the rooftops. He watched smiling as the black palace came into view in the distance. He knew Mordred was watching with anger rising inside him, he was satisfied.

With Rune and Meg at his side, he lifted Lee off the floor as explosions went off behind him, he smiled a sad smile at Meg. "Let's take him home where he belongs, you are one of us now, and you have already worked well with the best that Loxley had, come on Meg, follow me." Rune gave her a smile as they turned, and ran behind the others towards the grate and the way home. The floor shook as they slid down the tunnel and out onto the cleared area. Holding Lee close, Robbie came out of the hole and into Rune's window, all of them returned to the glade in Loxley. Robbie came through with Lee Sherman on his shoulder; he gently laid him on the grass and undid his cloak.

Robbie wrapped Lee in his own Loxley crested cloak as Hawk sat beside him with tears in his eyes. Robbie looked up at the others. "This man is the mould that we all strive to fit into, he will have high honour here. He has served this community for three generations; I will have his name spoken with honour on the lips of everyone." He looked at Fish and Rafe. "Go with Harry and Blades, and lead the people of the city to the main gates." They nodded and sped off into the trees.

Robbie lifted Lee and carried him to the cart very gently, he placed him down and he turned to Sapphire. "Take Keith and Lee to my father, tell him I want him to be placed in a box worthy of my grandfather, he will know what to do."

Sapphire nodded and he helped her up on to the cart, Rowan helped Keith, and slowly the cart drew away into the trees. Robbie turned and looked at his Specialists.

"That was wonderful work my friends, thank you, all of you have served Loxley well. The people of the black city are free of the grip of the dark hand. I am proud of all of you." They all smiled and nodded, Robbie looked at Meg. "We have a new recruit, this is Meg, she is one of us, treat her well. I am told she has shown extraordinary courage in our cause." Meg looked embarrassed and quickly raised a hand.

"Hi." Everyone smiled and nodded to her; Rune gave a smile and put her arm round her.

"Well Meg, if you intend to stay around with us, I think the colour green would be better than your grey. Come on in the house and we shall see what we have, you are about my size I think." Jade turned and followed and Rowan wiped the dirt off his face as he came up to Robbie's side. Robbie patted his back as the group gathered round.

"They will regroup and come fast; we must be on our guard now. We are back together again after a break, so I want all of you to go home pack your kit and tool up, first thing in the morning we leave to defend York. Mordred has had two tastes of the Specialists and he has lost one of his leaders, as of tomorrow we will show him the true measure of Loxley... Bear, Rowan, hang around will you, the rest of you, get a good night's sleep and be here by ten in the morning, it's going to be a wild time on the moors."

Jett beamed. "Yeah Robbie." She punched the air as everyone laughed, and broke apart and began to make their way across the glade to the trees. Una stood silent and Robbie sent Bear and Rowan into the house.

Robbie looked into her bright violet eyes. "I am sorry Una; I know he was your son. I had to act he would have taken any of them out if he could have."

Una took his hands in hers; two tears ran from her eyes. "I had my bow and was ready to fire; you and Rune are much quicker... He was my son, but he left me a long time ago. I wanted to thank you for acting swiftly, I am glad in the end it came from the lord he betrayed."

Robbie pulled her close and held her tight. "You are my family Una, Rune and I love you dearly, you are not without kin who care for you." Una pulled her arms round Robbie as she wept. Rune watched from the window above as she wiped her own eyes.

"I love you and Rune as my own Robbie; I have had such joy around here."

Robbie leaned back as she sniffled, and he looked into the violet eyes that held such love and devotion. "I mean what I say Una, you have been there for Rune and for me, you are family and loved dearly." She nodded.

"Thanks Robbie." She kissed his cheek, turned and picked up her bow and long holly staff. Ruby and Maddy stood smiling in the trees, and Robbie watched as she ran to them, Maddy put her arm round her and she walked into the trees and out of the glade.

Rune walked into the bedroom where Jade giggled as Meg turned around in front of the mirror, she had tight brown pants and long black leather boots, her blouse was emerald green and her long waistcoat olive green. Jade slid a belt of brown suede round her with a long silver sword and a small dagger on it. Meg looked at herself in the full-length mirror and smiled. "I can't believe I am here with the hooded man's family, look at me?"

Rune gave her a beaming smile. "You are not ready yet." She turned Meg to look at herself in the mirror, as she pulled the green hooded cloak on to her shoulders; Meg smiled as she lifted her hand and touched the Loxley coat of arms. Rune gave her a smile; she remembered her first time in her cloak. Jade lifted the hood up over her head and Meg gave a giggle. Rune pushed a Talisman into her hand with a violet on it. Meg's eyes seemed to sparkle with her tears as Jade gave her a huge smile.

"Welcome to the Specialists of Loxley my hooded friend." Her bright green eyes shone out from under her hood. Meg turned and threw her arms round Rune.

"Oh My Lady I have no words to thank you, you have made all my dreams come true."

Rune gave a smile as she looked down at Meg. "You are one of us now, I am Rune and this is Pebbles. We shall have to get Harry to find you your nick name, and then you will truly be a Specialist in the service of Loxley."

Robbie watched as Una disappeared under the leaves and he turned back towards the house. He slowly walked up to the small white gate and into the garden. Rowan smiled with Bear as he came up the steps. "Well my friends, we have a busy night of planning ahead of us, York has need of us and we cannot idle a moment longer than we need to. I fear our old friend in the black palace will be somewhat upset and he will want to even the balance, let's look at more ways to upset him." Robbie gave a bright smile as he entered through the glass doors and Rowan and Bear stepped in behind him.

CHAPTER TWENTY FOUR

THE FIRST DAYS OF WINTER

Robbie watched across the moors as the pictures of the funeral of Lee Sherman wandered through his mind. He had been given the full honours of a true man of Loxley and Robbie had been touched by the amount of people who had turned out to honour him. Without request people had thrown flowers into the road of the oncoming coach as a tribute to a loyal man. Robbie had never before witnessed such a mark of respect and it had moved him very deeply.

Megan had been distraught; Lee was very much a true hero and her role model, as she had fought side by side with him. She had taken the lead with the rest of the black city resistance and helped carry their fallen symbol of the hooded world from the cart to the open grave. Malcolm Prosper had spoken fine words, and stepped back as Robert Lox spoke for a family that Lee had shown tremendous loyalty to. No man had ever been honoured as highly. Robbie had been proud to have known him, and he found comfort in knowing that the greatest friend of his grandfather now sat beside him once again.

He enjoyed the feeling of knowing that maybe one day in the other realm he would sit beside Rowan and Bear, and enjoy eternity knowing that Harry or Jade would be with him. Knowing that in a funny way, all the Specialists would remain with their love in the other realm took away some of the pain and bitterness he had felt at losing Eric or Hog and Martin. Up on the cold bleak moor it was a comforting thought.

General Martin Jarrod had been in the city less than one hour from his long journey from Scotland, where he viewed the devastation of the night before from the attack of the Specialists of Loxley. He knew only too well the fear and panic that the hooded man could instill into young soldiers, he had viewed it himself recently at Dunnottar. He looked down from the high wall as the endless lines of the dead were laid out in long rows on the green grass. The huge crumbled wall still smoked, as the bricks were lifted and the remains of those crushed were lifted out to be counted. Over ten thousand had lost their lives during the time of the violet rebellion in the black city; it had been a hard lesson for the soldiers of the black city to learn.

Mordred had raged all night, and now five of his staff were laid out on the floor with the rest of the dead, he had screamed and bellowed across the war room and demanded and instant response. There was hardly enough time to place his bag on his bunk before General Jarrod, found himself back on a horse and accompanied by his old friend and colleague General Franklin, was out on the wild moors with his telescope scanning the area to look for the best ways to attack.

The wild wind was cold and bit hard at the face as they sat sheltered, as best they could in the trees. Martin Jarrod peered down the scope at the open land. "This is not a good place to fight my friend; it is open without much cover. A bowman of skill, which let's face it, is what we will face, could wipe out many men before we get within striking distance."

Franklin nodded as he shielded his eyes from the wind. "I have told the dark lord this; he just refuses to accept my opinions, and wants us to throw everyman we have got across the moor."

General Jarrod moved slowly along the horizon with his scope stopping occasionally to look at the lay of the land. In his mind he was already drawing up his picture of attack. "We could do as he asks, but if his goal is to wipe out York and then follow on through to Loxley, then we must hold our plans. Winter on this moor will kill more of our men than the hooded man will. Frost and bow will take at least a third of the force before we reach York. I cannot see a man as smart as Loxley not defending York; he knows that we will attack it."

"You think Loxley is smart, I heard he is just another uneducated woodsman." Jarrod smiled.

"Then my friend, you heard wrong. Believe me, he will run us ragged before this war is ended, do not under estimate him. He is the best they have and he will find ways of attack we never expected. I will tell you this much, he is my enemy but I do hold a lot of respect for him. With just a hand full of his men he brought Dunnottar to its knees, I would never have thought it possible, but he bloody well did it. No, we must not take a thing for granted, he can pop up just about anywhere, and always when you least expect it."

General Jarrod gave a large smile as he pulled the scope from his eye and handed it to General Franklin. "Like now for instance." He pointed across the moor and Franklin lifted the scope and looked across the barren wilderness of the moor.

Robbie stood on the high ground above the look out, as the wind buffeted him from behind, and blew his hood against the back of his head. His keen dark eyes stared out across the open moor and he saw the glint of the scope as it flashed

in the sunlight. He smiled and raised a hand in salute to his enemy, he was right
and he knew they were out on the moor watching to see when would be the best
chance of attack.

Rowan walked up by his side and pressed a hot cup into his hand. "Bloody hell
it is cold up here."

Robbie lifted the hot cup to his lips. "It will get a lot colder as we move into
January. We have company watching us on the edge of the tree line. They know
we are here preparing and waiting, that pleases me it might make them think twice
before rushing at us."

Rowan scanned the tree line looking for any sign of the enemy in the far
distance. "We need more time; we are nowhere near ready for them yet Robbie."

He slowly sipped his hot coffee. "I know, we will have it, Mordred may be in a
rush, but somehow I think his advisors won't be. We did a lot of damage in the
black city, and never forget the speed with which we overcame Dunnottar. I have
to admit Rowan; even I never expected to come out as quickly as we did. I thought
we would be months in Scotland, Mordred will calm down, and when he does
he will listen to what his advisors tell him. No one wants war in the snow, this is a
hostile place to be now, and it's hard to fight with frozen hands. We have until the
New Year to prepare." Robbie watched across the land as the heather swayed in
the strong wind, and the grass was whipped violently up and down.

"I want you to take a command as a General, it is important you are seen to have
my full authority Rowan. I have a pregnant wife now, and in my absence, you will
assume total command. This will not be a short war; we have to chisel and pick at
all his troops, and wear them away before the gates are opened. We have many
tools at our disposal and now is the time to use them." Rowan listened quietly as
Robbie spoke. He knew that Robbie was forming a plan of action for the coming
months, and he knew the outcome would decide the future of the green realm.
Robbie turned and patted him on the shoulder.

"Come my friend we have to prepare, we have Specialists to disperse where they
are needed, and I think Malcolm and his group should remain intact, if we strike
during the day, his men in black can strike at night. I mean to pound Mordred
day and night until he squeals with rage. It is time to bring the woodland world
into his nightmares, and I think we will start with our good friend Ox." Robbie
moved down the slope from the wooden platform on the hill, and a window of
shimmering violet opened, both of them walked through into the glade of Robbie's
mere.

They came up the steps as Rags came out of the house and smiled. "Hey
Robbie, I just brung you a stack of letters, they have kinda been piling up on your
desk while you was away."

Robbie smiled at her. "Rags just the person I wanted to see, tell me do any of
your riders know the east side of Scotland? I need to get a letter up there." She

shrugged.

"Not sure but if you show me a map, I will get you one there." He ruffled her hair.

"Follow me my wonderful little postie, get this through and you never know you might get to kiss your lord when Bobby isn't watching." He started to laugh and entered the house.

"Corr...! Now that is a challenge, keep your lips moist I will get it through." Rowan laughed at the look of delight on Rags face as she hurried behind them up to the office.

It had been a long day as Robbie walked down the grass to the water's edge and he stood with his hands in his pockets and looked out across the glass surface of the mere. He took a long breath as he stood in the early winter sunlight and watched the little Robin as it sang in the trees.

He felt like another chapter was over, now it was time to face the war that was looming on the doorstep of Loxley. He had struck when least expected and made his mark, yet he knew that the tall black fortress of Dunnottar still stood and the black city still had more secrets to reveal. Somewhere under the hills around Stonehaven, the last of the Scottish woodsman still survived. York was at great risk and if it fell, Loxley would be the next place to face a siege.

Winter was coming and he knew that the weather would help him. He also had Runestone, which was of course a benefit; she could at least swing the weather in his favour. Her arms came from behind as her head slipped onto his shoulder, he let his head slip back as she kissed his neck and he smiled. "Hey beautiful." She gave a soft giggle and whispered.

"Hi gorgeous... What you thinking?" Robbie relaxed as he felt her against him and he held her hands as his thoughts tumbled around.

"Courage... it is going to really get tough Rune, we will need all the courage we can muster."

"You will have it, you worry too much, just look what you did with your team in a few hours, if Mordred plans a long war, we will wear him out. Never forget your dream my love, the way of nature will win. Stone builders move fast and cut down to build with speed for profit. A tree grows slowly and strengthens itself; time will wear all things away even stone. It has never worn a tree away yet, they survive everything, as will your dream."

He turned and pulled her into his arms. Her face was pale as the winter sun, and the light illuminated her fiery eyelashes above her eyes, two bright glittering sapphire coloured eyes danced, and the whites of her eyes held a tint of lilac and he loved them, she was his world, he would never be parted from her. Her eyes sparkled and she smiled. "What?"

"Nothing, I just love you."

He turned with her on his arm and began to walk up the glade. "Oh yeah how much?"

"I thought you read my letters?" She giggled.

"I have Robbie."

"Oh yeah how many times?"

"Hundreds.. I love them."

"Wow that many times... I must write more."

"Oh Robbie, will you...? I would love that." She gave another giggle as he pulled her close.

"I shall write one tonight and hide it, if you find it you can read it."

"Ok." Rune giggled all the way up the glade and into the house, Robbie turned as the door closed, and he gave one last look at the mere for the day. "Thanks granddad."

The trees parted and a bald head appeared, movement at his side revealed the white thinning hair of the Old Scot. The convoy moved slowly out of the broken gates and on to the road where violets still grew in long thick rows up to the trees. The Old Scot winked at the bald head of Angus. "I reckon they think the laddie is not here, shall we show them his spirit is still very much in Scotland?"

Angus gave a smile and lifted his arm. "This is for the rose of our fair land." He dropped his arm and the arrows flew. Black soldiers dropped to the floor and screamed caught in the hail from both sides of the road. Panic rose inside them, as they turned unable to find cover, it was but ten minutes and the road was silent. The hooded figures drew back from the trees, and like the shadows of their leader, they disappeared. The fight for Dunnottar was not over yet. The men of the last Queen of Scotland smiled as they headed high into the trees of the ancient wood. Angus patted the Old Scottish Lord on his back.

"If Rose is watching us my old friend, she will be smiling." It was, her dream of saving her people that continued in the hearts of her brother and all of her men. Deep in the crystal cave, new woodsmen arrived as they returned from the west coast havens, to fight in the memory of the last true queen of their land. The dark castle was back, and bigger than ever before, but so were woodsmen who would fight to push it back into the sea.

The large table in the conference room was filled with papers as Angus walked in, the bright eyes of Grace looked up and she smiled. "We have word from Loxley dad." She beamed as she lifted a letter and handed it to him.

The wind blew cold across the moors of York; it had a raw edge to it that could bite at the face of men. The few silver birches now stood lonely and cold, their white bark peeling as the wind rubbed its long fine fingers under the soft layers, and pulled at it with mischief. The heather moved softly with its fine wiry heads of rough foliage, and the dark seed heads from a year of bright flowers shook out the seeds for years to come. It was open, empty and bleak, and yet the wildness of it made it beautiful. Winter was in the air and the quietness of the autumn lay down to sleep deep under the peat. A single woodsman sat high on the hill his cloak pulled tightly around him, his hood was just above the high line of the heather, as he looked down the long brass telescope.

He lowered it down, and his young dark eyes shone with something other than just life, as they watched out across the wide vast wild plain. He was young but he carried the wear on his face of an older man, his complexion was dark from his days of summer, and long strands of brown hair whipped out from under his hood and flapped in the constant relentless blowing of the cold wind.

He gave a long sigh and then rubbed his hands together. "I have seen enough." He rose out of the scrub, turned and walked over the hill; she looked up her eyes blazing blue in the eerie light of the winter day. Her smile brought a warmth that could warm the frozen heart of any man as he slid his hands inside her cloak and pulled her close. "Rune I am freezing." He shivered in her warm arms.

"I found it at last."

"What?"

"Your letter... You are so naughty hiding it in my pocket." She gave a soft giggle as she pulled him tight. "I love it... have you written anymore?"

"I might have?" He leaned down and kissed her softly as her eyes sparkled up at him. "You will have to keep looking... Come on it's getting late let's get back, you never know you may find something hidden." She giggled as she turned and waved her hand, the shimmering window appeared and they happily went through. The moors seemed suddenly bleaker, and the wind howled over the top of the bluff and the heather swayed.

LOXLEY 2039

The stockade of Loxley was set back from the road; it was not the easiest of places to find, set high in the moors on the border of Derbyshire and Yorkshire. It was even harder to find after a week of heavy snow, especially after the clock had ticked one hour into the start of New Year's Day.

At one hour past midnight, in a glade filled with soft snow, the sound of a small baby's cries echoed through the bare snow dressed trees around the ancient woodland that surrounded the house of the Lord Loxley and his wife. As if they all knew, the few animals that scratched in the snow for food stopped, and all of them raised their heads and looked in the direction of the wooden house. It was a sacred time when a power of the sight of the future was brought by Stephanie and Jessica into the world.

The house rang with cheers, laughter and the ringing of glasses of celebration, and somehow in the world of the woodland that was asleep for the winter, life seemed to tread round the trees and bring tidings to all of a new line to the line of Loxley. The glade fell silent as the snowflakes glistened as they fell from the sky. The glass doors banged, as a group of cloaked figures came out of the house and hurried through the deep snow, leaving a deep furrow as they rushed through the cold night air. Happy voices echoed through the dark of the empty woods and the group came through the trees and into the glade of the Sacred Oak. John Lox beamed as he looked at Robbie. "You are the lord of this land it should be you."

Robbie nodded and smiled. "You are her grandfather; her father is not here. This Uncle John is your duty."

John beamed as his eyes glistened with tears; he turned and gave a bow to the Sacred Oak tree, and raised the small bundle wrapped in blankets high in the air. Rune wiped a tear from her eye as Robbie pulled her close. The voice of John Lox boomed into the quiet night, as his love and his pride magnified it.

"Hear me My Lord of the forests and creation. Hear me a proud man of Loxley, as I offer you my praise for the birth of my granddaughter. She is our future and the prize of my house, take her into your realm and protect her. Show your love to her, for she will be known as Jessica Sapphire Lox."

He held her high in the air as the woodland felt calm, and Rune's eyes flickered as the breeze lifted and blew around the glade. The snow swirled around John and then fell; everything was still as John turned and gave a huge smile to Robbie.

"Thank you, Robbie"

Robert Lox pulled his brother into a huge hug. "Come on now John, it's bloody freezing out here; let's get her back to her mum." John nodded the happiest smile on his face Robbie had ever seen; they turned and began to walk back. Robbie pulled Rune back for a second and pulled her into his arms, his hand ran across the small lump in her stomach and she smiled.

"It will be my turn next; I will offer up two to our lord." She leaned forward and kissed him softly as he beamed with delight.

"At least it will be warmer." She shivered in his arms and he smiled.

"Come on let's get back, and get warm." They turned, and ran through the snow to catch up with the happiest pair of brothers Loxley had ever known. Robert and John laughed as they hurried back to the house.

Set back in the darkness of the trees, a tall stag turned, and walked slowly into the wood, and the wind lifted the soft flakes of snow, and danced with them round the ancient oak tree.

The Queen of the Violet Isle.

A new queen is coming, and so is a terrible and bloody war.

Heed my words and know that in the time of the golden arrow of the green world, a child will come forward to mark the start of the line of a new queen.

Her name will be given out of love from those who surround her, and it will be a gift. For to this world, she will be as such, and she will bring balance and have the power to protect kings.

Seek out the sage in the land of dragons, for he will have wisdom and know of this child, in him will then lie the keys to unlock her potential.

The time of the queen of the violet isle will come first, and through the line of her life will come the true king.

The violet stones will bring destiny south and on the right seat in the wood of a royal line the true king of the Britons will be revealed.

The lines of darkness will draw ever nearer so beware and defend the children in who all fate is relied upon, a new line of the moon will follow and the balance will come with great pain.

Heed my words and know that the world for a time will balance on the edge of fate.

(The last prophecy of Rhiannon goddess of the moon)

More Author's
From
Violet Circle Publishing

Mike Beale. (Children's Book)

Crumble's Adventures.
ISBN: 978-1-910299-06-7
Digital ISBN: 978-1-910299-08-1

Colin Smith (Play)

Heaven knows I'm Miserable Now
ISBN: 978-1-910299-16-6
Digital ISBN: 978-1-910299-23-4

Ted Morgan. (Poetry and verse)

Wordsmith's Wanderings.
ISBN: 978-1-910299-04-3
Digital ISBN: 978-1-910299-09-8
Peregrinations of the Wordsmith
ISBN: 978-1-910299-18-0
Digital ISBN: 978-1-910299-21-0
Silhouette Soldiers
ISBN: 978-1-910299-19-7
Digital ISBN: 978-1-910299-22-7
A Menu of Memories
Digital ISBN: 978-1-910299-32-6
Digital ISBN: 978-1-910299-33-3

Robin John Morgan. (Fiction/Fantasy/Slice of Life)

Heirs to the Kingdom.

Book One, The Bowman of Loxley.
ISBN: 978-1-910299-00-5
Digital ISBN: 978 1 910299-10-4
Book Two, The Lost Sword of Carnac.
ISBN: 978-1-910299-01-2
Digital ISBN: 978-1-910299-11-1
Book Three, The Darkness of Dunnottar.
ISBN: 978-1-910299-02-9
Digital ISBN: 978-1-910299-12-8
Book Four, Queen of the Violet Isle.
ISBN: 978-1-910299-03-6
Digital ISBN: 978-1-910299-13-5
Book Five, Crystals of the Mirrored Waters.
ISBN: 978-1-910299-05-0
Digital ISBN: 978-1-910299-14-2
Book Six, Last Arrow of the Woodland Realm.
ISBN: 978-1-910299-07-4
Digital ISBN: 978-1-910299-15-9
Book Seven, Bridge Of Sequana.
ISBN: 978-1-910299-17-3
Digital ISBN: 978-1-910299-20-3
Book Eight, The Circle of Darkness.
ISBN: 978-1-910299-26-5
Digital ISBN: 978-1-910299-29-6

The Curio Chronicles.

Part One, Abigail's Summer.
ISBN: 978-1-910299-27-2
Part Two, Curio's Summer.
ISBN: 978-1-910299-34-0
Digital ISBN: 978-1-910299-35-7
Part Three, Curio's Christmas.
ISBN: 978-1-910299-38-8
Digital ISBN: 978-1-910299-39-5

Other Works.

Rise Of The Raven
ISBN: 978-1-910299-30-2
Digital ISBN: 978-1-910299-31-9
The Countess Of Darkness
ISBN: 978-1-910299-40-1
Digital ISBN: 978-1-910299-41-8

Han's Cottage.
ISBN: 978-1-910299-36-4
Digital ISBN: 978-1-910299-37-1

Find out more about our authors and their books at
www.violetcirclepublishing.co.uk